R.A. McDougall

Maestros of the Anthymn

Dark Tide Rising

ATTUNED

Maestros of the Anthymn: Dark Tide Rising

This edition published in December 2023

Cover and Illustrations by Haiwei Hou
Edited by Lottie Hayes-Clemens
Maps by Jack Cutt

Attuned Entertainment
#142 – 757 West Hastings St.
Vancouver, BC V6C 1A1
www.attunedentertainment.com

This is a work of fiction. All of the characters, organizations, and events that are portrayed in this novel are either a product of the author's imagination or are used fictitiously.

Hardback ISBN: 978-17381436-3-4
Softback ISBN: 978-17381436-2-7

To Fran and Paul, the first
Maestros I had the honour
of knowing

And to those who may yet
one day spark

CONTENTS

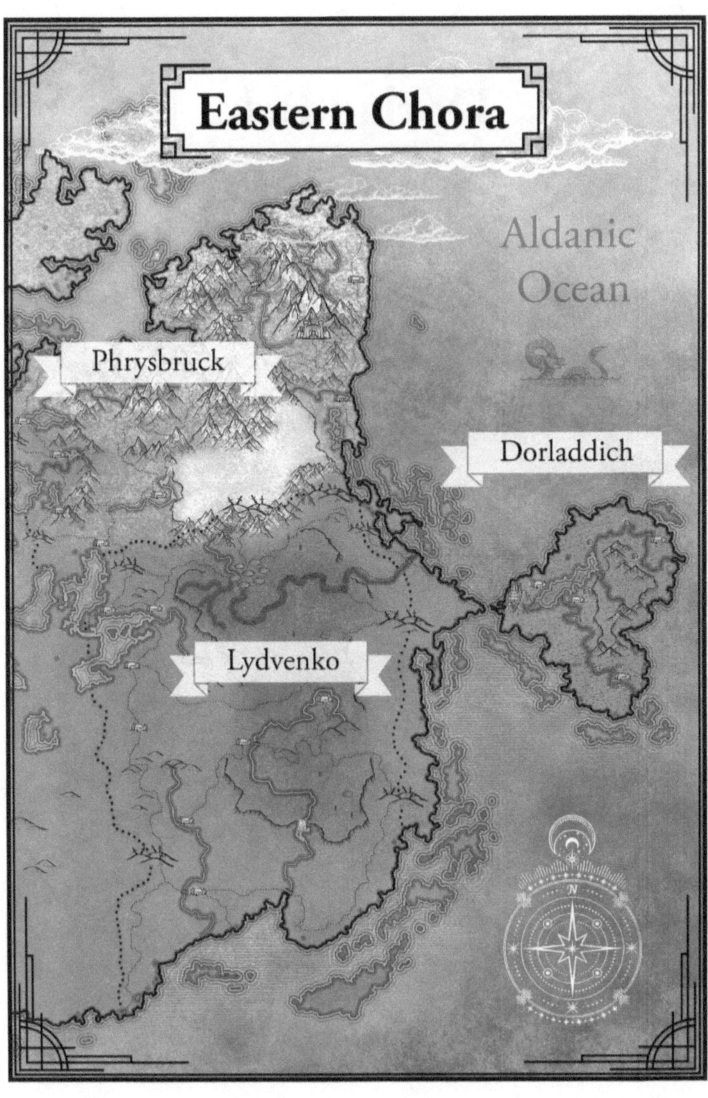

Eastern Chora
Aldanic Ocean
Phrysbruck
Dorladdich
Lydvenko
N

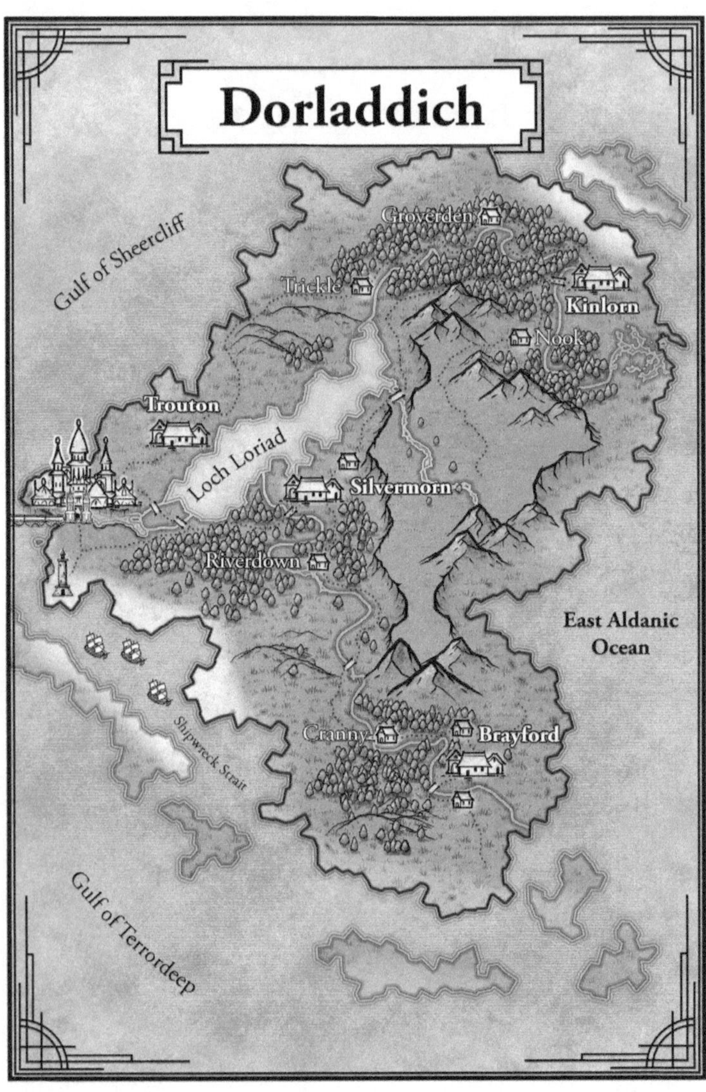

Dorladdich
Gulf of Sheercliff
Groverden
Trickle
Kinlorn
Nook
Trouton
Loch Loriad
Silvermorn
Riverdown
East Aldanic Ocean
Shipwreck Strait
Cranny
Brayford
Gulf of Terrordeep

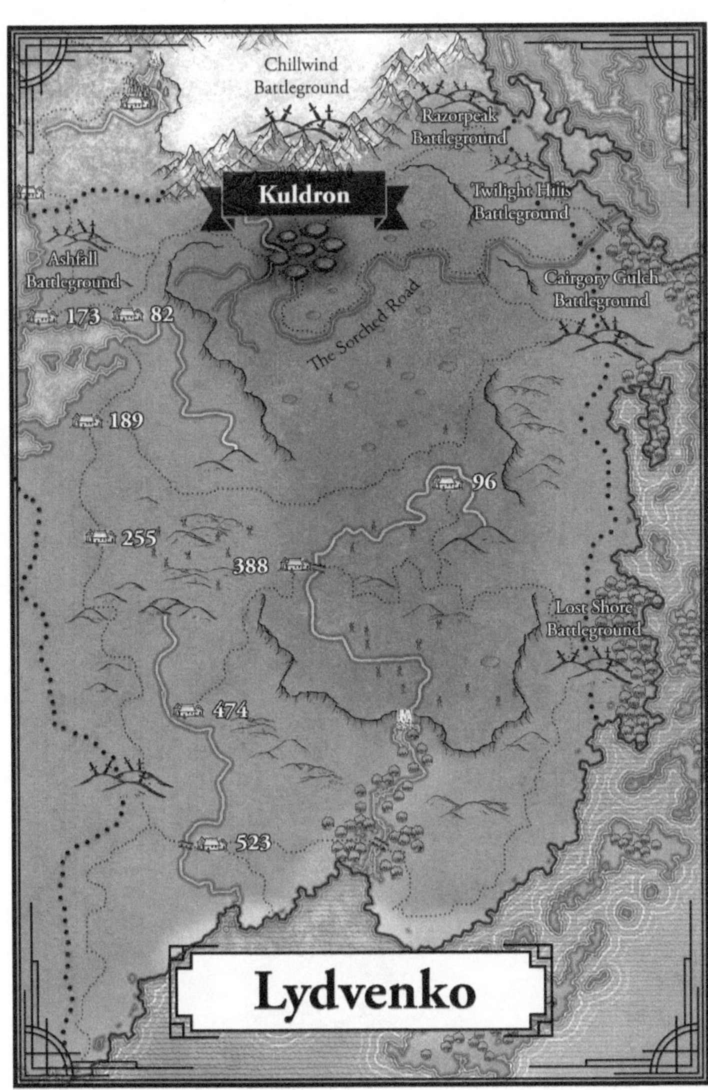

Chillwind
Battleground
Razorpeak
Battleground
Kuldron
Twilight Hills
Battleground
Cairgory Gulch
Battleground
Ashfall
Battleground
173   82
The Sorched Road
189
96
255
388
Lost Shore
Battleground
474
523
Lydvenko

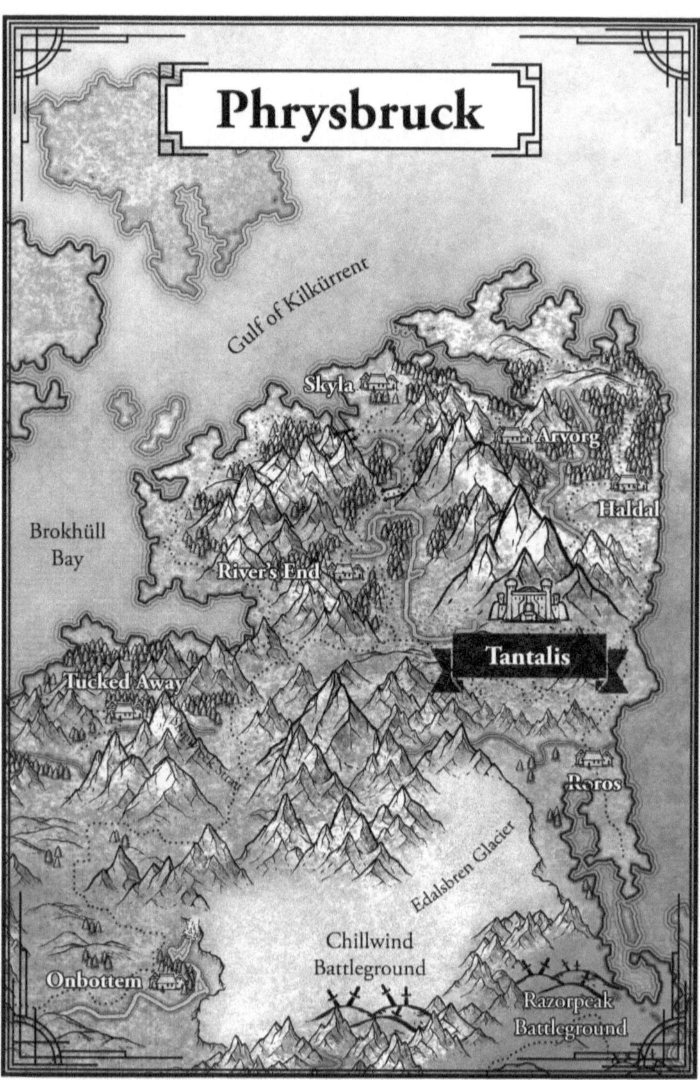

Phrysbruck
Gulf of Kilkürrent
Skyla
Arvorg
Haldal
Brokhüll Bay
River's End
Tantalis
Tucked Away
Roros
Edalsbren Glacier
Chillwind Battleground
Onbottem
Razorpeak Battleground

In a lost era of song and sword...

Chapter One

DAWNBREAKER

A heavy mist shrouded the island province of Dorladdich and covered its mossy highland hills, evergreen forests, and sheer coastal cliffs with cold morning dew. Nestled in a grove of fir trees at the mouth of Loch Loriad, Straveritas Manor was at the centre of Dorladdich's most luxurious estate. The manor's monumental granite columns and exquisite mouldings hinted at the regal wings inside that held four floors and countless rooms—each packed with opulent furnishings. Niera Straveritas, however, had chosen her bedroom not for its double walk-in closets, but because of the tall lancet windows that gave her a clear view of the eastern shoreline.

Standing barefoot in a grey nightgown and plush wool robe, Niera leaned against the frame of the middle window, rubbed her eyes, and tucked a thick curl back into the tangled mass of ashen blonde hair that framed her angular face. She looked up to see Brathlún and Sorolún high in the twilight sky. Like the hands of a clock, the two moons met several times each day. Brathlún always looked as though he might collide with the much smaller yet far brighter Sorolún. Instead, she passed by him only to begin their sibling chase again.

A sliver of daybreak crept over the horizon and drew Niera's gaze to the distant coast where the firs sloped down to a rocky beach that would be unreachable from the island if not for the colossal stonework Forth Reach bridge arching over the Aldanic Ocean strait. Though the landscape was breathtaking, Niera hadn't snuck out of bed to admire the scenery nor contemplate the devastating war raging across all of Chora.

Beams of buttery light suddenly flooded her bedroom—one falling onto an ornate music box resting on the nightstand.

Clink-clink... clink-clink... clink-clink... Click!

Iron gears turned and opened the lid. A tiny mechanical dancer popped up from inside, her arms arched above her head as she stood on a pointed toe with the other leg stretched into the air.

Clink-clink... clink-clink... clink-clink.

Usually, the metallic chimes emanating from the music box would wake Niera, but this morning, she was determined to make it a prelude to her private performance. Movement caught her eye, and she looked at her bedroom door. Just beneath it, a shadow from the guard standing on the other side faded away as he left to fetch her handmaidens. Seizing the chance she was waiting for, Niera quickly tiptoed across the cold floor and approached a small table in the corner where her ceramic instrument case was waiting. She ran her hand over the smooth, glossy surface, then pressed her thumbs against the polished silver latches. Niera felt her pulse quicken as she heard her father's voice in her head, *You are never to play this instrument without my explicit permission.* She knew better than to disobey him; as praetor of their province, his word was law.

Chick-chick!

The latches were released. Niera's fingers found their way underneath the lid, and she slowly raised it to reveal a pale maple-wood violin slumbering inside.

"Good morning, Dawnbreaker," she whispered with a wide smile.

Most musicians waited a lifetime to be honoured with an instrument that was half the quality of Dawnbreaker, but being a Straveritas, Niera was never left wanting. Reaching for the neck, her hand suddenly paused. She knew that she could close the lid, turn back, and hide under the down comforter until the handmaidens came to wake her. But what for? Just so another year could pass, wondering if she truly was the prodigal maestro everyone hoped she would one day become.

Given no choice, Niera was enrolled in Dorladdich's music mentorship program at age five, but instead of appointing her to a veteran member of the provincial orchestra like everyone else, she was placed under the direct mentorship of the current Maestro Dorian. Soon after, Niera found herself quickly overwhelmed by what seemed to be an endless abyss of music theory and complex instrument techniques. Even after an entire childhood of dedicated study and relentless practise, the numerous notes, chords, and scales remained mystical elements of expression to her. But one day, she realized that music had a structure very similar to language. Suddenly, the notes were akin to letters. If you put them together, they wouldn't form a word, but instead, a motif. Disconnected motifs, however, like words, were not enough to create meaning. Fortunately, when she placed motifs in sequence, they would create phrases, which, like musical sentences, carried an enormous amount of meaning. One interesting thing about phrases was that some could sound open and unresolved, as though asking an important question. It wasn't until a closed phrase followed that it felt like the question had been answered and a period formed. Often, phrases would repeat to create melodic themes, and it was these melodies that Niera found herself whistling without even realizing it. However, when she threaded motifs, phrases, periods, and melodies together, harmony conjured contemplation by enchanting her mind, rhythm summoned sensation by moving her body, and melody evoked emotion by charming her soul.

Only after completing her military training and demonstrating that she could perform each of Dorladdich's one hundred and fifty warsongs with perfect accuracy had Niera been allowed to take Dawnbreaker in hand. At first, every attempt to find the violin's voice failed. Her rest position was always wrong, bow hold constantly off, stance too narrow, or chin too low. But finally, with thousands of frustrating hours of rehearsal behind her, Dawnbreaker grew to be an extension of who Niera was. With this violin under her command, she became the youngest First String and Orchestra Lead in Dorladdian history, an achievement celebrated by the entire province.

Niera was often surprised by how little the provincials knew about the art that shaped and defined who they were. To her, understanding and performing music was as essential to life as breathing. Still, she had a soft spot for provincial children who would always ask her the same question in chorus: What was it like to perform in battle with *Maestro Dorian*? To them, music was still an arcane sorcery of limitless possibility. Magic, most provincials would say. A small part of her envied their naivety. The war was anything but enchanting, so Niera would simply tell them it was a privilege and an honour. Of course, none of the children disagreed, but that didn't stop their little faces from scrunching up in frustration because she hadn't revealed any of the rumoured secrets to illuminating a warsong.

As Orchestra Lead, Niera held the highest rank among all one hundred musicians in the provincial orchestra, which came with the expectation that she would one day succeed Maestro Dorian. There was just one problem: she hadn't yet illuminated.

Maestros were the only individuals in all of Chora who could materialize sound into glass—an ability unlike any other. According to Maestro Dorian, most maestros sparked around age thirteen, and the chaotic event felt like an ignition of emotional frisson so powerful that if you didn't channel it through your instrument, you might explode. Sparking was especially dangerous for young adepts because they hadn't yet learnt how to control their illumination or the lethal shards of glass it created. As a result, they would often end up severely wounding themselves—or worse.

As if the pressure wasn't high enough, Niera's family had held the title of Maestro Dorian for over sixty generations. Tiarnen, Niera's older brother, was meant to inherit the title after their mother died in battle, but he had never managed to spark and was thus considered a dud. Thankfully, their middle sister Reina had proved herself worthy and became Maestro before Dorladdich was left defenceless. Unable to move past the shame, Tiarnen had resigned himself to the harbour lighthouse as its resident lightkeeper and only returned to the orchestra when duty called. Niera was determined never to become a reclusive disappointment herself.

She pulled Dawnbreaker from its slumber to admire the polished maple-wood body and weightless bow in her hand. Then, she walked to the middle of the bedroom, stopping at the full-length mirror hanging against the west wall. Though there were no formalities here, she buttoned up her plush robe as if it were a maestro jacket—the signature piece of their uniform. She set Dawnbreaker on her shoulder and placed her chin on the rest. One by one, Niera's calloused fingers picked at the strings to test them: first G, D, A, and finally, E. The common ear wouldn't have been able to tell that the D string was out of tune, but to her, it might as well have been nails running down a chalkboard. She turned the D peg tighter and plucked the string once again, the tone finally pure. Straightening her posture, Niera gazed at the mirror and stared into her own green eyes.

"Septhembra the fourth, fifteen eighty-five," she whispered, convincing herself it would be a day to be remembered.

Her foot began to tap in rhythm. It was a simple motif, the beat causing her body to softly rock back and forth. Niera set the bow and blurred it across Dawnbreaker's strings to play a cresting rivulet that opened "Irinshaér in D Major." Though the composition was only a few minutes long, "Irinshaér" was specifically written to evoke intense emotion in three short movements: exposition, development, and recapitulation, where the themes are introduced, explored, and then enhanced, making it perfect for young adepts who were hoping to spark.

Niera's practised fingers scurried along the violin neck like spider legs as she progressed through the exposition, which was designed to introduce "Irinshaer's" spirited core themes. Motifs of ardent triplets roused her into pressing the bow harder, which only made Dawnbreaker sing louder and grow warmer. Transitioning with a trickle of arpeggios, the rest of the first movement brought cascading motifs that merged into an exhilarating, truculent phrase, which swept Niera up like a swift-moving current and cooled Dawnbreaker once more. Even though she knew it was intentional, Niera couldn't help but become inspired by the thematic contrast.

Then, the second movement darkened with descending phrases. The development plunged like a waterfall and made it seem as though Niera was free-falling. A sense of uncertainty took hold and deeply saddened her. However, before she could lament at the bottom of the scale, the themes became fervent and resurged to bring Niera hope once more. Yet, there still wasn't a flicker of the resonance she knew to be hidden inside of herself. *You just need to ignite it*, she thought. Niera closed her eyes and tried to push back the frustration—it would only distract and hurt her technique. Still, the fear of repeating failure, especially after taking such an enormous risk to play without permission, kept creeping into her mind.

Niera's grip tightened around the bow, and she pressed down even harder—channelling every ounce of determination into the exhilarating melody—developing it further by ornamenting the theme to burn herself from the inside out if it meant finally sparking. An eruption of arching figures brought her to the bridge, and after crossing it with a crescendo of undulating tonic leaps, the bedroom became incredibly humid. Niera took the fogging windows as a good sign. She had sacrificed her entire childhood—if anyone deserved to illuminate, it was her.

"*Miss Niera?*" shouted a female voice from the other side of the door.

Niera knew it was one of her handmaidens returning with the guard, but she couldn't afford a distraction, not when she was so close to finishing. All she had to do was prove herself, and there would be no reprimand, no consequences, only praise and celebration.

Sweat beading on her brow, Niera began the third movement with dazzling sonority. Watching the mirror completely fog over and her reflection vanish, she flourished her violin passionately—a last dance as an adept. But as she approached the end of the recapitulation, there was still no spark. And though she had performed perfectly, it was not resonance filling her heart, but panic.

Overwhelmed now with anxiety, she played the closing note with all her strength, accidentally forcing the bow down too hard and causing the E string to snap. Its death cry filled the bedroom, a distorted twang echoing and then fading into empty silence. Niera's entire body went numb as she realized the gamble had amounted to nothing except another failed attempt. Despite part of her wanting to look away, she kept staring at her silhouette in the foggy mirror with tear-filled eyes.

"Worthless!" she yelled, throwing Dawnbreaker and shattering the mirror into pieces.

Bam-bam-bam!

The bedroom door thundered.

"Miss Niera, *are you all right?*" asked the guard.

"Yes, I'm fine—just an accident!" said Niera. Carefully avoiding the glass shards, she retrieved Dawnbreaker, ran back to the case, and placed it inside. The bedroom door flew open just as she was about to close the lid.

"Stop," ordered a voice.

As though under a spell, Niera froze in place. All she could do was hide the bow behind her back and face the doorway where her father now stood.

Tharus was tall and thin, with lacquered salt-and-pepper hair. Contrasting with his unnaturally pale skin, a dark grey half-cape hung over his right shoulder, partially covering a tailored tunic underneath. Watching him slowly emerge from the shadows with a skeleton key in his hand, Niera could see deep hairline cracks running vertically along his gaunt face. They reminded her of the oil paintings hanging in the manor hallways that were in desperate need of restoration. Niera, much like the entire province, knew that Tharus was older than Dorladdich itself, but how time had somehow stopped for him, no one could say for certain. She believed that the relic chronograph around his wrist was part of the reason why.

"Father, I was—" began Niera, but Tharus only lifted a bony finger and took her voice away.

He pointed to her bed. She obediently walked to it and sat on the edge. Two handmaidens, both wearing simple dresses and aprons, rushed into the room to check her for any serious injuries.

"You had Imogen and Bridget worried sick," said Tharus.

"Indeed, we were, Praetor!" said Bridget, her plump cheeks turning rosy.

"All that noise at such an early hour!" added Imogen, pushing her thick spectacles back up her snub nose.

They had been tending to Niera's every need since she was a babe and so often blew the smallest things out of proportion—if only to prove to Tharus how dedicated they were to his favourite daughter.

"The guard said he heard music!" said Bridget, laughing off the idea as she took a seashell comb from the vanity and tried to brush it through Niera's hair.

"We knew it had to be a mistake. You would never think of playing alone," added Imogen, rummaging through a dresser and pulling out the ceremonial dress Niera wore every first Sunday of the month.

"Of course she wouldn't." Tharus shut the music box on the dancer with his finger. "Niera is well aware that disobeying my orders would be met with severe repercussions."

"I swear, you must have the thickest mane in all the province," said Bridget, trying to change the topic.

"And it was just cut a few weeks ago." Imogen's voice trembled. "Growing as fast as you are, we'll be lucky if these clothes still fit you by next summer." She rested a tartan dress of sea foam, sage, and forest green along with a cropped grey coat beside Niera in an attempt to cover the bow resting behind her on the bed.

Tharus wasn't having it. He marched over to Niera, pulled the bow from underneath the coat, and wrapped his sharp fingers around her jaw—forcefully raising her chin.

"What were you thinking?" he asked, his fingers digging in.

"I... I had to try," confessed Niera.

"And look what happened!" yelled Tharus.

"I'm sorry." Niera tried to blink back her tears as Tharus gripped so tight that she thought he might break her jaw. Instead, he released his grasp to gently wipe her wet cheek with his thumb.

"I know you are struggling."

"No matter what I seem to do. I just can't—" began Niera.

"But that is no excuse," finished Tharus.

"You're right." Niera let out a defeated sob.

"It may be hard to understand, especially when you are so frustrated. But my rules are in place to protect you, even if—"

"If it means from myself, I know," finished Niera.

A rapid knock sounded at the open door.

"If I may?" said Ignis, a tiny rat-faced man dressed in overly embellished ceremonial robes and struggling to hold a stack of ledgers under his arm.

"What is it, Executor?" asked Tharus, clearly annoyed.

"Given that we are running behind schedule, shall I tell Maestro Dorian to make her way to Noble Court and begin the Calling ahead of us?"

"No," said Tharus, "the maestro may rest."

"Forgive me, but who then will call the Houses?" asked Ignis, blinking with confusion.

Tharus turned back to Niera. "Am I foolish to keep my faith?" He held the bow out for her.

"Never, my Praetor," said Niera, taking the bow in hand and standing to her feet.

Following close behind Tharus and Ignis, Niera scrambled to replace the E string on Dawnbreaker while departing through the manor's double-door entrance. She carefully threaded the string through the tuning peg as they passed the forecourt and walked down the right side of a sweeping split staircase that had a massive freshwater aqueduct running down the middle.

Fed by Loch Loriad, the roaring river surged through a lush hedgerow garden until finally cascading over a wide lip into a colossal waterfall that vanished far below. Waiting beside the falls were five men. Four were praetorian guards who stood ready in glossy grey ceramic armour with a varying number of shark teeth embossed across their chest plates. Like Tharus, they wore half-capes on their right side but fashioned in the same tartan pattern as Niera's dress. The fifth man was boorish, sweaty, and in his early sixties. He should have been standing at attention, just as the guards were, but was too fixated on the nightingale perched on his finger.

Niera's expression soured with every step closer to the Inquisitor, not only because she had personally observed his ruthless inquiries—all apparently for the sake of provincial intelligence—but also from the gossip between Bridget and Imogen regarding his grotesque indulgences.

"Good morning, Praetor!" snorted Holgor, releasing the nightingale and then bowing as far as he could without splitting his trousers. "And Miss Niera, a pleasure as always."

"Inquisitor," said Niera.

"Maestro Dorian has not yet left the Conservatory," said Holgor, "I could send a messenger to—"

"That will not be necessary," interrupted Ignis. "The Calling will be led by Miss Niera this morning."

"Oh?" asked Holgor, puzzled by the news. "Well, an exciting surprise indeed! Will you allow Dorladdich's finest to lead you into Noble Court?" He gestured to the guards.

"Certainly," said Niera.

With a nod from Tharus, the guards surrounded Niera. Though being a praetor's daughter demanded the highest level of respect, she had never been escorted by her father's personal guard before and found herself revelling in the extra attention.

Holgor waddled over to the wide ceramic crossbar gate behind him and pulled a lever resting in the wall. Two slots on either side of the stonework opened, releasing heavy streams of water onto cogged wheels, which drew the gate open and revealed a cobblestone street descending into Noble Court. Despite the roar of the massive waterfall descending beside them, Niera heard Holgor strike up a tense conversation with her father.

"Praetor, there is something you should be aware of," he muttered.

"I take it the week's intelligence reports have arrived," said Tharus.

"They have."

"Was there anything of concern?"

"Yes, the one from Lydvenko, in particular," Holgor said nervously.

"Go on."

"It would seem Praetor Khazlokov deployed his entire legion several days ago."

"That's ten thousand legionaries," said Ignis, trying to insert himself into the conversation.

"What was their last known direction?" asked Tharus.

"Northwest," replied Holgor.

"They could be headed to Phrysbruck," interjected Ignis.

Tharus frowned. "Or any one of our battlegrounds."

"Shall I have the bridge watch doubled?" asked Holgor, ignoring Ignis's assessment.

Tharus pulled back his sleeve to look at the antique chronograph timepiece around his wrist. "No," he said, adjusting one of the many small brass dials surrounding its detailed face, "but you should endeavour to ensure critical information such as this does not take several days to reach me."

"Yes, my Praetor, apologies," croaked Holgor.

Dismissing the discussion since her father didn't seem at all worried, Niera continued down the stairs until they reached the plunge pool. Though she walked through Noble Court almost every day, she always marvelled at how the thundering falls splashed and frothed chaotically around the sculptures of alluring water nymphs sprawled against Ceirenor. The massive leviathan was fabled to be so large that a whale barely made a meal for it, which is why the monster circled Dorladdich in hunger and thus caused the waters surrounding the island to be so treacherous.

From the pool's edge, three aqueducts branched out, each of their rushing waters running underneath the arched foundation of a stunning estate home. If Straveritas Manor was the crown jewel of Dorladdich, the three noble houses were its garnets.

Identical in nearly every way, the sophisticated brickwork residences stood at six storeys, not including the chimneys, with clusters of deeply recessed windows along every side. Granite steps at the front led to towering twin doors that would have easily held the eye if it wasn't for the captivating tile mosaic covering most of the façade. Every amenity was available inside, including studies, galleries, parlours, smoking rooms, and even a grand ballroom. From each home, an aqueduct extended towards the perimeter of Noble Court and cascaded over the edge, where it descended into the districts far below.

Niera continued to the large fountain at the centre of the Court. Thousands of tiny silver shells rested at the bottom, all of them secret wishes made by noble children who dreamed of working in a branch of the War Office, becoming a praetorian guard, or even an orchestra member. Failure to do so meant working for one of their family's many businesses since the noble houses were responsible for all commerce throughout the province. By keeping their districts productive, they were ensuring that Tharus bestowed an enormous amount of privilege and prosperity on their house. However, it was the Premiership that they coveted most. Niera didn't care to understand the finer details, but she knew that whichever house won the annual Premiership could enact accords that changed anything from working conditions, transportation, education, and even medical care for all provincials. House Ashbrook, the oldest house by far, currently held the Premiership and was well known for enacting accords that put provincial interests first. The Roycrofts, a recently ascended house, detested the Ashbrook accords since their businesses were suffering greatly as a result. But

Niera didn't take much interest in noble drama since everyone always answered to her father in the end.

Niera was fairly isolated day to day for her supposed "protection," so she took every opportunity she could to leave the manor. Many thought that the Calling was a waste of time, or at the very least, took too long, but it was her favourite ritual because she had the chance to see all of the noble families at once. There wasn't very much socializing, but that still didn't stop Eimear Ashbrook from ignoring formalities and splashing a bit of sass around or the Finwicks from making delightfully inappropriate jokes.

"Niera, call the houses," ordered Tharus.

She stepped onto the intersection where the cobblestone pattern from each house met to form a swirling knot and readied Dawnbreaker, while Ignis held a ledger open for her to read. Written across the pages were the noble family names: Roycroft, Finwick, and Ashbrook. Just below each of them was a distinct melody and then a descending list of all family members.

Niera turned toward the Roycroft home. She liked their mural most of all; its tiles depicted a colossal squid rising halfway out of the sea with long barbed tentacles reaching for a cloudy sky. The Roycrofts owned Kilners' Row, a district where the province's ceramic weapons and armour were made; Trade Town, where the snobby merchants sold their goods and services at the highest price possible; and the Slick, a strip of foul refineries where oils of every sort were produced for heat and light.

She began playing the pompous Roycroft melody, and the front door immediately opened. Ten well-dressed family members marched out, playing string instruments in accompaniment to Niera. The women were draped in exquisite gowns with no shortage of jewellery adorning their necks, while the men wore tailored jerkins and trousers with fine pocket watches fastened by long polished chains. All of them donned fancy sea-foam green bycoket hats. Together, they followed their cobblestone pattern and took position on Niera's right, bowing deeply as she played the last note with them.

"House Roycroft! You have been called!" announced Tharus.

"And we have answered, loyally, Praetor!" said Earl Aran Roycroft, a handsome man in his early sixties with a thick moustache and more than a hint of loftiness in his voice.

Niera turned towards the Finwick house. Its mural featured a pod of dolphins racing along a cresting wave together. The Finwicks owned the Tavern Crawl, a district of ingenious distilleries and rowdy taverns where most provincials went after a day's work to spend their pay on spirits and ale; Punkworks, where the best engineers put wrenches to gears for all sorts of mechanical repairs, retrofits, and rebuilds; and Ler-ic, an inventive surf shop where the Finwicks had shaped the infamous Thrust Fin surfboard. Niera had never surfed before—not that she would be allowed, even if the desire were there—but she had to admit that the racing sport was quite thrilling to watch.

She played the rambunctious Finwick melody, and after many bars, the front door finally opened. Twenty family members spilled out, many playing percussion instruments in accompaniment with Niera, shoving and bickering incessantly among each other. Half were well-dressed in leather tunics, bodices, dresses, and doublets. The others wore similar attire but in a far more dishevelled and haphazard manner. Despite their differences, all were wearing sage-green leather boots.

"Move on, you worthless gobshites!" screamed Fiona, a wild-eyed waif in her early twenties with wiry black hair, who was banging on a large drum strapped to her hips.

"Put a bloody cork in it, Fiona," said Wendel, her equally thin broth-er, whose own black hair rested on his shoulders.

"He's right! Someone's gon-gonna think there's a bloody ba-banshee in the Court and call the pa-patrol," stammered Earl Liam Finwick, an eccentric man in his early seventies who looked like he had been pickled twice over.

They followed their cobblestone path and finally stood before Niera as she finished the last note of their melody.

"If they do, I'll shove this drumstick up their—" began Fiona.

"House Finwick!" interrupted Tharus. "You have been called!"

"And we ha-have answered, Praetor!" stammered Liam.

"By the Verse," said Aran. "Couldn't you have waited until after the service to finish a bottle?"

"No idea wha-what you're talking about," said Liam. "But if I had wai-waited, it would've been a waste of a fi-fine Dorladdian morning!" He finally straightened himself and then checked inside his coat to ensure his flask hadn't fallen out.

Niera faced the Ashbrook house. Their mural was a pair of entwined seahorses swimming together. The Ashbrooks owned Bilgewater Bay, a massive district just south of the harbour where kelp was farmed; Fisherman's Wharf, a bustling market where mongers sold every kind of fresh or canned seafood imaginable; and Shipshape, a small eclectic district of tackle shops and marine stores. Though the Ashbrooks were the oldest of the noble families, they still believed in getting their hands dirty, which kept them in high regard as the finest shipwrights and crewmen in the province.

Niera played the uplifting Ashbrook melody. After a few bars, the front door of the house swung open, and forty family members poured out. Most were casually playing woodwind instruments in accompaniment with Niera, and dressed in a simple attire of well-worn sweaters, pea coats, or shawls—though all their forest-green buckled belts had been polished to a respectable shine. Together, they followed their cobblestone path to stand on Niera's left, then casually bowed as she played the last melodic note with them.

"House Ashbrook! You have been—" said Tharus.

"Yes, yes, we are all here," remarked Earl Eimear Ashbrook, a stout woman in her early eighties with a mane of silver hair pulled up into a large bun. She was struggling to help Maeve, her youngest granddaughter, into a knitted sweater.

"Wait, where is Coniel?" asked Kaleigh, a freckled girl in her late twenties, the dark skin of her right arm tattooed with loch flowers.

"Swore he was right behind us when we left," said Saoirse, Kaleigh's teen sister, who had a voluminous afro and was pulling a loose thread from her shawl.

"Perhaps someone should check Sweet Salvation?" quipped Lachlan Roycroft. He stood just behind Aran, clean-shaven and already much taller than his father despite only being in his late teens. A spiteful expression contorted his narrow features.

"And why would I go looking for him at a bakery, exactly?" asked Kaleigh, turning to set a stern gaze on Lachlan.

"Oh, no reason. I just find it ironic that you've already lost a family member before midday," said Lachlan. "Especially since he's the largest one."

Half of the Finwicks joined the Roycrofts in laughing at Lachlan's remark, but all of them quickly clammed up when Kaleigh started marching toward Lachlan with her fists clenched. Just before she could reach for him, a ruckus erupted from inside the Ashbrook home. Muffled yells could be heard, followed by the sound of broken dishes. Then, with a final thud, the door flew open again, and Coniel barrelled out, caught in a tug-of-war with a large Dorladdian shepherd.

"Give it back, Dasher!" yelled Coniel, a rotund teen with light brown bowl-cut hair, who was pulling on something that the dog had in his mouth. Despite Coniel's best efforts, Dasher just wouldn't let go. He seemed to think it was a game and only pulled back harder to win. "Kaleigh, it's tearing! Help!"

"He won't let go of whatever it is until you do," sighed Kaleigh, as though for the hundredth time.

Coniel reluctantly eased his grip, and Dasher ran straight to Kaleigh, his tail wagging with pride.

"Thank you, handsome," said Kaleigh, pressing her finger to Dasher's wet snout as though it was a release button and gently pulling what was left of a drool-covered playing card from his maw.

"Tell that nosey beast to stop sniffing around in my room!" huffed Coniel, arriving in a sweat.

"No wonder he wouldn't give it up, you're not supposed to have Shatter cards in the house," said Kaleigh.

"But I need to win a match with it in order to complete the Blind Man's Bluff Achievement and get my Card Shark Seal!" From his belt satchel, Coniel pulled a small leatherbound book with *Year of the Wolf, 1585* embossed on the cover. He cracked it open, quickly flipped through the two hundred pages, and then stopped where a green ribbon was resting to mark the achievement description.

"Fishfeathers!" said Earl Ashbrook. "Grand Champion or not, I don't want you playing that game under my roof!"

"Which is why I taught Dasher to bring me any cards he finds so they can be thrown out," said Kaleigh. "Or... destroyed... in this case." She handed the card back to Coniel, who was clearly crestfallen after seeing that it was shredded.

Niera turned back to Ignis, who was double-checking the headcount on his ledger. "Is everyone accounted for?" she asked.

"Sixty-four... Sixty-fi—no! It seems we are missing... Pierce Finwick," said Ignis, looking up at the Finwicks.

"Right. It was Pierce's birthday last night," Wendel said rather casually. "Afraid the celebration left him in the bog wishing he was still a year younger." He chuckled, only to notice Tharus staring at him in silence. "But, on second thought," he said, with a hard swallow, "I'm sure I can get the skiver on his feet!" Wendel turned and sprinted back to the Finwick house, clearly in regret of letting his little brother sleep in.

"Now, before we make our way inside for the praetor's illustrious sermon," said Ignis, "there are a couple of recent achievements to award." Most of the younger children grew noticeably excited. "For those of you who haven't heard, Valis Roycroft achieved her grade six music conservatory level earlier this week."

Everyone applauded as Valis, a petite girl with frizzy red hair and wearing a dress that nearly rivalled Niera's in quality, stepped forward and stood before Ignis—staring up at him through her tortoiseshell glasses. "It is my pleasure to award you the Pin of Cogitation and grant you permission to join the Orchestra Entrance Corps under the mentorship of your cousin, Lachlan."

Everyone gently applauded again as Valis took the ceramic pin, embossed with a fountain pen and a tuning fork crossed atop a parchment scroll.

"Well done," said Niera, secretly revelling in the fact that she had completed the same exam two years younger.

"Thank you," said Valis. She bowed graciously, returned to the Roycrofts, and stood at Lachlan's side.

Kaleigh shook her head. "She would have better luck with Dasher mentoring her."

"Next!" proclaimed Ignis, trying to drown any further remarks from Kaleigh. "And I am not sure if she is even aware of this," he continued, "but our very own Earl Ashbrook is about to receive the prestigious Dearly Devoted Seal, as this is her seventy-fifth Calling anniversary!" The applause was much louder this time, along with a few embellished whistles from the Ashbrook troop and some barks from Dasher.

"Oh, dry up already," said Eimear, who seemed less than thrilled by the announcement and particularly annoyed as Ignis pinned a decorated ceramic heart embossed with *75* to her coat lapel.

"Quite an achievement, Eimear," said Tharus.

Eimear seemed like she had something to say to Tharus, but she held her tongue and instead returned silently to her family.

"Executor, if I might ask," said Aran. "How many prestige points does her seal come with?"

The Ashbrook whistles were replaced with audible groans.

"One thousand points," said Ignis, "which I believe puts the Ashbrooks slightly ahead for the Premiership this year."

"Only for the race to begin again next year," remarked Eimear, a hint of bitterness in her voice.

"As it always has and always will," said Tharus. "Unlike the rest of the provinces, nobility in Dorladdich must be earned."

Everyone fell silent. Niera had witnessed first-hand how intense the house rivalries could become. Last year, there had been an all-out brawl at the Pig and Whistle tavern that spilled into the whole of Tavern Crawl after a handful of Roycroft kilners accused the Finwicks of forging some of their yearbook achievements to gain extra prestige points.

She had once asked her father why tensions always ran so high in the city when it came to the Premiership. Tharus explained that it wasn't simply a case of the houses defending their prestigious titles and keeping privileges but also because the provincials knew that should one of the ruling houses be overthrown, a far crueler family might replace it and make their impoverished lives even harder.

"Niera, lead them on," said Tharus.

"Yes, Father."

She turned to face the mouth of a narrow bridge that stretched over the west quarter of the lower city. On the other side, a pair of tall doors led into the cathedral, which was as ominous as it was high. Every inch bore crockets, foils, and pinnacles spanning intricate marble masonry, especially the central tower, which housed both the Conservatory and Maestro Dorian's residence.

Niera put bow to string once again and played the house melodies in succession while leading the families ahead. As they crossed the bridge, she couldn't help but look over the north side and catch a glimpse of the shimmering harbour, only to notice a brilliant beam of light flickering chaotically through the fog. Passing through the doors and slipping inside the cathedral, her eyes narrowed in disapproval as she realized the beam was coming from the lighthouse.

Chapter Two

THE LIGHTKEEPER

A pack of surfers rode their twin-fin boards along a cresting wave towards Dorladdich's shoreline. They cut back and forth across the lip, racing each other while passing over the sharp reef just inches below the water. The wave began to close, but the pack kept riding until the last possible second, breaking off just before it crashed against the lighthouse's rocky foundations.

Seaspray erupted and rose twenty metres into the air, splashing the barnacle-encrusted stonework and finally dashing the lamp room windows. Though the surfers used the lighthouse to spot waves in the early hours, it was purpose-built to be a beacon for the province's mighty corsair ships.

Every morning the Riornath, Arabrae, and Calhoun returned from their nightly expeditions with holds full of fish and crustaceans beyond count—the lighthouse guiding them through the treacherous fog as they made their way to the harbour. These three ships were all that remained of the province's once-great military fleet, now reduced to trolling for sea life to keep Dorladdich fed.

Navigating the rough waters of Shipwreck Strait was dangerous enough with the lighthouse in working order, but this morning, its failing beam was making manoeuvres even more perilous. Inside the lamp room, the powerful chronolamp was struggling to retain its vibrant glow—the chaotic flickering giving way to growing periods of darkness.

Thunk!

A large ceramic jug fell to the floor, causing the cork to pop out and leaking kerosene oil everywhere.

"By the Verse!" yelled Tiarnen.

He crouched down to pick the jug back up with one hand while trying to carry another jug in the other. Standing, he hurried over to the narrow oil tank stairs and ascended, knowing he had no time to lose. Sweat dampened his dishevelled dark brown hair and beaded across his rugged late-twenties face that was defined by hazel eyes, a sharp nose, and an unshaven jawline. Finally reaching the top of the tank, he hastily set the jugs down, opened the oil hatch, and began pouring in the first jug in hopes that the pump valves wouldn't run dry. If they did, the lamp would go out, and the corsairs would be blind trying to cross the strait. Refusing to be the cause of the fleet's demise, Tiarnen hoisted up the second jug and poured it into the tank as quickly as possible, the clear, viscous oil glugging out as the lamp grew dimmer still.

"Come on, come on, come on!" he said, furious at himself for letting this happen.

With the last drops falling into the tank, Tiarnen waited nervously for the lamp to grow brighter, but it began emitting a metallic grinding sound.

The valves are seizing, he thought.

Tiarnen scrambled over the lamp housing, pulled a heavy wrench from his back pocket, and used it to twist open a pressure-release seal as fast as he could so the oil could flood the lamp before it went cold. If it worked, he would have one hell of a repair job ahead of him, but that was a small price to pay considering the consequences. After lining up the wrench and shifting his entire body weight down onto it, the seal cracked open, and he could hear the pipe fill.

"That's it, any second now," he said, trying to reassure himself. "Aaaaany second now," he repeated, his confidence failing as he watched the last of the wick's embers begin to fade away. "This cannot be happening!" In a panic, he stomped on the wrench as hard as he could, forcing the release valve to open all the way.

SHUNK!

The oil flooded the wick and fuelled the last dying ember, igniting it into a blaze. A blinding flash filled the lamp room. After a few hard blinks, Tiarnen regained his sight and hurried over to the windows where he could make out the corsairs nearing the shoals through the weather-stained glass.

"By the Verse, I'm too late," he said, bracing himself to witness the worst.

But at the last second, the Calhoun turned to starboard, and the fleet followed as the lighthouse guided them safely toward the harbour. If any of the ships had sustained damage or their crews any injuries, it would have been entirely Tiarnen's fault. He sighed in relief—only for a sudden sharp whistling to call him downstairs. He grabbed both empty oil jugs, hurried to the central lighthouse staircase, descended the upper section, and entered the service room.

Shelves filled with all manner of mechanical surplus and supplies lined its curved walls. Spare wicks, oil jugs, piles of rags, and tools took up the left side of the room, while canned shellfish, pickled herring, and tea filled the shelves on the right. Tiarnen set the jugs down and wiped his slippery hands with a rag, then pulled a couple of tea bags from a jar as he continued down the stairs to his living room.

He skipped the last few stairs and ran straight to the kitchenette, where an old kettle was boiling over on a small wood-burning stove.

"All right, all right—simmer down now," he said, wincing from the intense whistling sound.

Tiarnen pulled the kettle from the burner, tossed both tea bags into a large clay mug, and poured the steaming water over them, then walked through the living room. Ducking under a hammock made from an old fishing net with a colourful patchwork blanket draped over top, he passed his clawfoot bathtub, two small piles of books, a dresser, and a coat rack with a weather-stained cloak hanging off it and then arrived at a small table with an old leather lounge chair in the middle.

Tiarnen took a seat and carefully sipped on the steaming tea while looking over the table's contents: a scroll tied with a green ribbon, a well-worn piccolo, a thick card catalogue, and a large upside-down armoured helmet that had a turtle hatchling climbing over the edge.

"Haela, why is it always you trying to make a run for it, eh?" said Tiarnen, setting the cup on the table and carefully picking Haela up. "Just a few more months, and everyone will be strong enough for rougher waters." He set the turtle down in the bottom of the helmet pond among his three brothers, the quartet living a life of luxury among the rocks, water, moss, and dead crickets that Tiarnen had collected for them.

"Let's see what's new in all things Shatter, shall we?" Tiarnen wiped his hand on his trousers and then picked up the scroll. With a quick tug, he pulled on the ribbon, and the scroll immediately unrolled itself, emitting a mechanical-sounding fanfare from the top handle. "Apparently quite a bit," he said, reading from the top:

<u>The Shatterday News!</u>

Septhembra 4th, 1581 ADA

Welcome to your weekly Shatter news, covering all the latest in Dorladdich's coveted card game!

"Blah-blah-blah," said Tiarnen, taking a sip of tea and turning the scroll handles to read on.

This week, we interviewed current champion Coniel Ashbrook, better known as "Swiftsail," who talked about his winning deck from last season and how it helped in the Grand Tournament. As Swiftsail put it, "I like to think it's not the deck that makes the player, but the player that makes the deck!"

"You tell them, Coniel," Tiarnen chuckled as he turned the scroll a bit more.

*As promised last week, here is a sneak preview of the upcoming expansion **Blood in the Water** that will (rumour has it) introduce over thirty new cards, including five exclusive legendaries—*

"Which everyone will try to buy within the first day, per usual," said Tiarnen, scrolling on.

With very little time left in the current season, Moonlight Marauders, please remember to finish as many yearbook achievements as you can in order to receive your exclusive rewards and discounts for next season!

Tiarnen glanced past the scroll to his yearbook on the table, which was still in the original packaging. "Will get right on that." He took another sip of tea. "Ladder, ladder, where is the..." he muttered, turning the scroll until nearly reaching the end. "Ah, here we go." He leaned in closer to read the names.

Current Tournament Ladder

Swiftsail
Dreadgill
Kraitbane
Moondrop
Fogfisher
Kelpkeeper
Hookbeard
Shellshock
Reefclaw
Tipsytrawler
Gangplank
Sharptooth
Razorfin
Seawolf
Hookmaster
TheReelDeal
Crog

The final round of placement matches for the Grand Tournament is this Sunday! And, as always, the top sixteen players will be permitted entry, but only the top three finishers will receive prizes.

First Place
10,000 prestige points

Second Place
16,000 gold

Third Place
Next season's expansion for free

Tickets for the Grand Tournament are already selling fast, so make sure to buy yours today, and don't forget to dress in support of your favourite challenger on Novembra 26th!

Tiarnen closed the scroll, pulled his card catalogue towards the edge of the table, and opened it. On the first page were eight rectangular Shatter cards with breathtaking artwork.

Shatter was the most popular card game throughout the provinces by far, and for good reason; it was specifically designed to make the player feel like a maestro. Tiarnen had no real interest in being a maestro. He just loved to compete—so much so, in fact, that it sometimes posed a serious distraction from his responsibilities as the province's resident lightkeeper. Feeling guilty, he paused for a moment, listening for any sign of the lamp experiencing further mechanical problems, but everything seemed to be fine.

To his knowledge, Shatter had been around as long as anyone could remember—no one really knew how or when the game had originated. Much of Chora's history had been lost to the Provincial War, which was likely why each province had its own cards and rules.

According to Dorladdian legend, sailors invented Shatter to help pass their long weeks at sea. The game was eventually banned on deck, mostly because matches often resulted in someone being thrown overboard, or worse, returning to harbour with more debt than when they had left. Nonetheless, Shatter spread throughout Dorladdich, and several expansions had been released by the Office of Games to increase its depth. According to *Executor Ignatius's Almanac (Fourth Edition),* there were now over 2,200 unique collectible Shatter cards in Dorladdich alone. Tiarnen couldn't begin to guess how many more there might be throughout the rest of the provinces. When a new expansion was released, card shops sent their maidens to strut around the city and convince players to spend piles of coin in hopes of acquiring a new legendary card, the rarest and most powerful type. The provincials, often unable to afford new packs, relied on trading their common cards to construct decks with which they hoped to compete. The only other way to acquire cards was through victory: should you win a match, you could choose one card from your opponent's deck and add it to your personal collection.

Tiarnen first inherited his collection from his grandmother, and over the years, he continued to add as many common cards as he could due to their potential synergy. In his eyes, it was synergy that made a good deck *great*. Individual legendary cards were very strong on their own, but when simpler common card effects were combined in the right way, their synergistic effects benefitted each other and produced an even greater result—much like notes forming a chord. The problem was, as a deck's synergy increased, it became more complex to play, so the odds of getting the right cards on the right turn became very low. Tiarnen believed the risk was worth it because nothing felt better to him than pulling off a big synergistic play. Most players disagreed. To them, victory was the most important thing, so they constructed decks that didn't depend on synergy, ensuring they could always make a play no matter which cards were in their hand.

Tiarnen, however, was trying to make his *entire* deck synergistic, an effort that took an incredible amount of focus and thought. He had spent the last two weeks trying to connect all of his cards, striving to find the highest potential synergy while considering every possible outcome. The effort required an incredible amount of consideration, but given that he was utterly alone in the lighthouse, there wasn't much else to keep him occupied.

Tiarnen gulped the last of his tea and continued flipping through the catalogue. Page after page passed by, his eyes glancing over the Song, Ally, Trinket, and Talent card types. Song cards were used to build exciting warsongs which had either an attack or defensive effect. Ally cards were people, creatures, or monsters with their own fantastical abilities. Trinket cards were objects imbued with resonant qualities. Finally, Talent cards gave the player powerful maestro abilities, but usually for just a single turn.

A Song card caught Tiarnen's eye. He paused on the page, pulled it from its holding corners, and read the title: *Culrich's*. These opening cards immortalized maestros and memorable orchestra members. Tiarnen set *Culrich's* beside the four coordinating Song cards, thus completing the class two warsong and its title: *Culrich's – Crippling – Yet Refreshing – Catastrophic – Cloudburst.* Of course, this was not a real warsong name, just a sensationalized version to help the player feel more impressive.

Tiarnen only needed one more card to complete the deck; it was a choice between an Ally or a Talent. He turned the catalogue's pages, carefully contemplating each card that passed until finally stopping to pull a Talent card called *Quick Wits*. The card would allow him to reduce the amount of time his opponent had to make a play by half. People often made mistakes under pressure—mistakes on which Tiarnen planned to capitalize. Most players thought Shatter was simply a battle of cards, but he always believed that it was really a duel of minds. And there was no better place to test his theory than at the upcoming Grand Tournament, an event of fortune and glory that took place every year.

Last year's champion, Lachlan Roycroft, won "without any real challenge," according to himself. But that wasn't saying much in Tiarnen's eyes, as Lachlan came from one of the wealthiest families in the province. His deck was stacked with rare legendaries, all acquired by "noble" practices, Tiarnen was sure. Tiarnen had qualified for the tournament twice before but was defeated in the first round both times. However, he hoped that this year would be different—if only to humble Lachlan a bit. All Tiarnen needed to do was win his final placement match, and he would secure a seat in the Grand Tournament.

"And the *Hopestealer* deck is complete," he said with a smirk.

Satisfied, Tiarnen collected his cards, shuffled them into an organized stack, and slid them into a protective oak deck box. He stretched to his feet and put the piccolo into his back pocket, then pulled the tattered cloak from the rack as he headed down the bottom section of the spiral staircase to leave the lighthouse.

Chapter Three

STEEP ODDS

Tiarnen hurried down Harm's Way, a long, narrow street that had become a haven for shady establishments. Among them was Whelan's Wonderments, notorious for trading in stolen wares of every kind; Sheridan and Sons, a smoke purveyor that sold all manner of cured leaf and contraband herbs; The Widow's Mark, a nefarious financier that loaned money to desperate provincials who could never afford the interest; and the Pickled Prawn, a pub that sold cheap ale and bathtub spirits that would likely leave you blind the next day. Behind them, countless alleys snaked and intersected, all of which had their names scratched out so that the city patrol had a much harder time finding those engaged in darker dealings.

Normally, Tiarnen tried to avoid travelling this route through the broken bottles and reek of urine, but Harm's Way offered the shortest journey from the lighthouse to Cathedral Square. Fortunately, he didn't have to dodge any beggars or watch for pickpockets, as the patrol had already rounded everyone up to make sure they paid their respects at the service.

Turning a corner, Tiarnen arrived at Ardglen Street, where he was met by a long line of provincials waiting to get into the square. At the tail end, three children were chasing each other around their parents. They looked as though they hadn't bathed in weeks, their clothes ill-fitting and threadbare.

"Settle down, you three!" said the mother, attempting to catch the youngest one so she could brush his tangled hair.

"How much longer until we see *Maestro Dorian*?" asked the middle girl.

"As long as it takes for us to pay tribute," said the father, buttoning his shirt collar with one hand while holding a small basket of soda bread with the other.

Provincials never had much to offer as a tribute for Maestro Dorian. They either carved tiny soapstone effigies, made candles, or brought some sort of homemade food, all in hopes of receiving a blessing and some relief from their life of misery. What they didn't know was that only a few select tributes actually made it into the Conservatory where Maestro Dorian resided; the rest were thrown away. No provincials were permitted inside the cathedral, so they gathered around the front doors to listen to their praetor's sermon or socialize in the square.

Tiarnen's foot tapped as he looked down the line-up, watching impatiently as the city patrol inspected the provincials and their tributes. He knew they were only making sure nothing of ill intent made it into the square, but the search had slowed the line to a crawl. He couldn't be late for the Shatter match, or he would be disqualified. Accepting that it was a worthy risk, Tiarnen broke off from the line and hurried along the thick wall surrounding the square until reaching a corner that met with one of the city ramparts. There was a narrow gap in the eroded stonework that he remembered led to the other side. Unfortunately, a bramble thicket had long since grown over it—Tiarnen had last used the gap as a child. Left without much choice, he pushed through, his clothes and skin scraping along the countless thorns. Then, with a final push and a few minor cuts, he emerged on the other side of the wall, where he saw the groundskeepers sitting around a wheelbarrow just below.

Barry and Edna Gibbings were on the left, eating a sliced apple with their dirt-covered fingers; Dale and Agnes Tillman were on the right, cleaning sap off their pruning shears while listening to Herald Buckley announce the morning news several metres away. Everyone in the city referred to the foursome as "the Mill" because their incessant gossiping often turned into widespread rumours. In the end, it didn't matter much since most of the provincials believed ignorance was a virtue when it came to any developments outside of their own border. In fact, the less they knew, the purer they believed themselves to be.

"Lastly!" announced Herald Buckley. He was clad in a heavy burlap robe that carried the Office of News sigil on the front and was reading from a parchment scroll long enough to touch the ground. "Both Lydvenko and Phrysbruck have abandoned their glacial strongholds along their border! Reason for the withdrawal has yet to be confirmed by Inquisitor Holgor. And with that, your morning news is concluded!" The herald rolled up the parchment scroll, placed it under his arm, and made his way out of the square.

The foursome immediately turned to each other and leaned in close.

"Glacier must have collapsed," suggested Barry, chomping down on the last slice of apple.

His wife nodded in agreement. "All of that battling was only a matter of time before it became unstable."

"Last I heard, a terrible monster took residence inside," said Dale, putting the cleaned shears in the chest pocket of his coveralls.

Agnes scoffed. "Nonsense! Nothing could live in so much cold and darkness."

"Except for us!" retorted Barry. "Damn mist doesn't want to lift an inch!"

"No argument there. Could barely see my own hand in front of me face this mornin'!" agreed Dale.

"Be thankful. Lydvenko would probably be on our shores by night-fall if it cleared," said Edna.

Dale waved a hand dismissively. "Bah! It's too early for your worrying."

"She's right, though. We've been lucky with the weather," said Agnes.

"But it is no shield." Barry wagged a finger at them. "Be sure of that."

WHAM!

Tiarnen landed on top of the wheelbarrow, startling the foursome. "Pardon me!" he said.

"*Where did he come from?*" yelped Dale.

Tiarnen hopped onto the lush grass and continued ahead. Surrounding the massive crowd standing before the cathedral, a convoy of food carts awaited. He could smell the cauldrons of oats, brown sugar, and cinnamon bubbling up from the Solemn Oat. As delicious as a bowl would be, what he really needed was another cup of tea before the match. For that, the Loyal Trustea would do nicely—not owing to quality but because they made the strongest brew by far.

"Ah, good Sunday! What can I get you?" asked the brewman, peering over the counter at Tiarnen while stroking his long moustache.

"A Loch'd and Load'd, with spiced cream and a splash of maple, thanks," said Tiarnen. "Oh, with three bags."

"*Three bags*! Someone have a late night?" asked the brewman, who started filling three small linen bags with black loose-leaf tea.

"More of a rough morning."

"Well, this should fix you up nicely." The brewman dangled the bags into a tall clay cup, filled it with steaming water from one of his kettles, and added some heavy cream as well as a splash of maple syrup. "That'll be five copper, please."

Tiarnen reached into his pants pocket, pulled out a few gold coins, and tossed one to the brewman.

"I'm sorry," began the brewman, "but I only have a few silver and a pocket's worth of copper in my till, I can't possibly make change for—"

"Don't worry about it," said Tiarnen, waving the apology off and then making his way into the sea of provincials.

Leaving the brewman wide-eyed and shouting his thanks, Tiarnen tried to fight through the current of jabbing elbows. He hoped to reach the other side of the square where the Shatter matches always took place but was swept up as everyone pushed toward the front of the cathedral so they could hear Tharus's sermon. Before he knew it, Tiarnen found himself exactly where he didn't want to be—standing before the cathedral steps.

Despite having looked upon the façade countless times before, it never ceased to amaze him: the wide flight of granite stairs leading up to the triple arched marble entrance, tall double doors in the middle with an intricate tympanum above framed by pillars, and stained-glass lancet windows depicting stormy skies on either side. By any measure, it was magnificent, but much like most of Dorladdich, it had seen far better days. The stonework, having weathered many storms, was badly stained, and even though the provincials' tributes were piled high on the cathedral's steps, no amount of food or flowers could hide how badly chipped they were. A touch of sadness hit Tiarnen. He couldn't help but wonder how much longer the cathedral would endure—or Dorladdich itself, for that matter.

"SHATTERED!" yelled multiple voices from a short distance away.

Tiarnen snapped out of his dreary thought, his head turning to follow the cheers that were coming from the south side of the square. Knowing he didn't have a second left to lose, he pushed through the crowd and finally spotted the game table where a hundred or so provincials were watching the end of a Shatter match. As he walked closer, he caught sight of the loser swiping his cards off the table in anger.

"He doesn't look very happy," said a soft female voice.

Tiarnen looked over his shoulder to see a card maiden following behind him. She wore a top hat and a tight leather outfit, her several pockets filled with new Shatter card packs wrapped in decorative foil. It was the signature uniform that made card maidens very easy to spot and, at the same time, very hard to refuse.

"No one expects to lose," retorted Tiarnen, taking a sip from his tea.

"Wouldn't have happened if he had better cards," said the maiden, circling him.

Tiarnen tried to look straight ahead. "It's not about what deck you have; it's how you play it."

"True, but why make it any harder than it has to be? Especially when the odds can so easily fall in your favour." She ran her fingernails along Tiarnen's jawline to the edge of his hood. "And speaking of making things easy, I just so happen to have the full *Drumrunner* deck that Swiftsail won last year's Grand Tournament with."

"Not sure I want to know how much that costs."

The maiden leaned in a bit closer. "Can you put a price on victory?"

"You are far too good at your job, you know that?" Tiarnen pulled her hand away before she could pull his hood back.

"Yet you still haven't bought a single card," she said, wrapping her arms around his neck to give him a better view of her packs.

"Rainmaker! Is *Rainmaker* here?" said Cleary, a wild-haired old man dressed in pinstriped officiating robes. He was looking around frantically through his thick spectacles in hopes that someone from the crowd would answer.

"Coming!" yelled Tiarnen.

"Ah! There you are!" said Cleary, spotting Tiarnen and gesturing for him to hurry over.

"Last chance," purred the maiden.

"As much as the offer is tempting," said Tiarnen, gently pulling her arms away. "Seems that neither of us can say no to a challenge."

Tiarnen approached Cleary, who looked him up and down as though he had just washed in with the tide.

"Lucky I saw you," said Cleary. "I was about to award the match to Crog."

Tiarnen looked over at the brute of a crustapien who was taking a seat at the table while talking strategy with two friends of the same species, all of whom wore only tattered, salt-crusted shorts held up by thick belts. Crustapiens were the only other sentient species on Dorladdich. They dwelled in the northern lagoons and were permitted to labour aboard the corsairs or in the kelp farms. It was rare to see one playing Shatter—let alone climb the competitive ladder as Crog apparently had. With each step closer, Crog seemed to grow larger to Tiarnen. Like most crustapiens, his smooth skin was a mottled pale green that contrasted against his deep-set bright yellow eyes. Along either side of his jaw were a pair of gills, and a short spiny fin ran down the centre of his otherwise bald head. If his physique wasn't intimidating enough, Crog's left arm was twice as big as his right and covered in a dark green exoskeleton shell—the ridges and barbs ending at his sharp-nailed fingers.

Tiarnen arrived at the table, pulled out the bench, and took a seat, keeping his hood low.

"Don't much like anyone who hides their face," said Crog, his voice gurgling.

"Why not?" asked Tiarnen, gently putting his deck box on the table.

"Means they're untrustworthy."

"Luckily for me, Shatter isn't a game of trust."

Crog's eyes narrowed. "Wouldn't be so sure."

"How's that?" asked Tiarnen.

"Because you can *trust* my mates here will crush you like a tadpole if you cheat." Crog hammered his left fist down on the table.

Though taking a blow from either of Crog's companions would probably leave Tiarnen unconscious until the next day, his aggression was a welcome surprise since Tiarnen always tried to get a sense of his opponent as quickly as possible. This usually didn't happen until midway through the match, but using an intimidation tactic before it had even begun was a clear sign that Crog was insecure about something.

Judging by how rough and cracked Crog's hands were, Tiarnen guessed he was a longshoreman. Working the corsair ropes to secure the ships all day had a harsh and very distinct effect on crustapien skin. Longshoremen, much like all crustapiens for that matter, were very poor, but winning the Grand Tournament would bring Crog a small fortune and certainly allow him to escape his life of back-breaking labour.

"Your attention, everyone! Your attention, please!" announced Cleary.

Some provincials in the crowd around them immediately turned to focus on the table, while others were still in the midst of receiving betting slips from the lingering bookers who made sure all wagers on Shatter matches were properly secured—for a small fee, of course.

"The Office of Games recognizes Crog versus Rainmaker as the last placement match for the six hundred and sixty-fourth Shatter season! The winner will advance to the Grand Tournament; the loser will leave with nothing."

"Except a load of shame!" someone yelled from the crowd.

"Let me remind everyone that there can be no heckling, coaching, distractions, or interruptions of any kind during play!" Cleary continued, then turned to Crog and Tiarnen. "Do you both accept the rules and agree to an honest match?"

Tiarnen and Crog nodded in mutual agreement.

"Then present your decks," said Cleary.

Handing them over, Tiarnen noticed that Crog's box was an exclusive and obscenely expensive edition. He was confused, seeing as this was something the crustapien seemed unlikely to be able to afford. *Perhaps he stole it?* thought Tiarnen, looking up to see the intensity in Crog's face. The expression told him that this wasn't a match that Crog wanted to win—it was one he *needed* to win. Fortunately for Tiarnen, that genuine desperation was something he might be able to use to his advantage.

Cleary pulled Crog's cards out, quickly counted to fifty, and shuffled them with practised skill. All Shatter cards had the same back, which carried a signature *S* to prevent giving away which expansion they belonged to. Tiarnen listened intensely to the shuffle—older cards had a softer sound when they slapped together, while new cards were much firmer and slapped harder. From what he could tell, there was an equal mix of both. Cleary returned Crog's deck to its place on the table and swiftly counted and shuffled Tiarnen's cards.

"Count and composition meet all match requirements," said Cleary, placing the decks side by side at the end of the table. He then pulled out two player sheets, each with a health score of fifty and the players' names above them. Lastly, he searched his pockets and found a copper coin. "Crog, on account of punctuality, you may call the toss." Cleary held the common coin up for everyone to see: one side was engraved with a corsair ship with large sails, the other side featured a profile of Praetor Tharus's head. Cleary flicked it high into the air with his thumb.

"Sails!" grunted Crog.

The coin landed in Cleary's hand. He quickly palmed it against the top of his other hand, paused for a moment to build up the anticipation, and then slowly pulled his hand away to reveal the result.

"Heads!" announced Cleary.

"Tones," whispered Tiarnen, relieved that his hood was hiding his disappointment. Had Crog gotten the first turn, Tiarnen might have been able to guess which deck he was using. Most competitors used proven deck compositions, many with their own names, as it gave them a better chance of success. The sooner he knew which deck Crog was using, the better his chance of successfully countering it.

"Rainmaker, the first turn is yours," said Cleary.

Tiarnen drew eight cards. Crog followed and drew nine, the extra card making a full hand and countering Tiarnen's first-turn advantage.

"Let the match begin!" Cleary set a small minute glass on the table and turned it over. The sand inside began to fall as the crowd applauded lightly.

Tiarnen carefully arranged all eight of his cards at even height and distance from each other so as not to give away any pairings. His eyes glanced over his hand. He had a variety of Song cards, as well as an Ally, Trinket, and a Talent. As great as it was to have variety, it would take quite a few more cards to make any significant plays.

Taking everything into consideration, Tiarnen played his *Kalder "Forty-Six" Foolsworth* Ally. Its faded artwork showed a man in ridiculous argyle tights and a ruffled shirt. He had one foot up on a rock while playing a large bagpipe, his face full of pride. Kalder was once a well-known minstrel who had travelled the island over a century ago performing comedic limericks. Unfortunately, his bagpipe exploded mid-performance one day and left him in forty-six pieces, hence the name. Due to his abrupt and tragic end, the provincials wanted Kalder's memory preserved and so petitioned the Office of Games to add him to the next expansion. As far as cards went, *Kalder* wasn't much of a threat since it only limited Crog to playing one card at a time, but Tiarnen hoped it would provoke Crog into responding with a couple of Ally cards of his own, thus offering some insight into his deck.

"Turn," said Cleary, turning the now empty minute glass over and gesturing to Crog, who sucked his gapped teeth and drew another card to begin his turn.

Tiarnen watched Crog shift his seating position. He was obviously unhappy with the draw and placed the card at the end of his hand as though it were an outcast.

"Pass," said Crog.

Passing on a turn wasn't uncommon, especially in the early stages of the game. Players would rather miss the opportunity to make a play than be forced into making a bad one.

Tiarnen drew a card, then had to decide if he would put more pressure on Crog or pass on his turn and keep building his hand towards a bigger, synergistic play.

No, I need to see what he's holding, he thought.

Tiarnen played *Caitria Finwick*. The artwork showed a young woman in a full reefsuit riding her surfboard along a wave toward the horizon. Caitria shaped the first surfboard, and she was credited for inventing the sport itself. Though her card was low in terms of attack value, it had a very helpful attribute that allowed all other Allies to attack on her first turn. That meant *Caitria* and *Kalder* could strike Crog at the same time and bring his health down a notch.

As he watched Cleary cross off several health points from his player sheet, Crog whispered a profanity or two under his breath, knowing that he was about to be hammered again if he didn't come up with something quickly. Crog drew an Ally card and immediately played it. *Munificent Maiden* hit the table. The artwork showed an alluring card maiden. It was a card found in most decks, as it allowed the player to draw three additional cards. After doing just that and shuffling the new cards into his hand, Crog played *Plague Prophet*, removing all opponent Allies on the table. He grinned wickedly as he watched Cleary pull *Caitria*, and *Kalder* from the table.

Tiarnen was back to square one. Keeping his composure, he drew a new card, considered his options carefully, and played his *Dance of Lances* Talent card. Lances were long glass shards that maestros could illuminate with their music. Though they were simple blades in form, they could cut down an opponent like a propeller through water. In Tiarnen's case, he used the ability to strike Crog and lower his health points even further in hopes of taunting him.

Crog drew another card and ran it back and forth over his hand, finally placing it in the middle. This was it. Tiarnen was sure he would try and make a play.

"Pass," said Crog.

Tiarnen would have moaned, but the crowd beat him to it. Even they were growing frustrated with the match—not that Crog cared in the least. Tiarnen couldn't figure it out. Either Crog was having the worst possible luck with his draws and his hand was terrible, or he was building up to something massive. Tiarnen had had enough; he hated the idea of falling into a trap. He drew a new card and played the legendary Ally *Major Raghnall*—a brawny man in ceramic plate armour with a shaved head and full greying beard, holding a massive broad shield. What made the card so unique was that the good Major was alive today. It was incredibly rare for someone still breathing to have an honourary Shatter card in circulation, but the major's renowned acts of heroism in battle, including once saving the praetor's life, couldn't go unrecognized. On the table, the *Major* shielded Tiarnen from direct attacks while striking Crog for a fair amount of damage.

Crog scowled as Cleary took fifteen points off his player sheet, which was followed by a few whistles from the crowd. Tiarnen knew Crog was a bit dense, but even an amateur player wouldn't leave the *Major* unchallenged. In a few turns, this card alone could win the game for Tiarnen.

Snarling, Crog drew a card and looked at it, his sour expression immediately turning into a full gap-toothed smile. Tiarnen had seen that look countless times before when players "top decked" and got the exact card they needed for a big play.

Crog wasted no time slamming down three cards that formed a single *Marauding Mech* Ally. Their combined artwork showed a mechanical monstrosity of gears, cogs, rods, and springs that linked together to form an ancient chronomech built purely for battle.

That's why he was holding onto his cards for so long, mused Tiarnen. At least now he finally knew what he was up against: Crog was playing a *Mechmaster* deck.

Crog struck the *Major* with the *Mech* and instantly destroyed him. To make matters worse, he followed up with a *Tiny Tinkerer*. Its artwork showed a *Quindorial* Ally; an adorable furry little creature, no larger than a dormouse, who was tinkering with a large clock. The card itself wasn't much of a direct threat to Tiarnen, but its attribute—*Double the tempo of your opponent's next warsong*—would pose a serious problem.

Tiarnen drew a Song card, and even though he wanted to keep building his hand, he had to protect himself from what was sure to be a beating from the chronomech. Only a warsong would do the trick, but it meant trying to complete it at twice the normal speed. He took a deep breath and rearranged his cards to form a class one defensive warsong called *Balim's – Courageous – Barricade*, which would shield him for ten points of damage. Tiarnen set the three cards on the table, and as they slapped against the wood, they came to life.

The crowd stepped forward, everyone pushing and shoving to get the best possible view. The elongated diamond in the centre of each Song card pulsed with light as though begging to be touched. This is what made Shatter so exciting to watch, not to mention difficult to play. The warsong provided a sequence of rhythmic cues that had to be tapped in accurate order by the player for its effect to activate. If played correctly, the cards would ignite with luminous colour and sound, thereby activating the warsong's attribute. However, if too many cues were missed, the warsong would fail and be removed from play. How the cards came to life was one of the best-kept secrets in the province. There were, of course, countless theories. The most popular one being that it had something to do with the paint since the Office of Games allegedly locked its card artists in separate rooms under strict observation in case one of them accidentally discovered the classified alchemy.

Tiarnen gently tapped the first card with his index finger; the diamond in the centre instantly flashed in hues of green, simple musical tones emitting with each pulse. Despite the double tempo, he repeated the sequence perfectly, which triggered the second card. He watched the sequence of cues flash and pulse rapidly, then matched them as best he could, missing one. Luckily, the small mistake wasn't enough to stop the third card from activating. The sequence flashed by in what felt like a blink of an eye. Tiarnen attempted to match it, but this time, he missed too many cues. Upon the last tap, the cards flashed once more, went dim, and then went silent. Tiarnen let out a sigh. Without *Balim's Barricade*, he would be completely defenceless from Crog's next round of attacks.

"Shame for the match to end so quickly," said Crog, drawing a card and bursting into guttural laughter. "Just ain't your day," he continued, combining the newly drawn card with two more from his deck to create another *Marauding Mech*.

The crowd whistled in collective disbelief.

To make matters worse, Crog followed up with a class one attack warsong of his own, *March of the Mechs*. If activated, it would double their attack and unleash a powerful assault on Tiarnen. Crog waited impatiently for the first card to finish its sequence before repeating, mashing his bulging thumb on the cards like a child. To Tiarnen's dismay, Crog managed to clumsily match the cues of the warsong well enough to enhance both mechs, doubling their attack power. With a grin, Crog used his first mech to strike Tiarnen, bringing his health points down by twenty. He began pounding his meaty fists down onto the table, humming a celebratory tune that was echoed by both of his mates, humming along and pounding their chests in rhythm.

"No distractions, I said!" reminded Cleary.

"It's fine. Was a good play," said Tiarnen, watching as several provincials tried to change their bets with the bookers, who predictably refused them.

Crog smiled. "Their faith in you seems to be failing."

"I'm used to it, believe me."

Tiarnen drew a new Ally card. Thankfully, it was *Mendful Matron*, whose attribute would heal him for a fair amount of health. He looked at the rest of his hand and saw that he was at a crossroads once again. He could either continue to counter Crog play by play, which didn't seem to be working, or he could go on the attack and set a new tempo for the match. Tiarnen rushed to think of every possible outcome as the sand drained from the minute glass. He knew the *Mechmaster* deck was designed to become more powerful later in the game, but if he could just build towards—

"Time," announced Cleary.

Tiarnen snapped out of his trance.

"I said *time!*" repeated Cleary, pointing to the last of the sand emptying.

Tiarnen rearranged five of his cards to form a class two defensive warsong called *Culrich's – Inspiring – Deluge – of Calamitous – Discard*. The crowd leaned in even further than last time. He smacked the cards onto the table, and just like before, they came to life, flashing with twice as many queues at twice the speed compared to the class one warsong from his previous attempt. Nonetheless, he executed the complex sequence with precision and activated the attribute: *Remove the top four cards from your opponent's deck*.

"You can't delay forever," grunted Crog, watching Cleary take the cards from his deck.

"Coming from someone who passed on his first three turns," said Tiarnen. He drew three more cards, placed them into his hand, and played *Mendful Matron*, restoring himself to full health.

Cleary reached to turn the minute glass over.

"Oh, I'm not finished," said Tiarnen, putting down three more cards and playing another class one warsong: *Finnian's – Fervent – Flash Flood*. He performed the sequence perfectly and activated its attribute: *Wash your enemies away*. Tiarnen watched Crog's face redden as Cleary swept both of Crog's mechs from the table. The crowd applauded the tricky play, but he knew he wouldn't stand a chance of surviving another assault from Crog's *Mechmaster* deck. What he needed now was a way to get under Crog's skin in hopes of causing a misplay or two. Then, in a flash of inspiration, Tiarnen pulled the piccolo from his back pocket and aligned his fingers on the keys. "That little melody of yours, how did it go again?" he asked, bringing the instrument to his lips and playing the crustapien's celebratory theme as loud as he possibly could.

Chapter Four
THE SERMON

Tharus surveyed the congregation from his position in the centre of the elevated altar. He stood at a polished stone pulpit, which was decorated with clockwork gearing. Behind him was a backdrop of thick granite columns, with more gears turning between them. He pointed his emerald-tipped conductor's wand past the orchestra pit below to the noble congregation seated in their pews just beyond.

Split into three rows, the earls sat in the very front pews with their youngest grandchildren on their laps, while the noble family members who were not in the orchestra pit sat ranked by age towards the back.

Niera was sitting comfortably on her reserved balcony with Holgor, Ignis, and two praetorian guards. Normally, she would be in the orchestra pit leading the members, but being that she was maestro for a day, tradition demanded that she watch her father's sermon. Though Niera's position gave her the best view of the ribbed vaulting, flying buttresses, and beautiful clerestory windows, her eyes were fixated on the vast dome ceiling high above.

"And as we all know," said Tharus, already well into his oration, "song itself forged the great realm of Chor—"

A flurry of piccolo notes suddenly echoed throughout the nave. Niera, along with everyone else, looked around in utter disbelief to see who was foolish enough to interrupt the sacred service... but the offender couldn't be seen anywhere.

"—The great realm of Chora," finished Tharus, pretending as though the disruption had never happened. "Drums, temporal and earthen, hammered at the hollow darkness and gave it shape!"

He tapped the wand three times on the podium. The emerald tip began to glow and signalled a barrage of snare hits from the percussion section of the orchestra.

"Fer Dorrrladdich!" cried Earl Finwick, startling from his slumber and standing to salute, only for his wife, Aifric, to yank him right back down.

Ignoring the earl's enthusiasm, Tharus whipped his wand toward the ceiling. All eyes followed it up toward the immense cathedral dome, which was covered in thousands of black ceramic tiles that made it look like a desolate night sky.

Niera smiled as the snares continued in rhythm, each beat appearing to turn a single tile to mud brown or rock grey, making it appear as though a vast continent of mountains, hills, and valleys had been unearthed. Though it was the same story every month, she never grew tired of hearing her father preach. In fact, after embarrassing herself in front of him earlier, it was now a welcome distraction. The nobles also seemed to always share Niera's excitement, though part of her couldn't help but suspect that many of them were embellishing their reactions to reaffirm their loyalty and win Tharus's favour.

"Woodwinds, frigid and flowing, stormed as oceans, lakes, and rivers!" proclaimed Tharus. With a flick and swish of the wand, he conducted the flutes, clarinets, and oboes to howl and bellow.

All the tiles around the primordial land turned ocean blue and then flooded inwards to form veins of rivers, a cluster of great lakes, and streams beyond count.

"Strings, vibrant and dancing, flourished the forests and life within them!" Tharus pointed his glowing wand toward the string section.

Violins, fiddles, and cellos vibrated and hummed. Along the bodies of water, green tiles appeared to grow forests and fields.

"But when the first musicians discovered tone, chord, melody, and song, the heart of Chora truly awoke!" he said, carving the air and pointing towards the congregation.

In a rising wave, the noble children rose and sang. Tharus staggered as though he were overwhelmed by their enchanting voices, gripping both sides of the podium to hold himself up, which only encouraged them to grow louder.

"For generations, they explored and practised the art of music!"

Sweeping across the dome, all the tiles turned to form a mosaic image of a tribal war band performing with primitive instruments of bone and wood.

"Over the ages, theory was mastered and technique perfected."

The tiles transitioned over and over to show the band evolving through several historical eras, finally stopping at a classical renaissance, each member of the band now wearing a tailored jacket and proudly holding artisan instruments.

"Until one day, they discovered their performance did not simply resonate but—" Tharus paused, pulling down one of a few small levers on the pulpit.

Clack!

"Illuminate!"

Together, the orchestra reached a crescendo as the polished clerestory window shutters turned, directing daylight onto the dome. All of the once-dull tiles above the war band glimmered with vibrant colours of every hue which reflected onto the congregation below. The blinding kaleidoscope caused everyone to wince and look away—except Niera, who raised her chin and basked in the glow.

"In that moment of discovery, our musicians became *maestros*. But in the reckless exploration of their new abilities, they left Chora on the brink of destruction!" Tharus slammed his fists against the podium, which caused the luminous tiles to shake, turning the alluring glimmer into a turbulent radiance that made the noble children cower in their parents' arms.

"In response, the praetors were elected and compositional law written to protect Chora."

The praetors materialized in the mosaic behind the maestros, the turbulence calming and separating to form individual crowns of green, orange, blue, magenta, yellow, red, and purple above them. With the transition, the erratic light in the cathedral settled, inviting the children to risk looking back up at the ceiling once again.

"With their maestros governed, the praetors travelled with them across Chora and together forged a new era of peace and prosperity!"

Several tiles flipped to form the silhouettes of great capital cities behind each maestro and praetor pair.

Tharus lowered his head. "But this new age was never meant to last. For the maestros' pride inevitably turned into jealousy and then spite."

The maestros' crowns grew bigger and eventually collided with each other, the edges cracking and splintering under the pressure.

"Left with little choice, the praetors had to separate the maestros, thereby dividing Chora into seven provinces, each with their own musical genre and culture," said Tharus.

The colliding crowns continued to meld and expand, eventually covering the entire dome to form a map of the seven provinces.

"For over fifteen hundred years, the provinces have fought tirelessly to claim—"

The flurry of piccolo notes interrupted Tharus once again. Just as before, he said nothing. His face remained emotionless, except this time, his gaze met Niera's eyes.

"—To claim Chora as their own," he finished.

Though the entire congregation was still looking around the cathedral, Niera was now certain of the source. Glowering, she stood to her feet and left the balcony with two praetorian guards in tow.

"A civil war that must soon be won, lest it leave our realm shattered forever!" proclaimed Tharus, ensuring they were the last words Niera heard as she marched into Cathedral Square.

Chapter Five

IN PURSUIT

Crog snarled after tasting his celebratory melody for the second time. To Tiarnen's delight, it was the exact reaction he was hoping for because it meant he was getting under the brute's skin. With any luck, he could survive long enough to play it a third time and infuriate Crog to such a degree that he might make a severe misplay and give Tiarnen an advantage. Unfortunately, Tiarnen's newfound confidence in his master plan was immediately shaken as Crog's mates cheered and patted him on the back after seeing the card he had just drawn.

"Rule thirty-one of the Statute of Play forbids touching the players!" warned Cleary.

Crog shrugged off the premature celebration, rearranged the new card into his hand, and played it with three more to build another mech called *Caladrin's Colossus*. Several provincials whistled in disbelief, knowing that the mech would bring Crog certain victory in the next few turns. That was unless Tiarnen found a way to destroy it.

Taking a deep breath, he calmly drew a card and saw that it was his *Sing Ring* Trinket. These rare rings were coveted by maestros because, when spun, they emitted an extremely high frequency that stunned anyone within earshot. In Shatter, its attribute caused an opponent to lose their turn. Tiarnen wasted no time and played it.

Crog immediately slammed his fist down on the table. "You cheap piece of—"

"Crog! Rule forty-two forbids insults during a match," Cleary scolded.

Crog's face contorted as he strained to stop himself from finishing the sentence.

Tiarnen quickly drew another card which completed a class two warsong waiting in his hand called *Wendell's – Enthralling – Whirlpool – of Dizzying – Bewilderment*. He expertly matched its tricky sequence of tones, which activated the warsong's attribute: *Pull an enemy Ally under the sea to a crushing depth*.

Cleary brushed *Caladrin's Colossus* from the table and into the discard pile. Tiarnen's supporters erupted in applause, their sweaty hands squeezing tightly around their betting slips. Then, looking Crog right in the eye, Tiarnen lifted his piccolo and played the melody yet again. With each note, Crog rose an inch higher to his feet, looking as though he was about to lunge across the table to strike him.

"Rule five forbids players from standing during the match," said Cleary.

"I would have won already if you didn't top deck that stupid *Sing Ring*!" yelled Crog. "Trinkets shouldn't even be in the game!"

"Feedback regarding game mechanics can be submitted to the Office of Games *after* the match," replied Cleary, flipping the minute glass over to start Crog's turn.

Seeing that his posturing wasn't getting him anywhere, Crog slowly sat back down and drew a card with a huff. Grunting in frustration, he placed it at the beginning of his hand and played a class two attack warsong called *Amber's – Scornful – Scream – of Availing – Dismemberment*. Once again, Crog mashed the cards gracelessly but somehow managed to activate the warsong and release its attribute: *Wound your opponent with bitter vengeance for ten points of direct damage*. Tiarnen watched Cleary scratch the health points from his player sheet.

"Let's see you come back from that," taunted Crog, mimicking Tiarnen's piccolo-playing as his mates erupted in exaggerated laughter.

A glint of gold caught Tiarnen's eye as Cleary pulled Crog's warsong cards off the table. With only a second to get a closer look, he noted that the faded *Amber's* card showed a slim porcelain-skinned woman with wavy amber hair holding a piccolo. She was obviously a maestro, but as far as Tiarnen could remember, he had never heard of one named Amber before.

With the flip of the minute glass, she vanished into the discard pile, and Tiarnen focused back on what was left of his deck. Only a few cards remained, so the chance of him drawing what he needed was good, but if his luck had run out, there would be no surviving another mech attack, which Crog was sure to play.

Well, if you're going to go down, might as well go down fighting, decided Tiarnen. He played three Ally cards together, each showing a musician holding a two-string lyre, which formed *Six Strings*. They were in no way a direct threat to Crog, but their attribute: *Two is company but three makes it loud,* would amplify any warsong that Tiarnen played next. Hopefully, Crog would see them as a desperate play and ignore it in favour of striking Tiarnen down to his last few health points.

"That's your play?" chortled Crog, his spittle landing on the table.

"Just working with what I have," said Tiarnen, adding a tone of despair.

Smiling again, Crog drew and played the card with two more to form the first half of *Tiberian's Titan*. The vibrant artwork showed the left side of a legendary Ally mech breaking through the middle of a mountain. *Tiberian's Titan* was well-known in the Shatter community because of its attribute: *Lay waste to all who stand in play*. As far as everyone could tell, Tiarnen was headed toward certain defeat. Some of the provincials who'd wagered heavily on him moaned and threw their betting slips to the ground, which Tiarnen used as motivation for an overly dramatic exhale.

"Was a good match," said Crog, satisfied with himself.

Tiarnen nodded. "Indeed."

"Rainmaker, are you forfeiting?" asked Cleary.

"I could, but the crowd deserves to see this last card played," said Tiarnen, drawing the final card as though it were pointless. Thankfully, it was anything but. Lowering his head to hide a smirk, he put the new card at the front of his hand and then casually placed seven cards on the table to reveal the class three defensive warsong *Marifreth's – Adoring – Mirror – of Captivating – yet Fractured – Iridescent – Reflection.*

"Well, would you look at that," said Tiarnen, feigning surprise.

The crowd collectively gasped and came as close to the table as ever. Class three warsongs were the most difficult to activate by far, so much so that many top players didn't even carry them in their deck because they didn't want to take the risk of misplaying them. Tiarnen blew into his hands to warm them and then tapped the first card with his finger. As it flashed to life, he found himself quickly overwhelmed by the complexity and speed of the cascading cues. Hands dancing across the cards, he put everything he had into performing the patterns and sequences as he made his way through all sixty-three rapid-fire flashes of light and sound. Sweat beaded along his brow as he finally reached the last cue and struck it. The cards bloomed together with emerald luminance only to suddenly go dark with a faint fizzling sound.

Crog and the crowd both burst out laughing.

"So much for showmanship!" said Crog, slamming his last three cards onto the table and completing a *Titan* Ally. In a final indecorous display, he pounded his chest and hummed Tiarnen's melody with not only his mates but all of the provincials who had bet on him.

"Congratulations—" began Cleary, genuinely surprised by the clutch victory.

"You hear that, boys?" bellowed Crog. "We're going to the Grand Tour—"

"—To Rainmaker!"

"*What?*" Crog's head spun around to stare at Tiarnen's cards and read the warsong attribute.

"*Reflect half of your opponent's attack back onto them,*" said Crog.

Tiarnen sighed. "If you insist."

"But it only says *half!*" Crog pointed at the words. "I'm still alive!"

"Unfortunately, Six Strings doubles the reflection power for a lethal blow," said Cleary.

Tiarnen watched with satisfaction as Crog's smile faded. There was nothing he could do; he either had to finish his play and destroy himself or concede. Either option would be a complete embarrassment. Realizing this, Crog just stared at Tiarnen until the sand ran out of the minute glass.

"Crog, you are—" began Cleary.

"SHATTERED!" finished Tiarnen's supporters, elated at the victory. Many of them fell to their knees to crawl across the grass in search of their previously tossed betting slips.

Tiarnen slowly raised his piccolo to his lips.

Crog glared. "If you even think of—"

Not bothering to let Crog finish his threat, Tiarnen played the first few melodic notes as loud as he could. Crog lunged across the table to break the piccolo in half, only for another hand to yank it away from Tiarnen. He immediately turned to chase after the brazen thief but instead saw Niera standing over him with the piccolo firmly in her grasp.

"I should have bloody known," she said, pulling back his hood.

The crowd gasped at the sight of Lord Tiarnen Straveritas. Crog quickly and quietly sat down, looking at both of his mates, who were already trying to vanish into the crowd unnoticed.

"Oh, hello, Twinkles," said Tiarnen. "Is the sermon over already?"

"Thanks to you, brother." Niera shook the piccolo at Tiarnen.

"There, you see!" said Crog. "His music was a distraction for me as well!"

"Performing during a match isn't against the rules," said Tiarnen. "Strictly speaking."

"Then I'll be sure to have them amended," said Niera.

"You may submit a request to the Office of Ga—" began Cleary, stopping after seeing the piercing look Niera was giving him.

Crog banged his fist on the table. "I want a rematch!"

"A rematch can only be sanctioned by the victor," said Cleary.

"Sorry, Crog. Think I'll have to pass on the offer," Tiarnen replied, organizing his discard pile and returning the deck to its case.

"Don't forget to claim your card, my Lord... err... Rainmaker." Cleary spread out Crog's entire deck across the table like spoils of war.

"*Rainmaker*?" asked Niera. "That wasn't your name last year."

Tiarnen sighed. "I have to change it every season."

"Because?"

"Because if I don't, my opponents will either throw the match as a courtesy or because they think Father will have them killed for winning."

"As they should," muttered Niera.

"Anyway, it doesn't matter now. I'm in the Grand Tournament," said Tiarnen, carefully looking at Crog's cards. His finger slowly passed over them—then he spotted her—the maestro warsong card that had grabbed his eye earlier. He plucked *Amber's* from the table and looked it over—it was in far worse shape than he first thought. The paint was badly faded, which made the woman's face barely discernible. The gilding around the edges, however, was strangely pristine and in a style Tiarnen had never seen before. Looking closer, he also noticed that the top right corner had tiny lettering.

"Brightest of The Seven," read Tiarnen, squinting at the unusual wording.

"What were you thinking?" asked Niera.

"I know the mech seems more valuable, but look at how old this one is—"

"No, you dolt, I meant interrupting the sermon like that!" hissed Niera.

"Figured the nobles would be grateful if the match could save them a bit of suffering."

Niera shook her head. "Unbelievable."

"Now, may I please have my piccolo back?" asked Tiarnen.

"Sorry, but it's confiscated," said Niera, very matter-of-factly.

"For how long?"

"Until Maestro Dorian decides you can be trusted with it again." She glanced at the praetorian guards, who seemed satisfied with the decision and so began making their way back to the cathedral.

"Well done, you," said Tiarnen. "Now, let's have that back." He held his hand out for her to return the piccolo.

"I was being serious! You need to learn the difference between bending some stupid Shatter rules and breaking provincial laws." She slid the piccolo into the inside pocket of her crop coat and turned to leave.

"Where are you going?"

"To the Conservatory, as I said," answered Niera, not bothering to look back.

"It will be a long walk for nothing," teased Tiarnen.

Niera stopped in her tracks. "Why is that?"

"Because Maestro Dorian doesn't receive uninvited guests."

"She will once she hears that it's me."

"Ignoring the fact that the Conservatory is practically soundproof," said Tiarnen.

"Then I'll solve the knock-lock and let myself in," Niera said confidently.

Tiarnen tilted his head skeptically. "Despite never having done it before."

Niera turned to face her brother again. Her lips pursed in frustration.

"I have an idea," said Tiarnen, hopping off the bench and sliding *Amber's* into his pocket. "Since we both want to speak with her, perhaps a friendly race is in order."

"What are your terms?"

"If I reach the Conservatory first, Reina isn't bothered with any mention of this morning's transgressions *and* I get my instrument back."

"And if *I* reach the Conservatory first?" asked Niera.

"Name your prize."

Niera squinted in consideration. "Stormcaller," she finally said.

"What about it?"

"I want to play it," said Niera, lifting her chin.

"You want to sit at *the* mythical wind organ?" asked Tiarnen, circling around Niera now. "Place those finely manicured fingers on ancient keys that were carved from the granite heart of our island? Release the renowned voice that is breathed by the winds blowing onto our shores at this very moment?"

Niera couldn't help but raise her eyebrows with excitement at the idea.

"Instrument for an instrument, eh?" asked Tiarnen. "Seems fair to me."

"Good. Oh, and speaking of *fairness*—no shoving like last time. I'm half your size."

"Less than half, lately," said Tiarnen, poking at her ribs.

"Which way are we taking?" asked Niera, slapping Tiarnen's hand away.

"Through the sanctuary, of course."

"But the prayer pools will be packed with nobles by now."

"Guess we'll have to be careful not to disturb them," said Tiarnen, flaring his cloak behind him. Niera unbuttoned her coat and stood beside her brother, both now facing toward the cathedral entrance.

"Ready?" asked Tiarnen.

"Go!" yelled Niera, shoving Tiarnen hard and sprinting ahead.

"Piece of work, that one," muttered Tiarnen, regaining his balance and giving chase.

Looking on, he watched Niera vanish into the departing crowd—her smaller size making it easier to slip between the sea of bodies. Tiarnen, on the other hand, was once again caught up in the current and, despite his best efforts, took much longer to reach the cathedral steps.

Upon entering the sanctuary, his eyes took a moment to adjust to the darkness but eventually brought the long corridor into focus. Along the smooth limestone floor were three oval prayer pools with raised edges inscribed with a series of prayers. A noble family stood around each pool, softly whispering their morning prayers, as bioluminescent water droplets fell from holes in the ceiling. The rhythmic rainfall splattered inside one of many giant clam shells that were clustered together at the centre of each pool, causing a flash of light that shimmered up the walls and gave a percussive *thwamp!* Normally, everyone would be focused on their devotions to praetor and province, but Tiarnen could see that the Ashbrooks were taken aback by Niera, who was already running on top and halfway down the edge of their pool.

"Coming through!" bellowed Tiarnen, bounding past Kaleigh and Coniel and into the pool—splashing everyone who was standing near the edge as he blurred past.

"Tiarnen!" chided Earl Ashbrook, wiping the glowing water from her cheek.

"Sorry!" shouted Tiarnen. "Consider it a blessing!"

To his frustration, he saw Niera reach the other side of the pool, leap off the edge, dash between the Ashbrooks, and then immediately push her way through the Finwicks so she could hop up and continue running along their pool.

Tiarnen and Niera had settled more than a few arguments over the years with a friendly race. What had been coined as "Straveritas Marathons" started as small childhood chases through the manor and then grew into pursuits through the city, which often left behind a trail of destruction. This time, however, was without question the furthest Tiarnen had ever fallen behind. Niera was growing noticeably taller, and with the height apparently came a good bit of additional speed. If Tiarnen didn't find a way to make up for his sabotaged start, he might very well have to incur the wrath of Maestro Dorian. With a jolt of panic, he leaped over the edge of the Finwick pool as half of the family cheered him on while the others used words unfit for a sanctuary.

Hearing the commotion, the Roycrofts had figured out what was happening and cleared a path for Niera, who did not hesitate to seize the advantage and once again run along the edge of the pool. As Tiarnen approached, Lachlan made a weak effort to stand in his way but then quickly retreated when he realized Tiarnen wasn't about to slow down. There was no cheering or chiding from the Roycrofts while he bolted down the pool, only judgemental stares, to which he responded with flat-footed running that resulted in a lot more splashing.

With the pools and nobles finally behind him, Tiarnen watched Niera reach the end of the sanctuary and barrel around a newel post to quickly ascend the east staircase. Here, Tiarnen knew he had a chance to regain some ground. He had been climbing the steep lighthouse stairs for well over a decade. Taking two at a time, he bounded up the west staircase and finally arrived at the top, just as Niera did.

"Surprised the patrol... wasn't watching... the stairs," wheezed Tiarnen, his left hand pressed against his cramping side.

"Why bother... no one... is dumb enough... to actually use them," gasped Niera, leaning against one of the newel posts.

Tiarnen laughed. "Except for us." He took his eyes off Niera to wipe the sweat from his forehead, which she saw as an opportunity to dash into the narrow drip room just ahead of them.

Tiarnen chased her inside. A long, murky water tank filled with glowing algae ran overhead and down the length of the room. Countless spouts protruded from the tank, releasing gelatinous droplets that descended through holes in the floor. Niera ducked and dodged the luminous deluge as she sprinted to the far side of the room towards a passage that led to a pillared hallway. Losing ground yet again, Tiarnen didn't waste any effort to avoid getting wet, considering he was half-soaked already, and once he was on her heels again, he could tell that she was looking for a way to slow him down or stop him altogether. To his shock, he saw her reach for the thick chain dangling from the end of the tank.

"Don't even think about it!" he yelled.

But Niera grasped the chain and pulled down hard, leaping through the passage.

FLOOSH!

The drain plug popped out of the tank and released a waterfall of liquid light which instantly cut off Tiarnen's pursuit. He could only watch while the room flooded and screams erupted from below as the water poured down into the prayer pools and drenched everyone standing around them.

"Going to hear about that later!" shouted Tiarnen.

"One of us will!" replied Niera from the other side of the waterfall.

"By the Verse," muttered Tiarnen, seeing that there was no way to get around it. He paced back and forth in the rising water while considering his options: doubling back so he could take the standard route to the Conservatory was too far a distance to cover, and waiting around for the tank to empty would take too long. Tiarnen's pacing slowed, and his shoulders slumped as he began to accept defeat. Then, as he was about to turn away, the chain swung back through the waterfall.

"Probably a bad idea, Tiarnen," he said, grasping the chain. Taking several steps back, he gave himself half a second to reconsider... and then sprinted towards the waterfall.

SPLOSH!

Tiarnen burst through the other side—releasing the chain mid-swing—and landed right on top of Niera. They both crashed to the ground in a heap.

"How in the—" grunted Niera, struggling to free herself from under his weight. "I thought you turned back."

"On you? Never," said Tiarnen, grabbing onto her coat to pull himself closer so he could shake his soaking wet hair in her face.

"Stop!" Niera wailed, trying to fight him off. "I'll scream!"

"Shhh!" Tiarnen lifted his head. "I think I hear the patrol." He paused for a moment, looking down the empty hallway, but saw only the Conservatory door at the end.

"Not falling for it!" said Niera, shoving him off. Free of Tiarnen's weight, she scrambled back to her feet, rushed down the hall, and finally reached the Conservatory door. "Stormcaller is mine!" She turned to gloat but froze mid-spin as she caught sight of Captain Dansby approaching.

He was a handsome, clean-cut man in his late twenties with short sandy-blond hair who was wearing a fitted green leather tunic with polished ceramic spaulders and carrying a heater shield in hand. Two additional patrolmen, both dressed in similar but less illustrious uniforms, followed close behind.

"Afternoon, Captain," said Niera, trying to hide her irritation as they reached her.

"Afternoon, Niera." Dansby narrowed his eyes. "You wouldn't, by chance, happen to know anything about the sanctuary flooding just now?"

"*Flooding*? No idea what you're talking about, but it sounds like there might be a leak somewhere," said Niera, tucking a curl behind her ear.

"Mhmm." Dansby looked past her to the waterfall still pouring in the drip room. "And I don't suppose you've seen your brother anywhere?"

"He's skulking about, I'm sure. Funny that you should mention him, though," Niera raised her hand to knock on the Conservatory door, "because I just so happen to be on my way to report him for interrupting the sermon this morning."

"And I'm sure that our maestro will want to hear all about it when *she* decides to make herself available," said Dansby, standing in between Niera and the door.

"Funny, I didn't know that the Day Striders patrolled the Conservatory."

"I pass through from time to time."

Niera raised an eyebrow. "*Mhmm.*"

"Come on. Praetor Tharus is no doubt already inquiring as to your whereabouts." He gestured for her to start walking.

"Wait, you don't understand," pleaded Niera. "I really do need to—"

"Be reminded that the Conservatory is strictly off limits?" finished Dansby, his tone becoming more formal.

"Even for Orchestra Leads?" asked Niera, hoping that a reminder of her prestigious rank would sway the captain.

"*Especially* for Orchestra Leads, since they know better than *anyone else who might be within earshot of this conversation!*" Dansby glanced past Niera for any sign of Tiarnen.

Fuming at the fact that the captain was right, Niera pursed her lips and began following him down the adjacent hall, but not before catching a glimpse of Tiarnen, who was hiding behind one of the pillars. Refusing to accept total defeat, she reached inside her coat to remind her brother that she still possessed his piccolo—only to find the pocket now empty.

Tiarnen gave her a quick wink while tapping the piccolo to his temple, relishing the look of shock on her face as she vanished out of sight. He couldn't help but laugh to himself as he returned the instrument to his back pocket. Lifting it from Niera while she was distracted by a face full of his wet hair was easy enough, though he hadn't been sure if she would notice it was missing before they reached the Conservatory. Thankfully, the captain's arrival ensured that she remained unaware. It also brought him the unexpected opportunity to now speak with Maestro Dorian alone.

He remained behind the pillar until the sound of footsteps vanished and then cautiously approached the Conservatory door. Embedded deep within channels along its dull stone surface were interlinked gears, cogs, and rods, which converged to form the knock-lock on the right-hand side. The mechanism had an inset doorknob that could only be released with Tharus's key to the city or by solving a rhythmic challenge. Since Tiarnen was without his father's all-access pass, he rapped his knuckles three times on the pewter plate just above the doorknob. This triggered the gears and internal tumblers to turn and respond with a short rhythm of their own: *Knock-knock... knock-knock... knock-knock.*

"Three doubles, easy enough," said Tiarnen, confidently matching the same beats and tempo.

Below the knocking plate, a doorknob emerged a quarter of the way out of its hole.

He knocked three times again, and the gears and tumblers responded with another rhythm: *Knock-knock-knock... knock-knock-knock-knock... knock... knock-knock.*

"Triple, quad, single, and a double," said Tiarnen, matching the knocks and then watching as the doorknob emerged halfway out of the hole. Encouraged, he knocked another three times, to which the lock responded: *Knock... knock-knock-knock... knock... knock-knock-knock... knock-knock... knock-knock-knock.*

"Single, triple, single, triple, double, triple."

Once again, he matched the knocks, and the knob emerged three-quarters of the way.

Knowing the last response would be the most challenging, Tiarnen rubbed his hands together, took a deep breath, and knocked: *Knock-knock... knock-knock... knock-knock... knock-knock-knock... knock-knock-knock-knock... knock... knock-knock... knock... knock-knock-knock... knock... knock-knock-knock... knock-knock... knock-knock-knock.*

"*What?* No! How is anyone supposed to possibly—" blurted Tiarnen, who, out of sheer panic, stopped talking and started knocking in reply. Before he had time to think, the challenge was already over. Breathing rapidly, he took a step back and waited in anticipation... but nothing seemed to be happening, the door merely remained still and silent.

"Yeah, figured as much," said Tiarnen with a deflated exhale.

CLACK!

To his surprise, the knob extended, and the door unlocked.

Chapter Six

THE CONSERVATORY

Tiarnen crept into the Conservatory and carefully closed the door behind him.

CLACK-CLACK!

Unfortunately, the knock-lock reset so loudly it might as well have announced his arrival.

"By the Verse," muttered Tiarnen. He stood motionless, heart pounding, waiting for some elaborate defences to attack or for Maestro Dorian herself to arrive and throw him out. But the only other sign of life was an old broom just up ahead that was sweeping the polished floor of its own accord. He let out a sigh of relief, only to be bumped by another broom.

"Oh, I'm sorry. Am I in your way?" he whispered, stepping to the side.

The broom paused for a moment as though annoyed with him and then carried on.

Relieved that he wasn't about to be swept away just yet, Tiarnen looked down the massive oval hall, which was empty aside from a long banquet table in the centre. Several doors led off from either side, and a flight of stairs in the far back travelled up to the second-floor loft where there was a colossal pipe organ draped in shadow, as well as fifty-eight stained-glass maestro portraits in the wall high above it.

Stepping forward lightly, Tiarnen looked to his left and peered into the nursery where he could see row upon row of potted plants, vegetables, fruits, and herbs of every type basking in the daylight while luna moths fluttered between the rays. On his right, he saw the apothecary, which had numerous shelves filled with all kinds of exotic ingredients flanking a large c-shaped brewing station with three burners, mounted boilers, and drippers for concocting complex potions and tonics. Continuing ahead to the next two rooms, Tiarnen passed by the lounge on his left, which was furnished with plush couches, a card table, books shelves, oil paintings of Dorladdian scenery, and a beautiful chandelier. On his right, he peered into the galley, which contained a small stove built into the wall with pans and cooking utensils hanging above the inset shelves that were stocked with cured, canned, and jarred goods.

By Tiarnen's guess, a maestro could survive off the stores for at least half a year. Pressing on, he looked to his left again and peered into the observatory, which featured a large and small telescope, several astrolabes, a tea station, and a wide drafting table with dusty star charts clamped to it. Tiarnen was about to look into the stationary on his right, only to notice that the door was badly burned and hanging from one hinge. There was no light inside the room, only shadow, so he approached the long table.

By his count, it could have sat at least twenty people, but that would have meant moving the stacks of books, scattered parchment, sheet music, and dried inkwells. Walking past, he surveyed the mess for any sign of the Maestro Diary.

The diary had been passed down from maestro to maestro for generations, each page containing personal entries that described everything from musical discoveries, instrument techniques, combat strategies, and tonic recipes. Tiarnen was searching for it because he knew that his grandmother, Maestro Dorian LVII, had a keen interest in Shatter and spent most of her free time piecing its lost history back together.

If anything could provide insight into his new mystery card, it was the diary. Unfortunately, he couldn't see it anywhere on the table. There was, however, a large bowl at the end, which was emanating a strange smell. Tiarnen peered over it to see a half-eaten meal of boiled eel hearts and raw reef worms.

"Disgusting," he muttered.

Tiarnen touched the side of the bowl. It was still warm, which meant that Maestro Dorian was likely around somewhere, so he carried on toward the end of the hall, passing by a monolithic stone henge circle standing in the middle of the split staircase. Despite its crude circular design, each henge pillar had an elegant musical rune carved into it. There were countless theories about why the henge was built, but Tiarnen's personal favourite was that it was one of many scattered throughout Chora, which the early maestros once used to travel great distances. As he slowly trudged up the left staircase, his legs still burning from the chase, Stormcaller came into view.

The ancient wind organ seemed to be more sculpture than instrument due to the fact that its entire body was hand-carved from the island bedrock. Surrounding the black and white keys of the Great and Swell manuals, every inch of the curving console was covered in levers, dials, and clusters of round knobs. Tiarnen looked up at the various reed and flue pipes. There were thousands, all of them vanishing up into the vaulted ceiling. Just above the manuals sat a music rack, crowded with several notebooks and disorganized stacks of sheet music. Hopeful that the Maestro Diary might be buried somewhere, he pulled the bench out from underneath the console and took a seat. His optimism, however, quickly faded after briefly rummaging through the pile. The diary wasn't there.

"Suppose you can't expect her to just leave it lying around," Tiarnen said to himself. Accepting that he had no choice but to speak to Maestro

Dorian about the diary, Tiarnen pressed the middle key on the lower manual to try and rouse her, but only a frail C major wheezed out.

"Please tell me we can do better than that," said Tiarnen, a hint of disappointment in his voice. He blew the dust off the keys and aligned both hands on top. Knowing now that if C major was one of the white keys, the rest were also naturals, and the black keys were sharps or flats. It also meant that the keys to the right of C major went higher up the scale while those to the left went lower. Given that he understood the layout now, Tiarnen made an educated guess at playing a C major chord and pressed down hard on three keys. He braced himself to be blown off the bench by the fabled power of the mighty wind organ, only for another strangled whimper to issue from it.

Tiarnen leaned back, a baffled look on his face. "Maybe it's my hand—"

"It's not your hand placement," interrupted a voice, echoing out of nowhere.

"Ahhh!" Tiarnen startled, then quickly looked over his left shoulder to see Maestro Dorian tucked away in a clover-covered alcove at the far side of the loft.

She was in her mid-twenties, had pixie-cut dirty-blonde hair with clover-green streaks along the temples, and was sitting in a large velvet wingback chair with a leather-bound book open on her lap.

"By the Verse, Reina," panted Tiarnen, putting a hand on his pounding chest. "You just took a year away from me!"

"A small price to pay for entering without an invitation," said Reina, drawing a puff of smoke from the long pipe in her hand.

"What is the going punishment for trespassing these days?" asked Tiarnen.

"Loss of both hands." Reina stood to her feet, revealing her thick wool robe, and put the book in her side pocket before walking towards him.

"Seems appropriate," said Tiarnen, unconsciously crossing his arms.

"Not to mention an effective deterrent against unwanted visitors."

Tiarnen smirked. "Until now."

"Which is why it will be changed shortly after you see yourself out." Reina punched him in the shoulder, only to recoil in confusion. "Why are you *soaking* wet?"

"Long story."

"One that involves our little sister, no doubt," said Reina, exhaling a puff of smoke. "You need to stop encouraging her."

"Don't blame me."

"Why not? You're the oldest."

"Ah, but you're the *role model*, remember?" said Tiarnen.

"I wouldn't be so sure," said Reina. "It seems that admiration is fast becoming a competition with her these days."

"Runs in the family."

Reina nodded in agreement. "That it does."

"So what's wrong with this thing, anyway?" asked Tiarnen, trying to change the topic.

"Outside of being desperately out of tune and a little bit dusty, nothing serious."

"I would think you might have taken better care of it," Tiarnen paused, "considering—"

"*Considering* I was the one forced to sit here while mother hammered posture and technique into me every day?"

"Most would call that a privileged education."

"I called it *torture*."

"Flourishing lessons were the worst," groaned Tiarnen.

"Especially when *someone* was pretending to lop my head off with his imaginary shards most of the time." Reina elbowed her brother in the ribs.

"Practice makes perfect."

"How many imaginary duels do you think we had in here over the years?"

"Far too many to count." Tiarnen smiled wide and gazed wistfully over his shoulder at the main hall. "Still not enough for me to manage a win against you, though."

"Something tells me I should have lost more than a few times."

"Maybe once or twice."

"Considering nothing except Stormcaller can be heard from the Conservatory, it's no wonder Mom kept us in here most of the time."

"Yeah, well, she and I always knew that you would be the one inheriting all of this." He gestured to the Conservatory as though it was a prize Reina had just won.

"To be honest, I haven't spent a minute at these keys since she passed," said Reina, looking up at the portraits.

"Maybe it's time we changed that," suggested Tiarnen, scratching at the dust on a key.

"Maybe you shouldn't be touching things that don't belong to you." She slapped his hand away.

"Why? Afraid you might be outplayed, Maestro?"

"Please don't address me formally when we're alone."

"I could have gone with *Maestro Dorian the Fifty-Ninth*," Tiarnen said in his most over-the-top formal voice.

"Did you really break in here just to patronize me?"

"No, I'm sorry. I just need a quick look at the Maestro Diary."

"The diary?" asked Reina. "For what reason?"

Tiarnen pulled the Shatter card from his pocket to show her.

"Go back to the lighthouse," she said, turning to leave.

"Reina, wait! This is important!"

"Then we should discuss your priorities."

"I'm serious. Here, look!" pleaded Tiarnen, holding it out for her to see.

She glanced back to see both the card and Tiarnen's look of desperation.

"I've never come across a card with gilding along the edges like this! And have you ever heard of a maestro by the name of Amber before?"

"No," admitted Reina, "but given how ancient Shatter is, I'm sure there are countless cards that no one has ever heard of."

"Which is why I want to see if there is any mention of this one in the diary."

Reina's right hand unconsciously went to her robe pocket, drawing Tiarnen's attention. Taking a closer look, he could see the diary's badly burned edges.

"*Is that it?*" he asked, standing to his feet.

Reina's eyes narrowed. "Sit. Back. Down."

Tiarnen reluctantly sat back on the bench.

"You do realize that if you spent half as much time on music theory as you did cards, you would have been Orchestra Lead a long time ago," said Reina.

"There's nothing wrong with being First Wind," muttered Tiarnen.

Reina stared at him.

"Besides, Shatter helps me with my theory," he added.

"Is that so?" chuckled Reina. "Then you should have no problem proving to me that you're worthy of the diary." She sat to the right of Tiarnen and grabbed a handful of sheet music from the rack. One by one, she checked each page, placed any that were out of sequence back in order, and then returned the organized stack to the rack.

"Now, let's see if we can breathe some life back into the old man here," said Reina, pushing her feet down on a bar just above the pedals.

SHUNK!

All the clustered knobs retracted, becoming flush with the console.

"Grab the second lever on your left," she said.

Tiarnen reached to the far side of the organ and held the lever as Reina grabbed the matching one on her right.

"Three... two... pull!"

They both yanked down on the levers.

Clink-clink-clink!

Stormcaller's internal gearing sprung to life, and once again, Tiarnen grew excited for its awakening... but all that followed was what sounded like snoring.

"Someone doesn't want to wake up," said Tiarnen.

"He'll come around," said Reina, pulling another long puff of smoke from her pipe.

To his surprise, Tiarnen felt a rumbling—as though Stormcaller really was waking from a centuries-long slumber. With a last snort, the organ began taking deep breaths and a salty draft filled the Conservatory.

"All we need to do now is pull a few stops," said Reina.

"Which ones?" asked Tiarnen, eagerly looking over all the polished stop knobs on his side of the console.

"Let's see... How about tierce and tremulant for the Swell, as well as diapason for the pedals." She nodded to the cluster on Tiarnen's side again.

"Can I ask you something?" he asked, pulling the labelled stops.

"Do I have a choice?" Reina replied, pulling the Gemshorn and Prestant stops from the Great cluster on her own side.

"Why do you hate the title so much?"

"Look at those portraits. What do you see?"

Tiarnen looked up to the stained-glass windows inset along the brickwork above the organ, his eyes focusing on the highest one: a portrait of a man in his early twenties with high cheekbones and a full head of slicked-back fir-green hair. He was surrounded by dried fir branches and wearing an opulent maestro jacket with a high collar and two small pins on the left breast. One was the Dorladdich crest, and the other the numeral *I*. At the bottom of the portrait, a banner read: *Maestro Dorian I.*

"I see all of the maestros who came before you," said Tiarnen, gazing over the rest of the portraits.

Though each Maestro Dorian was unique in appearance, all wore similar maestro jackets—their war medals increasing in number as the banner number grew higher—and all were holding an artisan clarinet. His eyes finally fell onto the portrait at the bottom, *Dorian LVIII*. His mother, Marifreth, looked exactly as Tiarnen remembered her: long dark hair fading to sage green at the ends, a deep scar running along the right side of her cheek, and an inquisitive look in her brown eyes as she sat casually, surrounded by dried sage.

"Do not think for a moment that I need to be reminded of my inevitable place in history," said Reina.

"Yours will be different." Tiarnen looked away from Marifreth's scar to see Reina pointing at the area of brickwork that would one day be cut away for her portrait.

"Forgive me if I find it hard to believe that I'll somehow pass wondrously onto the shores beyond due to old age," said Reina, aligning her fingers on the keys again.

Before Tiarnen realized that she had started playing, Stormcaller was already bellowing. Never before had he heard, not to mention felt reverberating in his bones, such a rich and compelling sound. The power was, in a word, impressive.

"That's more like it!" Reina smiled. She pulled her hands off the keys, folded them on her lap, then nodded for him to read the title page of their sheet music.

"Oh, umm…" he stammered, pulling himself together. "'Quermorae in D Major.'"

"It's one of my favourite sonatas."

"Mum's too."

A sombre smile pulled at Reina's lips. "Now, tell me, what is the emotional difference between a major and minor key?"

Tiarnen slumped at the elementary question. If memory served, the last time he'd had to answer it was around eight years old.

"Posture," she said, pulling the diary out of her pocket and setting it on the bench beside her.

"Major keys tend to sound happy and uplifting, while minor keys sound sad and foreboding."

"Much like your personal life," jabbed Reina. She turned the title page to reveal the opening bar, which was comprised of three staffs: a treble, bass, and pedal. "Since you clearly found middle C already, I won't be going over the keys. I will, however, play the first movement, so I suggest watching my hand placement because you will be playing the second movement in its entirety."

"What about the third and fourth movements?" asked Tiarnen.

"We will perform them together, should you make it that far. Any questions?"

"How many chances do I get?"

Reina raised an eyebrow. "Fewer than you are hoping for."

"You do realize this is my first time?" asked Tiarnen.

"And very likely your last," remarked Reina, aligning her hands on the Great manual.

The opening bar of "Quermorae" was fast, bright, and formed a small tonic motif—like a tiny acorn exploding into life. Shortly after, a contrasting dominant motif of slow descending chords made Storm-caller gust with a frigid wind that rustled Tiarnen's damp hair and made him shiver.

Though it was hard not to be swept up by the exposition, he kept focus on Reina's hands and feet as they moved over the manual and pedals at speed, breaking the cobwebs in between and leaving finger and footprints in the thick dust. Watching his sister perform with practised grace reminded him that reading the sheet music wasn't going to be the real challenge—it was playing the right keys to ensure his performance met her high expectations.

Prestant phrases of triplets began the development and caused the air to warm. The acorn grew as the tempo accelerated and thawed the chilling minstrel into a gentle Gemshorn breeze. Then, Reina played several motifs of trills before finally decorating them with prevernal embellishments.

Arpeggios fluttered like hummingbirds, and Tiarnen swore they brought with them the sweet scent of pollen. He then heard the first movement recapitulated, but this time, the harmony was much higher, which helped the melody grow into a full equinoctial seedling and reach the top of the scale.

"Ready?" asked Reina.

The question startled Tiarnen, and he realized just how swept up he had become in the music. "Think so," he said, focusing back on the keys and placing his hands over the Swell manual as Reina turned the page to reveal the second movement. To his relief, the triadic downpour slowed to a soft drizzle of arpeggios, but Tiarnen found himself in trouble before he finished the first line. It had been such a long time since he had any instrument other than a piccolo in his hands that he had forgotten how hard it was to play without years of muscle memory guiding his fingers. Out of the corner of his eye, he could see Reina wincing as he kept accidentally pressing the keys together or missing them entirely.

"Stop, stop, stop," she said, laughing under her breath.

Tiarnen sighed, took his hands off the keys, and placed them on his lap. "Forgot how frustrating it is to play something new. It's like learning to walk again."

"And you keep tripping because you're trying to look in two places at once," said Reina. "Focus on the notation. Your hands will find their way to the keys."

Tiarnen nodded in agreement, straightened up, and attempted the second movement again.

Though he still had difficulty, Tiarnen managed to crawl through the first page, which Reina courteously turned. The next twelve bars were a sequence of harmonic chords that became more and more expansive until they parted with long rests. In between, the seedling melody grew and sprouted its first motif like a bright leaf. Then, the harmony began to rise and became hotter, with ascending fragments that made the entire conservatory feel like summer had just arrived.

"That's it. Much better," said Reina, turning to the next page.

As the tempo slowed, Tiarnen grew calm, his shoulders and hands loosening up, making it easier to find the keys. The next passage bloomed with vibrant leaf motifs, each with its own personality, as the serene harmony reached a solstice of extended chords.

Feeling a little more confident, he turned the last few pages of the second movement himself and played through a long, effervescent passage of descending half notes that cooled the Conservatory again and ended the development with a harvest of the leaf motifs.

Reina put her hands back on the Swell as he turned to the beginning of the third movement.

"I'll take lead," she said.

Happy to have a break, Tiarnen took his hands off the keys and admired how seamlessly Reina continued "Quermorae" despite the complex phrases. Under her command once again, the sonata gained a textural quality that reverberated not only against the stone walls of the Conservatory but in his own chest as well.

"Back to you," said Reina.

"Already?"

She answered by taking her hands off the keys, so Tiarnen did his best to keep the momentum and played what appeared to be another spurt of autumnal motifs. However, unlike the ones that came before, these were withering—their descending motion making it feel like they were falling to the ground.

"Now, together," said Reina, turning the page.

"*How?*" he asked, confused.

"You take the bass clef; I'll take the treble and pedals."

Tiarnen put his hands back on the Swell. There were a few bumped elbows, but he and Reina were smiling the entire time. In fact, he couldn't remember when they'd ever had the chance to play together outside of mundane weekly rehearsals or while entrenched in battle. Before he knew it, they were moving through the section of playful variations without missing a single note, smiles growing wider as their hands wove over and around each other with grace.

Reina closed her eyes and focused. After a moment, flashes of green light from above caused Tiarnen to look up and see tiny shards of clover-green glass illuminating the mouths of the Prestant and Gemshorn pipes. He never once grew tired of witnessing their birth. It was as if the split-second when oil ignited into flame had been crystallized. Reina made it look effortless, which was even more impressive because he knew it was anything but. Captivated by his sister, Tiarnen lost track of where he was on the Swell and missed a hibernal note... then another... and another, until he had lost his way in what had become a blizzard of eighth notes and rests.

Reina sighed, took her hands off the keys, and opened her eyes.

"I know, I'm sorry," said Tiarnen, frustrated that he had messed up again.

"Don't be. You're doing really well."

"Really?" A smile pulled at his cheeks.

"For a *dud*," she finished.

Tiarnen's grin immediately turned into a sneer. He hadn't heard the insult for a while but knew exactly what it meant: someone who had never illuminated.

"From the beginning," said Reina, aligning her fingers on the Great keys again. She started from the top of the page, and Tiarnen quickly followed, paying much closer attention to the notation as they found their way through the boreal passage and emerged into the fourth and final movement.

"Quermorae" quickly thawed into alternating refrains and contrasting couplets that swept Tiarnen up like a rushing river. The melody came round and round again, spiralling tighter and tighter, while the harmony grew to be more embellished with each measure. Just as he thought the sonata couldn't become more enthralling, it broke into several parts, each new motivic branch once again blooming with vibrant phrases.

The intensity of the growing form was inescapable. No longer was it in parts and passages of the previous movements; it was the sonata as a whole. The acorn was now a family tree that had been tempered by its first seasons. "Quermorae" finally made sense to Tiarnen. He was elated, but before he could reflect on the intense emotional journey, a flash of green light erupted again. Tiarnen glanced up at the Prestant and Gemshorn pipes. To his horror, the light was not flickering in them.

"Tiarnen?" asked Reina, confused at what she just saw.

Feeling like he was about to explode, anxiety flooded through Tiarnen and made his hands play of their own accord.

"Stay with me," his sister warned, covering the missed keys in Tiarnen's performance.

Instead, he went completely off-page, improvising something that didn't resemble the notation whatsoever, only to produce a piercing dissonance that tore through the Conservatory.

"No! You're going to—" yelled Reina, watching in horror as Tiarnen struck a final key with all his strength.

CRACK!

A shockwave erupted from the Swell manual, sending both Tiarnen and Reina back over the bench and crashing onto the floor. Key fragments and sheet music rained down around them as the Conservatory fell silent once again. Groaning, Tiarnen opened his eyes and blinked his vision back into focus to see Reina slowly standing to her feet.

"What in the Verse *was that*?" she scolded.

It had been a long time since Tiarnen had seen her so angry. Covered in a cold sweat, he slowly pulled himself up and prepared for Reina to tear into him. Instead, her eyes widened as they focused on his chin.

"You're cut!" She sat him on the bench and took a closer look at his wound.

"Just a scratch," he said, trying to wipe the blood away with the back of his shaking hand.

"You're lucky you still have your damn head!"

"Does that mean you're letting me keep it?" asked Tiarnen.

"After you explain what happened, perhaps," said Reina, crossing her arms.

Tiarnen shrugged. "I got a little carried away, that's all."

She stared at him.

"All right, the improvisation was a bad idea," he admitted.

"Improvisation? Sounded more like sabotage to me."

"Why would I intentionally—"

"Then tell me what I saw," interrupted Reina.

"How can I? You were the one putting on the light show!"

She stared at him silently again, but this time, her face softened with a hint of empathy.

"Fine. I'll see myself out. Thanks for the lesson." Knees shaking, Tiarnen stood to his feet and walked past her.

"Wait!" Reina called after him.

Tiarnen stopped and turned reluctantly to see her holding out the Maestro Diary.

"As promised."

"But we—" he began.

"Did finish the sonata... *technically*."

Tiarnen hurried back over and took the diary, the sight and feel of the burned edges in his hands causing him to pause for a moment.

"What's wrong?" asked Reina.

"Nothing," he said, breaking himself from his trance. He quickly opened the diary and began searching the pages. There were so many places he wanted to stop and read, but testing what little he knew was left of Reina's patience didn't seem like a good idea.

"Grandma's chapter is further towards the back," she said.

Tiarnen skipped to the last third of the diary and finally stopped on the title page he was looking for:

A Shattered History
Maestro Dorian LVII
Freyla Braithrach
1357–1440 ADA

He turned to the next page, and his eyes became so wide that even Reina had to see what he was gawking at. By the looks of it, their grandmother had filled every page of her chapter with sketches of long-forgotten Shatter cards. Significant time and effort had been spent carefully cataloguing each one, which was quite impressive considering there must have been over a hundred cards by his count, not to mention just as many attempts at finding historical connections between them.

"At least now we know where you get it from," said Reina.

"Get what?" asked Tiarnen.

"Your obsession."

"I think you mean *passion*."

Reina rolled her eyes. "Right."

"I remember mother telling me stories about how she and Grandfather used to hold tournaments here."

"Shatter matches in the Conservatory? I can't even begin to imagine that."

"Just my luck," said Tiarnen as he reached the last page of Freyla's chapter.

"Something wrong?" asked Reina.

"No. I mean, yes. Her cataloguing is honestly incredible. She even managed to go as far back as the fourth expansion, which was apparently released over six hundred years ago. But there's nothing in here that resembles my card."

"Then it will have to remain a riddle, for now," said Reina, taking the diary from Tiarnen and returning it to her pocket.

"Easy for you to say," he said sullenly.

Muffled noise suddenly filtered into the room, then quickly grew into what sounded like distant cheering.

"Are my ears still ringing," said Tiarnen, "or are those..."

They hurried over to the open lancet window beside the stairs and looked out to see a large crowd of provincials gathered in the cathedral gardens far below. With a deep look of regret on her face, Reina waved to the crowd, who cheered even louder at the sight of her.

"Look how many there are," said Tiarnen.

"You need to go," ordered Reina. She grabbed Tiarnen by the shoulder, pulled him away from the window, and hurried him down the stairs.

"I don't understand what the problem is," he said.

The mechanical movements of the knock-lock echoed through the Conservatory. Before Reina could hide them both, the door opened, and Tharus marched in with Niera at his side. An entourage of six prae-torian guards, Executor Ignis, Captain Dansby, and Major Raghnall followed close behind.

Reina rushed down the last of the stairs and immediately took a knee as Tharus arrived before her. "Father, allow me to exp—"

Tharus raised a finger, and Reina fell silent. He then signalled to the guards, who rushed up the stairs and began shuttering the windows. As each one closed, the Conservatory became darker and darker. Tharus waited for Tiarnen to stand beside his sister, but he crossed his arms and leaned against the railing instead.

"When I first heard the music, I thought it was coming from that lowly vagrant playing in Cathedral Square again," said Tharus, glancing at Tiarnen.

Tiarnen stared at Niera. "Traitor," he muttered.

"Cheater!" she spat.

"Enough, both of you!" shouted Reina.

"Then I realized it was coming from my very own Conservatory," continued Tharus.

Tiarnen stepped forward. "Before you go on, all of this was—"

"It was my mistake, Father," interrupted Reina. "I should have in-formed both you and the Executor that Tiarnen and I planned a lesson for today."

Tiarnen tried to hide his look of surprise at Reina for unexpectedly covering for him.

"This is the second time today that I have discovered my children performing in secret," said Tharus, kneeling to pick up a key fragment from the floor. "In Niera's case, I can understand. She bears an enor-mous amount of pressure being Orchestra Lead and next in line as maestro. But why would my son, whose interest in music seems to fade with each Shatter match, deserve a private lesson with our maestro?"

"Despite his distractions, he is still our First Wind," stated Reina.

"Yet will be nothing more. Why waste time on him?"

She shrugged. "Apparently, I have a soft spot for hopeless cases."

Tiarnen bit his tongue since he knew that the sarcastic rebuttal he had in mind wouldn't help matters.

"I think there might be some hope yet," said Raghnall. The major was exactly as his Shatter card portrayed: a brawny gentleman in his late fifties with a trimmed silver beard and shaved head. His massive physical presence was only made more daunting by his attire: a full suit of ceramic armour of the rarest quality. Everyone watched as Raghnall opened the window shutters, and daylight flooded back into the Conservatory along with the crowd's cheering. "It's been quite a while since we've seen the provincials gathered in such high spirits."

"Your point, Major?" asked Ignis.

"Since we already have a crowd, might as well strike up the band."

"What does Uncle mean?" asked Niera.

Reina grinned. "I believe he is suggesting a concert."

"*A concert?*" exclaimed Niera, her eyes widening.

"Is the orchestra not scheduled for drills this evening?" asked Tharus.

Niera nodded. "They are."

"But something tells me there won't be any complaints about taking the Orpheum stage instead," said Reina.

"The patrols could certainly use a bit of rallying as well," added Dansby.

"Please, Father, *can we?*" begged Niera.

Tharus raised his right arm and looked at the chronograph around his wrist. The complex timepiece featured the typical second, minute, and hour hands, but the device's face also had a calendar that tracked the days, weeks, months, and years. He turned one of the many dials and watched the calendars adjust until Niera grabbed his left hand affectionately.

"We'll give Dorladdich a performance to remember, we promise!"

Tink... tink... clink!

The chronograph chimed in response.

"I expect nothing less," said Tharus.

Chapter Seven

BUTTONING UP

Shortly after Tharus agreed to the concert, Ignis scurried to the Office of Provincial Affairs and informed his clerks to dispatch the heralds. Within the hour, the concert had been announced throughout the districts. This caused so much excitement that droves of provincials dropped everything they were doing to rush to the Orpheum in the hope of securing a clear view of the amphitheatre from its grassy knoll.

Tiarnen, however, couldn't have been less enthused. Still annoyed that Reina shared neither his curiosity nor enthusiasm for his relic mystery card, all he wanted was to return home, get out of his damp clothes, and rebuild his deck for the Grand Tournament. He departed the Conservatory with the lighthouse in his sights, though a grumbling stomach caused him to take a short detour to the Crusty Coffin. The Ashbrook's establishment was renowned for its incredibly tasty, not to mention oversized, meat pies. This was why, as a personal rule, he always bought two.

By the time Tiarnen changed into a pair of dry merino trousers and a waffle-knit shirt, he had already eaten most of the pie, which was packed with steak, carrots, onions, and stout gravy. Leaning forward in his lounge chair, his eyes landed on his deck case on the opposite side of the table. He glared at it in frustration. Part of him wanted to start to rebuild around *Amber's* card, while the other half hesitated because there were very few things Tiarnen hated more than unanswered questions.

Despite the inner conflict, he found himself grabbing the case and shaking the deck out with one hand while devouring the last bite of buttery pie crust with the other. He spread the cards over the table and started to think about where Amber might fit in. Being that she was a maestro, another would have to be removed from the deck. Tiarnen's eyes went to his mother's card. Though he always appreciated how well the illustration captured her likeness, it still paled in comparison to her portrait window in the Conservatory. He took a moment to consider if there were any other options, then decided the swap made sense since *Amber's* unique attribute made both the warsong and the deck stronger. With a heavy heart, Tiarnen slipped Marifreth back into his catalogue. He then placed Amber at the beginning of the warsong, reformed the deck—giving it a couple of taps on the table—and slid it back into the case.

Still famished, Tiarnen took the empty pie plate to the kitchen, grabbed the second off the counter, then sunk into the soft, worn leather of the lounge chair once again. The flaky pie crust broke under his fork as he carved off a large bite of rabbit, bacon, peas, and cream. Before long, half the pie had vanished, and his stomach was finally full.

Four muffled chimes emanated from the pile of laundry beside his dresser drawers. They not only reminded Tiarnen that he had left his pocket watch in his trousers but also signalled that his moment of satiated bliss was coming to an end as he would need to leave in a few minutes to meet everyone backstage at the Orpheum. Accepting that there was no way out of it, he threw his head back and let out a soft sigh... but before he realized his eyes were closing, the fork had already slipped from his fingers, and snoring filled the lighthouse.

*

BAM-BAM!

Tiarnen jolted up and looked around frantically to see what woke him. *Was the oil pump seizing again?* he wondered.

BAM-BAM-BAM!

He startled again.

"Tiarnen?" called a faint voice.

"By the Verse," he said, realizing what woke him—someone was at the door.

"Tiarnen? Are you in there?"

"Coming!" yelled Tiarnen, already rushing to the dresser. After a panicked search through his drawers, he threw on a cream formal shirt and dark brown slacks, fastening buttons and buckling his belt as fast as he could. Then, while trying to pull his boots up, Tiarnen grabbed an ascot, recovered his pocket watch from the laundry pile, shoved the piccolo into his back pocket, and then slid down the spiral staircase at breakneck speed.

BAM-BAM-BAM-BAM-BAM!

He whipped the front door open and almost caught Raghnall's armoured fist square in the face.

"Whoa!" blurted Tiarnen, dodging the gauntlet just in time.

"Ah, glad to see you're finally awake," said Raghnall.

"*Awake?*" Tiarnen gave a forced laugh. "Please, I just didn't hear you from the lamp room is all."

"Uh-huh." Raghnall glanced down at Tiarnen's unlaced boots.

Crouching to quickly tie them up, Tiarnen noticed several new dents in the door. "Exactly how hard were you knocking?"

"Apparently not hard enough," said Niera, stepping out from behind Raghnall. "We've been waiting out here forever!"

"Right... sorry," said Tiarnen, standing back up.

Though the dusky sky was evidence enough, he double-checked his pocket watch to see that it was just past five o'clock, which, to his embarrassment, meant that he was over an hour late.

Niera rolled her eyes, turned around, and stomped down the rocky steps.

"Come on. We're taking the canals to avoid the crowd," said Raghnall.

Together, they took the short winding trail to the lighthouse dock, where a gondola was moored. Niera climbed aboard and, ducking under the canopy, sat at the bow—immediately turning her back to Tiarnen and Raghnall as they carefully walked to the stern.

"Here you go, lad," said Raghnall, handing Tiarnen the end of a long oar.

"Is this the cost of my wake-up call?" he asked, grabbing onto the handle.

"A small price to pay, considering," Raghnall said while untying the mooring rope.

Tiarnen's eyes narrowed. "Considering what?"

"That someone was more than willing to let you keep sleeping." Raghnall nodded to Niera.

Unamused but also unsurprised, Tiarnen threw his weight onto the oar and pushed them off the dock. With a few clumsy strokes, he managed to steer them toward the mouth of the Grand East Canal and allowed the ocean current to push them into the city.

High walls rose on either side, and the canal began to turn, which caused the lighthouse and peninsula to vanish out of sight. Using the oar as a rudder, Tiarnen was thankful for how empty the waters were because his inexperience as a gondolier was showing. However, despite the rocking and a bit of splashing, he managed to keep the boat on course as the many arch bridges of Trade Town passed overhead and cast them in shadow. Tiarnen took the opportunity to quickly wipe the sleep from his eyes.

"You know, all of those double shifts are going to catch up with you one day," said Raghnall.

"Only if I let them," Tiarnen replied with a yawn.

"Have you thought about maybe focusing on more important things?"

"The lighthouse is important."

"You know what I mean."

"Are you asking me to join the patrol?" Tiarnen inquired sardonically.

Raghnall choked on his laughter. "You tried that once already, remember?"

"I don't see any reason to make a change." Tiarnen lowered his voice. "Besides, Niera is doing a great job leading the orchestra."

"Aye, no argument there. Sometimes I forget how young she is."

"That's why I'll just keep helping wherever I can."

"What are you two on about?" asked Niera, feeling their eyes on her.

"Nothing, my Lead!" said Tiarnen, clearing his throat. "Merely debating!"

"About?"

"Oh, about... if... the stage will be in working order by the time we get there."

"Speaking of which," said Raghnall, pointing to the approaching ferry dock where a squat older man stood, his overalls covered in grease and oil, with a small box in his hands. As the boat drew closer, Tiarnen recognized the province's chief engineer immediately.

"Permission to come aboard?" asked Garod, his walrus moustache twitching as he climbed onto the gondola.

"At your own peril," said Raghnall, nodding back to Tiarnen.

"I thought you said to be here at five sharp?" Garod grumbled, taking a seat beside Raghnall and resting the ornate box on his lap.

"I did, but we had a small delay."

"It's my fault, Chief," said Tiarnen.

"Not to worry," said Garod. "It's fashionable to take the stage a bit late anyway, right?"

"How about not at all?" Tiarnen grunted and caused water to splash into the boat as he struggled to push them off the dock again.

"All right, give it up," said Raghnall, taking the oar.

Tiarnen moved aside and sat across from Garod. "So, what has you risking such a treacherous voyage, Chief?"

"Normally, I would be happy to take the ferry, but I have a bit of precious cargo that needed escorting."

"Precious?" Tiarnen raised his eyebrows.

The question piqued Niera's curiosity as well, causing her to slide down the bench until she was beside Garod. Together, they watched him slowly open the lid to reveal a gold mechanical device that was about the size of a very large coin with many kinds of interconnected gears, sprockets, rotors, and tourbillons within its intricate framework.

"Is that a complication?" asked Tiarnen.

"Freshly wound," said Garod, with a hint of pride.

"I've never seen one up close before." Tiarnen leaned in to take a closer look.

"There are so many parts," said Niera.

"Indeed," said Garod. "In fact, this one has just over a thousand."

"A *thousand*?" replied Niera, genuinely shocked.

As if the intricacy of the device wasn't extraordinary enough, Tiarnen could see that much of it was fastened together by screws so small they were barely visible to the naked eye.

"How many complications are keeping the city running these days, Garod?" asked Raghnall.

"We are unfortunately down to six," lamented Garod. "I had to pull this one from Kilners' Row and shut the entire district down just so we could power the Orpheum stage tonight."

"Where are the others?" asked Niera.

"Second one is at Punkworks powering our tinkertables. Third is at the harbour controlling the cranes. Fourth is at Water and Sanitation flushing the canals clean. And the fifth is at the Refinery pumping heating oil to the districts."

"And the last?" asked Tiarnen.

"In your father's chronograph," said Garod. "Though I've never personally seen it."

"Why is that?" Tiarnen knew his father's timepiece was an antique, but he had no idea that a priceless complication was inside of it.

"Because it has never required any maintenance."

"Can't we just make some new complications?" asked Niera.

"Oh, we've tried. Numerous times, in fact," said Garod. "But the last attempt resulted in half of Punkworks being destroyed."

"What happened?" asked Niera.

"The challenge with complications is the tension coil inside. Because it's wound so tight and holds so much energy, every part of the complication must be built and calibrated perfectly, or it will explode without warning. As much as I hate to admit it, I'm starting to believe that the art of crafting them has finally been lost." Garod looked more than a little heartbroken at the idea.

Tiarnen couldn't help but also feel saddened by the news. Garod and his chronopunks specialized in all things chronotech and were so busy modifying and maintaining their mechanical contraptions for the war effort that they rarely left the Punkworks. But if Dorladdich's remaining complications eventually failed, then the city would certainly come to a grinding halt.

"I heard a rumour that you've trained the mice in Punkworks to be your assistants," said Niera.

"If we have, I would appreciate it if they showed up to work for once. I could use the extra hands!" chuckled Garod.

"Especially with broken-down relics like me coming in for a fix every week," added Raghnall, nodding to his gauntlet.

"Nonsense," said Garod. "Keeping you in working order is an honour. Besides, all we did was bring you back to full strength."

"Uncle, tell me how it happened?" asked Niera.

"You have heard the story," said Raghnall, brushing off the request.

"Only parts of it. And never from you."

Raghnall let out a long sigh. "When I was First Brigarch—"

"The most decorated Brigarch in military history," added Tiarnen.

Raghnall rolled his eyes. "—the Roycrofts ascended and became a noble house. Naturally, there was a city-wide celebration, but prior to the event, Holgor had been informed that an assassination attempt by Locarnia was planned for your father. The Praetorian Guard was, of course, placed on high alert, but the assassin used the bustle of the celebration to his advantage and managed to get close enough to make an attempt. However, for better or worse, I happened to be in the way and saw the glint of the poisoned dagger just in time to block the killing blow meant for our praetor."

"By the Verse," said Niera, her green eyes wide.

"Next thing I knew, a praetorian guard was tackling the Locarnian, and I had half a blade stabbed into my shoulder—not to mention a fair amount of aracula venom seeping into my veins."

"Enough to kill a horse is what I heard," added Garod.

"Luckily, Matron Halon was able to clean and dress the wound in time to save my arm," said Raghnall, looking at his gauntlet. "Well, what was left of it."

"I didn't realize Father came so close to death," said Niera.

"How in the Verse did you know to be there?" asked Tiarnen.

"I didn't," said Raghnall. "Truth be told, I was getting myself an ale."

Tiarnen burst out laughing. "*What?*"

"Just like you to thwart an assassination while questing for a pint," said Garod, joining Tiarnen in laughter.

"Please tell me the story ends with you sipping it victoriously as Matron Halon bandaged you up?" asked Tiarnen.

"Afraid I can't," chuckled Raghnall. "But your mother might have snuck in a few while I was kept at the hospital."

"Of course she did," said Tiarnen, shaking his head.

"Ignoring the injury, I'm glad that you were honourably discharged—can't imagine anyone else leading the patrol and keeping our streets safe," said Garod.

"Hear, hear!" said Tiarnen and Niera in chorus.

"Voices down!" hushed Raghnall, pointing upwards.

The three looked back in confusion as he pointed up at the canal ledge where a mob of provincials stood. Thankfully, the gondola seemed to go unnoticed since everyone was preoccupied with shoving their way into the Orpheum. Raghnall gave the oar a light push and turned them into a dark tunnel branching off the canal.

Niera covered her nose with both of her hands. "What is that *smell?*"

"Blackwater," said Raghnall, seemingly unaffected by the stench.

"Do we really need to take the sewer?" asked Tiarnen, taking short breaths.

"It's the fastest way backstage. There's a service entrance up ahead that no one ever uses."

"Can't imagine why," said Tiarnen.

After what felt like an eternity, another dock appeared just ahead of them. Raghnall carefully steered the gondola along it, but before Tiarnen had the chance to secure the mooring rope, Niera leaped past him, ran the full length of the dock, and pushed her way through the service door set in the wall.

"Typical," he grumbled.

"You better get going, too," said Raghnall, tying the boat to the dock. "We'll head up to the stage and set the complication."

Tiarnen gladly hopped off the boat, made his way down the dock, and opened the access door, which led to a narrow hallway.

"Oh, Tiarnen," said Raghnall.

He stopped and turned.

"Remind my niece that a little courtesy wouldn't hurt every now and again."

"Will do my best," said Tiarnen, letting the service door close behind him.

*

One hundred frazzled orchestra musicians fumbled and stumbled over each other in the humid dressing room as they fitted their formal attire, styled their hair, and tuned their instruments in preparation for the night's performance. Lining the right side of the room were twenty or so vanities that had small oil lamps running vertically in between them—the tops covered in all sorts of grooming and cosmetic products to make sure everyone looked their best. To no one's surprise, the Roycrofts had set up camp at most of the stations and were making it very difficult for anyone outside of their family to use them. Along the left side, most of the Ashbrooks were still getting dressed behind the heavy curtains while the rest were trying to help each other make themselves presentable. Down the middle, the Finwicks were already toasting to the event, although a few seemed to be having a row over when they were going surfing tomorrow.

Feeling like he was suddenly back at Cathedral Square, Tiarnen waited for an opening and entered the fray. Step by step, he managed to weave through the chaos of bodies and elbows until Coniel spun around with a large drum strapped to his chest and slammed into him.

"Steady on there, Second Drum!" said Tiarnen, regaining his balance.

"Tiarnen!" A worried look came over Coniel's freckled face. "Forgive me, I didn't see you!"

"No worries. Everyone seems to be scrambling at the moment."

"Yeah, bit of a mess, aren't we?" Coniel said with a chuckle. "Any idea what brought all of this about, anyway?"

"Haven't a clue." Tiarnen cleared his throat and peered through the crowd, trying to catch sight of Reina. "You haven't, by chance, seen our maestro anywhere?"

"On the far side of this gaggle, I'm afraid." Coniel pointed his drumstick towards the back of the room. "Here, allow me to clear a path!"

"Uh, that won't be necessary—" Tiarnen started, but Coniel had already begun a drum riff.

Boom! Boom! Ba-Ba-Boom!

The orchestra was startled by the booming solo—their heads turning to see Coniel proudly stamping his way through the crowd. "Make way, make way!"

Boom! Boom! Ba-da-Boom!

Tiarnen reluctantly followed Coniel through the mass of glares and sidelong glances.

"Oh! Congratulations on your victory this morning," said Coniel, butting Wendel out of the way with the front of his drum.

"Thanks," said Tiarnen.

"What deck were you up against?" Coniel pushed another musician to the side.

"Mechmaster."

"Oof, that must have been rough! Especially if they had the Titan."

"Which Crog did."

"*What?* Then how did you win?"

"I synergized *Six Strings* with *Mirror Image* to reflect his final attack."

"I didn't even know you could play *Strings* and *Mirror* together like that," admitted Coniel.

"Apparently, neither did Crog," interjected Lachlan, who was dressed in a lavish sea-foam formal suit and tuning his polished trumpet with no sign of moving out of Coniel's way.

"That's what happens when you buy a deck instead of building it," said Tiarnen.

"Acquiring the right cards shouldn't be a barrier to victory—simply a means to achieve it," stated Lachlan.

"Luckily for me, no amount of legendaries can make up for ignorance," said Tiarnen.

Coniel couldn't keep himself from chuckling at the insult.

"And overconfidence will simply bring you to your knees one card at a time," retorted Lachlan.

"I think *Dreadgill* here is trying to sound intelligent," Coniel said out of the side of his mouth.

Lachlan checked his hair in the trumpet's brassy reflection. "As reigning tournament champion, I would have guessed that you believed in a bit of game philosophy."

"I do. It's called *fair play*," said Coniel.

"I'm curious, what card did you claim?" Lachlan looked back at Tiarnen. "Please tell me it was that *Crooked Clockmaker*; it's worth a fortune."

"No, I took... Wait, how do you know he had a *Clockmaker*?" asked Tiarnen, a bit surprised by Lachlan's knowledge of the match.

Lachlan paled and suddenly became quite interested in a tuning peg on his trumpet.

"You know, now that you mention it," said Tiarnen. "I did find it interesting that a longshoreman could afford a deck that was easily worth twice his yearly wage."

"He must have been saving his copper," suggested Lachlan.

"Or someone sponsored him."

"But isn't sponsoring players in ranked matches illegal?" asked Coniel, though he already knew the answer.

Tiarnen nodded. "Very illegal."

"Why do I get the feeling that if I were to look for Crog on the corsair crew manifests they would show him serving aboard the *Riornath*?" said Coniel.

Lachlan leered at him, then slithered back into the crowd.

"It doesn't make sense. Why would Lachlan risk sponsoring Crog?" asked Coniel.

"To try and knock me out before I could place in the tournament," said Tiarnen.

"For someone with all the gold in the world, he certainly has no problem taking cheap shots."

"Earl Aran is as desperate as ever to win the Premiership, so I think it's a safe bet that the Roycrofts will continue to do anything they can to win."

"Business as usual," sighed Coniel, readying his drumsticks.

"Don't worry. It'll just make shutting down Lachlan while the entire city is watching all the sweeter."

Boom! Boom! Ba-da-Boom!

Coniel pushed through the last of the orchestra and finally reached the back of the room where Reina and Niera were being fitted and accessorised by Bridget, Imogen, and several tailors who were making final adjustments under the watch of Captain Dansby.

Boom! Boom! Ba-da-Boom!

"If this is your idea of making an entrance," began Reina, as Bridget applied dark green eyeshadow with a thin brush.

"Actually, we were looking for the exit," said Tiarnen.

Ba-da—

Tiarnen grabbed onto Coniel's sticks.

"Niera, if I may, you look incredible," said Coniel. He waited eagerly for a reply, but Niera only looked back at herself in the small vanity mirror that Imogen was holding.

"Thanks for seeing me through safely, Coniel," said Tiarnen, trying to spare him from the cold rejection.

"Happy to help," said Coniel, cheering up a bit from Tiarnen's gratitude.

"Where is that useless Second Drum of mine?" shrieked Fiona, somewhere deep in the crowd. "Coniel? Get over here and find my sticks!"

"Looking for them now, First Drum!" replied Coniel. "This is why I always bring a spare set." He pulled out a pair of drumsticks from inside his jacket, let out a sigh, and walked back into the crowd.

Reina turned to the tailors. "Could we please see to it that my brother is made presentable?"

One of them immediately brought over a chair, unzipped a garment bag, and pulled out a dark grey formal jacket for Tiarnen to try on.

"Remind me why we have to be so stiff about all this?" he asked.

"Does the word *tradition* ring any bells?" asked Reina, raising her chin as Bridget snapped the last of ten clasps running up the high neck of her emerald silk gown.

Tiarnen slipped the jacket on. Without hesitation, Reina and Niera started to laugh at the sight of him. Every inch of fabric seemed to stretch and crease where it shouldn't. The sleeves only reached midway down his forearms, and the waist was equally too short.

"I think you might need to let it out a little," said Dansby.

"It's fine." Tiarnen tugged at the cuffs. "Just been a few years since I last wore it."

Niera looked him up and down. "Not to mention a few pies."

"Luckily, there is another option," said Dansby. He picked up one of Reina's alternate dresses that was slung over a chair and held it up to Tiarnen.

"Certainly not," said Reina. "It would clash horribly with his eyes."

Tiarnen took in a deep breath and, with significant struggle, managed to get the middle jacket button through its hole. "See... fits like a... glove," he croaked, struggling to exhale.

"Remember, you play a woodwind," said Reina, loosening the ascot around his neck.

"Meaning?" wheezed Tiarnen.

"That you need to be able to breathe," said Reina.

"Orchestra to the stage! I said orchestra to the stage, now!" yelled Ignis, standing at the stage entrance door.

"That would be our cue," sighed Reina.

She turned to the table beside her, where an opulent ceramic and green leather instrument case was resting. The intricate wind symbols embossed over every inch glinted as Reina unhinged the latches and slowly opened the lid to reveal Windwalker resting inside. The artisanal basset clarinet was of the highest quality, its dark green maple-wood body contrasting against the glossy ceramic keys.

Tiarnen walked up to the table beside Niera, who was still fixated on Windwalker and opened the instrument case resting on it, pulling Dawnbreaker out. "This is your first concert, Twinkles. Nervous?"

"Maestros are never nervous," said Niera, reaching for Dawnbreaker.

Tiarnen lifted the violin just out of Niera's reach. "Is that true, Reina?"

"Oh, didn't you know? We maestros are incapable of fear," said Reina, testing Windwalker's keys to make sure they weren't sticking.

"What about forgiveness?" asked Tiarnen.

She shrugged. "It has been known to happen."

"On *very* rare occasions," added Niera, reaching again for her instrument.

"That so? Well, I believe we all know someone who deserves it." Tiarnen held the instrument further out of Niera's reach.

"Must you be so impossible?" she yelled, lunging and finally wrapping her hand around Dawnbreaker—only to be pulled into a hug by Tiarnen.

"I would have won!" said Niera, her declaration muffled by his embrace.

"Perhaps, but if you had, we might not be here right now."

Niera pushed herself off him. "How does that make any sense?"

"I believe he's trying to say that things happen for a reason," said Reina.

"Still mad at me?" asked Tiarnen, raising his eyebrow and lowering the violin.

Niera huffed and yanked Dawnbreaker from his grip. "Hard to be with this one, isn't it?"

"Don't get me started," said Reina. "Now, think you two can be on stage together without it turning into a competition?"

"Shouldn't make promises we can't keep, should we, Niera?" said Tiarnen, pulling his piccolo from his back pocket.

Niera nodded. "It would be disingenuous of us."

A patrolman walked up to Dansby, whispered in his ear, and then left just as quickly as he'd arrived.

"Sounds like we're secure," said Dansby, pulling the shield off his back. "But given how many jars of moonshine the patrol has confiscated already, we shouldn't be surprised if a few provincials try to get personal."

"Are you suggesting we deny Reina her adoring fans?" said Tiarnen. He and Niera both reached out for her. Dansby quickly stood in the way as though protecting Reina.

"Please, if we could only touch... just for a second... we'd finally be blessed!" Tiarnen and Niera said in harmony as they tried to stretch past Dansby.

"Consider it a blessing if I let you keep those grubby hands," said Reina, taking the chance to quickly grab Dansby's hand.

"Maestro!" Ignis scurried up to them. "I have the set list for tonight's performance."

Reina let go of Dansby, turned around, and reluctantly took the sheet music from Ignis with a look of confusion on her face. "I had assumed I would be choosing the songs."

"You were mistaken," Ignis replied.

Reina began thumbing through the sheet music and reading the titles. "'Thistle and Thorn'... 'Wolf Under the Wool,' and... 'Hey, How's She Going?'"

"Why would Father want us to play a bunch of stupid tavern ballads?" asked Niera.

"So that there's no chance of Reina illuminating," said Tiarnen.

"The praetor simply didn't want our maestro exhausting herself," said Ignis. "Also, he would like Miss Niera to be allowed some time at centre stage. It would be a good opportunity for her to—"

"I understand, Ignis. Thank you," said Reina.

"What? No, you do not understand!" said Tiarnen.

"Of course," said Ignis, ignoring Tiarnen completely. "And if there are any other services I might provide—"

Dansby took a firm step towards Ignis, partially blocking Reina from his view. "She will let you know, Executor."

Ignis's lip curled. It was obvious that he wanted to order Dansby out of the way, but he had no authority over the captain.

"I'm sure she will," said Ignis, skulking away with Lachlan and the last of the orchestra as they left the dressing room, slipped through the backstage curtains, and walked onto the stage.

"Didn't realize I needed protection," said Reina.

Dansby leaned in. "You don't. That's why it's so romantic."

A smile pulled at Reina's cheek, and Tiarnen cleared his throat.

"Right," said Dansby, putting his shoulders back and then turning to leave for the stage. "I'll see you three out there. Best of luck!"

"Reina, don't tell me we're just going to—" said Tiarnen.

"These are not suggestions." She spun to face him, holding the sheet music up. "They are orders, and we will follow them."

"Yes, Maestro," said Niera.

Tiarnen's jaw clenched as he fell in line behind his sisters, and they took the stage together.

Chapter Eight

THE CONCERT

A deafening wave of cheers erupted from the awaiting crowd and washed over Tiarnen. Though he knew all the excitement was really for Maestro Dorian, it was hard not to be swept up by the enthusiasm of fifty thousand people.

Along both sides of the grassy amphitheatre bowl, he could see countless provincial families sitting on tattered blankets with their children held close. In the middle stood a throng of ecstatic youths, many of them fighting to get to the front of the stage, where they usually ended up thrashing against each other, or as they called it: "dancing."

At the very back of the bowl, inside a brickwork enclave, Praetor Tharus, his usual entourage, and the earls were being attended to by servants. Their vantage point gave the best possible view of the stage as well as the monumental east city wall, which supported the back of the Orpheum and extended to the fortified gatehouse.

Tiarnen's boot slipped on a slug, and he looked down, noticing the dire condition of the stage. Every inch of the carved stonework was covered in dirt and mildew, and even some weeds were growing along the edges. He assumed there would have been at least some sort of attempt to scrub the stage down before they arrived, but given the short notice, he guessed that any effort would have probably been futile or, more likely, Tharus simply didn't care enough to give the order. Looking ahead, Tiarnen saw the orchestra already waiting in a semi-circle formation along the upstage, divided into their instrument sections. The woodwinds were standing upstage left, drums were in the middle, and strings were upstage right—all three arranged front to back in ranked lieutenant, sergeant, corporal, and private rows.

Tiarnen took position at the front of the woodwinds, with Kaleigh standing just behind him as Second Wind. He did his best to hide how taken aback he was by how beautiful she looked. Her dark hair was tied up with a forest-green bow, the ends reaching down her long neck to a simple but flattering off-the-shoulder dress. It was exciting to see everyone dressed up, but Kaleigh even more, since the Ashbrooks didn't exactly hold fashion in high regard.

"Everything all right?" she asked.

"Ye-yeah, why?" stammered Tiarnen, trying to play casual.

"No reason. Just that your eyes are bulging like a codfish."

"Suit is a bit snug, is all," he said, fussing with his top button.

"Is it now?" Kaleigh slapped Tiarnen's hand away and ripped off his top button, then slid it into his pocket.

"Hold it in place while I tighten the bolts!" said Garod.

His voice drew Tiarnen's gaze to centre stage where the Chief was kneeling with Jasper, his most promising chronopunk, while they struggled to set the complication in what appeared to be a small opening in the stage.

"How are we coming along, Chief?" asked Tiarnen.

"Slowly, which is why I told Ignis we weren't ready yet!" said Garod, turning the handle of a large socket wrench.

"Careful or you'll strip the bolt," warned Jasper. Though she was rather petite, Jasper had a strong build and look about her thanks to many years working at Punkworks. Much like the rest of the chronopunks, she had a wild hairstyle. Both sides of her head were shaved and a long, wavy lime-green mohawk ran down the middle.

"Is there a problem?" asked Reina.

"No... yes... possibly." Garod gave the socket wrench a last turn.

"We're sorry, Maestro," added Jasper. "Fitting the complication is turning out to be a little trickier than anticipated."

Clack!

"There, I think that did it!" said Garod. He turned to the side of the stage and gave a thumbs-up to Callum, another chronopunk with a wiry build and a row of tall lime-green spikes running down the middle of his head, who was standing at the control panel.

"Engaging the transmission!" said Callum. With one eye closed, he cautiously pulled down on the largest of several levers and then immediately took a step back as a high-pitched whining sound began to emit from the stage.

"Umm—is it supposed to be doing that?" asked Niera.

"Engaging the torque converters!" said Garod, paying no attention to Niera's question and running to the control panel to help Callum.

Tiarnen cautiously stepped forward and peered into the hole. Inside the stage, gears jutted out and interlinked with the complication, which immediately caused them to spin at high speed. Suddenly, violent tremors shot through the entire stage and caused everyone to nearly lose their footing.

"Not to worry!" said Garod. "Just need to dial the revolutions back a bit!" He nodded to Callum who adjusted six of the smaller dials. To everyone's relief, the tremors stopped, and the whining faded into a gentle hum as the complication seemed to calm.

"Old fool!" yelled Lachlan.

Tiarnen turned back to reprimand Lachlan for the unnecessary insult but then saw that he had been the only one to fall from the tremors. "Looks like someone needs to work on their sea legs," he quipped.

The Ashbrooks and most of the Finwicks didn't hold back their laughter as the Roycrofts leered at them in silence.

"None of you would be laughing if you knew how much this cost," spat Lachlan, pointing at his begrimed suit with a dirty hand. "Valis, help your First Brass up!"

"Belay that order!" said Raghnall. "You can quit the quailing and get off your own ass, Lachlan." Everyone looked up to see the major, holding a larger pewter pint of ale, glaring down at them from the edge of the east wall rampart with Patrolman Hiddleton standing at his side.

"You heard the major," ordered Niera.

Valis stepped back into formation, and Lachlan slowly pulled himself up but made sure to be as dramatic about it as possible before returning to first position in front of the brass.

"I'm surprised you chose the cheap seats!" said Tiarnen, nodding up at Raghnall.

"Someone needs to keep watch on the shoreline while you lot have all the fun." Raghnall gestured behind himself to the other side of the wall where the Forth Reach Bridge stretched across the ocean strait and vanished into the darkness.

"I believe that we're ready, Maestro!" yelled Garod, carefully turning a tiny dial on the control panel.

"If you say so," said Reina, watching as the complication vanished inside the stage. Despite still being skeptical of the stage mechanics, she turned with her head held high to address the orchestra. "Right, now that our technical difficulties are out of the way, I must say, all of you have cleaned up rather nicely."

A few whistles sounded from the Finwicks, followed by some scattered laughter.

"Double for you as well, Maestro!" said Kaleigh.

"Thank you, my dear," said Reina, bowing slightly. "I know this afternoon was a bit of a blur so please accept my apology for making our rehearsal, well, a bit more public than usual—but I really want us to use tonight as an opportunity."

"For what, Maestro?" asked Coniel.

Reina pointed back to the crowd. "To remind *them* what we're fighting for."

Most of the orchestra couldn't help but smile and nod in agreement.

"Does that mean someone's finally going to remind *us* what we're supposed to be playing?" asked Lachlan, trying to wipe his palms clean with a silk handkerchief.

"Orchestra Lead!" said Reina.

"Yes, Maestro!" replied Niera.

"Please review our set list with everyone."

Niera nodded. "Right away!"

"First Wind, walk with me," said Reina.

A little surprised by the request, Tiarnen followed behind Reina and walked with her to the front of the stage.

"Looks like the entire province showed up," he said.

"I expected nothing less." Reina waved to the crowd, causing them to start chanting.

"DORIAN-DORIAN-DORIAN!"

"Forgot how loud they could be," said Tiarnen, looking past the emaciated provincials and into the enclave where the nobles were filling their plates with food and their goblets with wine. Tharus, however, was seated in the middle, surrounded by his guard, and utterly motion-less.

"Listen, I know you normally hate the spotlight," started Reina.

Tiarnen shrugged. "Just the whole centre of attention part."

"Taking that into consideration, if you wanted to lead 'Wolf Under the—'"

"As you said, we have our orders. Niera deserves the chance to prove herself."

"Of course." Reina resisted the urge to argue. "Perhaps then, with a bit of luck, some sparks might fly tonight."

"In that case," said Tiarnen, realizing that the excitement might help Niera illuminate, "I will make sure to stoke the fire."

Reina put her hand on his shoulder. "She's lucky to have you, even if she won't admit it."

"We're the lucky ones," he said, placing his hand over hers.

"Maestro!" shouted Niera. "The orchestra is ready—once my First Wind decides to grace us with his presence!"

"Sorry, my Lead! On my way, my Lead!" Tiarnen chuckled. He let go of Reina's hand and made his way back to Niera, but in reaching for his piccolo, he split open the left shoulder seam of his jacket.

"Seriously?" asked Niera—in awe that her brother could possibly look more ridiculous.

"At least I can raise my arm now," he said, lifting his piccolo to his lips.

Niera looked him up and down. "Unbelievable."

Then, Reina raised Windwalker into the air, and the entire Orpheum fell silent.

"Forgive me!" she said. "It has been far too long since you were last invited here!"

The crowd applauded in agreement.

"I still remember when I stood on this stage with my mother as Orchestra Lead."

"Long live the fifty-eighth!" cheered the crowd.

"It never ceased to amaze me how she was able to come to the Orpheum and leave the war behind for an evening," reflected Reina. "But after I became a maestro myself, I finally learnt why... because this is where Dorladdich's true voice can be found. In this era of song and sword, it is not just musicians and military who sacrifice for the glory of our province, but every provincial I see standing before me now!" Reina pointed Windwalker towards the crowd. "Each day, you, your families, and your friends endure in *trust* that Dorladdich's bloodshed will finally come to an end! And I promise you, if we never forget who we are, where our music comes from, the last battle Chora ever sees shall bring us victory!"

Roaring cheers erupted from the crowd once again as Reina returned to the orchestra. She looked up to see Raghnall, who was leaning over the edge of the rampart now with a proud smile on his face.

"What is it, Major?" asked Reina, her eyebrow raised.

"Just never thought I would hear a better speech than *hers*."

Reina couldn't help but smile at her uncle's sentiment. Gathering herself, she nodded to Garod, who pulled down the first of a series of side levers on the control panel, causing the stage to vibrate as hundreds of small holes opened on its surface and broke the hardened dirt.

"Someone hold our First Brass!" joked Coniel, looking over to Lachlan, who was clearly unamused.

Reina turned to face the crowd, placed her fingers along Windwalker, and rested the reed on her bottom lip. She took a deep breath and began to play "Thistle and Thorn."

The intro notes were long and forlorn, each one accompanied by a stream of water that shot out from a hole in the stage, arched through the air, and then vanished into another hole. As Reina continued to play through the sombre melody, more and more streams leaped out and then vanished in perfect sync with her performance. From where the crowd was standing, it seemed as if their maestro was conjuring the aqueous effects, but it was really Garod, Callum, and Jasper working hard at the controls to keep them coordinated as everyone began to sing.

Last night I dreamt the rain had stopped
No longer had I a deck to mop
My pockets filled with shells I made
All of our debts finally paid

Mother and child find their way
Island and house rule our day
Thistle and thorn come what may

This morning I woke awash with mud
All of my rye had turned to blood
Truth be told, I am where I belong
Tones be judge, I will right all my wrongs

Mother and child find their way
Island and house rule our day
Thistle and thorn come what may

Today I hung from the sails till dusk
My hands were raw, my body a husk
The lighthouse beams, our course is bound
Once again my feet will know the ground

Mother and child find their way
Island and house rule our day
Thistle and thorn come what may

Tonight I'll drink the night to a blur
So my laments should never recur
When the bottom of the jar appears
I hope a smile replaces my tears

Mother and child find their way
Island and house rule our day
Thistle and thorn come what may

Stumbling as the district snores
Looking for a lass I might adore
The shore would fast become my bed
A pillow of stones to lay my head

Last night I dreamt the rain had stopped
No longer had I a deck to mop
My pockets filled with coin I made
All of our debts finally paid

Mother and child find their way
Island and house rule our day
Thistle and thorn come what may

Reina played the melancholy finale, the water streams descending with her last notes, and the crowd applauded in celebration because they knew the lyrics seemed like a tale of suffering but were really a reminder that they could endure anything together if it meant winning the war. Overcome with infatuation, a few enamoured teens tried to push past the patrol in a desperate attempt to climb up the stage and touch their maestro.

"That's far enough!" said Dansby, blocking two of the teens with his shield while the rest of the patrol tried to keep the perimeter secure.

Reina gave a soft bow and walked back to the orchestra, winking at Garod and the chronopunks along the way for a job well done. "Good work, everyone! I know most of you probably haven't played that one in forever."

"And for good reason," said Lachlan, not bothering to lower his voice.

Reina ignored Lachlan's comment and turned to the crowd once again. "Now, I don't know about the rest of you, but I heard that there might be a 'Wolf Under the Wool' nearby!"

Everyone cheered in recognition of the title.

"Ready?" asked Reina, looking at Niera.

"As I'll ever be."

"Niera..." began Tiarnen.

She turned back, expecting a jab from her brother.

"You can do this," he said, a rare tone of sincerity in his voice.

Garod turned up the torque dial, and the stage began to vibrate much more intensely. Tiarnen couldn't help but worry that the complication might explode and take half the Orpheum, not to mention the entire orchestra, with it. Instead, Garod pulled another lever, and the front quarter of the stage extended forward. Moving ahead with it, Dansby and the patrolmen walked further into the parting crowd, making sure no one tried to climb on top. After lengthening by about twenty metres, the stage settled, and now a catwalk ran down the middle between two pools of water that were underlit by oil lamps—their tiny exhaust bubbles rising to the surface and frothing on top.

Together, Reina and Niera crossed the catwalk and reached the front section of the stage, where they were greeted with applause. Reina stepped to the side so Niera could stand at the edge and greet the crowd, who fell silent with anticipation.

Though it seemed as if Tharus were half a league away, Tiarnen could tell that his father was penetrating Niera with his cold gaze. Even the nobles, who were casually moving about in the background of the enclave only moments ago, seemed frozen in place.

Niera raised Dawnbreaker to her chin, set the bow, and played the spirited intro to "Wolf Under the Wool." Just as before, streams of water leaped from the holes in the stage with each sprightly note, but the pool lamps now flashed in rhythm to her playful performance.

O' the flock is wet with morning dew
Though by count we have lost a few
There isn't a sign so I'll hazard a guess
As to what made the pen such a mess

By fang
By claw
By tail
By maw

There's a wolf over the mountain
There's a wolf across the pool
There's a wolf around the bend
There's a wolf under the wool
Awooo

O' one of the sheep has a strange gait
Every step closer seals its fate
Hiding in plain sight it leads astray
The grass will be red by end of day

By fang
By claw
By tail
By maw

There's a wolf over the mountain
There's a wolf across the pool
There's a wolf around the bend
There's a wolf under the wool

Awooo

Tiarnen could tell by the change in Niera's posture that by the time the second chorus of howling rang out, she had grown confident that the crowd was captivated. Her shoulders were further back, body movements more dramatic, and bow flourishes embellished. Callum and Jasper did their best to match Niera's fervour with brighter flashes of lamplight in the pools and rhythmic fountain eruptions. He knew Niera didn't want to slowly reveal what she was capable of. She needed everyone—here and now—to see why she was destined to be the next Maestro Dorian.

Her bow already a frayed blur, she reached the midpoint of the ballad and pressed even harder on Dawnbreaker's strings as the fountains rose higher and higher. Never before had Tiarnen seen her play with such determination. Even from a distance, he could tell she was pushing herself to the absolute limit. For the first time, he understood that being a maestro wasn't something his little sister wanted but something she *needed*.

"That's it. Keep it up," he whispered.

Caught in the moment, the very same frisson Tiarnen felt in the Conservatory washed over him now. He tried to ignore it, but sweat was already beading on his forehead, and both hands became so clammy that he thought the piccolo was going to slip through his fingers. A shimmering light began to dance around Niera, drawing his attention. It was hard to be sure, but it looked like she was sparking.

O' the time has come to begin our hunt
We'll find the menace and confront
Against all of us it won't stand a chance
And finally meet the end of a lance

By fang
By claw
By tail
By maw

There's a wolf over the mountain
There's a wolf across the pool
There's a wolf around the bend
There's a wolf under the wool

Awooo

Awooo

Awooo

The ballad ended with a crescendo, and Tiarnen expected gleaming glass shards to erupt from Dawnbreaker. But after the applause fell silent, so too did Niera. He realized that the shimmering was not emanating from his little sister but the lamplight refracting in the pool. Her head lowered, not in a gracious gesture to the crowd, but to give herself a moment to blink back the tears of shame. Reina went to take her hand and walk her back to the orchestra, but Niera only turned away and slowly trudged down the catwalk to return to her position. Tiarnen wanted to say something, anything, even if it was a sarcastic remark to help get her mind off what he knew she believed to be a complete and utter public failure. But his sweaty chills were starting to overwhelm him.

"Kaleigh?" Tiarnen's voice shook.

"What is it?" asked Kaleigh, perking up.

"Mind stepping in for me?"

"Sure. Everything okay?" She stood beside Tiarnen with a look of concern.

"Yeah, just need to catch my breath," he said, tugging at his restrictive jacket.

"Of course," said Kaleigh, taking position at the front of the wood-winds. "Maybe head up to the rampart and take in the breeze with the major?"

"Yeah, good idea." Tiarnen quietly slipped between the woodwind and percussion sections, hopped off the back of the stage, and walked up a flight of stairs leading to the top of the east wall. The cold ocean breeze immediately hit him as he stepped onto the rampart. Kaleigh was right about it helping—he could feel the sweat on his face evaporating, and with it, some nausea vanished from his swimming stomach.

"Don't you have a concert to finish?" asked Raghnall, noticing his nephew's sudden arrival.

"Think I need to sit the rest out," replied Tiarnen, taking his jacket off and sitting on the edge of a battlement.

"Not going to lie, you are looking a little green under the gills, lad." Tiarnen had practically sweat all the way through his dress shirt.

"I'll be fine," he said, hunching over.

"If you say so." Raghnall turned to Hiddleton, who was standing at a signal lamp. "Night watch check in yet?"

"I was just about to signal them, Major," said Hiddleton, pushing a lever back and forth which opened and closed the signal lamp shutter. A series of bright flashes cut through the mist and reached the other side of the bridge.

*

"Signal!" announced Patrolman Furley from inside the tiny brickwork guardhouse that only had room for himself and the signal lamp.

"You don't say!" proclaimed Patrolman Keaham, who was sitting at a small fire just outside of the guardhouse with Patrolman Watts to his left and Patrolman Bucklett to his right.

"Replying!" announced Furley, opening and closing the lamp shutter to inform Hiddleton that there had been no sign of the enemy along their shore.

"Must you inform us every hour, Furley?" asked Bucklett. "We can all see the damn signal!"

"Only following protocol. What's got your rope in a knot?"

The collective cheering of the crowd echoed from the city.

"That's what!" said Bucklett. "First concert in over twenty years, and we're stuck on watch."

"The Verse must hate us," muttered Watts, kicking a small rock off the edge of the high shoreline cliff only a couple of metres away.

"I say we're lucky to have such a view!" countered Furley. "Just look at her, finest city in all of Chora, without a doubt."

The patrolmen looked over their shoulders and couldn't help but admire how the long lamp-lit bridge faded into the mist and brought an ethereal quality to the moonlit silhouette of their city.

"Be lucky if we see anything at all soon. Fog only looks to be getting worse," said Watts. He tossed a piece of wood onto the fire, which kicked up a flurry of embers in response.

"Not to mention oddly warm," observed Keaham. "If anything, the temperature should be dropping about now."

"Just the fire kicking up again." Bucklett kicked at the log to settle it into the glowing coals.

"All the way into the forest, apparently," said Furley, pointing over to the nearby tree line.

The other patrolmen turned and saw three tiny orange lights floating and flickering within the dark pines.

"It's too damp." Watts narrowed his eyes. "Besides, the lights... they're moving."

"On your guard, men!" ordered Keaham.

The patrolmen grabbed their shields, stood to their feet, and formed a line, cautiously approaching the forest edge.

"By order of Praetor Tharus, whoever—or whatever—is there, show yourself!" demanded Keaham.

Instead, the lights went dim and vanished entirely.

"Scared them off, eh?" asked Bucklett.

Then, the three lights came back to life, along with three more. Before the patrolmen could blink, the six fiery lights had already darted out from the tree line. At first, any real shape was hard to make out, their movement so impossibly quick. But then the patrolmen suddenly found themselves staring at fairy-like creatures made purely of orange glass.

"What... what are they?" asked Furley.

"Haven't the foggiest," said Watts.

"I think they might be kyndling," said Keaham.

"Kynd-a-who?" asked Bucklett.

"*Kyndling*, you mud-head," corrected Keaham. "Remember my grandfather talking about them once, said they were made by music."

"You think Maestro Dorian is doing it?" asked Furley, holding his hand out. At first, the kyndling was hesitant, but then it slowly approached and landed softly on his palm, followed by a deep bow in greeting.

Bucklett cupped another kyndling with both hands and looked down at it. "Seems like that might explain your guest appearance, doesn't it, little fella?"

"I'll be. They are toasty!" Watts held a third kyndling closer, entranced by the countless little facets that made up its charming face.

"No complaints here," said Keaham, as the remaining kyndling landed on his shoulders.

More cheers erupted from the city. The kyndling startled, darted through the air for a brief second, and then hid under Keaham's armoured shoulder pauldrons. "Easy now, nothing to be scared about," he said, trying to coax one of the kyndling out with his finger. But the creature only burrowed further underneath—its pointed feet and sharp wings poking him like razors. "Ouch!" he shouted.

"What's wrong?" asked Furley.

"It's... it's inside my armour," said Keaham, now trying to forcibly pull the kyndling out with his fingers. "Tones!" he yelled, pulling his hand away to see his leather glove was slashed and his thumb and index finger bleeding. "Bloody things are as sharp as a knife!"

"Come here. Let's get your armour off." Watts leaned over and released the kyndling to help Keaham, only for it to swoop underneath the back of his own armour plating.

"Careful, that one went inside yours, too!" said Furley.

"They're burning me!" exclaimed Keaham, frantically trying to remove his armour as a bright orange glow began to emit from underneath.

Bucklett released the kyndling and rushed over to help Keaham as well, but he, along with the other patrolmen, were quickly brought to their knees as the winged menaces only dug deeper and grew hotter by the second.

"Send for help!" Keaham collapsed as the kyndling turned his armour into a roasting pan.

Furley tried to run back to the guardhouse, but the kyndling burned hotter and caused him to trip a few metres short. "Warn... we have to... warn," he gasped, his skin charring as he crawled. Only inches away from the signal lamp, Furley reached out for the lever... but his hand flaked away like burned parchment. Half cremated, he finally collapsed, his eyes closing on the sight of a tall female figure emerging from the forest.

She was like a shadow moving through the night—her burnt-orange leather maestro jacket dragging along the ground, its deep hood hiding her face. One by one, she walked through each patrolman's ashes like they were piles of dry leaves, and with her first step onto the bridge, the lanterns on either side extinguished.

*

"As much as it pains me to say this," said Reina, standing again at the front of the stage with Windwalker held to her chest, "we've come to our last ballad of the evening!"

The crowd booed.

"I know, believe me, I feel the same way," she assured them, "but you'll be happy to hear it's 'My Forever-After!'"

This immediately quelled the protests and turned them into applause. Reina, pleased to see she wasn't wrong, looked to the orchestra and made sure they were ready. Niera nodded in acknowledgement, her face pale and emotionless. Garod pulled down the third lever on the control panel, which caused the front of the stage to extend even further into the crowd and reveal another catwalk with underlit pools on either side. Reina put Windwalker's reed to her bottom lip and played the uplifting intro to "My Forever-After." Once again, the soft ascending scales seemed to bring the fountains and water streams to life as the crowd sang the first verse.

Tonight I was told that you fell
But refuse for this to be our knell
In the sky is where you belong
So I will fight to finish our song

No longer afraid to carve my trail
In your memory I will prevail

For the blade that wounded did not know
That you were my forever-after from long ago
For the shield that broke should not carry
My forever-after whom I would marry

Charge the oceans
Charge the dunes
Charge the mountains
Charge the moons

Tonight I was told that you fell
But refuse to despair nor to dwell
Many believe this quest too long
Yet our legend will prove them wrong
All our lives we were thought so frail
Yet in your honour a fleet sets sail

For the blade that wounded did not know
That you were my forever-after from long ago
For the shield that broke should not carry
My forever-after who I would marry

Charge the oceans
Charge the dunes
Charge the mountains
Charge the moons

Being the last ballad of the evening, Garod and the chronopunks turned every dial on the control panel wide open to give Reina every aquatic effect the stage could muster. The streamers shot overhead, and the fountains erupted higher than ever to surround her almost completely. As she was obscured from the crowd's view, it looked as though the lamps were now pulsing more vibrantly than ever, but from his vantage point, Tiarnen could see through the top of the fountain gaps—Reina was illuminating!

Brilliant sparks cascaded from the Windwalker's bell and formed vibrating diamond shapes a few inches long. One by one, they crystallized into brilliant shards of emerald-green maestro glass. Normally, every note would be intentionally illuminated, but the fact that it was happening randomly told Tiarnen that Reina was trying to fight her ability. Losing the battle, she began flourishing Windwalker to cast every shard into one of the pools, but they only made the water pulse brighter, and the fountains reach higher. The amplified display quickly raised the excitement and energy of the crowd, their voices growing so loud it felt as if all of Chora would hear them.

Tonight I was told that you fell
So that your sacrifice might cast a spell
On silent darkness where the lost grow strong
I pray your lesson will teach their throng
And at long last pull back the veil
To give hope a chance to avail

For the blade that wounded did not know
That you were my forever-after from long ago
For the shield that broke should not carry
It lost my forever-after whom I would marry

Dansby, now completely mesmerized by the light show, had forgotten about his duties and was instead standing in awe. Luckily, so was everyone else at the front of the stage. The crowd had stopped dancing and were simply singing the bridge together under the enchantment of the symphonic display.

Let it be known
Vengeance will come
My wrath unhinged
My ruin unleashed
My rebirth unbounded
Let it be known
Time will pass
A light released
A voice restored
A blade returned
Let it be known

Despite Reina's best efforts, the stage pools had now grown so bright and the fountains so tall that it was nearly impossible to conceal her loss of control. Tiarnen looked to the enclave and saw movement—Tharus was standing to his feet.

For the blade that wounded did not know
That you were my forever-after from long ago
For the shield that broke should not carry
My forever-after who I would marry

Charge the oceans
Charge the dunes
Charge the mountains

Charge the moons

A thousand times before
A thousand times again
My forever-after
Another chance
To begin again

In a final attempt to hide evidence of her lovestruck display, Reina cast the last shards of the evocative outro into the pool before they had fully glassed.

KA-FOOOOM!

All of the shards under the water shattered, releasing an acoustic shockwave that filled the fountains with blinding green light and shot them well over fifty metres into the night sky. Completely captivated by the unexpected climax, the crowd watched as the glowing fountain water sprinkled down onto their spellbound faces and took it as a sacred blessing from their maestro. After a few bewildered blinks, they leaped and embraced one another.

Reina, more than a little wet and weary, turned back to the orchestra and walked down the catwalk with a genuine smile of relief on her face. What evidence there had been of her illumination had been destroyed, and, just as she had promised, the provincials had been reminded that they were fighting for each other.

Applauding the performance, Tiarnen looked up to the enclave again and saw Tharus already leaving with his guard in tow. Though the provincials were easily fooled, Tharus certainly was not. Tiarnen knew their father was going to be furious at Reina for disobeying his command—not that he could prove it.

"Encore! Encore! Encore!" shouted the crowd, seemingly without end.

"Well played, everyone!" yelled Tiarnen.

The Ashbrooks and Finwicks cheered while the Roycrofts were already making their way backstage with sour looks on their faces. Niera, however, just stood in place and kept staring down at the stage.

"Well played, indeed!" echoed Raghnall, hoisting his pint up and taking the last gulp of ale.

"Not another…" whined Hiddleton.

"What is it?" asked Raghnall, only half interested.

"Nothing to worry about, Major. The bridge lanterns are blowing out, is all."

"Blowing out?" Raghnall glanced over his shoulder to see that the lanterns near the opposite shoreline had indeed gone dark.

Foof!

Another lantern died.

"Winds must be picking up with the tide," suggested Hiddleton.

Raghnall's eyes narrowed. He walked to the other side of the rampart where Hiddleton was standing and stared down the bridge, waiting for any sign of movement on the shore.

"Signal the watch again," he ordered.

Hiddleton grabbed the signal lever and shuttered the lamp in sequence, just as he did before. They waited for a reply.

"Why are they not responding?" asked Tiarnen, overhearing the conversation.

FOOF!

All of the bridge lanterns suddenly went dark.

"Take cover!" yelled Raghnall, pulling Tiarnen to the ground.

SHEEERUNK!

Tiarnen and Raghnall looked back to see Hiddleton now had a fiery orange shard of glass protruding from his chest. He staggered back in horror and, despite Tiarnen trying to grab onto him, fell over the edge of the rampart.

THUMP!

Before Tiarnen could warn everyone on stage, Niera had already been splattered with blood, and the patrolman's body was crumpled in a broken heap beside her.

Chapter Nine

GATE CRASHER

"Niera!" yelled Tiarnen.

"I've got her!" said Kaleigh, rushing to Niera and pulling her close as Reina ran to them from the front of the stage.

SMASH!

Two more fiery orange shards impacted the rampart and shattered.

"We're under attack!" announced Raghnall, pulling the broad shield off his back and raising it to protect Tiarnen from the lethal glass splinters streaking through the air. "Keep your head down!" he ordered, dragging Tiarnen towards the stairs as another shard exploded against his shield. Though Tiarnen tried to run with the major, it was rather pointless, given that Raghnall was practically carrying him under his arm as they hurried down to the stage.

"Is she all right?" asked Tiarnen, arriving just as Niera was pushing Kaleigh and Reina away.

"I'm fine!" she said, mad at herself for being stunned by the gruesome sight of the patrolman.

Relieved that none of the blood splattered across Niera's face was hers, Tiarnen focused on Hiddleton and knelt beside him with Raghnall. Together, they slowly rolled his corpse over to see the glowing orange shard still smouldering in his chest. A touch of grief in his eyes, Raghnall pinched the protruding end of the bloody burned glass with his gauntlet and carefully drew it from the wound.

"Lydvenko," muttered Reina.

Looking closer, Tiarnen couldn't help but notice some additional details: even though all shards had the same asymmetrical diamond shape, several characteristics gave insight into the maestro who illuminated them. In the case of this particular shard, the surface was dappled, which meant it was cast at the patrolman before it had time to anneal fully. Typically, that was avoided because it made the glass brittle, but in this case, it allowed for a surprise attack. His curiosity was further piqued by the shard's edges, since they often reflected the caster's emotion. As these were very jagged, it meant the shard was illuminated out of anger. He could see veins running through the inside of the glass; a characteristic Maestros couldn't intentionally control because it conveyed personality. Like a fortune teller reading a palm, he saw the veins were strangely erratic and broken, which meant the maestro was likely unstable.

Tiarnen sighed. "Why do I feel like we're in for a very long night?"

"Maestro Dorian?" called Dansby.

Reina looked back to see the entire crowd had frozen in fear behind the captain. "Send every provincial home and sound the alarm to warn the rest of the city," she ordered.

"Right away!" replied Dansby, turning and running back to the patrol.

"Orchestra!" yelled Reina, putting her shoulders back. "I believe a change of attire is in order!" Without hesitation, everyone broke formation and began making their way backstage. "Major, we'll meet you at the front gate shortly."

*

Clack-clack-clack!

Three rows of oil lamps ignited along the low ceiling of the subterranean Ready Room as Reina opened the door. "I want us on the bridge in five minutes!" she ordered.

"Yes, Maestro!" replied Niera, following in with the orchestra. "All right, you know the drill! Full regalia! Double time! Let's go!" She pointed to the three rows of tall beech wood wardrobes directly underneath the lamps.

Tiarnen and the orchestra immediately split into their instrument divisions, ran to their respective row, and flung their wardrobe doors open. Waiting for him on the top shelf was a pair of eel skin gloves and a ceramic vanguard helmet. The wardrobe was divided into two sections: hanging on the left was a heavy linen shirt, ceramic chainmail tunic, and reinforced trousers. Hanging on the right was a green high-collared military jacket with the Dorladdich crest, First Wind insignia, and a small cluster of victory pins on the lapels. Three ropes hung from the right shoulder, representing his military rank, which looped to connect at the back. A pair of double-thick whale hide boots and fuzzy wool socks rested on the bottom. Without hesitation, he and the orchestra stripped off their formal gowns and suits—using the wide wardrobe doors for privacy during the frantic change.

"How is everyone looking?" asked Niera, already putting on her jacket. Though it was standard issue, hers had a few extra embellishments such as silver-capped buttons, a jewelled ceramic leviathan pin resting in the middle of her medal cluster, and a braided silver rope that signified her position as Orchestra Lead.

"Halfway there," said Kaleigh, pulling the chainmail tunic over her curves, "but if Lachlan peeks at me again, the Lydvenkians won't have to bother killing him."

"Eyes ahead, Roycroft!" said Niera, looking past Kaleigh to see Lachlan spinning back to face his wardrobe. She reached for her helmet, only for Tiarnen, already in full uniform, to pull it down for her. "At least we know you can be on time when it counts."

"Good thing, too, since you still can't reach your own helmet," chuckled Tiarnen.

"Which is why I have you to fetch it for me." Niera punched him in the stomach and yanked the helmet from his hand.

"Easy! I don't want to go into battle injured." Tiarnen hunched over as he followed Niera toward the back of the room.

"Can I ask you something?" she said.

"Only if you promise to stop prefacing your questions."

"Why did you leave?"

"Leave?"

"After my solo."

"Oh! I left because..." He tried to think of an excuse that wouldn't raise more questions. "I was having problems with my piccolo."

"Problems?"

"The keys were sticking again," said Tiarnen, hoping she would buy it.

"That wouldn't happen if you actually cleaned the bloody thing once in a while," stated Niera.

"Instruments are supposed to be a reflection of their musician."

"Meaning?"

"Cleaning it would strip away all the character."

"Then you would be doing both of us a favour," said Niera, walking through an archway into the Maestro Chamber.

Tall pillars surrounded the small cylindrical room and curved towards each other at the ceiling, in the middle of which hung a large chandelier covered in hundreds of candles. They cast a column of soft light upon a small table in the centre of the chamber where Windwalker was resting. Beside it, a majestic full-length emerald-green maestro jacket hung from a mechanical coat rack.

"Listen, I'm sorry if the woodwinds sounded a bit diminished after I left. I didn't really think anyone would notice if I went missing," said Tiarnen.

"Well, I did, but… I thought maybe it was because…" Niera paused, running her finger over the shoulder of the maestro jacket in admiration. Though it was made of the finest merino wool, the jacket also had ceramic chainmail between the fabric layers. Every inch was held together by silver-stitch, the strongest thread in Dorladdich, which flowed from the seams to form woven patterns up the sleeves and over the back. Unlike Tiarnen and Niera's military attire, the jacket wasn't decorated with medals and ropes: there were only two small pins on the left breast—the Dorladdian crest and three numerals: *LIX*.

"*Because*?" Tiarnen pressed, nervous about what his sister might say.

"Because you were embarrassed of me." Niera's hand fell off the shoulder of the jacket to her side.

His heart sank at the realization that Niera thought he'd walked off stage because she had failed to illuminate.

"We could never be embarrassed of you, Twinkles," assured Reina. She emerged from her wardrobe in a fitted silk shirt, reinforced trousers, and thigh-high boots with elegant ceramic plating running up the front. A leather holster holding three small daggers was wrapped around her right leg.

"But I failed again, and this time in front of the entire city," said Niera, with more than a hint of disappointment in her voice.

"Your day will come," encouraged Tiarnen.

Niera's eyes watered. "How do you know?"

"Because you're a Straveritas," said Reina, popping the cork of a small bottle in her hand that was labelled *Fotentia*, then taking a sip of the glittery green elixir inside. Her face immediately contorted from the taste. "Which means somewhere, deep down, there is a spark."

"And what if I don't find it?" asked Niera.

"Then we only need to make sure it finds you," said Tiarnen.

"Which reminds me," said Reina, "the next time someone abandons my orchestra, they're going to find themselves spending a month in the dungeon."

"Will there be pies?" asked Tiarnen.

"*Am I clear?*" asked Reina, her stare piercing Tiarnen.

"As glass."

"Good." Reina gulped down the last drops of the elixir.

"Save me some?" asked Niera.

"You don't want to taste this, believe me," said Reina, shivering from the aftertaste.

Then, a tremor shook the entire chamber. They looked up to see dust falling from the chandelier.

"Why weren't we warned about the attack?" asked Niera, taking the empty potion bottle from Reina. She smelled it, only to instantly pull back in regret as the sting of alcohol infused with herbs, honey, ginger, and fermented cod liver oil hit her nose.

"Something tells me our watchmen weren't exactly given a chance," said Tiarnen.

"None of that matters now," said Reina, turning and facing the maestro jacket.

Tiarnen knew what she meant; much like Shatter, the Rules of Engagement were very clear when it came to the war; one of them being that whoever initiated battle had the right of *First Strike*, which allowed them to play the first warsong and set the tempo for the confrontation.

Reina shook her left arm, and a thin leather strap slipped out from under her sleeve. From it, a pair of keys dangled against her palm. She took the smaller key, slid it into a small hole in the centre of the jacket rack, and turned it clockwise.

Pop-click-ping-clack-click!

Several locking pins and springs released, causing the rack arms to retract and open the maestro jacket. Reina backed into it and slid her arms into the sleeves. With a roll of her shoulders, the jacket slipped off the rack and wrapped around her to fit perfectly. She fastened the clasps, fixed a cufflink, and took up Windwalker.

"Now, how about we show our uninvited guests a bit of Dorladdian hospitality?" said Reina.

*

VEERTHUNK!

Following behind Niera as Reina led the orchestra under the keep into the vast lower bailey, Tiarnen recognized the signature echo of maestro glass striking the colossal city gates where Raghnall was standing with his Night Ranger patrol. During the day, the bailey served as a popular social spot for provincials, which is why the well-worn cedar benches lining the perimeter had centuries of names carved into them, as well as countless clay cups and scattered months-old herald scrolls piled underneath them. Though they were washed off every week, Tiarnen couldn't help but admire the recent watercolour murals of corsairs sailing rough waters, leviathan sinking its teeth into the Roycroft sigil squid, and Maestro Dorian standing in a powerful pose along the walls.

"She looks good in that one," said Tiarnen.

"Yeah, but they always get her nose wrong," said Niera.

VEERTHUNK!

"How are we holding up, Major?" asked Reina, ignoring her siblings.

Raghnall turned around—his concerned expression fading to pride as he caught sight of his maestro and orchestra in full battle regalia.

"It'll take a lot more than a few shards to bring down our doors. But, truth be told, they can't hold up forever."

VEER THUNK-THUNK-THUNK!

As if adding an exclamation mark to Raghnall's warning, another volley of shards struck the granite doors.

"If we could only dredge up some reinforcements," said Tiarnen, already hearing a cacophony of footsteps arriving behind him.

"I might have found a few able bodies," said Dansby, marching towards the group with his Day Striders as well as Brigarch Costigan and an entire brigade comprised of just over three thousand legionaries.

"And in full armour, too. What are the odds?" asked Raghnall.

"Second and third brigade are suiting up as we speak," said Costigan.

Tiarnen didn't see the brigarchs much outside of combat but all three were poster boys for the Dorladdian legion; Costigan, especially. He had short chestnut-brown hair, a thick moustache, and heavy brows that shadowed his eyes, which had seen far too much bloodshed for someone in their mid-thirties. Costigan's amour was very similar to the rest of the legion as far as the ceramic plating and wool tunics, with the addition of oversized shoulder pauldrons from which a long green cape flowed.

Seeing the bailey packed full of ready and able Dorladdians at arms was always a sight to behold. The eager looks on their faces brought a welcome confidence boost for Tiarnen, especially since he knew that two more brigades were waiting in reserve.

The entire legion couldn't fit in the bailey, and that was the point; although it was a social area for the provincials most days, it was really designed to be a bottleneck for any attacking province should they manage to force their way past the gates. The doors of Dorladdich had only been breached twice before, but the enemy then had to fight against a sea of ten thousand shields. Thankfully, neither Lydvenko nor Phrysbruck had found victory, and Tiarnen certainly wasn't about to let that change tonight.

"Is the city secure?" asked Reina.

"Provincials are barring their doors as we speak," said Dansby.

Tiarnen looked up at the lower city tier—all the buildings along the east-facing districts were shuttered, and the streetlamps doused, making it appear eerily abandoned. A nightingale swooped through the air and drew his gaze as it landed on the window ledge of the upper gatehouse. Inside, he could see Tharus, wearing a heavy grey overcoat drenched in war medals, and his entourage arriving to gain a strategic view of the bridge.

VEER THUNK!

"By the Verse, Lydvenko could not have picked a worse night for an attack," grunted Raghnall.

"Then let's show them what we do with party crashers," said Reina.

"Costigan, what are our orders?" asked Raghnall.

"You tell me, Major," replied Costigan. "Our praetor has named you Battlemaster this evening."

Raghnall looked confused by this news.

"Makes sense. You know the city better than anyone," said Reina.

Tiarnen raised an eyebrow. "Looks like someone is coming out of retirement."

"It would be my pleasure." Raghnall grinned as he walked to a massive waterwheel on the left side of the gate and gripped a long handle extending from the gears in the centre. Usually, it would have taken three patrolmen to move it an inch, but the major had no problem pulling it down.

CLUNK!

Just above the gates, slots on both sides of the barbican opened, and heavy waterfalls poured down onto the waterwheels below. Slowly, they began to turn, and the colossal twin doors swung inwards, revealing numerous fiery orange shards, some still glowing, stabbed into the granite like daggers.

An ominous maw of foggy darkness devoured the bridge ahead, but Reina didn't hesitate for a second. Maestro jacket furling in the damp, salty wind, she stepped onto the bridge with Raghnall, Dansby, and Niera following behind. Tiarnen knew he was supposed to stay in formation with the woodwinds but thought it best to accompany them. They stared into the endless night, hoping to catch a glimpse of what they were up against... but nothing seemed to stir.

"Any sign of them?" asked Raghnall.

Dansby squinted. "None that I can see."

"Maybe they gave up?" asked Niera.

"Not likely, but we shouldn't provok—" began Reina.

"Cowards!" yelled Raghnall. "Has Lydvenko become so pathetic that it only strikes from the shadows these days?"

Reina shook her head. "Never mind."

A malevolent cackle emanated from the darkness.

"Shadow is all that vill be left of your city once I am finished vith it," said a foreboding female voice.

"Then step into the light, and you can get started!" said Dansby, drawing his shield and taking a step ahead of Reina.

"No need," hissed the voice. "For you vill find it is I who burns brightest!"

Haunting strings suddenly filled the air, and an orange shard chaotically flickered to life midway down the bridge to reveal Maestro Lydia standing by herself with a black harp shaped like a raven's wing resting on her hip.

"Appears we have a new Lydia to face," said Reina.

"The Sixty-... Fifth, it would seem," said Tiarnen, noticing the *LXV* numerals on Lydia's jacket.

"Why are you here?" asked Niera, surprised to see Tiarnen standing behind her. "Get back in formation!"

Tiarnen ignored her entirely. "Did we hear anything about the sixty-fourth being defeated?"

"No mention of it from Holgor," said Reina.

"I don't bloody care if she's the hundredth." Raghnall raised his voice for Lydia to hear. "You've come a long way to die, witch!"

Lydia's cracked, peeling lips stretched into a sinister grin as she flourished Ravenwing.

"So much for negotiations," said Tiarnen, watching the shard rise high into the mist, giving it a foreboding glow.

"Never was our strongest suit, anyway," said Raghnall, winking at him.

"Lead?" said Reina.

Niera turned to her. "Yes, Maestro."

"Bring up the orchestra."

"With pleasure."

Lydia rubbed the string harder, and the shard flared. Its fiery glow burned the mist away and pushed back the night to reveal Sivakosha, Lydvenko's renowned Orchestra Lead, standing behind Lydia, holding a double bell trumpet and dressed in a slim-fitting orange leather catsuit with iron spikes protruding from the shoulders. Further back stood the Lydvenkian orchestra, also in orange leather uniforms, which was split down the middle in ranked formation.

Waiting in between the orchestra rows, Praetor Khazlokov was mounted on a wrought iron mechanical chronosteed and wearing a heavy grey overcoat covered in war medals. Long, greasy, salt-and-pepper hair framed his sharp cheekbones, hooked nose, and deep-inset cracks running down his pale skin, much like Tharus's. On his right, stood Inquisitor Valchev. The stern-looking elderly man was quite tall and smartly dressed in military uniform, but his incredibly long black beard made it hard to see any finer details. On Khazlokov's left stood a dwelglin. The small, mischievous creature had mottled black skin, a thorny back, narrow orange eyes, long sharp ears, and hooked fingers, which helped it carry the heavy Lydvenkian warsong book that was bound in dark orange leather and reinforced with a rusty iron frame.

Just behind them, vanishing into the fading light was the Lydvenkian legion—the first row carrying tall banners of orange fabric, with the Lydvenkian sigil of a gear held by clawed hands burned into it. The next thirty rows of their first brigade waited behind impatiently, covered head to toe in rusted and spiked armour.

Khazlokov looked down at the dwelglin, and it immediately opened the warsong book to the first bookmark, presenting the title page. After reading the name of the warsong, Khazlokov reached inside his tunic and pulled out a long iron wand with an orange sapphire tip. He tapped the wand three times on the shoulder of his chronosteed, making it glow, and then flourished it as though writing cryptic letters in the air to Lydia as she glanced back at him.

"'Ferigni in F Major,'" said Lydia, lip curling.

"As you command, Maestro," said Sivakosha.

Lydia aligned her fingers along Ravenwing's strings. Then, her shadowed eyes looked up and narrowed with rage at Tharus.

Chapter Ten
FERIGNI
IN F MAJOR

One by one, Lydia plucked Ravenwing's strings and opened "Ferigni's" first movement with grim tonic phrases while Sivakosha led the orchestral trumpets, horns, and tubas in ferocious accompaniment.

Dansby grumbled under his breath.

"What's wrong?" asked Reina, watching Niera return with the orchestra in formation behind her.

"So much brass," said Dansby.

"Too harsh?" asked Tiarnen.

"Too Lydvenkian."

Tiarnen was hard-pressed to disagree. Each of the provincial orchestras had similar string, woodwind, brass, and percussion sections but used different combinations to best represent their musical cultures. He was sure that Lydvenko would have had just as much to say about Dorladdich's dominant woodwind section.

"It's not her orchestra we need to worry about," said Reina.

Together, they watched as Lydia effortlessly illuminated a scornful melody of contouring whole notes into a slew of rust-orange shards that leaped off the harp string like licks of flame and then streaked through the air. Ascending motifs conjured more arrays of glowing glass, which were made thicker and stronger by the rising orchestral harmony. They grouped together with the melodic clutch to form a glimmering nebula around Lydia by the time she finished "Ferigni's" exposition.

Her tempo slowing, Lydia transitioned seamlessly into the second movement. The orchestra diminished to let Ravenwing scream with a solo of scalic leaps and ascending triads that brought new variation to her melodic theme. "Ferigni" suddenly seemed eerily joyous, as though Lydia was now revelling in her attack on Dorladdich. With a flourish of her harp, the nebula drew inwards as if she had her own gravitational pull, the shards swirling at waist height until they looked like a spiral galaxy of glowing stars. Though it was still unfinished, the warsong wasn't any less dangerous—especially to Lydia. One misplayed note or accidental tilt of Ravenwing would cause the vortex to collapse and cut her in half. That, however, didn't seem to be risk enough to stop Lydia from lashing at Reina.

Three fiery shards approached fast, but Dansby jumped ahead of her and raised his shield in protection. Instead of striking the captain, the shards darted around him. The first curved to the left. The second, to the right. The third arced over top and shot through the middle of the orchestra, causing everyone in the woodwind section to duck—except for Wendel, whose contrabassoon slowed him down. Pierce managed to push Wendel out of the way, but not without the shard cutting the neck of his oboe and his bottom two fingers clean in half. Clutching his blood-soaked hand, Pierce fell to the ground as the other two shards stabbed into the brickwork around the gatehouse window from where Tharus watched.

"Get him to the infirmary!" ordered Reina.

With an amused smile on her face, Lydia finished the second movement and drew the last of her shards into a vortex. Tempo hastening, the orchestra rose up and accompanied "Ferigni's" third movement. All of the delight Lydia seemed to take in her solo was quickly extinguished by a return to the sombre melody she'd played at the beginning—only this time it was with additional sharp ornamentations that made it feel spiteful. She angled Ravenwing upwards and cast the vortex of shards high into the night, forming a cyclone of fiery light above her.

Tiarnen felt the air grow humid as he anxiously watched Lydia's shards align and collide to form the core of her lattrice. Though shards were formidable weapons on their own, when they were layered together in geometric patterns, they had a much more powerful effect. Just like everyone else, Tiarnen found lattrices difficult to describe in a way that did their abstract complexity and beauty justice. This time was no different; Lydia's lattrice was fast growing to become both captivating and intimidating. Her last odious note rang out and shot into the heart of the lattrice like an arrow. At the moment of contact, all of the shards fused together, and hundreds of jagged striations formed deep in the prismatic glass-like veins. The legion held their clawed gloves up to it in worship as the lattrice nova flashed with blinding brightness.

"Shields up!" yelled Raghnall, raising his to cover himself and Tiarnen.

Dansby defended Reina once again while the Night Rangers quickly formed a shield canopy over as much of the orchestra as they could. However, even the smallest gaps between shields, of which there were many, resulted in musicians being burned and blinded by the blazing light.

"Look away!" shouted Reina.

For a moment, Tiarnen felt like he had been trapped in a furnace, and even though Raghnall's broad shield provided adequate protection, he could still see the bones of his hands as they covered his eyes. The flash faded, and Tiarnen stepped out from behind Raghnall's shield to blink what little was left of the lattrice back into focus. Most of it had disintegrated after the climax, and what remained was flaking away and vanishing into the night with the offshore breeze. Everything around him that was left unshielded, including the bridge itself, was scorched and still searing.

"'*Step into the light,*' he said," remarked Tiarnen, looking at Dansby.

"'*And you can get started,*' he said," added Raghnall.

Dansby rubbed his brow. "Might have gotten a bit eager there for a second."

"My eye! I can't see anything!" yelped Fiona, looking around and blinking her left eye frantically.

"Let's avoid encouraging any further displays of power, shall we?" Reina stepped out from under Dansby's shield and looked over to Fiona. "Coniel, check on her."

Tiarnen glanced over his shoulder to see Kaleigh and the woodwinds standing ready. "How are the rest of us looking, Second Wind?"

"Some better than others," said Kaleigh, trying not to smile at the sight of Lachlan whose right eyebrow had been singed off.

"They should know by now that Dorladdich won't be intimidated," stated Niera, pushing the patrolman's shield out of her way.

Then, the bridge began to tremor.

"I don't think that was her intention," said Tiarnen, feeling the tremors grow stronger under his feet as a distant screaming filled the air. He looked down the bridge to see movement stirring in the darkness. To his horror, the Iron Legion's first brigade emerged from the shadows and charged ahead—their long iron claws glowing red hot with "Ferigni's" effect.

"Guardians of Dorladdich!" shouted Raghnall. The patrolmen raised their chins, hanging on his next words as they watched the Lydvenkian brigade fast approaching. "Ah, to hell with the bloody speech—this is as far as those wretches come, *am I understood?*"

"Yes, Major!" answered the patrol.

Raghnall turned the handle on his broad shield counterclockwise and released hinges on either side. Dansby arrived on the major's left. A patrolman arrived on the major's right. In unison, they linked their shields to the hinges, which then allowed an arriving platoon of patrolmen to continue linking to each other until the outermost man locked into a set of hinges embedded in the bridge walls to form a chain-linked barrier.

"Brace yourselves!" warned Raghnall as the legion crashed against them.

SMASH!

Hinges creaked under the strain, but the shields held strong, and the platoon stood their ground while hundreds of glowing razor-sharp claws tried to reach over and cut one of the patrolmen down, breaking a link in the barrier.

"Don't give them an inch!" yelled Dansby, ducking his head as claws swiped inches from his face.

Using his gauntlet, Raghnall grabbed the clawman by the throat and crushed it with ease. The platoon followed the major's example and struck any Lydvenkian who was close enough—sending them staggering backwards with cracked helmets, bloodied noses, or broken jaws.

"Gentlemen, get this garbage off my bridge!" shouted Raghnall.

The outer patrolmen unhinged their shields from the wall, and Raghnall led everyone forward as a single unit—forcing the clawmen back to the next set of hinges a few metres down the bridge and linking in again. Over and over, they repeated the effort, until the clawmen had lost over half the distance they gained in the rush.

Tiarnen could see Khazlokov watching his soldiers' failure with disgust. The praetor raised his wand, and before he had pointed it fully at the major, a second battalion burst forth from the darkness. As they ran up the bridge to support their comrades, Tiarnen noticed that these soldiers were wearing different armour. Instead of the thin, rusted plating of the first battalion, theirs was polished cast iron; the left shoulder pauldron three times as big and covered in long spikes. He turned back and looked to the gatehouse window where Tharus was flipping through the warsong book pages. Finding the one he was searching for, Tharus tapped his wand on the table to light the jewelled tip and, with a quick gesture, relayed the title to Reina.

"'Siathriste in D Major!'" she announced.

Chapter Eleven
SIATHRISTE
IN D MAJOR

Still trying to blink her vision back, Fiona opened "Siathriste" with a barrage of drum strokes that roused the rest of the percussion section. Though everyone knew their First Drum was erratic at the best of times, no one could argue that when Fiona's snare became her singular focus, few in the province could keep up with her riffs.

Nodding to the rhythm, Reina took a deep breath, pressed Windwalker to her lips, and brought the opening melody of "Siathriste" to life. Led by Niera, the orchestra accompanied their maestro—strings and woodwinds ornamenting every confident phrase she played with soulful harmony. As a result, Reina's emerald shards grew thicker and stronger while the light trailing behind them swirled like water vapour. Playing on with poise, the last few bars of "Siathriste's" uplifting first movement formed small ponds of glistening glass around her.

With another deep breath, Reina entered a spirited second movement of contrasting motifs stretched across several scalic sequences. In order to let their maestro's solo shine, the orchestra diminished, but Fiona and the drums doubled their tempo. Invigorated by the spirited pace, Reina closed her eyes and began to dance with Windwalker—flourishing it with graceful gestures as though the instrument were an extension of her body. In response, the glass ponds flowed into each other and formed a glinting vortex around her.

"Here they come!" announced Dansby, watching the battered Lydvenkian first battalion pull themselves off the Dorladdian shield barrier and split down the middle to allow the second battalion, now running at full speed, a clear line of sight.

"Brace yourselves!" ordered Raghnall, widening his stance as the second battalion drove their spiked shoulders into the front-line shields like battering rams.

WHAM!

The impact was crushing and pushed all but the outer patrolmen linked to the bridge back several feet. Yet, somehow, the Night Rangers kept the barrier intact, though it didn't deter the Lydvenkians from pressing on and straining the shields to their limits.

"*Major?*" said Dansby, panicking as the hinges of his and many other shields began to crack and break apart.

"Use your arms!" ordered Raghnall, hooking his free arm around the patrolman's to his right. The rest of the platoon did the same, but the stress on their bodies quickly became overwhelming.

Watching the front line struggling, Reina carried her melodic momentum into "Siathriste's" third movement. Wasting no time, she played through several sanguine sequences, then pointed Windwalker towards the night sky. The gesture raised the vortex around her high above the bridge, where it swirled and closed in on itself. One by one, with precise flourishes Reina aligned each shard until the lattrice core finally formed. Taking a deep breath, she illuminated the final note of "Siathriste" and carefully wove the long shard into the lattrice core, fusing it together. Instantly, it flashed with vibrant green light—smooth symmetrical striations running through it and blooming with resonant power.

As relieved as he was to see the gleaming lattrice complete, a strange sensation grew inside of Tiarnen. At first, it felt like tickling, but then he realized that every inch of him was suddenly vibrating.

The lattrice pulsed three times in rhythm.

WOM-WOM-WOM!

Reacting to the pulse, the left oscillator in Raghnall's broad shield reverberated and charged with kinetic energy. The major pounded his gauntlet against it in matching rhythm.

BAM-BAM-BAM!

On the last strike, the oscillator locked into place and filled the shield's carved linework with the same luminance that the lattrice was emitting. Though the aesthetic effect was brilliant, it brought no harm to the Lydvenkians. Instead, basking in the signature Dorladdian hue only angered them further and gave cause to press their spiked shoulders into the defensive barrier even harder.

Tiarnen and the orchestra could only look on helplessly, watching the front line bow and slide further back—the platoon using the last of their strength to hold their arms and the barrier together.

"Maestro!" yelled Tiarnen, instinctually taking a step forward.

"Stay where you are!" ordered Reina, watching the lattrice with confidence as it pulsed again.

WOM-WOM-WOM!

The right oscillator in Raghnall's shield responded and reverberated with kinetic energy until he pounded his gauntlet against it in matching rhythm, just like before.

BAM-BAM-BAM!

Once again, on the last strike, the oscillator locked into place. This time, the kinetic charge spread not only across Raghnall's shield but over the entire front line, lighting up the faces of the enraged clawmen as they clambered over top of their comrades so that they could leap down onto the patrol and shred them to pieces.

WOM-WOM-WOM!

"Together!" ordered Raghnall.

The front line struck their shields in rhythm with the major.

BAM-BAM-BAM!

On the last beat, Raghnall's middle oscillator locked into place and pulsed with luminance across the entire front line, their shields releasing a massive sonic boom together.

KABOOM!

The shockwave rippled down the bridge and levelled the battalions in its wake. Resonant power now completely drained, the lattrice flaked away and faded into the darkness. Everything became eerily silent as Raghnall slowly looked over his shield to see most of the Lydvenkians lying unconscious—their broken bodies piled on top of each other or hanging off the edges of the bridge.

"GOODNIGHT, LYDVENKO!" shouted Dansby, the patrol and orchestra cheering in proud support.

"Release!" said Raghnall, turning his shield handle clockwise and disengaging what little was left of the hinges. The front line separated, and the patrolmen were able to move freely once again, shaking out their strained and sore arms.

"Cut that a little close, don't you think?" asked Raghnall, walking back to Reina.

"You know better than anyone that 'Siathriste' takes *exactly* three minutes and forty-two seconds to perform," said Reina.

"Yes, well, felt like a lifetime from where we were standing."

"But we are standing," replied Reina, wiping the sweat from the sides of her cheeks.

"You all right?" asked Raghnall.

She smiled and nodded.

"Captain!" called a patrolman. "Looks like a few Lydvenkians are still up for a fight!"

"I would hate for them to leave disappointed," said Dansby.

"Wait for reinforce—" began Raghnall.

"Don't worry, Major. We'll make it quick!" said Dansby, taking his platoon down the bridge to deal with the handful Lydvenkians staggering towards them.

Eyes narrowing at the sight of her defeated forces, Lydia looked back to Khazlokov, who waved his wand furiously.

"'Morvistya in F Major'!" yelled Lydia.

Chapter Twelve
MORVISTYA
IN F MAJOR

A strange metallic sound filled the air. At first, Tiarnen couldn't place the source, but as it grew louder, he realized it was Lydvenkian cymbals grinding together. The deep rumbling of tubas soon followed, as did piercing trumpets, which blared with abrasive ascending scales—their sharp notes adding a high-pitched tension to "Morvistya's" first movement. Tiarnen's jaw unconsciously clenched. Then, Ravenwing cried out with a virulent melody of fiery quarter notes that quickly flickered into tiny copper-orange shards and swarmed around Lydia.

BOM-BOM... BOM-BOM... BOM-BOM...

A frantic heartbeat of timpani drums opened the second movement, their rapid rhythm shaking the bridge to rouse what was left of the stunned Lydvenkian battalions. To Tiarnen's dismay, many soldiers awoke—violas rising in support as they stumbled to their feet.

Despite regaining a significant portion of her forces, Lydia wanted her disappointment to be heard, and so made Ravenwing resound with bitter phrases—the sharp extended chords illuminating long shards that drew the flickering swarm into a glittering glass nebula around her.

Tiarnen watched Dansby and the platoon—their bodies silhouetted by Lydia's growing luminance—finally reach the disorientated battalions. Though the soldiers tried to fight them off, albeit like drunken brawlers, most were easy prey and quickly returned to their knees—the violas fading as each one fell.

"That's right! Crawl back to your hole of a province!" yelled Dansby, kicking a clawman who was inching down the bridge in the hope of returning to Lydia for protection.

But instead of showing empathy, Lydia only became more appalled by the weakness she was witnessing and entered her third movement solo by hitting the side of Ravenwing resentfully. Seeing their maestro's disgust grow, the orchestra quickly diminished until little was left of their harmony except for the ominous heartbeat of the timpani drums.

Lydia continued battering the harp in rhythm, her surrounding shards pulsing with each strike, until the few soldiers who had been able to stay on their feet made the mistake of choosing not to fight but retreat with their crawling comrades. She cackled malevolently at the display of cowardice, then doubled "Morvistya's" tempo.

BOM-BOM–BOM-BOM–BOM-BOM.

The drums quickened to keep pace while her fingers repeated the melody so furiously that it seemed as though she might break the harp strings. Despite the abuse, shard after shard leaped from the resilient Ravenwing while Lydia spun and caused the nebula to swirl into a glowing vortex of light and glass around herself.

Once again, Sivakosha led the tubas, trumpets, and grinding cymbals to begin "Morvistya's" rancorous fourth movement. Their caustic texture kept in time, while the timpani drums were ornamented with snares that added a piercing quality to the end of the now rapid heartbeat.

Lydia stopped twirling like a half-strung marionette and leaned back to tilt Ravenwing upwards—her flourish casting the vortex high into the night sky, leaving long, spiral streaks of titian light behind. She continued playing with perfect cadence, flourishing now with violent jerking. Her thrashes caused the shards to collide and form "Morvistya's" lattrice core.

Tiarnen felt the air grow hot again and expected the platoon to immediately fall back, but to his surprise, they continued chasing the soldiers further down the bridge.

"What is Dansby thinking?" asked Reina.

"He's not," said Raghnall. "Captain! Get your ass back in formation!"

But the captain was too far ahead and Lydia much too loud for him to be able to hear the major's firm order.

BOM-BOM–BOM-BOM–BOM-BOM.

The entire brass section of the Lydvenkian orchestra roared in full to open the fifth and final movement. Every horn was screaming now in refusal of Lydvenko's defeat while Lydia's melody softened with gentle leaps to become eerily inviting. Even her hands started moving delicately across Ravenwing as though trying to soothe it from the pain she had just inflicted.

Tiarnen couldn't help but wonder if Lydia had a change of heart after seeing her soldiers beg for salvation. He watched as she built up "Morvistya's" core to form an orange lattrice that almost resembled a pair of emblazoned wings, the sharpest tips extending like outstretched feathers to embrace her fallen comrades. Just as the platoon appeared to reach Lydia, Tiarnen realized how wrong he was about her forgiveness.

With a flash, the last shard shot into the core and fused "Morvistya's" lattrice together, but the warsong effect wasn't unleashed. Instead, Lydia held the finale by running her finger up and down the E minor string for so long that blood began dripping down her hand. The note now deafening, Dansby and the platoon stopped in their tracks—putting their hands over their ears to block out the painful amplitude. Even the lattrice succumbed to the endless reverberation. Cracks spread out through every inch of the crystalline structure until it finally shattered into thousands of prismatic splinters.

Tiarnen was utterly confused. Why would she intentionally destroy her own lattrice?

Lydia answered by pointing Ravenwing towards the bridge.

Though Dansby and the patrol raised their shields in protection, they quickly realized that she had no intention of wasting a single splinter on them. Instead, she made tiny but precise flourishes with Ravenwing to ensure every Lydvenkian soldier was turned into a pin cushion. Hundreds of times over, their bodies were pierced by the descending splinters. Those who still had breath used it to cry out for mercy as darkness swallowed the bridge once again.

Niera glanced grimly at Reina. "She's executing them?"

BOM.

"No," corrected Reina. "She's *resurrecting* them."

BOM-BOM.

Tiarnen watched uneasily as a soft, warm light pulsed to rhythmic life in the distance. It slowly rose up, swayed side to side, then started to move up the bridge, growing brighter.

BOM-BOM.

To his horror, he could now see that the pulses were emitting from one of the clawmen. The searing glass splinters protruded from every inch of his charred, bubbling skin as he twitched and lurched to the possessive beat.

BOM-BOM... BOM-BOM.

A second clawman began pulsing in rhythm behind the first.

BOM-BOM... BOM-BOM... BOM-BOM.

Before Tiarnen could swear at the gruesome sight, at least half of the Lydvenkians were back on their feet and marching towards the city again in full bloom—heartbeats and light pulses layering to become louder and brighter, while the platoon ran around them to return to the front line.

"Captain!" yelled Reina. "Don't touch their—"

BOM-BOOM!

One of the possessed clawmen exploded. The violent blast tore apart the patrolmen around him, throwing Dansby, as well as the rest of the platoon, against the north side of the bridge, knocking them unconscious.

"Night Rangers, with me!" ordered Raghnall, already rushing ahead.

Tiarnen wanted to follow the major, but much like the rest of the orchestra, he knew he would be of little use, so he stayed in position, praying that they could reach the captain before it was too late. After a hard sprint, the rangers reached the mid-bridge and vanished into the haze just as a few possessed Lydvenkians emerged. Tiarnen's stomach sank as they came into full haunting detail; their eyes, noses, and mouths were completely burned away—only empty glowing holes remained. The next few seconds felt like hours, but Tiarnen held hope that the major was heeding Reina's warning and finding a way to keep a safe distance from—

BOM-BOOM!

Another possessed man exploded—the bright flash revealing broken bodies and debris flying through the air. Determined to secure a safe return for both platoons, Reina turned to Tharus for her next warsong. Tiarnen looked to the gatehouse as well and saw his father already relaying the title with a quick series of wand gestures.

"'Archavral'?" asked Reina, confused by the choice.

"Can't be right," said Tiarnen, equally as baffled.

Reina waved her hand and signalled Tharus to repeat the title.

He relayed the exact same wand gestures again.

"'Archavral!'" announced Niera.

"But it doesn't make sense," said Tiarnen, "the effect will push all of us—"

"First positions!" commanded Niera, ignoring his concern.

Chapter Thirteen
ARCHAVRAL
IN D MAJOR

Tiarnen still couldn't understand Tharus's choice. "Archavral" was composed to flood the bridge and force the enemy back to the shoreline. However, with the Night Rangers still lost among the possessed Lydvenkians, he had no idea how the class two warsong wouldn't become a watery grave for both sides.

Niera didn't seem to share in his confusion, nor his concern for that matter, and loyally raised Dawnbreaker to slice her bow across the strings. With a slow ascending phrase of undulating chords, she led the orchestra into "Archavral's" first movement. The string section leaped to life. Violins and cellos accompanied her with chromatic scales that found harmony and called out for Maestro Dorian to join them.

With confidence, Reina put Windwalker to her lips and played "Archavral's" turbulent melody; clusters of triplets sprayed forth tiny jade-green shards from the artisan clarinet like a waterspout. After several more blustering phrases, the first movement was finished, and a shimmering nebula of shards hung in the air like a drizzle made weightless by the breeze.

Once again, Tiarnen looked for any sign of the major, but only more and more possessed clawmen emerged from the opaque smoke; by his count, at least thirty of them were approaching now.

Seemingly unworried, Reina focused intensely on the bridge—evolving "Archavral's" melody with sequences of cresting dyads and trills that illuminated crystal-clear shards, their gravity pulling the drizzle into streams of glimmering glass around her. The orchestra opened the second movement with riveting rhythmic figures. Ebbing refrains followed, as did accented motifs between the strings and woodwinds. Reina followed with rippling sequences that made Windwalker spill glass—the shards pouring into the many streams and making them grow brighter.

BOM-BOOM!

Splinters shot out in all directions from inside the billowing smoke and flame.

Though Reina was shocked by yet another sudden blast, she stepped forward—refusing to suffer interruption. Sweat beaded down her temples as her hands continued to dance over Windwalker's keys, opening "Archavral's" third movement solo with phrase after phrase of rolling trills—each of them illuminating a spiral of shards. Breaking form, she flourished her clarinet gracefully and wove the gleaming streams into a single vibrant vortex around herself.

As Reina's clover-green light washed over Tiarnen, he noticed that the ocean far below the bridge was becoming louder. In fact, each time the waves crashed, they grew in strength, while Reina leaned side to side in rhythm as though she was trying to rock a boat. In a burst of movement, she thrust Windwalker up at the night sky—the flourish casting her vortex high into the air where she wove together "Archavral's" intricate core. As she did so, her leg nearly gave out from the exhaustion she had been trying to ignore.

"Maestro?" asked Niera, noticing it too.

Reina did not reply and only kept performing as the partially formed lattrice core flashed chaotically.

Tiarnen was starting to believe that the concert had drained more of Reina's strength than she was letting on. Yet, to his relief, their maestro still managed to guide the last shard of the core into place and piece it together. Encouraged by her display of prowess, Lachlan and the brass developed the melody with swift, scintillating phrases as Tiarnen and the woodwinds accented them to begin the fourth movement.

Reassured by the orchestra's increasing amplitude, Reina stood tall again and played several cascading sequences that flung shimmering shards around the lattrice core.

The wind now gusting, Tiarnen looked ahead as the smoke from the explosions vanished into the night, revealing a heart-wrenching scene at the mid-bridge. Armour, bodies, and rubble were scattered everywhere, completely covered in soot and sparkling orange dust. Chunks of the bridge were missing, likely the exact spots where the explosions erupted. However, among the carnage, movement stirred with glints of green and grey. In utter disbelief, Tiarnen watched the major limp toward them with Dansby over his shoulder and two patrolmen following him through the corpse maze.

"There they are!" shouted Tiarnen, sincere relief in his voice.

"Orchestra! Into the courtyard!" ordered Reina, her voice noticeably strained.

Tiarnen and Niera looked at each other in confusion.

"*What?*" asked Tiarnen. "We're not just going to leave you—"

BOM-BOOM!

The last two patrolmen, so close to escaping, flew through the air like rag dolls, their lacerated bodies landing onto three more possessed clawmen.

BOOM! BOOM! BOOM!

Both the mid-bridge and part of the upper section were completely engulfed in flames and smoke—only for Lydia to emerge unscathed from the inferno.

"Now!" ordered Reina, turning to face them with sweat beading down her temples.

Niera grabbed Tiarnen by the sleeve, turned him around, and dragged him to the city gates. The entire orchestra reluctantly returned to the courtyard with bewildered looks on their faces.

"Why are we falling back?" asked Wendel.

"And how can we support Maestro Dorian from this *far away?*" asked Coniel.

"By giving her everything we have!" yelled Tiarnen, yanking his sleeve from Niera's grip to turn and face the front gate.

"Reform first positions!" said Niera.

The orchestra immediately reformed, and the drums unleashed a flurry of rhythmic strikes while the woodwinds called out to help open "Archavral's" tremulous fifth and final movement.

Grateful to hear the orchestra regroup so quickly, Reina blew a shallow breath through Windwalker and began an undulant melody. Lilting arpeggios illuminated shards several shades darker, which trickled out of Windwalker and then cascaded over the left side of the bridge. She repeated her melody, the shards again noticeably dim, and cast them over the right side of the bridge.

After repeating the effort several more times over, Reina began to sway back and forth—white sea-foam, normally hundreds of feet below, splashed up along both sides of the bridge as though the ocean itself was at her command.

Suddenly, she fell to one knee.

As much as Tiarnen didn't want to accept it, the combined fatigue from the concert and battle appeared to have finally overwhelmed his sister.

"Maestro, fall back!" yelled Tiarnen.

Hearing her brother's desperate plea pulled Reina from exhaustion's grip, if only for a moment. She looked up to see the gruesome Lydvenkian horde nearly in arm's reach of her, and so with a last desperate effort, she pointed Windwalker up at the sky. The defiant flourish caused a titanic wave to erupt on both sides of the bridge; the shards she had cast over the edges now pulsing as they rose like mountains and crested onto the core. "Archavral's" lattrice formed and surged with light to bring what looked like the entire sea down upon the bridge.

VOOOSH!

The roaring river of murky water turned the bridge into an aqueduct and flooded the bailey. Before Tiarnen could give warning, he was already tumbling head over heels in what felt like a whirlpool while clawmen exploded all around him. Violent flashes of orange light tore through the water, and glass shrapnel whizzed past from every direction.

After a short burst of panicked strokes, he finally broke the surface—taking a desperate gasp for air—to see Raghnall severing the gate chain with the edge of his shield. The waterwheel spun wildly, and the front gates slammed shut. With the river dammed, the bailey drained into the street and revealed a waterlogged orchestra spread out among steaming pieces of possessed Lydvenkians, as well as the few surviving Dorladdian legionaries from the first brigade.

Tiarnen frantically searched the chaotic scene—his stomach sinking a little further with each passing second that his sisters remained out of sight. Then, his gaze found Niera, who was sitting up against the south wall. Judging by the annoyed look on her face as she poured murky water out of Dawnbreaker, she seemed to be unhurt.

"We all in one piece?" asked Raghnall, slinging his shield onto his back.

The major's booming voice pulled Tiarnen's attention to the front gate, where he saw Raghnall limping over to Reina, who was on her hands and knees, with Dansby coughing up water only a few feet away.

"So it would seem," grunted Dansby, trying to bring himself to his feet. "Thanks to you."

"I'm afraid your gratitude is going to fall on deaf ears after disobeying my orders," said Raghnall.

"I honestly didn't hear you," argued Dansby.

"Wonder why," wheezed Reina.

"Remind me what the name of that warsong was?" asked Dansby.

"'Arch... Archavral,'" stammered Reina.

"Can we change it to 'Arching Wave of Idiocy?'" suggested Tiarnen, arriving from behind the major.

"I'll put in... the... request," said Reina, still struggling to get her breath back.

"Neither warsong titles nor their strategic application are up for deliberation," said Tharus, appearing with his entourage.

"Maestro Dorian, the warsong was not performed to standard," scolded Ignis. "You were to push the Lydvenkians away from the city, not use it for a retreat."

"It was a tactical withdrawal!" argued Raghnall.

Ignis snapped his fingers, and two praetorian guards yanked Reina to her feet.

"AHH!" she screamed, grimacing with overwhelming pain.

"But at what cost?" asked Tharus.

Tiarnen watched Reina pull her shaking hand out from under her tattered maestro jacket to reveal that it was drenched in blood.

"She's hurt!" said Niera, finally arriving.

Raghnall tossed the two guards holding Reina aside like they were toddlers and took her into his arms. "Easy," he said, slowly opening her jacket to reveal several glass needles protruding from deep in her ribs. Everyone looked at the grievous wound and then silently stared at each other for a moment.

"We need to get her to the infirmary now," said Dansby.

Raghnall gently picked Reina up and made his way through the bailey to take her to the infirmary bunker on the far side.

Tiarnen reached to grab Niera's hand, but she took Tharus's instead and paid no attention to her brother's consoling gesture. As the procession continued ahead, the orchestra and patrol stopped tending to one another and fell silent, watching their maestro being carried away. Tiarnen shared a concerned look with Kaleigh, who was unhooking Coniel from his broken drum harness, only to trip over something beneath the water.

He glanced down for a split second to find his footing and was about to keep walking but then saw a strange metallic glint under the rippling surface. Despite knowing that he should be following close behind the major, an eerie curiosity took hold, and he found himself reaching into the water. At first, his fingers found nothing, but then they brushed over what felt like leather and sharp metal. Cautiously gripping the heavy object, Tiarnen pulled it out of the water—his eyes widening at the sight of the Lydvenkian warsong book now resting in his hands.

Chapter Fourteen

DESPERATE MEASURES

Raghnall hurried down a short flight of stairs and into the infirmary while trying to keep Reina as still as possible. The subterranean bunker contained two long rows of stone tables stretching down either side, each covered in white linen sheets and with a headboard bordered by shelves that were stocked with surgical tools and all manner of medical supplies, as well as a bright oil lamp hanging overhead. The nurses were busy bandaging burns, setting bones, and stitching the wounds of thirty or so patrolmen and orchestra members.

"Matron! Over here!" yelled Raghnall, gently setting Reina on the closest available table as Dansby, Niera, Tharus, and Ignis arrived behind.

Matron Hallon, a kind-looking silver-haired woman in her late sixties, hurried over in a simple light cream shirtwaist dress and bibbed apron that was splattered with blood. "Major, I am not one of your patrolmen to be summoned! Every patient will be seen in turn—" She stopped dead at the sight of Reina. "Maestro? Forgive me! I never expected you would be..."

"Makes two... of us," wheezed Reina.

Matron Hallon carefully opened Reina's jacket to get a better look at the wound, but it only took a glance to turn her expression from hopeful to grim. A moment after, two more nurses arrived, drawing their surgical scissors to help cut Reina free of the jacket, but Matron

Hallon stayed their hands. "I believe the maestro will want the jacket to depart with her."

Reina closed her eyes and nodded, tears running down her cheeks as she accepted the news of her fate.

"There has to be something you can do!" implored Dansby.

"Believe me," said Matron Hallon, "if I knew of any procedure that could heal an injury as severe as this—"

"Then find someone else who can!" Dansby looked like he was about to leap over the table and throttle the matron.

"Captain," said Raghnall, gently gripping Dansby's shoulder to keep him in place.

"No!" yelled Dansby, fighting to free himself from the major. "I won't stand here and be told there isn't any chance of saving her!"

Reina looked past the argument to see Tiarnen approaching the group. As though no one else was in the room, she slowly held her hand out. "Tiarnen..." she said, her soft words calming the infighting. Everyone turned to see Tiarnen holding the songbook with a dumbfounded expression on his face.

Niera leaned in. "What is that?"

"Pretty sure it's Lydvenko's songbook," said Tiarnen.

The infirmary went completely silent.

"Can't be," said Reina, looking at it in disbelief.

"He's right. The markings are Lydvenkian," said Ignis, analyzing the cover as Tiarnen walked past to present it to Reina.

"But how?" asked Reina.

Tiarnen shrugged. "I don't know, must have washed in with everyone."

"Destroy it, immediately," ordered Tharus.

Ignis reached for the book.

"No!" said Reina. "He can... use it."

"*Use it?*" asked Ignis, his face souring at the suggestion.

"One way or another... Lydia will bring down our gates... which means Tiarnen is now our best hope of stopping her."

Feeling Niera's eyes on him, Tiarnen handed the songbook to Raghnall and sat down on the table beside Reina to take her hand in his.

"In the Conservatory... you misplayed on purpose," said Reina.

Fighting his every instinct, Tiarnen reluctantly nodded in agreement.

Reina's eyes became glassy. "I'm sorry, Tiarnen... I should have better prepared you for this."

"We both know I would have never agreed to it."

"Assuming I gave you a choice," said Reina, smirking at him.

Tiarnen wiped a spot of dirt from her brow. "Mum said we all have our talents. Clearly yours was patience."

"And yours... stubbornness."

They shared a laugh, only for Reina to cough up blood. Matron Hallon pulled down a clean linen cloth from the headboard and dabbed at Reina's chin.

Reina reached up and put her hand to Tiarnen's cheek. "If Dorladdich is to survive... you cannot hide anymore."

"I know." Tiarnen put his hand against hers.

"Then I pass my title to you, *Maestro Dorian the Sixtieth*." Reina smiled softly as her eyes shut and a final breath released through her parted lips.

His sister's hand now limp, Tiarnen carefully let it fall from his cheek and rested it on the linen sheets that were drenched crimson.

"Reina?" said Niera, pushing her way between Tiarnen and Dansby. "*Reina?* Please! You can't go!"

It broke Tiarnen's heart to watch Niera scream in the hope that their sister might open her eyes again, but after a long moment of tense silence, she took a jagged breath and threw herself into Tharus's arms.

Her desperate cries echoed throughout the infirmary and washed away what little resolve remained on everyone's faces.

Much like them, Tiarnen was in utter shock that Reina was now gone—even a few of the wounded sat up in disbelief at what they just heard. All he wanted to do was reassure Niera that everything would be all right, but he honestly didn't know if it would be.

KADUM!

A tremor shook the infirmary and made dust fall from the ceiling.

"Cover the wounded!" ordered Matron Hallon, hurrying with the nurses to pull the linen sheets over their patients.

"Major!" called a scorched patrolman who wasn't yet finished rushing down the stairs. "Maestro Lydia is setting fire to the lower districts!"

"We should retreat to the estate," recommended Ignis, panic in his voice.

"Which Lydia will burn to the ground as well if she breaks through our gate," said Raghnall, annoyed at the pointless suggestion.

"Not if *Dorian the Sixtieth* stops her first." Tharus turned to Tiarnen with an incredulous look on his face.

Tiarnen didn't know what to say. He rarely felt cornered, but this time, there seemed to be no escape from his father's piercing stare.

"Captain," said Raghnall.

"Yeah," mumbled Dansby, his wide eyes still locked on Reina.

"Tell Brigarch Geddings to rally second brigade to the bailey and then help the firefighters set up their water lines. Hopefully, we can douse the flames before they have a chance to spread."

"Right," replied Dansby, still unable to look away from Reina.

"Captain!" yelled Raghnall, his booming voice snapping Dansby from his trance and making everyone else in the infirmary straighten up.

"On my way," said Dansby, forcing himself to finally turn away and leave up the stairs with the patrolman.

Tharus took the Dorladdian songbook from Ignis and handed it to Niera. "'Obrenthium in D Major.'"

"'Obrenthium'?" asked Tiarnen. "But that's a class three warsong."

"And let us pray it will be enough to stop our enemy."

"How long do I have?"

"Given Khazlokov's determination," Tharus checked his chrono-graph, "dawn, at best."

*

Tiarnen swiped the stacks of dusty parchment and dry inkwells off the top of the Conservatory table onto the floor. He set the Lydvenkian songbook down while Niera, standing across from him, placed the Dorladdian songbook above it.

"Tiarnen, tell me we're going to wake from this nightmare," she asked, trying to hold back her sobs.

"One day, perhaps," he said, grabbing the iron-framed edge of the Lydvenkian songbook to open it. "But until then..."

Click!

"CAREFUL!" yelled Raghnall, arriving at Tiarnen's side.

Snap!

Before Tiarnen realized what had happened, the edges of the wrought iron frame sprung like a trap and released sharp, rusted teeth that closed around his hand. He slowly opened his eyes to count how many fingers he had left, only to see Raghnall's gauntlet over top of them—the songbook's teeth biting into the ceramic armour plating.

"Remove your hand. *Slowly*," said Raghnall.

Heart pounding, Tiarnen carefully slid his hand out from underneath the major's and then took a step back.

"All there?" asked Raghnall.

"Thanks to you, but we should still—"

Without hesitation, Raghnall tore the iron trap's jaws and most of the frame from the songbook.

"—preserve the frame," finished Tiarnen. He walked back to the table and cautiously opened the songbook with one finger—half expecting it to belch fire—to an unusually thick, textured cover page inscribed with dark orange ink.

"Almost looks like skin," said Niera.

"Knowing the Lydvenkians, it probably is," said Raghnall.

Niera peered at the book inquisitively. "What does it say?"

"It's tough to read; their writing style is so different." Tiarnen squinted as he attempted to make sense of the font. *"Be... behold and... despair!"*

"Charming," muttered Raghnall.

"For these... are the... warsongs of... Lydvenko." Tiarnen flipped through the first few pages. "Looks like the first section is all class one warsongs just like ours." He glanced over the compositions, trying to take them in as quickly as possible, becoming more and more intrigued with each page. All of the songs were incredibly angry and malicious. It was as though he was staring into the heart of Lydvenko itself.

"Look, that page is marked!" said Niera.

Just as Niera pointed out, a thin strip of orange leather rested on the warsong's cover page. *"Fer... Ferigni,"* said Tiarnen. He turned the page to read the sheet music and unconsciously began humming the notation.

Niera curled her lip. "Stop that."

He cleared his throat. "This is the first warsong Lydia used against us."

"There are two more markers," said Niera, seeing them poking out from their resting place in the second and third sections of the songbook.

Tiarnen flipped to the second bookmark and read the title page, "*Morvistya*." He quickly looked over the notation. "Definitely the second warsong she performed."

"Which means the last one should be—" began Niera.

"The one she'll perform next." Tiarnen turned to the third marker and read the title, "*Pyrozikar*." He studied the notation, but with each page that passed, his breath became more and more shallow with anxiety.

"Well, what are we up against?" Raghnall asked impatiently.

"Let's just say it doesn't look like I'll be getting the chance to play 'Obrenthium,'" said Tiarnen, stepping back in disbelief at the massacre "Pyrozikar" would cause.

"Then we need to slay Lydia before she can illuminate," spat Niera.

Raghnall sighed. "Easier said than done, I'm afraid."

"If we were to subdue her orchestra, 'Pyrozikar's' effect would be greatly diminished," said Tiarnen.

"I don't think our forces could reach them quickly enough." Raghnall began to pace. "What if you were to play at the same time she did and disrupt her performance?"

"You know the rules of engagement expressly forbid it," said Niera. "Two maestros performing different warsongs at the same time would cause catastrophic dissonance."

"There has to be a way to counter her!" yelled Raghnall, slamming his gauntlet down and breaking one of the table planks.

"Counter her..." whispered Tiarnen, the words drawing his gaze to Stormcaller—the memory of him and Reina sitting side by side and playing together already felt like a lifetime ago. "Niera is right," he said, pulling himself from his reverie. "Two maestros can't play different warsongs at once—"

"Maybe if I tried to spar—" interrupted Niera.

"But what if disrupting Lydia didn't cause any dissonance?" finished Tiarnen.

Raghnall crossed his arms. "And how do you intend to do that?"

"By performing the same warsong," said Tiarnen.

"The *same*?" asked Niera.

"Is he onto something?" asked Raghnall.

Niera pressed on her temples. "Madness, it would seem."

"Hear me out," said Tiarnen. "If I can perform *with* Lydia, I might be able to sabotage "Pyrozikar,' perhaps even diminish its power."

"There's just one small problem," said Niera.

"Which is?" asked Tiarnen.

"You can't illuminate!" said Niera, annoyed that she was the only one who hadn't forgotten the fact.

Tiarnen and Raghnall looked at each other.

"Right?" asked Niera, confused by their guilty look.

The conservatory became uncomfortably silent.

"*Right?*" she repeated, her green eyes now piercing Tiarnen's.

Flashes of orange light suddenly bloomed through the stained-glass windows above Stormcaller, reminding them that Lydia was still trying to force her way into the city.

"Major," said Tiarnen, clearing his throat, "could you please escort my sister out of the Conservatory."

Niera's jaw dropped as her brother focused back on the songbooks.

"Come on. Best give him some space," said Raghnall, making his way to the other side of the table.

"I'm not going anywhere until he answers me!" said Niera.

As much as Tiarnen wanted to explain, he knew it wasn't the time or place.

"Tiarnen!"

"Right then." Raghnall reached for Niera.

Niera took a step back. "Don't you dare!"

Ignoring the order, Raghnall scooped Niera up and hoisted her over his shoulder like a sack of potatoes.

"Put me down!"

"Need anything else before I leave you to it?" asked Raghnall, glancing back at Tiarnen while walking towards the Conservatory door.

"Just keep her safe for me," said Tiarnen.

"That I can do."

"You're the one who will need to be kept safe if you don't explain—" But before Niera had the chance to continue with her threat, the Conservatory door had already shut behind her.

Click-click-clack!

Finally alone, Tiarnen slumped over the table to put his head in his hands. So much was racing through his mind, it felt like it might explode. In fact, the more he thought about Reina passing, the battle ahead, and the conversation he would need to have with Niera after, if there was an *after*, the further his stomach sank.

"Slow down," he said, lifting his head. "Take this one step at a time." He slowly rose to his feet, grabbed the Lydvenkian songbook, and walked up the stairs to sit at Stormcaller. After pulling the piccolo from his back pocket and setting the songbook against the rack, he flipped through the pages until he found the third bookmark.

Reading over "Pyrozikar's" notation, Tiarnen realized it had been well over ten years since he had learnt a new warsong. By a league, the greatest challenge of entering the Dorladdian orchestra was memorizing all one hundred and fifty warsongs. The effort of putting just one to memory usually took days, if not weeks, but all he had now was the latter half of an evening. As if matters weren't complicated enough, he would also need to learn the flourishes, which were marked with tiny squiggles above the notation, if he hoped to control his shards. None of this mattered, however, if he wasn't willing to illuminate. The entire effort started to feel hopeless, but Tiarnen knew there was no other option, so raised his piccolo and attempted to play the first bar of "Pyrozikar."

Performing in the foreign F Major key felt so strange to Tiarnen, but that didn't matter much since he misplayed nearly every motif and phrase in "Pyrozikar's" first movement. "No problem, just first-time jitters," he said, shaking his hands to loosen them up and distract himself from the failed attempt.

Tiarnen flipped the pages back to the beginning of the warsong, aligned his fingers over the piccolo keys, and began the first movement again with as much focus and effort as he could manage. To his relief, the second pass proved a little easier, the challenging motifs and phrases feeling a bit more familiar. Though not without a few repeated mistakes and missed notes along the way, he quickly found himself swept up by the intensity of "Pyrozikar;" contempt and rage rushed through him on a level he never thought possible. In fact, by the time he finished the vindictive exposition, Tiarnen wanted nothing more than to bathe all of Lydvenko in fire. Despite understanding that "Pyrozikar" was intended to make him feel this way, it still surprised him how desperate he became for the next measure—as though he now had a thirst that could not be quenched. And so, he turned the page to begin the second movement.

A baleful melody of contouring whole notes and sharp ornamentations caused sweat to bead on Tiarnen's brow while also making the piccolo grow warmer. He was in disbelief at how incredibly powerful the warsong was making him feel, how unstoppable, how the only outcome while performing it could be absolute victory over Maestro Lydia. Once more, he was confronted with complex Lydvenkian phrases, unlike anything he had played before. Skipped notes and missed measures soon followed, but Tiarnen was so lost in "Pyrozikar's" bloodlust that he refused to acknowledge his deteriorating performance. The piccolo, however, wasn't as forgiving of the errors and grew hotter and hotter with each one until—

Tsss!

"Damn it!" blurted Tiarnen, yanking the searing mouthpiece away and tossing the piccolo onto the bench. "Idiot," he mumbled, checking his lip for burns.

Despite the shock, not to mention the pain, he seemed to be fine—the backfire a swift reminder of what would continue to happen if he didn't play the notation perfectly. Tiarnen pulled out his pocket watch to check the time. It was just after midnight, which meant he had roughly six hours before sunrise. Needing a short break, he stood and wandered over to the study, where he saw the well-worn leather chair surrounded by tiered shelves, most of them covered with wilting clover, curving along the inner wall. Piled on top were notebooks, novels, candles, trinkets, a variety of pipes, tins of smoked fish, a tray of butter cookies, jars of poached cinnamon pears, and a few rare bottles of Bubble Brew, a very strong and fizzy cold brew tea mixed with nut cream liqueur.

"Thank the Verse," he said, immediately grabbing one of the stubby brown Bubble Brew bottles and popping the cork. Part of him wanted to flop into the all-too-inviting chair, but he couldn't let himself do it. The memory of Reina sitting there was still much too near. Instead, he leaned against the arm and took a long sip, glaring at the Lydvenkian songbook in frustration.

"What were you expecting?" he asked, allowing himself a candid moment of reflection. As much as he didn't want to accept it, learning "Pyrozikar" to a standard that would contest Lydia's performance just wasn't going to be possible, given how much time he had left—no matter his determination.

"So now what?" he asked, taking another delicious sip. He would have to come up with an alternate way to counter Lydia.

Tiarnen spent the next hour thinking about when he had been so creatively stumped before, growing more and more frustrated with himself, but the only situation that came to mind was when he'd tried to build a new Shatter deck.

If you spent half as much time on music theory as you did cards...

"Shatter helps me with my theory," Tiarnen whispered to himself. Then—as though he had just lit the lamp in the lighthouse—a thought occurred. "Wait, what if... what if this is just like building a deck?" he asked himself. With renewed intensity, his mind went to the Dorladdian songbook still resting on the long table. "Hold on, don't get excited—think this through." He began to slowly walk out of the study. "When you're crafting a new warsong in Shatter, it is card by card... combining them to create the most synergy you can... but each card also has its own musical motif... so by the time they form the warsong... a new melody has been made!"

The realization sent him hurrying down the stairs, slamming the now empty bottle onto the table, and reaching for the Dorladdian songbook. In a blur, he opened the cover and frantically flipped through the pages until he found the title page for "Obrenthium."

"Now, the question is, can you use 'Obrenthium' to diminish 'Pyrozikar'?" Tiarnen fell silent. He wasn't sure if he was waiting for a sign from the Verse itself or for himself to come to the conclusion that what he was proposing was, very likely, going to be impossible to pull off. In the end, he knew it didn't matter—the only thing he was certain of was that he had to try. He grabbed the songbook, rushed back up the stairs, and opened it beside its Lydvenkian counterpart.

"All right," he said, taking a seat and feeling like he was about to sail the *Calhoun* into uncharted waters. "All you have to do is find the melodies and then see if you can make them work together."

For the next three hours, Tiarnen poured over both compositions in gruelling detail. Initially, he went through the warsongs together in parallel, his tired eyes darting back and forth while he turned the pages with both hands. He was sure it was the best approach to take, the most systematic, but to his disappointment, nothing stood out as being adaptable by the time he reached the end. He then tried again by working backwards in parallel, hopeful that reading the warsongs together in reverse might reveal a secret connection their notation was hiding from him. But just like before, it seemed that "Obrenthium" and "Pyrozikar" didn't want to cooperate. Now deeply concerned and admittedly more than a little desperate, Tiarnen resorted to skimming through the pages, stopping at random and then looking to see if any obvious motif pairings stood out.

"Curse it!" he yelled, hitting his fist on Stormcaller's keys. The organ let out a groan and a gust of wind that caused the songbooks' pages to turn. "Believe me, I know exactly how you feel," he muttered, his hands falling to his lap and shoulders slumping with discouragement. "Maybe they're just too different, or *we* are, for that matter." Tiarnen rubbed his bloodshot eyes and then reached for the songbooks to close them.

Wait. His hands froze on the pages as he noticed that the tenth-bar melodies on both warsongs were a potential match. "Do they really fit?" he whispered. Heart pounding in his chest, Tiarnen blinked a couple of times to make sure his vision was clear and then looked both melodies over—gently humming the notation to himself. Sure enough, he was right; the first half of the Lydvenkian melody dovetailed into the second half of "Obrenthium's."

"Yes!" he exclaimed, raising his arms in celebration only to remember that he was utterly alone. *But it's just a start—just threads,* he reminded himself. *We still have to weave them together.* Knowing now which melody he could use, Tiarnen looked for it throughout "Pyrozikar" and, to his delight, found that it recurred through most of the warsong, which meant he would have a few key opportunities to strip away its power and thwart Lydia.

"Now, all you have left to do is test it," he said, the words sending a chill up his back. Knowing what to play was one thing; *how* to play it was another matter altogether. Ignoring the fact that what he was about to attempt could easily get him killed, Tiarnen took a moment to clear his head and look the piccolo over. It didn't seem to have taken any damage from the heat, not that he could really tell given that the grimy instrument looked like it had washed up on shore yesterday. Letting out a long exhale, he wiped the mouthpiece with his sleeve and brought it to his lips. Fortunately, he didn't need to play all of "Pyrozikar," only the new melody he'd composed, so he took a deep breath and made his first attempt.

Though the Lydvenkian opening proved troublesome, Tiarnen found his way through it by the third try and then added the new "Obrenthium" ending. To his genuine surprise, it worked. The melody certainly didn't sound natural to his Dorladdian ear, nor a Lydvenkian either by his guess, but he didn't need it to be pleasurable—only practical. What the effect would be, Tiarnen couldn't say. From where he was sitting, performing the melody with Lydia would be no different from trying to blend fire and water together. However, even after taking that into consideration, he didn't see how the outcome could possibly be worse than what she was intending. He didn't want to mention it with Niera around, but if "Pyrozikar" went uncontested, Lydia would turn the entire city into a crematorium.

Tiarnen pulled out his pocket watch to check the time and saw that he only had an hour before sunrise. *An hour to illuminate,* he thought, a wave of guilt washing over and submerging him in doubt. Part of him wanted to run back to the lighthouse and hide, just as he always had, lying to himself every step of the way there. Knowing that was never going to be an option after tonight, Tiarnen took another long breath and reluctantly returned the piccolo to playing position. Exhaling carefully, he played the melody, but nothing happened. There was no spark and certainly no flash—just the tones slipping into silence. He cleared his throat and played again, this time a little louder, yet there was still no sign of a single shard. Tiarnen straightened his posture, took the deepest breath he could, and played the melody as loud as ever, but yet again, his overwhelming shame produced nothing more than a weak crescendo that fizzled throughout the Conservatory. He shook his head in disbelief. Even here and now, with everything at stake, he was acting like a scared child.

Bursts of orange light erupted from outside as Lydia terrorized the city, reminding everyone that she was just outside the gate. Tiarnen looked up at the stained-glass windows, his eyes falling onto his mother. Her inquisitive gaze filled him with a sense of pride for his melodic discovery, only for the guilt to return and make his stomach churn. His gaze dropped in shame, stopping on the empty space where Reina's portrait would soon rest.

"No more," he whispered.

Tiarnen closed his eyes and slowed his breaths—softening each one a bit more so his heart could find calm. Soon enough, it did, and he was able to gently rock to its steady rhythm. Caught up in the music, he put the piccolo to his lips and held it there, taking in the scent of oak, silver, oil, and sweat until the instrument felt like an extension of himself. Then, he gently filled it with his breath—as though he was blowing on embers to stoke a flame. With barely enough force to muster a note, his fingers moved along the keys—playing the melody over and over. At first, the tones were barely audible, but as he continued to perform, it felt like a grip that had been held for fifteen years was at long last starting to let go. Focusing now on each tone, he visualized them igniting and solidifying into glass shards—each melodic repeat an opportunity to see them grow brighter and stronger. Goose bumps covered Tiarnen's entire body, and his eyes flashed open to see the piccolo flickering inside with ivy-green light.

Chapter Fifteen
PYROZIKAR
IN F MAJOR

R aghnall knelt beside the bailey's aqueduct and dipped his hand in the frigid seawater to wash the soot off his face. But before he had the chance, Ravenwing's cry rang out.

"Shields!" he yelled, looking up to see yet another flock of Lydvenkian shards twinkling against the stormy morning sky.

Brigarch Geddings, a hefty woman in her late thirties with a dirty-blonde crew cut, raised her shield. Standing just behind, her entire second brigade followed suit to protect themselves from the incoming bombardment, while Dansby and the Day Striders rushed to protect two groups of provincials who were gathered around the aqueduct pumps. Though the pumpmen knew that hellfire was about to rain down yet again, they continued working the levers together. With each push and pull, the pumps syphoned water through large hoses that snaked to the bailey entrance, ran past the keep, and into Tavern Crawl, where the firemen were dousing a row of flame-engulfed pubs. A few shards managed to pierce the phalanx, leaving some of the pumpmen badly cut and one impaled.

After checking for a pulse he knew wouldn't be there, Raghnall lowered his shield and signalled the patrol to do the same.

"We can't keep this up forever, Major!" yelled Geddings.

KATHUD!

"Maybe a bit of Dorladdian weather will make Lydvenko reconsider their attack," said Dansby, as what he thought to be thunder drew his gaze to the storm brewing overhead.

KATHUD!

"Unfortunately, I don't think that was the storm," said Raghnall, turning to the front gates.

KATHUD!

Just as the major feared, a tremendous force struck the doors from outside.

"All of you, with me!" ordered Raghnall. Despite his limp, the major rushed to the barbican and met with the second brigade, who were watching in bewilderment as their supposedly immovable gate shuddered as though it were made of brittle wood.

KATHUD!

Once again, it shook, but this time, a hairline crack ran halfway down the length of the left door.

"Sounds more like metal than glass," observed Geddings.

"Maybe they finally brought up a battering ram?" said Dansby.

"Then the gate is definitely about to come down," said Geddings.

"Doesn't matter," said Raghnall, tightening the torsion bolt on his gauntlet.

"And how do you figure that?" asked Dansby.

"Because any Lydvenkian that makes the mistake of stepping foot in this bailey will be swiftly piled up with the rubble," stated Raghnall, giving the bolt a last turn.

KATHUD!

A hairline crack ran down the right door.

"And what about Lydia?" asked Dansby, bitterness in his voice.

"Tiarnen will be ready for her." Raghnall raised an eyebrow at the keep in the hope of seeing his nephew.

*

The cold limestone walls and low ceiling created an air of tension in the busy War Room. Along the floor was an elaborate tiled map of Chora covered in figurines that were being moved by intelligence officers under the observation of Holgor. Behind him, more intelligence officers transcribed their latest reports onto damp clay tablets that were then inset into one of many rows along the wall. Those that became outdated were pulled down and sent crashing to the floor so they would crumble and ensure the precious information could never be stolen.

Tharus and Niera looked down on the bailey from the keep's west balcony, flanked by praetorian guards with Ignis lurking just behind. Though Niera was still furious at Raghnall for removing her from the Conservatory, she was growing nervous watching him stand before the weakening gate.

"Father, couldn't we send a few guards down to help?" asked Niera.

Tharus ignored the question as Holgor appeared at his side and muttered tactical information.

KATHUD!

The gate shook again—a small chunk of the upper left door breaking off and falling to the ground.

"Executor, send for my son," demanded Tharus.

"No need," said a voice from behind them.

Everyone except Tharus turned to see Tiarnen standing in the doorway with a warsong book under each arm.

"I trust your evening was well spent," said Tharus, barely glancing over his shoulder at Tiarnen, who had bags under his eyes and hair like a bird's nest; his jacket not only covered in countless tiny cuts, but the sleeves singed as well.

"We're about to find out," said Tiarnen, walking to the only table in the room and setting the books down. "Niera," he said, turning to his sister. "I need you to bring the orchestra into the centre of the bailey and have them take positions."

Niera stood in place and crossed her arms in refusal.

Tiarnen walked over to her and took a knee. "I know you're angry with me, but I cannot possibly hope to do this without my Lead. Please?"

KATHUD!

The gate lurched further than ever—the cracks spreading everywhere now.

"On your way, *both* of you," ordered Tharus.

Accepting that she had no choice, Niera pushed past Tiarnen and stomped out the door. Without saying a word to each other, they made their way down a flight of stairs that led from the keep to the bailey entrance and then split up; Niera wrapped around the back of the keep to alert the waiting orchestra who were huddled in a bunker, while Tiarnen hurried across bailey to meet with Raghnall.

KATHUD!

The upper left gate hinge broke.

"At least they're polite enough to knock," said Tiarnen, arriving at the major's side.

"Ah, nice to have you with us again," said Raghnall, looking him up and down.

Tiarnen rubbed his tired eyes. "And just in time, it would seem."

Marching echoed from behind. Tiarnen, Raghnall, and the second brigade turned to see the orchestra, led by Niera, filing in and taking their positions at the centre of the bailey. Tiarnen nodded in thanks as he and Raghnall walked over to her, but Niera only responded with a scowl.

"Tell me he has some good news," muttered Raghnall, fastening the top button on Niera's jacket.

"Hard to when he hasn't told me a thing," said Niera.

"I do have news. It's just not exactly *good*..." began Tiarnen.

Raghnall glared at him.

Tiarnen put up his hand in defence. "But it's not that bad either!"

KATHUD!

A chunk of the right door broke off and fell to the ground, nearly crushing the nearest legionary.

"Well, get on with it then!" urged Raghnall, gesturing to the gate.

"After you two left, all of my initial attempts failed," admitted Tiarnen.

"Just like I said they would," stated Niera, feeling as though her brother needed a reminder.

"However, after a little experimentation," he presented his singed sleeves, "I think I found a way to counter Lydia."

"You *think*?" asked Raghnall.

"How?" asked Niera.

"I'm going to extend 'Pyrozikar's' melody with 'Obrenthium's.'"

"Will it be enough to stop her?" asked Raghnall.

"Don't pretend like you know," said Niera.

"I know that Lydvenko will lay waste to the entire city if we don't try," said Tiarnen.

"What's the plan then?" asked Raghnall.

"Just keep their Legion off our backs. Niera and I will take care of the rest."

KATHAM!

The gate finally buckled from the unrelenting strikes and began to collapse.

"Something tells me that will be easier said than done," said Raghnall.

Within seconds, all that remained of the once impassable doors were broken hinges and chunks of granite, now mostly obscured by a thick haze of dust.

"Geddings! I want second brigade in split divisions behind me!" ordered Raghnall.

Tiarnen turned to Niera. "Get everyone ready."

"But how will we know when to play?" she asked.

"When I rise," he said, raising his piccolo to play.

"And you want the harmony in full?"

"Might as well." There was more than a little uncertainty in his voice.

Niera looked like she had a thousand things to say but bit her tongue and returned to the orchestra to inform them of the so-called *plan*.

Tiarnen turned back and focused on the haze, expecting a swarm of Lydvenkian claws to emerge. Instead, a pair of massive iron boots strode out. Completely awestruck, Tiarnen watched as the rubble crushed into dust under the immense weight of a ten-foot-tall chronomech. Every inch of it appeared to be made out of interconnected gears, pistons, coils, and rods that were wrapped in thick iron armour plating etched with crude Lydvenkian markings.

Raghnall, however, wasn't as impressed and walked ahead to meet the hulking monstrosity—staring into the hollow eye sockets of its black metal skull. "General Mikavnik!" he yelled. "I was wondering if you were going to show your pretty face!"

VRRRRZZZZZZTT! replied Mikavnik, releasing a pair of long, jagged sickles from slots in its forearms.

At a speed Tiarnen did not expect, the chronomech's gears spun, and it rushed forward—the ground tremoring with each step. Closing in fast, Mikavnik swung hard to cut Raghnall clean in half, but he parried the deathblow—sparks erupting across his shield from the impact—and rolled out of the way. Then, just as Tiarnen had feared, hundreds of claws finally emerged from the haze as Lydvenko's second brigade poured into the bailey.

"Anyone else up for a dance?" asked Raghnall, striking his shield three times. *Bam-bam-bam!*

Their spirits renewed by the major's display of courage, half of the Dorladdian second brigade rushed in to help Raghnall fend off Mikavnik, while Dansby and the other half did their best to contain the clawmen and prevent them from reaching the orchestra.

"Tiarnen, she's here!" announced Niera, pointing towards the barbican.

Tiarnen peered through the battlefield to see Lydia and her orchestra approaching, with Praetor Khazlokov following on his chronosteed. The dwelglin was missing, so Tiarnen assumed that its punishment for losing the warsong book was most likely death. With the haze behind her, Lydia's eyes met Tiarnen's. For a brief moment, she seemed to be confused by the sight of him standing where Reina should have been, but then she smiled with wicked satisfaction after realizing what must have happened. Inspired by the unexpected victory, Lydia's gaze moved to the keep and then pierced into Tharus as she aligned her marred fingers along Ravenwing's bloodied strings.

With the Lydvenkian orchestra finally in formation, Khazlokov drew his iron wand and waved the jewelled orange tip at Sivakosha, who raised her trumpet obediently and opened "Pyrozikar's" intimidating first movement with a flurry of rapacious figurations. In response, the bass drums thundered. Their torrid tempo of bubbling rhythmic motifs roused the entire brass section; horns, trombones, and tubas simmered in harmony so Ravenwing could take flight on their warm breath.

Hearing "Pyrozikar" reverberating inside the high walls of his home should have struck terror in Tiarnen, but it brought an enormous amount of relief instead. Though the warsong was marked in the Lydvenkian songbook, there was a legitimate chance that Khazlokov could have changed his decision after it went missing. Unfortunately, Tiarnen's relief was quickly replaced with dread as he watched Lydia waste no time illuminating the first movement.

Several long sequences of pugnacious phrases erupted from Ravenwing to create hundreds of spessartine-orange shards, which formed a gleaming glass nebula that engulfed and slowly circled around Lydia. Tiarnen hoped that the embattled evening would have been just as draining for Lydia as it was for him, but she didn't appear to be showing signs of fatigue. If anything, she seemed more enthralled than ever with bringing about Dorladdich's downfall.

With confident chromatic leaps and truculent motifs, the Lydvenkian string section opened the ominous second movement. Shortly after, the brass followed in with intensifying refrains and accents that brought their simmering harmony to a boil. Using their accompaniment to her full advantage, Lydia played a long sequence of sharp trills that made Ravenwing scream with fiery glass—the shards pulsing with scorn as they cut through the air and sped up the nebula's rotation.

Knowing that "Pyrozikar's" melody was coming up fast, Tiarnen glanced over his shoulder to make sure Niera was ready. She nodded in acknowledgement, though he couldn't help but notice Kaleigh standing with the woodwinds behind Niera, a look of deep concern on her face.

"You can do this," he whispered, slowly putting the piccolo to his lips to not raise any suspicions as Lydia began the melody.

Each arpeggio she played felt like an eternity, and her seemingly unbreakable confidence was giving Tiarnen overwhelming feelings of hesitation and doubt. All he could think of was failing or somehow making "Pyrozikar's" effect even more disastrous. Just as Lydia was finishing the melody, the piccolo seemed to bring itself to Tiarnen's lips. He filled it with a nervous breath and dovetailed in "Obrenthium." Lydia's eyes fell on him before the third note was played, making him feel completely exposed. He expected that she would immediately lash her shards at him, but Lydia instead tilted her head in intrigue and then broke out with maniacal laughter as she assumed he was making a pathetic attempt to distract her. Her reaction was utterly unnerving, and Tiarnen tried not to see himself as she now did—like a cornered animal desperately trying to avoid a killing stroke. Keeping focus as best he could on his hand placement, posture, and flourishing, Tiarnen endeavoured to get all of it right in hope of releasing his resonance, but the piccolo barely flickered once with faint green light. Even before the last note of "Obrenthium" had a chance to fade away, Lydia was already playing on as though he didn't exist. Completely disheartened, he let his arms fall to his side in self-defeat.

"What was supposed to happen?" asked Niera.

Tiarnen sighed. "A lot more than that."

"*So now what?*"

Tiarnen was admittedly just as frustrated. Knowing it would be incredibly difficult to match a seasoned maestro's performance was one thing, but illuminating in the middle of battle was proving to be more daunting than he could have ever imagined.

"We try again!" said Tiarnen, hoping he would actually be able to make use of the next opportunity before Raghnall and the brigades were completely overwhelmed.

With bass drums rumbling, Lydia plucked Ravenwing and opened the third movement with a succession of grim tonic motifs—her orchestra's violins and cellos accenting each of them and creating a terrifying echo effect. The rolling harmony reinforced Lydia's serrated shards, making them grow thicker and bloom brighter as the string section's amplitude grew louder and louder.

Beholding her formidable nebula, the shards now in the thousands, Tiarnen felt his hesitation return. The fear of failing a second time took hold and flooded his mind with images of him and Niera running through the city as it burned to the ground around them; the corsairs sinking as hundreds of thousands of panicked provincials tried to climb aboard; Raghnall falling to Mikavnik's punishing assault; and Lydia finally razing the island to the bottom of the ocean.

As though calling him from a world away, "Pyrozikar's" melody pulled Tiarnen out of his horrifying daydream. This time, the piccolo didn't need to find its way to his lips; he raised it in outright refusal. Dovetailing just before, Tiarnen filled the instrument with more than just breath—he filled it with the regret of hiding in the lighthouse all these years and anger at the self-induced numbness he now swore he would never feel again. The release covered his entire body with goose bumps as Niera and the orchestra supported him in full so Dorladdich could be heard over Lydvenko.

And now it will be seen, he told himself.

His resonance igniting, the piccolo flickered brighter and brighter with each melodic note until the last one illuminated a disfigured shard of viridescent glass. Tiarnen could hardly believe what he was watching as the peridot-green shard arced chaotically through the air and shot toward the Dorladdian orchestra. *No-no-no-no,* he thought, flourishing to redirect the lethal shard away from everyone as it streaked overhead, only to accidentally lash it back at himself. After ducking out of its way, Tiarnen searched the fray but couldn't see where it had gone. Then, Mikavnik's left arm, its hand around the major's throat, fell to the ground—cut clean from its body as only maestro glass could.

Thunder clapped from the arriving storm as though to add an exclamation point. Raghnall looked at the still twitching mechanical fingers in disbelief... then blinked back at Tiarnen... then back at the twitching fingers... and finally at Tiarnen again.

"About bloody time you warmed up!" he shouted, the reprimand contrasting with a proud grin on his face.

The bailey suddenly filled with Dorladdian cheers.

"For Dorladdich!" shouted Coniel.

Tiarnen glanced back at the orchestra to see all of them screaming and leaping in elation, except for Niera, who was standing utterly still and emotionless. He didn't know if it was for better or worse, but before he could ask, Ravenwing's cry returned and pulled his attention back to Lydia, who wasn't making any effort to conceal her indignation. In fact, Tiarnen was pretty sure that if Lydia had fangs, she would have bared them at him. Instead, she opened the sombre fourth movement of "Pyrozikar" with broken chords and began her solo.

Picking and pulling at the harp with cruel intention, Lydia made her artisan instrument wail in agony again and again with predative phrases that illuminated thick, jagged shards. Sivakosha called on the cymbals and trumpets, which cross-faded with sizzling harmony while Lydia spun her body and flourished wildly. As though tied to a string, the shards followed and circled their maestro—the whirling momentum condensing the nebula into a blazing vortex around her.

Tiarnen tried to concentrate, but it was proving difficult while watching Mikavnik. Despite suffering a significant injury from his lashing, it now trampled through the battlefield, cutting down any Dorladdian legionaries within range. Most were able to duck or dodge out of the way, striking the chronomech in hope of finding a weak point in its armour, but a few who were unlucky enough to avoid its clutch found themselves tossed into Lydia's vortex and instantly cut to pieces. The only thing counteracting the gruesome sight was how well Dansby and his Day Striders were holding their ground against the clawmen. Ironically, the Lydvenkian orchestra was preventing their own third brigade from pouring into the bailey because they were taking up most of the front quarter.

In an attempt to remind Tiarnen that there was no escape from his impending demise, Lydia raised her amplitude and played the melody louder than ever, which not only pulled him from distraction but also steeled his heart. Watching her build the lattrice core, he felt a little more confident after managing to illuminate, and so he dovetailed in "Obrenthium," just as he did before. Sivakosha and the Lydvenkian orchestra immediately tried to drown him out, but Niera was having none of it and led the Dorladdian orchestra in a near-deafening response. Their coursing harmony washed away every Lydvenkian note. Invigorated by his sister's show of force, Tiarnen resonated and made the piccolo beam with vibrant light. Ivy-green shards splashed to life, and he could see they were stronger than before: the shape more symmetrical, glass thicker, edges smoother, and far sharper. Unwilling to lose control again, he made a couple of precise flourishes, using the angular momentum to spin them around himself and create his first vortex. For a brief moment, he felt a sense of nervous excitement as the shards picked up momentum and streaked past in pulsing ellipses. Confident they were now at the right speed, Tiarnen focused on Lydia's core and cast his shards toward it. One by one, they shot into the narrow gaps and locked into place. The core flickered chaotically with orange and green light as though in conflict with itself.

Furious at what had clearly become an insurrection against Lydvenko's rightful turn, Khazlokov shouted a few choice expletives at Tharus even though Tiarnen, *technically*, hadn't broken any rules of engagement. However, that small fact didn't mean Khazlokov was about to stand by and allow Tiarnen's experiment to continue without recourse.

"Forward!" he ordered, pointing his wand directly at Tiarnen.

Mikavnik and the Legion immediately began fighting their way down the middle of the battlefield so Lydvenko could advance directly on the Dorladdian orchestra.

Walking with the lattrice core following above her, Lydia unleashed several impassioned phrases of pulsating trills that made her shards leap like licks of flame and begin the feverish fifth movement. The bass drums rumbled again, and Sivakosha led the brass into accompanying their maestro with ascending scalic figures. The empowering harmony made Lydia's shards double in brightness and size as she arranged them to form several spiralling clusters. To make matters worse, with Sivakosha and the orchestra trailing behind their maestro, there was finally enough room at the front of the bailey for Lydvenko's third brigade to enter.

"Tiarnen," said Niera, looking past Dansby, "more of them are—"

"I can see that!" snapped Tiarnen.

"What do we do?"

"Stand our ground!" spat Dansby, eager for Lydia to approach.

Coming to the end of the movement, Lydia played the melody and used her shards to arrange another cluster, but just as she was about to cast all of them at the core, her right leg suddenly gave out. Though her recovery was almost instant, it was still a telling sign that she had finally become battle-weary. Pretending it was merely a misplaced footstep, Lydia quickly flourished and cast the clusters upwards to build the mantle around the core.

Watching Lydia weaken was all the encouragement Tiarnen needed to press on. In a breath, he committed every ounce of strength to dovetail in "Obrenthium" yet again, but it wasn't an emotional release like last time. It was with focused intent that he channelled his resonance. Translucent ivy-green shards erupted from the piccolo, and with a few awkward flourishes, he managed to arrange a cluster that he then cast at the mantle. Together, Tiarnen and Lydia both watched in equal astonishment as their mantles fused into place and made the lattrice refract with orange and green contradiction.

"Captain!" yelled Raghnall, crashing into Mikavnik again to stop the chronomech from stomping Geddings under its boot.

"We've got them!" said Dansby, certainty in his voice as he and the Day Striders braced themselves for impact.

The sound of iron spikes crashing against ceramic shields was like a thousand nails running down a chalkboard. Tiarnen's jaw clenched as he watched the captain do his best to stop Lydvenko from breaching their defence, but they were struggling to hold their ground against the daunting shoulder charges.

Incensed by Tiarnen's influence over her lattrice, Lydia screamed in anger while watching it flicker chaotically. Tiarnen couldn't blame her;

he had never seen a lattrice behave like this before, either. It seemed stronger but also far more unstable. He still couldn't guess what the effect would be, though his apprehension was growing fast. Lydia, however, wasn't showing any sign of hesitation, even though exhaustion had clearly set in. If anything, she seemed panicked by her waning energy, and so quickly began the calamitous sixth movement.

Ravenwing sang with elaborate figurations that created an unexpected heatwave around her. At first, the rippling air and lattrice light made it appear as though Lydia's face, neck, and hands were glowing orange, but Tiarnen disregarded what he assumed to be an illusion. That was until Lydia stepped out from the mirage and revealed the fiery light was indeed fulminating within her. From where he stood, it appeared as though she was burning alive inside—then he realized that Lydia was hollowing herself.

Tiarnen had never seen a maestro hollow themselves before, only heard of it, but he could now confirm that the stories did not do the gruesome sight justice. The effect on her music was just as frightful. Every note reverberated with haunting overtones that made her shards larger and brighter, but also caused the edges and tips to burn black. Normally, hollowing was a last act of desperation after a maestro had expended all their resonance. Perhaps Lydia's relentless assault throughout the night had finally caught up with her? At the moment, the answer didn't really matter to Tiarnen since all he could do was watch her arrange several charred clusters of shards to build up the second mantle and diminish "Obrenthium's" presence in the lattrice again. To make matters worse, the melody didn't occur in the sixth movement, which meant Tiarnen would have to wait for a final chance to complete what now seemed like an insurmountable task.

"Third brigade!" yelled Khazlokov.

The two words made Tiarnen's stomach sink as he watched the legion's fresh line of clawmen continue their way up the bridge. Even the mighty major, now with a swollen eye and bleeding nose, was showing fatigue as he tried to duck Mikavnik's sickle cutting through the air. The major parried, blocked, and dodged with impressive technique, but the relentless mechanical assault inevitably found a way past his defence—the sickle cutting deep into his right thigh. In response, Raghnall brought his gauntlet down hard onto the blade and snapped it in half as four patrolmen crashed into Mikavnik's side to provide a temporary distraction.

"Second brigade, fall back and regroup!" ordered Raghnall.

As much as they didn't want to give an inch, the front line had no choice but to retreat from the brawl. Unfortunately, the withdrawal made it easier for Lydvenko to gain more ground and reach the bailey's midpoint.

"Don't take this the wrong way, lad," said Raghnall, limping to Tiarnen's side, "but your efforts don't seem to be adding up to much."

"I know," admitted Tiarnen, "things aren't exactly going according to plan."

"Aye, somehow they never do."

"Any ideas?"

"Improvise."

"*Improvise?* But what if I can't?"

"That's the great thing about last stands." Raghnall put his hand on Tiarnen's shoulder. "You don't need to worry about making any more mistakes."

Tiarnen reluctantly nodded in agreement.

"Defenders of Dorladdich!" yelled Raghnall, turning to face his battered and bruised patrolmen. "Maestro Dorian needs us to clear a path!"

"You heard our Major! File in!" said Dansby, desperate to get within reach of Lydia.

Hearing Raghnall call him Maestro Dorian unexpectedly struck a nerve in Tiarnen. At first, he thought it might have been the same

dreadful inevitability Reina had described earlier in the Conservatory...
but then he realized it was something else... It was... an overbearing
sense of responsibility. Even though he hadn't yet accepted what he
was becoming, everyone else already believed that he would keep their
province and lives safe. To them, he was now and would forever be
Maestro Dorian LX.

"As one!" shouted Raghnall, running full speed ahead. The patrol and brigade followed with their shields raised, and together they
cut through the middle of the battlefield, pushing back and striking
down any clawmen or spikemen standing in their way. Just as Raghnall charged at General Mikavnik, Dansby and Geddings peeled off in
opposite directions—each taking half of the patrol and brigade with
them—dividing and pushing the legion against both sides of the bailey.

In the blink of an eye, Tiarnen's obscured view was replaced with a
clear path to Lydia who was now only about twenty metres away. To
his dismay, her hollowing didn't appear to have stopped—if anything,
it had become so intense that even her maestro jacket had begun to
burn away and reveal more scarred flesh, which now had a disturbing
underglow.

Confident that Tiarnen could no longer interfere, Lydia's glare returned to Tharus as she began "Pyrozikar's" seventh movement with
a barrage of scalic leaps and ascending triads that ignited clusters of
charring shards. She pressed the strings to their breaking point, making
Ravenwing scream in pain from the tense descending progressions of
quickening figurations that flared and unleashed yet another volley of
searing glass. Sivakosha and the orchestra accompanied her in full, their
domineering dynamic making it feel as though the fall of Dorladdich
was being announced.

With every note Lydia played, her body consumed itself—the already frail woman fast becoming little more than a husk. It had become
clear, for reasons Tiarnen couldn't explain, that she was more than

willing to sacrifice herself for this victory. Accepting that he would have to do the same if he hoped to save the province, Tiarnen did the unthinkable and began walking toward her.

"*Where are you going?*" asked Niera.

"I need to get closer," said Tiarnen.

"Orchestra!" yelled Niera. "Follow—"

"No!" interrupted Tiarnen. "Hold your position!"

Well aware that he was out of his mind for entering the fray, Tiarnen readied himself for a clawman, or ten for that matter, to seize the opportunity and attack, but none of them could get past the shield barricade. Mikavnik might have had the chance, but the chronomech was still engaged with Raghnall.

Only a few metres away from Lydia now, Tiarnen stopped as the melody arrived for the last time, and she fully immolated herself. He lifted the piccolo, trying not to vomit from the acrid smoke pluming off her body, and watched as she performed with ferocious passion as though welcoming him to die with her in a final moment of glory.

Taking her up on the demented invitation, Tiarnen didn't wait to play "Obrenthium" but instead heeded the major's advice and improvised, playing the beginning of the melody *with* Lydia. A surge of unexpected power shot through him—every inch of his body felt like it was being pricked with pins and needles as his first shard illuminated. He watched it pass by. The surface was slightly wavy, and the jagged edges at the top became smooth at the bottom. Inside, interlaced veins pulsated with light, leaving a slight halo behind the shard. There was no turning back now, so Tiarnen played the "Obrenthium" extension with what little resonance he had left, but Lydia took a page out of his book and played on with him. Just as he had feared, their last efforts made the prickling sensation unbearable and finally brought him to a knee as the final note was played.

"Tiarnen!" yelled Kaleigh.

Rain began to fall, and every drop felt like a dagger through Tiarnen's skin. He had never hurt like this—never experienced such complete and utter exhaustion before. It was as though his soul was evaporating. Yet, he somehow managed to flourish and cast his last shards with Lydia's into the core.

HERAAANG!

The lattrice fused and surged with resonant power—its dominant orange and diminished green glasswork flashing kaleidoscopically in the storm's downpour. Lydia, accepting a victorious demise, closed her eyes and held out her arms in wait for "Pyrozikar's" nova to consume her steaming body. Tiarnen also believed it was over... that he had failed... but the warsong did not unleash an inferno like it was designed to. Instead, his glass shards were containing the apocalyptic effect—somehow reflecting it inwards—melding the lattrice into a colossal blade of shimmering light. The captivating sight brought the battle to an abrupt stop; both sides were unable to help themselves from staring at it in confusion. Then, the lattrice descended upon the bailey like a guillotine.

Everyone scattered.

Tiarnen naturally wanted to leap out of the way, but even with mere seconds left, he found himself torn. Though "Pyrozikar" appeared to have been countered and Tiarnen had won the battle, along the way, he and Lydia somehow proved that two maestros could illuminate together.

Before realizing what he was doing, Tiarnen grabbed onto the sopping charred leather of Lydia's maestro jacket and pulled her towards him just as the blade passed inches behind her and stabbed deep into the ground.

KERSMASH!

Chapter Sixteen

A PROMISE MADE

A ribbon of light swayed in front of Tiarnen's adolescent eyes. He tried to focus through the narrow slit of his sweaty helmet but couldn't recognize the ground blurring beneath him. As much as he wanted to look up and see where he was heading, the punishing grip Raghnall had around the back of his neck made it impossible, but that didn't stop the aroma of cinnamon, apples, brown sugar, and butter from filling his nose.

"The door, Private," ordered Raghnall.

After passing through a doorway, the air became much more humid and carried the sound of casual conversations mixed with laughter—all of which suddenly went silent as Tiarnen found himself tossed forward like a petty criminal about to face sentencing. Aching pain running down his back, Tiarnen slowly raised his head to see that he was standing in To a Tea, the renowned upper district tea shop. All around him, nobles sat at small tables, sipping on cups of hot tea and spooning warm oats from tiered stands into their bowls. At the very back, several baristas worked a triple boiler that was filling rows of pots, while kitchenhands cleaned silverware and folded linen napkins, and waiters unloaded dishes from their trays after a sweep of their sections. It was a bustling scene for certain, but Tiarnen couldn't understand why the major had dragged him all the way—then he saw them: Marifreth and Reina sitting in the middle of the shop enjoying a rare afternoon together.

"Now, remember, pinkies out," said Marifreth, taking a last sip of tea from a dainty porcelain cup with her little finger pointed up at the ceiling.

"May I offer you another, Maestro?" asked a waiter.

"Two bags, with a splash of spiced cream and maple," said Marifreth.

The waiter turned to Reina. "Anything else for you, Miss Reina? Perhaps more of the apple-cinnamon?"

"No, thank you. Something tells me I'm about to lose my appetite," said Reina.

"Already?" asked Marifreth. "But you've hardly touched—" Her voice faded after noticing Reina was staring over her shoulder, and turning towards the shop entrance, she saw Tiarnen standing in a patrolman's uniform with Raghnall behind him and Private Dansby waiting at the door.

"Would you two like to join us?" asked Marifreth, turning back to spoon up some oats. "Major, you'll be happy to know there isn't a single raisin anywhere to be found in the butter pecan here."

"What I would like is for you to explain to me why I just caught my nephew skulking about Harm's Way in a patrolman's uniform," said Raghnall.

Marifreth took a bite and chewed thoughtfully for a moment. "Well, rumour has it that theft is on the rise there."

"Be that as it may, it doesn't give him the right to attempt an arrest!" Raghnall huffed.

"Did he really?"

"Yes!" said Raghnall, thankful that Marifreth seemed to disapprove of the news.

"How did it go?" She turned to him with a look of excitement on her face.

"Marifreth!"

"I mean, that was completely out of line, Tiarnen," said Marifreth, any sense of sincerity missing from her voice.

Raghnall shook his head. "Tell me you did not encourage this?"

"He was curious about the patrol. I told him that if he wanted to learn about duty and honour, taking a hands-on approach might be the best course."

"Should have bloody well known," the major muttered.

Tiarnen pulled off his helmet and glared back at Raghnall through his matted hair. "You should have also known that so-called *noble* was buying stolen wares!"

"Watch your tone! Just because she endorses this kind of behaviour doesn't mean I have to," said Raghnall.

"Please, we were no different at his age," said Marifreth.

"Aye, except whenever a certain someone found trouble, I was always there to get her out of it."

Marifreth tossed her spoon down in frustration and then stood up—her pregnant belly bumping the table. She opened her mouth to retort but, after seeing that everyone was watching, took a deep breath and calmed herself down.

"Reina," said Marifreth.

"Yes, Mother?" asked Reina.

"Please forgive me. It looks like our afternoon will have to be cut short."

"I understand."

"He'll make it up to you," said Marifreth, pulling out a gold coin from her purse and placing it on the table.

"Maestro, please, that is far too—" began the waiter.

"Private Dansby!" said Marifreth.

"Yes, Maestro!" Dansby hurried past Raghnall and pushed through the patrons to stand at attention beside Marifreth as though his life depended on it.

"Will you see to it that Reina makes it back to the Conservatory safely?"

"It would be my honour!" said Dansby, glancing at Reina.

"Had a feeling," muttered Marifreth.

Reina cleared her throat.

"Oh, see to it that all of this is spent along the way." Marifreth tossed Dansby her coin purse. "She passed her final music exam this morning, and we can't let that go without a bit more celebration."

"Thank you, Mother," said Reina, her cheeks going red.

"Think about stopping by Muin and Lustre; their reeds are far better quality than what we get from the Office of Instruments."

Marifreth gave Reina a proud kiss on the forehead and then made her way through the tea shop, though she didn't have to push past the patrons as Dansby did since everyone immediately stood to their feet and moved their chairs, as well as a few tables, out of her way. To Tiarnen's surprise, Marifreth grabbed his hand while passing by and left with him in tow.

"By the Verse, you didn't need to embarrass him like that," said Marifreth, glancing back to see Raghnall catching up as she and Tiarnen walked down a foggy Caledonia Street. "There's nothing wrong with him asserting a bit of independence."

"Except when he's in this uniform!" rebutted Raghnall.

"He's fourteen!" said Marifreth.

"And already a thorn in my side!" said Raghnall. "For some reason, you both seem to have forgotten that the actions of one patrolman hold *all* of us accountable."

"Meaning?" asked Tiarnen, feeling a bit more confident in pressing the matter now that his mother was defending him.

"Meaning that the entire patrol was pulled into the political mess you stirred up."

"*What mess?*" Tiarnen was irked by the accusation.

"Nobles are outside of the patrol's jurisdiction," said Raghnall. "We are not permitted to reprimand them, let alone take them into custody."

Tiarnen looked baffled. "So what happens when they break the law then?"

"Executor Ignis is informed of the discretion, and he determines the financial penalties," said Raghnall, raising a small gate to let them pass into the lower district of Bilgedale.

"But Ignis is a noble himself!" said Tiarnen.

"I didn't say I agreed with it!" A vein began to throb on the side of Raghnall's temple.

Tiarnen had never seen the major so agitated before. He looked to Marifreth, who silently shook her head in a way that told him to let the argument go.

"Who was it, by the way?" she asked.

"Lachlan Roycroft," said Tiarnen.

"Why doesn't that surprise me?" said Marifreth.

"I... I'm sorry, Major. I didn't know, honestly," said Tiarnen.

Raghnall took a long breath and regained his composure. "Yes, well, it's hard to make the right decisions when you aren't properly informed." He glared at Marifreth.

"Then I think it's time Tiarnen was brought up to speed on a few more things," said Marifreth, ducking down a short flight of stairs that led to a dock where several patrol boats were gently rocking back and forth along the waters of Kilmore Canal.

"I don't like the idea of you on a boat, given your condition," said Raghnall.

"I'm pregnant, not crippled! Besides, with all that armour, you'll be at the bottom of the canal well before either of us has dipped a toe in."

Trying to stifle a laugh, Tiarnen hopped into the boat and helped Marifreth to the front, where she took a seat. Raghnall followed in behind, his weight nearly sinking the stern.

"See," said Marifreth, elbowing Tiarnen to slide further up the bow to add a bit of counterweight. "I've been telling him to lay off the pies." She rubbed her belly and puffed out her cheeks.

"On second thought, a dip in the blackwater might do you both some good," said Raghnall, rocking the boat side to side.

Marifreth feigned shock. "How dare you put your maestro at such risk!"

"*Maestro*, indeed," the major muttered, settling the boat and gripping the oar to push them into the middle of the canal.

After a few quiet minutes of drifting with the current, they passed Kilners' Row, a busy district with well over a hundred kilns that were used to fire everything from basic clay bricks for mason work to the resilient ceramic shields carried by the major and patrol in battle. A tin whistle rang out to signal the end of the gruelling workday, and the kilnsmen, most of whom were covered in dry clay, wasted no time dropping their tools and trudging their way out of the Row.

"Cloaks on, both of you," ordered Raghnall, pointing at the weathered rain cloaks on the bench seat between Marifreth and Tiarnen.

"Best if we humour him," said Marifreth, pulling one on and raising the hood to hide her face.

Tiarnen casually tossed a cloak on as well but only pulled the hood halfway up so he could watch the arching upper-tier bridges pass by overhead. He felt the boat slow down and turned to see they were merging into a large roundabout with the evening traffic. Ferries, barges, haulers, and boats of every sort were now all around him—most of them doing their best to avoid a collision but not without a few inconsequential bumps along the way. Though Tiarnen and Marifreth were hidden well enough, Raghnall stuck out like a sore thumb.

"Good evening, Major!" shouted a ferryman.

"Good evening," grunted Raghnall, trying to keep his voice down.

"I'll be! What brings you to the slums, Major?" asked an emaciated provincial standing on a rickety raft.

"Just... transferring a... a couple of vagrants." Raghnall seemed quite satisfied with his jab.

"Over the south falls, we hope!" said the ferryman.

"Considering it, believe me," said Raghnall, steering the boat out of the roundabout and down Thuwar Canal, which led them into the lower east district of Karstown where most of the provincials lived. Even though their homes were little more than rudimentary sea caves eroded from the island's rocky foundation, all of them had been decorated in a unique way by their resident families. Some had grown barnacles in swirling patterns along the entrances; others used bright green paint to illustrate murals of the ocean or a Dorladdian crest—many also hung banners that carried a noble house sigil in the hope of gaining favour from their employer despite knowing the earls would never be caught dead there.

"Mam! Look! *Look*!" exclaimed a young provincial girl, who was washing laundry with her mother and recognized Marifreth passing by. Before the sighting could be confirmed, Raghnall gave the oar a powerful push and sped the boat ahead.

"Do you ever grow tired of it?" asked Tiarnen.

"Of the recognition? How could I? If they can still admire their maestro while living a life of worry, whisky, and the whip, I owe them every ounce of gratitude I can muster," said Marifreth.

Chanting, clapping, and whistling filled the air. Tiarnen looked ahead to see a group of teens playing air band with nothing but broken oars, brooms, and a barrel as instruments. He immediately recognized the warsong they were pretending to play and so pulled both flute pieces from his front pants pocket.

"I'm not sure that's a good—" began Raghnall, but the glare from Marifreth told him to focus on steering the boat.

Tiarnen put the flute together and then placed the tone hole to his lips. The first soft notes reverberated along the canal and immediately grabbed the attention of the teens, who looked upon the patrol boat in confusion. Tiarnen played on, the warsong motifs fluttering louder for them and becoming recognizable. Realizing that they not only had an audience but a sixth band member as well, the teens picked up where they had left off with even more enthusiasm. As the patrol boat passed, they kept in near-perfect sync and were so swept up by the end that one of them hadn't realized how close he was to the edge and fell into the water. Laughing and cheering, the rest of the band helped their friend out and then celebrated ecstatically.

"For Dorladdich!" they yelled.

Tiarnen raised his flute in acknowledgement, but then his proud smile faded as the band picked up the brooms, planks, and barrel.

Marifreth slid up next to Tiarnen and nudged him. "Your gears are turning."

"It's nothing," he said, watching the band fade into the distance.

Unconvinced, Marifreth kept staring at him.

"It's just... I can't help but wonder if music means so much to them because they have so little."

"Or perhaps they need so little because they have music," said Raghnall, rather philosophically.

"Which has only left them vulnerable to manipulation and abuse," said Marifreth.

"Here we go," muttered Raghnall.

"Oh, I'm sorry." Marifreth pointed her thumb back to the slums. "Did I mistake any of those provincials suffering from famine for thriving from the spoils of this war?"

"No, but their circumstances are completely out of our control," said Raghnall.

"For now," added Marifreth.

"All we have to do is win, and things will get much better," said Tiarnen.

"That's the spirit, lad," said Raghnall, navigating the cross waters of another canal junction.

"Not to mention the one that got us in this mess," said Marifreth.

"Where exactly are we going?" asked Tiarnen, trying to change the subject.

"The lighthouse," Raghnall replied, steering the boat south into an impossibly narrow tunnel.

"But nobody goes there."

"Exactly." Marifreth gave him a wink as they slipped into the darkness.

Barely able to see his hand in front of his face, Tiarnen could hear the side of the boat grinding against the stone walls.

"Watch your fingers," said Raghnall, following the tunnel's edge as it curved to the right and then finally opened up to a small cove. A beam of vibrant light suddenly passed overhead. Tiarnen blinked his eyes back into focus and looked up to see the lighthouse reaching into the misty sky like a spire.

"Here we are," said Marifreth, standing to her feet as Raghnall brought the boat to a stop against a wall of hanging ivy.

"What are you—" began Tiarnen, but before he could finish, Marifreth had already pulled herself through the ivy and into a hidden nook on the other side. Excited to see where it would lead, he grabbed the ivy and pulled himself through just as Marifreth began knocking on a mossy stone door set into the lighthouse's foundation. Expecting it would lead the three of them inside, he turned to help the major out of the boat, but Raghnall didn't appear at all interested in following.

"You're not coming with us?"

"Duty calls, I'm afraid," said Raghnall, tossing the patrolman's helmet to Tiarnen.

"I thought you didn't want—"

"Consider it a reminder in case she tries to encourage you again." Raghnall raised his eyebrow. "I'll pick you both up here in an hour. Do not be late."

"Yes, Major," said Tiarnen, saluting as Raghnall turned the boat around and vanished back into the tunnel.

"You mean a lot to him, Tiarnen," said Marifreth.

He rubbed the bruises on the back of his neck. "So I'm learning."

She knocked on the door again.

"Is there no one inside?" asked Tiarnen.

"Oh, there is," she said with a sigh. "Dear Haurel just happens to be older than the lighthouse itself."

Clack!

Marifreth pressed down on the door latch and then opened it to reveal a spiral staircase that appeared to go up forever. They both stepped inside—the musty smell of wet stone and kerosene oil filled the air.

"Careful, the stairs can be rather slippery," said Marifreth, who began walking up. "I took a tumble down them when I was a sprat and broke my left arm."

"You never told me that before!" said Tiarnen. "Did the Matron mend it for you?"

"Yes, but it took some time to heal, which your grandmother used as an opportunity to try and force me to become right-handed."

"But you're still left-handed."

"Indeed, I am." Marifreth suddenly grabbed the railing and came to a stop.

"Mum? *Are you all right?*" asked Tiarnen, rushing to her side.

"Just need to take a breath... here, feel." She took his hand and placed it on her belly. "Seems someone wants to race you."

"Don't think I could keep up with that pace," said Tiarnen, feeling the little kicks.

"You and me both," said Marifreth. "Come on. Not much further to go."

Side by side, they continued up the stairs, passing through a large hole in the first floor that led them into the circular living room. As they arrived, Tiarnen noticed a strange wheezing sound emanating from a small elderly man, frazzled white hair around an otherwise bald crown, who was fast asleep in a fishnet hammock hanging from the low ceiling.

"I take it this is Haurel?" whispered Tiarnen.

"The one and only," said Marifreth, giggling under her breath.

"I thought the sound might have been the lamp seizing up."

"Oh, no, he seized up years ago."

They both couldn't help but laugh.

"Should we wake him?" asked Tiarnen, keeping his voice low.

"Oh, there's no need to whisper."

"I don't want to startle—"

"Haurel!" yelled Marifreth.

"*Mom!*" hissed Tiarnen, only to notice the wheezing continued. "How in the—"

"He's as deaf as a clam these days. Still has great eyes, though. I swear he can see all the way to Locarnia. It's what makes him such a renowned lightkeeper."

"Is that why you brought me here? To meet him?"

"No, for that, we have just a few more stairs ahead of us."

"Do we have to?" whined Tiarnen, his knees still weak from the climb.

"It'll be worth it. Come on," urged Marifreth, continuing her way up the stairs again.

Trudging behind, Tiarnen followed her into the lamp room where the massive chronolamp was burning brightly—its gears and pulleys rotating the polished lens and casting a blinding beam through the water-stained windows all around him. He rushed over to look through the glass and watched as the corsair ships were guided through the treacherous waters far below. He had a thousand questions to ask Marifreth, so he turned back, but she had vanished behind the lamp mechanics.

"What could possibly be more interesting than this view?" asked Tiarnen.

"Come and see for yourself!" she said.

Curious, he walked over to see her pulling down a swath of fishing nets that were covering a pile of old crates. Before he could ask why the mess was there, Marifreth slid some of the crates over to reveal a large dusty trunk on the floor. "Uh, is that supposed to be here?"

"Not exactly," said Marifreth, shaking her wrist to let a thin ceramic chain slide out from under her sleeve. She knelt and inserted the smallest key into the trunk lock.

Click-clack!

The latches popped open.

"Go on then, have a look," said Marifreth, nodding at the trunk.

Tiarnen set his helmet down and cautiously lifted the lid to see the trunk was filled to the brim with countless unfamiliar trinkets.

"None... none of this looks Dorladdian," he said, eyes widening with shock.

Marifreth smiled mischievously. "That's because none of it is."

Tiarnen kept staring at the trunk in silence—his heart pounding at the thought of what would happen if he was caught anywhere near just one of the foreign objects.

Snickering at his apprehension, Marifreth took a thick, blood-stained leather glove covered in iron armour plating from the top of the pile and held it out for Tiarnen. "Don't worry. It's not going to bite."

Tiarnen reluctantly took the glove and carefully turned it over to get a better look at the interlinked gearing between the fingers, only for his thumb to accidentally press down on the palm.

Shkint-shkint-shkint-shkint-shking!

A jagged, rusty blade sprung from each finger.

"Okay, that one might," admitted Marifreth.

"What is it?" asked Tiarnen.

"An ironclaw—Lydvenkian infantry use them in battle to cut through enemies."

Tiarnen instinctually held the weapon a little further away.

"My love, I'm sorry," said Marifreth, taking the glove back. "Maybe this was a mistake; I thought you would want to learn more about the provinces."

"I do," said Tiarnen, "I just didn't expect all of..."

"This?" finished Marifreth.

"Yeah."

"Of course, I'll take you back home." Marifreth reached to close the lid.

"No, wait... what is that little box for?" asked Tiarnen, kneeling and pointing to the small rectangular metal box resting in the pile.

"Oh, that's a Lydvenkian music box," said Marifreth, pulling it out and opening the lid. A small spring-loaded dancer popped up and began turning while a simple melody emanated from inside. "What's amazing about it is that if sunlight touches—"

"Woah! What is *this?*" interrupted Tiarnen, already onto a curved horn with silver inlay.

"That is a frost-horn from Phrysbruck. In the hands of a well-trained maes—"

Tiarnen blew into it. The room suddenly chilled, windows fogged over, and a few delicate snowflakes fell from above. "Amazing!" he said, pulling a flake from Marifreth's hair to let it melt on his fingertip. "This looks heavy!" Tiarnen set down the horn and tried to pull a large hammer head with a broken handle from the pile.

"Ah, known as a foe-crusher, the cavaliers of Elihammer wield them while on horseback. Here, I can show you what happens if it is struck in rhyth—"

Before she could finish, Tiarnen struck the floor a few times with the hammer, which made the etched runes along the side glow magenta while also becoming feather-light.

"Feels as though it could almost float away!" he said, swinging it back and forth effortlessly. At once, the runic light faded, and the hammer regained its full weight.

Clunk!

Tiarnen didn't have much choice but to set it on the floor before he continued rummaging through the trinkets. Finding it hard to choose which one to look at next, he finally began to understand why his mother was so excited to bring him to the lighthouse. This wasn't merely a trunk; it was a treasure chest!

Tiarnen shook his head in disbelief. "How did you ever manage to collect all of this?"

"Oh, it wasn't just me; your grandmother also did her fair share of scouring for battle souvenirs while travelling the provinces."

"I wish I could see all of them, the provinces, I mean," said Tiarnen, still rummaging through the trunk.

"One day, perhaps," said Marifreth. "You might even breach the Tantalis, a mountain fortress in Phrysbruck that holds the largest musical archive in all of Chora."

Tiarnen raised an eyebrow. "How large?"

"Rumour has it a librarian once went searching the archives for a rare recording, took him over three days before finally returning with it."

"*Three days?*" Tiarnen's mind reeled at the idea of being lost for that long.

"Yes, but without question, my favourite province is Elihammer. It has leagues of endless wheat fields stretching in every direction. And high above them, ribbons of magenta light called *auroras* illuminate the night sky as far as the eye can see. I used to dream about what touching them might feel like," said Marifreth, her voice fading as she fell into memory.

"Mom?"

"To be fair," she continued, coming back to reality, "all of the provinces are equally as wondrous and unique as we are. That's why nothing in here should be feared. In fact, it should be celebrated."

Tiarnen was utterly intoxicated by her passion. He couldn't get enough, and so he kept rummaging through the trunk, where he found a thick leather-bound book with a Dorladdian crest embossed on the bottom of the cover.

"Ah, was wondering when we might find that," said Marifreth.

"It's Dorladdian?" asked Tiarnen, who felt it strange that the diary seemed out of place.

"The maestro diary, in fact."

"Can I look?"

"Of course."

Tiarnen unravelled the long leather strap around the cover, opened it, and read the first entry aloud: "*We have lost too much already. Those who follow me, let your ten pages never be the last. For Dorladdich! Roarke Raewan. Maestro Dorian II, 121–328 ADA.*"

"I can't believe that he lived for over two hundred years," said Tiarnen.

"And made the diary by hand. Every maestro who has succeeded Roarke followed his tradition of using ten pages," said Marifreth.

"Why only ten?" he asked, flipping through the diary.

"Probably because he knew how much maestros love talking about themselves," said Marifreth, sneering. "But in all seriousness, I think he simply wanted to make sure that the insights and experiences we passed on were truly important. Otherwise, the diary would have probably been full by the time that Dorian the Fifth was finished with it."

Tiarnen continued flipping through the pages, reading as many entries as his eyes could drink in before finally stopping.

Maestro Dorian XIV, Marendra 9th, 981 ADA

"Archavral" is finished and marks the completion of the Dorladdian warsong repertoire. I took great pride in making the announcement to the praetor, but only here will I express my sincere relief that no other maestros need to risk their lives by exploring its treacherous composition. May it wash away anyone who attempts to take our home. For Dorladdich!

Tiarnen skipped to the middle.

Maestro Dorian XVII, Junobra 15th, 1032 ADA

This is rather hard to explain, but I do believe I am beginning to better understand what animals are saying. Let me be perfectly clear, it isn't as though they are suddenly speaking words, and we're having lengthy conversations. Instead, I am gaining a deeper awareness of the nuance in their vocalizations and, thus, a stronger impression of what they're trying to communicate.

Absolutely enthralled, Tiarnen reached the second last chapter. "*A Shattered History. Freyla Braithrach. Maestro Dorian LVII, 1495–1540 ADA.*" He turned the page to see countless sketches of what looked like playing cards.

"Ah, yes, that would be your grandmother's chapter. She had a, how do I put this, *slight* interest in Shatter," said Marifreth.

"There are so many cards," observed Tiarnen.

"Which is why she spent the better part of her days cataloguing and documenting any that she found interesting. In fact, she used to host private matches in the Conservatory with your grandfather. Rumour was, she became one of the best players in the province."

"Shatter seems like a waste of time to me."

"Something tells me it won't stay that way," said Marifreth, ruffling his hair.

Tiarnen jumped to the last chapter. "*A Dream of New Days. Marifreth Braithrach. Maestro Dorian LVIII, 1540*—wait, this is yours!" he said, flipping past the title page. Every inch of the next page was covered in chaotic music notation, most of it crossed out or obscured with handwriting over top. He tried to read the unfinished compositions but couldn't make much sense of them. "It's hard to tell which warsongs these are."

"That's because they're not warsongs."

"Then what are they?" asked Tiarnen, his confusion returning.

Marifreth gave him a long look. "New compositions."

Tiarnen leaned back. "But we're forbidden to compose."

"I know." Marifreth sighed, taking the diary back. "But after House Roycroft seized nobility, your father had to let me compose a new melody for the Calling. I thought composing would merely be a fun challenge... however... after I finished the melody... I was compelled to keep writing. Before I realized what I was doing, ten more melodies were looking back at me."

"There's a lot more than ten in here, Mum." Tiarnen riffled through the pages. "I wonder if any of them could be used in battle."

"Tiarnen, this might be hard for you to understand but..." Marifreth took a long pause, considering her next words carefully. "I believe now that our ability to illuminate can be used for something greater than the war."

"Greater than the war?"

"Simply put, as an art."

Tiarnen's brow furrowed. "But how will that help us win Chora?"

"It won't, at least, not in your father's eyes," said Marifreth. "You see, with the warsongs in place, all they need are maestros who are willing to illuminate against one another and continue tearing Chora apart. If the other provinces are in the same dire state that we are, soon there won't be anything left to fight over."

"Has anyone honestly come close to victory?" asked Tiarnen.

"No, that's the problem—one that I don't think the warsongs can ever solve." There was more than a little bitterness in her voice.

Feeling like the conversation was going beyond his comprehension, Tiarnen looked at the notation again with nervous excitement—this time noticing how different it was compared to the standardized and perfectly executed penmanship in the warsong book. "The writing is so..."

"Messy?"

"I was going to say loose."

"How very kind of you," chuckled Marifreth. "The thing is, you're not exactly concerned with penmanship when music is pouring out of you. But, to be honest, I mostly just toil for weeks trying to find a chord progression that will help move a song forward."

"Is that why most of these are unfinished?"

"I like to think of them as works in progress, thank you very much," said Marifreth, raising her chin.

"Do they have titles?" asked Tiarnen.

"Not yet, but that doesn't mean I can't play one of them for you!" said Marifreth, rummaging through the trunk again.

Tiarnen couldn't believe what his mother was suggesting. She could already face life in prison for composing new music, but performing it was punishable by death—even for a maestro. Before he could come up with a reason to deter her, Marifreth pulled a badly tarnished piccolo from the trunk and turned to him with a wide smile on her face.

"This should do the trick," she said, wiping the mouthpiece with her sleeve. "Go on, pick whichever song you want to hear first." She aligned her fingers on the keys and quickly played through the piccolo's register.

"All right. How about this one?" asked Tiarnen, reluctantly pointing to the shortest song in hope that it would be over before anyone heard them.

"Ah, one of my favourites," said Marifreth, putting the piccolo to her lips.

"Wait!" Tiarnen pulled her hands back down. "How do we know it will be safe?"

"Safe?" asked Marifreth.

"To illuminate."

"My darling, none of these are meant to be illuminated. Which, in a way, makes them far more challenging for me to perform."

Tiarnen shook his head. "I don't understand."

"Despite countless attempts to understand resonance, we still haven't been able to explain why so few of us have it," Marifreth explained. "Some believe that we are born with it inside of us, while others have theorized that there is an external source empowering our ability."

"Which do you think it is?"

"Each hypothesis is as likely as the next, but what I can tell you for certain is that once you have sparked, illuminating becomes far more natural, which makes your resonance much harder to contain."

"Because of our emotions?"

"Exactly. And since emotion determines hue when we illuminate, all maestros attune themselves to a specific one and thus define their provincial colour."

"Dorladdich's provincial colour is green."

"For I am attuned to trust," said Marifreth, kissing Tiarnen on the forehead. "And since there are many kinds of trust expressed in our music, various shades of green are thus illuminated." She returned the piccolo to her lips to begin the song.

Though the intro, verse, chorus, and bridge were all rather simple to Tiarnen's well-trained ears, he still found it incredibly uplifting and playful—as though Marifreth was somehow threading joy through his worrisome heart. Before he knew it, she played the last note of the outro and finished with a whimsical flourish.

"Well?" asked Marifreth, leaning in closer.

"It was..." began Tiarnen, searching for the right words.

"Yes?" she pressed nervously.

Tiarnen smiled wide. "It was really good!"

"Just because I'm your mother doesn't mean you're obligated to say that," said Marifreth, putting a hand on his shoulder.

"No, I meant it!"

"In that case... would you like to hear another?"

"Definitely!"

Marifreth flipped to the next page, quickly read over the notation, and put the piccolo back to her lips. Once again, Tiarnen was astonished at how light-hearted and upbeat the second song felt. Even though a similar verse and chorus pattern repeated like before, there was a catchy hook this time that had him pumping his fist in the air enthusiastically. With the outro, he brought his other fist up, gave both a couple more exuberant pumps, and then applauded Marifreth as she brought the song to an end.

"Stop! You're embarrassing me," she said, pulling his hands down.

"You deserve it," said Tiarnen.

"But how did it make you *feel?*" asked Marifreth, her eyes widening with anticipation.

"I don't know... cheerful? Yeah, *really* cheerful."

"Exactly what I was hoping for! I've been trying to write each song with a specific emotion in mind."

"*Can I hear another?*"

"No, we should make our way back down to the dock, or I'll have to endure your uncle ranting about how I kept him waiting around for me *yet again,*" she said, finishing with her best Raghnall impression.

"Just one more, please?" begged Tiarnen. "If we're late, you can blame it on me."

"All right, *one* more, and then we're off." Marifreth turned to the last page in her chapter. She raised the piccolo to her lips but then paused... Her eyes went to Tiarnen, and then she handed the instrument to him like it was a sword of legend.

Tiarnen pursed his lips. "I don't know if that's a good idea."

"Only one way to find out," said Marifreth.

"Does it have a name?" he asked, taking the piccolo and looking it over.

"If it ever did, then I am afraid it has been lost."

"It's so much lighter compared to my flute." Tiarnen aligned his fingers on the keys.

"Luckily, the fingering is similar," said Marifreth, "but the mouthpiece is much trickier, which is why piccolos have a reputation of being notoriously difficul—"

Tiarnen played through the instrument's register just as she had.

"My little piper." Marifreth shook her head in disbelief as she held the diary up so Tiarnen could better read the notation.

"The higher octave takes a lot more breath," he observed.

"Just remember to stay relaxed," said Marifreth.

"Right." Tiarnen shook his hands out.

"Ready?" asked Marifreth, smiling to encourage him.

"Think so, yeah," he said, holding the piccolo to his lips again.

Marifreth started tapping her foot in rhythm. "And one, and two, and three—"

Tiarnen carefully brought the charming intro to life. A sequence of sirenic motifs made his heart leap as he navigated through the verse—knowing that he was incriminating himself with each note played. However, before Tiarnen could make it to the chorus, he lost the beat, and his performance fell apart.

Marifreth stopped her foot and smirked. "A bit harder than you thought?"

"That was awful," said Tiarnen, shoulders slumping.

"Because you're overthinking it."

"Maybe if I keep my fingertips more over the top of the keys, I'll have a better chance of—"

"Tiarnen, you have to stop listening to this," said Marifreth, pointing to his forehead, "and start following *that*." She put her finger to his chest.

Tiarnen nodded in agreement.

"Good. Now, from the top!" Her foot found a rhythm again, only this time, her heel stomped down harder.

With a look of determination on his face, Tiarnen took a deeper breath and blew through the piccolo—making the intro much louder and the motifs sparkle. He played through the intro again, but this time kept his momentum, trying his best to quiet his mind, and dove into the captivating verse.

"That's what I like to hear!" Marifreth encouraged him.

Wanting to impress her, Tiarnen stomped the floor in rhythm and transitioned into the entrancing chorus. The excitement of progressing further, of showing both his mother and maestro that he was more than capable, caused goose bumps to run all over his body. A flicker of light emanated from the piccolo. Before Tiarnen had the chance to glance at it, there was already a tiny shard of ivy-green glass streaking past.

"Tiarnen!" exclaimed Marifreth.

Though the shard was very thin, not to mention slightly misshapen, it still glimmered like a new star as it circled them. Tiarnen, awestruck at what he was witnessing, knew that he should have been elated to see he had sparked, but it was dread that gripped his heart. One wrong flourish of the piccolo or misplayed note, and the shard could cut them both to pieces. His hands trembled at the thought of causing his mother harm, which only made the shard vibrate chaotically in reaction—its trajectory becoming dangerously erratic.

"Listen to me. You can do this," said Marifreth.

Her confidence helped Tiarnen refocus and continue performing, but with his resonance now pouring through the piccolo, every note sparked into another shard and clustered with the first, only to circle mother and son faster and faster.

They were trapped.

Tiarnen was screaming inside, desperately wanting the nightmare to end as he played the thrilling outro—for it to have never begun in the first place.

"Now, finish it!" ordered Marifreth.

He played the last bar of the outro, ending it with a dazzling progression of ascending leaps while trying to flourish carefully in the hope of pulling the shards around himself. Instead, he accidentally fused them together and formed a shard that darted toward Marifreth, who somehow managed to duck out of the way. The shard struck the lamp lens and shattered it, causing a blinding flash of green light to shoot into the horizon. Just as quickly, the beam faded to half its normal brightness, and Tiarnen's senses returned.

Marifreth was slumped over the trunk, her body motionless.

"Mom!" he yelled, rushing to her.

"I'm all right," she said, slowly sitting up to reveal a long gash across her right cheek.

"You're hurt!" Tears welled in Tiarnen's eyes.

Marifreth pressed the back of her hand against the wound and looked at the blood-splatter. "I'll be fine, just as long as you're still in one piece?"

Tiarnen nodded, the tears streaming down his sweaty cheeks. "I'm sorry—I'm so sorry—I didn't think I would ever—or—or that I was even able to—"

"Slow down. This was not your fault!" said Marifreth, pulling him in close. "If anything, I'm relieved it happened here of all places."

"You are?" asked Tiarnen.

"Yes, because now we finally know..."

"That I could be a maestro," he finished, his sombre expression turning into a reluctant smile.

"But *should* you?" asked Marifreth. "Before you answer that, I want you to think about all of your years of training and hard work up until this moment. You have earned succession by every possible measure. However, that doesn't mean you're obligated to accept it."

"You're giving me a choice?" asked Tiarnen, sinking back in disbelief.

"One that I was never allowed," Marifreth said solemnly.

"How do I know that I'll make the right one?"

"You won't, but if you can't make it for yourself, be sure that the Verse will make it for you."

Tiarnen went quiet while he took everything into consideration. For a moment, he seemed torn—only for his eyes to focus on Marifreth's bloodied cheek. "No... I don't want to be a maestro."

"Then promise me, here and now, that you will never become one."

"I just said—"

"*Promise*," interrupted Marifreth.

"I... I promise," said Tiarnen, nodding in agreement.

"Tiarnen, you just made me the proudest mother in all of Chora," said Marifreth, drawing him into her arms.

"Wait, does this mean I have to give up music entirely?" asked Tiarnen, pulling back for an answer.

"Not yet." Marifreth slowly stood to her feet.

Tiarnen began moving the crates to obscure the trunk again. "But how do we make sure I don't accidentally illuminate again?"

"I will teach you how to control it," said Marifreth, tossing the netting on top of the crates. "However, as time goes on, your resonance will become harder and harder to repress." She made her way to the front of the chronolamp.

"Why?" asked Tiarnen, following her.

"As we grow older, we become much more resonant. Which means that you will need somewhere safe to practise."

He looked around. "This seems as good a place as any."

"True," said Marifreth. "In fact, Haurel will be retiring soon, and I can't think of someone with more reason to become Dorladdich's next lightkeeper." She undid the knot on her wrist strap, slid the trunk key off, and handed it to Tiarnen.

"Are you sure?"

"It will be our little secret," said Marifreth, a smile pulling at her cheek.

"But secrets are such a burden," said a cold voice.

Tiarnen and Marifreth startled and quickly turned to the stairway to see Tharus taking the last stair. "If kept for too long, even the smallest ones will eat away at you, slowly gnawing day after day." He walked towards them. "Until there is nothing left inside but lies and deception."

"*Lies and deception,*" chortled Marifreth, grabbing Tiarnen's hand and bringing them around the other side of the lamp to stand before Tharus. "Tiarnen, when did your father become so dramatic?"

"Or interested in the lighthouse, for that matter?" added Tiarnen, trying his best to act casual.

"The Inquisitor informed me that you took an unscheduled trip with the major. Naturally, I was concerned as to why, so he had you—"

"Followed," finished Marifreth, a lack of surprise in her tone.

"Apparently, Holgor has more spies in Dorladdich than all of Chora these days," said Tiarnen.

"If only for your mother's protection," said Tharus. His bony hand grasped Marifreth's chin and turned her head to the side, revealing the still-bleeding cut. "Which I am apparently failing at."

"It was my fault," she said, pulling her chin away.

"Is that why the lamplight turned green as I arrived? Or has our son finally—"

Marifreth cut him off. "No. Not yet. However, Tiarnen did choose to take up the piccolo today, so I thought our first rehearsal deserved a bit of inspiration." She gestured at the misty view of the ocean.

"Inspiration," said Tharus, taking the diary from Marifreth's hand, "will only lead us astray." He opened the cover and flipped to Marifreth's chapter. Then, his eyes left the music notation to stare at her. "As you have just proven." He gripped all ten pages of Marifreth's chapter and tore them from the diary.

"Stop!" yelled Tiarnen, rushing ahead to try and take the pages back from his father.

"Why you insolent..." Tharus backhanded Tiarnen across the face, sending him to the floor.

"Tiar—aahh!" screamed Marifreth, knees buckling as she clutched at her belly.

"*Mom?*" asked Tiarnen, "What's wrong?"

*

Niera's wails were deafening.

"Does she ever have a set of pipes on her," said Raghnall, helping Marifreth sit up in bed while Niera squirmed in her arms.

"Yelling has never been a problem for our family, *listening* on the other hand," said Reina, pushing past Tiarnen at the foot of the bed and then propping up a couple of pillows for her mother. "Better?"

"Yes, thank you, my dear," said Marifreth, smiling through a long, exhausted breath as she sunk back into the feathery softness.

Reina ran her fingers through Niera's thin wisps of curly blonde hair and then noticed her little sister reaching out for Tiarnen. She shook her head. "Already demanding big brother's attention."

"Something tells me that will be a recurring theme," chuckled Raghnall.

"Tiarnen, you better hold her or she'll make a fuss," said Marifreth.

"Is it all right?" asked Tiarnen, walking to Marifreth's side.

"Of course, just cradle her head." Marifreth carefully placed Niera into Tiarnen's arms.

"Hello, Twinkles," he whispered, staring into Niera's twinkling green eyes as he gently bounced her.

Niera smiled and cooed at the affection, running her hands over his face—only to pull hard on his ear.

"Ow-ow-ow!" chortled Tiarnen, removing her grip as Niera giggled at his winced expression. "This one is going to be a handful; I can already tell."

"Funny," giggled Marifreth. "Raghnall said the exact same thing about me."

"Aye, but I'll admit that I was off the mark," said Raghnall.

"How so?" asked Tiarnen.

"You proved to be far more trouble than I could have ever imagined."

Their laughter filled the bedroom, and though Marifreth didn't share in the humour, she couldn't help but begrudgingly smile at seeing all of them so happy together.

THUD!

The bedroom door flew open as Tharus and several guards stormed in.

"Show her to me," he demanded, his chronograph chiming.

Tiarnen turned to Tharus and reluctantly presented Niera to him.

"Healthy?"

"As could possibly be," Marifreth said proudly.

"Good," said Tharus.

"Praetor!" Ignis rushed into the bedroom. "The Inquisitor has just informed me that the Phrygians are about to reach our shoreline!"

Tharus smiled wickedly at the news. "And Maestro Dorian will be there to greet them."

"*Are you mad?*" asked Raghnall.

"Reina, help your mother to her feet," ordered Tharus, ignoring the major.

"Like hell, she will," said Tiarnen, stepping in between Tharus and the bed.

"I'll go instead." Reina stood at Tiarnen's side. "I'm ready."

"Our praetor decides who stands as maestro for this province," said Ignis.

"We only need to hold Phrysbruck until the tide comes in," said Tharus. "Once it does, Praetor Sturm will have no choice but to retreat."

"As you wish, Tharus," said Marifreth. Grimacing, she threw back the heavy wool blankets and, with the reluctant help of Raghnall, slowly put her feet back on the ground. Fighting back the overwhelming pain, she trudged over to Tiarnen, took a last look at Niera, and then kissed him on the forehead. "Take care of her, Piper."

Chapter Seventeen
TAKING STOCK

Tiarnen's blurry eyes slowly opened to daylight that was nearly too bright for them to bear. Body numb, he blinked the world back into focus and, to his confusion, found himself kneeling in the centre of Cathedral Square.

How did I end up here? he wondered.

Before Tiarnen could think of a possible explanation, he noticed there were charred black craters in the ground, and most of the wall surrounding the Square had been destroyed. Despite his vision still being a bit blurry, he could see that just beyond the wall were a few groups of provincials salvaging and stacking bricks into organized piles. Wisps of smoke rose from what was left of the badly burned and damaged shops along Ardglen Street.

"Parick? PARICK?" shouted a provincial woman, clearly distraught and searching for a loved one who had gone missing during the battle.

Even though there was widespread destruction and despair, Tiarnen exhaled a sigh of relief.

It worked, he thought.

A thousand questions flooded Tiarnen's mind, compelling him to stand up and figure out what had happened after he was knocked out, but something was holding him in place. Struggling with what little strength he had left, the numbness quickly faded to a painful, raw chafing around his neck and wrists, which he realized were secured in a stock. He turned his head to either side and saw that praetorian guards were flanking him.

"Remove—" began Tiarnen, but he immediately went into a coughing fit, his throat as dry as parchment from what felt like a year without water. "Get me... out of... this!" he wheezed. The guard on Tiarnen's left jolted and hurried towards him... but only continued past without any acknowledgement. A rush of rage cleared Tiarnen's spinning head, and he tried freeing himself, the struggle making the wooden stock shudder, which drew the provincial's attention.

"He's awake! Maestro Dorian is awake!"

The announcement reached everyone within earshot. Before a minute passed, a large crowd had gathered around Tiarnen, their tired and filthy faces contorted with spite.

"Unworthy!"

"Disgrace!"

Why were they yelling at him? None of it made any sense—the stock was only used to shame criminals who had committed a capital offence; they would be kept in the Square and made an example of until Tharus passed sentencing. Tiarnen searched his foggy memory, trying to recall what he might have done to warrant imprisonment, not to mention apparently turning the province against him. His mind went back to the battle: Raghnall taking on General Mikavnik, Niera rallying the orchestra, the lattrice coalescing with green and orange glass... then he realized that he had no idea what happened to Lydia after trying to pull her to safety.

Did she also survive? Her defiant scream seemed to echo through his mind, only for it to be quickly silenced by a cold shadow falling over him. Grimacing, Tiarnen twisted his head to glance up. His father stared back at him.

"Finally with us, I see," said Tharus, casually leaning against the stock.

"Why—" Tiarnen coughed, trying to open his dry throat. "Why am I in this?"

"What did he say?" yelled a voice from the crowd.

"Our maestro wishes to know the reason for his arrest!" announced Tharus.

"Conspirator!"

"Traitor!"

"*Traitor?*" asked Tiarnen, resentment stirring in his heart.

Tharus raised his hand to quiet the incensed crowd and then knelt beside Tiarnen. "Nobody understands what happened between you and Lydia," he whispered. "So they've naturally assumed the worst."

"But I saved—"

Tharus stood back up and faced the crowd. "I know it is my judgement which you have all been patiently waiting for, and be sure that I, too, share the same anger for our maestro, the same disgust, as we watched him poison the purity of Dorladdich with Lydvenko's music!"

The crowd hissed and shouted at the mention of Lydvenko while a guard knelt and let Tiarnen sip from a canteen.

"What? No! That is not what happened!" yelled Tiarnen, his voice returning.

Tharus raised his hand again to quiet the crowd. "No? Then how do you explain illuminating with Maestro Lydia?"

"There was no other choice!"

"Liar!" someone bellowed.

Tharus leaned down to whisper again, "Do not hope for them to believe you, Tiarnen, *make* them."

Tiarnen then realized that his father's question was an opportunity to convince the provincials. He tried to think of an explanation. How he wove "Obrenthium" into "Pyrozikar," albeit with an effect he could have never anticipated, but then he realized none of the provincials would ever be able to make sense of the technicalities. Discouraged,

Tiarnen looked back up at their spiteful faces—the only other time he had seen them so hostile was when Tharus spoke of the other provinces at the Calling. Tiarnen was always confounded by how his father could tell the same story year after year and still captivate Dorladdich without fail... then it dawned on him... it wasn't *what* Tharus said. It was the *way* he said it.

"Is there something you wish to confess, Maestro?" asked Tharus, projecting to his audience.

"I... I do!" croaked Tiarnen.

The crowd settled to listen.

"I confess that... I studied and learnt the music of Lydvenko," he said, with a note of shame.

The crowd collectively gasped at the admission.

Tharus feigned a look of shock. "And what could have possibly justified such a disgraceful act?"

"It gave me the insight I needed," said Tiarnen.

"*Insight*, you say?" asked Tharus, his voice growing louder to make sure everyone could hear him. "For what purpose?"

"To discover Lydia's weakness!" Tiarnen's voice now, matching his father's embellishment.

"Are you saying that you used the enemy's own warsong against them?"

He nodded. "Yes, exactly that."

"But how did you know it was going to work?"

"I didn't," admitted Tiarnen.

Tharus stared down at him and held a dramatic pause, letting the crowd see his exaggerated look of realization. "But that would mean you knowingly put yourself at risk of death to protect the city!"

"As your maestro, that is my duty!" exclaimed Tiarnen, his voice cracking.

The crowd fell silent in the wake of this revelation.

Tharus turned back to address them. "Then it would seem that Maestro Dorian's unyielding devotion has been mistaken for deception! Taking this news into consideration, I ask all of you, is such a selfless act worthy of my *forgiveness?*"

The crowd took a moment and whispered among themselves.

"Free him!"

"Forgive us, Maestro!"

"Long live Dorian the Sixtieth!"

"And so he shall!" announced Tharus, pulling the lock pin from the stock to release it.

Tiarnen instantly crumpled and fell backwards—only to be braced by Raghnall before he could hit the ground. Despite being shocked to see the major, Tiarnen couldn't help but notice every inch of him that wasn't covered in bruises was wrapped in bandages—especially his mangled right arm, which was free from his gauntlet and resting in a sling.

"Get him cleaned up," said Tharus, who was already walking away with both of his guards trailing close behind as the crowd dispersed.

It wasn't as though Tiarnen expected Tharus, as a father, to check on his son's injuries, but as a praetor who had a wounded maestro, he did anticipate *some* concern. Lamenting his own surprise, Tiarnen reminded himself that the ticking hands on Tharus's chronograph had replaced his father's heartbeat long ago.

"When did you get here?" asked Tiarnen, struggling to steady himself.

"Right as you were finishing your supposed testimony," said Raghnall, leading them toward the cathedral. "Would have arrived sooner, but I've been covering Dansby's duties while he's on bereavement."

The reminder that Reina was gone caused Tiarnen to push himself from Raghnall and stagger over to one of the cathedral's entrance pillars, which he leaned against to catch his breath.

"How are you feeling?" Raghnall pulled a canteen from his belt and handed it to him.

"All kinds of terrible," he said, his shaking hand taking the canteen.

"Can only imagine."

A thousand questions suddenly flooded into Tiarnen's mind. "Have I been out for very long? And where is Niera? The orchestra? Was anyone hurt? What's left of our forces?"

"Just over a day. Niera is fine. The orchestra had minor causalities—mostly in the brass section. We lost half of our legion—Brigarch Costigan included."

Tiarnen could only shake his head in disbelief at the dire news. "At least you don't seem to be much worse for wear."

"Speaking of which..." Raghnall reached into his pocket and pulled out Tiarnen's piccolo. "How this thing isn't a pile of charcoal is beyond me."

A wave of relief hit Tiarnen as he saw that his instrument had somehow survived. "Makes two of us," he said, taking it from Raghnall. The body and keys had a layer of burned dirt all over them, but it otherwise seemed completely intact.

"The city wasn't as fortunate, especially the lower east districts—they took the brunt of the attack."

"Just what the provincials needed," said Tiarnen, gulping down a long sip of water.

"Rain didn't stop until this morning, thank the Verse," said Raghnall. "Otherwise, I don't think we would have been able to put out all of the fires."

"Well, a storm was called."

"Luckily for us," said Raghnall. "Orchestra should be making their way to the *Calhoun* for brunch about now. Let's head over. Chef Auberdine will be happy to cook up anything you want."

"Wait!" Tiarnen held his hands out. "I still don't know what happened after I was out?"

"Once the dust finally settled, I found you lying on the ground with Lydia in your arms, which, as you can imagine, didn't exactly give the best impression."

"I imagine not," said Tiarnen, taking another sip of water.

"Aran demanded you be taken into custody until everything could be explained."

He laughed to himself. "So much for gratitude."

"The trick is to never expect it from the Roycrofts," quipped Raghnall. "For what it's worth, Niera demanded your release, but Tharus refused her."

"Of course, he wanted to make an example out of me."

"If you weren't his son, it would have been much worse."

"I think it has more to do with the fact that I'm now his maestro."

"Speaking of which." Raghnall carefully opened one of the pouches on his belt, reaching inside. "Figured you might want a souvenir to remember your debut." He held out a small leather wrapping.

Having a hunch as to what it might be, Tiarnen traded it for the empty canteen and cautiously unwrapped the leather to find a jagged sliver of the lattrice inside. He was immediately captivated by the coalescing orange and green glass—the colours were much like oil and water; they had mixed but never truly blended together.

"Thank you, Uncle," said Tiarnen, moved by the sentiment.

"Aye, least I could do."

"Did any more of the lattrice survive?"

"A fair bit, surprisingly. The scavengers wouldn't touch it, though, probably too afraid of what would happen if they were caught with something that could be considered Lydvenkian."

"Can't blame them."

"Ignis said all of it was headed for the kilns to be destroyed, so I snagged that piece there just as the carts were heading off to the Row. I'm still not sure how it has been holding up so well. Any maestro glass that I've seen is usually dust in the wind shortly after a battle."

"It's somehow stronger," said Tiarnen, giving the sliver another look.

"Any idea why?" asked Raghnall.

"No, I've never seen anything like this before, and by the look on Lydia's face, neither had—" Tiarnen suddenly realized that Raghnall hadn't told him what happened to Lydia. "Wait, is she *alive?*"

"Yes, unfortunately," growled Raghnall. "Come on. Let's get moving before Coniel eats all of the butter shrimp."

"Sure..." said Tiarnen, carefully wrapping the leather back around the sliver, "right after you tell me where Lydia is."

Raghnall sighed. "There's no point. Sentencing was already passed; she's waist-deep in the tide caverns as we speak."

"All the more reason to speak with her!" asserted Tiarnen, holding his arms out.

"No, absolutely not."

"I only have a couple of questions. Afterwards, we'll head straight for the harbour, and I'll see to it that Auberdine cracks a cask of Glindore 50."

"Glindore 50?" inquired Raghnall, taken aback by the mention of the incredibly rare rum. "Rumour has it there are only a couple casks left in the entire province, and they're held in reserve for the praetor."

Tiarnen raised his eyebrow. "Or a certain maestro."

Raghnall's eyebrow also raised at the suggestion. "It would be unlike the Ashbrooks to refuse a formal request."

"Certainly in their best interest not to. Besides, I can't think of a better way to celebrate your win against General Mikavnik."

A smile pulled at Raghnall's cheek. "I must say, it was rather satisfying to watch that abomination be strung up in Garod's workshop for disassembly yesterday."

"In that case, I consider us morally obligated to go further than victory pins to commemorate the achievement."

Raghnall stared long at him, taking the offer into silent consideration. "Fine, you get two minutes with her, not a second longer!"

"More than enough time. I just want some answers; that's all."

*

To Tiarnen's weak and shaking knees, each of the wet limestone steps leading down the narrow torchlit tunnel to the dungeon felt like stepping off a cliff. He had only been there once before, as a young boy, during one of the many city tours Marifreth used to drag him and Reina on so they could better understand the province.

Taking their last step into the dungeon, Tiarnen and Raghnall were greeted with shimmering daylight and laughter. Hundreds of glittering stalactites hung from the ceiling of the massive sea cavern, its jagged, rocky walls shaped by a millennium of tidal erosion. At the far end, a row of tunnels that had been converted into holding cells led to the ocean, each with barred gates at both ends to keep prisoners trapped inside. Two men were standing outside the furthest cave, both wearing chest-high waders and watching a prisoner being slammed against the bars by a series of heavy waves.

"Swear I could watch this all day," chuckled Warden Blublon, a whale of a man who was blowing his runny nose into a handkerchief.

"Just have to appreciate it while we can," snickered Bailiff Leary, stroking his salt-crusted beard.

"What my associate means," Blublon stepped closer to the bars, "is that by midnight, your new home here will be a little over ten feet deep."

"But most tenants are begging for a tight grip before that happens." Leary wrapped his hands around his neck and pretended to choke himself.

Drawing closer, Tiarnen could see they were speaking to Lydia, who was on her hands and knees coughing up seawater.

"Looking at the sorry state of her, she'd probably enjoy it," said Blublon.

"Speaking of which," said Leary, winking at Lydia. "Have to say I'm looking forward to opening the outer cell doors tomorrow morning and letting your cold, limp, *lifeless* body be carried out with the tide so the murgles can feast on it. I hear they fight over the eyeballs."

"Terrible way to go. But does make for easy cleanup."

"That it does, Blublon. That it does." Leary chuckled.

"Warden!" yelled Tiarnen.

Blublon and Leary both whipped around to see him walking towards them with Raghnall limping close behind.

"Maestro! Major!" said Blublon. "Good to see you both on your feet, we were just—"

"Leaving," finished Tiarnen.

Whalen and Leary looked at each other in confusion.

"With respect, Maestro," said Blublon, "the Inquisitor explicitly told us that we are to watch her until—"

Leary elbowed Blublon after seeing Tiarnen's expression sour.

"But with you both here now, we'll be on our way," finished Blublon.

Tiarnen waited for them to vanish up the stairs before turning back to Lydia, who had already slipped into the cave's long shadows—her sunken eyes reflecting what little light there was. "I would have come sooner, but it seems you recovered from our battle much faster than I did. If the Warden went beyond harassment—"

"Dorladdians," she interrupted, barely able to keep her skeletal body upright. "You are attuned to trust, yet have none for prisoners of var."

"You wouldn't know trust if it—" spat Raghnall.

"I think we can all agree," Tiarnen cut him off, trying to prevent the conversation from turning into an argument, "your treatment is appropriate considering Lydvenko's actions." His eyes met Lydia's. "Not to mention the murder of my sister."

"Is that vhy you saved me?" she asked. "To punish me for her death?"

"No," said Tiarnen. "After what happened between us, I couldn't just let you—"

"Die?" Lydia held out her bony hands as though presenting purgatory to him.

"Listen, we're both in uncharted waters here, but since you're clearly more experienced as a maestro, I thought you might have some idea about—"

Lydia turned her back callously.

"To be honest," he continued, unwilling to let her cut the conversation short, "I didn't expect we would make it so far as forging a lattrice. I only hoped that playing together might be enough to stop you."

"And so it vas," she said. "Now, if you both don't mind, I vould prefer to live my final hours vithout an audience."

"Come on, lad," said Raghnall. "She's not going to be of any help."

"No, I'm not leaving until we figure this out," stated Tiarnen.

Raghnall shook his head in confusion. "What is there left to discuss?"

"Oh, I don't know. Maybe the fact that we proved two maestros can illuminate together!" yelled Tiarnen, his voice echoing in the cavern. Hearing himself say those words a few days ago would have seemed unbelievable, but now they only reinforced why he was standing his ground. Unfortunately, Lydia didn't seem to share his interest and kept her back to him.

"But... maybe you're right... maybe it doesn't matter." He turned to Raghnall. "Sorry to have dragged you all the way down—"

"Your choice of melody vas—" began Lydia.

"Intuitive?" asked Tiarnen.

"Desperate," she finished, barely turning her head to look at him.

Tiarnen ignored the insult. "When did you realize I had recovered your warsong book?"

"After your first attempt. It vas the only explanation for you being able to time the melody so perfectly."

"I really didn't think I would be able to, let alone repeatedly challenge you, and playing the finale was nearly impossible."

"It's the arpeggios," they said in unison.

An awkward silence filled the cavern.

Raghnall cleared his throat.

"When we were illuminating," continued Tiarnen, "our shards were the brightest I have ever seen before."

"Because ve vere amplifying each other," said Lydia, turning all the way around to face him again.

Encouraged by her renewed interest, Tiarnen pulled out the leather wrapping from his pocket, unrolled it, and presented the jagged piece of glass to her. "Is that how the lattrice... well... I don't know if there's a term for what happened. Do you?"

Lydia stood up and trudged through the knee-deep water to inspect the glass. As much as Tiarnen was thrilled to have piqued her curiosity, seeing her in the daylight was horrifying. Hollowing herself had scorched most of her maestro jacket and leather bodysuit away to reveal severe scarring across every inch of her pale skin. However, as Lydia stepped within arm's reach, Tiarnen noticed that she seemed to be in her early fifties, had the lightest brown eyes he had ever seen, and was surprisingly taller than him. His eyes went down to the glass again, and he saw Lydia's reflection in it. Half of her face in Dorladdian green and the other half in Lydvenkian orange.

"Synestry," she whispered.

"Syn—synestry?" asked Tiarnen, making sure he hadn't misheard her.

But Lydia did not repeat the word. Instead, she returned to the shadows and braced herself for the waves rushing towards her.

Chapter Eighteen

A Delicious Manipulation

"**I**'m telling you, we can't trust a single word out of her mouth," said Raghnall, weaving his way through the busy harbour market with Tiarnen following close behind.

Once the province's great shipyard, the Public Market looked over Bilgewater Bay, where the corsairs docked and unloaded their daily catch to be sorted, gutted, and sold by one of the many specialty vendors clustered throughout the pavilion.

His mind still on the conversation with Lydia, Tiarnen couldn't help but feel a little distracted by the bustle around him: speckled pike and reef cod flew overhead as fish mongers traded with each other, shuckers were opening buckets of fanny oysters and noble scallops as fast as they could, all while crackers broke the claws off sand crabs and tails from spiny lobsters with matching mechanical pace. Tiarnen guessed that the corsairs had probably just returned with their holds full for the vendors to be unloading so much onto the cannery carts parked around them. However, something felt out of place. He was used to the market being a chaotic scene, but there was a strange air of tension, and everyone seemed overly fixated on their tasks at hand. Part of him wondered why they were working so fast, while the other half was relieved that heads were down. The last thing he wanted was to be noticed and bombarded with questions about the battle.

"What reason would she have to lie?" asked Tiarnen, focusing back on the conversation.

"She doesn't need a reason," said Raghnall. "Lydia has nothing left to lose. For all we know, she wants her last word to send you on a wild chase for more answers that likely don't exist, in the hope that you'll go completely mad along the way—just like she clearly has."

"I didn't get that sense when we were talking." Tiarnen ducked as another speckled pike flew overhead.

Raghnall rubbed his brow in frustration. "Because you're too bloody swept up to think straight."

"I am not swept up!" said Tiarnen, blowing off the accusation.

"No?" asked Raghnall, leaning in closer to lower his voice. "Have you even asked yourself yet how she knew it was called synestry if it's never happened before?"

Tiarnen admittedly found himself stumped by the question. He was so elated that Lydia knew of the term that he hadn't thought to doubt her honesty about it.

"My point exactly," said Raghnall.

They walked out of the market pavilion and made their way down the harbour seawall to the last of three piers, its weathered planks reaching over the sea for what seemed like a league. Along both sides ran staggered lamp poles that carried Ashbrook banners to the very end where the *Calhoun* was moored. Growing weary from the turbid morning and walk from the dungeon, Tiarnen was nearly blown over by the gusting winds. Even the seagulls were having a difficult time steadying themselves on the draught as they tried to steal from the crabbers who were pulling up their traps from the rough waters far below. Another strong gust pushed Tiarnen into an old crabber, causing him to lose his grip on his rope and watch in horror as the trap plunged back into the sea forever.

"There must have been at least ten claws in there!" barked the old crabber, who turned and immediately stuck his finger in Tiarnen's weary face. "You're going to pay for every last—" But he stopped cold after realizing who was standing before him. Despite looking like he had just been spat out of a sewer canal and left to dry in the mud, Tiarnen was still recognizable—if only from two inches away. "Maestro! Forgive me! I didn't know that—"

"You would be here to break my fall?" he interrupted, trying to make light of the situation.

"Well, no, but happy to help whenever I can!"

"You could start by lowering your voi—"

"Look! Everyone! Maestro Dorian is here!" yelled the old trapper, waving his hands wildly.

Raghnall turned around, his eyebrows furrowed in a sort of confused annoyance at the announcement. All Tiarnen could do was stand in place and give a tight-lipped smile as everyone on the pier swarmed him.

"Well fought, Maestro!"

"Thank you."

"Maestro, may the Verse protect you!"

Tiarnen gave a half smile in appreciation. "And you as well."

"We are all in your debt!"

"No, please, that's not necessary," he assured them.

"Long live the Sixtieth!"

"Long live *Dorladdich*," Tiarnen corrected.

After many years as First Wind, he was used to receiving a nod or compliment after battle, but receiving genuine praise was both new and uncomfortable territory for him. After shaking every outstretched hand and reminding himself to write a melody that would make him invisible, Tiarnen backed away out of the crowd and hurried to Raghnall, who was now waiting impatiently.

"I still think synestry is worth looking into," said Tiarnen, ignoring the last few cheers behind him.

"Of course you do," said Raghnall, continuing down the dock.

Tiarnen glowered. "What is that supposed to mean?"

"It means you have that damn look in your eyes."

"What *look*?" asked Tiarnen.

"The same—*one way or another, I'm going to figure this out*—look that Marifreth used to get when she wanted answers."

"Let's say you're right, and Lydia was trying to deceive me," said Tiarnen. "We still need to figure this out—"

"No!" shouted Raghnall, stopping in his tracks. "What we need is to rebuild half the city, not to mention most of our defences, before Phrysbruck decides to seize the opportunity Lydvenko has just given them."

Raghnall's foreboding assessment made Tiarnen look back at the city. Much of the front-facing buildings and district walls were burned black or missing sections, and wisps of smoke rose up from the still-smouldering detritus. It made him realize just how vulnerable Dorladdich truly was now.

"I know how much you want to understand what happened, but we have other priorities right now," said Raghnall.

"You're right," said Tiarnen, letting out a long exhale.

Raghnall looked up at the trailing storm clouds. "For what it's worth, I don't think even Marifreth could have made the stand you did."

"That's because she would have never let us get ourselves in this mess in the first place."

"Take the bloody compliment," said Raghnall, glancing at Tiarnen. "That's an order."

"Thanks, Uncle," said Tiarnen, his soft smile fading as a wave of nausea washed over him.

"What's wrong?"

"Not sure... feels like I'm going to be sick." Tiarnen clutched at his stomach.

"Been too long without a proper meal," said Raghnall, who put his good arm around Tiarnen and helped him walk the rest of the way to the *Calhoun*.

Despite white caps crashing hard along her two-hundred-metre stone hull and the figurehead of entwined seahorses, the *Calhoun* stood tall, with all thirty-three triangular sails furrowing up her four towering masts. Well over a hundred crewmen were scattered across the floating castle, dutifully securing ropes, moving crates, untangling nets, and preparing bait. Tiarnen noticed a few orchestra members standing on the mid-deck balcony at the stern—they seemed to be focused on plates of food in hand, laughing heartily about something. He took it as a good sign. Below the balcony, a handful of crewmen were suspended from cables attached to their multi-belts, patching a small crack in the stone hull just above the waterline.

"Sand the edges down first, if you have to!" said Admiral Donal Ashbrook, a stocky man in his late sixties with bushy salt-and-pepper eyebrows on a friendly face. He was wearing a thick pea coat and wool beanie and standing on the boarding plank that led from the pier to the ship's upper deck.

"When should I put on the sealant, Da'?" asked Blair, a freckled girl in a sailor's uniform two sizes too big—Donal's youngest of eleven adopted children. The Ashbrooks had a long-standing reputation for "*bringing in strays*," as the Roycrofts put it, most of whom were abandoned by their provincial parents due to tragic circumstances, which is why the *Calhoun* was often referred to as *the Orphanage*.

"Wait until the mortar dries, love," said Donal, watching his crewmen fit the last slate into the hole and fill the gaps with mortar.

"Why?" asked Blair, reluctantly lowering her dripping brush.

"Because if you don't, those little fingers will become a permanent part of the hull." Donal turned away from the wind to light his pipe with a flinter—only to catch sight of Tiarnen and Raghnall arriving. "Ah! There they are! Good to see you back on your feet Tiar—sorry—Maestro."

"You as well, Admiral," said Tiarnen, accepting that there would be some awkwardness when it came to his new title for a while yet.

"Fleet looks to have weathered the storm," said Raghnall, glancing over his shoulder at the other two piers where the *Riornath* and *Arabrae* were also crawling with crewmen.

"Where's your faith, Major?" asked Donal. "Rough seas are what the corsairs were made for! Though, I must say, Maestro, you gave all of us an awful fright. We could only hear the battle from the harbour, but after that last explosion of light, I thought we might have to raise anchors and leave the province behind!"

"Speaking of which, looks like the old girl took a hit there." Raghnall pointed at the *Calhoun's* hull. "Didn't think any debris would have made it this far out."

"Oh, it didn't—that was from grazing the damn reef last night," said Donal as he finally struck a match, lit his pipe, and exhaled a long breath of sweet vanilla smoke. "We were heading in from our second run when the lighthouse went cold—could barely see a metre ahead of us! The current swept us into the shoals. I barely had enough time to warn the other ships—luckily, they managed to make port no worse for wear."

Realizing he hadn't given a single thought to the lighthouse since waking up, Tiarnen looked past the *Calhoun* to see that it had indeed gone dark, just as Donal said. He couldn't begin to guess what sorry state the lamp must now be in; the entire valve assembly would probably have to be pulled apart and cleaned.

"Tiarnen!" barked Raghnall.

"Sorry," he said, pulling his head out of the damage assessment. "Were you saying something?"

"I was asking why the fleet made a second sailing last night."

"Oh?" asked Tiarnen.

"Orders from the Executor's office," said Donal, puffing on his pipe. "We figured it was to help feed the city restoration effort, but it looks like they're taking the entire catch to the cannery."

"Explains why the market is so busy," said Tiarnen.

Raghnall scratched his beard. "But if it's all for the labourers, why bother preserving everything?"

WHAM!

A massive stingray fell from the sky and hit the pier just beside them. Stunned by the sudden arrival, as well as the seawater splattering their faces, they looked up to see Gail Ashbrook—a tall woman in her late fifties with long greying hair pulled back into a bun, wearing a fitted officer's uniform. She stared down at them from the upper deck, her hand still gripping the pulley lever that had opened the net and released the stingray.

"Gail, I'm not sure if you noticed, but we're standing right here!" yelled Donal, his arms outstretched.

"Then move aside, you crusty old turtle!" shouted Gail. She hopped onto the deck railing, grabbed the pulley rope, and leaped off the side of the ship—using the heavy net as a counterweight to slow her descent onto the pier. Gail landed with grace beside Donal and looked as though she was about to hit him, but instead leaned in and gave him a hard kiss on the cheek.

"Word of advice, never make your wife a first mate," said Donal.

"Best decision you ever made, on both counts," said Gail. "I'm sorry, Tiarnen, should have warned you." She gently wiped the water drops from his chin with her thumb.

"Is that a kingray?" asked Tiarnen, finding himself captivated by the incredibly rare creature. By his measure, it was a bit longer than he was tall, minus the tail that resembled a lethal harpoon at the end, and its angular wings were at least twice his arm span. Every inch of the body was covered in a lustrous dark green skin that was rumoured to make the strongest leather in the province.

"Aye, saw one trailing our nets last night, and we managed to set a hook," said Gail. She whistled to a pair of crewmen who were securing another net—they immediately dropped everything and ran over with a wheeled cart to lift the kingray onto it.

"I thought they were off limits for hunting, though?" asked Tiarnen.

"They are, but your little sister made a personal request. We're supposed to have it gutted and brought to Christart Tailors before midday," said Gail, who gave the kingray a last shove to centre it on the cart.

"Looks like someone is getting a new maestro jacket," said Raghnall.

Tiarnen knew that he should have been elated to receive such a fine gift. Niera certainly would have been, but he couldn't help but feel incredibly guilty that something so majestic was killed just for him.

"Both of you better get aboard. Everyone is already into second helpings," said Gail.

"Any butter shrimp left?" asked Raghnall.

"Have you met our son?" chortled Gail, giving the cart a hard push and making her way back down the pier.

"You heard her; go on!" said Donal, focusing back on the ship repairs.

Raghnall helped Tiarnen walk up the long mooring plank and onto the *Calhoun's* top deck. Just as he saw from the pier, the crew was busy prepping the ship for their next run. Before anyone could notice them, Tiarnen and Raghnall rounded the first mast and reached a flight of stairs that led down to the mid-deck. Tiarnen pulled himself from the major, used the banister for support, and slowly descended into the dining saloon.

Eyes adjusting to the dim light, and with his nose filling with savoury smells, he could see the entire orchestra sitting around the edge of the ship on crates, barrels, and chairs. In the middle were several tables pulled together, topped with overcrowded serving platters and bowls of food. The cliques were evident as always; most of the Ashbrooks and Finwicks were socializing within their orchestra sections while the Roycroft brood whispered at the far end. Tiarnen spotted Niera sitting among them as Lachlan rambled on about how hard he'd played to make sure the warsongs were as powerful as possible. Thankfully, his bragging was drowned out by some boisterous cheering from the percussionists who were caught up in a match of Shatter that was being officiated by Coniel. The scene reminded Tiarnen of why his grandmother first started the brunch tradition: so the orchestra could reconnect on a personal level by sharing a rich meal and a few spirited drinks, all in the hope of leaving the battle behind and giving their fresh wounds, both mental and physical, a chance to heal.

Outside of the more serious stitches, slings, and crutches, Tiarnen noticed that most of the orchestra had small cuts, all of the same size, on their hands and faces. He knew they could have only come from one thing: maestro glass; likely when the lattrice had shattered. Despite accepting that there was nothing more he could have done, Tiarnen hated the fact that his actions played a part in harming them.

He trudged over to the buffet with Raghnall and saw that it held a variety of culinary choices ranging from scrambled eggs, soda bread, crab cakes, lime squid, twice-fried fish, and creamy dill clam chowder. Raghnall followed in theme with the orchestra and scooped generous portions onto his plate until reaching the last bowl, which was empty except for a shallow pool of garlic butter and a soggy shrimp tail floating on top. The major glared at Coniel just as Chef Auberdine arrived beside them with a steaming pot of chowder. Few people in Dorladdich could make the major seem average in stature, but Auberdine had grown to the size of a walrus, sporting a whiskered moustache to boot, after thirty years of sampling his own culinary creations.

"Auberdine, your galley never ceases to amaze," said Raghnall, dunking a clay mug into the fresh chowder.

"If there's anyone worth standing over ten boilers for, it's these brave souls, Major!" bellowed Auberdine, wiping heavy sweat from his forehead with the sleeve of his strained double-button chef coat.

Hearing the major mentioned brought the saloon's noisy chatter to a swift end as the orchestra realized he and Tiarnen were now among them. Unlike on the pier, there was no praise—just long, uncomfortable stares. Only then did Tiarnen remember how Reina always managed to have a little speech ready to reassure them that better days were ahead.

"I... I, um... I honestly don't know what to say," he admitted.

"*Thank you* would be a start," said Niera, her gaze piercing through him.

Tiarnen took a deep breath and accepted that there was no way of avoiding some sort of explanation as to what had happened on the battlefield. Uncertain of where to begin, he figured the best thing to do was be honest.

"You probably don't know this," he said, "but Niera opposed my idea to use Lydia's warsong against her. And she was right to do so. Not only because the decision meant putting myself at greater risk but all of you as well. I'm sorry that I didn't have time to explain everything, and I can't imagine what it must have been like to face defeat while the one person who was supposed to bring you strength only caused confusion and doubt. As someone who grew up in this orchestra, I know our faith in the maestro is expected, but I would much rather prove that I am, in fact, worthy of it. Maybe one day I'll be able to. All of that said, this was not my victory but ours, so *thank you*."

Raghnall held up his mug of chowder, and everyone followed in gesture with their drinks. "The Sixtieth!"

"The Sixtieth!" the orchestra exclaimed, minus Niera.

"Well said, lad," whispered Raghnall.

Once everyone focused back on their conversations, Kaleigh stood up from her chair and hurried over to Tiarnen. She didn't say a word, just wrapped her arms around him. As much as he wanted to stay in the warm embrace forever, her squeezing wasn't making his stomach any better.

"Careful, I'm damaged goods," he wheezed.

Kaleigh laughed. "Tell me something I don't know."

"Auberdine, think you could brew up a sea-spit?" asked Raghnall, dunking his mug into the chowder for another helping.

"Someone has been on shore leave for too long, eh?" asked Auberdine.

Raghnall nodded at Tiarnen. "It's for our maestro."

"Oh, in that case, right away!" Auberdine plodded his way behind the stairs and squeezed through a pair of double doors that led into the galley.

Putting a half step between them, Tiarnen looked over Kaleigh's shoulder and saw Niera staring at her plate.

"How has she been?" he asked.

"Keeping to herself mostly. Can't tell if that's good or bad," said Kaleigh.

"Only one way to find out."

Though the distance to Niera was short, the countless side glances and whispers made her feel like a league away. At his arrival, the Roycrofts broke their huddle, but not without Lachlan lingering for an extra second before stepping out of the way.

"You look awful," said Niera, spooning the cold food around on her plate to avoid looking at him.

"It has been a morning," said Tiarnen, sitting down on a crate beside her. He noticed that her forehead was badly scraped, but otherwise, she seemed to be without any serious injuries.

"How long ago?" asked Niera.

"About an hour or so, I think. At first, I had no idea where I was, but—"

"No, how long ago did you *spark*?" she asked, finally looking up at him.

"Before..." began Tiarnen, finding it incredibly hard to talk about. "Before you were born... the day before, in fact."

Niera gave a slow nod and then looked down at her plate again.

"I'm sorry... I would have told you... it's just that... it's complicated," he said, giving up on trying to make up an excuse.

Niera rolled her eyes. "Somehow, it always is with you."

Tiarnen did the only thing that made sense and pulled her into his arms despite overwhelming nausea. After a moment of resistance, she finally gave in and leaned her head against his shoulder.

"Nothing has to change," he said, "all I've done is ensure Dorian the Sixtieth has the shortest term as maestro in history."

"Why is that?" Niera looked up in confusion.

"Because your shards will be dancing around all of us well before I get a chance to blow up the other half of the city."

Soft smiles washed over the orchestra's faces as they watched their maestro and lead reconcile what was a tense moment for all of them. Then, the floorboards trembled as Auberdine returned to Tiarnen with a serving tray covered in clay jars and glass vials.

"Don't worry, Maestro. We'll have you fixed up in no time," said Auberdine, setting the tray on the nearest table. He handed Niera a large goblet and then proceeded to empty a portion from each jar and vial into it. The mixing happened so quickly that Tiarnen couldn't really tell what the ingredients were, but everything seemed to fall into the category of powder, liquid, or something alive. After the last vial was emptied, Auberdine pulled one of several tasting spoons from his breast pocket and put it in the brown liquid. "Two to the left and three to the right," he said, pulling the spoon out and watching with satisfaction as the sea-spit began to bubble and froth.

Niera looked at Tiarnen with genuine concern as she handed the fizzing concoction over to him.

"You're sure this is a good idea?" asked Tiarnen, looking into the murky mixture.

"Don't worry. I make them all the time for new crewmen to help settle their stomachs," assured Auberdine.

"*Was that a tentacle?*" asked Niera, certain she saw a little one reach out from the foam.

"Best to swallow it down before they get a grip," suggested Auberdine.

Tiarnen took a deep breath, put the goblet to his lips, and took as big of a gulp as he could manage.

"Now the real trick," said Raghnall, "is keeping it down."

The salty-sour flavour hit Tiarnen like a slap across the face. He lurched instinctually, but Raghnall tipped the bottom of the goblet up, forcing Tiarnen to drink the rest. For a moment, he thought it was going to come shooting back up, but the nausea quickly faded to a strange, cool tingling in his stomach. He exhaled a long sigh of relief as the colour slowly returned to his cheeks.

"Any better?" asked Raghnall.

"Loads," said Tiarnen, in disbelief at how fast it was working.

"There, you see!" exclaimed Auberdine, collecting the goblet and tray.

"What did it taste like?" asked Niera.

"I'll guess nowhere near as good as a glass of Glindore 50."

"No argument there," said Raghnall.

"Auberdine, would you please open a cask?" asked Tiarnen.

Auberdine's face dropped at the request. "I'm not sure if we should without the praetor's—"

"You can tell him it was on my orders," said Tiarnen.

"In that case, consider it cracked!" Auberdine beamed. "Oh, and speaking of orders, I hope you don't mind, but Miss Niera requested that we prepare Reina's usual menu, given that you were unable to make any personal choices."

"Sounds great. What will I be having?" asked Tiarnen, who was genuinely starting to feel hungry again.

"Boiled eel hearts, fermented roe, peppered spiny sponge, whipped shark liver, and raw reef worms."

"No wonder Reina always ate alone," muttered Tiarnen.

"Illuminating takes more out of you than just strength," said Niera, pointing at his chest. "You need food that will help replenish your resonance."

"Can't I just have a bit of chowder?" he pleaded.

Niera glared at him.

"Fine, peppered spiny sponge it is. But I'll be eating here, not in the Conservatory."

"As you wish, Maestro," said Auberdine, giving a slight but respectful bow.

Over the next hour, Tiarnen finally got the chance to take a breath and enjoy his first meal in days. Niera pushed for him to finish every dish that Auberdine brought out, which he did, except for the reef worms. Even if they tasted only half as bad as they smelled, there wouldn't be enough sea-spit in all of the province to stop him from vomiting over the edge of the ship.

Auberdine also cracked the Glindore cask and gave Raghnall the first pour, but the major made sure everyone was able to have a tasting. All things considered, it was as perfect a brunch as there could have possibly been. By the end, the only thing Tiarnen wanted was to return to the lighthouse, fix the lamp, and fall asleep in a hot bath. As he stood up to say goodbye, the thudding of heavy boots interrupted him, and two Day Striders awkwardly descended the stairs, carrying a long wooden case between them.

"Can I help you two?" asked Kaleigh.

"Just tell us where you want it," said the patrolman.

"No, there must be some mistake." Tiarnen recognized the Executive Office crest on the side of the case. "We can't have that—"

"Over here," said Niera as she snapped her fingers and pointed at her feet.

The patrolman brought the case over, released the legs that were tucked underneath, and stood the case up for Niera.

"What are you doing? We never—" asked Tiarnen.

"Father wanted to put the awards ceremony behind us since the funeral, and your coronation will take up the entire evening," said Niera. "This was the best time, considering we're already together." Before Tiarnen had the chance to argue, Niera unlocked the latches, lifted the lid, and picked up a small ledger that was resting on top of the contents. "First!" she announced. "A few notable statistics!" Everyone started gathering around. "The *Battle of the Bridge*, as it has now been titled, lasted for nine hours and forty-four minutes. One of our longest ever, according to Executor Ignis. Five and one-half warsongs were performed, a provincial first, as far as we know."

"And hopefully a provincial last," said Lachlan.

Tiarnen ignored the snide comment.

"Casualties on both sides were substantial," Niera continued. "First and second brigade suffered nearly five thousand deaths; eight hundred were severely wounded." Many of the orchestra hung their heads at the gruesome news. "Lydvenko, however, lost over six thousand legionaries." Whistles and claps erupted from the Roycrofts and some of the Finwicks while the Ashbrooks remained silent.

"Seems that what is left of their forces are camped along the shoreline," Niera finished.

"They're waiting for Khazlokov to be ransomed," added Raghnall.

Tiarnen's eyes widened. "Khazlokov is alive?"

"And being interrogated by Holgor as we speak," said Raghnall.

"Now, onto the awards!" said Niera.

From the right case compartment, she pulled out a small, medium, and large satin pouch. "As always, we'll be handing out noble marks first. For those of you who are recent members, noble marks can only be acquired by performing at the highest level in combat." To the eager anticipation of the youngest orchestra members, Niera opened up the small pouch and shook out a few polished white pearls for them to see. "Winners will be able to spend their marks at any of the designated Roycroft, Finwick, or Ashbrook speciality stores." She put the pearls back into the pouch and referred to the ledger once again. "The nominees for Best Form are Coniel Ashbrook, Fiona Finwick, and Saoirse Roycroft. And the winner is... Coniel Ashbrook!"

"*What?*" screamed Fiona.

"Not only for stepping in as First Drum temporarily but also for keeping a steady beat when it mattered most."

"Here-here!" said Tiarnen, applauding with everyone as Coniel stepped forward and accepted the pouch.

"The question now is, do I buy more drumsticks or get a new box of Shatter cards?" asked Coniel.

"Sticks!" shouted Kaleigh.

"The nominees for Noble Sacrifice," said Niera, holding up the medium-sized pouch, "are Rowan Roycroft, Pierce Finwick, and Afton Obare. And the winner is... Pierce Finwick!"

Hand heavily bandaged, Pierce approached Niera and carefully grasped the pouch with the three remaining fingers on his left hand, then gave a casual salute.

"A couple of nubs well spent, if you ask me!" said Wendel, hoisting a glass to Pierce as he returned to his side.

"And finally," continued Niera, "the nominees for Esteemed Execution are Kaleigh Ashbrook, Lachlan Roycroft, and Wendel Finwick. And the winner is... Lachlan Roycroft!" With the Roycrofts cheering loud enough for all of Chora to hear them, Lachlan sauntered over and, upon grabbing the pouch, pretended like it weighed a hundred pounds. "Executor Ignis also left a note praising *'your example of the highest skill and talent.'*"

"Not as much as he's praising himself," muttered Coniel.

"You hear that? *'The highest skill and talent,'*" said Lachlan, who raised the pouch to cue another flurry of embellished Roycroft applause.

"Moving on," said Raghnall.

Niera opened the middle case compartment to reveal three gleaming medals resting side by side. Everyone tried to lean in and get a glimpse, but she waved them back. Medals were a much more serious matter; if you were a recipient, many aspects of life changed for the better. You received a monthly stipend from the province, your uniform was kept in top condition, and there was always a reserved seat for you on canal ferries.

"The *Battle of the Bridge* yielded three medals, and it is an honour to award the Shield of Valour to... Major Raghnall!" said Niera. "For putting himself in mortal danger—"

"Yet again," added Tiarnen.

"—to save another. Namely, Captain Dansby," finished Niera.

Raghnall walked over and bowed as she held up a small silver shield dangling from a thin green ribbon and hung it around his neck. Everyone lightly applauded the major despite knowing it was his fifth time receiving the medal.

"Next, we are awarding the Cross of Bravery to... Maestro Dorian!" announced Niera. Tiarnen reluctantly took a knee as she hung a small but pure emerald cross dangling from a wide grey ribbon around his neck. "For showing resolve and cunning in the face of insurmountable odds." The orchestra erupted in enthusiastic applause as he returned to their company.

"And lastly, the Heart of Service." Niera pulled out a heart made of sparkling cream coral on a light brown leather ribbon. "And the award goes to..." But Niera's voice trailed off.

Wondering what might have caused her to clam up, Tiarnen walked back over to his sister and read the ledger. "The award goes to our Lead!" he said. Tiarnen took the medal from Niera's hand and hung it around her neck. "For unwavering service to both province and Maestro."

Niera looked up at him, smiling as wide as he had seen her in a long time. "It's beautiful," she said, admiring how it sparkled even in the dim light.

Tiarnen grinned back at her. "Nice work, Twinkles."

"I think that's enough formality for one day," said Raghnall.

"The major is right," said Tiarnen, who opened the left compartment of the case to see it was full of small pins embossed with the shape of the city bridge. "And it looks like our victory pins have already been pressed, so feel free to grab one before you leave."

Without hesitation, everyone rushed the case to take one.

"Maestro?" asked Lorna.

"What is it, Lorna?"

"With your recent promotion, doesn't that mean the First Wind position is now vacant?"

"You know, I do believe you are right."

"It will have to be filled immediately," said Raghnall.

"Kaleigh is the best choice," said Niera, rather matter-of-factly.

Kaleigh looked at her in disbelief.

"Hard to disagree," said Tiarnen. "You know the signals and flourishes better than anyone."

"Including our maestro," added Niera.

Tiarnen cleared his throat. "Which is why morale among the woodwinds should see an immediate improvement after she accepts my offer."

"I... I would be honoured," said Kaleigh.

Niera pulled the First Wind badge off Tiarnen's tunic, wiped the mud and dirt from it with her thumb, and pinned it to Kaleigh's lapel. Just as Tiarnen was about to announce her acceptance, a sour stench caught his nose and caused him to look back at the stairs. Inquisitor Holgor stood at the foot.

Tiarnen's expression hardened. "Something we can do for you, Inquisitor?"

"Your presence has been requested in the War Room," said Holgor.

"Can't be good," said Raghnall.

"Never is," said Tiarnen, taking the major's glass from his hand and gulping the last of the Glindore before making his way to the stairs.

*

Their footsteps echoing, Tiarnen, Raghnall, and Holgor walked down a long hallway deep within the keep. As they approached the guarded War Room door, Tiarnen could hear his father's voice emanating from behind it. Upon reaching the threshold, the praetorian guard stepped to the side and opened it so they could pass through—the motion interrupting Tharus, who was standing with the earls around a tiled map of Chora in the centre of the floor.

"As I was saying," continued Tharus, brandishing a long hooked staff in his hand, "a praetor's capture is exceptionally rare—we should not waste the ransom opportunity that Khazlokov has provided us." He began to walk behind the earls, clacking the staff against the stone floor, his long shadow passing over little stone figurines that represented the provincial legions—each one painted in their province's colour.

"Where is Khazlokov being held, anyway?" asked Tiarnen.

"Under lock and key," said Holgor, pulling a small scroll of parchment from inside his decorated coat and handing it to Ignis for transcribing. "And as for Inquisitor Valchev, he died yesterday of his wounds."

Knowing how brutal Holgor was with prisoners, Tiarnen felt an unexpected sense of relief that Lydia was half drowning in the caverns.

"In that case," said Aran, "Khazlokov's ransom should be a hundred carts of sunstone!"

"Are you mad, Aran?" asked Liam. "Even if Lydvenko has that much in reserve, what do you intend we do with precious gems that hold no value in Dorladdich?"

"Toss them into the sea for all I care!" scoffed Aran. "The point is, stripping that much wealth from Lydvenko's economy will cripple it."

"Only for the short term," said Eimear. "What we need are resources; ore, oil, and coal—as much as we can to help rebuild the city."

"Hear, hear," said Raghnall.

"You speak as though there's a way of bringing it all here," said Liam. "The city will have been rebuilt twice over before those supplies reach us, even if by the Scorched Road."

"Speaking of the Scorched Road," said Eimear. "We have yet to receive any explanation as to why Lydvenko was able to cross our border seemingly without detection."

"Earl, be assured that the intelligence I provide is as accurate and timely as possible," said Holgor, puffing out his chest. "My office, and our praetor, were well aware that Khazlokov had deployed his legion, but their exact destination remained unknown. However, Khazlokov's interrogation revealed that he was heading for the Cairgory Gulch battlegrounds when Maestro Lydia suddenly turned east, entered Twighaven Forest on her own accord, and proceeded to cut straight through our woodland with the help of several kyndling."

"Kyndling?" asked Tiarnen. He was stunned to hear this—the menacing creatures were known to be anything but obedient, even to the maestro who illuminated them.

"I'm surprised that Khazlokov allowed her to break formation and press on without his permission," said Eimear.

"Any objection was certainly forgotten once he saw that Lydia was providing him a direct path to our island," said Holgor.

"I don't blame Khazlokov for seizing the opportunity," said Tharus, "but that doesn't mean it wasn't a strategic error on his part."

"Be that as it may, if Khazlokov was able to cross the bridge uncontested, then we've lost far more control over our territory than we realized!" Eimear pointed at the borderline between Dorladdich and Lydvenko on the map.

"Then we should demand Lydvenko withdraw its border by a hundred leagues," said Aran. "At the very least, it will help ensure we are not caught off guard again."

"Lydvenko never retreats," said Tharus. "In fact, after he was taken into custody, Khazlokov had the nerve to accuse my son of breaking the rules of engagement by interrupting Maestro Lydia's performance and demanded that our victory be rescinded."

"I played *with* her, not against her," corrected Tiarnen.

"I know," said Tharus. "Khazlokov is merely desperate. Unfortunately, his ransom will not bring Dorladdich what it truly needs."

"Which is?"

Instead of answering, Tharus turned and walked onto the balcony.

Curious as to what had grabbed his interest, Tiarnen joined Tharus and peered with him over the edge of the west balcony to the bailey below.

To his amazement, the waterwheels, entire barbican, and gate were nowhere to be seen. Bridge repairs, however, were already well underway: a large group of labourers were transporting bricks in wheelbarrows over a basic wooden scaffold that spanned from the edge of the bailey to the fragmented second section of the bridge. Still, Tiarnen's jaw went slack at the realization that the lattrice had cleaved the whole front half of the bailey from the island itself.

"Quite a sight, isn't it?" said Tharus.

"I had no idea the lattrice would or even could..." stammered Tiarnen.

"No, but you knew there would be consequences of some kind. Tiarnen, I'm going to ask you something, and I need you to answer me honestly."

"All right."

Tharus turned and looked him in the eyes.

"Could you do it again?"

"If the circumstances were right... yes, I probably could."

Tiarnen didn't know if it was a trick of the light, but it appeared as though Tharus's expression softened for a moment and held the slightest hint of pride.

"I appreciate a dramatic pause as much as the next person," said Eimear, arriving with the rest of the party, "but I'm returning home if answers are ultimately going to be withheld from us."

"Along the shore, what do you all see?" asked Tharus.

Tiarnen focused on the misty coastline where rows of black fire pits smouldered along the wet beach, surrounded by what looked to be several platoons of legionaries.

"The remnants of Lydvenko's legion," said Raghnall.

"You mean the remnants of *our* legion," corrected Tharus.

"What use could Lydvenkian legionaries be for us?" asked Liam.

"The invasion of Chora." Tharus walked back inside the room, leaving everyone on the balcony completely dumbfounded by what he had just said.

"With all due respect, Praetor," said Raghnall, walking inside with the rest of the party to see Tharus circling the floor map. "Conscripting the Lydvenkians is one thing, but an all-out assault on Chora is something else entirely—especially since we don't yet know what happened between Maestro Dorian and Lydia."

Tiarnen glanced back at Raghnall in thanks for withholding what was obviously important information; he could only hope that it might make Tharus reconsider his announcement.

"Major, you're right," said Tharus.

Tiarnen exhaled with relief... but then noticed Tharus had begun clacking his staff against the floor faster and faster as though it were a countdown.

"It would be foolish of us to underestimate how difficult this journey will be," he continued. "Which is why we will occupy Lydvenko and use it as our staging point so that Maestro Dorian can once again unleash his newfound abilities and shatter Phrysbruck!"

SMASH!

Tharus drove the staff into the map, shattering the Phrysbruck tiles. "After they are conquered, we will conscript what is left of them, and he will take Elihammer!"

SMASH!

He plunged the staff into Elihammer, shattering it. "From their defeat, our forces will grow further, and he will march onto Ionima!"

SMASH!

"Then Mixylkhan!"

SMASH!

"Then with Locarnia's inevitable destruction..."

SMASH!

"...Chora will finally be mine, and by the grace of my son, nothing will remain of the provinces... not even a memory of them!" Tharus tossed the staff onto the decimated map and looked back to Tiarnen, who was already walking out of the War Room.

Chapter Nineteen
UNDER REPAIR

Every inch of Tiarnen was tingling. Laying back in his clawfoot bathtub, the fizzing soap bubbles rose to his chin and popped softly around him—releasing the light aroma of lemonwood. It had taken him well over an hour to scrub clean, the dirt and grease under his nails only coming off thanks to the rough bristles of his bath brush. The last thing Tiarnen wanted to do after brunch was fix the lamp, but after hearing how close the fleet came to wrecking along the shoals, the job had to be done. It took the rest of the afternoon to strip the pump, only for it to reward his hard work by causing the valve assembly to seize. There was no sense in trying to fix the assembly with the basic tools he had. It needed precision servicing at Punkworks. The idea of trekking across the city reminded Tiarnen of how sore he was, and so he decided to linger a little while longer in the soothing water and comfort of his solitude. Head leaning back against the edge of the tub, Tiarnen held up the Maestro Diary with one hand and turned the page with the other to continue reading the entries.

Maestro Dorian II, Aprolara 16th, 76 ADA

I delved deeper into the Wailing Caverns along the north shore and discovered a considerable deposit of resonant gemstones and precious metals. The Office of Supply was thrilled at the news as Praetor Tharus's conducting wand was beginning to dim, and the Office of Games was in desperate need of lumonium for new batches of Shatter paint. Regardless of the material benefits, the cavern itself is exquisite, and, thus, I have named it Dorian's Delve. May those who come after me enjoy its beauty.

As interesting as it was to learn about the Wailing Caverns and lumonium apparently being a key ingredient in Shatter paint, Tiarnen's intention to distract himself with the diary was proving futile since Raghnall's question continued to irk him.

Have you asked yourself yet how she knew it was called synestry if it has never happened before?

Tiarnen couldn't explain it, but in his heart, he knew that Lydia wasn't lying. He didn't know if it was the look on her marred face or her tone of voice, but she definitely wasn't trying to deceive him. In fact, it seemed like seeing the glass he brought from their battle had swept her up into a long-forgotten memory. The problem was that made Raghnall's question even more important and, if anything, it had now become a riddle. To make matters worse, if Dorladdich's invasion truly was moving forward, then that meant, as Tharus so eloquently pointed out with a stab through the heart of each province, Tiarnen would have to face Maestro Phrygus next. One way or another, the riddle had to be solved before then.

Frustrated by his racing mind, Tiarnen set the diary on the small table beside the bath and then submerged himself in hopes of washing away his anxiety. In the past, if there was something he didn't want to do, he would just lock himself up in the lighthouse until the obligation found a way of dealing with itself. However, as Niera had made clear in the Conservatory, that was no longer an option; all of Dorladdich was depending on him now. He poked his head out of the water, took a deep breath, and accepted that he would somehow have to find a way to—

"Ouch!" he yelped, a sharp pain running through his left middle toe. "What in the—" Tiarnen lifted his foot out of the water to see one of his turtles dangling from it. "Damn it, Haela. How did you get in here?" He gently pulled Haela off his toe, climbed out of the tub, and put him back in the helmet with his brothers.

Shivering from the cold air, Tiarnen rushed over to the dresser cabinet and grabbed a towel from the bottom drawer. After drying off, he opened the top drawer, ignored the dusty green velvet flute case, and pulled out a clean tunic and trousers to get dressed. Tiarnen kicked the towel onto the laundry pile beside the dresser, where his orchestra uniform was crumpled. Tattered, blood-stained, and mud-caked, it would certainly have to be thrown out. While clasping the last button on his tunic, Tiarnen grabbed his cloak and wrapped it around himself, then walked back to the table to pick up his piccolo and the valve assembly before hurrying down the spiral stairs.

Though the storm was now well over the horizon and the dusky sky rather clear, Tiarnen still pulled his hood up as he strode along the cobblestone path. Dodging the deeper puddles, he snaked through a tall hedgerow and arrived at the busy seawall. Like a piece of driftwood, he was instantly swept into the current of provincials who were overburdened with masonry supplies and equipment for the city-wide restoration effort. Not wanting to draw any unnecessary attention to himself, Tiarnen kept his head low and tried to blend in as best he could while making his way to the ferry dock just up ahead.

"Six for Woolerdon!"

"Taking five to the Patchway!"

"Three open for Elgrick!"

"Here!" said Tiarnen, emerging from the crowd after hearing his destination.

"Where you headed with that?" asked the ferryman, pointing to the assembly under Tiarnen's arm.

"Punkworks."

"That'll be my last stop, so it'll have to stay on your lap until we get there, can't take up any extra seats," said the ferryman.

Tiarnen nodded, climbed aboard, and took the last empty seat. Though the leaky double-decker ferry was roomy compared to most, he was still elbow to elbow with the rest of the passengers and nearly drifted off, staring down at his boots for over half an hour. The only thing that kept him from dozing was the provincials gossiping and bickering among each other.

"Explain the point of you crofties fixing up those precious shops when most of the lower east wall is a pile of rubble?" asked a provincial wearing an Ashbrook house pin.

"Mind your own business!" said another provincial, this one wearing a Roycroft house pin. "The Executor himself told us to make sure we reopened the stores as soon as possible."

"Thank the Verse!" said a Finwick-allied provincial. "I couldn't possibly handle another day going by without a noble being able to buy a fancy new hat!"

Everyone laughed, except the Roycroft provincials, as the ferry came to a stop against the canal where there was an inset of stairs and handrails.

"Aldermoore Quay!" announced the ferryman, grabbing his bucket and bailing water as all the passengers quickly shuffled out. Once emptied, the ferryman pushed them off again, and after a few minutes of welcome silence, they arrived at a wide dock with a large barge moored on the far side. The ferryman stuck his oar out to bring them alongside. "Last stop, Punkworks!"

There weren't many businesses that had their own waterfront in Dorladdich, but because the chronopunks were constantly moving mechanical contraptions in and out of their workshop, Garod was granted one to prevent roadblocks and canal congestion. Tiarnen tipped the ferryman, stepped onto the dock, and made his way down the waterfront, which had become a sprawling graveyard of abandoned inventions and industrial relics. He had forgotten just how dreary the massive workshop building was. There were no captivating stained-glass windows, fancy columns, or tile motifs, just heavy brickwork and double-thick roof tiles built around a massive sliding door at the front, which barely opened wide enough to let someone pass into what appeared to be complete darkness.

Pulling off his hood, Tiarnen cautiously stepped inside, hoping to find someone who could help him with the assembly repairs. Once his eyes adjusted to the dimness, he was overwhelmed by the industrious activity taking place. High overhead, six thick beams ran along the length of the workshop to support wheeled pulleys that suspended large mechanical components by thick ropes. Several chronopunks were pushing and pulling them over to their tinkertables on both sides of the workshop. The sound of rushing water drew Tiarnen's eyes to the very back, where a glimmering waterfall poured down from an aqueduct onto the largest waterwheel in all of Dorladdich. He didn't know the exact measurements of it, but by his best guess, the wheel was at least thirty metres high and created an immense amount of torque that powered the specialized tools on each tinkertable via a network of interconnected cogs, sprockets, and gears located in the floor. The chronopunks weren't just notorious because they were the best engineers in the province, they were also the fastest. What would normally take days for local servicemen would be repaired in a matter of hours here.

Wandering his way to the middle of the workshop, Tiarnen saw Mikavnik suspended in the air by several pulley ropes. Unlike Lydia in her precarious prison, he was relieved to see the monstrous chronomech mostly stripped of its iron armour plating; the endoskeleton a chassis of interlinked rods, hydraulic pistons, axial gearing, and actuators.

Stopping just before it, Tiarnen looked up and became transfixed by the empty sockets of Mikavnik's skull—could something so complex be capable of having a soul?

"Maestro?" asked a voice.

Pulling himself from the staring match, he looked over and saw Jasper sitting at her tinkertable with eyes five times as big due to the large magnifying lens she was looking through.

"Hi," said Tiarnen. "Is it a bad time to come by?"

"No, of course not, just tending to our guest here." Jasper pointed a wrench at Mikavnik.

"Looks like the tear-down is well underway," replied Tiarnen, walking to the table.

"The fact that it arrived in several pieces made things a lot easier—which I heard you might have had a hand in."

"If only by dumb luck." Tiarnen noticed that Mikavnik's left hand was lying on Jasper's table. "Anything interesting?"

"Where do I even begin?" Jasper moved the magnifying glass arm out of her way. "At first glance, the Lydvenkian armour makes Mikavnik seem crude as far as design, but underneath, it's hiding some of the most intricate gearings I've ever seen."

"Well, Lydvenko is the ironmonger of Chora."

"Even so, in my opinion, this level of engineering is more akin to the complications."

"Speaking of complicated..." Tiarnen set the valve assembly on the table.

"Ah—good to see I'm not the only one finding themselves outside of their expertise today," said Jasper, immediately noticing the problem with the assembly. "How many of the valves are broken?"

"Err—all of them, I think."

Jasper angled the magnifying lens to get a closer view of the assembly. "The good news is this isn't scrap just yet."

"But the bad news is?"

"We'll definitely need to replace all of the valve springs inside."

"Great," said Tiarnen, relieved it could be fixed.

"If you have better things to do, I can make these repairs and bring it back to the lighthouse," Jasper offered.

"Think I'd rather stay and lend a hand if it'll speed things up?" said Tiarnen, worrying about returning to the lighthouse before sunset.

"Of course, but even with your help, I think we're still going to need a bit of assistance."

"Oh? Is there someone you want me to find—"

"Quint!" shouted Jasper, "Are you around, love?"

Tiarnen figured Jasper was asking one of the chronopunks who were close by, so he looked over his shoulder. But none of them seemed to take notice of her question.

"I don't think they heard—" he began.

Clack-clack!

A slit of light behind Jasper caught Tiarnen's eye. Confusingly, it appeared as though a small hidden door had opened along the wall. To make matters stranger, a tiny pink nose surrounded by whiskers and cream fur poked out to cautiously sniff the air.

"What in the—"

"Don't worry. He won't hurt you, *right*?" asked Jasper, turning to look at Tiarnen for confirmation.

"Oh! Never. I couldn't bear the thought."

Then he saw a squirrel-like creature, except his ears were three times as big with tufts of fur at the ends, emerge from the doorway. Tiarnen had to blink twice to make sure he wasn't imagining the fact that Quint was wearing big round glasses and dressed in coveralls with a toolbelt around his waist. After checking to make sure no one was about to step on him, Quint closed the door and scurried over to Jasper, who picked him up and set him on the table.

"Go on, introduce yourself. We have a new maestro among us," said Jasper, focusing back on the valve assembly.

Quint cautiously made his way over, squeaked politely, and bowed to Tiarnen.

"Nice to meet you, Quint. I'm Tiarnen," he said, bowing his head in kind.

Quint immediately went back to Jasper, ran up her arm, and sat on her shoulder, where he squeaked excitedly.

"Well, you see, the springs have to be replaced," said Jasper. "That's why we need a little assistance."

Squeeeak?

"No, that was not a short joke," assured Jasper.

Squeak.

"There should be a whole bunch of spare springs in the second drawer from the left." Jasper pointed to her table drawers.

Tiarnen watched Quint run back down her arm, hop across the table, open the drawer, and then rummage about until he pulled out four tiny replacement springs.

"Yup, those should do," said Jasper. "Now, Maestro, would you be so kind as to hold the first and third valves open while I hold the second and fourth?" She handed Tiarnen two pairs of pliers and then grabbed two of her own to grip the tops of the valves.

"Sure thing," he said, using his pliers to grab the top of the valves on his side and pull them open just as Jasper did. Before he knew it, Quint had already squeezed his way through the small port in the assembly to begin replacing the springs.

"Just tell us when you're ready for us to release them," said Jasper, smiling at Tiarnen, who was trying to watch Quint use a screwdriver that was smaller than a sewing needle.

She giggled. "The look on your face right now."

"I had heard about Quint, but part of me didn't think he was real," admitted Tiarnen.

"We try not to talk about him much outside of the workshop."

Quint squeaked graciously.

"He likes his privacy," whispered Jasper.

Tiarnen lowered his voice, too. "But where does the door go?"

"To be honest, no one really knows," said Jasper. "A few of the punks apparently put a scope down it years ago, but the tunnel just seemed to go on forever. Not that it matters. He's usually here with us and helping wherever he can. I consider him my secret weapon for otherwise impossible repairs."

Squeak-squeak!

"Okay, you can release your valves," said Jasper.

Click-click!

Tiarnen opened his pliers and let the valves close. Relieved that they were making progress, he sat back, only to feel his piccolo digging into his backside. He pulled it out and set it on the table.

Jasper leaned in a bit. "That's definitely seen better days."

"Makes two of us," said Tiarnen, chuckling. He hadn't given it much thought, but by any measure, the instrument should have disintegrated while he was illuminating. "I don't think it took any real damage during the battle, but you're right. It's well overdue for a bit of spit and polish."

"Well, drivers and wrenches are on your left, cleaning solvents and rags are there on your right," said Jasper, pressing her foot down on a peddle in the floor, which brought the cogs, sprockets, and gears in the tinkertable to life, and made the torque wrench spin.

Since Quint seemed to need more time with the last two valves, Tiarnen grabbed both a medium and small flathead screwdriver and proceeded to loosen the pivot screws and hinge rods on the piccolo. With their removal, the keys easily slid off, allowing him to organize them into a pile on the table. Tiarnen then set the body down and grabbed a murky bottle of solvent as well as one of the rags.

"I strongly recommend putting those gloves on before using that stuff," urged Jasper.

Tiarnen raised an eyebrow and grabbed the heavy leather gloves resting on top of the table. With his hands better protected, he popped the solvent cork and took a whiff—his nostrils immediately burning and eyes watering. "Woah!" he exclaimed, yanking his head back and brushing the tears away with his sleeve.

"Still have your eyebrows?" asked Jasper.

"You tell me," said Tiarnen, moving them up and down to be sure. "What in the Verse do you use this for?"

"Degreasing torque converters in the tinkertables."

Tiarnen carefully dabbed some solvent on a rag and expected to have to scrub the heavy tarnish off the keys. All it took was a couple of careful wipes, and the brushed silver was completely renewed. "Wow. I'm officially a believer."

Jasper smiled. "Thought it might do the trick."

Tiarnen picked up the body of the piccolo, and he realized it was the first time he had completely stripped the instrument down. After a battle, he would normally just give the keys and mouthpiece a quick wipe with a soapy cloth, run a brush inside a couple of times, and then tighten any loose screws or pads. But seeing it bare for the first time made the instrument seem much more primal and strangely ancient.

"Raghnall!" said Jasper. "Hi—um, I mean—hello, Major," she stammered, her pliers slipping off the fourth valve.

SQUEAK!

"I *am* paying attention!" said Jasper, pulling the valve back up for Quint, who poked his head out to continue the reprimand but instead noticed Raghnall approaching and squeaked excitedly at him.

"Yes, *hello* to you as well, Quint," said Raghnall, giving a salute as he stopped just behind Tiarnen.

"You two know each other?" asked Tiarnen, who was starting to feel like he had been excluded from a secret circle of friends.

"Of course, who do you think helped Garod construct my gauntlet?"

"Which would be good as new already if everyone wasn't so busy with old numbskull over here." Jasper looked to Mikavnik, who was now surrounded by several chronopunks trying to pry off the last of its chest plating.

"The gauntlet isn't why he's here," said Tiarnen.

"How do you know that?" asked Jasper.

"Because whenever he's looking for me, he always walks on his heels in double time."

"I do no such—" began Raghnall.

"The question is," continued Tiarnen, "did he already search the entire city or somehow know exactly where I would be?"

"The latter, thankfully," said Raghnall. "The Paddleson brothers volunteered to split your lightkeeper responsibilities, so I brought them over to speak with you—"

"And why do the corporals need to take over my duties?" asked Tiarnen.

"Planning to manage the lighthouse on top of being a maestro, were you?"

"Well, I... no... I guess not," said Tiarnen, realizing that it would be impossible to do both.

"Which is why they are currently waiting in your living room."

"They better not fiddle with the lamp!"

"Would be hard to, considering we arrived with most of it spread across the floor. Figured you had a setback while making repairs and went looking for a bit of help."

Squeak-squeak!

Jasper released her valves.

Click-click!

"Nice work, love!" said Jasper. "I can tighten everything up."

They watched Quint wiggle backwards out of the assembly and wipe his grease-splattered spectacles on his coveralls. After putting them back on, he took a sudden interest in Tiarnen's piccolo.

"I didn't think my surrender of the lighthouse would be so urgent," said Tiarnen, trying to work around Quint, who was now looking over the instrument with growing intrigue.

"Well," Raghnall lowered his voice so no one could overhear, "you left the War Room before Tharus had finished his announcement."

"That was the point," said Tiarnen, dabbing more solvent onto the rag.

"Be that as it may, he set a date for your departure."

"Let me guess, a thousand years from now since that is how long it will take for us to embark on his delusion of grandeur." Tiarnen placed the piccolo in the soaked rag.

"You leave tomorrow," said Raghnall.

"*Tomorrow?*" asked Tiarnen, feeling like he just had the wind knocked out of him.

"At first light."

Tiarnen sat in silence.

"He said he couldn't risk giving the barons time to fortify Kuldron and make a stand against us."

"Of course." Tiarnen twisted the rag around the piccolo as though it was his father's neck.

"Once the capital is occupied, you'll be stationed there for eight weeks to prepare an attack on Phrysbruck," Raghnall continued.

Again, Tiarnen sat in silence.

"You all right?" asked Raghnall.

"Do I look *all right?*" shouted Tiarnen.

The shouting startled Quint and sent him running up Jasper's arm to hide behind her neck.

"It's fine, love," said Jasper, gently putting her hand on Quint to assure him. "Just a disagreement."

"Quint, I'm sorry for yelling," said Tiarnen, turning back to Raghnall. "Also, I'm not going."

"Afraid that's not an option, lad."

"Easy for you to say! You aren't the one being asked to lead us into oblivion!" yelled Tiarnen, his voice echoing throughout the workshop and drawing the attention of the chronopunks, who couldn't help but stop their work after hearing the news.

"Keep your bloody voice down," hissed Raghnall.

"For what? The whole province is going find out soon enough," said Tiarnen.

"Which is why you need to accept the fact that this is happening and take some responsibility," said Raghnall. "As much as I hate to admit it... Tharus is right... You have given us a very rare opportunity to take the provinces by surprise."

"Sure, all I have to do is start by facing Maestro Phrygus, who is far more powerful and experienced than I am." Tiarnen pulled the piccolo out of the soiled rag, pointing it at himself.

"If anyone is going to find a way to defeat him, it's you," said Raghnall. "In fact, I'll wager that by the end of this campaign, Maestro Dorian the Sixtieth will be wishing that he could have illuminated with all of the maestros together and been done with it." He gave a chuckle.

Tiarnen was about to dismiss the compliment, but he became utterly captivated by what looked to be someone else's instrument in his hand: the grimy stone body of the piccolo was now a glossy slate grey with a black opal inlay of cresting waves, spiralling around it and refracting every conceivable colour inside.

"Maestro, I believe your assembly is ready," said Jasper, giving the last bolt a final turn with her torque wrench.

"Best return to the lighthouse then. It'll be getting dark out soon," warned Raghnall.

"Wait—what did you say?" said Tiarnen, looking up at Raghnall in confusion.

"The lighthouse. It'll be dark soon—"

"No, before that, about the maestros."

"I just imagined that all of you illuminating together would make for one hell of a victory."

With those words, time seemed to stop for Tiarnen. Could synestry really allow all of the maestros to illuminate together? In his mind, Tiarnen saw the lattrice he and Lydia made together... then with some added blue... and a bit of magenta... until it was a kaleidoscope of all the provincial colours.

"Maestro?" asked Jasper.

"I'm... I'm fine," said Tiarnen, blinking himself back into reality. He quickly reassembled the piccolo, slipped it into his back pocket, and then stood up to take the assembly.

"Was there anything else you two needed?" asked Jasper, standing with Tiarnen and then walking him and Raghnall to the workshop entrance.

"No, thanks again. You absolutely saved—" began Tiarnen, turning back to Jasper, but Mikavnik's unsettling presence drew his gaze once again. Much like Lydvenko, each province would have just as many, if not more, unforeseen complications like the general. Not only would Tiarnen have to *find a way*, as Raghnall put it, to overcome them, but also somehow keep Niera safe along their treacherous journey. "You know what, Jasper," said Tiarnen, his eyes narrowing at Mikavnik. "There is one more thing you can do for me."

Chapter Twenty
LEAP OF FAITH

Jasper was right; the valve assembly slid back into place without any problems. However, Tiarnen still had to put the rest of the pump back together, and dusk was fast arriving. At least with the Paddleson brothers hanging around—both corporals apparently too scared to touch anything before Tiarnen returned—he had some extra hands. Tiarnen was worried that Nigel and Braig might slow him down, but they proved not only able and eager, they also knew when to keep out of the way. After a bit of casual conversation, he learnt that they were deckhands on the *Arabrae* before enlisting with the patrol, which explained the broad shoulders, deep tans, and mechanical sense—not to mention urgency since they knew all too well how important the lighthouse was to the fleet.

"Think we managed to reconnect all of the oil lines just like you showed us, Maestro," said Nigel.

"Does anything seem out of place?" asked Braig.

"Outside of you two?" jabbed Tiarnen, tightening a bolt on the lamp housing with his wrench and then walking over to the other side of the pump to inspect their work. "Looks like a job well done to me... assuming one of you knows how we ended up with a few extra screws?"

The brothers followed Tiarnen's pointing finger to see three small screws on the floor, which caused them to look back at him with panic on their faces.

"Don't worry," assured Tiarnen. "If there's one thing I've learnt about this place over the years, it's that whatever you manage to repair will usually cause something else to break a few days later, so you'll need all the extra hardware you can get."

"What should we do next?" asked Nigel, picking up the screws and tossing them into the dusty toolbox off to the side.

"Grab four jugs of oil from below," said Tiarnen. "Once the tank is refilled, we can pull the actuation lever, press the igniter, and hope the burner doesn't explode."

Braig pulled an anxious expression. "*Explode*?"

Trying to hide his laughter, Tiarnen made his way down to the service room. Truth be told, restarting the lamp was always finicky but fairly safe—he just wanted the corporals to err on the side of caution while he was away. Nigel and Braig followed him into the service room, and after showing them where the supplies and spare parts were, Tiarnen helped bring up the jugs, which they emptied into the tank.

"All right, looks like we're topped up." He closed and sealed the lid. "Nigel, grab that lever there and pull it down whenever you're ready." Tiarnen hopped off the side of the tank and walked over to the lamp while Nigel gripped the actuation lever and reluctantly pulled down.

Tunk-Tunk-Tunk-Tunk!

The repaired valve assembly brought the pump back to life, only for it to start vibrating chaotically.

"Ummm—Maestro? Should it be doing that?" asked Braig.

"Just shaking out the kinks," said Tiarnen, watching with growing concern as the vibrations quickly grew into shuddering. The two corporals instinctively took a step back. "Everything is fine," said Tiarnen, also taking a big step back. Then, to their collective relief, the pump settled into a jerky but consistent rhythm.

"See, nothing to worry about." Tiarnen forced a smile onto his face. "Now, all we need to do is light the burner."

"How many times do you have to press the igniter?" asked Braig.

"A few clicks usually does it." Tiarnen walked behind the lamp housing, turned the collar to expose the igniter, and pressed it three times... except nothing happened.

"Was that three?" asked Nigel, trying to look over Tiarnen's shoulder.

"Two and a half." Tiarnen started pressing the igniter rapidly until—

SHKOOM!

The burner ignited, and a flash of light erupted from the lens, shooting a blinding beam through the weathered windows.

"By the Verse, that is bright!" said Braig, turning his back to the lamp and stumbling behind it.

"Sorry," said Tiarnen, "should have warned you about the flash."

"Maestro, if I may, what should we do about all of this netting back here?" asked Braig, noticing the pile for the first time.

"Best to just leave it be. It's been there since before me, and I've heard growling coming from it on more than one occasion."

"As you say," said Braig, suddenly wanting nothing to do with the tangled mess.

With the lamp finally in working order again, Tiarnen checked for any oil leaks but, after a quick inspection, couldn't find any, so he brought the brothers down to the living room. After a casual tour of the kitchen, he cleared out the dresser cabinet drawers to make room for their personal items and, more importantly, showed them how to feed his turtles. Tiarnen still wasn't thrilled by the idea of Nigel and Braig moving into his home but told himself it would only be temporary—Tharus would surely break off the invasion after laying siege to Phrysbruck proved impossible. Confident that the brothers knew where everything could be found and had a bearing on their duties, Tiarnen left them to unpack their duffle bags and made his way back upstairs, grabbing a jar of pickled herring along the way, to sit out on the lamp room balcony one last time before leaving.

With a filet in his mouth and legs dangling over the edge, Tiarnen took in the captivating view of the white-capped Shipwreck Strait with a twilight expanse of glinting stars overhead. It was rare to see the constellations so clearly, but the tailwind from the storm was luckily keeping the fog away. An unexpected sense of relief washed over Tiarnen as he watched the fleet safely navigate the treacherous waters. All he wanted now was to draw out the moment of solace for as long as possible, so he leaned against the warm window, gulped down a delicious briny fillet, and then popped another into his mouth. Unfortunately, Niera seemed to be right about regular food no longer being enough to satisfy his hunger. It was so much deeper now; he could actually feel it in his bones. Already regretting another meal of peppered spiny sponge, he pulled the piccolo from his back pocket to get more comfortable but found himself captivated once again by the colours dancing inside of the renewed opal. His thumb instinctually ran over the cresting black waves, which seemed to make the tide crashing far below grow louder until it became a foreboding rhythm. His mind went to Lydia, her body slamming against the prison bars from the brutal force of the rising sea.

"Let it go," he whispered.

Then Raghnall's voice echoed in his mind.

All of you illuminating together would make for one hell of a victory.

Just like at Punkworks, Tiarnen was swept into a vision and saw all of the provincial maestros standing in a circle and illuminating, but they weren't fighting each other, like Tiarnen and Lydia had—they were performing *together.* Heart pounding, he shook his head and tried to push the vision away, but the repeated effort only made him feel a strange sense of guilt—as though he was somehow denying whatever the maestros were trying to accomplish.

"Get a damn grip on yourself!" he said, trying to make some sense of what he was imagining. The problem was analyzing the vision only raised more questions. *Why would they all wilfully illuminate a lattrice together? And for what, if not to win the war?*

Before he realized what was happening, Tiarnen stood to his feet, hurrying down to the living room where Nigel was putting the last of his clothes in the dresser while Braig attempted to make a pot of tea on the stove.

"Ah, Maestro! Braig has decided to take the night shift while I will take the day shift," said Nigel.

"Great, that's great," said Tiarnen, drifting past them to grab his cloak and quickly put it on.

"Are you off already?" asked Braig.

"I am sorry." Tiarnen checked his pocket watch, heading for the stairs. "Funeral in an hour and everything."

"Maestro, wait, there's one last thing!" Nigel called after him.

"What is it?" asked Tiarnen, his foot hovering over the first stair.

"We just wanted to say thank you for the opportunity," Braig said humbly.

"Right, well, I know the lighthouse will be in good hands," said Tiarnen, and he began making his way down the stairs. "And remember, don't let Haela climb out of the helmet!"

"We'll keep a sharp eye for any prison breaks!" shouted Nigel.

"Prison break..." muttered Tiarnen, the word stopping him cold and putting him at a crossroads with what he was setting out to do. There was a moment of pause as he gave himself one last chance to turn around, take off his cloak, and forget about Lydia. Instead, he pulled his hood up and rushed down the stairs.

*

Tiarnen couldn't remember the last time he had run so hard. Sure, racing against Niera was always intense, but their sibling rivalry kept him at a playful dash rather than the desperate sprint now carrying him down Water Street.

Clerical buildings blurring by on either side, he couldn't help but notice how most of them were a patchwork of light and dark grey—the new masonry bricks filling the holes, if not entire sections, left by Lydvenko's attack. Many of the broken windows still needed replacing, but the repairs were otherwise impressive, given that only a handful of days had passed. Someone hurtling down the street and weaving through the heavy construction equipment would have normally drawn unwanted attention, but the funeral had thankfully emptied the districts. Niera was also likely making her way to Caecius Cove with Tharus, which meant Tiarnen would have to come up with a plausible explanation as to why he was joining them so late.

Fast approaching Kilners' Row, he should have been surprised to see that work was carrying on as though it was an average day, but given that the campaign was moving ahead, the province would need a surplus of shields now more than ever, though the labourers didn't seem to be aware of that fact. He stopped in his tracks, pulled his hood up to hide his face, and tried to casually pass through unrecognized while looking for something that would be able to bend the prison bars or break the hinges. He walked over to the mud station where the mudders were scooping different kinds of wet clay from large troughs into mixing buckets. Trying to remain as inconspicuous as possible, he looked high and low for something, anything, that he might be able to use, but nothing stood out. Two mixers appeared beside Tiarnen, grabbed their mixing buckets, and brought them over to the station, where they poured in multiple pouches of sparkling powders and carefully stirred the clay to ensure everything blended together perfectly.

Tiarnen surreptitiously glanced at their station, but none of the tools seemed useful, so he followed the mixers over to the first of many kilns. There were eleven in total, all standing in a long row that reached the end of the street, which intersected with the seawall. The kilners took the buckets from the mixers, poured the clay into a variety of armour moulds, and then slid them into the top of the kiln while pulling out finished moulds from the bottom.

"Gimme some room here, would ya?" a kilner barked.

Tiarnen immediately sidestepped, watching as the kilner set the mould down on a table, then grabbed a long pry bar that was resting against the far side of the kiln to crack it open. If anything in the Row was going to work, that would be it. Seconds feeling like hours, Tiarnen waited until the kilner pulled the freshly baked ceramic chest plates from the moulds and walked them over to the polishing station. Tiarnen looked around to make sure no one saw him grab the pry bar, hiding as much of it as he could under his cloak. Then, he quickly weaved his way to the end of the Row and turned down the seawall to vanish out of sight. After another short sprint, Tiarnen hopped off the side of the wall and onto the narrow beach just below.

The soft sand made running far more difficult, but Tiarnen pressed on, passing a group of murgils who were feasting on the decaying corpse of a reef shark. Two of the frog-like creatures tumbled off the shark's head, fighting over an eyeball, and Tiarnen had to leap over them to continue sprinting. Finally, he reached the jagged bluffs high above the dungeon cells. He knew that freeing Lydia wasn't going to be easy; the warden would certainly still be there, given the fact he had a maestro behind bars and seemed more than excited to watch the frigid waters drown her. That meant Tiarnen had to approach from the outside if he wanted to remain unseen.

With the very last of dusk's light vanishing, Tiarnen could see the barnacle- and seaweed-crusted cell gratings in the far distance just above the waterline. As far as he could tell, the only way to reach Lydia was to climb up the narrow cliff ledges, traverse them until he was over the top of her cell, and then leap into the water just in front. Hugging the cliff face, he reached for the first ledge and pulled himself onto it. Despite Tiarnen's determination, his climbing was clumsy and not without falter; both his hands and feet slipped numerous times, which resulted in two close calls that almost sent him crashing into the rocky water below. Finally, and to his own disbelief, he arrived above Lydia's cell, though it was at least twenty metres below him.

"That did *not* look as far down from the shore," muttered Tiarnen. After quickly surveying the turbulent waters to make sure there weren't any more rocks peaking above the surface, he accepted that it was now or never and leaped off the cliff face.

SPLOOSH!

The sea's icy temperature shocked his entire body. Tiarnen swam with panicked strokes toward the surface, but the swift current dragged him further down and tossed him around like a leaf in the wind. Slamming against the reef, he lost his breath, and the pry bar nearly slipped from his failing grip. Everything grew dim as his vision narrowed and his lungs begged for air. He felt his feet land on the coral, so with a panicked effort, he kicked off hard and managed to break the surface.

Cold air passed over his purple lips and his chattering teeth, and Tiarnen gasped for breath. He wiped the sea-foam from his eyes with his free hand and then grabbed onto a long piece of driftwood to keep himself above water. Before he even had the chance to get over the fact that he had just nearly drowned, a set of waves rolled in and pushed him towards the cliff wall at speed. Tiarnen tried his best to paddle and steer himself toward Lydia's cell, which seemed to work, but there was no way to slow down. Bracing himself for impact, the driftwood broke into pieces as his body slammed against the cell door. Winded and grimacing, he gripped the bars and held himself steady—giving a moment to recover from the impact. His eyes opened to see there was only a couple of inches between the top of the cell and the waterline. He looked inside: a sliver of light on the other side backlit a pair of hands splashing frantically. The same feeling of conviction that overtook him at the lighthouse suddenly returned and pushed the frigid exhaustion to the back of his mind. Tiarnen set one foot against the grate and another along the rock face so he could try to pry the prison bars apart, but they wouldn't budge—the bars were simply too thick. Unwilling to give up, he looked over the door again and noticed there was a thin, eroded gap where both sides of the door met. Tiarnen drove the end of the pry bar into the gap and put every ounce of strength he had left into forcing it open. A strained creaking began to ring out. He couldn't tell if the door was about to release, or the pry bar was about to break.

CRUNNNNNNK!

The gap widened.

Encouraged, Tiarnen kept prying it further and further until there was enough room for him to push his body through. With barely an inch left between the water and the cell ceiling, he took several deep breaths in a row, holding in the last one, then ducked under the water and swam through the murk as fast as he could. Never in his life had he been this cold before. In fact, his hands were so numb now that he didn't know if he would be able to feel Lydia even if he managed to reach her in time. Stroke after kick took him deeper inside the cell; he could hear the waves crashing ominously behind him, but something else began to echo as well. At first, it seemed like a strange pulsing, but then it grew into what Tiarnen realized was laughing.

Warden Whalen and Bailiff Leary, as they promised, were clearly enjoying the sight of Lydia's demise. Tiarnen worried that he might already be too late and started reaching out—hoping to glance or grasp any part of Lydia he could. After what felt like an eternity, he found her. Initially, he didn't know where his hand landed, but then he realized it was her upper arm. He followed it down to take her hand, but as his fingers moved, she pulled away—no doubt in shock at what she'd just felt. Tiarnen reached out and found Lydia again, only for her to try and pull away once more. With barely enough air in his lungs to escape the cell alive, Tiarnen stretched out one last time, grabbed a hold of Lydia, and pulled her to within an inch of his face. Despite the lack of light, he could see her eyes widen in bewilderment—yet she still tried to pull away. *What in the Verse?* he thought. Tiarnen couldn't believe she was struggling against what was clearly a rescue. Unless, for some reason, she wanted to die here. But even if Lydia had accepted her fate, Tiarnen would be damned if he was about to let it come true. He yanked on her wrist and started swimming back towards the cell door with her in tow. Once he finally passed through the gap again, his vision became darker with each desperate stroke toward the surface. Just as he was about to lose consciousness, Tiarnen broke the surface, gasping for air.

Vision fast returning, he looked around frantically for any sign of Lydia. At first, he couldn't see her anywhere, but then a flash of orange near the rocks caught his attention. It was Lydia. He took a couple of deep breaths and swam over to find her draped across a large piece of driftwood. Side by side now, they stared at each other for a moment. Then, as though coming to a silent agreement, Lydia and Tiarnen broke their gaze and began swimming back to shore together.

Chapter Twenty-One
THE SHORES BEYOND

"I was hung up at Punkworks... Training the corporals took longer than expected... There were complications with the lamp... I had to go by the Conservatory first... No, don't mention the Conservatory!" said Tiarnen, scolding himself.

Catching heat for his poor time management was old hat, but given that Tiarnen was now over an hour late to the funeral, he knew his father would want a good reason why. Tiarnen hadn't yet decided if a short justification or long-winded excuse would be the better alibi. Either way, he had to make sure it didn't raise any suspicions.

After reaching the shore, both he and Lydia had collapsed on the beach and tried to recover from the rescue. Watching his panting breath rise into the night sky and listening to Lydia cough up half the sea, Tiarnen realized that he hadn't thought of what to do with her should he be successful. Hiding Lydia somewhere safe was, of course, the highest priority, but the only place he considered secure enough was the Conservatory, which meant escorting her through the lower west districts and then into the cathedral without being seen.

Tiarnen recovered his filthy cloak and draped it over Lydia to make her appear as though she were nothing more than a lowly provincial who deserved no interest. He wasn't too far off, either. Soaked to the bone and covered in sand with hair matted against his face, he probably wouldn't have recognized his own reflection given the state of himself.

Though he was confident that they wouldn't be easily identified, he still made sure they crept through every shadow along the empty side streets and back alleys that led them closer and closer to the Conservatory.

Finally arriving, Tiarnen pointed Lydia to the study and told her to hide there until he returned. The last thing he saw while closing the door was her slowly walking up the stairs towards Stormcaller and vanishing into the darkness as the knock-lock set. Given that his legs were about to give out, Tiarnen decided that taking the rowboat to the funeral was the best option, so he quietly sneaked out of the cathedral and made his way down to the dock where it was waiting.

The swift current of Luathel Canal was speeding Tiarnen along nicely, but it was still rather eerie to see one of the largest waterways so empty. He tried to use the moment of calm as an opportunity to regain his composure, but that was proving much harder to do than he expected. Then it dawned on him: the reason he was still so nervous was because he didn't yet have a plan. Yes, Lydia was secure for now, but even if he managed to get the truth about synestry out of her, she was still an enemy of the province and no less dangerous than before. That meant someone would need to watch over her while Tiarnen was away, someone he trusted implicitly but also believed capable of keeping the city safe should she turn on him. Raghnall was the obvious choice. The trick would be to return to the Conservatory with the major alone and then somehow protect Lydia long enough so Tiarnen could explain himself. Passing into a pitch-black tunnel, it felt like the foreboding darkness was whispering worry into his ear. *What if Lydia was, in fact, lying, and I rescued her for nothing? What if she took this as a second chance to regroup with the legion and return to Lydvenko? Or worse, try to finish what she started!* he thought. His heart started pounding again, and he could no longer tell if his tunic was still wet from seawater or sweat.

"Stop it. You did the right thing," he scolded himself. "And you'll see this through to the end, no matter what it takes." With that promise to himself, Tiarnen left the tunnel and his self-doubt behind, spotting the crescent beach of Caecius Cove a short distance ahead. From what he could tell, the entire ferry fleet, as well as three noble catamarans with their house banners flapping high in the wind, were anchored at the pier. Instead of mooring among them, Tiarnen rowed on and beached the boat. As much as he wanted to hop out and run up the pebbled strand, his knees were so weak that he didn't have much choice but to clumsily slide off the port side and hobble through the ankle-deep water until finally reaching dry land. Approaching the fringe of the crowd, he was met by the weeping of widows and the sobs of grieving friends. He then saw that everyone was holding small soapstone lanterns with flickering green candles inside while standing around one of several hundred mourning skiffs where the fallen loved ones of Dorladdich's residents now rested. Recalling the unwanted attention he'd received at the harbour, Tiarnen lowered his head, trying his best to find a way through the prayers and recollections of fond memories, but made the mistake of trying to slip between two elderly provincials. As they turned to scold whoever dared be so inconsiderate, their wrinkled faces quickly shifted from anger to confusion at the sight of him. Realizing that he looked far from presentable, Tiarnen ran his fingers through his messy hair and promptly fastened the top button of his tunic as though it would all somehow make an improvement.

"He's here!"

"Our maestro has arrived!"

"What happened to him?"

Before Tiarnen had the chance to apologize for the disruption, the crowd quickly shuffled to clear a path that led down the middle of the beach. At the far end, he could see Tharus, Niera, Ignis, Holgor, Raghnall, Dansby, and the Earls, all standing in their finest attire around a large opulent skiff where he knew Reina was resting.

Unfortunately, the parting of the crowd also caught Tharus's attention, and his cold gaze fell onto Tiarnen. Steeling himself as best he could, Tiarnen walked ahead as though he had nothing to hide, but with each wobbly step, his father's stare was like a dagger stabbing deeper into his chest as he drew closer. A couple of metres away now, the group noticed him approaching, and their widening eyes made it feel as though he was standing naked before them—utterly transparent—already giving away the lie he was about to tell. Even worse, he could no longer remember any of the excuses he had prepared—his mind had gone completely blank with fear. Though, as he reached the skiff, he caught a glimpse of Reina, and all of Chora seemed to melt away.

If it wasn't for her ghostly pale complexion and the small fact that she was lying on a bed of water lilies, Tiarnen would have guessed that Reina had simply fallen asleep in her maestro jacket. He slowly exhaled, and the next breath filled him with a strange sense of acceptance. A sniffle pulled his focus to Dansby, who was standing on the opposite side of the skiff, dressed in formal uniform; the captain had dark circles under his bloodshot eyes that were likely from equal parts lack of sleep and an abundance of drinking. No one could blame him. He and Reina were always incredibly secretive about their long-running romance, especially since Tharus had voiced his disapproval on numerous occasions. Tensions eventually boiled over, but after a shouting match that put the soundproof walls of the Conservatory to test, Tharus allowed Reina to pursue the relationship so long as they kept it under wraps.

"*Where have you been?*" asked Niera, staring up at Tiarnen with tear streaks down her cheeks. She wore a formal dress with a dark grey cape that hung down from her shoulders, a bouquet of water lilies in her hands.

"Bottom of the bloody sea, looks like," said Raghnall, who, for only the second time in Tiarnen's life, was also wearing formal a uniform but still had an arm sling over top.

Tiarnen cleared his throat and was going to begin rambling on about how training the corporals took much longer than expected because the lamp was so problematic—only to remember that Reina never responded to questions she didn't believe deserved an answer. Following her lead, he remained tight-lipped. Tiarnen expected Tharus to force the issue, but his father only kept glaring at him from the bow of the skiff as though they were in a match of Shatter and looking for a tell. Tiarnen couldn't decide if his choice made things better or worse. At this point, he no longer cared. He just wanted to say goodbye to his sister. Looking to Niera's bouquet, he pulled out one of the water lilies and gently put it between Reina's clasped hands.

Feeling her cold skin against his unleashed a flood of memories. First, how she always managed, without fail, to fill one of his shoes with salmon roe on his birthday. When Tiarnen turned nine, they had snuck into the kitchen, and, despite Reina's warning, he ate an entire bowl of roe, becoming violently sick afterwards. Though Reina stayed by Tiarnen's side while he puked up streams of bright orange eggs for the rest of the evening, she refused to let him live the mistake down. He tried to remember to check his shoes each year but always forgot, and whenever they saw each other next, she would just break out into laughter and a little victory dance.

Another memory featured them training together as children. There was no particular moment, just images of them being side by side and working themselves to the bone in the hope of showing their mother that they might one day be worthy of becoming maestros.

A final, playing with Niera together when she was a babe; how she was always reaching for Reina's clarinet as though demanding succession even before she could walk.

Tiarnen always figured that Reina would become a maternal figure to their little sister, but Tharus kept Niera too close to ever let it happen. Still, Reina showered her in love and affection whenever there was a chance—in little paper notes that she would write and hide in Niera's pockets to discover later. Tiarnen had only caught a glimpse of one and saw that it said: *You will always be my little sister.* After that, he didn't need to see another because he knew the rest were just like it, a simple gesture of her affection and a reminder that even though they worked and fought together every day, they were, above all else, a family.

"She has never looked more beautiful," said Tharus, running his thumb over Reina's cheek and then pulling down her veil.

Rage stirred from somewhere deep in Tiarnen and quickly dried up his tears. Even he was a bit taken aback by the intensity, but those words—his father's complete disregard for seeing any real value whatsoever in Reina—reminded him that maestros had become—or perhaps always were—utterly disposable to his father so long as he had another waiting in line.

"Tonight, as a praetor," began Tharus, turning to face the waiting crowd. "I must put to rest yet another maestro. Tonight, as a father, I must say goodbye to my eldest daughter." He trudged among the provincials as though he were in serious emotional pain.

Tiarnen's brow furrowed at the pathetic performance, knowing his father was incapable of feeling anything these days.

"But death does not care about title, rank, or role, nor does it show pity even for those who have suffered immeasurable loss," continued Tharus. "I will confess after Reina fell... I, too, began to wonder how many more years of pain Dorladdich would have to endure before we claimed victory. One more? Ten more? *A thousand more?*" He stretched his arms out dramatically and looked up at the night sky as though he were waiting for a reply from the distant stars. "Like all of you, I too wanted an answer... I *needed* an answer... Then, in our darkest hour, my very own son showed me, through his devotion and sacrifice, that victory is nearly in our grasp!" The provincials looked at each other in confusion. "I am sure you have heard many rumours, if not elaborate stories, from those who saw what happened in the bailey—of how the *Battle of the Bridge* was won. It is true, a discovery was made; a unique ability only Tiarnen possesses—one that he will use to bring the provinces to their knees!"

As much as Tiarnen had anticipated the announcement, his heart still wasn't ready to hear it, and his stomach sank as he watched the provincials stir with intrigue and excitement.

"However, my son cannot possibly do this alone," continued Tharus. "No! He will need the help of every man, woman, and child standing here before me. A choice lies before us now, perhaps the most important one that Dorladdich has ever made. I know how tired you are and how impossible it might seem to give more, especially when it seems as though everything has been taken away. But if we cannot find it in our hearts to rally, to take what could very well be our last chance, each sail we set tonight will have been in vain!" Tharus pointed at the skiffs and paused to let his words sink in. "So, I will ask this only once... Is Dorladdich ready to conquer Chora *at long last?*"

For a desperate moment, Tiarnen hoped there would be a divide among the provincials or at least signs of hesitation. Instead, everyone erupted in cheers as though they were back at the concert.

"Then it is time for my son to step forward and receive his title!" Tharus said with a wide smile.

As all eyes fell on him, Tiarnen had no choice but to walk over to his father.

"Kneel," said Tharus, his finger pointing at the ground as though his son was a disobedient pet.

Clenching his jaw, Tiarnen did as his father ordered.

"Every descendent of Dorian the First has sworn an oath to praetor and province. Are you, Tiarnen Straveritas, finally ready to do so?"

"I... I am," said Tiarnen, the words like jagged glass in his mouth.

Ignis hurried over and pulled an antique scroll from inside his tunic, then carefully unrolled it for Tiarnen to read. The old parchment was badly cracked and yellowing, every inch covered in faded cursive handwriting. Just as Tiarnen was about to speak the first word of the oath, a heavy sob pulled his attention to Niera, who had more tears streaming down her face. As much as he wanted to believe it was from sadness, part of him couldn't help but think a few were shed in envy.

Ignis cleared his throat and drew Tiarnen's gaze back to the scroll. Looking upon the words again, he wondered if Reina felt the same conflict speaking them, if she had doubts as well, or felt the weight of the entire province on her shoulders just as he did now. Though it seemed like only yesterday that she was kneeling in the exact same spot at their mother's funeral, Tiarnen remembered being taken aback by the conviction in Reina's voice; how it made him feel protected and safe despite Marifreth resting in a similar skiff. He realized it was now his responsibility to do the very same for Niera.

"Hear me Dorladdich, and witness my vow!" read Tiarnen. "Tonight, I will become your maestro! As such, it is my honour to stand against those who threaten the sanctity of our great province. For our praetor, I will be loyal. For our nobles, I will be cunning. For our provincials, I will be brave. For our music, I will be... pure." Even though Tharus was right about every maestro speaking those exact words, the oath was still Tiarnen's promise to make, so he made one small amendment. "And for my family..." he said, returning the stare his father had been giving him since he arrived, "I will be vengeful." It was subtle, but Tiarnen could see Tharus's eyes narrow. "I swear this, for I am Maestro Dorian."

"The Sixtieth," finished Tharus.

"The Sixtieth!" cried a provincial, who was followed by another cry—then another—until Tiarnen's title was being shouted across the strand.

"Now arise, Maestro Dorian, and accept your gifts of fealty!" said Tharus, gesturing for Tiarnen to stand. As he did, two tailors from Christarts approached from the perimeter of the crowd, together carrying a long garment bag.

"On behalf of the Roycroft family," said Earl Roycroft, "I present your new jacket, Maestro!"

The tailors unzipped the bag, and Tiarnen immediately recognized the dark grey leather hanging inside; it was from the kingray he'd seen on the pier earlier in the day. The bag was removed, hanger pulled out, and the jacket held open for Tiarnen, who slipped his arms into the green silk-lined sleeves so the tailors could pull it over his shoulders. It was undoubtedly the softest leather he had ever felt and the cut was absolutely perfect, but that didn't stop Niera from walking over and double-checking every inch.

"I told them to keep it simple," she said, making sure the decorative stitching running over the arms and across the back was up to her standards. "I know how you hate embellishments." She buttoned the jacket up, and Tiarnen immediately felt a snug warmth envelop him.

"It's exquisite, truly," he said, admiring how the collar sat high around his neck, and the length ended exactly at his knees.

Ignis handed Niera a small ceramic pin of the letters *LX*, which she then pressed to his upper right chest.

"On behalf of the Finwick family," slurred Earl Finwick, stumbling his way over to Tiarnen. "I presssent your... your... where did I put it?" he asked, patting himself all over.

"Inside your front pocket, you pickled paddy!" shouted Wendel.

Liam blinked slowly and managed to find his inside pocket, from which he pulled out a fine ceramic flask embossed with the Dorladdich crest. At first, Tiarnen thought the earl was offering him a drink, but then he realized the flask was, in fact, the gift.

"Oh!" said Tiarnen. "Well, I'm sure I'll find something to put in—"

"No need. It's already full," Liam said with a wink. "Figured you... you'd miss us too much and want a ta... taste of home." He clanked his flask against Tiarnen's. "Cheers, Maestro!"

"Cheers!" Tiarnen unscrewed the cap and sipped with the earl. Expecting there would be something that closely resembled Glindore dancing over his tongue, he was shocked by the sharp bite that resulted in a harsh cough after somehow managing to swallow it down.

"I know wha... what you're thinking!" said Liam.

"Which is?" asked Tiarnen, feeling like he was exhaling solvent fumes.

"*Liam! Nothing could pos... possibly taste worse!* That might be true but noth... nothing burns like it either and that's ex... exactly what you want when your spirit nee... needs lifting!" Liam gave a satisfied laugh.

"No arguments here," wheezed Tiarnen, watching with watery eyes as the earl stumbled back to join the rest of the Finwicks.

"We don't have anything to help remove paint," said Earl Ashbrook, giving Liam a side glance as she approached. "But the Ashbrooks thought this might come in handy along your journey."

Tiarnen immediately recognized the multi-belt in Eimear's hands. The coveted device was only issued to corsair officers who used it to hold their compass, gloves, small tools, tackle, freshwater ampules, and sardine snack cans, while the buckle housed a hook and cord mechanism that allowed them to climb, repel, or swing from one part of the ship to another. Looking closer, Tiarnen could see that his buckle was made from a mollusc shell, containing the internal spools and gearing for what should have been a common metal hook but had instead been fashioned from whalebone.

"I can't accept this, Eimear. I'm not crew."

"No, you're much more than that now," said Eimear, giving it to Tiarnen. "Besides, sometimes a bit of hook and line is all that's needed to get out of a tough spot, and you certainly have a few of those on the horizon."

He knew there was no arguing with her, so he pulled off his tattered old belt, handed it to Raghnall, and then slipped in and fastened the multi-belt.

"Thank you... *all* of you!" said Tiarnen. "I could not have wanted for anything more!"

"Yet there is one gift you have yet to receive," said Tharus, already opening the familiar instrument case that was being held by Holgor.

Tiarnen didn't need to look inside. He knew exactly what he was about to be handed.

Tharus pulled Windwalker out and presented it to Tiarnen, who could see it had been polished to a shine. If tradition had been upheld, Tiarnen would have begun training with it the day after he sparked, just like Reina, his mother, and all their predecessors did.

"Windwalker has been wielded by Maestro Dorian since the first days of Dorladdich," said Tharus. "It has no equal in the province and now belongs to you."

"Though I respect legacy and tradition," said Tiarnen, pulling out his piccolo, "I have chosen to keep..." He paused, realizing that his instrument needed a name. Tiarnen searched his memories for a past event, a defining moment, anything to inspire one. He looked back at Niera and thought about the long road ahead of them—of what it would mean not if they should fail but if the invasion was success-ful—of the untold death and destruction that would wash across all of Chora because of him. Though instrument names were supposed to feel heroic and demand renown, Tiarnen wanted it to carry an omen of what was to come. "*Darktide*," he said. Tharus's eyes flashed at what was a direct public refusal by his maestro but everyone else seemed to be so captivated by the piccolo's chromatic shimmering that they didn't even notice.

"And you believe that it will be able to endure our journey?" asked Tharus.

"It has just as much of a chance as I do," said Tiarnen.

"In that case," grumbled Tharus, placing Windwalker back in the case. "We will mark tonight as the campaign's commencement and rising of our Dark Tide!"

The crowd erupted in cheers, and though Tiarnen shouldn't have been surprised, he was still admittedly impressed at how fast his father turned Darktide's reveal into a rallying cry for the province.

"Now," said Tharus, putting his hands up to quiet the crowd, "we must say goodbye to—"

Boom... Boom...

Tremors shook the ground and cut Tharus off.

Boom... Boom...

Tiarnen looked over the crowd as everyone turned back to see a towering shape approaching.

Boom... Boom...

Screams and shouting erupted, but before panic completely took over, the chronopunks, led by Garod, stepped into the candlelight.

Boom... Boom...

With General Mikavnik following behind.

The crowd gasped and cried in horror at the sight of the looming chronomech, despite the fact that it was wearing a half-cape made from a large Dorladdian flag. It was hard to make out all of the details in the dim light, but Tiarnen could tell that the general's armour had been altered—the jagged Lydvenkian elements sanded away to allow for smoother Dorladdian lines—while the black skull was hidden underneath a closed jousting-style helmet. Most of Mikavnik seemed to be repaired or retrofitted, but some areas still needed significant work—one of which being the left shoulder joint, which Jasper was elbow-deep in while trying to straddle the pauldron. She finally realized that Mikavnik had come to a stop, so she looked around, spotted Tiarnen, then waved hello with a wrench in hand and a proud smile on her dirty face. Tiarnen chuckled and waved back; it was beyond impressive that the chronopunks were able to get the general back up and running so quickly. Understandably, Jasper was more than a little shocked by Tiarnen's unexpected request just before leaving Punkworks, but she was confident that they could deliver Mikavnik in some form of working order.

"Abomination!" yelled Raghnall, instinctually standing in front of Niera and reaching for his shield that wasn't there.

"Stand down, Major! You have nothing to worry about!" assured Garod.

"Chief, explain yourself!" ordered Ignis. "Our praetor gave a direct order to dismantle this monstrosity!"

"And we did, for the most part," said Garod. "But Maestro Dorian requisitioned a retrofit shortly after."

"Oh, he did, did he?" Tharus stared back at Tiarnen, who paid no attention to his father but instead walked over to Niera, took her hand, and led her towards Mikavnik. The crowd split to let them pass, but as Tiarnen brought Niera closer to the towering sentinel, he could already feel her pulling away.

"No, I don't want to go any closer!" she said, coming to a full stop as her eyes widened with fear.

Tiarnen raised an eyebrow. "You might want to reconsider."

"Give me one good reason to," said Niera.

"It's waiting for your command."

"What?" asked Niera.

"He's right," said Garod. "We reset—"

"Wait!" interrupted Jasper, reaching deeper inside Mikavnik's gearing. There was a short pause and then a quiet *click* that caused the general's head to tilt to the left for a moment, then straighten, as did its posture. Jasper pulled her arms out and gave a thumbs-up to Garod.

"We *just* reset its recognition switch, which means that whoever introduces themselves will become its commander," said Garod.

Niera furrowed her brow at Tiarnen with suspicion.

"Do you honestly think I'm about to let you leave the city without proper protection?" he said.

"Isn't that what *you* are supposed to be providing?" asked Niera.

"Like the major has been reminding me, I can't always be in two places at once." He tucked a curl behind her ear.

Niera's skepticism quickly turned to intrigue. "So you're telling me... that this thing... is now my personal bodyguard?"

"Correct."

She looked up at the general as though it were a new toy. She began cautiously approaching until she was about a metre away, the top of her head only reaching its knee. "He... hello," she said.

Mikavnik lowered its head to look upon her.

BRRRRRZZZZTTTTTTT!

Niera jumped back from the mechanical cacophony.

"Sorry! Thought I fixed that!" exclaimed Callum. He immediately climbed up Mikavnik's leg, pulled out a long screwdriver, and shoved it into a small circular port in the side of the general's chest.

Tiarnen rubbed his chin. "Still working out a few problems there, Callum?"

"More like a hundred," admitted Callum. "The first being that someone decided to tear out all three of its vocal coils."

"Why would they do that?" asked Niera.

"Not sure," said Garod. "But we were able to cobble a few parts together and replace one of them—just needs some fine-tuning."

"That should do it!" said Callum, giving a last turn of the screwdriver and hopping down.

Niera swallowed hard and stepped forward again. "Hello, I'm Niera."

The vocal coil emitted a surprisingly soulful vibration. "Mik-av-nik."

"Unfortunately, one coil means one-word answers for now," said Garod.

"Any chance of replacing the other two?" asked Niera.

Garod gave half a nod. "Perhaps, if there are any to be found in Lydvenko."

"I didn't think you would be coming with us," said Tiarnen.

"Not exactly my idea of a good time," muttered Garod, "but there's still a fair bit of work to be done before I'm confident that it will be combat ready—"

"*She*," interrupted Niera.

"She?" asked Tiarnen.

"Before *she* is combat ready," repeated Niera.

"Until then," said Tiarnen, smiling at his sister's decision, "at least you have someone trustworthy watching over you again."

"It is time to say goodbye," said Tharus.

Tiarnen nodded in agreement, took Niera's hand, and they walked back to the skiff together.

"Do you remember the dirge?" asked Tharus.

"Like it was yesterday," said Tiarnen, pulling out Darktide.

Ignis approached Niera with a small scroll and opened it. After a quick review of the simple lyrics written on the parchment, she looked back to Tiarnen and nodded.

He ran his thumb over the mouthpiece, put the piccolo to his lips, and aligned his fingers along the keys. With a deep exhale, the notes cried out in lamentation and wove into a forlorn melody as Raghnall and Dansby began to push Reina's skiff down the beach and into the sea. The rest of the provincial families followed with their own skiffs—making it look as though an entire fleet was being launched. Tiarnen watched sorrowfully as many mothers, fathers, and siblings held on for as long as they could, still in denial. Long after Raghnall had let go, Dansby continued wading out until he was almost neck deep and inches away from being swept up by the cove's notorious rip current. With no choice but to let go, Reina left his hand and led the casket armada into open moonlit waters. Niera's mournful voice cut through the air as she wove the first words of the dirge with Tiarnen's sombre performance.

Those we deliver are never adrift
May the waves carry them
Those we love are never lost
May the winds guide them

Our hearts go with you
Onto the shores beyond

Though Reina was deep within the flotilla, Tiarnen's eyes didn't leave her skiff for a second; he refused to let himself blink before she was gone forever. *Gone forever.* The foreboding thought made his heart leap, which in turn caused a green glow to emanate from within Dark-tide. In no way was he attempting to illuminate, but now that he didn't have to consciously bury his talent, it seemed to manifest on its own. Watching the shards spark around him, anyone standing near Tiarnen instinctually took several steps back.

Those we hold are never far
May the moons warm them

> *Those we cherish are never forgotten*
> *May the rain cleanse them*
>
> *Our hearts go with you*
> *Onto the shores beyond*

The dirge was never meant to be illuminated, but Tiarnen was too heartbroken to care about restraint. He played the last few notes as loud as he could, channelling his resonance through Darktide with intent, and illuminated three shards so bright that they cast the cove in emerald light.

> *Those we honour are never forsaken*
> *May the stars bless them*
> *Those we remember are never gone*
>
> *Our hearts go with you*

With a quick flourish, Tiarnen sent the shards, spiralling into the air, streaking over the water, and reaching high above the skiffs. His last ounce of breath nearly spent, he closed the keys halfway and intentionally soured the notes, causing the shards to explode and disintegrate into glimmering green dust that covered the fallen and made them glitter wondrously while finally fading from sight.

"Onto the shores beyond, Reina," said Tiarnen, tears filling his eyes. After what felt like an eternity of silence, Niera took his arm and put it around herself to hug him.

"I can't lose you, too," she whispered.

"You never will," Tiarnen whispered back.

Turning, he noticed Tharus speaking with Ignis, Raghnall, and Holgor, who had a devious grin on his face. Head shaking in disagreement with something the inquisitor said, Raghnall excused himself from the heated conversation and walked over to Tiarnen.

"Do I want to know?" asked Tiarnen.

"Just departure details," said Raghnall. "Despite my objections, it looks like I'll be remaining here with our reserves while the rest of you will be leaving for Lydvenko at first light."

"*First light?*" blurted Tiarnen. "But that's in a few hours!"

"Which should be more than enough time to make final preparations," said Tharus, appearing in front of them.

"In that case," said Tiarnen, "I need to get a couple of things from the Conservatory."

"I can help—" began Niera.

He shook his head. "No."

"Why not?" she asked.

"Because someone needs to make sure Imogen and Bridget pack the right hairbrushes," he said, which was followed by a punch in the arm from Niera. "Besides, I'm sure the good major can lend me a hand."

"If only one at the moment," said Raghnall.

"Maestro, if I may?" asked Dansby.

"Of course, Captain. What is it?" asked Tiarnen.

"There's also an... item... that I would like to retrieve from the Conservatory," said Dansby, a hint of desperation in his voice.

Tiarnen's stomach sank. He tried to think of something, anything, that would give him a valid reason to decline the captain's request but found himself entirely out of excuses. "Of... Of course," he said, already regretting the agreement.

"So long as the *souvenir* is personal rather than provincial," added Tharus.

"I'll make sure of it," said Raghnall.

"Which reminds me," said Tiarnen. "Given that half the city is still being restored, I would like Stormcaller to receive the same care while I am away."

"And who do you propose leads the effort?" asked Tharus.

Tiarnen raised an eyebrow at Raghnall.

"As much as I enjoy fixing a violin or flute every now and again," said Raghnall, "restoring Stormcaller is well beyond—"

"Your usual ambitions, I know," interrupted Tiarnen. "But if Dorladdich becomes the capital of Chora—"

"*When*," corrected Niera.

"*When* Dorladdich becomes the capital of Chora," he continued, "our iconic organ should reflect its illustrious position. Wouldn't you agree?"

Raghnall raised his eyebrow back at Tiarnen. "I do."

"Well then, given how tight security is around the Conservatory, I don't see how you're not the best man for the job," said Tiarnen, raising his eyebrows higher at Raghnall.

"I will make every effort to have it ready for your return," said Raghnall, noticing Tiarnen's expression growing more urgent by the second.

"Excellent." Tiarnen turned back to Tharus. "Oh, and it will probably be best to bestow a particular key to Uncle so that he doesn't have to deal with the knock-lock resetting every day."

Tiarnen sidestepped to put Raghnall and Tharus directly in front of each other. Tharus's eyes narrowed at Tiarnen and a long, uncomfortable pause followed, but he eventually pulled the skeleton key from his pocket and held it out.

"We should get going," said Tiarnen, watching Raghnall take the key. "The Ashbrooks can drop us off at the Conservatory on their way back to Noble Court."

"Tiarnen, one last thing," said Tharus, waiting for the major and captain to walk out of earshot. "Given the circumstances, I am willing to tolerate small amendments to oaths and forgoing a tradition here and there. However, should you illuminate without my consent again, Dorian the Sixtieth will only be remembered as the shortest-lived maestro in history. Do we have an understanding?"

"We certainly do, Praetor," said Tiarnen, turning away to leave.

Chapter Twenty-Two
HOSTILE NEGOTIATIONS

Thanks to the Ashbrooks, Tiarnen made a swift return to the cathedral, but it didn't leave him enough time to come up with a reason as to why Dansby couldn't be allowed inside. Standing now at the Conservatory door, his heart pounded as Raghnall slid the skeleton key into the knock-lock.

"What did you need to get exactly, Captain?" asked Tiarnen.

"A... a ring," said Dansby.

"*Ring*?" asked Raghnall, turning the key and pressing down on the latch.

"It was an anniversary gift for Reina, but she was never able to wear it."

"Why not?" Raghnall frowned as he pushed open the door.

"Have you met my father?" said Tiarnen, his heart sinking as Raghnall led them inside.

"I know she kept it in her study," said Dansby. "Didn't think anyone would mind if I held onto it."

"No, of course not," said Tiarnen, quickly shutting the door and then double-checking the lock to make sure it had set. Trying not to make it too obvious, he hurried to catch up with Raghnall and Dansby, then walked ahead of them in case they saw Lydia before he had the chance to explain the situation. Since she was approaching Stormcaller when he last saw her, Tiarnen assumed that Lydia had probably spent a moment looking the organ over and then made her way into the study just as he told her to. "Listen, before we go any further," he said, looking back at them over his shoulder. "I really need to tell the both of you someth—"

Thunk!

"By the—" said Tiarnen, tripping over one of the brooms, which had unexpectedly crossed his path. As though it was Tiarnen's fault, the broom swept at him twice in agitation and then continued to clean the floor.

"You all right?" asked Raghnall.

"Sure," said Tiarnen, looking up to see Dansby had continued trudging up the stairs as though in a trance.

"Think we should just let him search for it himself?" asked Raghnall, helping Tiarnen to his feet.

"That's probably a bad idea." Tiarnen bolted to catch up with Dansby and warn him. "Dansby, just give me—" As he reached the top of the stairs, he saw that not only was the worn leather chair empty, but the entire study as well.

"Give you?" asked Dansby.

"A..." began Tiarnen, his mind reeling at where Lydia could possibly be, "...a second to move the chair out of the way for you."

"It's fine. I have a good idea where it will be," said Dansby, walking into the alcove. As he began looking over the top shelf, Tiarnen started frantically glancing around the Conservatory as though he was tracking one of Holgor's nightingales through the air.

"What has gotten into you?" asked Raghnall.

"Me?" asked Tiarnen. "Nothing, just making sure I'm not forgetting anything."

"Found it," Dansby said with a hard swallow. He pulled the velvet box off the shelf and then walked over to Tiarnen and Raghnall while slowly opening it to reveal a beautiful pearl ring.

"It's lovely," said Raghnall, leaning in. "Tiarnen, you should see how stunn—" But the major stopped his question after turning to see Tiarnen was still nervously searching the Conservatory. "Maestro...?"

"Hmm?"

"The *ring*," stated Raghnall, clearly miffed that Tiarnen wasn't paying attention.

"Oh! Yes, you're right, absolutely stunning!" he said, checking under the organ bench out of desperation, then sitting on it to stare at the torn warsong sheet music and pretend that he wasn't sweating over the fact that Lydia was missing. As much as he didn't want to, Tiarnen started considering the idea that she might have fled despite the fact he saved her life. He knew he shouldn't have felt betrayed, but a small part of him couldn't help but brood over the fact that his actions meant nothing to Lydia.

"Guess I should let you two make preparations." Dansby closed the ring box, leaving the study to walk back down the stairs.

"Yes, the clock is unfortunately ticking," Tiarnen said with more than a hint of desperation in his voice. Following Dansby and Raghnall down, Tiarnen tried to convince himself that he should be relieved Lydia was no longer his responsibility.

"Before you go, Captain," said Raghnall, stopping just before the henge. "I think you should take leave from active duty. It doesn't have to be long. Maybe a couple of weeks aboard the *Calhoun* with your family to put some wind back in your sails?"

Dansby turned, already shaking his head in disagreement with the major. "I appreciate the offer, truly, but have to formally decline."

"Why's that?" asked Tiarnen, leaning against a henge pillar.

"Given what little is left of the patrols, the major can't afford to lose a single able body—especially since our entire military force is about to leave the city behind," said Dansby.

"Be that as it may," said Raghnall, looking at the ring in Dansby's hand, "a wound this deep needs proper time to heal."

"I know, sir," said Dansby, stepping out of a broom's way. "But I think staying on will help keep me focused. Otherwise, I'll probably just find myself—" His eyes suddenly went wide, as though he had just seen a ghost—only for his entire face to fill with rage. "TAKING HER HEAD!"

Stomach plummeting, Tiarnen followed the captain's eyeline into the henge and saw Lydia sitting at the very back, knees against her chest, bathed in the cold moonlight. Everyone froze, unsure what to do, to say, how to react—then Dansby burst forward—pushing past Raghnall—sprinting into the henge.

THUD!

Tiarnen tackled the captain to the Conservatory floor.

"What in the Verse are you doing, *Tiarnen?*" yelled Raghnall, rushing into the henge as well.

"Explaining this!" Tiarnen pulled himself to his feet and stood in front of Lydia with his arms stretched out in defence.

"Get out of the damn way!" yelled Dansby, standing up.

"Not until you hear why I did it," said Tiarnen.

"*Did what?*" asked Raghnall.

"Rescued me," croaked Lydia.

Raghnall and Dansby both looked at each other in utter disbelief.

"*Rescued?*" asked Raghnall, pulling himself out of the shock. "Have you lost your mind?"

"My mind?" asked Tiarnen. "This was your idea!"

"*My idea?*" asked Raghnall.

"'*Imagine all the maestros illuminating together,*'" said Tiarnen.

"So you could defeat them!"

"No, so we can *save* them!"

Raghnall and Dansby just stared at Tiarnen in shock.

"Tiarnen..." said Raghnall, the tempo of his voice slowing, "You need to listen to me... whatever truly happened between you two has somehow poisoned your mind."

"No, it's been opened." Tiarnen lowered his arms. "Don't you understand? Chora is at war because the provinces believe they could never be united in song, but Lydia and I proved that's a lie."

"We've been over this!" said Raghnall, fast losing the sliver of patience he had left. "There's no way of her knowing about synestry if it's never happened before!"

Tiarnen glanced over his shoulder to Lydia in the hope that she would finally explain herself.

"Much like Dorladdich, Lydvenko has many musical myths of its own," she said.

"If you're expecting me to trust you because of some legend—" said Raghnall.

"Before the rules of engagement vere enacted," continued Lydia, "our predecessors vere often playing at the same time in an attempt to overpower each other."

"This is already known," said Raghnall. "Dissonance is one of the reasons the rules were created."

"True, but there vere also rare occasions vhere two opposing var-songs had harmonious elements vhich vould cause their lattrices to merge. This vas entirely accidental, of course, but the early maestros saw fit to call it *synestry*."

"Has this been mentioned anywhere in the Maestro Diary?" asked Raghnall.

"Not that I have read so far," said Tiarnen.

"Nor vill you, since synestry vas outlawed by the praetors shortly after the provinces formed," said Lydia, resting her head back against the pillar.

"Even if that were true, I find it hard to believe that other maestros haven't rediscovered synestry over the last fifteen hundred years," said Raghnall.

"How could they when playing by the rules makes it impossible to achieve."

"I believe she's calling me brave," Tiarnen smirked, turning back to Raghnall.

"Or stupid," added Lydia.

"*That*, we can agree on," Raghnall grumbled.

"Now it's a matter of what to do with synestry," said Tiarnen.

"You already have that answer," said Raghnall.

"I will not use it against the other maestros."

"What other choice do you have?" asked Raghnall.

"If I can synestrify... synes—" fumbled Tiarnen.

"*Synestrize*," corrected Lydia.

"Synestrize with them. I think there might be a chance of ending the war peacefully."

Raghnall looked long at Tiarnen, who couldn't tell if the expression on the major's face was hope or disappointment. For the moment, it didn't matter. Dansby was still trying to make his way around the henge to Lydia, so Tiarnen opened his jacket and pulled Darktide from his pocket.

"Put your instrument away, right now!" ordered Raghnall, concerned that Tiarnen would take such an aggressive stance against the captain.

Tiarnen shook his head. "I can't do that."

"Because you're confused," said Raghnall, slowly stepping towards him.

"More like mad," said Dansby.

"Maybe both, but it doesn't mean I'm wrong."

"How can you be certain?" asked Raghnall, still cautiously approaching while Dansby continued to flank.

"Because I... I saw... I saw them," said Tiarnen.

"Saw who?" asked Raghnall.

"The maestros."

"Where? In a dream?"

"It felt more like an old memory... They were standing in a circle... performing together..." Tiarnen stared into Darktide's chromatic shimmer.

Lydia burst out laughing, her condescending cackle filling the Conservatory.

"And their colours... all of them were synestrizing... I think they were trying to build a lattrice together," said Tiarnen, turning and showing Darktide to Lydia.

Her eyes widened as though she had seen a ghost. "The *Anthymn,*" she whispered unconsciously.

"*Anthymn?*" asked Raghnall, confused by Lydia's apparent suggestion. "Each of the provinces already has its own."

"But Chora doesn't," said Tiarnen.

"And why would Chora need one?"

"Because the provinces will be united."

"Not if every maestro is long dead before you have the chance to attempt it," said Raghnall. "Or were you planning to somehow save them from *our* own invasion?"

"You're right. I can't avoid the battles ahead—" began Tiarnen.

"Exactly," said Raghnall, stopping just before him. "Now, you need to step aside so the captain and I can clean up this mess—"

"Which means I would need to make it appear as though the maestros were killed," finished Tiarnen.

"And how could you ever convince Tharus of that?"

"We saw it ourselves in the bailey. Lydia and I could have easily been destroyed, but now that I know how to synestrize, I just need to put on one hell of a show."

"There's a small detail you still haven't considered," said Raghnall.

"Which is?"

"The fact that you won't be here when you face them! And last I checked, the journey from Phrysbruck, let alone Locarnia, is a bit longer than a swim from the dungeon."

Tiarnen was stumped. The major was right; there was no possible way of sneaking the maestros back to Dorladdich without being recognized at some point along the way.

"He could use the henges," suggested Lydia. "Travel betveen them is said to be nearly instantaneous."

"Even if they really do work," said Raghnall. "We only know the key tones for ours." Raghnall pointed to the runic notation carved along the henge pillar to the left of Dansby, who was still trying to close in.

"Those are all I need. It'll be a one-way trip for them!" said Tiarnen.

"Every capital city vas built around or near their henge," said Lydia. "Phrysbruck's is atop the Tantalis. It von't be difficult to reach should you manage to infiltrate the city."

"Then I just have to make sure the battle takes place there." Tiarnen shrugged as though it were the easiest task he had ever been given.

"Right!" chortled Raghnall. "Just so I'm perfectly clear, your plan is to lure each maestro into their own henge, synestrize to make it look like they've been killed during battle, and then send them back here to the Conservatory in secret?"

Tiarnen quickly reviewed the order of events. "Correct."

Raghnall bellowed with laughter. "And what do you expect our honoured guests to do while patiently waiting for your glorious return?"

"The *Anthymn* will have to be an entirely new composition, one that the maestros need to write together," said Tiarnen.

Lydia nodded in reluctant agreement.

"And what happens when Tharus eventually learns the truth?" asked Raghnall.

"We will stand against him," said Tiarnen.

Raghnall went silent in consideration.

"Or end this now!" said Dansby, finally lunging again for Lydia.

"Stand down, Captain!" yelled Tiarnen. He was about to hold Darktide to his lips when Raghnall stepped in the way, grabbing onto Dansby.

"Get off of me!" said Dansby, trying to push his way past the major without any luck.

"I know you don't want to hear this—and I sure as hell don't want to say it—but... Tiarnen is right... We have to give them a chance," said Raghnall.

"*What?* How can you trust this woman after what she has done to us?" screamed Dansby, his face glowing red.

"We are all guilty of the same crimes," said Tiarnen. "But if the maestros see that I can forgive Lydia despite what she has done to us, maybe they can do the same for each other." He slipped Darktide back into his pocket and closed his jacket.

Accepting that he wasn't getting any closer to Lydia nor convincing Tiarnen and Raghnall to reconsider, Dansby took a step back—though he was still seething with hatred.

Over the next few hours, Raghnall did most of the talking. He agreed to keep watch over Lydia while she remained in the Conservatory and composed a first draft of the *Anthymn* so the maestros would have a clear explanation as to why they had been unexpectedly saved from certain death. Weekly progress reports would be sent to Tiarnen disguised as casual letters between an uncle and nephew.

"I still have a concern," said Raghnall.

"Which is?" asked Tiarnen.

"The fact that she hasn't agreed to any of this." Raghnall pointed at Lydia.

"She hasn't disagreed either," said Tiarnen.

Raghnall raised his eyebrow, which was more than enough to get Tiarnen to approach Lydia and kneel beside her. "We have to try," he said. "If not, nothing will remain of Lydvenko."

Lydia leaned her head back against the pillar. "Perhaps the time has come for it to fall."

"You can't mean that," said Tiarnen, baffled that a maestro would say that about her own province.

"Vhy not? Lydvenko is but a shadow of its former self. Vhat is there left to save?" she spat.

"You, for one," said Tiarnen. "The rescue didn't end with me pulling you out of that cell. It was only the beginning."

Lydia clenched her jaw as though wanting to spit venom in Tiarnen's face.

"We can do this," he whispered.

"Do not give me hope," whispered Lydia.

"Then I'll give us a chance instead." Tiarnen stood, holding his hand out for her to take. Tension filled the air as Lydia stared at it. He waited patiently, but she didn't show any sign of accepting his offer, so he began turning away, only to feel her hand grip his tightly. With a look of relief, Tiarnen turned back and helped Lydia to her feet.

"Let's keep some distance, Maestros," said Raghnall.

"So much for having a moment," said Tiarnen, letting go of Lydia's hand and stepping out of the henge.

"Vhy do I sense a theme?" said Lydia.

Raghnall's face hardened. "The only theme you need to worry about is the one that will convince Maestro Phrygus of our plan before he tears the Conservatory, along with all of us, apart."

"Who knows, if my battle against Phrygus is anything like ours, then he might be excited to find himself arriving here in one piece," said Tiarnen.

"Forgive me if I don't count on it," said Raghnall.

"How long will it take to reach Lydvenko?" asked Tiarnen, walking to the long table where Dansby was sitting.

"Nine days by the scorched road," said Raghnall. "You'll station in Kuldron, likely until early spring, and then deploy for Phrysbruck. All things considered, you should be facing Maestro Phrygus in a few months."

Tiarnen looked back to Lydia. "That's a long time to be kept in here."

"I've spent much longer in far vorse," said Lydia.

"And what about you, Captain?" asked Tiarnen.

"Like the major said, a wound this deep needs proper time to heal," said Dansby.

Tiarnen nodded in agreement, but he didn't know if Dansby meant forgiving Lydia for taking Reina's life or Tiarnen's betrayal. "Lydia, is there anything you can tell me about Maestro Phrygus?" he asked, scouring the random objects scattered along the table.

"Only that he follows history to a fault," said Lydia.

"Well, I don't expect that composing the *Anthymn* will be easy, so my Conservatory is at your disposal." Tiarnen made a last survey of the table, then picked up a tuning cone, reed puller, and key weight and put them in his jacket pockets. "As is the major."

"Excuse me?" asked Raghnall, unimpressed by the offer.

"Whatever you might need, just ask him," said Tiarnen, making his way to the door.

"Ravenving," said Lydia, "as a star—"

"Out of the bloody ques—" interrupted Raghnall.

"And a change of clothes. I vould prefer—"

"Whatever I damn well bring you!" Raghnall finished.

"I'm sure you'll reach an agreement." Tiarnen chuckled under his breath at the preview of what life was about to be like in the Conservatory. Truth be told, his laughter came from an overwhelming sense of relief. He did his best not to think about the innumerable ways their negotiations could have taken a turn for the worst; a misspoken sentence or misunderstood answer would have likely been enough to cause the armistice to unravel and his rescue to ultimately fail. If the major had chosen to do so—even with his injury—he could have tossed Tiarnen aside and just as easily snapped Lydia's neck with his bare hand.

Considering it further, Tiarnen wondered if, in the end, it was facing death yet again in such a short time that it became the deciding factor for Lydia rather than the *Anthymn*'s noble cause. She seemed to have been ready to embrace her last breath in the cavern, but when they spoke of the *Anthymn* it was as though the life in her eyes returned for a moment. At this point, Lydia's commitment was all Tiarnen could ask for. But despite their music being stronger together, he would not underestimate the fragility of their accord, which would only be strained further if Maestro Phrygus was successfully delivered to Dorladdich. And Dansby was a wildcard Tiarnen could not have anticipated. Putting Lydia's life in the major's hands was risky enough, but the captain's involvement made things much more complicated and worried him deeply. As much as Tiarnen empathized, he was still concerned that it might not be a matter of *if* the captain would eventually enact revenge on Lydia but when.

"Maestro," said Raghnall.

"What is it?" asked Tiarnen, opening the door.

Raghnall looked long at his nephew. "Good luck."

Tiarnen wasn't sure why, but the major saying goodbye made reality sink in; unless a key part of the mission failed or the campaign ended before reaching Locarnia, he wouldn't be returning to the Conservatory for nearly two years.

"To us all," said Tiarnen, his eyes meeting Lydia's as he closed the door.

Chapter Twenty-Three
BANNERS EAST

Tiarnen hurried down the cathedral steps—passing melted candles, scattered tributes, and rotting food—to step into the vacant square. Daybreak warmed his face as he took in what looked to be a perfect Dorladdian morning. The misty air was damp and fresh, everything was covered in dew, and birds were chirping melodically in the trees. Unwilling to let the unexpected moment of solace go to waste, Tiarnen closed his eyes and tried to clear his mind, but it proved easier said than done. He could feel the anxiety of the mission trying to creep into his heart—whispering the countless ways it might fail.

"You made the right decision," said Tiarnen, opening his eyes to glance up at the Conservatory. He knew it was impossible to run back upstairs and help Lydia compose the *Anthymn*, especially since he still didn't know what to make of the vision or, as the major alluded to, his apparent lapse in sanity. Either way, it didn't seem to matter to Lydia, perhaps because she, too, understood that they had no other choice now but to try.

"Maestro!" called a distant voice.

Tiarnen blinked himself into the present and looked across the square to see Holgor's sweaty face peering out from an unfamiliar carriage that was coming to a stop on the other side of the entrance. Tiarnen let out a long exhale and accepted that he couldn't avoid the inquisitor after being spotted. He put on a surprised expression and began making his way over, but not without running his finger over the stock he woke up in. Tharus's speech echoed in his mind, particularly how his father's political performance manipulated the provincials into rallying for his release. Then it happened again at the funeral when his father put up the same seductive façade to sell what could be the end of Dorladdich. The scariest part was that the provincials bought into it without question. Watching him perfect the art of coercion made Tiarnen thankful that the talent seemed to have skipped a generation, but it also reminded him that there was much he still needed to learn about Tharus Straveritas—if only to understand where the praetor ended, and his father began. Given that they were embarking on a journey across the entire continent, Tiarnen didn't know what to expect as far as their relationship was concerned. Would they grow closer or even further apart? The question raised a critical point Raghnall made in the Conservatory: Tharus would eventually learn the truth about the *Anthymn*, and nothing could ever make a praetor forgive his maestro, let alone his very own son, for betraying him.

Tiarnen finally reached the regal carriage and took in its peculiar details: the enormous pentagonal coach rested on springs that were attached to an elaborate skeleton frame with four large wheels at each corner. A coachman sat high up at the front on a narrow bench, holding onto taught reins that harnessed a pair of draft horses. Tiarnen had never seen bronze metalwork fashioned in such a way before, and its green patina made the metal seem as though it was from another age.

"On your way to the bailey?" asked Holgor, a nightingale swooping in and landing on his shoulder.

"Indeed I am," said Tiarnen.

"Well then, allow me to give you a lift," said Holgor, opening the door.

"See! I told you I heard his name!" screamed a provincial girl, already running to the carriage from the other side of the street.

Tiarnen quickly hopped inside as every provincial youth within earshot seemed to take a keen interest in his sighting as well. After Tiarnen slid across the leather bench seat, Holgor closed the carriage door, then rapped his knuckle on the frame. The coachman cracked the reins, and the horses pulled the carriage ahead.

"Bring me with you, Maestro Dorian!" pleaded the girl, running beside the carriage.

"No, it should be me—I'll protect you!" declared a boy, following just behind.

"Charming," commented Holgor.

"Don't think this is something I'll ever get used to," said Tiarnen.

"Too bad. I'm sure a few adoring fans could be put to very good use," Holgor said with a smirk.

Tiarnen didn't know what Holgor meant, but he certainly didn't like the Inquisitor's tone. He tried to ignore the heartfelt pleas by looking over the carriage interior. Every inch was covered in quilted grey velvet that made the air feel close, including Holgor's sweaty stench, which Tiarnen tried not to breathe in too deeply. In between them was a polished marble table covered in tiny scrolls, a quill and inkwell, and a large map book covered with what looked to be thousands of tiny handwritten symbols.

"Lucky that we ran into each other," said Tiarnen.

"Oh, it wasn't luck," said Holgor. He wrote a series of numbers on a tiny parchment scroll, rolled it up, and then slid it into the nightingale's leg holster.

"How is that?" inquired Tiarnen.

"I received word that you had just left the Conservatory, so I brought the carriage around since you normally take the east cathedral entrance." Holgor watched his feathered messenger hop from his shoulder onto his hand.

A small pit formed in Tiarnen's stomach at the realization that Holgor seemed to be a little too familiar with his habits.

"Expect that you haven't been inside a carriage before," said Holgor, holding his hand out the window so the nightingale could flutter away.

"No, only heard about them when I was young," admitted Tiarnen.

"Understandable, especially since it hasn't been used since your grandmother set out for Phrysbruck."

"This is what she rode in?" asked Tiarnen, taking a second look around.

"Your mother too, well, not this one exactly, of course. The maestro carriage has far better amenities."

Tiarnen's eyes widened. "There's more of them?"

"Twelve, to be exact—though I believe the convoy originally had eighteen."

"Convoy?"

"Yes—sorry—already ahead of myself," said Holgor. "The twelve carriages link together to form a convoy so that you, our praetor, Miss Niera, and a privileged few can move freely throughout while we travel."

"That should make my sister happy."

"Because she won't have to travel on foot?"

Tiarnen shook his head, chuckling to himself. "Because I won't have the chance to be late to appointments anymore."

Holgor clasped his hands and leaned forward. "Considering you were able to be a lightkeeper and First Wind while still making it to every Shatter match, I can't help but think that your long-running streak of missing military meetings or family events was more statement than accident."

"At least someone noticed," said Tiarnen, pretending not to hate the fact that it sounded like he had been regularly shadowed by Holgor's agents.

"Don't take it too personally, Maestro." Holgor reached into a small basket on the bench beside him, pulling out a thin can of salmon roe and a tiny fork. "It's my job to know everything about everyone." He peeled the top of the can open and then forked some of the bright orange fish eggs into his mouth.

"So, outside of providing accommodations, what are the rest of the carriages used for?" asked Tiarnen, trying to ignore the fact that his privacy had been invaded for longer than he would like to consider.

"Mostly storing supplies, weapons, water, food, and the like," said Holgor, taking another bite of roe. "However, you'll be pleased to hear that one carriage is a full kitchen, and Chef Auberdine will be aboard to prepare our meals. As for myself, if you ever need to find me, I'll likely be in here gathering intelligence and trying to ensure that none leaks while we're away."

"I can see how withholding information is just as important as acquiring it," said Tiarnen, casually glancing over the scrolls on top of the map book.

"Indeed." Holgor followed his gaze. "By all means, take a look. You now have the second-highest security clearance in the province."

"*Second*?" asked Tiarnen.

"Praetor Tharus is above you, of course."

"Of course," said Tiarnen, annoyed at himself for not making the guess. He casually unrolled one of the scrolls with his fingertips to see three lines of tiny numbers. At first, they seemed random, but then he realized what they were. "Date, time, and..." he paused, looking back down at the city map, which he saw was divided by a symmetrical grid. "... location?"

"Well done," said Holgor, a note of surprise in his voice.

"But why such little detail?" asked Tiarnen, rolling the scroll back up.

"Anything more than *where* and *when*, and we risk exposing valuable information."

"Like what?"

"Exactly," said Holgor. "Or even worse, *why* and *how*." He pulled on a thin metal lip at the top of the window frame, bringing down a slated blind that blocked out the light and muffled the youths' pleading. "For instance, shortly after your father announced the campaign, we caught two Lydvenkian spies attempting to depart the city."

"They were trying to inform Lydvenko," said Tiarnen.

Holgor nodded. "And give the barons a chance to prepare for our arrival with whatever forces might be left in Kuldron."

"But if no word whatsoever has reached the capital, wouldn't they be preparing for the worst already?" asked Tiarnen.

"Here we touch on the incredible value of *mis*information," said Holgor, shifting in his seat with excitement. "As you may have heard, Inquisitor Valchev was killed in battle, and his absence has significantly weakened Lydvenko's intelligence office."

"Won't the barons try and step in?"

"Without any doubt. Fortunately for us, Yavor, Ferotov, and Grensky are not exactly known for their military leadership—even with Executor Kizik helping them make every decision."

"Hence the misinformation," said Tiarnen, pointing at Holgor.

"Which is why Lydvenko believes that it won the battle and is now expecting Khazlokov to return with what is left of the legion in the coming days," Holgor said with a look of satisfaction on his face.

A smile pulled at Tiarnen's cheek. "Buying us the element of surprise."

"Precisely. When we arrive, it will already be too late for the city to take up arms. However, I don't believe that I will be able to prevent Phrysbruck from receiving word that we have occupied Kuldron."

"That means Praetor Sturm and Maestro Phrygus will know we are coming."

"Indeed they will."

"I remember my mother mentioning how impressed she was by the Tantalis," said Tiarnen, flipping the pages of the map book until he found one of Phrysbruck where he could see the enormous mountain city.

"The fabled Phrygian military academy is certainly a sight to behold—especially the library. But make no mistake, it is just as much of a fortress and the very reason why Dorladdich has never once been able to cross into Elihammer. However, given your accomplishments as maestro already, I expect that history is about to change."

"We still have a very long road ahead of us before that might happen," said Tiarnen, riffling through a few more pages to see Phrysbruck's vast Laurenian mountain range abruptly end at Elihammer's eastern border, where it quickly flattened into the Great Plains which had several branching rivers and what appeared to be bell towers with enormous barns scattered along them. Before Tiarnen could ask for details, the carriage came to a stop, and Holgor opened the coach door once again. Tiarnen emerged, and his eyes didn't even have the chance to adjust to the bright morning light again before both ears were ringing with the sound of his name and title being shouted from all directions. After a couple of blinks, he could see a few of the youths who were chasing the carriage had now collapsed at his feet in a sweat-soaked, panting mess.

"By the Verse," he muttered.

"Maestro, at last!" shouted Ignis.

Tiarnen turned to see Ignis emerging from the crowd and scurrying over with the usual number of ledgers in hand, one of which had Holgor's messenger perched on top and a secretary following close behind. However, it was the scene behind the executor that made it difficult to reply. The entire city seemed to have filled the bailey. In the middle was the convoy; all the carriages interlinked just as Holgor had described. Just ahead of it stood the entire orchestra, and then further on was Dorladdich's entire military.

"We were relieved to hear the inquisitor was escorting you here," said Ignis, the nightingale fluttering off his ledger and returning to Holgor's shoulder.

"As was I," said Tiarnen, focusing back on his loyal followers.

With a hint of disgust in his voice, Ignis asked, "Was this lot giving you some trouble along the way?"

"As a matter of fact—" began Holgor.

"Just the opposite," finished Tiarnen. "However, they would better serve their province by dedicating all of that energy towards rebuilding the districts rather than chasing after me."

"Forgive us," pleaded the young boy.

Tiarnen noticed the boy's feet were blood-soaked from running the entire way in his now shredded socks. "No, the mistake was mine." He knelt before them. "I should have greeted all of you before the carriage left the square. Please allow the executor to find you something to drink and new boots as an apology for not doing so."

"New boots? I am a little busy at the mo-moment..." stammered Ignis, his voice trailing off after Tiarnen stared long at him. "I'm sure we can find something suitable for them." With a snap of Ignis's fingers, his secretary sprang ahead and gestured for the youth to follow her.

"Praise you, Maestro Dorian!" said the provincial girl who had first spotted him.

"We are forever devoted!" added the young boy, hobbling on his sore feet.

"Now," said Ignis. "If we're about finished with charitable gestures, our praetor is waiting."

Tiarnen followed Ignis and Holgor down the left side of the carriage to see the horses being unhitched so it could be coupled to the end of the next carriage just ahead. Curious to learn what was actually inside the rest of them, Tiarnen peered through the open windows as he passed by.

Carriage eleven looked to be a supply hold since they were full of barrels and crates with *Fresh Water, Charred Eel, Oysters in Herb Oil, Salted Cod, Pickled Herring, Kelp Mash,* and *Clam Juice* labels on them. Carriage ten was undoubtedly for catering since Chef Auberdine was inside, cursing at what looked to be an ancient stove of some kind. Carriage nine was stocked with every instrument part imaginable for the orchestra. Carriage eight was its own armoury filled with replacement pieces and shields for the battalion. Carriage seven seemed to be for medical treatment since Matron Hallon was barking orders at a nurse organizing bandages on the shelf above an operating table. Carriages six, five, and four were residences, which Tiarnen took an extra moment to look over. Lavish interiors were filled with full-size beds as well as plush lounge seats and ottomans. Carriage two appeared to be for meetings as it contained several chairs around a large table in the middle. The last carriage had no windows at all, only a series of port holes that exposed an intricate gearing and pulley system that led up to the front, where four horses were bridled.

"Four horses can't possibly pull so much weight," remarked Tiarnen.

"I said the very same thing when I first saw the convoy," said Holgor. "But according to Garod, the lead carriage here is a transmission of sorts that does most of the work. We only need the horses to get it turning."

Tiarnen would never question Garod's mechanical expertise, and so let go of his doubt. If anything, he was even more excited to travel in the convoy now.

Continuing ahead, he passed the horses to find himself flanked on both sides by the orchestra, who were standing at attention, wearing long green peacoats, large backpacks with sleeping bags on top, and carrying or rolling their protective instrument cases.

"He would have barked the entire way!" said Coniel.

"You don't know that!" said Kaleigh.

"Are we all accounted for?" asked Tiarnen.

"No, Maestro, we most certainly are not *all* accounted for," stated Kaleigh.

"Who is missing?" Tiarnen glanced over the woodwinds to see if he could tell who it might be.

"Dasher!" said Kaleigh, a hint of desperation in her voice.

Tiarnen looked back at her in confusion. "Sorry?"

"I'm not allowed to bring him with us," said Kaleigh.

"Good thing, too," said Lachlan. "Last thing we need is a mangy mutt sniffing around."

"Then why are you coming?" asked Kaleigh.

"Easy, now!" said Tiarnen, trying not to laugh. "I'm sorry to be the one to say it, but Dasher belongs at home."

"So do we," muttered Kaleigh.

"That said," continued Tiarnen, raising his voice to make sure Lachlan heard him, "expectations will be much higher during the campaign and so must our standards of respect."

Kaleigh gave an accepting nod to Tiarnen, so he left her side and caught up with Ignis and Holgor as they began walking through the military ranks.

"What was the final headcount?" asked Holgor.

"After calling up our reserves, we have six thousand enlisted legionaries, four hundred stewards, and just under two hundred horses."

"My last report has the Lydvenkian forces at just under three thousand, although there were a fair few lifeless bodies lying on the beach as of this morning," said Holgor.

"Still, that should be enough to bring us up to full strength," said Ignis.

Seeing the full might of Dorladdich standing at the ready should have filled Tiarnen with pride and confidence. However, there were so many young faces scattered among the ranks, especially the second brigade, that he couldn't help but worry for them. In contrast, the senior officers stuck out like sore thumbs due to their hastily repaired armour, bandages, and fresh stitches. Up ahead, Tiarnen saw Tharus mounted on the chronosteed. There was something eerily foreboding about the sight—especially since his praetorian guards had Khazlokov shackled and kneeling to the right of the steed's hooves while he shouted up at Tharus. To his father's left, Niera was standing with Mikavnik and appeared to be teaching her new companion the name of her instrument.

Though Tiarnen knew not to expect to see the familiar high stone walls, hulking waterwheels, and towering front gate, the fact that there was nothing but temporary scaffolding stretching over the chasm to Forth Reach bridge was still a sight to behold. Ignoring Khazlokov's ranting, Tiarnen walked past everyone and stood at the cliff. He took a knee and looked over the edge to find himself confounded by the perfectly sheer rock face leading down to the ocean far below. Chunks of rubble peeked out of the turbulent blue waters as orange and green glass glimmered among the detritus.

"You've kept me long enough, Tharus!" shouted Khazlokov. "Return me to my legion!"

The praetor's demand pulled Tiarnen from his bewilderment and brought him to Niera's side. Khazlokov, as far as Tiarnen could tell, didn't seem to have been mistreated, but judging by the frazzled hair, dirty face, and badly singed robes, he certainly hadn't been living his usual life of luxury. A glint of brass drew Tiarnen's eye to the chronograph around Khazlokov's bony wrist as he shook his finger at Tharus. It was identical to his father's.

"You are in no position to be making demands," said Tharus, amused by Khazlokov's barking.

"Then tell me vhat my ransom is!" said Khazlokov.

"Ah, yes, the ransom. Now that I'm thinking about it, I don't know if you'll be willing to pay the price of your release."

Khazlokov was the one laughing now. "Let me guess, a cart of uncut sunstones from Indrilka crater? A bar of pure malachite ore? Or have you run short of goats—" His laughter abruptly ended with a phlegmy cough.

"As enticing as those offers might be, I simply need you to provide me but a small gift," said Tharus.

"Gift?" asked Khazlokov.

Instead of clarifying, Tharus nodded to his guards, who pulled Khazlokov to his feet and then turned to Tiarnen.

"Did the captain find what he was looking for?"

"He did," said Tiarnen.

"And did you give Raghnall clear instructions?" inquired Tharus.

"Instructions?" asked Tiarnen, his heart leaping into his throat.

"For your restoration effort," said Tharus with obvious irritation.

"Oh! Yes, he knows exactly what needs to be done," assured Tiarnen.

"Good. Now, to the shore!"

The praetorian guards picked up Khazlokov and dragged him across the scaffold. Seeing that it was safe to cross, Tharus followed, as did Holgor and Niera.

"After you," said Tiarnen, gesturing for Mikavnik to go ahead. He heard as much as he watched the chronomech cross the scaffold, which creaked with strain under the enormous weight.

"Forward!" yelled an officer.

Marching feet made the ground tremor and told Tiarnen to get a move on, so he, too, passed over the scaffold and reached the bridge. After fifteen minutes of walking through strong crosswinds and stepping over what was left of the possessed, Tiarnen felt a lump forming in his throat when he saw that it hadn't been driftwood that the legion was burning in their fire pits along the beach, but the bodies of their dead. Upon seeing Tharus approaching with Khazlokov in custody, the Lydvenkians stood to their feet and amassed at the mouth of the bridge. Tiarnen unconsciously reached for Darktide in anticipation of an attack, but after seeing their exhausted faces, he could tell that all they wanted was to return home.

"Tiarnen, look," whispered Niera, pointing to the Dorladdian watchmen who had the misfortune of meeting Lydia's kyndling.

"Explains why we never received any warning," whispered Tiarnen, pushing away the thought of how different things might have been if they had.

"Our praetor has returned!" shouted a clawman, every inch of his broken armour covered in dry blood and sand.

"And who might you be?" asked Tharus.

"I am Davmir, First Brigarch," stated the clawman, removing his helmet. Despite the scarred, shaved head, formidable build, and branding down his right arm, Davmir was much younger than Tiarnen expected. If he had to guess, the third commander couldn't have been a day over twenty.

"Where are the other commanding officers?" asked Tharus, looking over the legion.

"Somevhere in fourth and fifth pits," spat Davmir.

"Then I suppose you will have to do," said Tharus, dismounting from the chronosteed.

"Release him!" demanded Davmir.

"As you wish." Tharus stepped behind Khazlokov to remove his shackles. "It would seem the hour for you to depart has finally come, Khazlokov."

"And not a minute too soon," said Khazlokov, shaking the shackles off and turning to face Tharus. "Now, for the last time, vhat is it you vant?"

"Only this," said Tharus, holding up Khazlokov's chronograph as though it were a prize he had just won.

Though they had never discussed it directly, Tiarnen always understood that the rare timepiece was important to his father and that the unique chimes constantly emitting from it seemed to tell him far more than what the hour was. But the way Khazlokov reacted, the genuine panic on his face as he clutched the rotting flesh around his wrist, proved that Tiarnen didn't have a clue as to its true significance.

"*Vhat are you doing?*" yelled Khazlokov, "Put it back on! Put it back—" He tried to lunge at Tharus, but even before the guards could step in between them, Khazlokov's knees gave out and he fell to the ground. No one could make sense of what was happening as the cracks along Khazlokov's face grew deeper, his body wilted, and his skin sloughed off. Even the legion took a collective step back as their praetor screamed incoherently at Tharus, who stood like a statue and watched Khazlokov wither until there was nothing left but a pile of dust in his crumpled clothes.

Everyone stood in shock.

"I can't imagine what it must feel like," said Tharus, "to watch your maestro and now praetor both be destroyed within a few short days." He brushed some of Khazlokov off his sleeve. "To know that *you* are the ones to blame, *you* are the ones who failed, *you* are the ones who caused the greatest defeat Lydvenko has ever seen." Tharus pointed at the legion. "Is it disbelief? Guilt? Or perhaps shame?" He waited for a reply even though he knew none would come. "*Disbelief*, I can understand.

Guilt, seems only natural. *Shame*, however, is something I do not wish for you to endure. Do you know why?" Tharus walked to the nearest Dorladdian soldier and took the provincial banner from him. "Because I want you to take pride in returning home, in welcoming the next battle, in carrying our banner to the Tantalis!" He walked to Davmir and held it out for him to take. "The question is, will you allow shame to steal that bright future away from us?"

"And if your offer is refused?" asked Davmir.

"Then I promise you that every last man, woman, and child in Kuldron will have pits of their own," said Tharus, gesturing to the beach fires.

Bam-bam-bam!

The praetorian guards struck their shields as if adding an exclamation mark.

Davmir looked up at the banner, clenched his jaw, and reluctantly accepted it from Tharus.

"Now, *First Commander*, tell your comrades whom you fight for," said Tharus.

"For... for Dor..." stammered Davmir, struggling to say the words. "For Dorladdich."

"And who do they fight for?" asked Tharus, nodding to the legion.

Head low, Davmir turned to his comrades and raised the banner as high as he could. "For Dorladdich!"

It wasn't long before the renewed Dorladdian legion was marching down the Great East Shoreway with the Lydvenkians taking up the rear. Deep in the Shadowpine Forest now, the convoy rounded a bend and came upon what looked to be another convoy. Tiarnen could hardly believe what he was seeing. Sure, Khazlokov's convoy only had five carriages, but as they approached it, Tiarnen noticed many similarities to their own. For instance, the metalwork was painted orange, but it still had a very close resemblance in structural design. In fact, when they finally reached the convoy, Tiarnen saw that they were an exact match.

"Where are the horses?" asked Niera.

"Perhaps wolves got to them?" suggested Holgor.

"Not before the legion did," said Tharus, glancing at Davmir, who looked down at the ground with embarrassment.

"Unhook the transmission carriage and link it to the back," said Tharus.

It was only a few minutes before a handful of legionaries had unhinged the Lydvenkian carriage, turned it around, and linked it to the rear of the convoy. From what Tiarnen could see, they linked up perfectly.

*

Chef Auberdine waddled his way around a square table where Tiarnen, Tharus, Niera, and Holgor were sitting in the middle of the common carriage. Unlike the heavy shadows and close air of the conference carriage that Tiarnen found himself trapped in earlier, the common carriage was larger, more luxurious, and with a glass dome roof that filled it with daylight. Despite hitting many bumps along the Shoreway, it was riding smooth enough for Auberdine to balance three large plates that were piled with cured sausage, eggs, brown beans, and soda bread while also holding a bowl in his right.

"Apologies for the simple fare. Best I could do given that sorry excuse for a stove in the galley carriage," said Auberdine, setting the first plate down in front of Tharus.

"I'm sure we can arrange something better for you while stationed in Lydvenko," said Tiarnen.

"The palace kitchen in Kuldron will be more than adequate," said Tharus, carefully adjusting a dial on Khazlokov's chronograph. "You will simply have to make do until we arrive." Tharus glanced at his plate and then pushed it away.

"Of course, Praetor. Thank you," said Auberdine.

The savoury smell of the sausages hit Tiarnen and made his mouth water while he watched Auberdine come around to set the bowl in front of him.

"I know that brunch was somewhat of a miss, Maestro. But I hope this is a bit more to your liking."

Seeing how delicious everyone else's meals looked, Tiarnen was about to tell Auberdine not to worry, but then he peered into the bowl and saw that it was full of slimy sea slugs covered with fermented kelp flakes.

"Maybe with a bit of toast..." said Tiarnen, reaching for Niera's plate only to have his hand slapped away.

"A pleasure to cook for all of you on this auspicious morning!" said Auberdine, bowing to the table and then stepping out of the carriage.

"Have you chosen our route to Lydvenko, Praetor?" asked Holgor, taking a large bite of sausage.

"I would normally avoid the Scorched Road, but given that anyone who might attack our convoy is marching alongside us, I think taking it should be safe enough—barring a few pairs of melted boots," said Tharus.

"Does that mean I'm going to see the *Fire Tongue?*" asked Niera.

Tharus nodded. "Indeed. Campaign permitting, I'll make sure you don't miss any of Chora's more notable sights along the way."

"How far is it to Kuldron?" asked Tiarnen, reluctantly stabbing a slug with his fork.

"Right now, the distance doesn't matter. Only time does," said Tharus. "And I want us there within six days."

"Why?" asked Tiarnen, forcing himself to take a bite of the slug and immediately regretting it.

"As Holgor informed you earlier, the barons still believe that Khazlokov is alive but will no doubt be trying to scrounge every last ounce of power and influence over the provincials while they can. The longer we give them to continue doing so, the deeper those wretches will be entrenched when we arrive," said Tharus.

"With all due respect," said Holgor. "If we are to reach Lydvenko by the thirteenth, our legion will be on a loaded march for over twelve hours a day."

Tiarnen's face contorted as he swallowed the slug. "They won't be able to keep that pace up."

"They will if their maestro inspires them to do so," said Tharus, locking the chronograph dial in place and then staring at Tiarnen.

Tiarnen tossed his fork back into the bowl. Not only did his father's unrealistic expectations cause him to lose his appetite, but even if they hadn't, there wasn't enough sea-spit in the province to get him through the rest of the slugs.

"What are we going to do about Sivakosha and her brass section?" asked Niera.

"I'm sure they will make a fine addition to the labour force in Kuldron," Tharus said callously.

"You're integrating the legionaries into our military. Why not the brass as well?" asked Tiarnen.

"You know exactly why."

Tiarnen bit his bottom lip for a few seconds.

"Niera, when I passed the orchestra in the bailey, I couldn't help but notice that our headcount looked a little thin."

"We'll manage," Niera said dismissively.

"How many active members do we have exactly, my Lead?" asked Tiarnen.

Niera huffed. "Seventy-six."

"Last I checked, the rules of engagement specifically state that a provincial orchestra must be comprised of one hundred members."

"Niera assured me that there are enough cadets to fill the vacant positions before we depart for Phrysbruck," said Tharus.

"None of whom will be ready for battle—especially one so decisive," said Tiarnen.

"What would you have us do, Maestro?" asked Niera.

"There are at least thirty proven Lydvenkian musicians just outside that door. We should fold them into the orchestra and begin rehearsals to see if they're capable of performing up to standard. If they do, we'll be able to face Maestro Phrygus at full strength. If they don't, we put them in the labour force, and our cadets are promoted as Niera suggested."

"Will the warsongs be affected by expanding the brass section?" asked Tharus, looking to Niera.

"Unfortunately, there's only one way to find out," said Niera.

"I'll consider it," said Tharus.

Frustrated that he didn't get an answer, Tiarnen pushed the bowl away and stood to his feet.

"Where are you going?" asked Niera.

"To *inspire*, apparently," said Tiarnen, stepping around the table and making his way out of the carriage.

Whomch!

Before Tiarnen even had the chance to close the door behind himself, Mikavnik's heavy iron foot had nearly crushed him.

"Maestro!" shouted a praetorian guard. "Forgive me, I should have warned you! Didn't expect this... thing... to get so close."

"Makes two of us," said Tiarnen, looking up to see Garod and Jasper still hard at work.

"Probably want to keep a bit of distance!" said Garod.

"Thanks for the warning! When do you think she'll be finished?"

"At this rate, probably mid-Novembra," said Garod, turning a socket wrench in the side of Mikavnik's neck.

"Of next year," added Jasper.

"If anyone can have her ready for Phrysbruck, it's you two," said Tiarnen, slipping in behind Mikavnik as she stomped ahead. With a safe enough distance between them, he looked back at the convoy, which was being followed by the orchestra and then the legion close behind. Spotting Kaleigh, he stopped walking to let the orchestra catch up and began marching with her.

"Nothing like a brisk morning walk to start the day," said Tiarnen.

Kaleigh glanced down at her boots. "I just need a few more blisters to make it perfect."

"One benefit of being on the island was that the enemy always came to us."

"I know that I always said that we needed to get you out of the lighthouse more often, but this wasn't exactly what I had in mind."

"My mistake," said Tiarnen, putting a hand to his chest. "I'll tell the praetor that we're turning around immediately."

They both shared a chuckle.

"How are you feeling?" asked Kaleigh.

"Has Sivakosha said anything?" he asked, ignoring the question.

"Not a word," she said, accepting that she wasn't going to get an answer from him.

Tiarnen knew Marifreth or Reina would have waited for Tharus to make his decision, but the campaign changed everything—even his father seemed to recognize the fact. "Something tells me we'll be getting the silent treatment from our new brass members for a while."

"*New brass members?*"

"*Shhhh*. It's not official yet."

Kaleigh lowered her voice. "When are you planning to tell the orchestra?"

"Soon enough. But since we're discussing promotions, did you have any questions as far as yours?"

"Only about a hundred."

Tiarnen laughed. "Don't worry. I did, too."

"In that case, I'm just a bit confused as far as the chain of command since you never really listened to Niera, so I didn't know if—"

"All orchestral commands should come from our Lead."

"And what about rehearsals?"

"What about them?" asked Tiarnen, a bit confused.

"Well," began Kaleigh, "you rarely attended, and Niera would normally lead the wind section herself—"

Tiarnen rubbed his brow.

"I'm sorry," said Kaleigh. "I didn't mean to make you feel as though—"

"No, you're right," admitted Tiarnen. "I really was rather awful at all of it."

"I wouldn't say *awful*, maybe just absent."

A soft smile crept onto his face. "And I would say that you are being far too kind, per usual."

"Don't give me that look," warned Kaleigh, shaking her head.

"What look?" said Tiarnen, smirking.

"Your *come-hither* look."

"I have no idea what you're talking about."

"One way or another, we have to figure it out!" shouted Coniel.

Tiarnen and Kaleigh both turned to see what Coniel's problem was.

"Figure what out?" asked Tiarnen, noticing that Coniel and Lachlan were in an argument.

"The Grand Tournament," said Coniel.

Kaleigh shook her head again. "I cannot believe you're worried about cards at a time like this.

"That's because you haven't seen the latest house standings," said Coniel.

"What about them?" asked Fiona.

"It seems my family is currently tied with the Ashbrooks here," said Lachlan.

"Why is that a problem?" asked Kaleigh.

"Normally, it wouldn't be," said Lachlan, "but given the current situation, it seems likely that the Grand Tournament will be the only event left this year that can award enough points to decide the premiership."

"As much as I hate to say this twice on the same day... Lachlan is right," said Tiarnen. "But, for now, we need to keep our focus and especially our pace!" Tiarnen looked at the drums. "Fiona, would you do us the honour and set a tempo?"

Fiona nodded and reached for her drumsticks, but after patting at her pockets, she realized they were either lost or forgotten. She turned to yell at Coniel for another pair, but she didn't have much to say since he was already holding a spare set in her face. Fiona snatched the sticks out of his hand, twirled them, and then struck her drum in rhythm. Coniel and the rest of the drum section quickly accompanied her, and together, they set a tempo that hastened the march.

For the next eight hours, the convoy continued along the Shoreway, and despite the captivating view of the ocean, Tiarnen had to try his best not to let his thoughts dwell on Lydia. Casual conversation with Kaleigh helped pass the time, but it was only when Tiarnen and Coniel started talking about the latest Shatter expansion that he was finally distracted enough to stop ruminating about what could be going wrong in the Conservatory.

"Wow, I just realized something," said Coniel.

"What's that?" asked Tiarnen.

"We'll get to see what Shatter is like in Lydvenko."

"I heard they use a Weapon card type," said Tiarnen.

"Why are you encouraging him?" asked Kaleigh.

Coniel's eyes widened with excitement. "What kinds of weapons?"

"I don't have a list on me," said Tiarnen. "But if I had to guess, claws would definitely be one of them."

"Tiarnen, look!" said Niera, hanging out of a carriage window and pointing excitedly at a massive plume of steam rising high into the dusky sky.

Emerging from a last bend in the trail, the convoy arrived at the coastal Caeladas Cliffs. Before them, a thick waterfall of molten lava poured out like a flaming tongue and plunged into the sea far below. Niera burst out of her carriage and ran over to join Tiarnen, who was already peering over the edge and taking in the wondrous sight of the Fire Tongue.

"Is this the end of the Scorched Road?" asked Niera.

"It is indeed," said Tharus.

"But where does it begin?" asked Niera.

"The heart of Kuldron."

Tiarnen and Niera both looked back to see that Tharus was now standing behind them.

"Mining the depths of Elvarok crater caused it to crack and its molten pour out," said Tharus.

Tiarnen looked past Tharus to see the wide road snaking into the distance. Its hard surface was smooth and glossy black, but the edges had hairline cracks that were glowing orange from the magma flowing beneath. The ground along either side was charred and split as though the road were some poisonous wound festering in the earth.

"Can the convoy really travel along this?" asked Tiarnen.

"The crust is more than thick enough," said Tharus.

Despite Tharus's assurance, Tiarnen carefully stepped onto the road. His boots immediately warmed but, to his relief, never grew too hot to bear. Niera, however, avoided walking altogether by climbing up Mikavnik and sitting in the crook of her neck.

Before long, the convoy had sloped down into Morlow Valley, where the Scorched Road kept slithering along the rolling lowlands. Tiarnen hopped onto the side of the galley carriage to look back and get a last look at Dorladdich. Knowing that it would be a very long time before he returned, Tiarnen tried putting the sight to memory, the now distant island glinting green against the dusky sky thanks to the sibling moons in a race to claim the night once more. The lighthouse was flashing in rhythm, a beacon he worked so hard to keep lit. He just never thought it might one day light *his* way back home. *Maybe it doesn't have to?* he thought. Tiarnen's stomach sank at the realization that this was his last chance to turn back. If he waited for the legion to gain enough distance, he could return to the city and stand against Tharus with Lydia. *But what of the other maestros? What of the Anthymn?* he wondered. Part of Tiarnen wanted to pull Niera off Mikavnik and tell her the truth. No, the less she knew, the better, he decided. Tiarnen had seen first-hand how Tharus valued life, even when it came to his own family. Niera's ignorance might be the one thing that would keep her innocent in Tharus's eyes should everything go wrong.

"Homesick already?" asked Niera, arriving with Mikavnik.

"Just wanted a last look, is all," said Tiarnen, forcing a smile.

Niera followed his gaze. "It already feels so far away."

"And how different it will be when we return."

"For the better," added Niera.

"For the better," echoed Tiarnen.

With the last of the sun setting behind them, the convoy contin-ued along the Scorched Road until they were deep within the mossy mounds of Morlow Valley. Even though the temperature was dropping fast, the natural heat rising from the road was keeping everyone quite warm. Tiarnen couldn't see a Dorladdian face that wasn't glistening with sweat, but he didn't seem to be experiencing the same effect. In fact, the maestro jacket was keeping him strangely cool. The Lydvenkians, as should have been expected, were marching along without any sign of discomfort or fatigue—their iron boots kicking up fiery orange sparks with each step.

"We make camp here!" announced Holgor.

Groans and sighs resounded as everyone stepped off the road and dropped their packs on the charred earth.

"Is it going to be this bloody hot the entire way?" asked Lachlan, pulling at his collar.

"No," said Holgor.

"Thank the Verse."

"It'll be far worse by the time we reach Kuldron."

Lachlan let out a dramatic moan.

"I heard the city is nothing but a cluster of desolate craters," said Fiona.

"And the Lydvenkians just throw any *unwanteds* into them," added Lachlan.

"I have no doubt that there are just as many rumours about us," said Tiarnen, looking over to Sivakosha.

"I vould rather not say," she said.

"You have to tell us at least one," said Tiarnen.

Sivakosha shook her head in refusal.

"Consider it an order."

"You..." began Sivakosha, already regretting her next words. "You drown children who cannot play music."

"Drown our own children?" blurted Kaleigh, horrified by the suggestion.

"That's clearly a lie," said Coniel. "Lachlan is proof."

"Why you insolent—" began Lachlan.

"He's kidding, Lachlan," said Tiarnen, staring at Coniel.

"If you say so," muttered Coniel.

Everyone but Tiarnen abruptly stood at attention as Tharus arrived.

"The convoy is secure," said Tharus. "Auberdine should have a pot on and your bowls full within the hour." He took Niera's hand as she hopped down from Mikavnik. "Come, dinner is already waiting in the common carriage."

"I'll be eating with the orchestra," said Tiarnen.

"Suit yourself." Tharus turned and led Niera away.

Cha-chak–cha-chak–cha-chak!

Hearing unexpected mechanical sounds behind him, Tiarnen turned around and saw that not only had the convoy formed a circle and thus a protective fortification for those residing inside, but the sides of the carriages themselves were also expanding to double their width.

Clink-clank-clunk!

"By the Verse! Who put all the pots on the top shelf?" yelled Auberdine.

"Come on," said Tiarnen, pointing to the galley carriage. "Let's give our chef a hand. We have a lot of mouths to feed!"

By the time Brathlún stole the night sky from his lunar sister, Auberdine—thanks to Tiarnen and Kaleigh's help—had filled almost every Dorladdian belly with warm clam chowder. Tiarnen never thought he would find himself working a food line, but the effort was well received by the legion who were more than a little taken aback by seeing their maestro wearing oven mitts and holding a ladle. Tiarnen knew that Auberdine had prepared a feast of maestro-appropriate, albeit revolting, fare for him, but he was more than willing to suffer a bit of malnourishment if it meant getting all the herbed clams and golden potatoes that were left at the bottom of the chowder pot.

To his surprise, there was enough for two bowls, and even though he would have happily taken on the challenge of devouring both, he looked across the road where Sivakosha was sitting with her brass, chewing on something that looked like shoe leather. Tiarnen knew he'd have to be careful about showing too much empathy, but he picked up a pair of spoons from the cutlery tray, tossed one into each bowl, and walked over to Sivakosha with them in hand.

Seeing that Tiarnen was approaching, Sivakosha stood to her feet while the brass seemed to hold their breath as though waiting to hear bad news.

"That doesn't look like it's meant to be supper," said Tiarnen, nodding to the strands of dried meat in their hands.

"Is last of rations," said Sivakosha.

"Dare I ask what it's made of?"

"*Chevrae.*"

Tiarnen shook his head in confusion.

"Goat," she explained.

"And that's all you have been eating since you reached our shore?" he asked.

"Khazlokov said ve vould only be fed if ve von," said Sivakosha.

"Of course he did," grumbled Tiarnen, offering Sivakosha a bowl.

She shook her head. "I cannot."

"I know it probably won't taste like anything you're used to," said Tiarnen, "but the broth is really good—"

"No, I cannot because there is not enough for all of them," said Sivakosha, glancing back at her brass.

Realizing he had put Sivakosha in an awkward position, Tiarnen reluctantly handed her his bowl as well. A bit taken aback by the unexpected generosity, she subtly nodded her head in thanks and then handed them both to the nearest brass members, who waved the rest of their comrades over.

"Vhat vill you do vith us?" asked Sivakosha, turning back to Tiarnen.

"I have decided to integrate you and your members into the orchestra."

Sivakosha was shocked by the news and stared at Tiarnen in silence.

"As such, you'll receive the usual perks—including regular meals, of course. I only ask for two things in return. One, you prove to be as capable as I hope you are. Two, you do not, in any way, sabotage our efforts to take Phrysbruck."

Sivakosha looked back to her brass, saw their desperate faces, and then nodded in agreement.

"Vhen vill ve receive our manuals?"

"Manuals?" asked Tiarnen.

"In Lydvenko, ve are self-taught, so ve have manuals for everything. Orchestra manual has all varsong positions, formations, terms, and military orders."

"Oh!" said Tiarnen, intrigued by the insight. "Well, we use a mentoring system that has a ranked progression of... you know what... Niera will be able to fill you in on all of the details tomorrow."

Sivakosha lowered her head. "As you vish, Maestro."

"Great," said Tiarnen. "Then, welcome to the Dorladdian military."

*

Camp didn't take long to set up; the army and orchestra pulled sleeping bags and personal tents from their backpacks, which proved simple enough to set up around the convoy. The Lydvenkians, however, were kept under close watch along the roadside with nothing as far as shelter or comfort, for that matter.

Tiarnen knew Sivakosha and the brass weren't about to complain that they had to use their instrument cases as pillows—especially since Lachlan was intentionally moaning loud enough about the flat spot in his down feather liner for everyone to hear.

Cla-chak.

Tiarnen pressed his thumb down on the door latch of his carriage and drew Mikavnik's gaze.

"General," said Tiarnen, opening the door.

"Mae-zzztro," replied Mikavnik.

"No one gets within ten metres of her," said Tiarnen, nodding to Niera's carriage. "Understood?"

"Under-zzztood," said Mikavnik.

Confident that Mikavnik would keep her word, Tiarnen stepped inside the candlelit coach to see that it was filled with opulent furnishings. To his right was a reclining leather lounge chair, ottoman, and oak side table, all with a closet door behind them. To his left was a twin bed with a merino wool comforter and down pillows. Opposite him was a large vanity table with a wide washing bowl, a pitcher of warm water, and a bar of soap, as well as folded clothes and plush towels.

Compared to the lighthouse, it was especially lavish and brought a twinge of guilt, given that Coniel and Kaleigh were sleeping a couple of centimetres above bare dirt. Tiarnen took off his maestro jacket and draped it over the chair—suddenly feeling as though he was now radiating heat. Ignoring the strange sensation, Tiarnen peeked inside the closet and saw that it was packed with new clothes, ranging from the finest linen shirts and pants from Christarts, as well as merino breeches and heavy wool socks. Without skipping a beat, he stripped down, washed off the sea salt and sand still stuck to his body, and then put on simple linen loungewear.

The bed was as comfy as it looked, although he couldn't help but think of where he might hang a hammock as he pulled the Maestro Diary from his jacket pocket and then climbed underneath the soft covers. Accepting that he would have to get used to riding in the lap of luxury, Tiarnen let his head sink into the down pillows and flipped to the last page he'd gotten to—his tired eyes glancing across the cursive handwriting.

Maestro Dorian IX, Julifra 28th, 294 ADA

An argument with my brother escalated into a physical altercation in the Conservatory today. I am making note of it because my resonance seemed to surge while I was defending myself. The sensation is difficult to describe... thoughts were much sharper... reflexes were far faster... emotions much stronger... Everything bloomed in a way I had never experienced before. There is no previous mention of it in the diary from what I have read and so will refer to it as "blooming" should it happen again.

By the time Tiarnen finished reading the entry, darkness had already begun to swirl and make his eyelids grow heavy—leaving him a last drowsy moment to guess that the next five days on the Scorched Road were about to melt together.

Chapter Twenty-Four
A FIRST DRAFT

Lydia had already been awake for over an hour but still couldn't bring herself to move from the cold stone floor of the Conservatory. Bones stiff and muscles sore, her bleary eyes watched the brooms sweep their way down the hall to the rhythm of Raghnall's snoring. At first, Lydia thought the thunderous cacophony might have been wind passing through Stormcaller's bowels, but when the major grumbled an order in between snorts, it became clear that he was asleep somewhere on the upper balcony behind her.

After Tiarnen left, Raghnall told Lydia to remain in the henge while he and Dansby decided what should be done with their new guest. As far as Lydia could remember, the captain hadn't agreed with a word the major said, but she must have fallen asleep from exhaustion since she didn't recall much of anything happening afterwards. Judging by the steep angle of the rays pouring in from the stained-glass windows, she guessed it was around mid-afternoon. Grimacing, she slowly sat up as the damp leather suit clung to her body like an oily film that made moving all the more uncomfortable. Lydia leaned back against the nearest henge pillar and shivered in agony at just how badly everything hurt. Pain might have been a very old friend, but even she had to admit that taking on two maestros, hollowing, and then nearly drowning had pushed her to her limit. As far as she was concerned, there was no recovering from her current state, not that she had any desire to.

Lydia tried to stand—keeping most of her weight against the henge pillar—and slowly rose to her feet. Head dizzy, she turned back and looked up to see Raghnall lying flat out on Stormcaller's bench. Lydia sneered at his apparent disregard for her presence and foolishness for leaving her unwatched, though she knew just as well as he did that she didn't pose much of a threat. Her tired eyes continued up to the maestro portraits and paused on Dorian I. Swallowing hard, she broke her forlorn gaze and then looked around for the captain but couldn't see him anywhere. However, the door to the nearest room on her right was wide open. She stumbled forward to peer inside and saw that not only were the floor-to-ceiling shelves crammed with instruments, but Windwalker was secured in its own protective alcove at the very back. A lancet window just above was casting light down upon the clarinet, giving it a hallowed glow. Then, in the heavy shadows to the left, Lydia recognized the shape of something even darker. To her disbelief, Ravenwing was resting in a nook between the alcove and shelves. Lydia's pulse quickened. She had assumed her harp was either lost or destroyed during battle, yet there it was waiting to be reunited. Instinct took over as she realized there might be a second chance to escape.

But what of Tiarnen?

The fact that she gave him a second thought shocked her. It wasn't in her nature anymore to take someone else into account, but after another look at Ravenwing, the moment of concern was burned away by bitterness and spite. Lydia fought her stiff muscles and traipsed over to the room while Raghnall's snoring drowned out the sound of her footsteps. She managed to reach the doorway but had to lean against the frame for a moment to catch her breath. Ravenwing was only ten yards away now, and she could see that even though it had somehow survived, much like herself, it wasn't without a few battle scars. Many of the feather-like tips were bent, there were deep gashes all over the wrought iron body, and several strings were broken. But it didn't matter. With Tiarnen so far away, nothing would be able to stop her once the renowned instrument was back in her hands. Steadying herself, Lydia hurried ahead and finally reached out for—

SHING!

Before she knew what happened, Lydia had fallen to the floor. Pain racked her once again. She thought she might have tripped but then felt something cutting into her right ankle. She rolled over and looked at her foot to see an incredibly thin ceramic chain looped around her ankle, leading all the way back to the henge. Lydia scrambled to sit up and clutched the chain in the hope of pulling it off, but the noose was too tight. Out of desperation, she tried to break it, but the effort only caused the chain to cut into her hands. Suddenly feeling like a trapped animal, she screamed in overwhelming frustration.

"Good morning to you as well," said Raghnall, yawning as he walked down the balcony stairs.

"Explain this!" demanded Lydia, pointing to the chain.

"Do I really need to?" he asked, nearing the doorway.

"I thought Tiarnen had already broken me out of prison," spat Lydia.

"Which is why you are now on parole." Raghnall nodded at the chain.

"You mean a leash."

"Don't worry. There's enough slack to allow you access to most of the instrumentry here, and the lavatory, of course," said Raghnall, pointing to the doorway directly opposite them.

"This vas not a part of the agreement!" she shouted.

"You agreed to compose the *Anthymn*. But the conditions under which you do are determined by me."

Lydia's eyes pierced into Raghnall like daggers, but the major paid no attention as he walked past her to pick up Ravenwing.

"Don't touch it!" spat Lydia, clawing at the shelves to pull herself up.

For what it's worth, I don't blame you for being tempted," said Raghnall, looking the instrument over. "If there's one thing I've always admired, it's the connection between a maestro and their instrument."

"Vhich is vhy it vill be impossible to perform the *Anthymn* vithout Ravenving."

"Then you better do everything possible to earn it back. Until then, I am sure we can find something here that will be adequate for a first draft." Raghnall set Ravenwing on the table and then began looking over the antique instruments.

"None of these vill last beyond a day."

"Good thing we have plenty to spare then," said Raghnall, grabbing a dusty recorder from the nearest shelf and holding it out for Lydia to take. Her expression quickly soured as she grabbed the recorder.

"Tiarnen might as vell have left me to die."

"That can still be arranged. Oh, speaking of timely demises, you should know that Khazlokov is dead."

"Dead? *How?*" asked Lydia.

"I wasn't there to see it myself, but after Tharus removed his time-piece, he apparently turned to dust right then and there."

Lydia just stared long at Raghnall, her face a strange mix of relief and concern. "Vhat... vhat did Tharus do with Khazlokov's chronograph?" she asked.

"As far as I know, he kept it for himself," said Raghnall, finding the specific question a little strange.

CLACK-CLACK!

The knock-lock echoed throughout the Conservatory and drew their attention. Raghnall quickly made his way into the hall, and Lydia followed to see Dansby arriving at the end of the long table.

"Afternoon, Captain," Raghnall said cheerfully.

"Major," replied Dansby, making no effort to hide his disgust at the sight of Lydia.

"How was the evening?" asked Raghnall.

"Quiet," said Dansby. "Unless you count a few brats moon-dipping in the kelp pools again."

"Think we can skip the report on that one." Raghnall chuckled forcefully to help lighten the mood.

"Night Rangers are checked in, and your Day Striders just began making their first round of the lower districts. I told them you would join them once you had the chance," said Dansby, handing Raghnall the skeleton key back.

"Appreciate it. Anyone ask where I was?"

Dansby shook his head.

"Good, if we can keep this rotation, I can't see why any suspicions will be raised," said Raghnall, reaching out to take the key from Dansby, but the captain's fixed focus on Lydia was preventing him from letting it go. "Why don't you wash up and get some rest, eh?"

Dansby didn't reply; he only kept staring at Lydia.

"Dansby..." said Raghnall, putting a hand on the captain's shoulder.

"Right, good idea." Dansby let go of the key and then made his way into the lounge.

"Do you really trust him around me?" asked Lydia.

"Do you really think I have a choice?" asked Raghnall.

"His grief vill consume—"

"He'll pull through," interrupted Raghnall, certainty in his voice.

"Time vill tell."

"I would think you might want to keep a bit more faith."

"Vhy is that?"

"Because if you're right, that chain will likely end up around your neck," warned Raghnall.

Lydia leered at the threat.

"Now, is there anything else you need?" asked Raghnall, pointing at the mess of cobwebbed stationary supplies on the table.

Lydia hobbled over to see that the unorganized piles of parchment were as dusty as they were creased, the chipped clay cups were filled with broken pencils and crumbled bits of rubbing eraser, and in between lay a few bent rulers and half a protractor. "As if this vasn't going to be difficult enough," she said. Lydia then noticed the torn warsong sheet music on the other side of the table, so she walked around and took a seat to read over them.

"Where are you going to start?" asked Raghnall.

"That has already been determined for me," said Lydia, flipping through the ragged sheet music until she found the pages with Tiarnen's handwriting all over them. She looked closer and analyzed his synestric melody.

"Still can't believe Tiarnen managed to figure it out," said Raghnall, a hint of pride in his voice.

"The question now is, can I replicate synestry on my own?"

"Verse willing, you'll find a way."

"Do me a small favour, Major?"

"That depends on what it is."

"Spare me your naive convictions," spat Lydia. She swiped over a cup to spill out the stationary supplies, found one of the only usable pencils, and began to make notes of her own around Tiarnen's.

*

The sky darkened behind Raghnall, and his attention was pulled from the shift roster to Dansby as the captain emerged from the lounge. Seeing the major sitting on the balcony steps, Dansby ignored Lydia's presence and made his way over.

"I could have finished that up," said Danby, nodding at the roster.

"Had to keep myself busy with something," said Raghnall.

"Any headway?" asked Dansby, rolling his eyes at Lydia.

"None that I can see yet," said Raghnall, making sure Lydia heard him.

"Forgive me if I don't share in your disappointment," said Lydia.

Raghnall handed the roster to Dansby, stood to his feet, marched over to Lydia, and spun her chair around to face him as though she were a disobedient toddler. "Let me make this perfectly clear; I will be writing a letter to Tiarnen on Saturday informing him of your progress. Should he receive news that there hasn't been any, it will not bode well for you."

"*Bode vell*," repeated Lydia, not bothering to hide her laughter. "Do you have any idea how many years vere spent perfecting *Pyrozikar*?"

"Probably hundreds of—" began Raghnall.

"Four hundred and eighty-two! And I expect somevhere around the same for this Dorladdian dribble given its similar length."

"Your point being?"

"It took nearly a millennium to compose these pages, and yet here you stand, threatening me after a few short hours!" shouted Lydia.

"Because we don't have a bloody millennium!" said Raghnall.

"Then all of this should be put to an end now," stated Dansby.

Raghnall stared long at Lydia while taking the captain's words into consideration. "Tiarnen risked everything to give you a second chance," he said. "Like it or not, you are in his debt, but if, at any point, I believe you are unwilling to repay his trust... your life will be forfeit."

"I assumed it already vas," said Lydia, turning her chair back to the table and focusing on the sheet music again.

Seeing that his point was made, Raghnall walked up the balcony stairs, grabbed his shield off the organ bench, and then made his way downstairs again. "Keep an eye on her," he muttered, handing the roster to the captain.

"Yes, sir," grumbled Dansby.

"I'll return with some supper," said Raghnall. "Craving anything?"

"Whatever you can find, that is cask strength."

"Noted," said Raghnall, walking past the table.

"And a change of clothes," added Lydia.

"Once you have a draft ready." The major continued to the door and cracked it open just a hair to make sure no one was outside, then quietly slipped out of the Conservatory.

CLACK-CLACK!

Alone together for the first time, Lydia pretended to read over the sheet music while wondering if Dansby might seize the opportunity to avenge Reina right then and there. A tense silence filled the air. Instead of attacking her, the captain trudged up the stairs and then into the study, where he flopped into the leather chair to review the shift roster. Confident that she wasn't about to be strangled just yet, Lydia returned to her analysis of Tiarnen's notes. After reading through all his creative approaches to making what should have been a last stand, she saw that there was real ingenuity, and so she continued adding insights of her own until there wasn't a blank space left on the torn pages.

CLACK-CLACK!

Lydia startled from the door opening again and whipped her head around to see Raghnall returning.

"I trust the evening was productive," he said, approaching with a crate under his arm.

"The evening?" asked Lydia, glancing up at the windows, which were now dim and shadowed against the night sky. She had completely lost track of the time.

"I'll take that as a *yes*," said Raghnall, setting the crate onto the table and pulling out two bottles of ale as well as two pewter thermoses as Dansby made his way down from the study. "Sorry to say I couldn't get my hands on something stronger, but I figured a bit of ale would go nicely with these mussels." Raghnall opened the thermoses—the air suddenly filling with the scent of garlic butter and the ocean—but

Dansby was already banging the edge of a bottle on the table to pop the cap off.

"Something tells me I von't be joining you two," said Lydia.

"Certainly not," said Raghnall. "But since I am in no position to let you starve just yet." The major reached into the bottom of the crate, pulled out a stack of sardine cans, and set them on the table in front of her.

Lydia picked a can up and sneered at Raghnall. "If this is your idea of a joke..."

Raghnall held out a can peeler for her to take. "Do you see me laughing?"

Lydia tossed the can into the sack and sat back down.

"Suit yourself," he said, setting the peeler onto the cans and then taking his meal to the lounge with Dansby.

As much as Lydia wanted to resist giving into Raghnall's insult forever, her growling stomach and light-headedness simply wouldn't let her. She grabbed the peeler, opened a can, scooped a fillet up with her fingers, and begrudgingly devoured it. Three cans emptied, she wiped her hands clean on some parchment and then returned to analyzing the sheet music. However, after a couple of minutes, she found her eyes becoming heavier and heavier until they began closing of their own accord. Accepting that nothing more could be done as far as the *Anthymn* nor her escape, she crossed her arms on the table and rested her head upon them.

*

Lydia had no desire to watch the brooms sweep away Tuesday morning as well. In fact, she was already in the lavatory and standing under the warm waterfall shower when dawn arrived. She wasn't one to indulge in lavish amenities, mostly because Lydvenko didn't have many of them, but the lemonwood soaps were lathering up nicely as she tried to scrub the foul sea stench out of her leathers. Soaked to the bone now, Lydia turned the water valve closed and stepped out of the shower. Steam rose off her body as she towelled off in front of the foggy mirror, trying to avoid her murky reflection. But after seeing how little was left of her thin, wet hair, Lydia couldn't help but look up and meet the eyes of what resembled a pallid cadaver. Staggering forward in disbelief, she wiped the fog off the mirror with her skeletal hand—only to meet the eyes of someone she no longer recognized.

"You vere so close," she muttered.

Disgust bubbled over into a rage that caused her fists to clench.

SMASH!

Lydia struck the mirror and cracked it.

"*Lydia?*" shouted Raghnall, his heavy footsteps fast approaching. The major barged into the Lavatory, ready for a fight, only to see she was sopping and staring silently at her fractured self in the mirror. "What are—oh—I didn't realize you were—" he stammered, realizing that Lydia had seen just how badly she had deteriorated since the battle. "If the pain is affecting your ability to compose, I could check the infirmary for something that might help—"

"Don't you have a roster to be filling out?" snapped Lydia. She turned, threw the towel onto the floor, and then walked past the major to leave the lavatory. Sitting back down at the long table, she picked up the sheet music and began reviewing her notes, but before she had the chance to distract herself, Raghnall was already looking over her shoulder and reading them aloud.

"Why do you need to *shape the melody into a core theme*?" asked Raghnall.

Lydia ignored him.

Raghnall yanked the page out of her hand and continued reading over it. "*Modulating between keys throughout Anthymn only option but effect is unknown.* Explain," he ordered.

Accepting that the major wasn't going to take her ongoing silence for an answer, Lydia glared back at him. "Dorladdian music is alvays in the key of D major, Lydvenkian is alvays in the key of F major."

"I'm quite aware, and Tiarnen clearly solved that problem already."

"For a single melody. But now I alone need to synestrize the entire *Anthymn* and define its effect."

"Have you figured out how?"

"I can potentially use Tiarnen's melody as a core theme and build the *Anthymn* around it, but that vill require testing several variations."

Raghnall stroked his beard. "What effects will the variations produce?"

"There's only one vay to find out," said Lydia, standing and grabbing the recorder as well as the music stand.

"Shouldn't we make preparations of some kind first?" asked Raghnall, following Lydia into the henge.

"You can hide behind one of the henge pillars if you like. Don't vorry. I von't tell the captain."

Raghnall scoffed and handed her the sheet music, then pulled his shield off his back.

"Suit yourself," said Lydia, putting the sheet music on the stand.

"What about you?" asked Raghnall, readying his shield.

"If everything goes vrong, I von't need to vorry."

"Why not?"

"Because I'll be splattered across the valls before it's over," said Lydia, wiping the mouthpiece of the recorder with her sleeve and then aligning her fingers on the tone holes.

Taking a shallow breath, she began the music with gentle, warm motifs from *Pyrozikar*; the spluttering figurations in between them, bringing the opening to life. Despite Ravenwing being a string instrument, Lydia seemed to have no issue playing the rudimentary recorder, but it, not to mention her weakened state, could only illuminate a sparse, flickering nebula of tawny-orange shards. Then, she played Tiarnen's melody and modulated into "Obrenthium"—the uplifting Dorladdian phrases dousing her anger and filling the nebula with an equal number of sage-green shards.

With a listless flourish, Lydia drew all the glittering glass into a vortex around herself, but the contrasting shards proved difficult to align. She watched as they repelled against each other, so she played harder in the hope that she could force them to merge. The rejection only grew stronger with each new shard that she illuminated, and those that accidentally touched released tiny bolts of static electricity.

Seeing now that she was about to lose control over her chaotic vortex entirely, Lydia flourished the recorder in panic and sent the shards above her to form the *Anthymn*'s core. She had intended to forge a sphere, but the shard's refusal to cooperate was making it far more complicated than anticipated. Growing frustrated, Lydia stabbed the shards into each other and forced them to form a partial sphere.

Despite the recorder's wooden body charring under Lydia's fingers, she pressed on, and ignited a ferocious sequence from "Pyrozikar." Rust-coloured shards spat from the instrument, which she quickly cast to fill in the gaps of the core. Hoping it would synestrize, Lydia flourished the last shard into the lattrice and watched as it partially fused—releasing a blast of kaleidoscopic light—only to break apart and fall to the floor in malformed clumps.

KATHUD!

Silence filled the Conservatory, and Raghnall stepped out from behind the henge. "Can't say I saw that coming," he said, cautiously walking over to get a closer look at the chunks of smouldering glass.

"Nor I." Lydia scowled at the nearly disintegrated recorder in her hands. "The lattrice is going to be a significant challenge."

"Changing your attunement seemed easy enough," observed Raghnall.

"It's not so difficult for a seasoned maestro. All you must do is abandon everything you stood for."

Dansby raised an eyebrow. "Lots of experience with betrayal, eh?"

"How many more variations do you think we'll need to test?" asked Raghnall.

"As many as it takes," said Lydia.

*

Wednesday afternoon brought nothing but frustration and crumpled parchment for Lydia. The repelling force of the shards was completely unexpected, and without Tiarnen there to help her control them, Lydia didn't know if she would be able to overcome what was proving to be a serious problem.

She spent every waking minute trying to compose a second variation, but it was fast becoming overly complex. With barely anything left of the recorder, Raghnall had no choice but to replace it with an equally common fiddle. There wasn't much to admire about the chipped body, though she did notice how the arch had been trimmed down, which would make it easier for her to perform some elements of the new variation on its steel strings. Still, Lydia kept glancing past it to stare at Ravenwing in the instrumentry, and even though her harp was only twenty or so metres away, it felt like a hundred leagues. Accepting that there was nothing to be done about it, Lydia tried to focus and finish the last few bars, but Dansby's return from his shift couldn't be ignored.

Judging by his stumbling, the captain had a few drinks while on patrol, which only made his boisterous rant about how the Roycrofts were bribing two patrolmen for favours all the more unbearable. However, one thing that did catch Lydia's ear was Dansby's mention of Executor Ignis asking why the major and captain didn't seem to be as attached at the hip as of late. Raghnall dismissed the comment and said that he would visit Ignis in the evening to quell any suspicions with an exceptionally long and boring explanation of their rotating shifts.

"I have a second variation ready," said Lydia, standing to her feet.

"Should we be excited or horrified?" asked Dansby.

Lydia pretended that she didn't hear the question and made her way into the henge with the major and captain, each taking position behind a pillar. She stacked the composition neatly on the music stand and then tucked the fiddle's rest as far as she could under her chin to put more of the instrument's weight on her shoulder so her hand could easily glide along the well-worn neck.

Lydia set the bow and began the *Anthymn* with motifs from "Pyrozikar," the spluttering figurations in between them coming to life. Despite the fiddle's sound being rather shallow, it was also clean and especially precise—which Lydia hoped would allow her better control over the shards.

Fragile glass ignited and leaped off the strings with each fiery motif, soaring through the air and forming a glittering coral nebula that began to slowly orbit her—this time, moving in an oval shape instead of the usual circle. Tiarnen's melody soon followed, and the fiddle squealed in pain. Realizing that playing Obrenthium had caused her to tense up and press the bow down too hard, Lydia eased off and let it sing once again to allow the viridian shards their chance to swoop into their own oval ellipsis. By any measure, trying to control a vortex with two independent yet intersecting paths was a recipe for disaster, but Lydia couldn't think of another way to try and arrange the shards, given their refusal to cooperate. Though controlling the double ellipse was awkward, it was proving somewhat successful—until two contrasting shards scraped along one another as they passed by.

ZZZAP!

A powerful bolt of static electricity erupted and licked one of the henge pillars, turning it black. Despite being surprised by the unexpected after-effect, Lydia pulled herself together and completed the upbeat Obrenthium sequence, which filled the second ellipse until the vortex had an equal amount of green and orange glass pulsating within it.

ZZZAP! ZZZAP! ZZZAP!

"Lydia?" asked Raghnall, deep concern in his voice.

"Stay there," she hissed. Seeing that she was about to completely lose control of her vortex, Lydia flourished the fiddle back and forth between the ellipses to cast them above her in a spiral, forcing many of the shards together and synestrizing most of the *Anthymn*'s spherical core.

Watching it fuse and crackle with unstable power, she illuminated searing motifs from "Pyrozikar" and arranged the vermillion-orange shards as a ring to form a mantle around the core. Modulating to Obrenthium again, she tried to add another layer of jade-green shards to the mantle and complete the lattrice, but the repelling force had grown too strong. The fiddle now burning and becoming brittle in her hands, Lydia flourished as hard as she could and tried to stab the last few shards into the mantle, but as they passed by each other, another static bolt erupted.

ZZZAP!

Instead of licking one of the henge pillars like before, it struck the core, causing it to fracture. The vortex disintegrated before her eyes, and Lydia let the fiddle fall to her side as the mantle came crashing to the floor like a broken chandelier.

KERSMASH!

She barely turned her head away before jagged splinters and blackened chunks whizzed past from the impact. After the moment of defeat passed and the dust finally settled, silence filled the air again.

"Still in one piece?" asked Raghnall, emerging from the pillar.

Lydia blew out a small flame on the bow hair. "So it vould seem."

"The bolts were unexpected," said Raghnall.

"Indeed, they vere," said Lydia, leaving the henge with a smile of satisfaction on her face.

*

Thursday morning was nothing but a long, exhausting argument between Lydia, Raghnall, and Dansby at the long table. The major had confiscated the fiddle, and what little faith he had in Lydia's intentions all but evaporated with the explosive finale of yesterday's performance.

"Neither of your variations have convinced me that we're any closer to proving the *Anthymn* will work," stated Raghnall. "If anything, they're showing us how much more dangerous it will become!"

"That is the risk ve agreed to take," said Lydia, rummaging through the pencil cups.

Raghnall pulled the cups out of her reach. "There's a difference between risk and *reckless*."

"Be that as it may, I still need to take vhat ve have learnt and use it to compose the first draft," said Lydia.

"First draft?" asked Raghnall. "I don't see how we could possibly be ready to—"

"But in order to do that," interrupted Lydia. "I'm going to need more than useless nubs and rubs." She tossed what little was left of her short pencil and crumbling gum eraser onto the table in frustration, only for the pencil to roll off the edge and across the floor. Following it, her gaze landed on the room on the other side of the hall—her eyes narrowing at the door, which was hanging off its broken hinges.

"Where are you going?" asked Raghnall.

Lydia ignored the question and continued towards the room.

"Stop!" said Dansby. "You don't have perm—"

Lydia grasped the tarnished door handle and pushed her way inside the room to see that every inch of it was in shambles. Nearly all the shelves lining the round walls had been torn down into piles on the floor and several burned tables were turned over. In the centre stood a stone plinth that came to a tiered point with hundreds of broken glass vials resting on each level.

"That's far enough!" said Raghnall, finally arriving behind her.

"Vhat happened here?" asked Lydia.

"Tharus. He destroyed the room shortly after the last warsong was written."

Lydia, noticing a glint of metal beneath one of the broken shelves by her feet, bent down and reached under to pull out a badly damaged fountain pen. "And just like him to leave the job unfinished," she said. Lydia looked over the delicately carved ceramic and wood body, which was cracked open. Tiny gears and rods were mangled inside, the nib bent beyond repair. "Ve need to find vhat's left of these pens."

"What use will that be?" asked Raghnall.

"If there are enough parts, I should be able to piece a new pen together," said Lydia, looking under more shelves.

After a few minutes of rummaging, Raghnall and Lydia found five more broken pens while Dansby did nothing to help.

"Tell me there are some ink vials still intact," said Lydia.

Raghnall walked around the stone plinth, carefully looking at the stacks of crushed ink vials. "Found one... make that two... and a third!"

"That vill have to do," said Lydia, leaving the room.

Arriving back at the table, she began stripping them of their cases as though she had done it a thousand times before.

"What makes these pens so special anyway?" asked Dansby.

"Accurate musical notations require many details that only these composition pens can produce," said Lydia.

"Like what?" asked Raghnall, setting the ink vials on the table beside her.

"Flourishing, as an example," said Lydia, grabbing a page of the "Pyrozikar" sheet music to show Raghnall and Dansby the incredibly fine lines above the notation. "The subtle thickness and length of every arc, curve, spiral, and dash tell a maestro vhen and how to flourish so that our lattrices are pieced together properly."

"Don't forget, we've had to endure your music—there's nothing subtle about it," jabbed Dansby.

Lydia took the parts, which were still in working condition from each composition pen, discarded what couldn't be saved, and then began piecing them back together. Before long, she was holding her hand out for Raghnall to give up the ink vials.

"Major, I vill be needing that ink."

"Not until I get some assurances," said Raghnall.

Lydia set the quill down. "Those being?"

"I don't care how you want to spin it; we got lucky yesterday," said Raghnall.

"Perhaps," admitted Lydia.

"So, if we are going to continue exploring uncharted waters, I want to, at the very least, know what direction we're headed."

"As I said before, I have to compose a first draft in order to answer that question."

"And I have an entire city to keep safe." Raghnall gazed at the ink in the vial.

"You can't have it both ways."

Raghnall looked up at her and crossed his arms in disagreement.

Seeing that the major wasn't willing to negotiate, Lydia tried to think of what she could do to appease him. "I suppose there is something ve could try," she said.

"I'm listening," said Raghnall.

"Each varsong was composed vith a specific effect in mind," said Lydia. "Pyrozikar, for example, uses themes that feel angry and resentful because it is supposed to cause desolation."

"You're saying that we should decide what the *Anthymn*'s effect will be first?" said Raghnall.

"If ve do, then I can compose to achieve it," said Lydia.

Raghnall looked at the ink vials in his hand. "Dorladdich, Lydvenko, Phrysbruck, *all* of the provinces... we have been at each other's throats for so long that there's barely anything left of us." His eyes went to Lydia. "I know Tiarnen dreams that the *Anthymn* might one day unite the provinces, but there might not be anything left of Chora by the time Tharus's campaign is over."

"What are you suggesting?" asked Dansby.

"We're here under the guise of a restoration effort. I can't think of a more noble effect for the *Anthymn* to have," said Raghnall.

"*Restoration*, it vill be then." Lydia held out her hand to Raghnall, who nodded in cautious agreement and then handed over the ink vials. She set them on the table except for one, which she slid into the rebuilt pen, closed the top, and then pressed down on the cap—

Clink!

A pin released inside and cracked the vial—ink filled the reservoir. Lydia grabbed a piece of blank parchment and ran the nib along it, leaving a smooth curve of wet onyx behind. "That should do nicely," she said.

For the rest of the afternoon and well into the late evening, Lydia composed tirelessly—only taking breaks from the meticulous flourishing details to inhale the last tin of sardines or berate herself for making notation mistakes. "No, that's too fast. It needs to build up right until the end," she hissed at herself, crumpling the parchment into a ball and tossing it onto the floor with the others. She grabbed another piece of parchment, rewrote the last page, and then blew on the ink to dry it quickly.

"Major," said Lydia, stacking the sheet music in order.

"Ready?" asked Raghnall, emerging from the lounge with Dansby. Lydia nodded.

"Grab a pillar, Captain," said Raghnall, walking to the henge and taking his usual position while Dansby stood behind the one on the right.

Lydia followed in and set her music on the stand. She slid the fiddle under her chin, set the bow, and opened, as usual, with "Pyrozikar." Honey-orange shards quickly formed a flaring nebula that, accompanied by a quick flourish, curved through the air to swoop around her and form a much tighter vortex than usual. Then, Lydia modulated into "Obrenthium" and illuminated another nebula of myrtle-green shards. The bow started to smoke, but Lydia paid no attention and flourished the Dorladdian shards to build a second outer vortex around her.

ZZZAP! ZZZAP! ZZZAP!

Just as she had hoped, static bolts erupted, but they did not lash at the pillars like before. Instead, they bounced between the two vortexes and made the shards glow even brighter.

"Major?" asked Dansby, unsure what to make of the light show.

"We hold!" ordered Raghnall.

Seeing that the major wasn't about to stop her just yet, Lydia flourished the fiddle to cast the shards in pairs—one from each vortex at a time—to build the lattrice just above herself. As each pairing fused into the next and formed the wreath-like core, it surged more and more with synestric power. Encouraged by the success thus far, she illuminated more searing motifs from "Pyrozikar" and arranged the topaz-orange shards around the wreath to build up its inner mantle. She modulated into "Obrenthium" again, finishing with undulating motifs that formed the outer mantle with juniper-green. Without missing a beat, Lydia flourished aggressively and closed the mantles around the core together.

KATHOOM!

A blast of wind and a pulse of prismatic light tore through the henge as the mantles interlinked and vibrated precariously. With a last flourish of the now smouldering instrument, Lydia raised her bow hand into the air, fused the mantle into the core, and synestrized.

HERAAAANG!

Half blinded, Raghnall stared in shock at Lydia's upper arm, which seemed to be trapped now in the *Anthymn*'s lattrice.

"By the Verse," he muttered.

The glass started to turn black and crumble—falling around Lydia into piles of ash along the glossy granite. In a matter of seconds, nothing remained of the lattrice, and she was left doubled over, clutching her hand.

"What happened?" asked Raghnall, emerging from the pillar. Lydia remained silent.

"She failed is what happened," said Dansby.

"Is that true?" asked Raghnall.

"You... tell... me," grunted Lydia, slowly sitting up to show Raghnall her arm.

Raghnall arrived at Lydia's side and saw what appeared to be a glass bracelet around her wrist. Slack-jawed, he kneeled and took a closer look at the green and orange synestrized shards that were still pulsating with resonant power.

"Is this what you were expecting?" asked Raghnall.

"No..." said Lydia, watching as the bracelet's light began to bleed into her veins—a surge of invigoration rushing through her body. "It is far better."

"What do we do now?" asked Raghnall.

"This is only a glimpse of vhat the *Anthymn* might become, the first piece of a much larger puzzle." Lydia stood up.

"Sounds like we're going to need more parchment," said Raghnall.

"No, the next draft vill have to be painted," said Lydia. "At full scale."

"I'm not sure where we can find canvas that big."

"Not to vorry." Lydia ran her hand along the pillar. "I believe ve already have."

"Is there any ink left in that pen of yours?" asked Raghnall, standing back to his feet.

"A little, vhy?"

"I have a letter to write."

Chapter Twenty-Five

HEART OF IRON

For better or worse, Niera had become much bossier now that there was another qualified Orchestra Lead among their ranks. While travelling along the Scorched Road, Tiarnen played a wide range of Dorladdian tavern tunes, even though Sivakosha and the brass were confused by his educational approach to their indoctrination. According to Sivakosha, as children, the Lydvenkians were provided training manuals and had to learn all the material on their own. Tiarnen couldn't wrap his head around how anyone could possibly excel without mentorship, but given what a formidable enemy Lydvenko had been, there was substantial proof that their education system worked quite well. Hearing the drinking ballads with new trumpets, trombones, and tubas was not only invigorating for Tiarnen—despite Niera chiding Sivakosha for missing a few notes—but the brass's ability to learn them so quickly also gave him hope that they might really become a permanent part of the orchestra.

Tiarnen glanced back at Niera to tell her the next tune but noticed how tired she looked. It wasn't her fault. The past few days had been a gruelling march for everyone. Unfortunately, there were more than a handful of legionaries who succumbed to their previous injuries and needed to turn back or simply collapsed on the side of the road. Niera, however, had never before come close to pushing herself physically like the journey had so far, and as much as she was trying to keep her chin up, Tiarnen could tell she was struggling this morning.

"My Lead!" said Tiarnen. "How about some refreshments before the next—"

"Maestro!" said a guard, approaching from the convoy.

"What is it?"

"A letter from Major Raghnall for you!" said the guard, holding an envelope out for Tiarnen.

"Oh, thank you." Tiarnen took the envelope, noticing it had already been torn open.

"Praetor Tharus is also requesting both yours and Miss Niera's presence up front with him," said the guard.

"Of course he is," muttered Tiarnen, taking a few steps away from Niera. He wasn't surprised that the letter had been opened since Holgor would undoubtedly be checking every piece of correspondence for critical information—whether it was intended to be read by him or not. Thankfully, the major had done a good job of choosing his words carefully and made the letter seem nothing more than a casual update as far as how the past few days back home had been. Nearing the end of it, Tiarnen worried that Raghnall might have hidden the real message all too well since he couldn't find a single hint regarding the *Anthymn* or Lydia anywhere. Until the very last line.

As you well know, I was skeptical about the restoration effort. However, I must now admit that we're making far better progress than anticipated.

Tiarnen's heart leaped at the news.

"What does it say?" asked Niera.

"Let's not keep the praetor waiting," said Tiarnen, folding up the letter and trying to hide his smile.

They began making their way to the front, but not without Mikavnik following, while Garod and Jasper continued making repairs. Her footsteps made the road tremor and announced their arrival to Tharus, who was riding on the chronosteed just ahead of the convoy horses.

"Ah, perfect timing," he said.

"Why is that?" asked Tiarnen, already wanting to get back to the orchestra.

Tharus pointed to the onyx hills ahead that sloped down into an endless valley of scorched earth. "Allow me to present Palenyon Valley."

Tiarnen focused and saw nothing but rolling volcanic barrens that seemed to go on forever; every metre appeared to have melted and ebbed over itself thousands of times over. In the distance, impact craters were scattered everywhere with raw iron ore boulders resting in the middle of them; some were the size of a fist while others were larger than Mikavnik, but all were covered to some degree with orange rust.

"It's so desolate," said Tiarnen.

"Lydvenko wasn't always like this," said Tharus. "Khazlokov's mechanical obsession inevitably brought ruin to Lydvenko. If left to his devices, all of Chora would have suffered the same fate."

"Do you think there are many more chronomechs like Mikavnik?" asked Niera, looking up at her bodyguard with pride.

"Difficult to say," said Tharus. "The first chronomechs were Colossus class or *Earth Movers* as many named them. They did everything from clearing forests, diverting rivers, and even moving mountains so the early cities could be built."

"They must have been enormous!" Niera's eyes widened with intrigue.

"And took half a century to build just one of them," said Tharus.

"So why have we never seen any?" asked Niera.

"After the key cities were established, the Colossuses no longer had a purpose and so began roaming Chora of their own accord—causing far more destruction than they were worth," said Tharus. "Most of them were eventually captured and disassembled; their parts and pieces were used to build the Titans, which were smaller and certainly much more reliable in comparison. These *Long Haulers* travelled along trade routes to deliver goods and supplies. '*Sure as a Titan's tempo,*' they would say. Unfortunately, after the war began, all of the routes were closed, and the Titans eventually found themselves rusting away in one of the countless chronomech graveyards throughout the provinces."

"But what about our new addition to the family?" asked Tiarnen. "Mikavnik definitely isn't a Colossus or a Titan."

"It is a Wraith class or *Blade Buster*," Tharus said with disdain. "They were designed specifically for combat but were also over complicated and prone to... behavioural issues."

"Remind you of anyone else we know?" Tiarnen glanced back at Niera.

"Mikavnik, they're being mean to me," said Niera.

Mikavnik immediately scooped Niera up and sat her in her nook.

"Two pearls in an oyster already," said Tiarnen.

"You only have yourself to blame," said Niera, patting the top of Mikavnik's helm.

"Maybe if the barons see that pair approaching, they will surrender Kuldron out of sheer intimidation," said Tiarnen.

"I want more than just surrender," said Tharus. "Inquisitor!"

Holgor, who was sitting beside the driver on the bench of the transmission carriage, looked up from his reports. "Yes, my Praetor!"

"How many gatemen are stationed at Elvarok crater?" asked Tharus.

Holgor quickly flipped back through his papers and pulled out the one he needed. "By our last count... there were only... six. However, I strongly suggest that we enter through Volomira crater instead as the main gate is significantly larger and would allow our forces—"

"Most of the legion will remain outside the city until called for," said Tharus.

"Of... of course... Praetor," said Holgor, glancing back at Tiarnen with a vexed look on his face.

*

Since that fateful night at the lighthouse with his mother, Tiarnen had always wanted to explore the provinces, but after a couple of hours of marching in Palenyon Valley, he was starting to seriously question that desire. Already missing Dorladdich's damp breeze, he looked up to the hazy sky; the sun peered back as a dim yellow globe. His respect for the Lydvenkians was growing by the minute; to endure under these harsh conditions day after day, let alone an entire lifetime, would surely make any Dorladdian welcome death. *Perhaps that is why the legion was always so eager to fight,* he thought.

"I can see Kuldron!" exclaimed Niera, pointing ahead.

Tiarnen squinted and looked to the horizon, where he saw seven massive craters, the rims of which were interlinked and protected by a jagged, rusted iron city wall.

"What in the Verse could have made craters that big?" asked Tiarnen.

"A meteor shower long ago, nothing more," Tharus said dismissively.

"Father, won't the barons see us coming?" asked Niera.

As though answering the pertinent question, a faint chime emitted from Khazlokov's chronometer. As though on cue, an explosion erupted from the furthest crater, belching smoke, ash, and rubble high into the air. Tiarnen watched in awe as the debris hurtled through the haze with glowing lava trailing behind.

"Take cov—" he began.

"Forward!" interrupted Tharus, kicking his heels into the chronosteed's rib actuators to make it walk faster.

"Protect the orchestra!" ordered Niera, bringing her knees to her chest as Mikavnik raised a hand overhead.

Hellfire rained around the convoy as the legion raised their shields in protection of the Dorladdian orchestra members, but Tiarnen couldn't help but notice that the Lydvenkians were seemingly unfazed by the pandemonium. Suddenly, a few frightened Dorladdians broke formation and scattered into the valley.

"Stay on the road!" yelled Davmir.

But it was too late. The straying legionaries were pulverized by some of the larger boulders before Tiarnen could echo the order. Stomach sinking at the gruesome sight, Tiarnen looked up to see if more debris was headed directly for the convoy, and to his surprise, none appeared to be. Davmir was right. Outside of a few small rocks pelting the roof of the caravan, everyone who kept to the Scorched Road didn't have a scratch to show for it. Kuldron, however, had now completely vanished in the rapidly expanding smoke and ash.

"That is going to make reaching the city a lot harder," said Tiarnen.

"And being seen from it nearly impossible," said Tharus.

Moments later, the convoy was enveloped by the approaching smog. Tiarnen's eyes began to water with irritation, and he couldn't help but cough from the overwhelming stench of rotten eggs. To make matters worse, the road had all but disappeared from sight—only the glowing orange cracks along it guiding the convoy through the last league until they finally reached the perimeter of Kuldron.

"Halt!" ordered Tharus.

Tiarnen looked west to see the opaque silhouette of Volomira crater. A narrow gate was carved deep into the side of the ridge. Six guards, three on either side, stood at the gate, Lydvenkian banners gently rippling in the putrid breeze above them.

"Looks like Holgor was right about the gatemen," said Tiarnen.

"Then you may take Sivakosha and her brass to dispose of them," said Tharus.

"Shouldn't I take Davmir and some clawmen instead?"

"It is too much of a risk. They could subdue you and alert the city."

"But Davmir gave his word—" began Tiarnen.

"Trust is earned, not given," said Tharus. "If Sivakosha betrays us, you will at least have a chance of making your way back here in one piece."

Tiarnen found it hard to argue the point.

"Oh, another thing, we need the gate opened first," said Tharus. "The gatemen should unlock it when they see their orchestra returning."

"And once it is opened?"

"Relieve them of their heads before the alarm can be sounded."

Knowing that there wasn't any other choice, Tiarnen looked to Niera, who was climbing down Mikavnik. "Can you grab my cloak from the carriage and then send Sivakosha with her brass up to the front?"

"Yes, Maestro," said Niera, vanishing into the smog.

"Davmir," said Tharus.

Davmir arrived to stand at Tiarnen's side. "Praetor."

"Do you know where the master control is for the labour district?" asked Tharus.

"I do," said Davmir.

"Then, once we are inside, I want you to take a Dorladdian squad and lock the entire district down. Under no circumstances are the provincials to be released until I give you the order. Understood?"

Davmir nodded in acknowledgement.

"What exactly is going on?" asked Tiarnen, still confused as to what the plan was.

"Kuldron comes to a grinding halt during these eruptions, so the provincials return to their burrows and rest until they're over," said Tharus, glancing back to see Niera returning with the brass and Tiarnen's cloak. "If we're lucky, all Davmir must do is pull down a few levers, and the entire city will be under our control before anyone has woken up."

"And if we're unlucky?" asked Tiarnen.

"The craters will be brimming with blood," said Tharus.

Still skeptical that it could really be so easy, Tiarnen took the cloak from his sister and put it on while explaining the plot to Sivakosha. The brass then surrounded him, and together, they made their way toward Volomira crater.

As they drew closer, Tiarnen couldn't help but marvel at the colossal iron wall. Seeing it now in detail, he could tell that it had not been made by hand but instead seemed to have accumulated naturally over time—as if a thousand years of molten iron had bubbled up and layered itself into a razor-sharp crown. Equally as interesting was the gateway itself since there was no door of any kind—just a long corridor through the crater rock that was blocked by hundreds of criss-crossing iron bars.

"Announce yourselves!" yelled a gateman.

"Sivakosha Ovamelik Bolgarin, First Bra—Orchestra Lead!" said Sivakosha.

As Tharus predicted, the gateman stood in shock at the sudden sight of the orchestra members.

"Open the gate!" ordered Sivakosha.

Two gatemen closest to a pair of large rotary combination locks spun around and began to turn the heavy dials in synchronous combination.

Tiarnen, his head low to protect his face, glanced up to see the four other gatemen cautiously approaching.

"Vhere is Praetor Khazlokov?" asked the first gatemen.

"And rest of legion?" asked the other.

"Ve vill explain everything to the barons once inside," said Sivakosha.

Tiarnen risked lifting his head a little further to see the gatemen making their last turn of the combination locks. He tried to think of a way to subdue all six without taking their lives, but there was just too much distance between them.

"Who is that vith you?" asked a gateman, looking through the orchestra and pointing at Tiarnen.

CLAK-CLAK-CLUNK!

"Vait!" ordered the first gateman. "Don't open the—"

But before the gateman could finish shouting his order, the jagged iron bars had already begun retracting to open a clear path down the corridor. Seeing now that there was a wolf among the sheep, the other four gatemen shoved the brass members out of the way and rushed for Tiarnen, who knew there was nothing else that could be done to stop them.

"Get down!" yelled Tiarnen.

VEEEERANG!

Just as the brass dropped to the ground, a single shard ignited from Darktide. In a streak of ivy-green light, it cut both of the lunging gatemen's heads clean off. Tiarnen flourished his piccolo and cast the shard at the other two beside the gate—their headless bodies falling limp just before they could sound the alarm. Standing silent, Tiarnen looked over the bloody scene and felt a strange sense of shame and nausea mixing into a cold sweat.

"Well done," said Tharus, arriving with Davmir and a squad of legionaries. "Now, come, I want to show your sister the palace."

As if walking down the narrow corridor while the sharp iron crossbars were still retracting wasn't foreboding enough, the walls were plastered with layer upon layer of Lydvenkian propaganda posters, most of which portrayed Khazlokov, Lydia, and the general, all standing tall in heroic poses with victorious battle scenes behind them. Truth be told, Tiarnen thought the design and print quality were rather impressive. Passing the last poster, he reached the end of the corridor to take in the full sight of Volomira crater.

He was genuinely at a loss for words as he looked upon what he assumed was the palace. It resembled a ten-story inverted pyramid of meshed iron that was suspended in the middle of the crater by three chain-link bridges. The enormous structure was underlit with flickering orange hues from the bubbling lava lake far below, which caused the concave walls of the crater to glitter with what he could only guess was some kind of mineral. The crater itself was divided into three sections, each with a towering relief sculpture of provincial men and women collectively holding the palace chains while their faces grimaced.

"On your way," said Tharus, pointing down the east ridgeway that led to the next crater.

Davmir signalled his squad of legionaries to follow him, and together they left.

"Inquisitor, you may hold here for now," said Tharus, dismounting from his chronosteed. "Once I return, we will secure the war offices and accommodations."

"Excellent, Praetor," said Holgor, bowing slightly.

Tharus held his hand out, and Niera immediately took it. Together, they stepped onto the chain-link suspension bridge with four praetorian guards following and began to cross it while Tiarnen and Sivakosha trailed just behind.

Although Tiarnen was used to the height of the bridge back home, looking down to see a lake of bubbling lava rather than foamy waves was far more nerve-racking. His eyes unconsciously darted ahead to focus on Tharus and Niera, who continued towards the open entrance. At first, Tiarnen found it strange that there were no guards preventing them access to the palace, but after finally entering and giving his eyes a moment to adjust to the dim light, he could see why: the iron mesh walls were moving and shifting into themselves. Where there was one doorway, suddenly two more appeared on either side and then there were none at all.

"This place is a labyrinth," said Niera.

"A deadly one at that if you don't know which way to go," said Tharus.

"I can lead us through—" began Sivakosha.

"No need," said Tharus, taking Niera's hand and leading her through a doorway as it began to close in on itself.

Sivakosha nodded for Tiarnen to follow. "Quickly."

Tiarnen hurried down the passage with everyone as it snaked. Despite the countless twists and turns, Tharus continued ahead as if he knew them by heart. Still, being able to partially see through the mesh ceiling, walls, and floor, only to see more ceilings, walls, and floors, was incredibly disorientating to Tiarnen—so much so that he ended up running face-first into a corner.

"Maestro?" asked Sivakosha.

"I'm fine," said Tiarnen, checking his nose for blood.

Pressing on, they made a last turn and finally entered the reception room. Hanging from the low ceiling and wrapping around the perimeter was a bright orange tapestry depicting Colossus mechs toppling mountains, Titan mechs carrying trees, and Wraith mechs battling each other. It was just as Tharus had described. In the middle stood a massive gear that looked to have been turned into a banquet table since it was hosting several platters of food.

Tiarnen didn't recognize any of the delicacies except a charred black goat—or a *chevrae,* as Sivakosha had called it—in the middle that was surrounded by baked snails which three men (all of whom were balding, pudgy, drenched in jewellery, and draped with embellished orange robes) were devouring while servants refilled their goblets from large decanters. Then, Tiarnen noticed a very old and pale-faced man dressed in similar attire to Ignis standing only a few feet away, ledgers in hand—his jaw now completely slack at the sight of the group's unexpected arrival. If Tiarnen had to guess, this was Executor Kizik.

"Certainly looks like a meal fit for a praetor, if I do say so myself," said Tharus.

A servant shrieked at the sight of him, dropped her decanter, which smashed on the metal floor, and ran down the doorway opposite in panic.

"I didn't think anyone was allowed to dine in the reception hall without Khazlokov being present." Tharus let go of Niera's hand and walked towards the men as though he owned the palace. "Not even you barons."

The barons flushed, eyes wide.

"If you are here..." said Baron Yavor, licking his iron lip piercings, which had tarnished his mouth black. "Then... Khazlokov must be—"

RIPPPPPPP!

Grabbing onto the soft fabric, Tharus tore the tapestry from its hooks in the ceiling. "Oh, please, don't let me stop you from enjoying the braklova. It looks delicious," he said, continuing to walk around the room with the tapestry tearing behind him.

"Should ve consider this our last meal then?" asked Baron Grensky, snorting through his pierced and blackened nose.

"That depends," said Tharus.

"On vhat, exactly?" asked Baron Ferotov, the adorable chevrae kid on his lap trying to bite at the iron studs in his ear.

"How many provincials you convince to work for me," said Tharus, pulling down the last inch of the tapestry and tossing it to the floor.

The barons laughed in defiant chorus.

"They vill die before putting pick to rock for Dorladdich," chortled Yavor.

"Then I see no reason to spare your lives after we leave." Tharus pointed to his guards to remove the barons.

"Vait," said Ferotov, brushing a guard's hand off his shoulder. "Vhere are you going?"

"Phrysbruck, naturally," said Tharus.

"And then?" asked Executor Kizik.

"Ah, there, you see," said Tharus. "That glimmer of intrigue in the eyes, the hope that there might be an opportunity to prosper—perhaps one far greater than Khazlokov could have ever offered you. Well, barons, I assure you, there is."

"Ve are listening," said Ferotov.

"Then I will keep it simple," said Tharus. "Kuldron will be Dorladdich's staging point for the invasion and occupation of Phrysbruck. Those who contribute to my victory will be rewarded beyond their wildest dreams. Those who attempt to stop me will be shown no mercy."

Grensky set the chevrae kid on the floor and then stood to meet with the other barons so they could discuss their decision. The kid noticed Tiarnen, tilted its head to the side with curiosity, and then hurried over. He had never seen a goat quite like it before: the little orange horns poking out of the top of its head sparkled brilliantly, and its rectangular pupils were just as vibrant. Even more strangely, it smelled like vanilla. Even Niera couldn't help but be a bit enchanted and knelt to scratch its chin.

"It's softer than a rabbit," she said.

The chevrae bleated warmly and pushed its chin into her nails.

"Ve accept your offer," said Grensky. "The provincials, however, vill be—"

"Awoken with a rousing performance by our maestro," said Tharus. "I have no doubt it will set the perfect tone for your speech."

"Speech? Vat speech?" asked Yavor.

"The one that you are about to write to win over every man, woman, and child," said Tharus.

"Vith respect, Praetor," said Kizik, finally mustering the nerve to speak. "Considering the circumstances, nothing could vin *all* of them over."

"You're right," said Tharus. "Given the prevailing fanaticism, I think it's fair to expect some losses. But if more than... let's say... ten thousand provincials choose to throw themselves into Indrilka crater rather than return to work, I can promise that one of you three will be joining them." Tharus pulled out a chair and took a seat at the table as the barons lost colour in their faces.

"And what am I to wake the province with, exactly?" asked Tiarnen.

"Maestro's choice," said Tharus, plucking a snail from a serving plate and stabbing into it with a fork.

"Is there somewhere I can go to prepare?"

"I can show you to the Maestro Chamber," said Sivakosha.

"Father, can I go?" asked Niera.

"As you wish." Tharus gestured for a guard to go with her.

After making their way down the adjacent hallway, it wasn't long before Tiarnen found himself standing in the Maestro Chamber. As far as accommodations went, the chamber was nothing compared to the Conservatory. In fact, it was rather austere; only a basic music stand and a side table to one side, a wardrobe and a small iron frame bed on the other. Tiarnen's eyes were instantly drawn to the countless orange roses that had grown behind the bed—they reached to the high ceiling and were long since dead—some of the wilted petals resting on the thin bed pillows and blanket, which appeared to have a loaf-sized lump in the middle.

"Cozy," said Tiarnen.

"Is every inch of this cursed place designed to be cruel?" asked Niera, running her finger over the sharp edges of a bedpost.

"Lydvenkians pride themselves on living in unforgiving conditions," said Tiarnen.

"Is true," said Sivakosha, a bit taken aback by the accurate insight.

"A lot of good it did you," said Niera.

"Something to be said for their resolve, though," said Tiarnen, seeing Sivakosha's jaw clenching.

"That sounds like admiration," said Niera.

"*Appreciation*. The short time I had with Lydia's songbook helped me better understand who they are."

"*Were*," said Niera, walking over to the bed and pulling back the thin wool blanket to reveal a barely there mattress and a startled feline.

HISSSS!

"Ahh!" yelled Niera, backing away from the bed.

The guard immediately leaped in between them—ready to throttle the hairless feline.

"Vait! Is just Persol!" said Sivakosha.

"*Persol?*" Tiarnen leaned in to get a closer look.

"Yes, is—vas Maestro Lydia's cat. She is very old."

"I'll say," said Tiarnen, unable to count the number of wrinkles.

HISS!

"Has lived in palace for centuries and kept maestros company. Also excellent at catching mice. Right, Persol?" Sivakosha leaned in and gave Persol a couple of pets on the top of her head, which she seemed to enjoy, given the light purring.

"Talk about a change in attitude," said Tiarnen.

"Only pet tvice, though, no more," said Sivakosha.

"Why only *twice*?"

"Pet three times and find out."

Tiarnen laughed and then nodded in agreement. "All right, two pets it is." He turned and met Persol's gleaming yellow eyes. "Looks like you and I will be spending some time together. But, just so you know, I prefer the left side of the bed."

Persol grumbled and then buried herself back under the blankets.

Tiarnen continued looking over the chamber and saw a massive tree along the far wall behind him that seemed to be interwoven with portraits at the ends of the branches. "What is this?" he asked.

"Maestro family tree," said Sivakosha.

Tiarnen approached it and knelt to look closer at the base of the trunk, which bore a stained-glass portrait of a beautiful young woman, presumably in her early twenties, with high cheekbones and a full head of long orange hair that was parted down the middle. She was wearing a spiked orange leather maestro jacket that had two small pins on the left breast; one was the Lydvenkian crest, and the other was the numeral: *I.* At the bottom of the portrait, a banner read: *Lydia the First.* Tiarnen continued up the trunk and slowly rose to his feet with each generation as they branched off.

"Sixty-Third... Sixty-Fourth... Sixty..." said Tiarnen. His voice trailed off; he couldn't find Lydia's portrait anywhere. "Where is *Lydia the Sixty-Fifth*?"

Sivakosha walked over to the tree and pointed to a portrait with no connection to any of the branches.

"Why is she on her own?" asked Tiarnen.

"Is not from any of these families," said Sivakosha.

"How did she become maestro, then?"

"Killed sixty-fourth herself to take title."

"That explains the scars."

"No, vas scarred before becoming maestro."

"*Before?*" said Tiarnen, surprised by the news, "But how?"

"No one vas told."

"If we're about done with the history lesson, can we please decide what song we are playing?" asked Niera, leaning against the wardrobe with her arms crossed.

"We have to remember that whatever song we choose will set the tone for the barons' speech," said Tiarnen.

"Then it should be a warsong," said Niera.

Grumbling resounded from under the covers.

"I agree with Persol," said Tiarnen. "The provincials will think they are under attack and likely riot."

"Playing something familiar might lessen shock of vaking up to invasion," said Sivakosha.

"The only way to do that would be to play something Lydvenkian," said Niera.

"Great idea," said Tiarnen.

"That wasn't a suggestion."

"Nonetheless, it might be our best option."

Niera shook her head. "I refuse to. And so will the rest of the orchestra—present company excluded."

"Good, that saves me from having to explain why I'll only be needing Sivakosha and the brass."

"You are making this far more difficult than it has to be!" spat Niera.

"That's rich coming from you," said Tiarnen.

Seething, Niera waved at the guard, and together, they left the chamber.

"Maestro, if I may?" asked Sivakosha.

"Go ahead."

"Provincials have many simple vork songs, like ones ve learnt vith you on Scorched Road. It vill not be hard to teach you most popular one."

Tiarnen nodded in agreement but then fell silent for a moment.

"Is something vrong?" asked Sivakosha.

"Do you think we'll lose many families?" asked Tiarnen.

"Hard to say," admitted Sivakosha. "Here, blood does not mean much."

"What does?"

"Brands," said Sivakosha, pulling her collar to the side to show three small symbols seared into her collarbone.

Tiarnen recognized the first one; it was the crest of Lydvenko. The second was three sets of double digits, which were likely her birthday. The third looked to be Ravenwing.

"So you really don't know who your parents are?" asked Tiarnen.

"No," said Sivakosha. "Whoever has same brands is brother or sister and must vork together to keep Lydvenko strong."

"What happens if you can't work?"

"Even if sick or injured, ve must still try or be punished."

"And your elders?"

"They sacrifice themselves so they are not burden on province."

"Well, hopefully, the barons can convince everyone that Lydvenko has become stronger now," said Tiarnen, swallowing hard. He realized that he was trapped; the news of the Anthymn showing genuine potential meant that there was no choice but to complete the mission—he just didn't yet know how many lives it would cost to do so.

"Like us, as long as provincials are promised a future most vill fight for it," said Sivakosha.

"Then let's get started," said Tiarnen, pulling Darktide from his back pocket.

*

Ding... Ding... Ding!

Khazlokov's chronograph chimed as a warm breeze picked up around Tiarnen, Tharus, Niera, Davmir, the barons, and the brass, who were all standing on a large metal platform at the end of an iron peninsula that reached into the middle of Indrilka crater. Tiarnen glanced over his shoulder to see Holgor, Mikavnik, and most of the Dorladdian army standing ready at the heel of the peninsula, waiting for pandemonium to ensue. A gust of sweltering wind dispersed the haze to reveal Kuldron's immense labour district. If Tiarnen had to guess, Indrilka was at least three times the size of Volomira, and he could now see why it was chosen to house the province's entire workforce; there had to be over a hundred thousand gated communal burrows carved into three tiers along the crater wall, and outside of every gate sat countless leather work boots.

"How many provincials are inside each burrow?" asked Tiarnen, staggered by what he was seeing.

"A hundred or so," said Baron Grensky, tightening a bolt on the strange-looking staff in his hand.

"Ve can fit more in child burrows," said Baron Ferotov, as if it were an achievement.

Suddenly feeling sick at the thought of nearly a million people living in such close quarters, Tiarnen stepped to the very edge of the platform to get a better look inside one of the burrows, but the shadows were far too heavy. Further down the crater wall, he noticed movement. What Tiarnen thought to be a rocky outcropping just above the molten was instead a ringed cluster of subspecies he had never seen before. They appeared to be about his size, covered from head to toe in dark orange scales and had long tails which were curled around their eyes as they slept. Completely intrigued, he unconsciously leaned over the platform to get a better look.

"Careful, Maestro," said Sivakosha.

The warning pulled Tiarnen from his bewilderment.

"What are those?" he asked.

"Pavolkins," said Sivakosha. "They love the heat so vork near molten to skim for minerals."

Ding... Ding... Ding!

"It is time," said Tharus.

"Sivakosha, will you do the honours?" asked Tiarnen.

Sivakosha and her brass formed a semi-circle at the front of the platform, readied their instruments, and began to play "Ulavolet." She had offered Tiarnen a wide range of songs to learn in the Maestro Chamber, but he chose "Ulavolet" after learning that elderly women traditionally sang it to calm children after they joined their work group.

As Sivakosha and the brass played the soothing intro, Tiarnen saw the first sign of movement in one of the communal cells: a child pressing her dirty face against the bars of the door. It took her a moment to figure out where the music was coming from, but once she did, her eyes grew wide with excitement. Shortly after, each conciliatory note seemed to conjure a hundred more faces until every provincial was eventually staring in shock at what was left of their orchestra.

Applause, cheering, and singing reverberated throughout the crater—even Tiarnen couldn't help but smile as they sang.

We live together
Fire raging in our hearts
We work together
Ore piling in our carts

We fight together
Picks strike and whips bite
We bleed together
Strike

When Tiarnen and Sivakosha were rehearsing earlier, they agreed that she and the brass would play the intro and first verse to put the labourers at ease—then he would step in to begin the chorus and reveal the truth of what had happened to them. A pit growing in his stomach, Tiarnen drew Darktide as the brass faded, and he began the chorus to announce himself to Lydvenko.

Tears will fall
The picks dig deeper

Embrace our cause
We sweat together
Embrace our cause
We eat together
We dream together
We sing together
Embrace our cause
We sleep together
Embrace our cause

Part of Tiarnen was hoping, knowing it was naive at best, that they might give him the chance to prove that not all was lost. Unfortunately, it only took a moment before the provincials realized it wasn't Maestro Lydia standing before them. Their confusion swiftly turned to outrage. Tiarnen played on, but even with the brass in full support, not much of their performance could be heard over the shrieks of terror and incoherent, rage-filled screams.

We live together
Fire raging in our hearts
We work together

Ore piling in our carts

We fight together
Picks strike and whips bite
We bleed together

Tiarnen watched in concern as, one by one, the children were pulled away from the cell bars—their scared faces and voices vanishing into the shadows only to be replaced by snarling adults who were now striking at the door locks with their mining tools or throwing them in hope of hitting him. He'd had enough. Unwilling to put the children at further risk, Tiarnen closed his eyes and let his resonance spark the last few notes of the final verse.

Strike, strike, strike, strike, strike!

VEEEEERAAAAAAAANG!

Three shards illuminated with vibrant ivy-green light, and Tiarnen flourished them high into the air. Together, they swirled and spun in a tight spiral until they reached the top of the crater and collided. A vivid flash erupted from the explosion and startled the provincials into silence.

"That would be your cue, barons," said Tharus.

The barons stepped to the front of the platform, and Grensky put the base of his amplistaff into a slot in the platform floor.

"Lydvenko! Fear not, for our revolution has begun!" said Grensky, the large brass cone at the top of the amplistaff increasing the strength of his voice a hundred-fold. "When you voke today, it vas not under the long shadow of Khazlokov but in the light of Praetor Tharus!"

The news did not go over well. Many provincials were screaming louder than ever as well as throwing everything they could find out of their burrows. Fortunately, none of the cups, bowls, or boots had any chance of striking the platform—it all simply fell into the bottom of the crater, where it vanished with a puff of smoke after touching the bubbling magma.

"Dorladdich has defeated us!" continued Grensky. "Mercifully, they are not bringing annihilation but salvation—an opportunity we could have never before dreamed of receiving!" He took a step back so that Ferotov could take his place at the amplistaff.

"The opportunity is that of transformation," said Ferotov. "One that will shape us into the new province of *Niervalia*!"

Tiarnen's mouth hung open in shock at what he just heard. *Did Father seriously rename Lydvenko after her?* he thought. He looked at Niera, who had a satisfied smile on her face. Then, the sudden cacophony of metal banging drew his attention to the burrows again, where he saw many men and women striking their heads violently against the bars in protest.

"Like you are now, I found myself asking how can ve possibly repay such a priceless gift?" asked Ferotov. "I heard of how Davmir swore to serve our new legion and so vas bonded." Ferotov pointed to the green fabric around Davmir's arm. "Next, I heard of how Sivakosha swore to serve in our new orchestra and so vas bonded." Ferotov pointed at the same material around Sivakosha's arm. "Ve too must swear ourselves by vorking harder than ever before. If ve do, all helonists, anvilmars, and minoroks vill become heroes of Niervalia so that our bonds may be received."

Three praetorian guards walked up to the barons and tied matching green bonds around their right arms. Baron Yavor then stepped up to the amplistaff.

"Ten veeks!" said Yavor. "That is all ve have to prepare supplies and armaments for our assault on Phrysbruck! Ever have ve tried to seize the Tantalis. Ever have ve failed. But should ve all bond together just as

Praetor Tharus believes ve can, Phrysbruck vill finally be ours! Now, I ask you, are you ready to be heroes of Niervalia?"

Davmir turned to a small control panel on the platform railing, pulled a short lever down, and unlocked the labour district.

CLUNK... CLUNK... CLUNK!

Silence filled every inch of the crater... and then... battle cries reverberated as the labourers poured out of their cells and ran across the tiered walkways with mining picks and shovels in hand. By Tiarnen's guess, there were a thousand of them, maybe more, wrapping around the crater towards the platform.

"Defend the praetor!" shouted a guard.

"There is no need," said Tharus, waving the protection off.

The fact that Tharus and the barons were remaining so calm about the impending attack worried Tiarnen even more. But wait they did as the horde continued to rush closer—some of them even clambering over each other in the hope of being the first to draw their usurper's blood. Out of the corner of his eye, he saw Tharus casually step beside Davmir to reach the control panel. His heart sank as Tharus reached for one of the many levers just as the first few labourers were about to reach them.

SHUNK!

Tharus pulled the lever down, and the walkways fell out from underneath the protesters. Tiarnen turned away as the screams of horror faded with their doomed descent.

"By the Verse," he muttered.

Without a second thought, Tharus pushed the lever back up to raise the walkways and lock them back into place.

Ding-ding... Ding-ding... Ding-ding

Once again, Khazlokov's chronograph chimed.

"Niera, call them," said Tharus, checking the dial.

Niera walked to the amplistaff with her head held high. "Helonists! You have been called!" she said.

It took a moment, but the snail farmers slowly stepped out of their cells. They were dressed in rags while carrying a large bucket and long hooked stave.

"Anvilmars! You have been called!" said Niera.

Another moment passed, and then the blacksmiths emerged from their cells, wearing thick leather coveralls and holding a heavy hammer and prongs.

"Minaroks! You have been called!" said Niera.

Tiarnen expected most of the now Niervalian labour force to emerge, but it was still a sight to behold as a wave of emaciated, dirty, branded bodies filled all three of the tiered walkways with pickaxes and shovels in hand. Before he could fully take in the shocking sight of an entire province standing ready to begin their workday, a vibration began running through the platform.

Klack-klack... Klack-Klack... Klack-KLACK... KLACK-KLACK!

Tiarnen looked back to the northern ridgeway, where three chrono-trains were arriving at breakneck speed. He would have given anything to see the look on Garod's face as the mighty trains shot along the gleaming rails and then curved like cast-iron snakes around the stone walls of the crater.

After coming to a screeching halt at their respective stations, it took but a minute before the provincials had trundled aboard one of the numerous passenger cars. With the walkways now empty, the conductors pulled on chains hanging from the roof of their cabins, and the trains lurched forward. Tiarnen watched as they wrapped around the other side of the crater and couldn't help but worry that Dorladdich's heart would soon be made of iron.

Chapter Twenty-Six

A DIVISIVE DEPARTURE

CHUK-CHUK

Much like the rest of Kuldron, what was Khazlokov's private train had become Tharus's. For all of Octavora, Tiarnen, and Niera had been taking the Praetavain through the city every day to meet the orchestra for rehearsals.

Closely resembling the palace as far as being a marvel of meshed ironwork, countless bars wove together to form the train's structure and then spiralled inwards, creating a rigid framework of furnishings that ran down both sides of the passenger car. On the right, Tharus and Holgor sat across from each other in cushioned chairs while Executor Kizik and six praetorian guards stood ready at their side. On the left, the barons were huddled side by side on a bench, whispering while sipping on their tea. In the middle, the ends of the ironwork met and formed an oval table that was hosting a small banquet of Lydvenkian breakfast dishes. Tiarnen assumed they smelled delicious, but the warm breeze blowing through the thousands of tiny gaps in the compartment's structure obscured it with the strong smell of eggy sulphur from Zhelavos crater. Eyes watering, he turned the page of the Maestro Diary to read a couple more entries.

Maestro Dorian XV, Decembra 22nd, 858 ADA

Due to my most recent battle against Maestro Phrygus XIV, a new maestro jacket had to be made. Given that winter is already upon us, I am having the tailors at Christarts add an "all weather" layer to better shield myself and any future maestros from the elements. In addition, I am also updating what has been a long legacy of rather drab fashion choices by my predecessors with a bit of glow-thread embroidery.

Maestro Dorian XV, Janura 3rd, 859 ADA

The whistle weave responds very well to whistling.

"More tea, Maestro?"

The question broke Tiarnen from the diary and made him look up at a young servant girl who was holding a cast-iron teapot.

CHUK-CHUK

"Yes, thank you," he yawned, holding out his ornate cup so she could more easily refill it. As she did, the train rocked, but her practised hands countered the movement so perfectly that there wasn't a single drop spilled.

CHUK-CHUK

"Conductor! Vatch our speed!" yelled Yavor, shaking tea off his hand.

The conductor, a frail old man dressed in ragged, oil-stained coveralls, frantically pulled one of the many control levers down in his open cab to reduce the speed of the regal Praetavain. "Apologies, Baron! Easing throttle now!"

CHUK-CHUK

"May I ask you a question?" inquired Tiarnen, trying to breathe through his mouth.

"Of course, Maestro," said the servant.

"Is there any chance we could make the tea stronger?"

"I vill double leaves for next pot." She bowed her head and then turned to Niera, who was sitting on the padded bench beside Tiarnen.

"You might as well just put a straw in it for him, too," added Niera, checking the new collar around the chevrae's neck.

Tiarnen rolled his eyes and gulped half of the tea back. Though the black brew reminded him of ripe berries and fragrant roses, he still would have traded it in a heartbeat for a creamy Loch'd and Loaded. The chevrae bleated and drew his attention. "Seems like someone has made a new friend," he said.

"Father mentioned that a chevrae is worth as much as a corsair's monthly haul," said Niera, proudly.

"I was talking to the kid," said Tiarnen, chuckling and then taking another sip. "But I can see why given how cute the damn thing is." He reached out to pet its soft fur only to have his hand slapped away by Niera.

"She was just groomed. Apparently, they have four stomachs and only eat once every twelve weeks."

"*Twelve weeks?*" The thought suddenly made him very hungry. "What do they feed on?"

"According to Baron Yavor, a rare type of grass high in the mountains."

"Well, hopefully, there is something a bit more appetizing at the breakfast table this morning."

He stood up, arching his sore back for a moment—thanks to the incredibly uncomfortable bed in the Maestro Chamber—and then walked over to the breakfast table, the soles of his boots sticking to the floor from the glue spots that were left behind after Tharus had the orange carpet ripped up. Tiarnen was greeted by large bowls of baked snails and goat seven ways: bacon, sausage, fried liver, marrow, crumbled cheese, yogurt, and whipped cream with blackberries.

All of it looked delicious, but he was still stuffed to the gills from yet another putrid breakfast that Auberdine had forced upon him only an hour ago. As much as he knew that keeping his strength and resonance up was crucial, Tiarnen would have happily traded a few eel hearts for some sausage if it meant losing a bit of speed in his step. Unwilling to leave the table empty-handed, he snatched a handful of blackberries and then walked over to Davmir, who was standing at one of the many windows and midway through a yawn.

"Couldn't agree more," said Tiarnen, popping a blackberry into his mouth.

"Maestro, forgive me. I didn't mean anything by—" began Davmir.

"It's all right," said Tiarnen. "You're not the only one struggling with these early mornings. In fact, I'm usually going to bed around this time in Dorladdich." He stepped closer to the window and took in the sight of the hazy morning light, cutting a sharp line through the heavy shadows in Zhelavos crater. "Still, this view alone has made the past month of bleary trips to rehearsal worthwhile."

Tiarnen looked over the edge of the window and down into the crater. He saw thousands of provincials working far below—his stomach sinking a little as he watched them standing on the tiered walkways, wearing nothing but rags and striking at ore veins in the crater wall with their pickaxes. At the very bottom, the pavolkins were skimming the surface of the molten with large ladles, their long tails wrapped around metal hooks which had been secured into the crater wall.

"How are the other brigarchs treating you," asked Tiarnen, looking back to Davmir.

"As vell as can be expected," said Davmir, forcing a smile.

"That bad, huh?" asked Tiarnen, popping another blackberry into his mouth.

Davmir glanced at the barons. "I am in no position to complain," he whispered.

"You didn't exactly sign up to be paraded around the city with us every day, either."

"It is a pleasure to serve Niervalia in any vay I can."

"I heard from Holgor that some of the labourers formed a small rebellion and have been attacking the railway."

Davmir nodded. "Some resistance vas to be expected. They are hiding in crater fissures, but I am vorking hard to stamp out quickly."

"Wait, you're leading the mission?" asked Tiarnen, a mix of disgust and confusion making him wonder who would have told Davmir to hunt down his own people.

"Praetor said I vould be made Third Brigarch if I completed extermination."

"Of course he did," Tiarnen muttered bitterly.

"Entering Olienovok tunnel!" announced the conductor.

Shortly after, the train descended into darkness, the musty scent of warm rock replacing the sulphur. Then, the subterranean tunnel opened again to a vast cavern, and the train announced itself.

Clang-clang—clang-clang-clang—clang-clang—clang!

Tiarnen didn't understand the exact mechanics, but he overheard Executor Kizik explaining to Tharus that the rail ties were notched to produce the chimes. Each train had its own unique melody so that anyone waiting at a station would know which one was arriving. The Praetavain, however, was at least twice as loud as the rest.

Flickering torchlight revealed a complex network of smaller railways on either side of the train with hundreds of mining carts speeding along them. As Tiarnen watched them pass by, some looked to be filled with chunks of ore, coal, and glittering orange sunstones. Thanks to Garod, he had learnt that Kuldron's rail system was powered by two large complications that operated in tandem at either end of the city.

SHHHAAAAACHUK-CHUK-CHUK!

Tiarnen jerked back as another train passed within inches of the Praetavain. Normally, he would have seen passenger cars full of provincials blurring past, but this time it was his own image. Painted murals of Maestro Dorian standing in a ridiculous hero pose with the words *We work to win!* at his feet. It was more than enough to make Tiarnen cringe. As if the blatant propaganda wasn't embarrassing enough, his mural alternated between one of Niera standing elegantly with the orchestra and then another of Davmir holding the Dorladdian banner. To make sure all of the provincials saw the posters, the barons had them placed on the passenger and food trains.

Seeing how the provincials ate was probably one of the most depressing things Tiarnen had ever witnessed. The trains would arrive at the burrows once in the evening—each of the cars shaped like a trough that was filled with a type of warm soupy slop. Apparently, the top of the slop was covered in baked snails that were rich in nutrients, so when the burrow doors opened, the provincials fought with everything they had to reach the troughs first. This was, of course, the intention since the barons only wanted the strongest to thrive and transfer into the military, while the weakest were left with the scraps that remained, if not left for dead after being trampled. Thankfully, the children didn't have to endure dinner by combat each day and merely had to wait in line.

After the last flash of his face finally passed, Tiarnen became mesmerized by the view of the cavern and suddenly felt self-conscious at how surreal it was being in Kuldron.

"Maestro! If you would be so kind as to join us?" asked Holgor.

Tiarnen walked over to Holgor, who was looking over a large map of the Niervalian and Phrygian border with Tharus. There were three battlefields marked, but the northern one, titled *Galvalok*, appeared to be in the middle of a large glacier that was crossed off.

"We were just discussing the strike plan for Phrysbruck," said Holgor.

"As I was saying," said Tharus, "winter will be upon us in under two months, and given that Praetor Sturm is pulling most of his forces out of the Lurvask and Urvensk battlefields, he is no doubt preparing for our arrival."

"If that's the case, shouldn't we wait until the spring to attack?" asked Tiarnen.

"The longer we give Sturm, the harder it will be to breach the Tantalis," said Tharus. "Besides, late autumn always brings strong northern winds, which will put his otherwise formidable squalls at a disadvantage."

"My latest report says that Major Svante has just over a hundred in his air force," added Holgor. "If we keep our legion off of the main roads, the city residences and buildings should act as adequate cover from their arrows."

Tiarnen had never personally seen a squall before since they were kept as a last line of defence for the Tantalis, but he'd heard them described as winged wolves that could easily fly away with a horse and make a meal of it.

"What day do we depart?" he asked.

"Novembra twenty-eighth," said Holgor. "Which should have us at Sturm's door on Decembra first around midday. Weather holding, of course."

"Five weeks left," Tiarnen muttered to himself.

"Arriving at Anvalin crater!" announced the conductor.

Clang-clang—clang-clang-clang—clang-clang—clang!

The Praetavain emerged from the cavern only to pick up more speed and curve along the inner wall of the smallest crater in Kuldron. What it lacked in size, it made up with ferocity—the glowing molten bubbling and spitting high into the air as thousands of provincials along the lower ridgeline skimmed the top with long ladles. Their job seemed to be to remove the crust so the magma could flow into several culverts that had been carved into the crater wall. Taskmasters paced back and forth with leather whips in their hands, eagerly flogging those who were letting the crust build up or accidentally melting their ladle from leaving it in the molten for too long.

After noticing that Anvalin was spitting out fire and brimstone every morning at exactly eight-thirty, Niera had asked Tharus why it kept happening, but he waved the question off, muttering something about a demon likely stirring at the bottom. Unsatisfied with the answer, Tiarnen had tried to get some insight from Davmir, but even he didn't seem to have a plausible explanation—other than it had simply been occurring like clockwork since anyone could remember.

SCREEEECH!

The train began to brake and slow.

"Why are we stopping?" asked Tiarnen.

"To pay a quick visit to the anvilmars," said Tharus, standing to his feet and walking to the car doors with Holgor as the train came to a complete stop.

"Anvilmars?" asked Tiarnen, looking back to Niera for more insight, but she was already hurrying to grab her father's outstretched hand. The double doors slid open, and Tharus's entourage walked out of the train with the barons following behind.

"They are blacksmiths," said Davmir. "Best in province."

Trailing behind Davmir as he stepped into Anvalin Station, Tiarnen was immediately taken aback by the incredible scale of the torchlit crossbeam iron columns rising up from the stone floor, which then branched into a series of trusses that looked to be supporting the jagged rocky ceiling high above.

"Out of vay!" snapped Kizik.

The provincials quickly crawled to make sure there was a clear path for Tharus and his entourage to continue ahead.

As Tiarnen followed, he noticed many of the younger provincials were wearing a long chain loop over their shoulder that hung down to their hip and carried several thick books hanging on binding rings. He assumed they were the training manuals that Sivakosha mentioned before they had arrived in the city.

CL-CLANG! CL-CLANG!

Before Tiarnen could ask what exactly was making all the noise, Executor Kizik pushed the large station doors open and answered his question. Up ahead, the shadowy blacksmith district was a continuation of the cavern with a long row of smith stations running along either side. Down the middle was a train of mining carts that were half filled with a wide variety of forged items. There were no torches or lanterns of any kind because they weren't needed. Much like the Flame Tongue, thick streams of glowing molten were pouring out from openings high in the cavern walls and cascading down into cauldrons at each smith station. Tiarnen guessed that this was what the crater workers were ladling. It was hard to tell just how many stations there were in total due to the smoky haze obscuring the alcoves, but he estimated around a hundred in total.

CL-CLANG! CL-CLANG!

"Velcome to the Iskroval," said Davmir, more than a hint of pride in his voice.

Approaching the first smith station on his right, Tiarnen could see that the anvil was on the edge of a turntable in the floor, which slowly rotated so the blacksmith would pass by several sections along the alcove wall, which contained different tools for the various stages of whatever they were trying to make. From what Tiarnen could tell, the smith was forging an armour chest piece.

Tiarnen looked to his left and saw the blacksmith on the other side hammering a new link to a heavy chain. He was reminded of Kilners' Row, except it didn't appear that the chest amour and chain were moving from station to station at different stages like they would there. Instead, the blacksmiths would start and finish the pieces themselves.

He saw movement at the smiths' feet and realized they weren't without a little help; lurking in the shadows at each station was at least two, if not three, dwelglins. Their narrow orange eyes were the only clear feature in the haze as they assisted their smiths by handing them tools or simply cleaning up. After catching sight of Tiarnen passing by, they startled and vanished completely behind the anvils or water basins. Moving on, he watched the smiths forge everything from mechanical parts, utensils, horseshoes, and—as he and Davmir finally arrived at the last station where Tharus, Holgor, Niera, the barons, and Garod were standing—even railway ties.

"Tell me, how long does it take for each tie to be forged?" asked Tharus.

"Three hours by Farovas's hammer," said Yavor, gesturing to the muscular female smith who was holding the tie for Tharus.

"That means *six hundred thousand hours* of forging in total," said Holgor.

"Why do we suddenly need thirty leagues of new track?" asked Tiarnen.

"As we expected, it is taking roughly one week for supplies and equipment to arrive from Dorladdich. However, that will soon turn into *months* as we continue further west—unless we start laying track now."

"We're going to build a train to Dorladdich?" asked Tiarnen.

"The first transprovincial train of its kind," said Tharus. "When the campaign is finally over, it will reach across all of Chora."

Tharus's ambitious proclamation left everyone in uncomfortable silence.

"Chief, you must be very—umm—excited," said Tiarnen.

"That's an understatement, to be sure," said Garod, "Though, I can't help but feel a bit of professional sympathy for whoever is taking on the effort."

"I wouldn't start feeling sorry for yourself just yet, Garod," said Tharus.

"*Myself*?" The colour quickly drained from Garod's face. "But I don't have any experience with trains."

"Which is why Farovas here is now promoted to forehammer, and the entire Pyrovarog will be at your disposal. Once the legion is finally re-armed, of course," said Tharus.

Garod and Farovas looked at each other in disbelief.

"Speaking of which," began Tiarnen, trying to give Garod a moment to gather his thoughts, "how are combat drills progressing?"

"About as well as your rehearsals from what I have been told," said Tharus.

Tiarnen shot a look at Niera. "Taking our new orchestra members into consideration, I don't think that successfully performing two war-songs is something to be disappointed about." Truth be told, he was rather proud that only after a handful of rehearsals, Sivakosha and the brass were able to learn the warsongs while also outperforming Lachlan, despite his intentional sabotage, in more than a few sections.

"That's because you're ignoring the fact that we still have one hun-dred and forty-eight left," said Niera.

"Is anyone here actually under the impression that our conscripts are going to adopt the entire Dorladdian repertoire within the next two months?" asked Tiarnen.

"If they don't, you will be putting the campaign at a severe disad-vantage," said Tharus.

"Not if you select the warsongs before we set out for Phrysbruck."

Tharus stared through Tiarnen, his eyes narrowing as though he were trying to contain a violent outburst. "How many in total can the conscripts realistically learn before we depart?" he asked, looking to Niera.

"Twenty," said Tiarnen.

"Twenty-*five*," said Niera.

"Luckily for us, Praetor Sturm is rather predictable as far as his warsong choices, so I will at least have some certainty as to which ones we should prepare for," said Tharus. "That said, I want no less than three options for each designation and class."

"But that means twenty-seven," said Tiarnen.

"With some extra motivation, I'm confident that the orchestra will have no problem making it a reality—which is why I will see you both in a few hours."

"We look forward to it, Father," said Niera, grabbing onto Tiarnen's jacket and turning him around with her. They made their way back down the Pyrovarog with three praetorian guards trailing close behind.

"You know, Holgor mentioned having numerous informants in the city, but I didn't think my own sister would be one of them," said Tiarnen, walking back into Anvalin Station.

"Stop making it seem like I'm picking sides," snapped Niera.

"Then exactly what are you doing?" asked Tiarnen. "Besides airing grievances behind my back."

"Reina and I reported to Father every day while you were hiding in the lighthouse. If anything, she encouraged me to speak my mind."

"So do I," said Tiarnen. "Just with your inner voice."

Niera rolled her eyes.

"To be honest, I thought the hardest part was going to be integrating Sivakosha and her section, but it's our own members that are posing the biggest challenge," admitted Tiarnen.

"We can't blame them for not wanting to play nicely," said Niera.

"Be that as it may, they still have a job to do—which Lachlan isn't making any easier given the way he has been treating the conscripts."

"Meeting standards shouldn't come as a surprise to anyone in his section—he is their First Brass."

"Maybe that needs to change then," said Tiarnen, stepping onto the train.

*

After arriving at Farosha crater, Tiarnen and Niera made their way from the station to Karadrel Sulka, which was the Lydvenkian version of Cathedral Square. Earlier in the week, they'd passed by tributes of small iron figurines and bowls of fresh water along the karadrel steps while on their way to explore the first floor.

To Tiarnen's surprise, the layout was nearly identical to the cathedral all the way down to the podium and tiled dome. However, there were some key differences: the flowing Dorladdian masonry was replaced with jagged layers of oxidized iron sheet metal. Where the prayer pools should have been, there were three fire pits—their sparks fluttering up from the glowing coals and licking the high ceiling, turning it not black but metallic orange; instead of pews, there were just waist-high semi-circle dividers of serrated metal which forced you to stand in very tight rows between them. Overall, the sense of inspiration that the cathedral evoked was replaced with cruelty and oppression by the karadrel.

Finally passing into the square, Tiarnen and Niera found themselves standing before the orchestra, who were casually hanging about in groups. Sivakosha and her troop were far removed from everyone except Kaleigh and Coniel—while the Roycrofts skulked and leered in a corner together. Tiarnen took a warm breath and was about to get everyone's attention when—

"I want first positions for 'Orniach!'" shouted Niera.

"Wait!" shouted Coniel, turning away from a conversation with Sivakosha to face Tiarnen and Niera. "There is something the maestro will want to know about before we start!"

"What's so important?" asked Tiarnen, walking over with Niera.

"See for yourself." Coniel held his hand out for Tiarnen.

Tiarnen took what looked to be a Lydvenkian Shatter card from Coniel and looked at the title. "*The Fang of Svar.*"

"Are you serious?" said Niera.

"I assure you that a new Weapon card class is *very* serious," said Tiarnen, eyes widening as he looked over the painted image of a menacing blade made from molten metal.

"Sivakosha said that one is a legendary," Coniel said enthusiastically, "and it can be used for multiple turns. Oh! And they also apparently have playing tables that light up with the cards!"

"*Really?*" asked Tiarnen, staring at Coniel as though he was just told a third moon had been discovered.

"Maybe we could get the barons to show us one?" asked Coniel eagerly.

"Are you two about finished?" asked Kaleigh, arriving beside Coniel.

"Right, thank you, Second Drum, this was very informative," Tiarnen said formally.

"No, thank you, Maestro, for allowing me to present this recent discovery," said Coniel, just as formally.

"First. Positions," ordered Niera.

The Roycrofts sauntered over as the groups dispersed to form their sections, and Tiarnen walked to the front of the courtyard, where the rocky earth looked to have been stabbed a million times over—some of the tiny wounds still glinting with ivy-green maestro glass deep inside.

"After two days of practise, I expect *all* of you to know 'Orniach' by now," said Niera. "Which is why today will be full play-throughs only. Once our Maestro has been able to illuminate the lattrice and approves our performance, we can get out of this cursed heat—so don't waste his resonance. Nor my patience. Understood?"

"Yes, Orchestra Lead!" shouted the members.

Niera turned and nodded to Tiarnen, who nodded back and put Darktide to his lips.

'Orniach' was one of the more complicated class one defensive war-songs in the Dorladdian repertoire, but it was well worth the effort to perform since the lattrice effect filled you with restorative energy.

Opening the first movement with confident ascending phrases, Darktide sang, and from it Tiarnen illuminated a splash of verdant shards that soared through the air above himself. The orchestra rose up in support, making the next splash of shards much thicker and stronger. Tiarnen kept a keen ear on the brass. From what he was hearing, there were a few missed notes in their sprightly scalic sequences, but as they transitioned into the second movement, it began to fall apart. He couldn't tell who it was specifically among the brass, but instead of flourishing to expand the nebula, Tiarnen cast the shards into the ground.

THUNK-ING—THUNK-ING—THUNK-ING!

"Unacceptable!" shouted Niera. "Brass, keep it together!"

"Yes, Orchestra Lead!" shouted the brass.

Niera turned to Tiarnen and nodded again.

Opening the first movement once again, Tiarnen illuminated and cast the shards. As before, the orchestra joined him. While expanding the nebula, he focused on the brass. Thankfully, there were fewer missed notes in their sequences this time, which allowed them to transition into the second spirited movement.

Fiona struck her drums fiercely as Tiarnen played "Orniach's" melody—the surging phrases illuminating vibrant shards—their addition to the shimmering glass nebula causing it to slowly rotate around him. Before he could continue with the contrasting figurations, a shrill misplay from the brass filled the courtyard... then another... and yet another. Left with no choice, Tiarnen dropped his shards to the earth.

THUNK-ING—THUNK-ING—THUNK-ING!

"First Brass!" shouted Niera, her head practically spinning around to stare knives into Lachlan. "I want an explanation!"

"I can assure you the problem is not Dorladdian in nature," said Lachlan.

"You know what? Let's test that theory," said Tiarnen.

"Does that mean we're finally dropping all of this dead weight?" asked Lachlan, nodding to Sivakosha and her troop.

"No, unfortunately, I still need to keep you around."

Kaleigh and the woodwinds laughed under their breath.

"So what's going to be different, then?" asked Fiona.

"Our wise Lead reminded me this morning how important it is to be honest, not only with ourselves but with each other," said Tiarnen, walking to Niera and standing at her side.

"Meaning?" asked Lachlan, adding a yawn.

Tiarnen looked long at him. "*Meaning* we need to admit that this entire situation is complicated, frustrating, and simply put... uncomfortable as hell." He turned to Sivakosha. "The fact is, no two provincial orchestras have ever been forced together like we are now. However, given the incredible amount of talent standing before me—I can't help but believe that we can not only perform up to standard but perhaps that with our new members, there is a chance of even going beyond it. Which is why I am going to let Sivakosha lead the brass today."

Niera looked back at Tiarnen in disbelief as the rest of the orchestra muttered among each other at the news.

"I'll be dead before I give up my section to a—" began Lachlan.

"It's not yours to give up!" snapped Niera, turning to face the orchestra again. "Our Maestro has made his decision. Sivakosha and every Niervalian to the front!"

The order pulled Sivakosha and her troop out of their shock, and they hurried to reorganize themselves at the front of the brass.

"Thanks," muttered Tiarnen.

"I really hope you know what you're doing," said Niera.

"Yeah, me too," said Tiarnen, leaving Niera to return to the front of the courtyard.

Truth be told, he had been struggling just as much as the orchestra most days since he had never once performed any of the warsongs as a maestro before. To ensure he wasn't the problem, he had been practising well into the evening while alone in his Maestro Chamber just to get a handle on the flourishing so that nobody would be injured or worse during rehearsals the next morning. All in all, it was a considerable challenge, both physically and mentally, that left his resonance nearly drained every night. He was fast learning that the two were entangled in a very intimate way, deeper than he ever realized, but he still didn't know why. He had so many unanswered questions. The diary had provided a bit of insight. There were observations and then warnings about exhaustion in Reina's chapter as well as what she called "burn out" when she pushed herself too hard, but the only consistent recommendation for recovery was rest and most of the Dorladdian cuisine that Auberdine was already preparing.

"Maestro, the orchestra is ready!" announced Niera.

Tiarnen blinked himself out of the reflection and then gave her a soft smile. He knew that Niera was screaming inside but was impressed at how well she kept her resolve. He looked over Darktide, watching the prismatic colours refracting inside the instrument's black opal inlay. His mind tried to wander back to the Conservatory and how things might be progressing for Lydia, but he pushed the thought away and lifted the piccolo, ready to play.

Once again, Tiarnen began the first movement with ascending phrases that illuminated ivy-green shards that he cast high into the air. The orchestra rose with them in chromatic support, making the rest of the shards thicker and stronger, just like before.

With the nebula expanding, Fiona struck her drums fiercely to begin the second movement. Tiarnen played "Orniach's" melody—the ascending phrases of cresting dyads and trills igniting into vibrant shards—their addition to the glass nebula causing it to slowly rotate around Tiarnen. The orchestra then developed several sets of rhythmic figures followed by descending motifs between the strings and woodwinds. But then, Lachlan.

Tiarnen immediately knew it was Lachlan misplaying due to the especially rich timbre of his artisanal trumpet.

THUNK-ING—THUNK-ING—THUNK-ING!

"Lachlan!" shouted Tiarnen. "You mind explaining what I just heard?"

"Apologies, Maestro. I'm finding it difficult to follow her performance," Lachlan said acrimoniously.

"That's not what it sounded like from here."

"I am astonished that you can make sense of anything over that racket." Lachlan casually pointed his trumpet at Sivakosha.

"Again, from the top!" said Niera.

Tiarnen raised Darktide and then looked long at Sivakosha, who, given her spiteful expression, was just as furious with Lachlan as he was. It was hard to tell, but she seemed to acknowledge Tiarnen's stare with a very subtle nod.

Opening the first movement for what he was hoping was the last time, Tiarnen illuminated a splash of ivy-green shards and cast them into the air. The orchestra accompanied his performance perfectly, enhancing the nebula while Fiona struck her drums fiercely to begin the second spirited movement.

Tiarnen played "Orniach's" melody—the addition of the vibrant shards causing the glimmering glass nebula to rotate. The strings and woodwinds developed several sets of rhythmic figures, followed by supporting refrains and then descending motifs. Excited by the fact that they had made it halfway through the warsong, Tiarnen flourished gracefully and drew the nebula into a spinning vortex of glass around himself.

Normally, it would have been his chance to shine as he carried the melodic momentum into the third movement, but Sivakosha and her troop were suddenly drowning out everyone, including Niera. Tiarnen tried not to smile at the unexpected effort, as it would have made it hard to keep his lip placement on the piccolo, so he gave her a raised eyebrow instead. Encouraged, Sivakosha and the Niervalians played several passages as though they were standing alone with Tiarnen, which allowed him to illuminate some of his thickest shards yet. Feeling their weight pull against Darktide, he threw his shoulders into a strong flourish, which left him pointing the piccolo at the hazy late morning sky. The gesture raised his vortex high where it swirled in on itself to forge the lattrice. With a final breath, Tiarnen illuminated and cast a last shard into the heart of the lattrice, which fused it together and released a sudden flash of vibrant virescent light. The bloom of resonant energy filled the courtyard and the hearts of the orchestra.

"I almost forgot how good this feels!" exclaimed Coniel, looking over his hand as the veins pulsed with a green glow.

"Enjoy it while it lasts!" said Tiarnen, looking over the orchestra as they all enjoyed the surge of restorative power coursing through them.

"Probably our best performance yet," admitted Niera, her eyes greener than ever.

"Maybe we make the change permanent." Tiarnen looked at Lachlan, who was fuming—when suddenly his face dropped.

"Praetor!" exclaimed Lachlan. "Thank the Verse you are here!" He shoved his way to the front of his section, nearly pushing Sivakosha over, and then rushed to stand before Tharus. "All week, I have been trying to educate and set the example for our conscripts, but they are proving to be incapable of meeting your standards!"

Tharus said nothing in response. He simply walked ahead and then stood before the brass with a praetorian guard on either side of him. Inches away from Sivakosha, he reached out and then ran his finger over the bond around her arm. "These were given in good faith that you would take every opportunity to earn your position in my orchestra. Davmir has done so by working tirelessly these past six weeks to prove that he is worthy of a legion rank. In fact, I dare say that most of his brigade has fit in rather nicely and will play a key role in our swift victory over Phrysbruck, which is why I have made him Third Brigarch."

Sivakosha swallowed hard. "Ve too have been vorking, Praetor."

"Is that so?" asked Tharus. "Lachlan."

"Yes, Praetor!"

"Has anyone from your section failed to earn their bond today?"

"Yes, Praetor!"

Tharus's cold gaze fell upon the brass section. "Bring them before me."

"Gregar and Lodbrok!" yelled Lachlan, pointing at the ground in front of his feet.

Two Niervalian men emerged from within the orchestra and reluctantly made their way over to stand before Lachlan.

"Both have shown a complete lack of discipline, dedication, and, above all else, talent," said Lachlan.

"Liar!" said Sivakosha. "They are vorking harder than—"

WHAM!

The blow seemed to come out of nowhere, and before Sivakosha realized what had happened, she was on her knees and bleeding from her mouth. Half of the orchestra gasped aloud while the other half remained silent. Wiping the crimson with the back of her hand, she glared at the praetorian guard who was already returning to formation behind Tharus.

"I will only say this once," shouted Tharus, making sure the entire orchestra could hear him. "If you are stripped of your bond, you have nothing, you are nothing, because there is no place for you in Dorladdich's new age."

RIPPPP!

Lachlan tore the bonds off Gregar and Lodbrok.

"Kneel," said Tharus.

Gregar and Lodbrok fell to their knees as the guards approached while drawing their shields off their backs.

"What are you doing?" asked Tiarnen, realizing there was about to be an execution. "We can't afford to lose any members!"

"Executor, what is the current orchestra headcount?" asked Tharus.

"One hundred and thirty-three, Praetor," said Kizik.

"We can, in fact," said Tharus. He raised his finger, which signalled the guards to lift their swords.

"Maestro! With all due respect," said Kaleigh. "If Niervalia truly is under the domain of Dorladdich, does that not mean our house laws apply here as well?"

The question brought a smirk to Tiarnen's face. "I believe they would, yes."

"Then, according to the Ashbrook accords, *no orchestra member can be executed without a trial,*" said Kaleigh, helping Sivakosha back to her feet.

"A trial? For this filth? You can't be serious," said Lachlan.

Tiarnen looked to Tharus who was deeply unimpressed with Kaleigh's effort to spare the lives of the Niervalian members but knew that he had to enforce the accords.

"Taking time and resources into consideration, we will forgo the trial," said Tharus.

Lachlan smiled with satisfaction.

"And place them in one of the labour districts. Perhaps they at least be of some use there."

As Lachlan's smile faded, the guards pulled both men to their feet and shoved them at Kizik, who had his secretary take them away. Tiarnen and Niera waited for a moment to see if there were any other reprimands to follow, but Tharus seemed a bit lost in thought, staring at Kaleigh, so they nodded to the orchestra to get back to rehearsals.

"Maestro, remind me," said Tharus. "When was the Grand Tournament supposed to take place?"

"Novembra the twenty-sixth," said Tiarnen, a bit taken aback by the question. "Why?"

"Given the state of morale," said Tharus, nodding to the orchestra. "I would hate for the campaign to upend something that was so highly anticipated."

"As... As would I," said Tiarnen, glancing back at Coniel, whose eyes were as wide as the moons.

"Excellent, then I will tell the Office of Games to host it here," said Tharus. "Oh, and let's be sure to invite the barons as well. Seeing how they would otherwise feel put out."

"We certainly wouldn't want that," said Tiarnen, turning again to Coniel, who was already staring back at him with his mouth hanging open in shock.

*

Tiarnen entered the Maestro Chamber sweaty, exhausted, and still in utter disbelief that the Grand Tournament was suddenly back on. How they were going to include the barons as far as the match order, Tiarnen didn't know, but at the moment, he didn't much care. His guards closed the door behind him, but the mesh walls didn't make it feel as though he had gained much privacy.

HISSSS!

"I missed you, too," remarked Tiarnen, watching Persol's yellow eyes blink from within the swirled bed blankets that were covered in fallen rose petals. He walked over to the coat rack, unfastened the buttons on his maestro jacket, and slid it off his damp back. The heat of the room immediately hit, swiftly reminding him of how well the jacket protected him from the elements. He carefully hung it on the rack and looked it over for any wear and tear but couldn't yet find a single fraying thread nor even a crease in the supple leather. Overall, he was quite happy with the design, especially the high collar and stitching, and still remained grateful for Niera's request to keep it simple—especially since so many maestro jackets in the past were incredibly ostentatious.

The green of the jacket seemed even brighter against the backdrop of the Lydvenkian family tree, and although it was a brilliant piece of art to behold, Tiarnen's eye would always go to the singular portrait of Lydia—the most recent addition with no branch of her own. He had already spent far too many hours wondering how someone could arrive seemingly from out of nowhere and seize the title. Tiarnen had even asked the barons a few more questions about what exactly happened, but all of them simply repeated the same, "She vas Orchestra Lead and challenged the Maestro." An answer that didn't offer much more insight than before.

Swallowing dryly, Tiarnen turned to the corner table where there was both a large and small pitcher; the taller one was filled with fresh water while the smaller one was filled with a spirit called Vosok. As much as Tiarnen liked the cooling effect the Vosok had on his mouth, he chose the water pitcher and poured himself a large glass—all of which he quickly gulped down. Setting the cup on the table, he noticed a bowl filled with his usual dinner of Auberdine's hand-selected "delicacies," which Tiarnen knew he had to devour at some point before bed, but the paper package and open letter beside it stole his attention. He snatched up the envelope and parcel, made his way over to the bed, sat down, and pulled out the folded letter to see Raghnall's handwriting.

Tiarnen,

I trust the journey to Lydvenko was both challenging and inspiring. You'll be pleased to hear that I checked on the lighthouse yesterday, and everything seems to be in order. However, even with all the lights on, Dorladdich still feels empty without you and Niera here. That said, the captain wanted me to relay his thanks for having to file fewer incident reports.

With the extra time on our hands, I'm relieved to inform you that the first stage of the restoration effort is now complete! There is, of course, a large amount of work to be done, but I am growing more and more optimistic that it will be ready when you return home.

My very best,
Raghnall

P.S. Smelts are included per your request.

Tiarnen sat on the bed and read between the lines of Raghnall's letter twice over with his heart pounding in his chest. "*The first stage is now* complete." *What did it sound like? What did it look like? How did Lydia manage to make it stable on her own?* Knowing that he wasn't going to receive answers any time soon, Tiarnen tried to push the questions out of his mind and slipped the letter back into the torn envelope. He was naturally concerned that the wax seal had already been broken, but then he realized there was no possibility of the Inquisitor allowing any direct maestro correspondence to go unchecked. Thankfully, Raghnall seemed to anticipate Holgor's prying eyes and didn't give anything away as far as the "restoration," but Tiarnen would have to make the same literary effort or risk exposing their mission.

"What are you going to do now, Tiarnen?" he muttered to himself. It wasn't as though he didn't have faith that Lydia would find a way to complete a first draft, especially since her life depended on it, but if she was moving ahead, that meant he would have to find a way to as well.

Mowwwwww!

Tiarnen looked down to his side to see Persol had made her way over to sniff the package curiously. He gently tore the paper wrapping off to reveal three cans of smelts. Tiarnen grabbed the top one and pulled it partially open—the scent of salty fish quickly filling the air around them.

MOWWW! Persol raised a paw at the can.

"Now, wait," said Tiarnen, standing up with the smelts in hand. "You and I need to come to an agreement first."

Mow.

"That's right. These aren't just smelts—they are a peace offering." He pulled the lid off the can completely. "Should you accept said offering, I promise that more will come, *but* I expect you to be a little nicer in return."

Persol paused in consideration.

Moww.

"Then we have an accord," said Tiarnen, setting the can onto the bed. Persol wasted no time and buried her face into the smelts. After devouring the first of many, she raised her head, licking her lips, and Tiarnen slowly lowered his hand to give only two pets, heeding Sivakosha's words. He took his hand off the surprisingly soft skin, and Persol went back to eating with her tail straight up. "Well, if I can win you over, maybe I really do stand a chance of convincing him."

After a short walk down the west corridor of the palace, Tiarnen found himself standing at the entrance to Tharus and Niera's private suite. One of the praetorian guards flanking the door nodded and then knocked.

"What is it?" asked Niera from the other side.

"Maestro Dorian has arrived," said the guard.

A few moments passed, and then the door opened, but Niera was already walking away by the time Tiarnen had stepped into the luxurious living room. It must have been at least ten times the size of the Maestro Chamber. A wide variety of ironwork tables and furniture were carefully arranged throughout, but none of them had the cruel design Tiarnen was used to seeing in Niervalia. Instead, the pieces were much more elegant—even the couches had plush chevrae fur cushions and soft wool blankets draped over the side. He looked up at the ostentatious chandelier in the middle of the ceiling, which had countless glowing sunstones perched on top, giving the living room a glimmering orange glow.

"Father, Tiarnen is here," said Niera, sitting on one of the loveseats.

"This is unexpected," said Tharus, emerging from his bedroom and looking at Tiarnen like he was an uninvited house guest.

"I know, but I need to speak with you," said Tiarnen.

"About?"

"Phrysbruck."

"Be specific."

"Our departure date—" began Tiarnen.

"Is not changing," finished Tharus, turning away.

"Which is why I must leave ahead of the legion."

"I do believe I have lost the plot." Tharus stopped and turned to face Tiarnen again.

"The reason I was able to defeat Lydia was because I was able to learn her music," said Tiarnen. "If I am to defeat Maestro Phrygus, I will need the same access to his warsongs."

Tharus paused for a moment in consideration. "Let's say by some miracle you do manage to make your way to the Tantalis on your own—what then?"

"Infiltrate the Great Library and study as much Phrygian music as I can before you arrive." All of this was true. He just left out the small part about also finding the henge and ensuring the battle with Maestro Phrygus ended up there at the end.

"Even if you did somehow survive travelling the frostlands on your own, you would be caught the moment you stepped foot in the library. Our campaign will be lost if you set out alone," said Tharus.

"It already is if I don't," said Tiarnen.

"What makes you so certain?" asked Niera.

"Maestro Phrygus has held the title for over fifteen years; he is far more experienced and powerful than I am by every possible measure," said Tiarnen.

"So was Lydia," said Niera.

"Exactly my point! The only advantage I had over her was surprise. If that is taken away from me when I face Phrygus, we won't be marching into the Tantalis but a slaughterhouse!"

"Just as Lydvenko proved when they attacked us, the siege will create a fair bit of chaos, and with that will come unexpected opportunities," said Tharus. "Once Phrysbruck's forces are preoccupied, there should be a chance for you to—"

"I can't read sheet music while fighting on the front line!" shouted Tiarnen.

"Nor can our spies steal what you need before we set out," said Tharus, making his way to the door.

"Maybe we should ask Holgor before assuming—" said Niera, standing back up.

"I don't need my Inquisitor to point out the obvious!" snapped Tharus, turning to Tiarnen. "Your request for an early departure is denied." He opened the door and left down the hall with Niera in tow.

Chapter Twenty-Seven

THE GRAND TOURNAMENT

The day before the Grand Tournament, Tiarnen and Coniel took a train to Joriska crater, which was far more wondrous than he expected. Running all along the interior were open veins of glittering orange citrine. Apparently, the crystal didn't carry much value, but it was still beautiful to behold. Each of the barons had taken a third of the upper crater for themselves—their lavish residences carved deep into the ridge, while the war offices they were responsible for took up the descending lower ridges.

When they arrived at the Office of Games, Tiarnen anticipated the usual sparse, stark Lydvenkian décor, only to see that the barons had indulged themselves with opulent furnishings. Surrounding the triangular lounge were three glass cabinets, and in the middle stood three plush leather chairs as well as a massive brass gear that had been converted into a Shatter playing table.

Seeing the countless Shatter cards inside the cabinets, Tiarnen let the excitement push away his overwhelming frustration regarding Tharus's denial of an early departure to Phrysbruck and strode over to one of the cabinets.

There were so many to look at. As far as artistry and style, he noticed that they were very similar to the cards in Dorladdich—though taking the opportunity to add orange wherever possible. According to Baron Grensky, his Office of Games held to the same season and deck format as Dorladdich. The Weapon class cards, as late as they might be, would merely be an addition to the Grand Tournament. Tiarnen learnt it was only the barons and their small court of nobility that could afford to play competitively, given that the provincials were intentionally kept in poverty. There wasn't a yearly Grand Tournament either. Instead, the barons held smaller high-stakes invitationals every month, of which Grensky was usually victorious, according to him, since there were conveniently no officials to referee the matches.

Tiarnen and Coniel were offered any cards they wanted, which Tiarnen assumed was a gesture of loyalty on Grensky's part but enticing nonetheless. He continued looking over the cards, and even though many of the weapons were intriguing as far as their features and potential synergy, part of him was hoping that he might also find another card similar to *Amber's*. Unfortunately, there didn't seem to be any that were close. Coniel had also begun to feel a strange sense of disappointment when he realized that cherry-picking the exact weapon he wanted greatly diminished the thrill of the game.

Confused by their change of heart, Grensky began rambling on about some of his favourite legendary weapons, but Tiarnen and Coniel assured him that they would be happier with a handful of card packs instead. Despite finding their decision very odd, Grensky made sure they left with two boxes of cards each and promised that the other contenders would receive the same.

Tiarnen and Coniel returned to the palace, desperately needing something to eat—not to mention a fair amount of table space to open their new card packs—and so made their way to the kitchen, where Auberdine was arguing with his Niervalian line cooks. At first, Tiarnen couldn't tell what the commotion was about, but then he noticed that Auberdine had singed his left eyebrow off—likely due to the open-flame stove that was roaring behind him. After assuring him that no one would notice—despite knowing full well that everyone would notice—Tiarnen and Coniel sat at the large prep table and started to tear open their packs. Auberdine took the opportunity to teach his cooks how to fry up a couple of "proper" Dorladdian crispy sardine sandwiches.

As Tiarnen and Coniel devoured their delicious meal and tried not to get oily fingerprints on their new cards, the grocery train arrived. Tiarnen hadn't asked himself just how supplies made it to the palace, but the six-cart train reminded him that nearly everything ran on rails in Niervalia.

Stomachs full, they continued to build their decks with the new Weapon cards until the early morning hours. Sunlight piercing through the mesh walls of the palace, Coniel was finally satisfied with his build and left to get a few hours of much-needed sleep. Tiarnen kept trying to discover as much synergy as possible before the tournament began.

That afternoon, Tiarnen, Tharus, Niera, and their usual armed escort took the Praetavain to the arena where the Grand Tournament was being held. To Tiarnen's delight, many of the Dorladdian food carts had made the journey from home and were parked out front, but, unfortunately, the Loyal Trustea had apparently broken a wheel hub and wasn't able to make it. Admittedly disappointed, he was still excited to see that the house vendors had twice the apparel selection compared to last year and at half the price. He guessed it was because they wanted to make Dorladdich's presence felt as much as possible in Niervalia. Or, they were simply ordered to by the War Office. While browsing, Tiarnen was, of course, offered anything he wanted for free, but he had no interest in bringing more attention to himself—although part of him did want to put on an Ashbrook belt but knew full well that it wouldn't help with political tensions.

After entering the arena, Executor Kizik greeted their party and took them to a private balcony where the barons were waiting with twelve or so high-ranking officers from both the Dorladdian and Niervalian War

Offices, who did not look pleased to be in such close quarters. Tiarnen took a seat in between his father and sister and looked out. Below, the massive square stage was surrounded on all four sides by tall torches and at least two hundred ranked rows, where thirty thousand provincials were eagerly waiting.

Tink!

The sharp tip of a polished iron pointe shoe struck the stage floor. Tiarnen watched the sinewy principal dancer balance on pointe while raising the other leg high above to form an elegant arc. Despite the impressive feat of strength and grace, he had to blink his bleary eyes hard a couple of times to keep focus and stop last night's deck-building from catching up with him. From his vantage point, it almost looked as though the principal dancer was floating just above the square stage in her glossy patent-leather catsuit. Enthusiastic applause erupted from the audience, most of whom were dressed in tabards with their faces painted, and those who came directly from Dorladdich wore either an embellished Roycroft hat, Ashbrook belt, or Finwick boots. Ten more dancers—*vilmiras* as they were called—arrived on either side of the principal dancer and took position. Then, Sivakosha and the Niervalian portion of the orchestra opened a spirited rite from the stageside, which inspired the vilmiras to spring, turn, and saunter in practised choreography.

"They're pretty incredible, eh?" whispered Tiarnen.

Niera, sitting beside him, didn't respond and only kept watching.

Tiarnen wasn't sure if she hadn't heard him or was too captivated by the performance to notice what he said. Either way, he couldn't blame her. He didn't want to discount any of the dancers in Dorladdich. They were certainly skilled, but he was willing to bet that none of them were capable of what the vilmiras were on a physical or technical level. As though to prove him right, the dancers leaped into the air, landed with grace, and then rose onto their toe point to spin. The synchronous revolutions seemed to strike a chord in Niera since she looked to Tiarnen with bright, wide eyes.

"What is it?" asked Tiarnen.

Niera looked as though she was about to ask a question but then seemed to give up on it. "Nothing," she said.

The dancers made their tenth turn and then finished with a collective bow that received overwhelming applause from everyone.

Baron Grensky stood to his feet, walked to the metal amplistaff at the front of the balcony, and then held his hands up, which quickly settled the crowd. "Once again!" he said, the amplistaff making his voice reverberate throughout the entire arena. "Ve must thank our vilmiras for opening the tournament vith such artistry!"

Cheering and whistles resounded from everyone.

"However!" continued Grensky. "Just as Niervalia has seen many changes these past few months, so must our cherished card game!"

Tiarnen looked around the arena to see that many Niervalians had suddenly lost their enthusiasm.

"I know some of you vere looking forward to playing this evening, but being that ve are now hosting the six hundred and sixty-fourth *Dorladdian* Grand Tournament, only the barony have been invited to compete."

Some of the Niervalians were naturally outraged by the news, as Tiarnen predicted, and a few provincials threw their decks into the air out of spite—the paper cards fluttering down like dead leaves from a tree.

"Be sure that the barons and I are proud to represent all Niervalians this evening!" said Grensky.

Niera turned to Tiarnen. "Aren't there only sixteen challengers allowed in the tournament?"

"Indeed, there is," said Tiarnen.

"So, how did we make room for the barons?"

"*Someone* cut the bottom three qualifiers," said Tiarnen, nodding to Tharus.

"They were compensated handsomely," Tharus said dismissively.

"But what do the barons have to gain if they're not competing for the Premiership?" asked Niera.

"I promised a minor house should one of them win," said Tharus.

"And what did it cost them to enter?" asked Tiarnen, knowing there had to be a catch.

"Every chevrae to their name," said Tharus. "And since the herd is the most valuable commodity in Niervalia, I would guess that the barons will be taking the tournament very seriously."

"Vith your permission, Praetor." Grensky looked over his shoulder to Tharus, who nodded in approval.

"Let the Grand Tournament begin!" yelled Grensky.

The arena's torch lights ignited, and most of the audience leaped to their feet with signs bearing various challenger's names held high or waving a miniature provincial banner. Tiarnen took in the magnificent sight and then looked down at the stage to see the vilmiras hopping off as standing tables rose from each corner.

"Please follow us, Maestro," said Grensky, walking to the back of the balcony with the barons following close behind.

Arriving stageside, Tiarnen met the other twelve challengers who were already standing around and sampling from the long refreshment table.

"Careful not to mix up the voligar vith the vater, or you'll be vaking up tomorrow vondering vhere you are," said Grensky, with a phlegmy laugh as he raised a glass of the crystal-clear spirit.

Looking over Coniel, Tiarnen could see an impressive selection of Niervalian and Dorladdian delicacies as well as enough spirits to pickle the entire legion. Tiarnen tapped Coniel on the shoulder, and he turned around with a small plate piled high with salted prawns.

"Are there any left?" asked Tiarnen.

"I see one at the bottom of the bowl," chuckled Coniel.

A servant handed Coniel an iron stein of spiced mead and then looked at Tiarnen. "Can I get you anything, Maestro?"

"Actually, I wouldn't mind a tea with some cream and maple if there is—"

"*Tea*?" scoffed Lachlan, a polished goblet in his hand. "Come now, the best our provinces have to offer is at your fingertips, and all you want is a cup of dishwater?"

"As much as I can appreciate the spread, I never was one for spirits, really," said Tiarnen.

"A little too strong for your tastes, eh?" asked Lachlan.

"Dreadgill talking about taste, that's fresh," said Coniel.

"Now that we're all here," said Cleary, arriving at the side of the stage with four other Office of Games officials from Dorladdich. They were all dressed in their usual striped officiating robes, but Cleary's was glittering. "I would like to review the tournament rules. Do pay attention because they will only be told once, and breaking any of them, even if by accident, will result in your certain disqualification."

The challengers were suddenly very interested in what he had to say.

"The Grand Tournament, as always, is single-turn elimination," said Cleary. "Only fifty card decks allowed, no duplicates. Card substitutions are forbidden. There will be four rounds: group, quarter, semi, and the final. Four matches will play at a time on the stage until each round is complete. Winners will return to this area and wait for the next round to begin, while losers will see themselves to the first-row seats behind you."

The challengers glanced back to the empty row.

"Any questions?" asked Cleary.

"The barons, as well as some of us, are playing with Niervalian cards. What happens if there is a unique interaction that we have never come across before?" asked Tiarnen.

"As expected, we'll have to make some potentially divisive decisions regarding those unforeseen interactions," said Cleary. "But let me remind all of you that an official's decision is indisputable." His eyes went to the barons. "However, should you still disagree, feel free to make a formal complaint to the Office of Games, where it will be ignored for the next ten years."

Everyone gave a laugh.

"Understood," said Tiarnen.

"It looks like there is some kind of shuffling mechanism on the side of each table?" asked Coniel.

"Yes," said Grensky. "They help prevent *sticky* fingers."

"Speaking of cheating," said Cleary. "Let me remind all of you that should anyone be caught doing so, they will receive a lifetime ban from all ranked matches and thus the tournament itself."

"Noble or not," added Coniel, looking straight at Lachlan.

"Relax, Swiftsail. No one here needs to cheat to beat you," said Lachlan.

Cleary looked over the match list in his hand. "If everyone is ready, the group round will start with Ferotov versus Rainmaker at table one... Kelpkeeper versus Grensky at table two... Hookbeard versus Yavor at table three... and Shellshock versus Dreadgill at table four."

The challengers who were called began making their way to the stage stairs.

"Maestro!" yelled a voice.

Tiarnen looked over his shoulder to see Kaleigh and Sivakosha standing behind the stageside rail. Both had their faces painted with Ashbrook seahorses and were holding steins.

"Think about having some fun, eh?" said Kaleigh, holding up her stein.

"Care to make a bet, ladies?" asked a booker, arriving beside Kaleigh with his quill and pad of blank betting slips at the ready.

"Why not," said Kaleigh, "I'll put a hundred gold on Rainmaker."

"You sure that's a good idea?" asked Tiarnen.

"That would be up to you now," said Kaleigh, handing the coin pouch to the booker and receiving a betting slip in return.

The crowd applauded as the challengers and officials walked onto the stage and made their way to the assigned tables, then stood across from each other. Decks were handed to the officials, who gave them a quick inspection and then placed them into the shufflers.

Thwip-thwip-thwip-thwip-thwip-thwip-thwip!

The cards blurred as they mixed in the spinning tumblers.

Click!

With the decks and challengers now ready, the officials flipped their coins, and the calls were made. Opening cards shot out of thin slots at the bottom of the shufflers, and a hushed tension filled the arena as the challengers looked at what fate had brought them.

To Tiarnen's dismay, Ferotov quickly gained the advantage with his *Runaway Train* deck. He was lucky enough to draw both of his Conductor Allies that synergized with his Express Train Allies two turns later and wiped out half of Tiarnen's health. Tiarnen had never faced such a powerful early game-board presence before, so he countered with *Major Raghnall* to mitigate more train damage and then healed himself fully with a class one defensive warsong called *Galagar's – Curative – Drizzle*. Unfortunately, Ferotov drew his *Complication* Trinket, which doubled the speed of the trains and thus their damage. His back against the wall on turn ten, Tiarnen unleashed a brutal offensive with three Vilmiras Allies, equipped his *Prokiev's Pointe Shoe* Weapon, which doubled their damage, and then played a class two attack warsong called *Eowahn's – Encouraging – Sails – of Propitious – Propulsion* that gave him lethal. Given the snarl and long stare, Tiarnen could tell that Ferotov wasn't used to losing, so he waited patiently for the official to announce—

"Ferotov, you are shattered!"

A deafening mix of cheering and cursing erupted throughout the arena. Tiarnen thought he was prepared for the noise, but it hit him like an anvilmar's hammer and was well beyond anything he had ever heard before. He looked to the crowd and saw the Niervalians who had bet on Ferotov burning their slips in the arena torches, as was apparently tradition.

"Please remain at the table until the other matches are decided," said the official.

Left with no choice, Tiarnen stood in place and watched Kelpkeeper try to defeat Grensky. Her *Mean and Green* deck tangled his Allies in kelp and caused them to skip every other turn, while she used a *Tempting Lure* Trinket to set many a *Snap Turtle* Ally upon them. Unfortunately, it wasn't enough. Grensky's *Craterous Cretins* deck eventually overwhelmed Kelpkeeper by using *Dwelglin* Allies that stole the lure and turned the turtles against her.

"Kelpkeeper, you are shattered!" announced the official.

Once again, roaring cheers and curses erupted from the crowd, but it was mostly the Dorladdians burning their betting slips this time.

Yavor's *Thousand Lashes* deck was proving to be incredibly effective against Hookbeard. The *Barbed Whip* Weapon empowered his numerous Raven Allies to not only attack each target but also Hookbeard himself as many times as his Allies had been lashed. Hookbeard's *Bad Form* deck was using a crew of *Surly Pirate* Allies that were still a major threat to Yavor until he misplayed a class three attack warsong, which made them mutiny against him.

"Hookbeard, you are shattered!" announced the official.

Dorladdian groans could be heard from all directions.

With the last table in play, Tiarnen watched Shellshock assault Lachlan with his *Pickled Twice Over* deck. Despite it being incredibly popular, Tiarnen still enjoyed this deck since it had a *Pressurized Flask* Trinket that made attack warsongs twice as powerful but also twice as dangerous if misplayed because they backfired at full strength. Becoming more and more frustrated with Dreadgill's *Crushing Depths* deck—since he had used the powerful *Diving Belt* Trinket to sink and destroy most of Brigarch's Allies—Brigarch attacked with a class three warsong called *Irial's - Astonishing - Geyser - of Deleterious - yet Memorable - Lustrous - Revenge*, which he unfortunately misplayed and gave Dreadgill lethal.

"Shellshock, you are shattered!"

An overabundance of cheering came from the Roycroft house supporters as the tables emptied so the next group of challengers could take the stage and begin their matches.

Standing at the refreshment table while the defeated challengers were escorted to the first-row seats of the south section, Tiarnen sipped on his still-warm tea and watched Coniel make short work of Reefclaw. Moondrop then defeated Gangplank a few turns later. And Fogfisher clutched victory against Sharptooth on a near record-setting fortieth turn.

The victors arrived at the refreshment table and took up their drinks.

"From what I've seen so far, the quality of the Niervalian cards is nowhere near that of Dorladdich's," said Kraitbane.

"Goes for the rest of this cursed province," muttered Lachlan, sipping from his goblet.

Kraitbane chuckled at the remark but then fell silent after noticing that the barons were staring at him.

"Nonetheless, there have been some impressive decks and plays already," said Tiarnen.

"Even if most of them are from last season," added Coniel.

"Can't blame us for using what works," said Kraitbane. "Tournament stakes are too high to risk unproven combinations anyway. Well, for most of us, that is." Kraitbane raised his glass to Tiarnen.

"Happy to be at a disadvantage if only to keep Swiftsail here entertained," said Tiarnen.

"Perhaps if he was less fixated on everyone else, the Premiership wouldn't be such a close race this year," said Lachlan.

"It's funny that you have *Dread* in your name because even if it was a *one-point* difference, I still wouldn't be worried about you," said Coniel.

Tiarnen laughed into his mug and then took a last sip as Cleary raised his arms to the crowd and drew everyone's attention.

"The quarter-finals are now commencing!" announced Cleary. "It will be Fogfisher versus Grensky at table one... Dreadgill versus Kraitbane at table two... Moondrop versus Swiftsail at table three... and Rainmaker versus Yavor at table four!"

The challengers handed their empty drinks to the servants and then made their way onto the stage, where decks were once again shuffled, coins flipped, and minute glasses turned.

Fogfisher was the first to win by gaining an early advantage on Grensky thanks to his *Ravenous Shark* Ally synergizing with the *Tempting Lure* Trinket and devouring the board. However, Grensky's *Craterous Cretins* deck wasn't so easily defeated thanks to his *Dwelglin* Allies that not only stole the Lure but also modified it with the *Rusty Ratchet* Trinket and turned Fogfisher's *Shark* against him.

"Fogfisher, you are shattered!" announced the official.

Unfortunately for Kraitbane, he didn't last much longer against Dreadgill. By turn five, Dreadgill had already drawn his *Diving Belt* Trinket and used it to sink Kraitbane's Allies, leaving him open to a powerful class two attack warsong called *Faelan's – Admirable – Plunge*

– *of Booming – Innervation*, which dragged Kraitbane down to a lethal depth.

"Kraitbane, you are shattered!" announced the official.

Moondrop wasted no time unleashing her *Jellyfish* Allies on Swiftsail. In fact, by turn eight, Swiftsail's *Seaman* Allies were overwhelmed and made useless after being stung. Luckily, Swiftsail was able to piece together a class two attack warsong called *Anrahan's – Zealous – Gust*, which blew all the *Jellyfish* back into Moondrop's deck. He was then able to revive his *Seamen*, who danced to the beat of the warsong and struck Moondrop for lethal.

"Moondrop, you are shattered!" announced the official.

Tiarnen was nervous about facing Yavor, and the board was proving he had good reason. Yavor had six *Raven* Allies in play as well as his *Barbed Whip* Weapon equipped, which meant that whenever he attacked Tiarnen with the *Whip*, all the *Ravens* would attack as well. By turn eight, Tiarnen already found himself down to half health and didn't have much to counter with. Luckily, he drew *Tuathal's* and was able to release a class three attack warsong called *Tuathal's – Rousing – Starlight – of Advantageous – yet Detrimental – Beaming – Retribution*, which caused enemies who inflicted damage on him to also hit themselves with the same amount. Needless to say, the *Ravens* didn't survive their own damage, and the board was cleared. Yavor tried to quickly rebuild another flock, but the draw wasn't in his favour, so Tiarnen hit for lethal.

"Yavor, you are shattered!" announced the official.

Those who had bet on Tiarnen shouted accolades as he walked off the stage to the refreshment table with Lachlan, Coniel, and Grensky while their defeated opponents left in the opposite direction to take their seats.

"Have to admit, I vas not sure if I vould make it this far," said Grensky, taking another drink off the servant's tray.

"A little luck goes a long way in the tournament," said Coniel, looking back to see Kaleigh making yet another bet. "Kaleigh! Where are the odds landing for the semifinal?"

"Apparently Lachlan and Grensky are favoured to move on," she said, taking her betting slip from the bookie.

"We'll see about that," Coniel said confidently.

Kaleigh gave her brother a big smile, but Tiarnen could see the worry in her eyes.

"The semifinals are now commencing!" announced Cleary. "Grensky versus Rainmaker will be at table one, and Swiftsail versus Dreadgill will be at table three!"

Tables two and four retracted and became flush with the stage floor as the challengers paired up and made their way to their assigned tables with an official trailing behind. Decks were shuffled, coins tossed, minute glasses turned, and the first hands were drawn. All four players carefully rearranged their cards, knowing that this might very well be the last match they played tonight.

Tiarnen won the coin toss and so used his *Dance of Lances* Talent to strike Grensky and put him on his heels. Despite the early provocation, the baron wasn't fazed and returned the gesture with his own *Ebon Claws* Talent, which cut into Tiarnen for an equal amount of damage. For the next few turns, they built up the board with a variety of Allies, but the one Tiarnen was most concerned about was the *Loyal Minion*, which closely resembled the dwelglin Khazlokov had chained to his side at the *Battle of the Bridge*. Reason being, it allowed Grensky to pull whatever Song cards he needed from his deck to complete the one in his hand.

Worried about what was about to come, Tiarnen played *Balim's – Courageous – Barricade* to put up some defensive protection and then braced himself. As expected, Grensky pulled the five cards he needed from his deck and then laid down *Velisav's – Petulant – Breath – of Vi-*

cious – and Noxious – Sparkling – Cremation, which he played perfectly and set Tiarnen ablaze for ten damage per turn. Given that Tiarnen only had twenty health left, that meant he had two turns before he was shattered. Back against a wall, Tiarnen looked over his hand and noticed that there was potential to make a complicated play that might save him, but first, he needed to see what his next card was. Tiarnen drew from his deck and placed the card in his hand to see that it was his *Sing Ring* Trinket.

"Opponent health check, please," said Tiarnen.

"Grensky stands with thirty-two health points," said the official.

Tiarnen nodded in understanding and then played his *Caitria Finwick* Ally, who empowered the three *Wakerider* Allies to strike Grensky for ten health. Excited for what he thought would be a decisive turn, Grensky shifted in his seat—only for Tiarnen to play his *Sing Ring* Trinket.

"Vhat is this?" shouted Grensky, reading the Trinket trait to learn that he had to skip his turn.

"Good question. Let's find out," said Tiarnen, drawing a card from the shuffler. He wanted to hide his smirk after seeing that it was *Radovir's* since it completed the class two warsong he needed, but he couldn't help himself. One by one, he placed the cards down and then played *Radovir's – Dreadful – Magma – of Provoking – Spoilation*. Despite missing one queue, Tiarnen completed the performance and unleashed the warsong effect, which caused Grensky's Allies to not only catch fire but also enter a panicked frenzy and swarm him for lethal.

"Baron Grensky, you are shattered!" announced the official.

Grensky looked up from the table and stared directly into Tiarnen's eyes as the crowd shouted both praise and scorn. There was no movement from the baron as the betting slips with his name on caught fire throughout the arena—he simply held his gaze on Tiarnen.

"You played well, Baron," said Tiarnen.

"Vell, if I am to lose," said Grensky, his demeanour suddenly relaxing. "I am glad it is by your hand."

Waiting at the table, Tiarnen looked up to Tharus, who gave him a subtle nod of satisfaction that ruined the victory for him. He knew the barons couldn't be allowed to hold so much economic power in Niervalia, but Tiarnen still hated the fact that he contributed to any part of his father's agenda. Desperate to give himself something else to think about, he glanced back at Kaleigh only to see that she had gone several shades paler while watching Coniel's match unfold. Tiarnen wanted to reassure her that Lachlan would be defeated, but the arena suddenly filled with gasps and groans.

"Swiftsail, you are shattered!" announced the official.

"No!" sighed Kaleigh, her head dropping.

Tiarnen turned to see Coniel standing at the table in a total state of shock.

"Some... something has to be wrong with the shuffler!" said Coniel, looking at it as though he had just been insulted. "The odds of me drawing that last card are—"

"The same as any other," interrupted Lachlan.

"I still want it checked!" demanded Coniel.

"I am sorry, but there has been no tampering," said the official. "It was a clean match."

"I would say *well played* but..." said Lachlan, already walking away with his deck.

Coniel pounded his fist on the table and then swiped his cards off it as the betting slips and his hope of securing the Premiership went up in smoke. Accepting that nothing else could be done, he turned and followed Dreadgill down the stairs to the refreshment table.

"The shattered are not permi—" began Cleary.

"It's fine," interrupted Tiarnen, raising his hand to the official.

"It most definitely is not *fine*," said Coniel, looking up at his sister. "I'm sorry, Kaleigh. Just had the worst draw ever."

"There's nothing more you could have done," said Kaleigh. "The fact that you made it to the semis is more than admirable."

"If you say so," said Coniel, his shoulders slumping.

"Hey, she's right," said Tiarnen.

Coniel turned back to Tiarnen. "You have to beat him. If the Roycrofts take the Premiership, then the provincials will be made slaves again and—"

"I am aware, Coniel," Tiarnen said sternly.

Coniel nodded reluctantly and then climbed over the aisle railing to stand beside Sivakosha, who seemed to be more interested in the Grand Tournament flyer than the dire situation, given her perplexed expression.

"Something wrong, Sivakosha?" asked Tiarnen.

"Yes, these tournament rules, they don't make sense," said Sivakosha.

"Which one in particular?"

"Rule eleven, it says *second place keeps all prizes*."

"It's to ensure that whoever wins the tournament values the prestige above all else."

"Then whoever places second vill have to value getting up very early tomorrow morning."

"Why is that?"

"*Sheprevniak.*"

Tiarnen shook his head in confusion.

"It is seasonal chevrae migration through mountains so they can feed before vinter," said Sivakosha.

"*Through the mountains...*" repeated Tiarnen, remembering that Niera had mentioned something about it in Praetavain. "How far do they have to migrate?"

"All the vay to grove at glacier stronghold."

Tiarnen's stomach sank as he realized what this meant. *If you take second place, the chevrae herd is yours, and you can leave for Phrysbruck tomorrow.*

"The finals are now commencing at the high table!" announced Cleary.

"*High table*?" asked Tiarnen.

As though the stage was answering his question, the first and third tables retracted into the floor, leaving the stage flush until an entirely new and much larger table began to rise from the centre. Tiarnen and Lachlan set their drinks down and made their way over to the stage stairs once again. Upon their arrival at the high table, it locked into place. Lachlan took the left side, and Tiarnen took the right. They both looked over it to see the usual shufflers and minute-glass turner, but that was where the similarities to the other tables ended.

The top itself was very wide and resembled a stained-glass window. Each player side had an area to place cards down, from which an ornate pattern of about three hundred tiny glass panels spread out and merged in the middle. At the far ends, the table's raised edges were inset with mirrors that looked to be positioned so they could reflect the card light onto the board.

"This will do nicely," said Tiarnen.

"Present your decks, please," said Cleary, arriving at the end of the table.

Tiarnen and Lachlan handed their decks to Cleary, who did a quick card inspection and then placed them into the shufflers.

Thwip-thwip-thwip-thwip-thwip-thwip-thwip!

"Dreadgill, the call is yours." Cleary pulled a coin from his pocket and flicked it into the air.

"Heads!" called Lachlan.

The coin landed in Cleary's hand. He palmed it against the top of his other hand and then slowly revealed the result. "Heads!" he said. "Dreadgill, the first turn is yours!"

Lachlan and Tiarnen drew their cards while Cleary turned the minute glass over.

Tiarnen carefully arranged all nine of his cards at even height and distance from each other so as not to give away any pairings. His eyes glanced over his hand to see a variety of mismatched Song cards, as well as an Ally, Weapon, and a Talent. There wasn't much to make any big early plays with, but he wasn't overly concerned since he would rather be building a foundation for a strong mid- or late-game push anyway.

Lachlan finished organizing his cards and then played a *Morey Eel* Ally card. Although it didn't hit for much damage, its handy attribute would allow Lachlan to draw three cards on each turn and choose from them.

Tiarnen didn't have a card to counter the *Eel* with, so he drew and added a new Song card to his hand. Left with few options, he played his *Kalder "Forty-Six" Foolsworth* Ally, whose attribute would only allow Lachlan to play one card at a time while he was present on the board.

Annoyed by Tiarnen's play, Lachlan drew three cards, picked the one he wanted, and then slipped it into his hand while Cleary put the discarded ones back into the shuffler. He then struck Tiarnen for a single point of damage with the *Morey Eel* but didn't play any other cards.

Cleary crossed a health point off Tiarnen's player sheet and flipped the minute glass.

Happy to have quickly made up for the turn disadvantage, Tiarnen drew his *Dance of Lances* Talent card and immediately played it to destroy the *Morey Eel*. Knowing that Lachlan's *Crushing Depths* decks also had a strong mid-game ramp, Tiarnen played *Balim's – Courageous – Barricade* to give himself a bit of protection. He slapped the three cards onto the table, and the stained-glass panels around them began to glow. The entire arena leaned in as he gently tapped the first warsong card with his index finger, making the shard shape flash in green and emit simple tones. The light show, however, didn't end there. Pulsing in a rhythmic pattern, the high table flashed with Tiarnen's performance and cast a dazzling display of light over the entire arena. Even Tiarnen himself was somewhat distracted by the unexpected and nearly overwhelming splendour, but he managed to finish the warsong and empower its defensive attribute, which would shield him for ten points of damage.

HARAAAH!

Tiarnen's supporters shouted and applauded in celebration.

Wanting all the spotlight for himself, Lachlan drew a card and then played a class two attack warsong called *Liadaine's – Brazen – Font – of Refreshing – Retaliation*. He set the five cards on the table, and just like before, the glass panels came to life. Lachlan tapped the first card and made the table pulse in sync. The arena filled with light and sound as he played the complex sequence and empowered the attribute, which ensured that any damage his Ally's inflicted would return an equal amount of health to himself for the next two turns.

HARAAAH!

Lachlan's supporters—especially his family—shouted in support.

Tiarnen tried to conceal his concern and drew another card, but he was disheartened to see that it wouldn't contribute to any type of synergistic play. Left without much choice, he played *Major Raghnall* in anticipation that Lachlan was about to put down a few more Allies, given his warsong choice.

Sure enough, Lachlan drew and then played three *Tyrannical Tentacle* Allies.

As much as Tiarnen didn't want to believe it, he was in trouble. Lachlan now had an active warsong protecting him as well as three Ally tentacles that would seize *Major Raghnall*, not to mention any other Allies Tiarnen might play, and drag him off the board once Lachlan had his *Diving Belt* Trinket equipped. The only way out of the situation was to draw the last card he needed for Finnian's Fervent Flood. Tiarnen took a card and, to his relief, saw that it was his *Flood* Song. Instinct kicked in and had him pulling the other two cards from his hand, but just as he was about to play the warsong he thought of the Sheprevniak. Tiarnen kept staring at his cards as though reconsidering his play, but in reality, his heart was quickly filling with dread. He knew he needed to leave the city tomorrow if there was any chance of reaching Maestro Phrygus before the attack on Phrysbruck, and as far as Tiarnen could tell, the Sheprevniak was his only way there.

"Time," warned Cleary, seeing that only a quarter of the minute glass was left.

Tiarnen took a deep breath to try and calm his nerves. It didn't work. Heart pounding now, his eyes left the cards and looked over Lachlan's shoulder to Kaleigh and Coniel who were leaning over the guard rail in anticipation of what they were hoping would be a winning play.

"Turn lost in three... two..." warned Cleary, pointing to the last of the sand emptying.

Tiarnen played his *Mendful Maiden* Ally, which healed him for the one point of damage on his card. By every measure, the play was a complete waste since the *Maiden* could have healed for much more.

"Oh, come now, you can do better than that," said Lachlan.

"Easy with the taunting, Dreadgill," warned Cleary.

"I am merely concerned for my opponent here since he seems to be cracking under the stress already," said Lachlan, gesturing to the *Maiden*.

Tiarnen remained silent as a cold sweat began to cover him.

Lachlan drew a card, which turned out to be his *Diving Belt* Trinket. More than satisfied with his luck, Lachlan attacked *Major Raghnall* and the *Mendful Maiden* with the *Tentacles*, which meant the *Diving Belt* would crush and remove them next turn.

Realizing how careful he needed to be, Tiarnen tried to think of a way to make it look like he wasn't throwing the match—especially since he still had the right warsong to remove the *Tentacles* and save his Allies. Tiarnen drew a card, and to his dismay, it completed the class three attack warsong in his hand that would destroy Lachlan's Trinket. Never before had he cursed such a clutch draw, but with two complete and viable warsongs now in hand, he knew that he had to play one of them or risk drawing far too much attention to himself. Left with no choice, Tiarnen put down *Ruarc's – Intoxicating – Surge – of Mischievous – yet Thoughtful – Pearly – Liquification*.

The table flashed and pulsed with an intensity not yet seen. As the entire arena was cast in kaleidoscopic light and filled with amplified tones, Tiarnen made a strong effort to seem overwhelmed by the complex card queues. He tried his best to make misplays seem erratic and then buckled under the supposed pressure by missing the last three queues at the very end. Much like the Ashbrook's hopes, the table faded with Tiarnen's failure, and his turn came to an end.

The minute glass flipped, but Lachlan did not draw a card right away. He paused for a moment, looking at Tiarnen in confused disbelief at what he had just witnessed.

"The turn is yours, Dreadgill," said Cleary.

Still staring at Tiarnen, Lachlan drew a card and then finally looked at it. Unwilling to turn down the opportunity that Tiarnen's supposed blunder had provided him, he went all in and played every card in his hand. First, *Major Raghnall* and the *Maiden* were sunk with his *Diving Belt* Trinket and removed. Next, he played two *Shock Wave* Talent cards that broke *Balim's Courageous Barricade* and destroyed its defensive attribute thus leaving Tiarnen open to direct attack. Lachlan sniffed and then pressed on with his legendary *Admiral Kardinic* Ally.

The artwork portrayed an elderly man in a lavish naval uniform standing at a captain's wheel. *Kardinic* was the last of the Dorladdian fleet admirals, who made his name by hunting down the notorious *Cardinal Cove* pirates by ramming his ship into theirs and sinking both. *Kardinic* hit for significant damage alone, but his attribute also allowed him to strike again for each enemy Ally that had already been sunk. It was a lethal play, and Lachlan took great pleasure in watching Cleary cross off the rest of Tiarnen's health points.

"Rainmaker... you are shattered!"

Half of the arena went wild while the rest burned their betting slips, tore up signs, and shouted in anger at the loss. To make matters worse, a few fights broke out in the lower rows.

Tiarnen felt like he was going to be sick.

"Looks like someone could use another sea-spit," said Lachlan, smiling.

Cleary turned away from the table to face Tharus's balcony and gestured to Lachlan.

Grensky, sour-faced, arrived at the amplistaff. "It gives me... great pleasure... to announce that Dreadgill is our new Grand Tournament champion!"

Most of the arena cheered this time, but those who took on heavy losses remained in their seats—if not hunched over in them.

The other officials made their way onto the stage, holding a massive jewelled ceramic cup with thick handles on either side and the last fifty champion names engraved around it. Tiarnen knew he was supposed to stick around for the closing ceremony and what was sure to be an indulgent after-party, but he wanted none of it. As Grensky continued to announce the victory details, Tiarnen gathered his deck and walked off the stage to make way for the arena exit.

Chapter Twenty-Eight
THE SHEPREVNIAK

Drips of green wax fell on the back of a small parchment envelope. Just above it, Tiarnen held a candle to a small sealing stick—his tired eyes watching the wax slowly melt and secure the letter that he had been up all night trying to write.

Finding what very well might be his last words to Raghnall was much harder than he expected; informing the major of his plan to reach Phrysbruck alone was one thing, but saying a proper goodbye should his infiltration fail was another. He was confident that the hidden message in what was otherwise a mundane update about life in Niervalia would be understood, but, in the end, what he really wanted to express was his gratitude for all that Raghnall had risked for him.

The wax pooled over the middle of the envelope flap, and Tiarnen set the sealing stick down on the desk, grabbed the stamper, and then pressed into the wax, embossing it with a Dorladdian seal. He knew full well that the letter would be opened by Holgor before Raghnall received it, but he didn't want to further risk anyone outside of the Inquisitor glancing over the sensitive information. Tiarnen gently blew on the wax to harden it—catching movement out of the corner of his eye.

Mowww!

Tiarnen turned to see Persol emerging from under the bed covers. "Just because I'm up doesn't mean you need to be."

MOW!

"I'm actually hungry, too, now that you mention it," said Tiarnen, setting the letter on the table and then peering at his pocket watch to see it was nearly six in the morning. "*Already?*" he asked himself, standing to his feet in surprise. Panic filling his empty stomach, he hurried over to the wardrobe and quickly changed into his formal maestro attire. After locking the buckle on his multi-belt, he stepped into his combat boots, strapped on the leg holster, slipped Darktide into his back pocket, put on his jacket, and then shoved the cloak under his arm.

"Well, looks like this is goodbye," said Tiarnen, kneeling to Persol, who tilted her head in confusion. "Thanks for keeping me company... and not eating me in my sleep." He chuckled and cautiously gave two gentle pets. He was about to pull his hand away per usual but instead held it above her head. "Since this is probably the last time we get to do this?"

Persol's eyes narrowed in distrust, but then she lifted her tiny pink nose up towards his palm, which Tiarnen took as a sign and gave her a third pet.

"At least you get the bed to yourself again." He stood up, opened the chamber door, and was met by two sleepy praetorian guards who jolted to attention.

"Everything in order, Maestro?" asked the first guard.

"I'm fine," said Tiarnen, "just getting Persol something to eat—keep an eye on her for me, will you?"

The guards looked at Persol.

HISSS!

"Oh, and there's a letter on my desk for Major Raghnall that needs to go out with today's mail."

"Of course," said the second guard.

As the guards entered his room, Tiarnen quickly made his way down the hallway, passed through the reception hall, and then snuck into the kitchen, which was empty save for a dishwasher scrubbing a pile of cast-iron pans.

"H-hello," said the young dishwasher.

"Good morning," said Tiarnen, sauntering over to the grocery carts to see that one of them still had a crate of dried ingredients of some sort in them. "Looks like Auberdine forgot a few things." He pulled the crate out. "Mind taking this for me?"

The dishwasher, stunned that he was standing near, let alone speaking with a maestro, walked over and took the crate. Tiarnen then threw his cloak on and hopped into the last of the grocery carts but realized he couldn't reach the release lever.

"Would you be so kind as to pull the lever there for me?"

Completely bewildered by what was happening, the dishwasher reluctantly walked over to the lever.

"Appreciate it," said Tiarnen.

The dishwasher pulled on the lever, and the grocery train started to speed down the tracks.

"You're doing a great job on those pans, by the way. Absolutely spotless!" said Tiarnen.

"Th-thank you, Maestro!" said the dishwasher.

Keeping himself low, Tiarnen pulled his hood up and watched the palace tunnel blur past—opening to the crater as the train continued along the top of the chain rail.

Wanting one last look, he risked raising his head and peered over his shoulder to see the palace basking in the orange magmatic underglow while Mikavnik stood at the entrance like a sentinel. A strange calm washed over him as though something inside had accepted that he was now past a point of no return, and with that realization, darkness enveloped him once again as he vanished into another narrow tunnel. Tiarnen looked ahead, but there was nothing to be seen. He could only feel the train shuttering and swerving as it continued east for what felt like an eternity. Rounding a sharp corner, he emerged from the darkness and found himself racing along the ridge of Elvarok crater, where countless provincial dockers were tending to other grocery carts at the market docking stations.

"Davmir, you could have mentioned this part," muttered Tiarnen, trying to figure out how he wasn't going to be seen. As his train began to slow, Tiarnen noticed the first docking station was empty and readied himself to leap out. When the station arrived, he vaulted out of the cart, landed hard on the docking platform, and then slammed into the station-dividing wall.

He grimaced from the hard impact and slowly drew himself up, peering around the corner to see two emaciated dockers hurrying over to fill the carts. Needing a distraction, Tiarnen pulled the release lever on the train, which sent it shooting down the track and crashing into the next train—

WHAM!

Which caused that one to hit the next train—

WHAM!

And then the next—

WHAM!

Chaos ensued as all the trains rocked and spilled much of their food down into the lava below.

The foremen cracked their whips at any provincial within range—yelling randomly at everyone since they had no idea who'd caused the accident.

Tiarnen seized the moment and dashed into a gap between the nearby piles of grocery crates. Using them as cover, he quietly wove his way through and then crept along the crater wall until he reached a long flight of stairs, which looked to lead up to the stables. Flyers and betting slips from the Grand Tournament were still everywhere and made him think about his decision to throw the match. With the Roycrofts seizing the Premiership, Aran finally had the power to dissolve the Ashbrook accords and make life much harder on the provincials. *Are things only going to get worse because of you?* The thought made Tiarnen's heart sink, and he imagined each page in his chapter of the Maestro Diary being filled with nothing but remorse for causing everyone more suffering. However, as he took the last stair and finally reached the surface, Tiarnen saw the stable just ahead and reminded himself that if he didn't press on then the cruel malice that his father was already inflicting upon Chora would never end.

Tiarnen walked past the holding pens which were filled with every chevrae he now owned. He didn't know much as far as their behaviour, but they seemed to be excited, given the frantic tail wags and rapid bleating. Continuing past and finally arriving at the east entrance of the ironwork barn, Tiarnen came to stand before the barons who were holding long crooks while mounted on the strangest animals he had ever seen. They were much like horses as far as size and character except with greasy dark orange hair, a stubby tail, long spiral horns that had a lantern hanging from each one, and hooves so narrow it almost looked like they were walking on spear tips.

"Ah, Maestro, ve vere starting to believe you vould not be joining us," said Grensky.

"Happy to disappoint," said Tiarnen.

"I am surprised that you are villing to risk leaving the city so close to Legion's departure," said Yavor.

"Right, well…" Tiarnen tried to think of a reasonable excuse. "… I like to clear my head before a battle."

"Some fresh mountain air should help vith that," said Grensky.

"My thoughts exactly, Baron," Tiarnen agreed, turning his attention to the barons' mounts. "I take it these are what we will be riding to the glen?"

"Yes, ostrop are only mount that can climb mountain trail," said Ferotov, patting his ostrop's long neck.

"And we're not bringing an armed escort along with us?" asked Tiarnen, noticing there weren't any guards to be seen.

"Never have to, Sheprevniak is vell vithin borders," said Yavor. "But ve should be on our vay. I vill get a hand to bring your mount—"

"It's all right," interrupted Tiarnen, "I'm sure I can manage."

"Here, you must vear to lead Sheprevniak," said Ferotov, handing Tiarnen a rather tall cap made from ostrop fur with several randomly protruding horn tips and thin chains dangling in between them.

"Let me guess, something to do with tradition?" asked Tiarnen, looking the cap over as he made his way inside of the stable. After walking past numerous empty stalls, some being cleaned by stable hands, he reached the shadowy far end where his ostrop was waiting. Curious about Tiarnen, it leaned its horned head over the shoulder-high gate, sniffed at him, and then shook its head.

"Yeah, well, you don't exactly smell great either, so how about we both agree not to stick our noses where they don't belong, eh?" asked Tiarnen, grabbing the reins and opening the stall.

The ostrop reluctantly followed his lead and stepped out. As it did, Tiarnen set the fur cap in the rigid iron-frame saddle that was secured over a thick woollen blanket. He noticed a leather satchel on the back filled with canned Dorladdian rations as well as a large canteen, which he assumed was full of water.

"Should have asked Auberdine to pack you a lunch."

Startled, Tiarnen spun around on the spot to see Niera standing a couple of metres away with her arms crossed.

"By the... is anyone else with you?" asked Tiarnen.

"Just Mikavnik, but I told her to wait by the pens," said Niera.

He sighed in relief. "How did you know where to find me?"

"After rehearsals were cancelled this morning, I figured it probably had something to do with you recently acquiring every goat in Niervalia."

"Don't worry. It's only a day trip."

Niera rolled her eyes.

"I have to go," said Tiarnen. "There's no other way."

"I know."

"And even if—wait—you do?" asked Tiarnen, realizing that Niera had just agreed with him.

"Before dinner the other night, you were right. I should have said something. It's just that..."

Niera's voice faded, and the stable filled with an uneasy silence.

"He is going to ask where I have gone to," said Tiarnen.

"Which is why I'll make sure I'm not around to answer that question until later this evening," said Niera. "That should buy enough distance so that no one can reach you before we have to leave tomorrow."

"Thank you."

"This is the part where you tell me how exactly we're supposed to find you in Phrysbruck."

"I'll try to lure Maestro Phrygus to the top of the Tantalis."

"Why?"

"The henge is supposed to be there, and I—" said Tiarnen, stopping cold after realizing that he was about to give himself away. "I figured that would be the best landmark to regroup at."

Niera stared at Tiarnen as though she saw through him. "Attacking the city without you is going to pose a serious problem for the legion."

"Not if they have the finest orchestra in Chora rallying them," said Tiarnen. "Besides, it'll be far worse for Praetor Sturm."

"How do you figure that?" asked Niera, baffled at his statement.

"Because he'll expect Phrygus to be at his side. When he isn't, the Phrygian legion will be confused, if not entirely lost, as to what to do."

"No maestros means no turns."

"Exactly," said Tiarnen. "Our legion can just keep pressing into the city."

Niera nodded in agreement but then looked down at the ground and gave a sniffle.

"Come here," said Tiarnen, walking over to Niera and pulling her into a hug.

"Keep an eye on the barons," said Niera. "They just lost everything, and I don't see them as the type to forgive easily."

"Don't worry. I'll be fine."

"Good." Niera pushed him away. "Because if all of this goes terribly wrong, I don't want them killing you before I get the chance."

"I love you too," said Tiarnen, chuckling. He walked back to the os-trop, stepped into the stirrup, and pulled himself onto the saddle—the rigid iron bars immediately biting into his sides.

"That does not look comfortable," said Niera.

"Just like everything else Niervalian," said Tiarnen, trying to adjust his seating position to find some relief.

"Careful, you're talking about my city."

"Then how about you start making some improvements around here," said Tiarnen. "Oh, that reminds me, I need you to add a little something extra to Sivakosha and Davmir's bonds."

"Their bonds? What for?"

"So Lachlan knows that they're under my personal protection after his father dissolves the Ashbrook accords."

"I'll come up with something," said Niera, nodding in agreement.

Tiarnen put on his fur cap and fastened the chin strap. "How do I look?"

"Let's just say it's fitting," said Niera, her laugh quickly turning into a look of concern.

"What's wrong?"

"Nothing. It's stupid."

Tiarnen stared at her.

"Last night... I noticed something... about the vilmiras," said Niera. "They are the same dancers as the one in my music box back home."

"It would seem so," said Tiarnen.

"Why would Mother give it to me then?" asked Niera.

"She was... complicated... but I can promise you that her decisions were always made with best intentions in mind—especially when it came to our family."

"Maybe she had a feeling that Lydvenko would one day be mine," said Niera, the idea bringing the smile back to her face.

"Then it looks like you proved her right, Twinkles."

"Tiarnen, do you think she would be proud of us?"

"One of us," said Tiarnen, leaning down to tuck a curl behind Niera's ear. "I'll see you soon." He sat up again and cracked the reins, then left the stable.

*

With the city behind them and ravens following high above, Tiarnen's ostrop travelled a well-trodden trail that, within a few hours, had already led the herd out of the Adogon Valley and then between the sharp granite toes of the Olvuruk mountains. Along the way, a few chevrae wandered off, but the barons were swift to use their long crooks and yank them back into the herd. The barons hadn't said much to Tiarnen after they departed, although he could still hear them occasionally laughing, which he guessed had something to do with his ridiculous fur cap. They eventually arrived at the mountain face, where the terrain changed just as quickly as the gradient did. Seeing that the trail came to a dead end, Tiarnen was about to look back and ask the barons how they were going to continue ahead, only for his ostrop to suddenly leap onto the steep rock.

"A little warning would have been—" began Tiarnen. But before he could finish his sentence, the ostrop leaped up the face again... then again... and yet again—its sharp hooves landing on the narrow ridge-lines in the stone. Since his mount clearly knew the way, Tiarnen let go of the reins and gripped both sides of the saddle frame so he could hold on for dear life as they continued to climb while the chevrae followed close behind.

It was around midday when they reached the first plateau, and Tiarnen could make out the seven craters of Niervalia through the acrid haze. They looked like a constellation of smouldering stars. In fact, from his vantage point, the craters didn't seem to have erupted from the earth as Tharus had told. Instead, they looked to be caused by enormous impacts that rippled outwards like waves—their crests becoming the very mountains Tiarnen was now navigating.

"Maestro, ve should keep going," said Grensky, arriving on Tiarnen's right and lighting his ostrop's lantern with a flinter.

"Are we in a hurry?" asked Tiarnen.

"Have to reach canyon before nightfall or vill be stuck on mountain ridge," said Yavor.

"Doesn't sound like a great way to spend an evening," said Tiarnen.

"I vould not recommend," said Grensky.

With Tiarnen leading again, the herd climbed up the second ridge, the mountain face becoming even steeper along the way. In fact, it became so steep that Tiarnen was instinctually holding his hand against the face after a few chevrae had lost their footing and fallen to a bone-crushing death in the ravine far below. The ravens then proved why they were following so closely by swooping down moments after to feast on the fresh carcasses. Given the losses, Tiarnen thought the barons would have said something, perhaps to slow down, but they only continued to ostracize him, so he assumed they merely expected some fatalities during the treacherous journey.

Evening arrived, and with the sun setting fast behind the rocky western peaks, Tiarnen felt the air grow cool for the first time since he could remember. He opened up his jacket and breathed a long sigh of relief as Niervalia's relentless heat finally released its grip. However, the dryness in the air seemed to worsen. Assuming it had something to do with the altitude, Tiarnen grabbed his canteen as the ostrop turned off the ridgeline, and he sipped away while the herd entered a gap between the mountains.

Lantern lights danced, and bleats echoed against the snaking canyon walls, which finally opened up to reveal the fabled glen. Tiarnen went slack-jawed at the unexpected, tranquil sight of lush green grass and the sweet smell of yellow honeysuckle flowers, which contrasted against the colossal gleaming blue glacier on the far side, while Brathlún and Sorolún chased each other in the dusky sky above. All he could do was take another gulp from his canteen and continue to stare in awe while the famished chevrae hurried past him to gorge on the grasses.

"Vell done, Maestro!" said Grensky, arriving along Tiarnen's left side. "Vas like you had been on Sheprevniak a hundred times."

"Let's be honest, all I did was hold on," said Tiarnen, patting his ostrop in thanks as he took another long sip. "How long will the chevrae need to feed?"

"By morning, there vill not be a single blade of grass left." Ferotov arrived along Tiarnen's right side.

"Should we be worried about Phrygrian scouts?" asked Tiarnen.

"No, they don't have reason to venture this far since stronghold vas abandoned," said Yavor, arriving along Tiarnen's left side and then pointing to the glacier where the stronghold entrance was.

Tiarnen tried to focus through the dim lantern light. From what he could see, there was a pair of tall iron doors set in the ice with several piles of empty supply crates on either side.

"I overheard rumours in Dorladdich, but no one seemed to know exactly why the glacier was abandoned."

"Neither do ve," admitted Ferotov.

"What did the legionaries say after they returned?" asked Tiarnen.

Grensky shrugged. "Nothing."

"How could that be?"

"Because none made it back alive," said Grensky.

"Only thing to cross glacier these days are natterhorns," said Ferotov.

"I don't think I have ever heard of—"

"They are like rabbits, except vith horns, and more fur—make very good roasts," added Grensky.

"Come, there is place for us to make fire and rest," said Yavor, cracking his reins and leading his ostrop towards a small maple tree grove along the west side of the glen.

Tiarnen followed the barons, but as they passed through the glen, the glacial entrance became clearer. He could see that the stronghold doors weren't locked. In fact, they weren't even closed. A wave of relief washed over him. He had done it. He had found a way to Phrysbruck, and given that it was nearly dark, all he needed to do now was let the barons fall asleep and then quietly make his way inside the glacier.

Everyone arrived at the maple grove, and the barons dismounted so they could tie their ostrops to the trees which surrounded a large iron-frame cabin that had a deep fire pit at the front. Tiarnen was about to climb down as well but a series of thunderclaps echoed and drew his attention to the nearby glacial wall. Deep vertical cracks ran down the ice. Many of them were wide enough for him to fit through, but as he stared into the voids, they only seemed to lead to a frozen oblivion. For some reason, his head was spinning at the thought, so he turned his ostrop toward the nearest tree and then hopped out of his saddle. The moment Tiarnen's feet touched the ground, he knew something was wrong. Nearly falling over, he tried to steady himself by grabbing onto the saddle again. But his hand slipped, and he slammed against the tree.

"Are you all right, Maestro?" asked Grensky.

"Perfectly fine," said Tiarnen. "Legs are just numb from sssitting all day."

Yavor pointed at Tiarnen's feet. "Looks more serious than that."

"Nothing I can't walk off," said Tiarnen, pushing himself off the tree only to stumble for a few steps and then trip over.

THUD!

The next thing Tiarnen knew, he was flat on his back and staring up at the moons, which were circling above him at a hundred times the speed.

"Oh, look, the maestro fell over," muttered Ferotov.

"I must have mistakenly put voligar in his canteen instead of vater," said Yavor.

"Was no missstake," said Tiarnen.

"Ah, see, he is fast learner," said Grensky.

"Here, let us help you up, Maestro," said Yavor, holding out his hand for Tiarnen.

With the entire glen now spinning around him, Tiarnen took Yavor's hand and tried to pull himself up.

CRACK!

Yavor struck Tiarnen clean in the jaw and sent him crashing back to the ground.

"Yavor, how dare you treat him vith such disrespect," said Ferotov, walking past Yavor to hold a hand out for Tiarnen. "Come, let's get you on your feet."

Blood dripping from his split lip, Tiarnen grasped Ferotov's hand and began to pull himself up.

WHAM!

Ferotov kicked Tiarnen square in the ribs and knocked him back down.

"Maestro, you must get up," pleaded Ferotov, holding his hand out again.

"Please... just let me... go..." wheezed Tiarnen, clutching at his ribs and ignoring Ferotov's second attempt to pull him back to his feet.

"He von't take my hand again; I'm insulted." Ferotov drew a dagger from his belt.

"No... no more," begged Tiarnen.

"Maestro, don't beg, is embarrassing," said Grensky, putting his boot on Tiarnen and pushing him over.

"Why... why are you doing this?"

"Vhy?" asked Yavor, laughing with the other barons. "*Vhy*, he asks!"

"You take our province, our city, our music, and then if that vas not enough, you take everything ve are vorth," said Ferotov, pointing his dagger at the herd.

"Phrysbruck... you don't understand... I must go to Phrysbruck," coughed Tiarnen, turning onto his stomach and beginning to crawl along the grass.

"Unfortunately, your tragic fall vill prevent you from ever reaching the Tantalis," said Grensky.

"The look on Praetor Tharus's face vill be priceless vhen he sees your broken body in the ravine," said Yavor.

"Little sister vill no doubt be heartbroken, too," said Ferotov, kneeling beside Tiarnen and then raising the dagger into the air.

The idea of Niera seeing him crushed and folded over suddenly steeled Tiarnen and made his resonance bloom. It only lasted for a brief moment, but the second of clarity allowed him to flip over and strike Ferotov clean in the face before he could plunge the dagger.

"Grab him!" yelled Grensky, stepping over Ferotov, who was grasping his broken nose.

But before the barons had the chance to seize him, Tiarnen had already scrambled to his feet and was sprinting through the darkness. He didn't know what direction he was headed. All of Chora seemed to be spinning now—it was only the tree branches cutting his cheeks that told him he hadn't yet fallen over. The barons' shouting suddenly grew louder as their pursuit closed what little distance Tiarnen had gained. He didn't know what could be done. There wasn't anywhere else to go—until he saw a shadow within the shadows just ahead. Tiarnen realized it was one of the glacier cracks, and with a desperate leap, he threw himself into the void.

Chapter Twenty-Nine
ICY DEPTHS

Tiarnen lay motionless on the frozen glacial floor, his splayed body cast in a dim pool of daylight. Ominous thundering echoed from deep within the surrounding shadows, pulling him out of unconsciousness. After a few blurry blinks, his cavernous prison came into focus, only for the thundering to erupt and echo once more. Tiarnen jolted up, looking around frantically for the barons' next attack yet... no one was there... He was completely alone. Eyes wincing, Tiarnen looked up the twenty-metre wall of ice beside him and then stared at the fissure opening where he had apparently made his grand entrance. All he could remember of the assault were a few flashes of the barons striking him, a muddled conversation, and then darkness.

Steadying himself with one hand while holding onto his aching ribs with the other, Tiarnen managed to get a knee up and then finally rise to his feet. Every inch of his body hurt, but it was his swollen jaw and bruised ribs that were causing him to grimace and grunt.

"What a mess," he wheezed, sliding his hand under the maestro jacket to check for blood. Thankfully, there wasn't any, though saying those few short words felt like shards stabbing into his lungs. Given his battered condition, Tiarnen guessed that the barons had assumed that he perished from the fall since there didn't seem to be any sign of effort on their part to climb down and confirm his death. Still, he paused in silence to listen for bleating chevrae, ostrops snorting, or the barons themselves celebrating his supposed demise. For better or worse, there wasn't any, which meant they were already on their way back to Niervalia. He had no idea what the barons were going to tell his father when they returned—outside of the fact that it would certainly be a lie. The question now was, would Tharus believe them, call off the campaign, and delay the attack until the spring in the hope that the pressure might cause Niera to spark? But Tiarnen knew his sister wouldn't give up on the chance that he might still be alive. He suddenly felt so ashamed by the situation. He was foolish not to take Niera's advice about the barons more seriously. He should never have assumed the canteen was safe to drink from. It was arrogant to believe he could simply traverse the glacier and navigate his way to Phrysbruck. This was all his fault. His stomach turned at the realization, but the fact remained that he had managed to breach the glacier—all he had to do now was somehow find a way through it.

Tiarnen reached into his front pants pocket and pulled out his watch to see that the lens was badly cracked, but the hands seemed to be unaffected and told him it was just after four in the afternoon. Knowing that what little daylight there was would soon be gone, he put the watch back and began to look around for anything that appeared to be a tunnel or passage through the ice.

"There has to be... a way... out of here," he wheezed, his foggy breath drifting through the air as though being pulled along a thread. *Odd*, he thought, watching as the last of it trailed into the shadows. Curious, Tiarnen let out another shallow breath, and it, too, drifted in the exact same direction, only this time he followed close behind. *Is something drawing it? A draft from another part of the glacier, perhaps?* He carefully walked over the uneven, slippery ice with only the ambiance of the fissure light to guide his footing. Despite it becoming harder and harder to see while inching forward, Tiarnen knew it was his only option, so he kept his free hand along the frigid glacier wall as it gradually curved and soon led him into total darkness.

Now, without any sense of direction, he became incredibly nervous and let go of his ribs to reach out with his other hand... but nothing was there. Nervousness quickly grew into desperation. Tiarnen remembered the diary entry about the whistle weave and endured the sharp pain of whistling a short melody in the hope that his jacket might reveal where he was. Unfortunately, the weak tones were easily devoured by the endless gloom. Tiarnen repeated the melody with more effort, and as his eyes watered in agony, the jacket embroidery bloomed with ivy-green light that pushed back the darkness and revealed the massive cavern he was standing in. At the top of a sloped wall of ice, just beneath the high cobalt-blue ceiling that rippled like ocean waters, he saw a ledge.

Tiarnen put his boot on the slope and tried to climb up it but immediately slipped and found himself on his hands and knees. He stood back up and tried to approach from a different angle, only to slip and fall again. Tiarnen rose once more and surveyed the slope for another angle, but there didn't seem to be a better way up. Exhaling in frustration, he put his hands on his hips and felt the multi-belt under his jacket. Remembering that he had tools at his disposal, Tiarnen looked down at the buckle and detached the whalebone hook. He gazed at the slope and saw that there were some smaller ridges that the hook might be able to bite into, so he pulled at it and drew several metres of slack. Taking a few steps back, Tiarnen began to spin the weighted hook in the air and then tossed it towards the first ridge—

Climp!

It struck the ice and slid off.

"Second time's the charm," said Tiarnen, pulling up the slack, spinning the hook, and then tossing it at the ridge again—

Climp!

Once again, it struck the ice and slid right off.

"My fault. It's definitely the third time," he said, spinning the hook and tossing it again.

Climp!

A few more minutes passed, as did another thirty or so tosses until—

CLIMP!

"As far as anyone else is concerned, that was the fourth time," said Tiarnen, tugging on the line to confirm that the hook had indeed bit into the ice. He slipped on his leather gloves and gripped the cord tightly. "Just take it slow," he said. Inch by inch, he began to step up the slippery slope while pulling himself along at the same time, but not without nearly slipping on more than a few occasions. Eventually, he reached the top of the first ridge and took a knee to pull the hook out of the ice. It seemed sharp as ever, and there weren't any cracks from holding the weight, so Tiarnen stood back up, looked to the second ridge, and began to spin it in the air again.

Five more ridges and an hour later, Tiarnen finally pulled himself onto the highest one to be greeted by nothing but a small dark tunnel ahead. The climb, having taken far longer than expected, he wanted to keep pressing on but needed a moment to recover some strength and a bit of breath. If there was one thing he was grateful for, it was how rich and cool the glacial air was. After twenty minutes, Tiarnen felt some stamina return and so made his way over to the waist-high tunnel mouth. He knelt and investigated the shaft inside—it seemed to go on much further than his jacket's glow could reach.

"Why am I regretting this already?" he asked himself, dropping to his hands and knees. Crawling along the ice quickly became uncomfortable, but Tiarnen had no other choice but to slither along. As he did, he noticed how smooth the tunnel wall was—as though something perfectly round had shaped it. *Water, maybe? Or perhaps a Phrygian device to explore the glacier with?* he wondered. Contemplating the answer, Tiarnen followed the tunnel as it took any and every direction, and the next few hours blurred together.

Eventually, he became exhausted again and was left with no choice but to stop crawling. He lay on his back, forcing his legs up, but he didn't mind since he needed to give his knees a rest anyway. Lying in complete stillness, Tiarnen listened as his laboured breathing echoed up and down the tunnel. A growing uneasiness overtook him as reality set in. *What if the tunnel has no end? What if you're going to die in here?* he thought.

Despair crept into Tiarnen's heart and whispered to him that maybe this was where his mission, his life, was fated to end. The jacket glow began to fade, and with it, so did much of Tiarnen's resilience to the dreadful thoughts. Tears crept into the corners of his eyes, and he let out shallow sobs that reverberated down the tunnel. It was like he was hearing himself break over and over again, but instead of falling to pieces, something else welled up in him—something he had never truly allowed himself to feel before. Rage. His heart started pounding as the image of Niera alone with Tharus for the rest of her days entered his mind, Raghnall and Dansby being discovered and executed for treason, and Lydia succumbing to torture all over again before finally drowning. All because he had been too cocky and careless to foresee the barons' attack. Before Tiarnen knew what he was doing, he was already scream-ing—screaming harder and louder than he ever had before—the jacket glow turning from green to fiery orange. He thought the tunnel might crack from the reverberation, and the glacier would come crashing down upon him. Instead, it seemed to respond by pulsing with little yellow lights of its own.

Tiarnen thought he was seeing things, but after wiping his eyes with his sleeve and then looking down the tunnel again, he saw that he wasn't imagining it—the pulsing yellow lights really were there. He scrambled onto his hands and knees again and scuttled ahead as quickly as he could, hoping it might be a way out. Reaching the end of the tunnel, he slid from the mouth and suddenly found himself lying in a small cave that was filled with hundreds of small translucent yellow sacks embedded along its walls. Confused by what exactly he was looking at, Tiarnen stood to his feet and cautiously walked over to inspect one of them. As he got closer, he could see it was an egg of some kind that was filled with gelatinous yellow fluid and had something moving inside.

"Do you *really* need a closer look?" Tiarnen asked himself, leaning to within a few inches of the sack.

SLAP!

The mouth of a grotesque pale larva struck out from the yellow fluid and pressed its rows of jagged black teeth against the egg sack—tongue flicking underneath.

"Definitely not!" shouted Tiarnen, stumbling back.

SCREECH!

The high-pitched cry pierced his ears as the larva struck at the wall of its egg sack, except this time, it broke through and spilled out onto the ground along with the glowing gooey fluid. Tiarnen thought that might be the death of it, but the larva twisted and sprung forward to try and bite his boot.

"Get off!" said Tiarnen, raising his foot and then instinctively stomping down hard.

SCREEEEELLLLCH!

The crushed larva let out a blood-curdling death cry before twitching rapidly and then going limp.

"How can something so small scream so lou—"

As though answering Tiarnen's question before he could finish it, thunder echoed throughout the crater again. He was about to shrug off the coincidence, but when all the other sacks began to pulse and grow brighter in response, Tiarnen came to a terrible realization. He wasn't standing in a cave—it was a *nest*! He turned back to the tunnel to escape, only to see that there was a far brighter yellow glow in the far-reaching shadows approaching him at speed.

"That can't be good," he said, backpedalling and looking for another exit. With all the larvae now pulsating excitedly, the cave was very well-lit and allowed Tiarnen to see that there was another tunnel at the far end of the nest. There was just one problem: it looked to be pointing almost straight down. He rushed over, larvae gnashing at him as he passed by, and stood at the edge, contemplating what horrible fate might be awaiting him below. As more thunder echoed and the cave began to fill with a horrible stench, Tiarnen stepped into a free fall. Only after the shadows swallowed him did he realize his jacket light had faded away, but he couldn't whistle the melody again because of the air rushing past him. To make matters worse, the pitch-black hole became so narrow that he couldn't move a muscle within it—just shoot along helplessly at what was becoming breakneck speed. Spiralling down, he tried to press the toes of his boots against the ice in the hope of slowing himself, but it was of no use.

Suddenly, Tiarnen was flying through the air and then plunging into frigid meltwater—his body slamming against the icy edge of the pool. Battered and more bruised than ever, he rose to the surface while drawing Darktide to defend himself against whatever monster made those eggs. Although the piccolo was pressed firmly against his lips, Tiarnen's hands were shaking violently. He had never been in this kind of pain before—everything was numb yet excruciating at the same time. What felt like an eternity passed and made every ice glint or water droplet along the tunnel mouth seem like a sign that his battle was about to begin, but nothing sinister emerged. Accepting the fact that he might have gotten away, Tiarnen cautiously pulled himself out of the pool and then lay on the rocky ground to give himself a minute to recover.

There was nothing to do but stare at the dappled ceiling in soaking-wet agony, so Tiarnen watched as the moons shone through the thick cyan ice—their cold white light just strong enough to bounce off the pool water and cause an enchanting ripple effect over the entire cavern. He couldn't explain why, but seeing the moons unexpectedly brought him not only a sense of calm, perhaps because they were a sign of the outside world, but he also felt his pain subside and some warmth return to his body. Tiarnen tilted his head up a bit while buttoning the maestro jacket and noticed several support trusses secured in the ceiling towards the back of the cavern. Seeing that they were made of wood instead of iron, he guessed it was of Phrygian design. Tiarnen rolled over for a better look and saw two ice sculptures of Phrygian archers with their longbows drawn on either side of a tall open doorway.

"Thank the Verse," he sighed, standing to his feet.

Darktide in hand, Tiarnen hurried to the doorway, which he quickly realized was the fabled stronghold entrance, given the detailed provincial sigil of a mountain surrounded by books and wings carved into the ice above it. Treading lightly under the archway, Tiarnen saw that the doors themselves had been completely broken off their thick hinges and were lying on the ground in several pieces. Just beyond, frozen Phrygian and Lydvenkian soldiers were strewn everywhere, but as Tiarnen cautiously entered the fray, he noticed that some didn't look to have suffered wounds from weapons. They had been crushed while still inside their armour, which was punctured with numerous holes. If he had to guess, they almost looked like bite marks. Nothing about the eerie scene was making any sense. There had obviously been a defining battle, but he couldn't think of what might have caused this level of carnage. Pausing for a moment, he glanced over his shoulder and realized that whatever was chasing him might have truly had a part to play here. A twinge of panic in his chest now, Tiarnen continued on and saw that the stronghold was a fortress carved from the glacier itself and made up of three arcading levels—each with ramparts, inset corner towers, and an extended balcony in the middle that likely acted as defence platforms since several ballistae were positioned at the edges of them.

Passing by more frozen corpses, Tiarnen entered the lower-tier gatehouse and considered the large ward further inside, but something was telling him to keep putting one foot in front of the other. He climbed the stairs leading up to the middle tier and, upon arriving, saw that it was nearly identical to the first, except for the ballistae on the balcony, which he couldn't help but linger on because they weren't pointed towards the battlefield like he expected. Following their line of sight, Tiarnen looked to the west wall of the cavern, where he could see their long arrows had pierced into the ice.

"Why would they waste—" he began, only to notice a familiar sickly yellow fluid splattered around the points of impact.

"Tiarnen, you need to get out of here," he said, turning back to the stairs again and climbing them as quickly as he could. He arrived at the upper tier, but he simply kept ascending and finally reached the roof. Despite being out of breath, he gasped audibly at the horrific sight before him. There must have been well over two thousand bloodied chest plates, helmets, pauldrons, and greaves haphazardly piled up twice as high as he was tall. It was a graveyard. As if the scene wasn't terrifying enough, Tiarnen saw that every piece was drenched in dry yellow fluid.

"Just keep moving," he said, weaving his way through the heaps while making sure he didn't touch a single piece of armour in fear that he might knock one over and tell whatever might be slithering through the shadows where he was. Tiarnen continued moving ahead, but despite his best effort at keeping quiet, he began to notice a low-level rumbling that was becoming louder and louder. After rounding several more piles, Tiarnen finally emerged from the graveyard and saw that the end of the cavern opened to a wide cave mouth, which was covered entirely by a massive waterfall. Had he really found an exit? He noticed that the falls were not only backlit by direct moonlight but also crashing down upon a wooden bridge in the middle. Hurrying towards it, Tiarnen spotted a crossbeam roof that had been built above the bridge to block the water for anyone crossing, but it had either collapsed over time or been intentionally destroyed. Either way, he was more than willing to leverage his experience at leaping through waterfalls if it meant leaving the glacier behind at long last. Nearing the bridge now, he readied himself to sprint down the last few metres—then something glinted brightly along the west wall of the cavern.

He almost didn't want to look. It couldn't be more important than escaping, but his curiosity convinced him otherwise. Tiarnen turned to see shadowy figures inside the ice. Expecting to be mistaken, he quickly approached the wall and wiped the frost away. The moment his hand touched the surface, he knew it wasn't ice at all; it was glass. Stunned at the realization, he peered inside to see that deep within the azure glass, Maestro Phrygus LXII and Lydia LXI were locked in battle along with many of their soldiers. It was clear that Maestro Phrygus was the one illuminating since it was his lattrice that was glinting, but Tiarnen had never imagined this type of warsong effect was even possible. *But what could have made him go to such lengths, to encase himself, to condemn all of them to a tomb of his own making?* he wondered.

To Tiarnen's shock—Phrygus's eyes stared directly at him. Muffled yelling suddenly reverberated, and the lattrice became brighter, revealing that Phrygus and Lydia were battling not only each other but countless worms far larger and more mature than the larvae in the nest. Mouth agape, Tiarnen took a step back from the wall and was so overcome with dread that he began to imagine the terrible stench again. A yellow glow bloomed all around him, and he realized that the stench was all too real. At a flash of movement reflected on the surface of the icy wall, Tiarnen instinctively rolled out of the way as an open maw filled with jagged black teeth blurred past him. Turning back around, he took in the full sight of the monstrous hagworm queen. There were no eyes at the head, only a snarled and wrinkled mouth, from beneath which glowing yellow veins ran over the belly of its pale serpentine body. Tiarnen could tell the hagworm was stunned from the unexpected impact with the wall, so he tried to seize the opportunity by dashing for the bridge.

THWUNK!

The hagworm's tail struck Tiarnen across the chest and sent him hurtling back into the nearest armour pile while Darktide flew out of his hand. Shocked and winded, he looked up to see the hagworm queen raising herself up to her full twenty-metre height and opening her maw again at him. Terror gripping him, Tiarnen clambered back to his feet, drew two daggers from his leg holster, and stabbed them as deep into the queen's ghastly flesh as he could.

SCREEEEEECH!

The volume of the hagworm's wounded cry was deafening and sent Tiarnen falling to the ground once again. The effect made the entire cavern spin, but he fought back the dizziness, picked himself up, and managed to dash behind a larger pile of armour just as the hagworm ploughed through a neighbouring one in search of him. Realizing that he needed to somehow circle back and cross the bridge, Tiarnen picked up a greave and tossed it as far as he could into an adjacent pile. The hagworm immediately tore through the piles in its way and lunged into the one where the greave landed as Tiarnen circled around to regain ground.

SCREEEEEEECH!

Tiarnen covered his ears, but it was of no use. He dropped to a knee while his stomach lurched, and the cavern spun around him again. Feeling the powerful effect first-hand, he could only guess the queen's scream had been what made slaughtering the soldiers in droves possible, given that he was nearly debilitated by it. Pulling himself together,

Tiarnen picked up a helmet and threw it toward the front of the stronghold as hard as he possibly could. After a long arc through the air, it crashed into one of the furthest piles and toppled over.

SCREEEEEECH!

Already running in the opposite direction, Tiarnen would have made a clean getaway if the scream hadn't made his knees buckle and caused him to fall into another pile, which drew the hagworm's attention. He looked back to see her slithering towards him—the yellow veins growing brighter with ferocious excitement. Knowing that this truly was about to be his end, Tiarnen stumbled to his feet and ran like he had never run before. Heart pounding, he sprinted directly for the bridge. Still, it wasn't enough. He could see the yellow glow getting closer and closer, to the point where he thought it alone might consume him. Nearly at the bridge now, he picked up Darktide and glanced back to see the queen rising to strike. This time, her maw opened and continued to spread vertically down her belly, appearing like a barbed coffin ready to close on his corpse. Tiarnen felt his foot touch the first wood panel of the bridge and leaped brazenly into the air.

SPLASH!

The chilling, heavy water of the falls hit him much harder than he expected, but Tiarnen kept focus and tried to ready himself for landing on whatever was left of the bridge. After bursting through the waters and opening his eyes, he saw that there was in fact nothing left of the bridge whatsoever. Time slowed while he looked down to see only an endless canyon abyss below. The queen erupted from the falls behind him—her lunging strike closing the distance between them. Tiarnen focused ahead and saw the other side of the chasm had a wide ridgeline as well as stairs leading up to an open night sky just beyond. In a desperate last effort, he reached for the side of his multi-belt, grabbed the whalebone hook off its clip, and flung it forward as the queen came baring down onto him.

CLIMP!

The hook landed on top of the ridgeline but only dragged back across the surface as Tiarnen plummeted. With only a few inches of slack left, it finally caught on the ice, bit in, and made the line go taught, nearly snapping Tiarnen's neck while swinging him out of the queen's maw as she tried to devour him.

WHAM!

Tiarnen's body slammed against the canyon wall—the impact knocking the wind out of him. Gasping for breath, he watched the queen free fall and let out a bone-chilling death cry before vanishing into the darkness. Tiarnen hung limply from the line for a while in utter disbelief as to what had just happened. Then he worried that the cord might not hold him forever, so he turned himself around and placed both feet against the canyon wall. Step after pull, he climbed his way toward the top of the ridgeline, and with a last desperate reach, he managed to get his hands over the ledge. Feet dangling now, he used the remainder of his strength to grab onto some of the rocky outcrop, lifted his leg onto the ledge, and finally pulled the rest of himself over.

Tiarnen rolled onto his back and lay still—delirious from the shock of, well, all of it. Feeling like he should celebrate his survival, he reached inside his jacket and pulled out the flask that the Finwicks had gifted him. His hands shook violently as he unscrewed the top and let the rum pour into his mouth. *Liam couldn't have been more right,* thought Tiarnen, swallowing hard and then laughing in between coughs as his eyes teared up. The burn was exactly what he needed.

Chapter Thirty
ON THE HUNT

*K*ERSNAP!

Bleary-eyed and beyond sore, Tiarnen slowly emerged from the narrow glacier entrance to see what had made such a violent sound. The stark morning light might have been blinding, but feeling the warm sun on his bruised face was so comforting that he paused to soak it up. After a few long breaths, Tiarnen raised a hand and looked between his dirty fingers to see a deserted Phrygian garrison set against the backdrop of an evergreen forest covered in snow.

KERSNAP!

"Are the branches breaking?" he asked himself, seeing how the heavy snow was weighing down the younger trees.

KERSNAP!

Hearing the sound for a third time, Tiarnen got a better sense of where it was coming from: slightly to his left and probably fifty metres or so into the forest. At best guess, anyway. A dirt road led from the garrison and wound into the woods, so Tiarnen buttoned up his maestro jacket, checked to make sure there weren't any Phrygian scouts lurking about, and began following it towards the greenbelt. The snow crunched under his boots as he passed the first pine trees, their sharp, oily scent quickly filling his nose, and he noticed that the air was beginning to feel strangely close.

After a minute or so of following the road further into the forest, Tiarnen slowed his pace in anticipation of hearing the sound again, except he was only met with more silence. A bit lost as to what to do next, he stopped walking and leaned against a tree, waiting patiently. Several more minutes passed, but there was still no sign of the sound's source among the thick trunks and pillowy snowbanks. Not that he was complaining, the forest was rather majestic, and he was more than happy to soak in the tranquillity. Then, just up ahead, Tiarnen saw movement. Whatever was approaching him was burrowing under the snow, pushing little hills up to the surface at a rapid pace. He reached for Darktide, but just before pulling the piccolo from his back pocket, a small creature burst out of the nearby snowbank and stared at him inquisitively.

"Good... good morning," said Tiarnen.

He, too, stared back curiously at what looked much like a common Dorladdian rabbit except the fur was far thicker, and the ones back home definitely didn't have little antlers sticking out of their heads.

"You must be a natterhorn."

Snowflakes still on its tiny snoot, the natterhorn sniffed at him.

Squeak!

"Yeah, I know I'm not supposed to be here," said Tiarnen, slipping Darktide into his back pocket again.

The natterhorn hopped a little closer.

He knelt to greet his new friend. "You don't happen to know what was causing that soun—"

KERSNAP!

Before Tiarnen could finish his sentence, a pair of polished steel jaws sprung from the snow and crushed the natterhorn between its sharp teeth.

"By the..." said Tiarnen, wiping the blood splatter off his brow. Opening his eyes again, he took in the gruesome sight of the still-twitching natterhorn, which was making the snow around the lethal contraption turn crimson. "Looks like a hunter's trap."

KRAW!

Tiarnen jolted up and stared further down the trail, his eyes searching for whatever made the distressed—

KRAAW!

This time it was much more forceful, as though in self-defence. His eyes going back to the trap, Tiarnen realized that he might not be standing in just a forest—he could very well be in the middle of someone's hunting grounds. He hurried down the trail, and as the pines grew thicker, the sound of shouting voices and flapping wings became louder.

KRAAAW!

"Oleg, Fausi, Gulry—watch the clawz!" yelled a voice.

The trail turned sharply around an enormous elder pine, which Tiarnen pressed himself against so he could risk looking down the path again without being seen. Carefully peering past the peeling brown bark and lush needled branches, he saw a small glade about thirty metres ahead. Three canaurians, dressed in ragged leathers and dirty wool coats, were surrounding what appeared to be a cross between a crow and a grey wolf that was the size of a horse and had a wingspan three times as long.

"It's a squall," whispered Tiarnen, his eyes widening with excitement.

The regal squall flapped its massive fur-lined wings, snapping its sharp beak at the three canine-like trappers, despite them gnashing their teeth and poking back at it with spears. To Tiarnen, the canaurians most closely resembled the tawny coyotes that roamed Dorladdich's lowlands, and despite being only half as tall as he was, their feral ferocity more than made up for it.

"Damn thing is fearless," he muttered, wondering why the squall didn't simply fly away from the attack. But then he saw that its back left paw was caught between the same kind of steel trap that crushed the natterhorn. To make matters worse, every time the squall managed to get airborne it sunk the trap teeth deeper into its ankle. Despite the squall kicking up a blizzard with its frantic flapping, a fourth trapper, this one human, braved the gusting winds and made his way closer, approaching with confidence in a plush fur coat and holding a spear much longer than the canaurians'.

"What-t-t do we do now, Bruek?" asked Oleg, a lanky canaurian who was foaming at the mouth.

"Bring the wagon over zo we can put thiz overgrown chicken in itz cage," said Bruek, sucking air through the wide gap between his front teeth.

Oleg rushed to the west corner of the glade beyond Tiarnen's line of sight, which motivated him to start inching up the road again and get a better angle.

"Protezt all you want," laughed Bruek, "but the next time you zpread thoze furry featherz, it'll be for the Phrygian air force. I can promize you that!"

Doing his best to stay close to the pines, Tiarnen managed to approach the mouth of the glade unseen. The squeaking of rusted wheels cut through the air, and then he saw a large wagon roll back towards the squall thanks to the effort of two hulking frost rams that Oleg was steering from the riding bench with a pair of reins.

"What zay we wrap our prezent, eh boyz?" asked Bruek, kicking some snow to the side with his boot.

The trappers cheered in agreement and took another step forward, which forced the squall over the trap.

Bruek stabbed the end of his spear into the ground.

CLITCH!

The walls of a steel cage sprung up out of the snow and formed a prison all around the squall before it knew what had happened. Equally as stunned, Tiarnen expected the squall to go wild now that it was imprisoned, but it went unnervingly silent instead and began to examine every inch of the enclosure.

"Not zo tough now, are you?" said Fausi, making a fake stabbing motion with his spear.

"How much you think he'z worth?" asked Gulry, the shorter canaurian, stepping onto the bed of the wagon. He grabbed a thick rope at the back which was threaded through a rudimentary pulley system.

"Lazt one I brought to the Roozt fetched a hundred gold," said Bruek.

"A *hundred*?" exclaimed Fausi. "That'z more than we made all of lazt year!"

"Don't get t-t-too excited," said Oleg, a long drip of foam falling from his maw. "We ztill only get four percent-t-t."

"Zplit four ways," grunted Gulry, tying the pulley rope to the tow loop on the cage.

"I'll be zplitting you mongrelz four wayz if you keep complaining about it," said Bruek, turning the pulley handle which began to drag the cage along the snow and then finally onto the wagon where he and Fausi secured it.

Gulry grabbed a tarp from under the riding bench and threw it on top of the cage—the trappers working together to pull down the corners and conceal their prize.

PLINK! PLINK!

To their surprise, the squall had already turned itself around and was pecking at the cage lock with the tip of its beak.

"Oi! Enough of that!" said Bruek, letting go of his corner of the tarp to grab a small lit torch on the side of the riding bench. He rounded to the back of the cage, climbed up, and waved the flames over the lock to force the squall away. It worked for a moment, but then the squall attempted to break itself free again.

PLINK! PLINK! PLINK!

Having enough, Bruek stuck the torch deep into the squall's neck plume and burned it.

KRAAAAAAAW!

With some feathers smouldering, the squall retreated so fast that the entire wagon rocked.

"Put. The torch. Down."

The trappers turned to see Tiarnen now standing in the glade with them.

"Where in the zix peakz did he come from?" asked Oleg.

"Shut it," barked Bruek, keeping the torch in hand and hopping off the wagon to get a better look at Tiarnen. "Lizten here, thiz iz my catch, and I'll do with it az I pleaze."

"The more you hurt it, the less it'll be worth," said Tiarnen.

"After what he'z cozt uz in natterhornz and trapz thiz zeazon, you can be sure we're willing to loze a little coin for zome retribution," said Bruek, with a cruel smile.

"Burn him again, and you'll be losing far more than coin," said Tiarnen.

Fausi, Gulry, and Oleg gnashed their teeth and pointed their spears at him.

"But since you seem so keen to sell the squall, how about I take it and the wagon off your hands?" asked Tiarnen.

"You must have zomething very valuable to offer uz in return," said Bruek, looking Tiarnen up and down as though he was about to put him in the cage as well.

"Indeed I do. Your lives."

The trappers broke into collective laughter, and even the squall tilted its head in surprise at the direct threat.

"Take it you don't make dealz often," said Bruek, pulling himself together.

"Don't often have to," said Tiarnen, drawing Darktide from his pocket.

"Oi! Look boyz, drifter here, thinkz he'z a maeztro," said Bruek.

"*Drifter?*" asked Tiarnen, looking at himself. Sure, his cloak was torn to pieces, he was admittedly filthy, and in need of a shave, but he still looked like a maestro in his humble opinion.

"Go on then, *Maezt-t-t-ro*, play uz a t-t-tune," said Oleg, maw now frothing over as he closed in on Tiarnen with the other trappers.

Seeing that he had no other choice, Tiarnen put Darktide to his lips as the trappers rushed at him. Little did they know that it was already too late. Tiarnen only illuminated a single note, then soured it, which caused the shard to explode with a concussive blast that knocked them out cold. It was so intense, in fact, that even Tiarnen had to wait a moment for his ears to stop ringing. The glade, now eerily quiet, he returned Darktide to his pocket and approached the trappers.

Kraw?

"No, they're not dead," said Tiarnen. He kneeled to Bruek, pulled his tattered woolly coat off, and then walked over to the wagon.

PLINK!

"I'm sorry, I can't let you go."

KRAW?

"Because as far as I can tell, you're my only way into the Tantalis," said Tiarnen. "But if there's a chance of releasing you after we're inside, I promise that I will." He pulled the tarp over the back of the cage, covering it completely.

Kraaaaw.

"Don't worry. Apparently, I'm becoming an expert at freeing prisoners." He put on the fur coat, trying to ignore the pungent smell of Bruek's body odour, and pulled himself onto the riding bench. "I really hope you two know the way back," he said to the rams, unwrapping the reins and giving them a light crack. With a slow first few steps, the rams pulled forward and rolled the wagon out of the glade and down a wide trail. Unfortunately, there was no suspension on the wheels nor springs under the riding bench, which meant that every rock they ran over felt like it would send Tiarnen flying from his seat.

Kraw!

"No backseat driving," said Tiarnen.

After an hour of riding along the trail, Tiarnen looked past the rams and saw that there was a main road up ahead. Coming to the crossing, the rams didn't hesitate and immediately turned right, which boosted Tiarnen's confidence as far as them being his unspoken guides through hostile territory. He looked up to the powder-blue sky, the forest canopy falling behind him, and saw that he was surrounded by grey stone mountains with veins of permafrost running through them—their jagged peaks almost piercing the little fluffy white clouds hanging just above. The forest itself was nestled in a vast bowl of rolling hills, which the main road looked to cut straight through. Peering further ahead, Tiarnen noticed other wagons that were also making their way up and down the road, as well as long sleds with children sitting at the front bundled in blankets, pulled by packs of dogs very similar to Dasher except they were mostly black and white. Along both sides, there were also provincials on foot, so Tiarnen cautiously pulled up his woolly hood to better hide his face.

The day waned on, and despite passing through many intersections, all with hand-carved signposts pointing and naming the alternative routes they might take, the rams simply kept to what Tiarnen had learnt was called the *Homstraz*. Seeing that the sun was starting to slip behind the mountains, he guessed that the trappers had likely woken up by now, albeit with their heads pounding. He realized that even if he did manage to fool the city guards with his pathetic disguise and gain entry into the Tantalis, the trappers would eventually inform the very same guards that a *"maeztro"* attacked them, and everyone in Phrysbruck would be searching for him by this time tomorrow. *Maybe you should have killed them?* he thought. Tiarnen couldn't believe what he had just considered and shook his head at himself as the rams pulled the wagon up another rolling hill.

Expecting to see yet more swathes of frosted pines as they reached the top, Tiarnen was pleasantly surprised to instead be greeted by a wide snowy valley and the Tantalis itself. Curved around the base of a mountain greater than he could have ever imagined was a colossal ice wall, which looked to be protecting thousands of homes nestled within its defensive perimeter. Though their angular blue-tiled roofs, wide balconies, and carved façades were of architectural interest to Tiarnen, he couldn't help but stare beyond them to the pair of stained-glass doors inset into the mountain itself. He guessed that he was still a league or so away, but given the sheer size of them, he felt certain that the sapphire-blue doors were as tall as the cathedral back home.

"At last," said Tiarnen, cracking the reins.

Chapter Thirty-One
CLOUDSTRIKE

The wagon slowly came to a stop as the frost rams reached the back of a line-up for the Tantalis city gate. Tiarnen could see that they were breathing heavily from pulling the wagon for the past six hours straight. A few provincials, annoyed by the squeaking wagon wheels, looked over their shoulders and gave him a displeased look. He suddenly felt even more aware that he shouldn't be there, not so much for being a foreigner, but because he realized that he was the only wagon in line. The provincials turned ahead again and focused their attention on the ten or so gatemen who were dressed in polished metal armour with blue tunics underneath and holding long polearms. To Tiarnen's dismay, they were searching and interrogating everyone before allowing them to pass into the city. Seeing that he had a couple of minutes before reaching them, Tiarnen gazed upon the ten-metre-high defensive ice wall, which he now saw was also an endless relief sculpture. There were archers with bows drawn, much like the ones protecting the glacier stronghold entrance; squalls similar to his partner in crime but they were saddled and covered in armour themselves; and sleds akin to the ones he saw on the Homstraz but much larger and with three times as many dogs, which were pulling a full platoon of soldiers holding their polearms high.

"Next!" shouted one of the gatemen.

Tiarnen focused on the gate again, and his mind began racing with questions he might be asked. *Where are you coming from?* Tiarnen thought back to the signposts and remembered one had the name *Andelstäd* on it. He didn't know if that was the name of the crossroad or a nearby town, but it was all he had to work with. *How did you hunt down a squall?* Tiarnen knew that the trappers were using natterhorns as bait, so he could just say that the squall was caught in one by accident. *Where are you going with it?* The trappers had planned on taking it to the Roost, though he had no idea where that was exactly.

"Roozt... roozzzzzt," whispered Tiarnen, trying to make himself familiar with the accent and already regretting that he hadn't been practising it while on the road. Knowing first-hand what the hunters sounded like at least gave him a reference point, although he couldn't help but think about how Holgor had caught many well-trained spies in the past due to subtle inconsistencies in their Dorladdian accent. He didn't expect the gateman to have the same ear training but that didn't mean they would be easily fooled either.

"Fahri! Can we hurry thiz up? It iz freezing!" said a provincial man.

"*What did you zay?*" asked Fahri, a burly gateman who opened the provincial's fur coat and searched him. "Turn around, armz up!"

Tiarnen's stomach sank. If he was searched, then the gatemen would certainly see his maestro jacket, which would likely lead to him being pulled from the riding bench and then held until he could be placed in chains. Even if he did manage to break free, he had nowhere to run—there was nothing but open valley behind him for well over a league.

"Oi! Urich! What iz thiz trapper all about?" asked Fahri.

Tiarnen didn't know what Fahri was asking and naturally looked around in confusion.

"Don't give uz that!" said Urich, a squat gateman who was approaching the other side of the wagon. "You know wagonz are not permitted through the front gate!"

Tiarnen took the reins in panic.

"Where you coming from, exactly?" asked Urich.

"Andels—Andelztäd," said Tiarnen, stammering on the accent.

"And what buiznezz bringz you to the Tantaliz?" asked Fahri, nodding at the tarp.

"Yeah, what are you hiding under—" began Urich, grabbing a corner of the tarp and lifting it up to take a peek.

KRAW!

The squall snapped at Urich's fingers, causing him to leap back and fall over.

"How did you manage to capture a zquall?" asked Fahri, looking up at Tiarnen. "No chance you trapped it by yourzelf."

"Yeah, you trapperz are alwayz in packz, so where'z the rezt of your lot?" asked Urich, picking himself up.

"Idiotz almozt got me killed trying to trap it, zo I made them walk back," said Tiarnen. "Getting harder to find good help theze dayz." He risked a nod over to Urich as though making a point to Fahri.

"Tell me about it," said Fahri.

WOOSH!

Out of nowhere, winged shadows flew past overhead. Tiarnen and the gatemen naturally ducked, then looked up to see three squalls fly past and bank hard, revealing a rider on each of their backs with a bow slung over their shoulder. They shouted something down to the gatemen and then ascended towards the top of the Tantalis in perfect formation.

"Typical airborne!" shouted Urich. "Alwayz thinking they're better than uz juzt because they can fly!"

"If you azk me, bootz on the ground iz what matterz!" said Tiarnen.

"At leazt thiz one haz zome zenze to him," said Fahri, looking to Urich and pointing at Tiarnen.

"Fine, let him pazz!" said Urich, pulling a small pad of paper out of his chest pocket and writing on it quickly. He tore two slips off the pad and handed them to Tiarnen.

"What are theze?" asked Tiarnen.

"Firzt one is a pazz to the Roozt," said Urich. "Zecond one iz a fine."

"A fine?"

"Conzider yourzelf lucky we're not zeizing the wagon and your prize here," said Fahri.

Kraw.

"Head ztraight up the north road," said Fahri, pointing to the road leading on from the gate and into the city.

"No ztopz!" added Urich.

"And no detourz!" added Fahri.

"Wouldn't dream of it," said Tiarnen. He cracked the reins, and the rams pulled the wagon through the gate.

Kraaaw.

"Don't you dare start now," he said firmly.

Tiarnen couldn't believe it; he had managed to infiltrate the city. Even better, the north road appeared to lead straight to the Tantalis.

Shhhhhwip! Shhhhhwip! Shhhhhwip!

Before Tiarnen could guess what was making the odd scraping sound, a provincial wearing a large empty backsack blurred past him on the left. He hadn't noticed until now, but a narrow path of ice appeared to be running between the road and a line of bustling specialty shops, to which the young man was gliding on metal blades attached to the bottom of his boots.

Shhhhhwip! Shhhhhwip!

Another provincial, also wearing a large backsack, except this one was filled with parcels, glided past, drawing Tiarnen's gaze to Tic and

Toc's Finest Clocks. The narrow building looked like a whimsical grandfather clock, complete with a pendulum bob swinging just above the door. Tiarnen read a little sign in the front window: *From single face to the tallest case, we have what you're looking for!* The door opened with a Phrygian family of six—all dressed in heavy but well-tailored blue- and cream-coloured clothing—pouring out while the mother clutched what looked to be a wall clock with well over a dozen hands on its face.

"*Almozt broken beyond repair*, I waz told!" said the mother, more than a little annoyance in her voice. "Can you imagine if they didn't have the partz and we were late to zomething thiz week? We would loze our houze!"

"But Mama, we didn't mean to drop it!" said the oldest daughter.

Tiarnen was taken aback by what he heard. How could a family lose their home simply for being late? But before he could think of a logical reason, the rams had already pulled him to the next shop, where numerous provincial teens crowded around the open front window.

"I want all of the young go-abouterz in the back to give the little onez zome room to breathe, or you won't be getting a zingle lick!" shouted a stern female voice.

Tiarnen risked standing up a bit to peer over their heads and saw a rotund woman inside who was dipping waffled pastry cones into a steaming vat of chocolate, then topping it off with a scoop of frozen vanilla cream.

"*Charla's Creamery,*" said Tiarnen, reading a wooden sign mounted on the azure-blue tiles of the shop roof.

A sweet vanilla smell emanated from inside, and the children who managed to get a cone were apparently loving the taste, given that they were wearing much of the frozen cream on their faces. Tiarnen's mouth watered, and his stomach grumbled deeply—reminding him that it had been empty for a few days. Unconcerned with his hunger, the rams continued up the road while Tiarnen's head kept swivelling back and forth to try and take in more passing shops like Selvard's Sleds, which looked to sell the dog sleds he saw on his way to the city. The location was fitting since Poskar's Performance Pups was next door, with several sled puppies bounding wildly in the double front windows as though they wanted nothing more in life than to play in the snow outside.

Music suddenly caught Tiarnen's ear. He looked to his right and saw that it was coming from Reverb Records.

"*Finest Recordings and Players*," said Tiarnen, reading the bottom half of the shop sign which was hanging from the second-floor balcony. He looked through the front window and saw a strange device which was comprised of a polished wooden box with a flat metal disc spinning on top and a curved arm pressing a needle down upon it, causing little blue sparks to shoot out. Sticking out from the side of the box was a spiral metal horn that opened like a flower, which Tiarnen realized was playing the music.

"How in the—"

"Cheeze dip, zir?"

The question drew Tiarnen's attention, and turning to his left, he saw a young man walking alongside the wagon. Over his shoulders and around his waist was a strange harness that held several candlelit simmer-pots of bubbling cheese as well as an open back sack filled with countless cubes of bread.

"*Cheeze dip*?" asked Tiarnen.

"Yez! Only a zilver for a ztick," said the merchant. He waved a long wooden skewer in his hand, stabbed it into the sack, and then pulled it out again with several cubes skewered along it.

"Why not," said Tiarnen, excited to finally get something to eat. He reached into the woolly jacket and searched the deep pockets. After pulling out a small rusty switch knife, keychain, several pine cones, and a flinter, he found a few random coins—one of which was silver. He leaned over and handed it to the merchant. It went straight into his coin purse, and Tiarnen became even more excited as the bread skewers then went straight into the gooey cheese pots. Watching the process was only making him hungrier and, once the skewer was handed over to him, a bit worried that he might have been foaming at the mouth.

"Thank you," said Tiarnen.

"A very good evening to you!" said the merchant, tipping his hat and then making his way over to the Owlery, where numerous provincials were sitting on the open patio around small round tables. Barely chewing the three cubes now stuffed in his mouth, Tiarnen swallowed the savoury cheesy garlic bread while watching them sip on steaming cups of tea and trading what looked to be Shatter cards. Shoving three more cubes into his mouth, he instinctually stood to get a better view of the cards.

"Keligräth iz worth at leazt two Archedez!" said a provincial, pointing at his friend sitting across from him.

"One at bezt, look at the cornerz—mozt of them are bent," said the friend as a waiter refilled his coffee.

"Then I'll trade you Diedrelk and Haelbärth for it!" The provincial held up two new cards.

As he shoved more cubes into his mouth, Tiarnen saw both cards had a shimmering foil to them, which meant they were legendaries. He squinted at them in the hope that he would be able to make out some details.

"You there! Halt!"

Tiarnen looked up to see another gateman standing at the crossroads ahead with his hand held out as though he was the foremost authority in Phrysbruck. Unwilling to chance that the rams would listen, Tiarnen pulled on the reins and brought the wagon to a stop.

"You better have a pazz for that wag—"

Tiarnen grabbed the pass off the bench and held it out for the gateman. Annoyed that Tiarnen had an answer before he could finish his question, the gateman snatched the pass out of his hands and quickly read it over. To his relief, the gateman pocketed the pass and then walked over to the heavy crossbar which was blocking access to the other side of the road that, as far as Tiarnen could tell, snaked up the side of the Tantalis.

"Air Marshall Gryzilva iz on duty in the Roozt," said the gateman. "Juzt look for her feather cap. Once you are paid, you are to come right back down or face arrezt."

Tiarnen nodded in acknowledgement.

With the pull of a lever, a set of gears turned along the gate and raised the bar, and the gateman waved his arm for Tiarnen to get a move on. Wasting no time, Tiarnen cracked the reins, and once again, the rams began pulling the wagon ahead.

After a few minutes of travelling up the road, he found himself gazing upon the largest pair of doors he had ever seen in his life. *They must be as high as the Dorladdian cathedral itself!* he thought. At first, the stained-glass panes looked to be cerulean-blue, but as Tiarnen got closer, he could see that because of their incredible thickness, there were many shades darker and brighter refracting within. Both the left and right doors were a complex framework of brushed steel that curved upwards from the very bottom to create motifs of snowflakes, pine trees, and mountains—all highlighted and backlit by soft firelight coming from within the Tantalis itself. Tiarnen was mesmerized; the scale and detail of the glass imagery were far beyond anything he had ever seen before. But just like the shops, it slowly passed from view as the rams continued along the north road, which began to quickly steepen and wrap around the mountain.

Tiarnen gripped the reins with one hand and the bench with the other as gust after gust of frigid wind tried to blow him off the wagon. Despite the maestro jacket's protection from the elements, he was starting to believe that he would become an ice sculpture himself if it weren't for the woolly coat layered on top. The rams, however, seemed to be having no problems braving the treacherous conditions and simply continued ahead. Tiarnen was already impressed by their tireless pace, especially given the long day, challenging climb, and size and weight of the wagon, particularly with the addition of the squall.

Another sobering gust hit him as though the Tantalis itself saw through Tiarnen's disguise and was trying to blow him off its shoulder. He wasn't about to give up so easily, but the tarp accepted defeat and tore off the cage, leaving the squall exposed as it vanished into the night. Expecting a protest of some kind, Tiarnen glanced back at the cage to see that his passenger was instead raising its sharp beak as though it were enjoying the wind.

With the last turn of the road, the rams pulled the wagon onto a long plateau that led into a vast cave mouth at the end. Tiarnen lifted his hood a bit to get a better view and saw that there were stables running down both sides of the cave with squalls resting inside each of them.

"This must be the Roost," he said, as though announcing it to himself.

"Oi!" yelled Grysilva, a tall silver-haired woman who was wearing a straight-cut blue military uniform and a fedora with two long feathers sticking out the left side and waving her hands at Tiarnen frantically.

"Uhhh, hello there!" he replied, waving back awkwardly.

"What are you doing in the middle of the landing ztrip?" screamed Grysilva, pointing up to the sky.

Confused by the question, Tiarnen looked over his shoulder to where she was pointing and saw the same airmen that passed overhead earlier—only this time they were about to land on top of him.

"You heard her! Move!" he yelled at the rams, pulling the reins hard to the right. Thankfully, they must have sensed either the danger or Tiarnen's urgency because they didn't hesitate to lead the wagon off the strip and onto the snowy shoulder as the airmen descended and missed the top of Tiarnen's head by what felt like centimetres.

VOOOOOSH!

The airmen landed on the strip and slid into the Roost with practised skill. They immediately hopped off their saddles to pull their squalls into a stable, but not without giving Tiarnen a two-fingered salute first.

"I'm sure it's a sign of respect," he told himself.

"Damn fool!" yelled Grysilva, marching toward Tiarnen. "You're lucky they didn't run you over!"

"Apologiez, itz my firzt time up here."

"And your lazt if you don't have a good reason for dragging that heap all the wa—" Grysilva's words came to a dead stop as she saw the caged squall.

"Well, I'll be," said Grysilva, her eyes widening. "Never thought I would zee a royal again."

"*Royal?*" asked Tiarnen.

"A very rare bloodline among the zquallz. In fact, it iz the oldezt one as far az we know."

"How can you tell?"

"Zee the zilver glinting in hiz featherz there?" Grysilva pointed to the squall's left wing tip.

Tiarnen hopped off the wagon and walked to the cage to get a closer look. Sure enough, Grysilva was right—along the edges of the squall's dark blue feathers was a metallic sheen he hadn't noticed before.

"It makez them sharper and ztronger—letting them manoeuvre in ze air far better," said Grysilva.

"When waz the lazt time you zaw a royal?" asked Tiarnen.

"Over fifty yearz ago. But they are impozzible to break, let alone train."

"What are you going to do with him, then?"

"Breeding ztock. Which meanz he haz seen hiz lazt dayz in the air."

KRAW!

"Good newz for you iz that he fetchez ten timez the price of the uzual zquall," said Grysilva.

"Yeah, good newz," said Tiarnen, feeling awful that he wasn't going to get the chance to free the squall.

"Now, all you have left to do iz name him," said Grysilva, gesturing for Tiarnen to follow her into the Roost.

"Name him?"

"Yez, every zquall muzt be named and registered."

"Right, how could I forget?"

They arrived at the Roost control station, which was a very large semi-circle desk where three control officers were sitting and either looking through large binoculars with multiple lenses or double-checking what looked to be flight schedules. Grysilva walked to the far end, opened a drawer, and pulled out a thick registry book.

"If nothing iz coming to mind, juzt go with zomething that fitz hiz character," said Grysilva, opening the book and setting a pencil on top of the page.

"Character, huh?" asked Tiarnen. "In that caze, what about... *Featherface?*"

The squall's eyes narrowed at Tiarnen.

"Or... *Dullbeak?*"

Krawwww.

The squall snapped its beak in anger.

"All right, all right... *Littlewing*, it is."

KRAW!

Furious at the insult, the squall began to breathe heavily as Tiarnen picked up the pencil.

"I'd be careful about the teazing if I were you," said Grysilva.

"Why iz that?" asked Tiarnen.

"Hear the way he'z zniffing? Zquallz ztalk their prey by zcent. Once they have it memorized, there izn't anywhere within a hundred leaguez that you can hide."

Tiarnen looked back at the squall, who was now staring straight into his eyes.

"I should get uzed to being a marked man anyway," he said.

"Be that az it may, he ztill needs a name," said Grysilva. "If it helpz, the airmen alzo uze onez that convey action of zome kind—you know, to inzpire."

"Inzpire, huh? In that caze..." said Tiarnen, writing on the blank line in the registry.

Grysilva took back the pencil and turned the book around so that she could read it. *"Cloudztrike."*

Krrrraw.

She put the registry away and pulled out a pad much like the ones the gatemen had, using the pencil to fill out some of the checkboxes as well as add her signature at the bottom.

"You can take thiz to the mazter of coin on the firzt level," said Grysilva, handing the torn slip to Tiarnen.

"Thankz."

"Your keyz," said Grysilva.

Tiarnen looked at Grysilva in confusion.

"For ze cage, we'll need to tranzfer him to a holding ztable," said Grysilva, confused as to why Tiarnen was confused.

"Right. Zorry, haz been a bit of a long day."

Tiarnen reached into the woolly pocket, found the keychain, and handed it to Grysilva. He then made his way through the roost, ignoring the glares from the airmen, and finally passed through a large archway at the back to enter the Tantalis.

Chapter Thirty-Two
THE TANTALIS

*C*uckoo!

As though he were being warned by it, Tiarnen found himself gazing upon the largest chronoclock he had ever seen in his life. Hanging from the mountain ceiling, the clock house was made from stained pine wood and was bigger than Tic and Toc's entire shop. An angular blue roof covered the very top, and a large silver face took up the centre, with around thirty or so black hands pointing at just as many outer rings—some of which had numbers and others foreign symbols. A large double door sat above the face, and a row of three smaller doors at the bottom. Much like the city wall, carvings of trees, natterhorns, squalls, soldiers, and a very strange creature that resembled a long-legged fox filled every centimetre in between the ornate mechanical features.

"This is incredible," muttered Tiarnen, watching the upper doors swing open, and a wooden squall emerged from the shadows.

CUCKOO!

In frantic fashion, the squall flapped its pine wings, and with its second warning chime, the enormous brass gears at the bottom of the clock house began to turn, which caused the thick ropes hanging from them to move up and down. Wanting to see where they led, Tiarnen stepped out of the archway entrance and onto the perpendicular staircase, which wrapped along and spiraled down the entire wall of the Tantalis. In small alcoves all the way up burned cream candles with blue flames flickering from their wicks—the cobalt light dancing over centuries worth of built-up wax that had poured down and layered onto the steps. He reached an open balcony opposite the staircase and looked over the edge to see multiple small platforms secured to the clock's ropes. Each of them was carrying a mix of crates, containers, sacks, and supplies to more balconies between three vast, open levels carved into the mountain. Tiarnen leaned over further and saw the ground floor of the mountain where hundreds of provincials were socializing in groups—all of them cast in the blue glow of the stained-glass doors. Then he noticed that a few ropes kept going even further down to what looked like a shadowy subterranean labyrinth.

CUCKOO-CUCKOO-CUCKOO-CUCKOO-CUCKOO-CUCK-OO-CUCKOO-CUCKOO!

The squall chimed in series a third time and then quickly retracted as the platforms locked into place along the balconies.

Kla-klack!

"Guessing that means it's eight o'clock," said Tiarnen.

Every door along each level swung open simultaneously, and Tiarnen watched the countless officers, cadets, professors, and students flood onto the staircase like rivers breaking through their dams. Many of the cadets hurried to the platforms so they could grab arrows for their training bows, while several students dropped off their instruments so they could pick up textbooks. A librarian shoved past Tiarnen so that she could reach the platform secured to his balcony.

"Excuze me, I muzt drop off theze recording albumz for the library," she said, pulling a stack of leather album covers out from under her arm. She placed them into one of the empty crates and then hurried down the stairs.

"Recordings?" he asked, pulling one of the albums back out of the crate to see that the front was embossed with the title: *The Battle of*

Shädek – 22AP. He then turned the album over and saw that there were three warsong titles listed as well as time durations beside them.

"How do the Phrygians transcribe their music onto these?" he whispered to himself, pulling out the thin metal disc. As far as he could tell, it was very similar to the one that he saw spinning at Reverb Records. He brought it closer, focusing on the countless circular grooves—each of them etched with thousands of tiny notches.

Cuc-koo-koo-koo!

He glanced back up to the clock and saw that the three windows below the face had opened and released carved natterhorns which were chiming in succession. All the doors along the lofts closed simultaneously, and Tiarnen found himself alone once again.

Kla-klack!

The platform in front of his balcony began to descend, and since the record in hand was supposed to go to the library, Tiarnen hopped off the edge and onto it. Hiding among the crates and supplies, he tried to keep himself out of sight, though he didn't know from what exactly—there weren't any guards posted as far as he could tell. Maybe the Phrygians were so confident that the Tantalis could never be breached that they didn't see any reason to waste valuable resources on the idea.

Hints of leather and pine filled the air as Tiarnen passed through the upper loft where leatherworkers were stitching bridles and oiling leather saddles. On the other side, aviarists turned squall eggs in warming baskets while their assistants pressed stethoscopes to the snow-white shells.

Passing into the mid-loft, a cacophony of grinding and sanding reverberated through the air. Tiarnen looked over his left shoulder to see bowyers stringing and testing new recurves while fletchers feathered a variety of arrows and arranged them in leather quivers. On the other side, luthiers strung their violins, windsmiths hammered their silver horns, and drum makers sanded their sticks.

"We're coming, Profezzor!" yelled a young voice.

Descending through the lower loft, Tiarnen saw an elderly professor wearing a long blue jacket, somewhat like his own, holding a heavy door open for two students, who were clutching their musical instruments and running towards him as fast as they could. He guessed the students were late for their lessons since the doorway led to a classroom full of other students making a racket as well as some strange wooden figures in the far back.

"Thiz will be going on both of your report cardz!" shouted the professor, smacking one of the students in the back of the head while letting the door close behind them.

Tiarnen snickered at the discovery that music education was apparently far more formal here than in Dorladdich. Then, a bright blue glow cast over him, and his amused heart suddenly sank. Hand reaching for Darktide, Tiarnen turned and expected to see Maestro Phrygus illuminating an attack but was instead greeted by the moonlit doors of the Tantalis.

"Take a breath, Tiarnen," he scolded himself.

Stretching between them, the ground floor's Grand Hall was filled with groups of military officers, secretaries, orators, and scribes who were conversing and socializing as they wandered between open court and War Rooms on both sides.

Shadow swallowed both Tiarnen and the platform whole.

The cool, dark air brought the scent of damp stone and dust to Tiarnen's nose. His eyes slowly adjusted to the dim and began making out the shapes of what appeared to be enormous bookcases just below.

Kla-klack!

The platform came to a stop, and Tiarnen could hear voices approaching. Still barely able to see much, he tried to creep out from behind the crates but accidentally tripped over one—the cacophony echoing as he scrambled behind the nearest bookcase.

From the bookcase across from him, two librarians emerged with a rolling cart that had a large lantern on the end.

"Zee, I told you, waz juzt a crate falling over," said the taller librarian.

"Good, the lazt thing I am in the mood for iz chazing down more ztudentz again," said the shorter librarian. "Anyway, what were you zaying about the praetor?"

"That he wanted uz to rearrange the entire library bazed off recording datez rather than battle namez, but I told him we couldn't begin without firzt deciding where to put Aridaz or we rizk her running amok again," said the tall librarian.

"But can't we work around the zecure area she iz protecting?" asked the short librarian.

"Zure, but that meanz we would have to do the work," chuckled the tall librarian.

Both laughing, the librarians arrived at the platform and loaded the crates onto their carts. Seeing that he had made a clean getaway, Tiarnen turned back and leaned against the bookcase, which he noticed wasn't holding books but instead packed with nine rows of records. He read the little label on the edge of the shelf nearest his face: *BoP.MP35vM D34.452AP.* He was perplexed. *What could the random numbers and letters possibly mean?* Then he remembered what the librarian had said about the names of the battles and recording dates. He looked at the label again and tried to decipher it.

"First part might be the *Battle of Phrysbruck*?" Tiarnen whispered to himself. "If so, that means the middle part is probably *Maestro Phrygus the Thirty-Fifth versus Maestro Dorian the Thirty-Fourth*," he said, a bit more confidently. "And the last part is definitely the date." Happy with his first attempt, he stood to his feet and looked over the other shelf labels, but he didn't see anything that was recorded recently—and there was no sense learning warsongs that might be out of date.

"Do you want to wait for more or head back to control?" asked the short librarian.

"Letz go back to control and put theze in circulation," said the tall librarian, turning the cart around.

Tiarnen waited until the librarians' voices faded a bit before poking his head out again. Seeing that they were at a safe enough distance, he began following their lantern light through the darkness while keeping close to the bookcases. He kept glancing at the closest shelf labels in the hope that he might find some recent recordings. He wasn't having any luck, so he continued to trail his unaware guides until they vanished around a bookcase. Panicked, Tiarnen sprinted ahead to catch up. He rounded the bookcase expecting to see the lantern light again but was instead nearly blinded by a large chandelier hanging above the library control station.

Blinking away the bright lamp spots in his vision, Tiarnen retreated behind the bookcase again to watch the librarians join at least ten more colleagues who helped pull the crates from the cart, stack them on the circular sectional desk they were all in the middle of, and then begin organizing them into ordered stacks under the many tall stained-glass lamps. Creeping to the other side of the bookcase, he got a better view of the control station and saw that there were also multiple brass dials and levers protruding from the gaps between the desk sections.

"Calling caze number four hundred and fifty-two!" said the tall librarian, turning the dial a few times and then pulling down the largest lever at his station.

Tiarnen didn't know what was supposed to happen, but given that the announcement was only followed by silence, he figured it might have been more about protocol than—

FWOOOOOF!

If he had been leaning his head out any further, the bookcase that flew past him would have removed his head. Seeing now that thin rails were inset along the stone floor, Tiarnen caught his breath and watched the bookcase arrive in front of the tall librarian, who then put a few records on the shelf, pulled the lever again, and sent it speeding back to whatever dark corner of the library it came from.

"Calling caze number two thouzand and ninety-four!" said the short librarian.

"*Two thousand?*" muttered Tiarnen, in disbelief that there were so many.

FWOOOOOF!

Another bookcase arrived from the other side of the library, and the short librarian began stacking his records on the shelf.

THWAP-THWAP-THWAP.

Swooping down out of the darkness, a brown moth that was almost the same size as the librarian tried to steal one of the records from his hand.

"Get off!" shouted the short librarian, whacking the moth with the record and sending it fluttering away in retreat.

"Damn mothz are worze that ever thiz year," said the tall librarian.

"Lukeiru muzt be getting zlow in her old age."

"Thatz it for me." The tall librarian unbuttoned his robe. "Oh, can you put the lazt of thoze on caze zeventy-three, for me?" He pointed to the last two records in the otherwise empty crate on the floor.

"Shouldn't it be two hundred and twelve?" asked the short librarian.

"No, everything recorded in the lazt fifty yearz waz tranzferred to the north zector lazt week."

"Why am I alwayz the lazt one to be told about theze thingz?" asked the short librarian, begrudgingly grabbing the two records and then dialing in the case.

"Probably becauze you're alwayz the firzt to complain," chortled the tall librarian.

The rest of the librarians didn't bother hiding their laughter either as the bookcase arrived from the northern shadows.

Knowing now where he should be headed, Tiarnen skulked through the darkness until he was facing the north side of the library. There he waited, and when the short librarian released his bookcase, Tiarnen leaped onto the side of it and held onto the shelves for dear life. He didn't know the exact speed he was going, but given how badly his eyes were watering, it was well beyond a sprint, and the ride wasn't nearly as smooth as he would have guessed since his teeth were chattering uncontrollably. Rows upon rows flew past him, and then his bookcase abruptly turned to speed towards a gap in another row just ahead. Tiarnen swung himself onto the front of the shelves as it filled the row, but the abrupt stop sent him flying through the air.

WHAM!

If it wasn't for the thick woolly jacket, Tiarnen would have certainly been winded, if not worse, when his body slammed hard against the next row over. Still, he took a moment to lie still on the floor and let his head stop spinning.

"Give it here, Evzen!" said a young voice.

Tiarnen blinked a few times and then looked down the row to see that he wasn't imagining the voice—there really were some students down here with him.

"I'm not finished yet!" said a second young voice.

Tiarnen rolled onto his side and saw three boys dressed in dark blue student robes, about twenty bookcases down, sitting around a large candle.

"You never will be at thiz rate!" said the third boy, grabbing the strange headband adorned with brass trumpet bells that was over the second boy's ears.

The moment it was pulled off, Tiarnen could hear music. *Did they really bring a record player with them?* He leaped to his feet and was about to dash over, but then realized that the boys would certainly be scared witless by a trapper's unexpected arrival and likely run away with the record player. He had to find a way to keep them around and help him, so he took off the fur coat, removed the *LX* and provincial crest pins from his maestro jacket lapel, and began to slowly make his way over to them. As he got closer, Tiarnen recognized the boy's robes: they were identical to the ones the students wore in the lower loft.

"Gentlemen!" he said, channelling Major Raghnall as best he could.

The boys startled, jumped to their feet, and turned to face him.

"I expect you three have a very good reazon to be down here."

"We... uhh..." started the first boy.

"We were lozt!" finished the second boy.

"You don't look very lozt to me," said Tiarnen, gesturing to the third boy who still had the headset on.

The second boy elbowed the third, and after he saw what was happening, he quickly pulled the headset off and stood to his feet.

"What are your namez?" asked Tiarnen.

"I am Jonefa," said the first boy.

"I am Evzen," said the second boy. "And thiz my little brother, Baztien."

Bastien gave an embarrassed wave.

"Might we know yourz?" Evzen asked suspiciously.

Tiarnen stepped out from the shadows. "*Profezzor* Keligräth."

Looks of remorse washed over the boy's faces, and Tiarnen breathed an internal sigh of relief that they weren't Shatter players.

"We're dead," muttered Bastien.

"Forgive me, Profezzor, but I have never seen you before," said Evzen, taking a step closer.

"I am newly appointed," said Tiarnen.

Jonefa looked him up and down. "Why are you zo dirty?"

Tiarnen followed Jonefa's gaze. Where he wasn't splattered with mud, he was covered in dirt, and though the maestro jacket was practically unrecognizable as a result, it seemed to still be in excellent condition. "Ah, that would be thankz to a particular zquall I waz dealing with in the Roozt before I came down here," said Tiarnen. "Now, forgetting that you juzt lied about being lozt—how about you give me an honezt explanation, and I might conzider letting you return to clazz without your parentz hearing about thiz."

The boys looked at each other and subtly nodded in agreement.

"We wanted to ztudy here overnight for the examination," said Jonefa.

"Examination?" asked Tiarnen.

"Yez, for tomorrow'z apprentice placementz," said Bastien.

"We are third-year ztudentz in Maeztro Phryguz'z conzervatory program," added Evzen.

"Then you are well aware that the library iz off limitz to you," said Tiarnen. He knew he was taking a risk assuming that rule was true, but given how sweaty and pale the boys had become, it felt like a safe bet.

"It waz my idea. I take full rezponzibility," said Evzen.

"Well then, Evzen, you'll be relieved to hear that I don't believe leadership is zomething we should dizcourage amongzt our youth."

The boys didn't know how to react to the statement.

"That meanz your zecret iz zafe." Tiarnen winked.

"Thank you, Profezzor!" said Jonefa, his face dropping in disbelief.

"However! Zince you three zeem to be expertz at locating reztricted materialz, perhapz you can help me find zomething I am looking for?"

"Of courze!" said Bastien.

"What waz it exactly?" asked Evzen.

"A recording of Maeztro Phryguz'z lazt battle," said Tiarnen.

CUCKOO-CUCKOO-CUCKOO-CUCKOO-CUCKOO-CUCK-OO-CUCKOO-CUCKOO-CUCKOO!

The tension rose as the chimes tolled after his request.

"Zure, it'll be in hiz vault," said Evzen.

"We know where it iz!" said Jonefa, kneeling to take the record off the player. After pulling up the needle, he slipped it back into its album cover and returned it to the shelf.

Evzen then opened a canvas backpack for Bastien, who stuffed the player as well as the headset inside and then slung it around his shoulders.

"Come on, Profezzor. Thiz way!" said Evzen. He blew out the candle, crammed it into the cargo pocket of Bastien's pack, and then all three of the boys jumped onto the bookcase beside them.

"Not again," muttered Tiarnen, dashing over and climbing onto it.

"Wait, are we zure thiz iz the right one?" asked Jonefa.

"It's ninth period," said Evzen. "The librarians alwayz call for *BOP*—"

But before Evzen could finish his sentence, the bookcase lunged from the row and was speeding through the darkness. Tiarnen held on as tight as he could and tried to hide his concern while the wide-eyed boys looked to be elated about streaking through the library with a professor.

"Get ready!" yelled Evzen, pointing to the shelves that were pulling up beside them.

"Are we there already?" asked Tiarnen, relieved that it was going to be a short trip this time.

"Not even cloze!" said Bastien, leaping off the bookcase.

Tiarnen watched in disbelief as Evzen and Jonefa sailed through the air after Bastien and landed on a passing bookcase with him. Not wanting to be left behind, Tiarnen followed shortly after, but not without his foot slipping off the shelf, which nearly sent him tumbling across the blurred floor. Fortunately, the shelf his hands were gripping was rather sticky. Realizing how odd the feeling was, he pulled a hand off to see glossy black webs of, well, he had no idea what it was, but something told him the clusters of tiny red eyes between the records had something to do with it.

"On our left!" said Evzen.

Tiarnen didn't hesitate to leap with the boys onto the next passing bookcase. Excited to get away from the webs, he realized things might have just gotten worse when he noticed that the tops of the shelves were surrounded by billowing dark clouds, which flashed chaotically with light and brought the familiar smell of the sea. There were some wide gaps between the tattered albums, allowing Tiarnen to read one of the titles.

"*Dirges of Dorladdich – 192AP*?" he said, confusion causing him to reach for the album. However, just before his fingers could touch it, a tiny lightning bolt shot out from the clouds and struck his hand.

"Ah!" shouted Tiarnen, shaking the pins and needles from his hand.

"Careful, Profezzor, foreign recordingz are well-protected," said Jonefa.

"You don't zay!" said Tiarnen.

"On our right!" said Evzen.

Tiarnen and the boys leaped from the stormy bookcase and onto another as it passed just like before. Thankfully, there was no sticky webbing or lightning bolts to worry about on this one, as far as Tiarnen could tell. In fact, the hundreds of soft little mushrooms, adorable tiny snails, and glimmering yellow butterflies living along the shelves brought him an unexpected sensation of tranquillity despite still racing through the library.

"Thiz iz uz. Jump!" said Evzen.

Everyone leaped off the case and either slid, rolled, or came to a running stop. They were in a very different area of the library; instead of rows, there was a grid of stone pillars, around six metres high, that contained several inset rows of records locked behind ornate glass windows.

"Are we in the zecure zection?" asked Tiarnen, helping Bastien to his feet.

"Yez, Maeztro Phrguz'z vault iz juzt on the other zide," said Evzen, keeping very close to a pillar with Jonefa.

"What'z wrong?" asked Tiarnen, noticing Evzen's apprehension to move.

Evzen scratched his temple. "Well, normally Lukeiru iz wandering around here, but I can't zee her."

"She's probably juzt zleeping in a corner zomewhere," said Jonefa.

WOMPF!

An enormous furry white paw with curved blue claws longer than Tiarnen's forearm stamped on the ground beside him. A splatter of blood followed. Tiarnen swallowed hard and slowly looked up to see Lukeiru. As far as he was concerned, she looked like an overgrown fox save for the missing left eye and front right leg and the glowing blue fur at the tip of her tail. Another splatter of blood hit the floor, and Tiarnen noticed that it wasn't coming from Lukeiru but something that resembled a moth—its wings still flapping in an effort to escape her clenched teeth.

"Well, at leazt she got one of the mothz that waz eating away the wezt zection," whispered Bastien.

"Who carez!" hissed Jonefa, smacking Bastien on the back of the head.

"What now?" whispered Tiarnen, shuffling to hide behind a pillar.

"Ztick to the pillarz and follow me," whispered Evzen.

Together, they peeled off from the direction that Lukeiru was headed, using the pillars as cover. Luckily, Lukeiru became occupied with feasting on the moth, so the company made their way to the end of the section uninterrupted while the sound of crunching echoed around them.

"There'z the vault," whispered Jonefa.

Tiarnen looked past the last few pillars to see a perfectly round vault door with a large wheel knob, which stood partially open.

"It'z not locked?" asked Tiarnen.

"There'z no need," said Evzen.

"Why not?"

FWUMP!

Lukeiru flopped down between them and the door while still chewing on a bit of moth wing.

"Right," muttered Tiarnen.

Jonefa sighed. "We need to find a way around her."

"Think I have a better idea," whispered Evzen. "You three wait here."

"Where are you going?" asked Bastien.

Evzen ignored the question and vanished back into the pillar shadows.

The next few silent minutes felt like hours, and after Lukeiru swallowed the last of the moth, she licked her lips with her blue tongue, let out a satiated sigh, and then seemed to grow sleepy—her eyes closing and tail growing dim.

Fweeeeep!

A sharp whistle echoed, and Lukeiru sprung back to her feet—her tail swooshing with vibrant blue luminescence now and leaving a light trail of glowing fur dancing in the still air.

Fweeeeep!

"Iz Evzen out of hiz mind?" hissed Jonefa.

Lukeiru lowered her head with ears perked and eyes narrowed to determine what direction the whistle was coming from.

Fweeeeep! Fweeeeep!

Her head turned slightly to the left, and she sprung towards the sound, leaving the vault unguarded.

"Will she kill him?" asked Tiarnen, reaching for Darktide as he watched the blue tail fade away.

"No, she'z trained to take anyone she findz back to the librarianz," said Jonefa.

"A far worze fate, if you azk me," said Bastien.

Fweeeeep!

"Thiz iz our chance. Come on!" Bastien left the safety of the pillar shadow and ran towards the vault door.

Tiarnen and Jonefa followed close behind, sprinting hard across the stone floor, and then finally passing into the vault.

"He'z coming!" yelled Bastien.

Tiarnen turned to see Evzen emerging from the pillars and running like his life depended on it. Given the ferocious look on Lukeiru's face, as she gave chase behind, Tiarnen understood and shared Bastien's doubts that she only intended to take Evzen back to the librarians in one piece.

"Hurry up!" yelled Jonefa, turning to the door and putting his hands on it. Bastien and Tiarnen followed suit, and after Evzen threw himself into the vault, they pushed together and closed the door.

THUD!

WHAM!

Scratch-scratch-scratch-scratch.

"Zorry, Lukeiru," chortled Bastien, listening to the pawing against the door. "There'z only enough room for four!"

"Ztill have all your limbz?" asked Tiarnen, holding his hand out to Evzen.

"Lookz like," said Evzen, taking Tiarnen's hand and pulling himself up.

Tiarnen looked around the ostentatious vault. The curved wall of the round room was covered with carved motifs of Phrygian maestros in dynamic poses. To his left, there was a grand record player with a table, plush couch, and a lounge chair in front of it. To his right, there was a simple bench seat and a small refreshment bar containing multiple ornate bottles of what he guessed were spirits. What grabbed Tiarnen's attention, however, was the glass column standing floor to ceiling in the middle of the room, which appeared to be protecting an archive of jewelled record albums.

"What makez theze albumz zpecial compared to the rezt of the library?" asked Tiarnen.

"They are conzidered to be perfect performancez," said Jonefa.

"Of Maeztro Phryguz?" asked Tiarnen, trying not to show too much enthusiasm that he had finally found what he was looking for.

"And hiz opponentz, by Phrygian ztandardz, anyway," added Jonefa.

Bastien's wide eyes kept gazing at the albums. "I don't even know which one to chooze."

"The mozt recent recording would be bezt," said Tiarnen.

Bastien nodded in agreement and stepped over to the archive console at the base of the column, which had a curated list of album titles and shelf designations beside the control panel. "Found it!" he said. After a bit of fidgeting with the levers and dials, he figured out how to work the selection claw, pulled the desired album from its shelf, and then deposited it into the retrieval slot at the bottom. Tiarnen pulled the slot open and grabbed the album, noticing the plush leather and intricate title embossing.

"*Battle of Zigrizberg, 1579*," said Tiarnen, flipping the album over to see the warsong list. "'Primiznix in E Major', Maeztro Phryguz the Zixty-third... 'Ziathrizte in D Major,' Maestro Dorian the Fifty-ninth...

wait, that'z my zi—" Tiarnen bit his tongue, realizing that he was about to reveal his relation to Reina.

"Your *zi*?" asked Evzen.

"My, ughh... *zingle* most hated Dorladdian warzong," said Tiarnen, quickly looking back to the album. "'Hoarthur in E Major'... 'Galatlas in D Major'... 'Länulinge in E Ma'—"

"Oh! 'Länulinge' iz one of my favourite warsongz!" interrupted Bastien.

"Apparently, Zturm'z az well, zince Maeztro Phryguz performz it in practically every battle," said Jonefa.

"Iz that zo?" asked Tiarnen, his eyebrow raised.

"Zix hundred and twenty-two timez to be exact," said Evzen.

"All right, the exam hazn't begun yet," said Jonefa, dismissively.

"Remind me, what time iz the exam tomorrow?" asked Tiarnen.

"Zeven o'clock, az alwayz," said Evzen, looking at him suspiciously.

"Right," said Tiarnen, handing the album to Bastien.

Bastien made his way between the plush blue velvet couch and lounge chair and then approached the record player. Much like the rest of the vault, the player was in a class of its own: there was not one but four spiral horns curving out of the oversized gilded case, soft blue felt covered the turntable, and the needle arm was in the shape of a large natterhorn antler. Bastien pulled the polished metal disc from the cover and set it on the turntable. After a few rotations of the hand-crank set in the front of the case, the record began to spin, and Bastien carefully brought the needle down onto it.

A flash of blue sparks erupted, followed by a brief second of distortion. Then, Tiarnen heard what sounded like voices... No, they were cries... *battle cries*! The clashing of weapons and armour filled the vault, making Tiarnen look around as though the fight was happening right then and there.

"'Prizminix in E Major'!" announced a confident voice.

Tiarnen guessed it was Maestro Phrygus shouting, and he was proven right when the bone-chilling woodwind tones of Frostfang opened the class one warsong.

"I love the way he announcez the warsongz," said Bastien, flopping onto the couch beside Evzen.

"*Shhh!*" hushed Jonefa, also collapsing on the couch and taking up the last of the cushions.

Accepting that he wouldn't have any sheet music to reference, Tiarnen listened intensely to the haunting phrases of "Prizminix" and immediately noticed how sorrowful they were. Each ascending motif was unquestionably uplifting, but the descending motifs that followed created a deep sense of loss in Tiarnen. He didn't even know what for exactly, though by the time the first movement was over, he was forlorn like he had never experienced before—to the point where part of him just wanted to lay down Darktide and forget about the *Anthymn*. The effect was unbelievably powerful, and then Tiarnen realized that was the intent of "Prizminix": to cause the enemy to lose all hope and accept defeat. Aware now of what was happening, Tiarnen was even more impressed by the recording—how it allowed Phrygus to still have a strong impact on susceptible listeners like himself. He looked over to the boys, who seemed to be feeling it as well, but they were taking a strange comfort in the despair since their feet were tapping to the beat of the drums.

As the warsong continued, Tiarnen pulled himself out of its emotional clutches and tried to focus back on the mission. "Prizminix" was proving to be fairly simple as far as compositional standards, and he could think of at least two Dorladdian warsongs that might be able synestrize with it. Then he remembered Evzen mentioning how Sturm constantly chose "Länulinge." Tiarnen was at an impasse. He could either adopt a warsong that would be easier to work with but risk it never being performed by Phrygus, or plan for "Länulinge," which was much more complex but would likely be used against him.

As much as Tiarnen didn't want to admit it, he knew "Länulinge" was the right choice. He let out a long breath and took a seat in the lounge chair. There the four of them sat for most of the evening, listening to the album on loop, which meant hearing Reina's voice over and over again. Pushing the pangs of sorrow aside, Tiarnen tried to think of a Dorladdian warsong that he might be able to synestrize it with.

"'Siathriste' is probably the best choice," muttered Tiarnen.

"Profezzor?" asked Evzen.

"Hmm?" Tiarnen looked over at the boys on the couch, who were staring at the record player intensely.

"At the end of that lazt motif, what iz Maeztro Phryguz doing?" asked Evzen.

"He iz applying an extended technique called *pitch bending*. Mozt Maeztroz don't uze it very often because they rizk malformed shardz."

Evzen crinkled his nose. "I don't think I underztand."

Tiarnen stood up and raised the needle off the record to quiet the room so he could explain.

"Zome inztrumentz allow you to move up or down an octave without having to change your fingering."

The boys looked at each other in confusion.

"Here," said Tiarnen, instinctively pulling out Darktide.

"Woah!" exclaimed Bastien. "I have never zeen a piccolo like that before!"

"It... uhhh..." stammered Tiarnen, realizing the potential mistake he just made. "It haz been in my family for a long time now."

"I really like the colourz!" said Bastien.

"Needz more blue," added Jonefa.

"Couldn't agree more, Jonefa," said Tiarnen. "Now, what Phryguz iz doing iz changing hiz tongue plazement on Froztfang'z reed to bend the pitch of the note either up or down to enhance hiz shardz. I can create the zame effect by rolling my lipz acrozz the piccolo plate like thiz." He put Darktide to his lips, rolled the mouth plate along his bottom lip, and bent a few pitches.

The boys gave an obligatory light applause.

"Making zenze?"

They nodded in agreement.

"Good." Tiarnen quickly returned Darktide to his pocket and then placed the needle on the record again.

The album looped twenty more times, and even though Tiarnen was still listening intensely, his eyes were trying to close. Allowing himself a yawn, he casually pulled out his pocket watch to see that it was two o'clock in the morning. "Already?" he whispered, looking over to the boys. To his relief, they were draped over each other and fast asleep on the couch. Knowing that this was the last chance he would get, Tiarnen slowly got up and quietly walked over to the record player again. He examined all the dials, levers, buttons, and gauges in the hope that he would find something that would allow him to loop only "Länulinge." Thankfully, there appeared to be. Beside the turn lever, there were two dials labelled *start* and *end*. Tiarnen set them both to where "Länulinge" began and ended on the album and then pressed the *set* button. Sure enough, it worked.

"All right, now onto the hard part," said Tiarnen, pulling out Darktide again.

As "Länulinge" began to play, he sat on the edge of the lounge chair and held the piccolo at the ready. He had no intention of illuminating, but he could at least try and get the fingering down for synestrizing with "Siathriste." The problem was, unlike with Lydia, he wouldn't be able to test any of his attempts at fusing the warsongs together before facing

Phrygus. There would only be one chance, and Tiarnen knew it would be in the heat of battle.

Chapter Thirty-Three
STONE CANVAS

A long brush licked the henge pillar with black paint. Lydia pulled the wet bristles off the stone and then dipped them into a paint bucket held in her other hand—the cuff of her sleeve soaking with onyx, which only added to the matching stains already there. To her surprise, Raghnall had delivered on his promise of new attire after she had completed the first draft of the *Anthymn*. The simple tunic and kirtle dress were far too long, though she was still begrudgingly thankful as it covered the maestro glass bracelet around her right wrist.

She pulled the brush out of the bucket, pressed it to the pillar again, and finished the arcing line.

"Looks like the contouring is finally coming together," said Raghnall, observing from the long table.

"Forgetting the fact that ve still don't know vhich colour—ahh!" screamed Lydia, an excruciating jolt of pain running along her right arm and causing the brush to slip from her hand.

"Dare I ask?" inquired Raghnall.

"It's nothing," said Lydia, shaking her hand and then picking the brush up from the henge floor.

"Sure seems like a lot of pain for *nothing*."

Lydia ignored the major's assessment and painted another long arcing contour line along the pillar.

"Speaking of colour, I think the first batch of green is ready," said Raghnall.

Lydia walked back to the table to see Raghnall standing over a large marble board that had a thick roll of vibrant green paint on it. Shortly after Lydia had completed the first draft, she put together a list of supplies that she would need in order to move forward with her composition.

Orange paint

Green paint

White paint

Black paint

Walnut Oil

Solvent

Round brushes

Flat brushes

Pallet knives

Marble slab

Mullers

Rags

Raghnall mentioned that everything could be found at the Office of Supply, but he worried that the seemingly odd request might raise a lot of questions—perhaps even from Ignis himself. The executor didn't need to be given any more reason than he already had to take an interest in Raghnall's comings and goings, especially since he wasn't allowed in the Conservatory to check on the "restoration." All things considered, Raghnall decided it would be best to source each item from individual merchants. The green pigment was easy enough to acquire since the kelpers were producing dry seaweed by the ton every day. The white pigment came from the island's cliffs, thanks to the rich chalk deposits that regularly broke off in clumps and collected on the decks of the corsairs when they were retrieving crab traps. The black pigment came from the charred wood piled up in Kilners' Row. Orange pigment, however, proved very difficult to find. Fortunately, much of the iron armour left behind by fallen Lydvenkian soldiers was rusting badly in a heap behind Garod's shop, and the major could scrape off as much as he needed.

Lydia grabbed a fresh brush from the table, dipped it into the green paint, and then walked back to the henge, where she made a couple of quick strokes inside one of the shard contours.

"How is it?" asked Raghnall.

"Lumpy," said Lydia, walking back to the long table.

"But I mulled the pigment over a hundred times," stated Raghnall.

"Doesn't matter if it vas a thousand given the vay you're doing it."

"Well, I didn't realize there was a standard to be met."

"I suppose standards are a new concept to you, Dorladdians."

"Just as *manners* are to you, Lydvenkians."

Lydia ignored the remark and grabbed one of two corked jugs of walnut oil.

Pop!

She tilted the mouth of the jug and poured a heavy glob of golden oil onto the paint, grabbed the muller, and then mulled until the oil had been absorbed.

"If I could illuminate a few kyndling to help…" began Lydia, but Raghnall's immediate laughter told her it wasn't worth finishing the sentence.

"I'll be a praetor myself before I let you bring one of those winged menaces to life," said Raghnall.

Lydia scooped some paint into a small bowl with a pallet knife and then returned to the henge. After a quick dip, she pressed the green brush bristles onto the pillar and made a couple of glossy strokes. "Much better," she said.

"That looked like practised skill," said Raghnall. "Did you paint before you were a maestro?"

Clack-Clack!

They both looked to the door and saw Dansby already closing it behind him. After the lock reset, the captain turned around with a slight stumble and then made his way over to the henge. As he got closer, Lydia could see that he was looking worse than ever; his hair was unkempt, heavy bags silhouetted his bloodshot eyes, and there was now a patchy beard stealing what little youth was left in his face.

"Mail for you, Major," said Dansby, arriving beside the major with an envelope resting on top of a new shift roster for him to approve.

"Thank you, Captain," said Raghnall, seeing that it was from Tiarnen. He set the roster down and immediately opened the letter to read it. "*Dear Raghnall... I hope this letter finds you well... Legion and orchestra both ready to depart... However, I will be leaving ahead in hope of infiltrating the Tantalis... With a bit of luck, I should meet Maestro Phrygus in combat on Decembra first.*" Raghnall looked up at Lydia in disbelief. "*Decembra first?* That means Phrygus will be arriving here tomorrow."

"*If* Tiarnen is successful," said Lydia.

"He'll find a way," said Raghnall, folding the letter back up and putting it in his pocket.

"Roster for the week is finished," said Dansby, ignoring the news.

"You had time to do it on shift?" Raghnall picked up the roster again and looked it over.

"Took a long lunch at the Stag's Hollow," Dansby said casually.

"Captain, wait," said Raghnall, noticing the sloppy handwriting. "You have Edmond down twice on Tuesday... and I don't see Selmar or Breck anywhere."

"Just take Edmond out and replace him with either of those two then," said Dansby, continuing to walk away.

"Captain!" shouted Raghnall.

Dansby stopped.

"Finish the roster properly and re-submit it to me."

"Don't know why we're being so formal about this," said Dansby, trudging back and taking the roster from Raghnall.

"Because it's important that we maintain standards," said Raghnall, side-eyeing Lydia. "More than ever."

"If that were true, she would have been composing this whole time instead of painting a useless mural like some child," grumbled Dansby.

"This mural *is* composition," said Lydia, walking back into the henge.

"That so?" chortled Dansby. "Major, do you see music anywhere here?"

"I see... pattern," said Raghnall.

"At least one of you has an eye," said Lydia, filling in the shard with more green paint.

"It's easy enough to make out the individual shards," added Raghnall. "And I'll guess that the larger repeating shapes they are forming will be recurring themes in the *Anthymn*."

"Correct," said Lydia, trying to hide her surprise.

"That said, I have never seen composing approached this way before."

"It seemed like a sensible approach to test the next iteration. If I can glimpse the *Anthymn* in full—"

"Then you can extrapolate the composition required to illuminate it."

"Precisely. The contouring defines vhere the shards vill be placed but the colour determines vhich tones are played."

"This is nothing but a deception," said Dansby.

"What makes you say that?" asked Raghnall.

"Because her bracelet was made without a single brush stroke."

"That vas merely a sketch, a glimpse, of vhat the *Anthymn* vill need to be," said Lydia.

"You mean another step closer to betraying us," said Dansby, marching over to Lydia only for Raghnall to step in between them.

"We don't know that," said Raghnall.

"No?" asked Dansby. "Then why has she been hiding her hand?"

Realizing that Dansby had a point, Raghnall turned to face Lydia and nodded at her wrist. "Go on."

Lydia looked at Raghnall with refusal in her eyes.

"I'll be damned if—" said Raghnall, marching over and grabbing Lydia's bony arm. He yanked the stained sleeve back and expected to see an infected wound, only to find himself looking upon porcelain skin—the scars and marring that once covered her gnarled hand almost completely gone.

"By the Verse," muttered Raghnall.

"Now, unless either of you has a better idea of how to finish the *Anthymn* vith only a day left," said Lydia, yanking her arm away from Raghnall and hiding her hand once again. "Please see yourselves out of the henge."

Raghnall and Dansby did as she asked and walked to the long table, where the captain picked up the roster.

"Are we really going to sit back and let this doomed experiment continue?" whispered Dansby.

"With Phrygus arriving tomorrow, we don't have any choice," said Raghnall. "Just have to keep a closer eye on her in the meantime."

"I don't care what theoretical explanations she tries to sell us on, that witch can't be trusted," said Dansby, pencilling in changes to the roster.

"Agreed."

"Do you?" asked Dansby, handing the roster to Raghnall once again and then leaving to the lounge.

An hour passed, and Lydia finished brushing small swatches of colour in all the contoured shards.

"Major," said Lydia, setting the empty green and orange paint bowls down on the table where Raghnall was sitting. "I vill need you to bring me Ravenving."

"There are plenty of other instruments to choose from," said Raghnall, gesturing to the instrument room.

"As I have already proven, none of them vill be able to vithstand my performance," said Lydia, looking past the major to catch a glimpse of her harp.

"Yet you were still able to complete the first draft. I'm sure we can find you something that will be a worthy sacrifice for this iteration as well."

Lydia looked at Windwalker.

"Don't even think about it," growled Raghnall.

"Then give me Ravenving, damn you!" shouted Lydia, the bracelet blooming with light under her sleeve.

"Pick another instrument," said Raghnall, standing to his full height and looking down at her. "Or I will melt that cursed harp down and make your urn out of it."

They stared at each other in silence for a moment, and then Lydia turned to walk to the instrumentry. "Vhat is there for strings?" she asked.

"Third shelf to your left has a double bass."

Lydia entered the instrumentry and glanced at the double bass. "It von't have the right timbre," she yelled.

"Verse, give me strength," said Raghnall, making his way over. After arriving, he stepped on the ladder, reached the top shelf, and then descended with a violin in hand. "Be gentle with this one; it's—"

Lydia snatched the violin, placed her chin on the rest, and set the bow. As though she had been playing it her entire life, she performed a quick melody and then looked over the instrument again. "It'll do." Chain dragging behind, Lydia made her way back to the henge and took position in the middle of it while Raghnall drew his shield and chose the nearest of the nine pillars to stand behind.

"Anything I should be warned about?" he asked.

"Probably," said Lydia, setting the bow to the strings and opening the second draft with a scintillating motif that quickly brought the first movement to life. Jagged honey-orange shards illuminated and leaped from the violin to hang in the air above her until a flickering nebula of firelight had formed. At the midpoint, she repeated her performance in retrograde and with it, doubled the nebula with smooth myrtle-green shards. Lydia slowly spun her body and flourished, the flowing move-ment drawing the nebula down and around her into a vortex. Bolts of lightning crackled and leaped between the contrasting shards, but Lydia only flourished again to increase the rotational speed and better conduct the static charge. It was working. The bolts condensed and drew the shards to each other, which divided the vortex into three groups. Lydia then cast them against the first, second, and third pillars, thus matching the mosaic patterns.

The violin bow was already beginning to smoke as Lydia transitioned into the second movement with renewed conviction and illuminated more bright juniper-green shards that leaped from the strings and hung in the air until a glittering nebula had formed. Then, she repeated the passage and doubled the nebula with topaz-orange shards. Lydia spun her body and mirrored her flourishes from before, casting the three groups of shards against the fourth, fifth, and sixth pillars.

Without hesitation, Lydia began the third movement and formed a fulvous-orange nebula. She then inverted the passage again, which doubled the nebula with shimmering pine-green shards. With a spin of her body and a flowing flourish, Lydia pulled the nebula down and around herself into a vortex. As expected, bolts of lightning crackled and leaped between the shards while she conducted the static charge and then cast the groupings against the seventh, eighth, and ninth pillars.

In a grand finale, Lydia flourished and drew the first three pillar mosaics towards her. As they approached, she fused them into a crescent mantle and then stopped it at about an arm's length away. She then turned to the next three pillars and did the same to form another crescent mantle. With careful gestures, she tried to align the patterned edges in the hope of fitting them together. The moment they touched, the mantles joined and made a partial cocoon structure that bloomed with synestric energy. Satisfied, she turned to the last three pillars and tried to repeat the process, but the cocoon was already beginning to fracture.

HISSSSSSSS!

Seeing the glass burning black, Lydia then dashed out of the henge and ducked behind a pillar at the last second, as the cocoon lattrice collapsed in on itself and exploded with violent prismatic light.

KARAAANG!

Silence returned to the Conservatory. Raghnall and Lydia both slowly emerged from behind their pillars and looked upon the graveyard of charred glass.

"Are you hurt?" asked Raghnall.

Lydia shook her head and walked back into the henge to survey the detritus.

"What went wrong?" Raghnall pressed.

"The shape of the movements, overall structure, this vorthless driftwood you call an instrument!" said Lydia, tossing the broken violin onto the floor like a dead thing.

"From where I was standing, it looked like you intentionally broke it."

"Easy enough, given that it vasn't even fit for a second-rate minstrel," spat Lydia.

"I spent months rejuvenating the wood—even the bow was reinforced!"

"And your pathetic effort vould have been better spent on a tavern stool!"

Raghnall was taken aback by the insult. "Perhaps you're right," he said, slinging his shield over his shoulder and leaving for the door. "Perhaps I am a fool for wanting to try and preserve what little we have left."

It took most of the evening for Lydia to repaint the henge, and even though she was satisfied with the second version of the composition, she still had no idea if it was going to work. Seeing that all she could do now was wait for the paint to dry, Lydia made her way to the table and began to clean the brushes.

Clack-clack!

She jumped at the unexpected opening of the door and turned to see Raghnall arriving with two crates in hand.

"Vhy are you back so soon?"

"*Eraduile*," said Raghnall, setting the crates on the table.

Lydia shook her head in confusion.

"It is a Dorladdian holiday that celebrates the last sailing of autumn—usually with a dinner among friends and family." He began pulling out several jars and small baskets from the crates.

"She is neither," stated Dansby, emerging from the lounge.

"Couldn't agree more," said Raghnall. "But one of the rules is that *no one* eats alone, so I'm going against my better judgement and spending it with her."

"Vill the captain not be joining us?" asked Lydia, watching as Dansby made his way to the door.

"He and the rest of the patrol will be filling their plates at the Stag's Hollow," said Raghnall, setting out plates and cutlery.

Clack-clack!

Dansby exited the Conservatory, leaving behind a moment of awkward silence.

"Now, I'm not sure what you'll want to try." Raghnall looked over all the seafood. "I'll just give you a bit of everything." The major served up hearty piles of steamed mussels, fried prawns, raw urchin, poached salmon, smoked haddock, lobster tails, and scalloped potatoes. Lydia reluctantly took the overloaded plate and set it down in front of herself as he did the same with his. After choosing an angle of attack, Raghnall dove into his meal while Lydia scowled at the foreign fare for a minute and then finally began to pick away at it. They sat together in silence for a few minutes, which was more than enough time for Raghnall to clear half his plate. "How is it?" he asked.

"The fish is dry, and the mussels have too much salt," said Lydia.

"You know what? Never mind, this was a bad idea," said Raghnall, standing again to take Lydia's plate away from her.

"But the yellow... stuff... is rather delicious," said Lydia, pulling the plate out of his reach.

"That would be urchin," said Raghnall. "Most people never touch it, but Marifreth couldn't get enough either." A soft smile pulled at the major's cheek but then faded to a subtle sadness.

"It is a loneliness unlike any other after your siblings are gone."

"What would you know of siblings lost?" asked Raghnall, sitting back down.

Lydia pushed her food around the plate for a moment. "Tell me, vhy did you never become a maestro yourself?" she asked.

Allowing Lydia to change the subject, Raghnall took a large bite out of his lobster tail and then wiped the melted butter from his mouth before replying, "According to my parents, I had all the skill but none of the talent for the position. My father was the major at the time, so he offered me a second chance in the military."

"A dud then?" asked Lydia.

"Proudly," said Raghnall.

"And vhere is the pride in that, exactly?"

"Because it took just as much work to prove that I wasn't a maestro."

Lydia rolled her eyes. "Now I see vhere Tiarnen gets it from."

"Gets what?" Raghnall raised his eyebrow.

"His sickening optimism."

Raghnall huffed and took another bite of lobster tail.

"You vere lucky to have supportive parents," continued Lydia. "In Lydvenko, duds are disposed of to reduce any chance of abnormalities in the maestro's bloodline—strength being yours, apparently."

Raghnall nodded to the sheet music on the far end of the table. "Have you discovered anything unexpected about Dorladdich while learning our music?"

"Outside of your misplaced pride?" asked Lydia.

Raghnall scoffed at the insult and went back to eating.

"I suppose one thing I have learnt is that you are... resilient," said Lydia, lip curling at the admission.

"Given what Tiarnen mentioned in his letter, he would probably say the same thing about Lydvenko," said Raghnall. "Perhaps we're not quite as different as we might think."

"I vouldn't go that far."

"Why is that? After all, everyone speaks a common tongue."

"Your point being?"

"That we likely came from the same place before the provinces."

Lydia stared long at Raghnall as though lost in a memory. "Even if that legend vere true, all it serves now is a reminder that nothing lasts forever."

"Including the provinces," said Raghnall.

"Just as Tharus intended," said Lydia, tossing her fork onto the plate.

"Your intentions, however, remain vague at best."

"I intend to compose the *Anthymn*."

"To what end, though?" asked Raghnall, gesturing to her healed hand.

"If it makes you feel any better, that question has been plaguing me as well," said Lydia, pulling her sleeve back slightly.

Raghnall shifted in his seat. "I realize that my music theory is a little rusty, but it was hard not to notice that the *Anthymn*'s lattrice seemed to be missing a core."

"The *Anthymn* is not a varsong, therefore its lattrice structure vill naturally be different," said Lydia.

"Is that why you're putting yourself at the centre of it?" asked Raghnall.

Lydia's cackle suddenly filled the Conservatory. "You're afraid. Even in my pathetic state vhile chained to a pillar—you're still afraid that I might somehow break free."

"No, I am certain that you will. The real question is, what happens after you do?"

Lydia stared at him.

"It's ironic that you warned me about Dansby's grief consuming him," Raghnall continued.

"Vhy is that?" asked Lydia.

"Because your rage might very well do the same to you."

"Are you forgetting that ve Lydvenkian maestros are attuned to it?"

"Oh, I remember every battle against your predecessors, how they used anger to ignite their shards and lay waste to my friends and family," said Raghnall. "But none of them had the kind of hatred I see in your eyes every day."

"And vhat do you think could possibly be inspiring that?"

"If I had to guess... betrayal."

Lydia clenched her jaw.

"Whatever happened, I am sorry. But if you use the *Anthymn* for revenge... Lydia... it will only bring ruin to us all."

Clack-clack!

The chamber door unlocked.

Raghnall leaped to his feet and stood ready but saw that it was merely Dansby returning.

"You weren't due back for hours, Captain," said Raghnall.

"Sorry, sir... I... I was," stammered Dansby, struggling to close the door while still holding onto a stein in his hand. "I was... I was asked to leave... the... the, uhh... the Hollow!"

"Can't imagine why," said Raghnall.

"I, too, found... found it very odd," said Dansby, walking at an angle to the table and spilling his drink everywhere. "So I took... a... a detour through Harm's Way for a... a last celebratory drink before returning."

Raghnall took a sniff. "Well, if we run out of turpentine, I know what we can clean the brushes with instead."

"Fitting, since this tastes... almost as bad... as... as the *Anthymn* sounds," said Dansby, laughing to himself and then taking another long sip.

Lydia stood to her feet and began making her way to the instrumentry. Raghnall was going to follow, but she quickly returned with a mandolin and walked straight into the henge.

"Lydia, we can wait until he is—" began Raghnall.

But she was already opening the new draft with flowing phrases that ignited the first movement. Just as before, the shard groupings were cast against the first, second, and third pillars. The second movement saw more groupings cast against the fourth, fifth, and sixth pillars. Without hesitation, Lydia transitioned into the third movement and cast the shard groupings against the seventh, eighth, and ninth pillars.

Flourishing feverishly, she fused the first crescent mantle and then stopped it about an arm's length away. She then formed the second mantle, drew it towards herself, aligned the edges, and joined the two mantles together. The partial cocoon lattrice bloomed with synestric energy. With a final effort, she turned to the last three pillars and fused the last mantle. Lydia focused intensely and flourished—pulling the mantle towards her. When it was inches away from the cocoon, she made a tiny gesture to adjust its angle, only for the mandolin neck to snap in half. The mantle drifted, and the edges misaligned with the cocoon, causing the synestric power to misdirect and begin burning the glass.

HISSSSSSSS!

For a moment, Lydia stood in denial of her failure, but as the lattrice began to collapse on top of her, she was left with no choice but to retreat behind the henge yet again.

KARAAANG!

A blast of violent prismatic light filled the Conservatory. After a moment, silence returned, but it soon gave way to Dansby's condescending applause.

"Encore, encore!" he exclaimed, emerging from behind a pillar. "I would say tha-that it's getting a bit... predictable... even boring... but for some reason, I just ca-can't get enough of watching her fail so miserably."

Lydia tossed the instrument at Raghnall's feet and raised her eyebrow at him.

"You know... you might as well leave that there si-since Phrygus will probably pile our bodies up beside it aft-after he arrives here tomorrow," said Dansby.

"We don't know that," said Raghnall.

"No?" scoffed Lydia. "Once he is over the disorientation of his sudden arrival, Phrygus vill be in no mood for a lengthy conversation as to vhy ve brought him here. Vhen he attacks, I cannot hope to defend us vithout Ravenving."

"Then we destroy the henge and stop Phrygus from ever coming here," said Dansby, sitting on the table.

"We can't," said Raghnall.

"*Why in the Verse not?*" asked Dansby.

"Because that would prevent Tiarnen from returning safely as well."

"He made his choice," Dansby said dismissively.

"What did you say?" asked Raghnall.

"I said Tiarnen made his bloody choice!" yelled Dansby, standing to his feet, "In fact, he made it for all of us, and we are no better for it!"

"I don't believe that."

"Because your loyalty ha-has blinded you." Dansby pointed a finger in Raghnall's face. "And may-maybe if you would have shown Reina the sa-same devotion as your nephew, sh-she would still be alive!"

"Captain..."

"Go on, te-tell me I'm wrong, Raghnall!" shouted Dansby.

"Captain, you are... relieved of duty."

Chapter Thirty-Four
A NEW APPRENTICE

"Ztudentz!" shouted a rather tall woman wearing rectangular glasses, with her grey hair pulled into a tight bun.

"Yez, Profezzor Kohlder!" the students replied in chorus.

"Pleaze chooze your inztrumentz and then gather yourzelvez here." She gestured to the tiled floor on her left. "Maeztro Phryguz will be here shortly."

Watching from the heavy shadows of the long oval classroom, Tiarnen looked past the other six professors standing in front of him to Bastien, Jonefa, and Evzen, who were joining ten other students in picking their preferred instruments from the many resting on a long wall shelf. Together, they walked over to stand between Professor Kohlder and a circular rostrum which had a music stand and control panel inset along the handrail. Tiarnen could see three channels in the floor that extended from the rostrum all the way to the far side of the classroom, where they ran through separate archways which led into a short hall. At the end of each hall stood a wooden dummy that was painted in Dorladdich green, Lydvenko orange, or Elihammer magenta. Given that there were parts and pieces of other dummies piled on the floor of the halls, he guessed they were used for some sort of target practice.

Tiarnen blinked his tired eyes and then focused back on the boys, who looked as though they hadn't quite woken up yet, either. It was his fault. He almost lost track of time in the vault while trying to figure out how to best synestrize "Länulinge," and it wasn't until the record player stopped that he thought to look at his pocket watch again. To his horror, they only had twenty minutes before the exam started, so he woke the boys, returned the album to the archive, and then carefully opened the vault door to leave. Half expecting that Lukeiru's snout was going to be the first thing they saw, Tiarnen was relieved to find her off to the side and curled up with her tail over her eyes. According to Evzen, she hunted during the evening when the moths were out and slept most of the day, so they quietly tiptoed their way to the library stairs, which, after three hundred or so steps, brought them to the second level of the Tantalis and finally into the classroom where the examination was being held.

"Iz everyone az excited az I am?" asked Maestro Phrygus, arriving through the doorway with an artisan bassoon in hand.

The students whistled and krawed like squalls in response.

Tiarnen saw that Phrygus was in his late forties, had well-kept sandy blond hair framing his friendly but lined face, and blue eyes with heavy bags underneath which were behind a pair of round chronospecs on his turned-up nose.

Clink... clink... clink.

Like a long shadow, Praetor Sturm trailed behind Phrygus. He closely resembled Tharus and Khazlokov: gaunt and pale with the same hairline cracks running down his stern face. Ignoring the terrible comb-over, Tiarnen noticed that Sturm, too, was wearing the signature dark grey tunic and half-cape that Tharus and Khazlokov preferred, but the jewelled cane in his right hand made him stand apart.

"Good to hear," said Phrygus, stepping onto the rostrum and standing tall in his knee-length bright blue double-breasted maestro jacket with a fur-lined collar and cuffs. The silver *LXIII* pin on his left lapel was glinting brightly, as was the Phrygian crest made up of a mountain with wings on either side. "Letz ztart this auzpiciouz morning off right with 'Beyond the Froztland,' shall we?" Phrygus straightened his posture and held the bassoon reed to his lips as the students took deep breaths.

Wonder, beyond the froztland
Our heartz yearn
Our mindz forgot

Our zecret hope to remember
There in a warm mountain
There are our lozt dreamz
There the recordz zpin
There iz our beauty

Though the way back iz long
Znowy and narrow
The froztland dreary and gloomy
It doez not matter
When hearing a memory'z voice
We forget the hardship

Our heartz yearn
Our mindz forgot
There iz wonder
Beyond the froztland

The students and professors lightly applauded, which pulled Tiarnen out of the melancholic daze the song put him in. He didn't know if it was the lyrics, the student chorus, or the sorrowful bellows of Frostfang, but he suddenly yearned to be back in the library and studying every record he could get his hands on. He couldn't help but imagine what Phrygus would add to the *Anthymn* in terms of emotion—the green and orange mixing with blue—how each maestro would influence and augment its quality, shape, and power.

Everyone quickly became quiet again as Phrygus lowered his bassoon. "I know that I need not remind you, but your performancez thiz morning will be one of the mozt decizive momentz of your life."

"No pressure," mumbled Tiarnen.

"Over fifty generationz of ztudentz once ztood where you are now in hopez of graduating from our preztigiouz muzic academy, but it haz only been the very bezt of them who have tried to win the coveted apprenticeship for Orcheztra Lead!" said Phrygus.

The students looked at each other with excitement.

"All right, let'z begin," said Phrygus.

Bastien took a step forward.

"And your name iz?" asked Phrygus.

"Baz-Baztien, Maestro," said Bastien, bowing slightly.

"Pleazure to meet you, Baztien. Are you ready?"

"I am."

"Excellent. The firzt part of the exam will be zimple. I shall perform a zingle motif and all you must do is tell me *which* warzong it iz from and *where* it firzt appearz."

"Yez, Maeztro."

Phrygus put his lips to the reed of Frostfang and played a handful of short notes.

"'Primiznix in E Major,'" said Bastien. He paused for a moment to think. "Tenth meazure of the firzt movement."

"Well done," said Phrygus.

Bastien exhaled in relief and then walked to the back of the line while everyone applauded.

"The bar haz been zet!" said Phrygus. "Let'z zee how the rezt of you fair."

"Jonefa, my Maeztro," said Jonefa, arriving at Phrygus, bowing, and then standing tall.

"Ready, Jonefa?"

"Yez, Maeztro."

Phrygus put his lips to the reed of Frostfang again and played another handful of short notes.

"'Hoarthur in E Major'... zecond measure of the... third movement," said Jonefa.

"I'm sorry, Jonefa," said Phrygus. "But the motif arrivez on the zecond meazure of the *fourth* movement."

Jonefa slouched in disappointment.

"Give him another chance, pleaze Maestro!" begged Bastien.

"There are no zecond chancez on the battlefield, and zo there will be none granted in thiz room," Sturm said bluntly.

Tiarnen didn't bother hiding his scowl.

"I underztand, Praetor," said Jonefa, leaving the line with tears in his eyes.

It wasn't long before the rest of the students were challenged, most of whom failed, leaving Evzen to be last.

"Ah, Evzen, isn't it?" asked Phrygus.

"It iz, Maeztro. Thank you for remembering."

"Being that your older brother iz currently leading my orcheztra, I can imagine you muzt be feeling an enormouz amount of prezzure right now."

"I am, but hopefully, the extra ztudying will pay off."

"Let'z find out," said Phrygus. He took a breath and played a new motif.

"'Länulinge,' eleventh meazure of the first movement," Evzen said confidently.

"Correct," said Phrygus.

Everyone applauded, and Phrygus smiled in acknowledgement of the four remaining students standing before him.

"Onto the practical half of the examination. I will perform a pazzage from each warzong you identified, and together we will hopefully make short work of our provincial opponentz." He gestured to the target dummies. "Bastien."

"Yez, Maeztro."

"Whom would you like to face thiz morning?" asked Phrygus, pressing a button on the rostrum control panel, which caused the dummies to jolt forward along their rails to the front of archways.

"Lydvenko," said Bastien.

"Then let uz show Maeztro Lydia what you have learnt," said Phrygus, stepping down from the rostrum. He took position in the middle of the classroom to face the Lydvenkian dummy waiting in the left hall.

Bastien walked over and took position behind Phrygus, his flute at the ready.

"I will be diminishing my performance greatly, which meanz my shardz will be very fragile and thuz incapable of deztroying the dummy unlezz you, Baztien, accompany me perfectly. Underztood?"

"I'm ready," Bastien said nervously.

Phrygus put Frostfang's reed to his mouth and opened "Prizminix" with the now all-too-familiar forlorn phrases. Bastien's accompaniment made Phrygus's ice-blue shards grow thicker and stronger, though he had already missed two notes due to his nerves getting the best of him. Tiarnen knew the feeling well. Practising and rehearsing was one thing, but only when eyes were on you was your resolve truly tested. Reaching the end of the passage now, Phrygus flourished and drew the shards into a vortex around Bastien and himself. Then, he cast them with practised accuracy at the dummy. Blue light trails streaked behind as the shards tore through the air and stabbed into the wood—except for two, which shattered on impact.

"Fail," Phrygus said coldly.

Heartbroken, Bastien reluctantly nodded in acknowledgement and trudged over to the rest of his peers. Tiarnen wanted to say something to him, give reassurance but knew he had to remain hidden in the shadows, and so he watched as the two other students made their best attempt to accompany Phrygus and inevitably failed just the same. Last, and who Tiarnen hoped would not be least, Evzen took position with his clarinet in hand.

"Ah, our lazt hope it would zeem," said Phrygus. "Who shall we ztrike down together, Evzen?"

"Maeztro Dorian," said Evzen.

Tiarnen couldn't help but feel a little betrayed.

Phrygus turned to face the green dummy, readied Frostfang, and opened "Länulinge" with a chilling sequence of phrases that made the entire classroom quickly grow cold. Tiarnen was pleasantly surprised to get a live performance of the warsong, even if it was just a part, and so he paid close attention to Phrygus's technique, as was Evzen judging by how he was matching his maestro note for note. Once a sparkling ice-blue nebula swirled above them, Phrygus flourished and cocooned himself and Evzen in its vortex.

"Come on, Evzen," muttered Tiarnen.

Frostfang sang the last note of the passage, and with it, Phrygus cast the shards at Tiarnen's dummy. Once again, countless streaks of blue light cut through the air, and the green wood was stabbed a hundred times over—the last shard cutting deep into the centre of the dummy's chest. Phrygus lowered Frostfang and watched as the dummy froze solid, then broke into pieces which came crashing onto the floor. He turned to Evzen and paused—his face emotionless. "Full markz," he said, a smile finally breaking. "Apprentizeship granted."

The students cheered, and professors broke into applause while Sturm made his way over to Evzen.

Clink... clink... clink.

The room quickly fell silent as the praetor reached into a belt pocket, retrieved a small pin in the shape of a snowflake, and pressed it into Evzen's sweater.

"Congratulationz are zertainly in order, Evzen," said Phrygus. "But, tell me, how were you able to match my ztylization zo well?"

"Oh! Profezzor Keligräth waz generouz enough to help uz review your latezt album in the vault lazt night, and he taught uz all about pitch bending," Evzen said cheerfully.

"*Keligräth*?" asked Phrygus, looking back at the professors in confusion.

"Yez, *newly appointed*." Evzen pointed to the professors. "I can't thank him enough for the opportunity."

"I'm sure." Phrygus's eyes locked on Tiarnen's silhouette. The other professors felt the sudden tension and cautiously put some distance between themselves and Tiarnen as he stepped into the light. "Tell uz... Maeztro Dorian... did you come to be tezted az well?"

Evzen, Jonefa, and Bastien looked at each other in disbelief.

"I'm a firm believer that you're never too old to learn something new," said Tiarnen, finally able to drop the accent.

Ting-ting! Ting-ting! Ting-ting!

As though called by the third chime of Sturm's chronograph, Major Svante, a short, slim man with a glorious windswept moustache and eyebrows, barged through the classroom door with a large bow in hand. "Praetor! Maeztro! We're under attack!"

"Thank the Verse," muttered Tiarnen, exhaling in relief.

"Let me guezz... Dorladdich?" said Phrygus.

"And what remainz of Lydvenko'z forcez appear to be with them az well!" exclaimed Svante.

"Launch the airborne immediately!" yelled Sturm.

"Profezzorz, zee the ztudentz to the bunkerz," said Phrygus.

There wasn't a moment of hesitation; most of the classroom cleared out in a flash, but not without Tiarnen giving Evzen a wink before he left.

"What shall we do about our guezt?" asked Phrygus.

"Thiz iz where hiz little tour endz," said Sturm, following Svante out.

"And here I thought you might have been dumb enough to come alone," said Phrygus, setting Frostfang against the rostrum railing and then opening up his maestro jacket.

"Happy to disap—" began Tiarnen, but before he could finish his sentence, Phrygus drew his tin whistle and illuminated a quick motif of shards.

VEER-VEER-VEERSH!

Tiarnen ducked out of the way as they streaked overhead and shattered against the stone wall as he rolled behind the rostrum.

"I waz told that you deztroyed Maeztro Lydia a short while ago," said Phrygus.

"Don't believe everything you hear," said Tiarnen, looking for a way to escape the classroom without losing his head and lure Phrygus up to the henge. He needed a diversion. His eyes went to the control panel, and he quickly pulled down as many levers as he could reach. The doors at the back of the halls cracked open, and target dummies swiftly emerged—their arms swaying and rotating in jerky mechanical motions, making it nearly impossible for Phrygus to find a clear line of sight on Tiarnen.

"A pathetic diverzion," said Phrygus. He illuminated with his tin whistle again and cut down the dummies that Tiarnen was using for cover while trying to make his way to the classroom door.

"Your speed is impressive, but that aim could use a little more work!" said Tiarnen, already regretting the taunt.

"I will show you imprezzive, coward." Phrygus reached the rostrum, tossed the burned tin whistle to the side, and picked up Frostfang.

Tiarnen could tell by Phrygus's tone that he was done humouring him and watched as a flurry of shards ignited from the bassoon, making the classroom grow cold. Frost began to appear and expand on the dummies, then the floor, and even up the walls. Seeing that evasion was no longer an option, Tiarnen sprinted for the door as Phrygus released his shards.

VEEER-BOOM!

The dummy to Tiarnen's left instantly froze solid and then exploded—the wood and ice chunks ripping through the air. He kept running as fast as he possibly could as more dummies froze and exploded around him.

VEEER-BOOM! VEEER-BOOM! VEEER-BOOM!

His right cheek now slashed and bleeding from the splinters, Tiarnen dashed through the doorway, rolling onto the second-tier stairs and into a river of foot traffic: airmen, soldiers, professors, students, librarians, and orchestra members hurrying to answer the chronoclock's call to arms.

KOO-KOO-KOO! KOO-KOO-KOO! KOO-KOO-KOO!

Tiarnen scrambled back to his feet and began running up the stairs. He pushed against the crowd like a fish trying to swim upstream and reached the nearest balcony, but there wasn't a platform docked. His stomach sank as he peered over the edge to see the platforms rising and falling. With a quick look over his shoulder, just as Phrygus emerged from the classroom, Tiarnen leaped off the balcony, sailed through the air, and landed hard on one of the rising platforms, but not without pushing off most of the crates, which descended and broke against other platforms or vanished into the darkness of the library far below.

Not wanting the chase to end, Tiarnen stood up and gave Phrygus a casual Dorladdian salute as he ascended in the hope of encouraging the pursuit.

It worked. Phrygus immediately began running up the stairs again at a blistering pace—the forty or so years of traversing the Tantalis clearly paying off—and ran past the last balcony to continue towards the maintenance door in the side of the cuckoo clock. Knowing now that Phrygus would be inside the clock house waiting for him, Tiarnen looked around frantically for anything that might serve as another distraction.

KRAW!

The familiar call drew his attention to the passing Roost, which appeared to be in complete disarray. Squadrons of airmen were trying to prep for takeoff while the ground crew was in the middle of moving several squalls out of the stables.

"I don't care where their armour iz, Gryzilva, I need all our zquadronz in the air now! Dorladdich juzt broke through the gate!" yelled Svante, grabbing onto the reins of his majestic squall and pulling himself onto the saddle.

We're already in the city? thought Tiarnen, his heart jumping and stomach sinking at the same time.

KRAW!

Tiarnen looked past Major Svante and saw the trapper's wagon exactly where he left it, except the cage was open, and two crewmen were trying to secure Cloudstrike with long poles that had nooses at the end. Knowing it was probably a very bad idea, Tiarnen lifted Darktide and played a sharp note that echoed through the whole of the Tantalis and immediately grabbed Cloudstrike's attention. His eyes narrowed at Tiarnen, and he sniffed the air.

KRAAAAAAW!

Enraged, Cloudstrike tossed the crewmen to the side like rag dolls and then lunged out of the cage—running at full speed through the Roost in hunt of Tiarnen.

"Definitely a bad idea," said Tiarnen. He looked up to the clock house and saw that there were still twenty or so metres before the platform would stop inside. Knowing that Cloudstrike would tear him apart well before that, he put Darktide back to his lips and illuminated another single shard that cut the platform rope in half.

Snap!

Tiarnen grabbed the end of the rope, and with the platform detached, he shot up at blinding speed.

SMASH!

Before he even realized what had happened, his body broke through the rope slot and then slammed against the massive gears inside the clock house. After collapsing in a heap, he caught his breath and then rolled onto his back to see a ladder leading up to the roof and then through a stone tunnel. He hoped it might finally take him somewhere close to the henge.

KOO-KOO-KOO! KOO-KOO-KOO! KOO-KOO-KOO!

Being so close to the clock's internal mechanics, its call to arms was nearly deafening, and the sudden movement of the soldier characters caused Tiarnen to lift Darktide, ready to play—except the piccolo wasn't in his hand. He looked around in panic and saw it resting on the floor a few metres away. He crawled over, feeling every one of the new bruises on his battered body, and reached out—only for a fine blue leather boot to step on his hand. Tiarnen glanced up to see Phrygus standing over him. "I don't suppose you would mind passing me—"

"I think not," interrupted Phrygus, readying his bassoon.

This is it, thought Tiarnen. All he had worked for was about to end, in a clock house of all places.

KRAW!

Chunks of wood panelling suddenly hit both of them as Cloudstrike pierced through the house wall with his sharp beak—the debris sending Phrygus flying back. Though Tiarnen was grateful that Cloudstrike didn't give up his chase, the squall wasted no time and started pecking at him as though he were a trapped natterhorn. Tiarnen rolled out of reach, grabbed Darktide, and then sprinted to the ladder as Cloudstrike clawed and pecked the breach in the wall wider and wider. Rung after rung passed under Tiarnen's hands and feet as he frantically made his way up the ladder and into the stone tunnel where he found himself in near-total darkness.

Thunk!

"Ow!" he yelped, hitting the top of his head on something metal and coming to a dizzying stop. He ran his hand over the cold surface, searching for any clue that might help him out of what now seemed to be a dead end. Then, a series of bassoon notes resounded below, followed by a burst of blue light, which revealed that it was a hatch above him.

Krawwwww!

As Phrygus's luminance faded, Tiarnen pressed his upper back against the hatch plate. Slowly, he began stepping up the few remaining ladder rungs. "Come on! Give, damn you!"

Creeeeeek.

The frozen hinges finally gave, and, with a last push, Tiarnen saw snow falling around him as he heaved the hatch open. Knowing that Phrygus was about to be on his heels again, he climbed the rest of the way out to find himself looking upon the snowy mountain summit. As his eyes adjusted to the flat morning light, Tiarnen saw that the henge was nestled into the side of the Tantalis peak only a short way ahead. Boots crunching in the snow, he hurried along the ridgeline and couldn't help but look down the sheer cliff face to see the battle unfolding far below.

Just as Major Svante had said, the legion was already well into the city, and only rubble remained of the main gate. Several Phrygian battalions were trying to slow the legion's assault at the end of the north road but were quickly losing ground. Tiarnen watched both sides' orchestras following close behind, trying to hold formation for their maestros, who would likely never arrive. Svante and his squadrons flew into view, banked hard, and then dove while loosing their arrows at Mikavnik. Tiarnen's stomach sank at the thought of Niera being hit since he knew she would be close by, but he told himself to stay focused and press on to the henge.

Only metres away now, he saw that it was nearly identical to the one at home. The pillars and upper ring were the same width and height. However, instead of stone, they were made of dark indigo ice with frost-white veins running out from the runic notes carved into them. Walking into the centre, Tiarnen saw that there was no escape thanks to how the mountain peak wrapped around most of the henge, so he double-backed over his footprints and then hid behind the first pillar. With a bit of luck, Phrygus would follow them into the henge, and then Tiarnen could cut him off. Seeing the maestro finally emerge from the hatch, Tiarnen took a knee and waited patiently for him to arrive—the unexpected moment of calm making the weight of the situation feel all the heavier. He hadn't given synestrizing a second thought since leaving the vault. Evzen's examination at least confirmed that "Länulinge" really was a favourite, but Tiarnen still had no idea if he could survive long enough to synestrize with it. Doubt tried to creep into his heart as he watched Phrygus cautiously follow the footsteps into the middle of the henge—laughing as he noticed that they had come to an end.

"I zuppoze I should thank you for thiz little chaze! It haz left uz with no Praetorz, orchestraz, or military to worry about," said Phrygus, his frosty breath hanging in the still air.

"Not to mention rules of engagement," said Tiarnen.

"And yet ztill you hide, why?" asked Phrygus, readying Frostfang.

"Because…" Tiarnen paused just as he was about to taunt Phrygus. *Maybe he could be convinced to go to Dorladdich willingly?* "Because… we're *both* in far greater danger than you realize."

"Iz that zo?" said Phrygus, chuckling. "Then by all meanz, ztop hiding and tell me about our impending doom."

Tiarnen took a breath, stood up, and stepped out from behind the pillar.

Phrygus smirked. "Am I zuppozed to feel trapped?"

"Yes… but not for the reason you think," said Tiarnen, lost in the fact he suddenly had an opportunity to explain himself.

"If you're about to tell me that all of thiz iz zome zort of elaborate ruze."

"No… well… it actually is," said Tiarnen, trying to pull his thoughts together. "I came here to tell you that my father—"

"—Will fall," said Phrygus. "Along with the entire Dorladdian legion, shortly after I take your head!"

"Wait!" pleaded Tiarnen.

It was too late. Phrygus had already illuminated a pair of shards and cast them to his left and right. At first, Tiarnen was confused. Then he watched them impact the icy henge pillars and ricochet towards him at twice the speed. He ducked out of their path, causing them to shatter against the rocky mountain face.

"That's new," muttered Tiarnen. He pulled Darktide from his pocket and returned to his feet as Phrygus played another malicious short motif and illuminated six shards that he cast at the pillars again.

Tink! Tink! Tink! Tink! Tink! Tink!

Unwilling to duck away like before, Tiarnen played his own defensive motif and illuminated six shards, which he spun around himself, blocking Phrygus's attack—except for one shard. The pain was unlike anything he had ever felt before. Stunned as much as he was hurt,

Tiarnen leaned back against the nearest pillar and looked down to his right shoulder, where he saw a glowing blue shard pierced deep within it—frost already spreading from the wound.

"You may find that shiver-lance to be a touch on the colder zide, Maeztro," Phrygus said proudly.

"R-r-r-really? Hadn't n-n-n-noticed," said Tiarnen, shivering uncontrollably from the lance's freezing effect.

"It'z a shame we muzt bring thiz to an end zo quickly, Dorian. You have, at the very leazt, been quite entertaining." Phrygus began walking towards him.

"T-tell me, how w-would Phrygus the Sixty-First d-destroy me?" asked Tiarnen. He raised Darktide and attempted a searing phrase from "Pyrozikar" but failed due to his trembling hands.

"He would have cut down that pillar you're leaning againzt and crushed you with it," Phrygus said confidently.

"And P-Phrygus the Sixty-Second?" asked Tiarnen. Allowing his anger at the injury to rise, he played the phrase again—this time successfully illuminating three tiny copper-orange shards.

Phrygus stopped dead in his tracks, completely baffled by what he was seeing. "She... she would have kept you here until you froze to death."

Tiarnen flourished, fused the three shards together, and then stabbed the searing blade of glass into the wound. He screamed out in pain as it charred Phrygus's lance into dust and cauterized the wound.

"You would play Lydvenkian muzic to zave yourzelf?" asked Phrygus, disgusted by what he was witnessing.

"To save *both* of us," grumbled Tiarnen, smoke rising from his wound as he stood to his feet. Channelling the excruciating pain through Darktide, he went on the attack—illuminating another blistering motif from "Pyrozikar" and casting the shards at the henge pillars.

Tink! Tink! Tink! Tink! Tink! Tink!

They ricocheted just as Phrygus's did, but Tiarnen's lack of control sent only one of them streaking at their intended target.

Phrygus laughed, illuminated a single note, and parried Tiarnen's attack with ease.

The Lydvenkian shard had imbued Tiarnen with so much rage that it was intoxicating. All he wanted to do was cut Phrygus to pieces, so he played the motif again.

Tink! Tink! Tink! Tink! Tink! Tink!

This time, he managed to direct two shards at Phrygus, but they were just as easily parried.

He played his motif yet again with more determination.

Tink! Tink! Tink! Tink! Tink! Tink!

Phrgyus parried the four shards with ease.

Enraged, Tiarnen played the motif for a fourth time and flourished fervidly.

Tink! Tink! Tink! Tink! Tink! Tink!

All six streaked towards Phrygus, and he parried all but one, which cut through his jacket and across his left thigh.

"You learn quickly," said Phrygus, checking the wound and then looking at the blood on his fingers.

"Spending all of that time in your vault is paying off," said Tiarnen.

"Then you can chooze which warzong I will deztroy you with," said Phrygus, standing back to his full height. "Zince we are not bound by formalitiez."

"In that case, 'Länulinge,'" Tiarnen said confidently.

Phrygus smiled. "Zo be it."

Chapter Thirty-Five
LANÜLINGE
IN E MAJOR

Tiarnen watched with trepidation as Phrygus put Frostfang's reed to his lips and opened "Länulinge's" sombre first movement. From several mournful motifs, Phrygus illuminated glossy ice-blue shards, and as they flew from the bassoon's bell ring, Tiarnen could see how perfectly smooth they were. With a quick flourish, Phrygus cast the cluster high above himself and continued into the next passage of frigid figurations—more shards ascending to build his nebula.

Transitioning into the second movement, Frostfang howled a scalic sequence of contrasting motifs that illuminated more vibrant blue shards and expanded the nebula. Knowing that "Länulinge's" melody was coming up soon, Tiarnen slowly readied his piccolo in anticipation. As expected, Phrygus played the woeful theme—its last note a calling, which Tiarnen answered with "Siathriste." Just as before with Lydia, he felt completely exposed and expected that Phrygus, too, would laugh off what appeared to be a pathetic distraction. Instead, Phrygus seemed to be perplexed.

Tiarnen was admittedly relieved—not that it mattered because Phrygus merely continued playing into the bleak third movement. A full section of melancholic phrases followed and tripled the mass of the nebula. Shards now in the thousands, Tiarnen dovetailed with "Siathriste" once more. Phrygus watched him intensely while he played, but this time, there was no confusion on his face—it was a look of pure curiosity.

Unwilling to be distracted, however, Phrygus opened the fourth movement with ascending broken chords and then made his artisan instrument sing a solemn section that he flourished with a precise downward movement. The shards followed his gravitational pull and circled their maestro—the swirling momentum condensing the nebula into a glistening vortex.

Tiarnen focused as Phrygus began the wistful fifth movement by casting his vortex into the centre of the henge and building

"Länulinge's" core. As it formed, the snow kicked up around them and swirled around the outskirts of the henge. In an attempt to remind Tiarnen that there was no escape from his impending doom, Phrygus raised his amplitude and played the warsong melody louder than ever. The posturing only steeled Tiarnen's heart, and so he made Darktide glow with ivy-green light in response. He used the angular momentum of several precise flourishes to quickly spin the shards around himself and then cast them towards the core. One by one, they shot into the narrow gaps and locked into place, making the core flicker chaotically with blue and green light.

Phrygus had no idea what exactly Tiarnen was up to but clearly wasn't willing to lose control of his own warsong, so he pressed on and began the sixth movement with a long dolent section. Tiarnen waited patiently, fingering set on the piccolo already. Phrygus's eyes narrowed at him as he arrived at the melody once again and played it louder than ever. Appreciating the effort, Tiarnen played Darktide without hesitation and illuminated—flourishing as fast as he could so that his shards could give chase to Phrygus's and overlay them as they shaped a malformed mantle around the core together.

"You fool!" shouted Phrygus. "Whatever you're attempting, it won't work!"

"Only one way to find out!" said Tiarnen.

Incensed by Tiarnen's smugness, Phrygus began the seventh and final movement, which made the veins along his temples and hands glow blue. The artistic carvings along Frostfang pulsed with icy light as a gust of shards flew out of its bell ring and streaked through the air. His resonance now pulsing, Phrygus repeated "Länulinge's" melody one last time. The amplitude from Frostfang was nearly deafening, but Tiarnen refused to be drowned out and played with all his heart to ignite for what he knew could very well be the last time in life.

Phrygus flourished with conviction and cast his shards to form the second mantle. Tiarnen followed in pursuit, casting his teal-green shards in between and over the top of the mantle just as Phrygus closed it around the core and thus fused the lattrice together.

HERAAAAAANG!

Phrygus looked up to see the blue-green lattrice hanging high above the henge as its effect unexpectedly swirled the snow around them and turned the countless flakes into a cyclone of glass razors.

"What... *what have you done?*" asked Phrygus, watching the glass flakes cut through the air.

"Don't worry. She'll explain everything!" said Tiarnen, turning and running into the whirlwind. Hands over his face, he pressed through while screaming in pain as the glass flakes streaked past and left behind what felt like a thousand cuts across his exposed skin. With a last desperate effort, Tiarnen leaped and finally emerged from the cyclone.

Thud!

His bloodied body landed on a snowbank.

"Tiarnen!" screamed a voice.

Face nicked and bleeding, he looked back to see Niera in the far distance with Tharus, Davmir, and what remained of the legion—all arriving at the summit. *Please, let this work,* he thought, raising Dark-tide and quickly playing Dorladdich's key tones.

VEEEEEROOOOF!

The rune notes flashed, and an unexpected blast of air dispelled the cyclone to leave a clear view of the now-empty henge.

"By the Verse... I did it," muttered Tiarnen.

But before he could celebrate Phrygus's departure, the lattrice came crashing down and exploded with a blinding shockwave that struck the mountain peak—causing an avalanche to descend upon the entire summit.

Chapter Thirty-Six
REBIRTH

Lydia swirled her brush at the bottom of the paint bowl and then, with a gentle stroke, ran the bristles along the naked stone and filled the shard contour with orange.

Raghnall quickly surveyed the henge. "Is that the last of the changes?"

"Yes, as vell as the last of the paint," said Lydia.

"Good. Means you can give me a hand with this," said Raghnall.

Lydia looked back to see Raghnall standing with Ravenwing in hand. The bowl nearly fell out of her hand as she stood there, stupefied.

"Don't get too excited," said Raghnall. "Some of the strings need to be replaced."

He walked over to the long table, pushed some of the empty supplies to the side, and set the harp down as well as a pair of leather gloves, a thick roll of wire string, pliers, and some cutters. He looked Ravenwing over and tried to make sense of how the broken strings were threaded through its neck and eyelets. "Now... I don't exactly know how to..."

"Thread the new strings from the bottom, knot them, and then tie each one around their tuning pin," said Lydia. "Here I can—"

"Oh, no," said Raghnall. "You're not touching this yet."

Lydia started to snarl but fought off the impulse and instead stood and watched as the major began pulling out the broken strings.

"I don't know which idea I hate more," said Raghnall. "Phrygus coming here or putting this back into your hands."

"I suppose it depends on the outcome you're expecting."

"Is there one where neither of you tries to seize Dorladdich?"

Lydia remained silent.

"My point exactly," said Raghnall, pulling out the last broken string and then slipping on the leather gloves. He grabbed the cutters and began to measure out the wire for the First String. Lydia watched him intensely as he measured, cut, and replaced the strings one by one. He didn't say it, but he hated being near the cursed instrument—unable to stop thinking about how many Dorladdian lives it had taken and how many more it might yet. Looping the last new string around its tuning peg, Raghnall heard the Conservatory door open. Knowing that it was Dansby, he didn't bother looking back—the last thing he wanted was another confrontation, given how much tension there was now between them.

"Good morning, Major!" Dansby said cheerfully.

Raghnall was a bit taken aback by the friendly tone and then even more surprised when Dansby arrived beside him clean-shaven, his hair styled, and armour polished. The captain held up a steaming mug in greeting and took a long sip while Raghnall stared at him in confusion.

"Don't worry. Just a cup of grey," said Dansby.

As much as Raghnall was relieved to hear it, he still didn't like what he was seeing as far as the sudden change in appearance.

Dansby laughed. "Try not to look so relieved."

"I see that you're still in uniform," said Raghnall.

"Yes, well, that's because I'm ignoring what you said last night," said Dansby, taking another long sip.

"I will admit that maybe I went too—" began Raghnall.

"No," interrupted Dansby, "it was I that went too far."

Raghnall put his hand on Dansby's shoulder and nodded in agreement. The captain glanced at Lydia and then made his way into the henge.

"Have to admit, the detail is quite impressive."

Lydia remained silent.

"Still, it could use a bit more green, wouldn't you say, Major?" said Dansby.

"In this case, I think we're aiming for balance," said Raghnall.

"Speaking of which, my head is already spinning from the fumes—we should let some air in here," said Dansby.

"Is that why you left the door open?" asked Lydia.

"*Open?*" asked Raghnall, his face dropping. He turned to rush back and close the door only to see that it was too late—Ignis was already walking into the Conservatory with a patrolman following at either side.

"Well... well... well," said Ignis.

"Executor..." said Raghnall.

"I see that the *restoration effort* has been very productive," said Ignis, arriving at the end of the table and looking over the mess.

"Ignis, let me explain what is happening."

"Oh, there's no need. The good captain saw fit to find me late last night and fill me in on every little detail."

"Did he?" asked Raghnall, glaring back at Dansby.

"As you can imagine, I was rather shocked to hear that Maestro Lydia was not only still alive but in our very own conservatory under *your* protection. Naturally, my first reaction was to inform Maestro Dorian—only to learn that it was Tiarnen himself who'd rescued her and then convinced you to commit treason as well. At that point, I thought the months of drinking had pickled his mind, but part of me had to be sure."

"And now that you know the truth?" asked Raghnall, trying to slowly circle back to his shield, which was propped up beside a chair on the other side of the table.

"I can only agree with Dansby. The detail is quite impressive," said Ignis, gesturing to the henge.

"Ignis has assured me that if you surrender, no harm will come to you," said Dansby.

"You forget, I have seen first-hand what the Executor's assurances really mean," said Raghnall.

"Major, this is your last chance," said Ignis.

"No, it is yours!" spat Lydia, tossing her brush and bowl down and rushing out of the henge for Ravenwing.

As though he were pulling in a fish, Dansby yanked on Lydia's chain and sent her crashing down.

"Captain, stop!" said Raghnall, rounding the table and picking up his shield.

"No!" yelled Dansby, kneeling over the top of Lydia and grabbing her by the throat. "You and Tiarnen have forgotten who she is!" He squeezed tighter around Lydia's neck, looking dead into her eyes. "But I know what you really are."

"If that vere true," said Lydia, leaning into his grip and choking herself further, "you vouldn't be holding me so close." Her upper lip curled into a cunning smile.

Dansby's face filled with rage. He stood, pulled Lydia up with him, and threw her emaciated body against the nearest pillar. Raghnall turned to rush into the henge.

"Seize him!" ordered Ignis.

The two patrolmen chased down Raghnall and tried to subdue him. "Major, please, stand down!" one of them begged.

Dansby pulled on Lydia's leash again, dragging her back towards him. "Your worthless life, the cursed *Anthymn*, my pain, *all* of it ends here!" said Dansby, raising his shield to kill Lydia.

WHAM!

Raghnall blindsided Dansby and sent him crashing to the floor, then grabbed the captain, dragged him out of the henge, and tossed him into the two patrolmen who were clutching their broken noses.

"Stand down!" said Raghnall, engaging his gauntlet and pointing a finger at Dansby as the patrolmen helped the captain get back on his feet.

Ignis's laughter filled the Conservatory. "Do you honestly believe that you can still get away with this, Major?"

Raghnall looked long at Ignis... then readied his shield.

"Day Striders!" yelled Ignis.

Ten patrolmen rushed in and arrived on either side of him.

"Seize them!"

The patrolmen rushed Raghnall as he raised his shield not in defence but—*CLANG*—to break Lydia's chain. Raghnall then rose, grabbed Ravenwing, and tossed it to Lydia, who—watching it soar through the air—raised her hands and caught it. She paused for a moment in disbelief that it had finally been returned to her, but the crashing of the patrolmen against Raghnall's shield pulled Lydia from her daze.

She hurried to the middle of the henge, set Ravenwing on her hip and aligned her fingers over the strings, then opened the *Anthymn*'s first movement. Inspiritive phrases illuminated vibrant myrtle-green shards and brought with them a blast of wind that shut all the windows and doors. The entire conservatory was swallowed by darkness, but as Lydia continued to bring the *Anthymn* to life, each new shard flashed with stark brilliance that gave split-second glimpses of the brawl unfolding just outside the henge. Once the nebula was twinkling above, she repeated her performance in retrograde while Raghnall protected her. Smooth honey-orange shards flew off the strings and ascended. Lydia flourished and pulled the nebula into a vortex—bolts of lightning crackling between the contrasting shards—then cast them against the pillars to form the mosaic patterns.

As Ravenwing sang, Lydia saw Raghnall fending off the patrolmen while she transitioned into the second movement. Knowing this would be her last chance, she played with absolute conviction and illuminated a glittering juniper-green nebula. Then, she inverted the passage with fervour and doubled the nebula with sparkling topaz-orange shards. Lydia spun her body and mirrored her flourishes from before, casting the three groups of shards against the fourth, fifth, and sixth pillars.

Intensely focused, Lydia transitioned into the third movement with blazing sequences that illuminated and formed a flame-bright nebula. Once again, she inverted the passionate sequence, which doubled the nebula with shimmering sea-green. With a twirl of her body and a fast flourish, Lydia pulled the nebula around herself into a vortex. More violent than ever before, bolts of lightning erupted and crackled between the shards while she conducted their static charge to cast the groupings against the pillars.

With quick flourishes, Lydia fused the first three pillar mosaics into a crescent mantle and then stopped it about an arm's length away. She then turned to the next three pillars and did the same to form another mantle. Flourishing precisely, she tried to align the patterned edges in the hope of fitting them together. The moment they touched, the mantles joined and made a partial cocoon structure that bloomed with synestric energy.

KARANG!

She turned to the last three pillars and fused the mantle together. This time flourishing as delicately as she possibly could, Lydia drew the third mantle towards herself and, with a final effort, aligned its edges to seal herself within the cocoon.

KARAAAAAANG!

"Face me!" screamed Dansby, ducking past Raghnall and rushing into the henge as the cocoon flashed like a newborn star. Blinded by the light, he had no choice but to stop and raise his shield, but it was futile, for no shadow in the Conservatory was safe from the radiance nor ears from Lydia's horrific scream.

And then, it was over.

The smell of burned stone and glass filled Raghnall's bloodied nose as he rose and blinked his vision back into focus. His eyes followed the sharp rays of daylight cutting through the broken window shutters to the henge. He tried to make out what little seemingly remained of the cocoon: a smouldering halo of synestric glass embedded in the floor. Movement stirred in the middle of it, so he cautiously approached until he saw Lydia on her knees at the centre. Watching the steam rise from her body, Raghnall could tell that she had transformed: her frail body had somehow recovered its muscle and renewed its flesh. Much like her hand weeks ago, the scars that once covered her were now barely visible. Even her hair had changed: the long-frizzled strands looked to have burned off to make way for short amber waves.

"Ly-Lydia?" asked Raghnall, stepping into the henge. "Are... are you—"

"Restored, it would seem." Lydia slowly raised her head to reveal a seraphic face with elegant features.

"Then your slaughter will be all the sweeter!" screamed Dansby, rushing out of the darkness and leaping towards her with his shield held high for a killing blow.

Left with no choice, Raghnall turned, grabbed Dansby by the throat with his gauntlet, and slammed the captain's body down onto the floor.

WHAM!

Upon the moment of impact, Raghnall knew that he had broken Dansby's neck and so tried to loosen his grip as gently as possible.

"I'm sorry, lad," said Raghnall, bottom lip quivering. "I didn't want it to come to this."

Lydia kneeled beside Raghnall and put her porcelain hand on Dansby's cheek while he struggled to breathe. "Vondrous are the shores beyond," she said softly. "Go to her, Captain. She is vaiting."

Dansby's eyes went to Raghnall, and a soft smile pulled at his cheek as they closed for the last time.

A sorrowful silence filled the Conservatory.

No longer able to fight back the tears, Raghnall sobbed, and so Lydia pulled him into her embrace. They said nothing to each other; she merely held onto him until he was able to regain his composure.

"Major?" Ignis asked cautiously.

Raghnall slowly stood up with Lydia, and they walked together to meet the snivelling Executor.

"Forgive me!" begged Ignis, already cowering. "The captain, he said that you were committing treason!" Ignis continued backpedalling until he bumped into the overturned long table and had nowhere left to go. "Please, please tell me, what is truly happening here?"

VEEEEEROOOOF!

The henge flashed with synestric blue and green light as a draft of frigid wind blew through the Conservatory. Snowflakes falling between them, Raghnall and Lydia turned to see Maestro Phrygus now standing in the henge.

"A new beginning," said Lydia.

Chapter Thirty-Seven
BEYOND REACH

A dense, chilling fog had swallowed the Tantalis summit and brought an eerie stillness with it. The henge could no longer be seen, its pillars now buried under a heavy cloud of snow and ice.

Suddenly, a hand broke through the surface and reached out—frantic for something to grab a hold of. Pale fingers outstretched, it found a large chunk of ice and took hold—pulling as hard as it could. With a gasp, Tiarnen surfaced from the snowpack, heaved himself from the frozen entombment, and then lay there for a moment to catch his breath.

When the avalanche hit, it felt as though he had the entire weight of the mountain bearing down on him. Luckily, the slide kept pushing him to the surface, though not without tossing him head-over-boots so many times that he lost consciousness.

"Maestro Dorian, can you hear us?" yelled Davmir.

Shaking the disbelief that he was not only still somehow alive but could also remember his own name, Tiarnen raised his head to see any sign of movement in the fog.

"I'm over here!"

"I heard someone!" yelled Kaleigh.

Tiarnen put his hands around his mouth. "Follow my voice!"

"Tiarnen, is that you?" shouted Niera.

Having a general idea of where they were coming from, he pulled himself up and tried to trudge through the dense powder.

"Where are you?" asked Tiarnen.

"Just keep talking!" yelled Niera.

"Remember you said that!" yelled Tiarnen.

"It's definitely him," said Kaleigh.

After what felt like an eternity of plodding on, the wind picked up and began to move the fog out of the summit. As though making some grand stage entrance, Tiarnen emerged from the last of the haze and saw Davmir, his armour badly dented and dirt-caked; Mikavnik, her left arm missing completely and chest punctured by what looked like a thousand arrows; Niera, somehow with barely a scratch to be seen; Kaleigh, her uniform and hair blood-splattered; Tharus and part of the legion waiting in formation in the far distance behind them.

"Look, there he is!" shouted Niera, her eyes widening at the sight of her brother.

"Told you he vould make it!" said Davmir.

Without hesitation, Niera ran to him. Relief washed over Tiarnen. Despite the victory, he didn't know what he would have done if she had been hurt, or worse.

Thud!

Niera nearly tackled him in an embrace. "Easy," he said.

"After the avalanche, I thought maybe—" began Niera.

"Makes two of us," finished Tiarnen.

Niera looked up at him, her smile fading a bit as she saw all the cuts and the wound in his shoulder. "Wow, you look terrible."

"Just need a shave." He winked.

Niera started laughing—then her eyes were suddenly drawn to the sky. "T-Tiarnen, behind you!"

KRAW!

Before Tiarnen knew what was happening, he found himself hurtling through the air and landing hard on the icy ground. Blinking his blurred vision back into focus, he looked up to see Cloudstrike approaching. The squall had a deep gash over his beak, platform rope tightly wrapped around his body, and his eyes were burning into Tiarnen.

"All right, you're angry. I get it," said Tiarnen. "And you have every right to be, but that's because you didn't see what *we* just pulled off!" He pointed back to the henge despite knowing it was nowhere to be seen. Cloudstrike, however, was having none of it. He snapped at Tiarnen over and over, trying to bite into any part of him he could.

"Help him!" screamed Niera, looking back to Davmir and Mikavnik.

They both sprang into action, but not before Cloudstrike extended his razor-sharp talons.

"Dorladdian filth!" yelled a voice from high above.

Tiarnen and Cloudstrike both looked up to see a squadron of airmen descending upon them, with Major Svante leading their chevron formation.

"We will have retribution!" yelled Svante.

Fweeeeet!

The airmen loosed a volley, and Cloudstrike vaulted forward, fleeing from the deadly arrows. Tiarnen would have run as well, but he didn't have to—his ankle was caught up in the pulley ropes as Cloudstrike blurred past, and now he was being dragged in tow. Tiarnen tried to reach up and free himself while the ground raced underneath. Hand almost on the rope, he saw the edge of the summit fast approaching, and then, to his horror, Cloudstrike's wings extended.

"No-no-no-no!" pleaded Tiarnen, his voice fading as they vanished over the edge together.

Although he had never flown before, he could tell they were spinning out of control. Cloudstrike tried to counter the momentum by angling his wings, but Tiarnen's off-centre weight was making it impossible. With what little strength he had, Tiarnen started hoisting himself up the pulley ropes as the ground sped towards them. Finally able to get his hand on the rope around Cloudstrike's neck—he heaved himself onto the squall's back and then gripped it like a rein.

KRAAAAW!

"Stop whining and get control!" ordered Tiarnen.

With Tiarnen's weight finally centred, Cloudstrike extended his wings fully and then pulled hard to the left to counter the spin. It worked, but despite flattening out, their rapid descent wasn't slowing. In a matter of seconds, they were going to crash through the city rooftops below.

"Pull up, damn you!" shouted Tiarnen, hauling back on the rope.

Instead, Cloudstrike lowered his head and turned their stall into a dive. Wind passed over his glinting feathers and filled them with lift as Tiarnen closed his eyes in anticipation of the fatal impact. His entire body pressed down onto Cloudstrike's back with incredible force. He felt them level off, and so he opened his eyes just as they were shooting over the rooftops—the squall's talons kicking up some of the bright blue tiles.

"YES!" shouted Tiarnen, celebrating the close call, only for Cloudstrike to start bucking and trying to shake him off. *"Really? After all that?"* Tiarnen wrapped his other leg in the pulley ropes and secured himself. "Now, take me back to the peak so we can talk about—"

Fweeeeet!

Two arrows shot past them, drawing Tiarnen's gaze over his shoulder where he saw the squadron, which was still in perfect formation and giving chase. Gripping the rein, he tried to steer Cloudstrike to the left.

KRAW!

Cloudstrike gave another buck.

"Fine! Just remember that you have a very valuable passenger on-board!" said Tiarnen.

Cloudstrike snorted and dove between the taller homes, trying to prevent the squadron from getting a clear shot. Despite holding on for his life, Tiarnen couldn't help but notice the city's devastation: fires were burning everywhere, the north road was barely recognizable, and the streets were in chaos as the legion hunted down the last of the Phrygian forces.

Fweeeeet!

Despite Cloudstrike powering through the turns, the squadron's well-practised manoeuvres kept them in close pursuit.

"We won't last much longer out in the open!" said Tiarnen.

Cloudstrike banked hard around the last tall house, pumped his wings furiously, and then straight-lined. Tiarnen wiped the tears from his eyes to look where they were heading: a narrow canyon running between the Tantalis and a neighbouring mountain.

"Uhh, can we talk about this first?" he asked.

Cloudstrike snorted again and pumped his wings harder, the leagues passing by in what felt like seconds. Fast approaching the canyon mouth, the squall turned sideways to fit between the rocky walls as they shot inside. Tiarnen glanced back to see the squadron skillfully break formation and follow in a single file. After a quick series of turns, the canyon opened and became much wider, allowing the airmen to take aim again. Tiarnen looked ahead to see a fork in their path fast arriving, and just as the airmen loosed their arrows, Cloudstrike veered left at the last possible second, leaving the squadron no choice but to sepa-rate. Two airmen managed to follow, while Svante and the remaining squadron vanished down the right ravine.

"Think we can shake them?" Tiarnen asked.

Rattling in acknowledgement, Cloudstrike dove for the ravine floor and then levelled off close to the ground. Tiarnen expected him to slow as they approached what seemed to be a series of sharp turns, but he was proven very wrong. After a hard left, they twisted right, then left again, and barrel-rolled into two more right turns, which Cloudstrike navigated with absolute precision. The first airman tried to match their line exactly, but his squall wasn't quick enough and ended up clipping the corner of the ravine, which sent them crashing down into a broken heap. The second airman kept his pursuit and drew another arrow, but before he could release the kill shot, Cloudstrike dragged his talon in the snow to kick up the powder and mask the turn ahead. Engulfed and blinded by the snow screen, the airman missed his mark as Cloudstrike wrapped around the corner.

CRUNCH!

Tiarnen didn't need to look back to know what happened.

Kraw.

"Nice work," he said, patting the side of Cloudstrike's neck.

The chase now seemingly at an end, Cloudstrike slowed his speed, and Tiarnen could feel him taking deep breaths. Wanting to give him a moment to recover, Tiarnen remained silent as they glided along a wide turn, which then opened to hundreds of frozen waterfalls on either side of the canyon. Awestruck by the unexpected moment of serenity, he took in the sight of the ice arcing down from the frosty mountains while drenched in late afternoon sunlight.

SHUNK!

An arrow pierced into Tiarnen's thigh. His teeth clenched as the pain radiated through his leg.

"For Phrysbruck!" yelled Svante.

Tiarnen looked up to see the major and his squadron descending upon them. Once again, the airmen aimed and released their arrows. Cloudstrike was quick enough to bank left and evade most of them, except for one, which found its mark and pierced the side of his chest. Carrying his momentum, Cloudstrike dove and fled—his wings pumping furiously in panic. He tried to pick up speed once again, but the arrow was already taking his breath. Instead, he ducked under the waterfalls to find cover. Tiarnen leaned in closer, riding Cloudstrike like a horse at full gallop to try and let him fly as naturally as possible into what seemed like an impossible gambit. The squall continued to duck and dive impressively around the frozen falls, but with Svante and the squadron still in the open air, all they had to do was continue taking shots between the gaps. Losing speed now, Tiarnen could feel Cloudstrike's breathing become more and more strained. As a result, the squadron was able to catch up, and one of the airmen ducked under the waterfalls to arrive on their right. Another airman swooped underneath them and arrived on the left. With airmen now on either side of him, Tiarnen was suddenly caught in the middle of a crossfire. He expected Cloudstrike to dive out of the way, but instead, the squall held the line as the airmen drew their bows.

"What are you doing?" yelled Tiarnen, pushing down onto Cloud-strike's back. Then, a chill ran down his spine as he realized that perhaps the squall was finally taking his revenge.

The airmen aimed and took their shots, but Cloudstrike collapsed his wings and dropped like a rock—the arrows flying overhead and mortally piercing into the unsuspecting targets. Both airmen went limp and slumped over—their squalls breaking off pursuit and fleeing from under the falls.

"Never do that again!" shouted Tiarnen, realizing that he was just used as bait.

FWEEER-BOOM!

He didn't know what flew past him, but its sonic explosion shattered the nearby falls and rained down colossal chunks of ice onto them. "Climb!" he yelled.

Cloudstrike lifted his head and ascended through the debris. Leaving the chaos behind, they shot up from the ravine and into the open sky, with Svante giving chase.

"Keep going, as high as you can!" said Tiarnen, looking back to see the major drawing his great bow with a whistle-tipped arrow knocked. As much as he didn't want to admit it, Tiarnen knew they were exactly where Svante wanted them: wounded and out in the open so they would make easy prey.

FWEEER—

The artisan arrow tore through the air just as Cloudstrike tried to vanish into the thick clouds.

BOOM!

The sonic boom was as violent as it was deafening and made the surrounding cloud disperse from the blast. Tiarnen and Cloudstrike suddenly found themselves tumbling through the air, but they were able to recover, only for Svante to be ready with another arrow.

FWEEER-BOOM!

Just as before, the concussive blast hit them like a hammer, but this time, Cloudstrike was barely able to right himself.

"These skies belong to me, Maestro!" shouted Svante.

"I don't know about you," said Tiarnen, tilting to the side to look Cloudstrike in the eye, "but I'm about done with this bloody chase!"

Cloudstrike snorted in agreement and began to turn back down towards the ravine.

"No, I have an idea," Tiarnen said, grabbing a handful of feathers on both sides of Cloudstrike's neck and trying to pull him up towards the clouds—but he resisted.

Kraw.

"You need to trust me!"

Cloudstrike rattled... then... Tiarnen felt the muscles in his neck relax to give control. Once again, he pulled back on the feathers, and

Cloudstrike, his breath now rapid and gargled, pumped his wings as purple blood spluttered out of his beak. Climbing straight up, Tiarnen lay low since he knew the predictable flight path would make them an easy target for Svante, who was already taking aim again.

A confident smile crossed the major's lips, and he unleashed his last arrow as Tiarnen and Cloudstrike were about to vanish into the clouds.

FWEEER—

Now hidden from sight, Tiarnen yanked back hard on Cloud-strike—forcing him into a reverse loop.

BOOM!

The arrow's impact busted the cloud wide open, revealing nothing but an empty sky behind it. Svante shouted in victory and then looked down to watch what little must be left of Tiarnen and Cloudstrike vanish below—except there was no sign of them anywhere.

KRAAAAAAAW!

Svante glanced back up to see Tiarnen and Cloudstrike breaking out of the next cloud at full speed, the squall's talons outstretched.

WHAM!

The impact snapped the back of Svante's squall like a tree branch, while the major was torn from his saddle.

"This is... not... the end!" proclaimed Svante, the talons piercing through his armour and body. "Phrysbruck... will have... rev—"

Cloudstrike released his grip, and Svante plummeted.

"Yeah, I wasn't interested in hearing the rest either," said Tiarnen.

Krawlllchh!

More blood sputtered out of Cloudstrike's beak.

"Well, aren't we a pair," said Tiarnen, looking down at the arrow still deep in his thigh. He wasn't sure that anything could be done for either of them, and removing the arrows might only make matters worse.

A strong gust allowed Cloudstrike to stretch his wings, relax for a moment, and glide—the stillness bringing a welcome moment of calm.

Tiarnen took a long breath and tried to think of what they should do next as the last of the sun set behind the mountains. He could, of course, return to Tharus and try to explain himself if only to reunite with Niera, but the punishment for his direct disobedience would undoubtedly be severe. Dread began to creep into his chest, and then... a soft smile pulled at his cheek at the realization that he had done it: he had proven that the maestros could be sent back to Dorladdich. All he had to do now was reach the rest of them, and the *Anthymn* might truly stand a chance. A westerly gust came, and Cloudstrike began to instinctually lean into it.

"Wait..." said Tiarnen, his stomach sinking at what he was about to ask of his companion. "I... I need you to take us east... into Elihammer."

Krawlch.

"Please," Tiarnen said desperately.

Cloudstrike didn't move, and for a moment, Tiarnen thought he might ignore the request... and then... they began banking eastward.

"Grysilva was right. You are a rare breed, my friend."

Cloudstrike rattled in recognition.

Brathlún and Sorolún now shining brightly above them, Tiarnen buttoned up his jacket and popped the collar—its insulation returning some comforting warmth to the parts of him that weren't racked with pain. His sight now set on the last few leagues of the mountain range, Tiarnen's thoughts went to Lydia in the hope that she had somehow successfully performed the *Anthymn* and convinced Phrygus to join their cause. His eyes grew heavy from the exhaustion and blood loss, but Cloudstrike made one last turn through the ravine, emerging from the mountain range to a striking view of Elihammer.

The province was just as Marifreth had described: an endless valley of wheat fields with glistening streams running through them that reflected the vibrant light of the *aurora borealis* flashing high above. Seeing them now for himself, Tiarnen finally understood why his mother had been so enchanted by the wondrous phenomenon. With the memory of their last night together in the lighthouse filling his heart, Tiarnen slowly reached up and ran a finger along the glowing ribbon of magenta as he vanished inside of the aurora—wondering if his broken promise could be mended by her dream fulfilled.

MUSIC TERMS

A

Accent: Momentarily emphasizing a tone with a sudden dynamic increase.

Acoustics: The properties of a physical space and how sound behaves within it.

Arpeggio: The separation of a chord or series of tones into individual notes so they can be played individually.

Ascending: Rising in pitch.

Augmentation: Lengthening of a tone or rhythmic value so that a melody, theme, or motif can be extended.

B

Ballad: A common provincial song designed to tell a story.

Beat: A steady pulse usually from a drum.

Brass Family: Instruments made of brass tubes formed into different shapes like the trumpet and the tuba.

C

Cadence: A melodic or harmonic punctuation mark at the end of a phrase, section, or entire piece of music.

Chord: More than two tones played at the same time to produce a richer and more complex sound.

Chromaticism: Harmony or melody that uses pitches beyond the central key of a piece of music.

Clef: A clef is a written compositional symbol that determines which notes will be played. The three main types of clefs are the treble, bass, and C clef.

Counterpoint: The combination of two or more independent melodies to form a complex harmony.

Crescendo: Gradually getting louder.

D

Descending: Falling in pitch.

Development: The dramatic section of a warsong that expands or progresses the musical effect.

Dissonance: Tones that create tension and sound as though they need resolution.

Dynamics: The relative loudness or quietness of a performance.

E

Ensemble: A group of musical performers.

Exposition: The opening section of a warsong.

H

Harmony: The vertical layering and simultaneous playing of complementary tones.

I

Interval: The measured distance between two tones. When measuring vertically, it is referred to as a harmonic interval. When measuring horizontally, it is referred to as a melodic interval.

Intonation: The pitch accuracy of a musical instrument or singer's voice.

Inversion: When the intervals of a melody are turned upside down.

K

Key: The central note, chord, or scale of a musical composition often designated as major or minor.

M

Major Scale: A select pallet of brighter notes, or scale, that provide specific sound values for a maestro to compose with.

Measure: A rhythmic grouping of notes to make reading music composition easier.

Melody: A phrase that is emotionally iconic in a piece of music and often repeated to make memorable.

Meter: The number of rhythmic beats in a measure (2/4, 3/4, 4/4, etc.).

Minor Scale: A select pallet of darker notes, or scale, that provide specific sound values for a maestro to compose with.

Modulation: The transition from one key to another.

Motif: A small group of tones or chords equivalent to a word in a sentence.

Movement: A complete, independent section of a warsong.

N

Note: The written representation of a tone in a musical composition.

O

Octave: An interval between two tones in which the upper tone vibrates twice as fast as the lower tone.

P

Percussion Family: Instruments that produce sound from being struck like the drums, cymbal, or gong.

Period: Two phrases that often resolve much like how a question is followed by an answer.

Phrase: A group of tones, chords, or motifs that build and form the equivalent of a sentence.

Prelude: An introductory movement to a larger piece of music.

R

Range: The distance between a singer or instrumentalist's lowest and highest possible notes.

Refrain: A repeated section in a piece of music.

Rest: A marking used to notate space where music isn't being played within a composition.

Reverberation: An echo-like effect caused by sound reflections against surfaces.

Retrograde: A melody presented in backwards motion.

Rhythm: A repetitive pulse that forms a pattern in time.

S

Sequence: A passage of music where a melody is played at a higher or lower pitch.

Slur: To blend multiple tones together.

Staff: The lines that a piece of music is written on where you will find the time signature, tempo, and notes.

String Family: Instruments characterized by having a carved, hollow wooden body like the violin, viola, and harp.

Syncopation: Shifting rhythms to create an offbeat groove.

T

Tempo: The speed at which rhythm repeats.

Texture: How tempo, melody, and harmony combine to create the overall sound in a piece of music.

Theme: The main musical idea that is the focus of a composition or warsong and is often repeated throughout.

Timbre: The distinct characteristic of an instrument's sound quality.

Time Signature: How many beats per measure exist within a musical composition. Common time signatures include 4/4, 3/4, and 6/8.

Tone: A class of recognizable sound frequency. Tones are identified as written notes which make up the provinces musical alphabet: A, B, C, D, E, F, G.

Tonic: The first note of a scale or key.

Triad: A chord that consists of three notes.

Trill: The rapid alternation of two close tones to create a "shaking" effect.

Triplet: A rhythmic grouping of three equal-valued notes played in the space of two.

W

Woodwind Family: Instruments that produce their sound from a wooden read and need air blown into them like the flute, piccolo, and oboe.

Please note: these are not all of the conventional music terms but merely a reference list for the ones used in the story.

Shard Arcanum

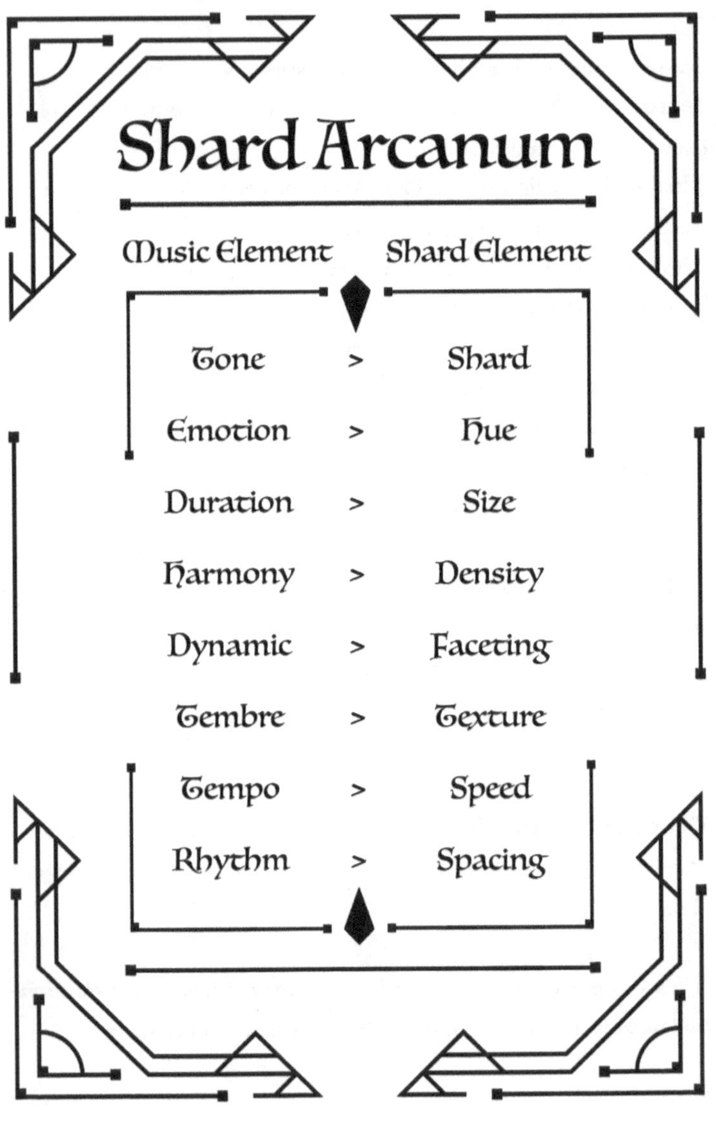

Music Element		Shard Element
Tone	>	Shard
Emotion	>	Hue
Duration	>	Size
Harmony	>	Density
Dynamic	>	Faceting
Timbre	>	Texture
Tempo	>	Speed
Rhythm	>	Spacing

Core Shatter Rules

1. A deck can have no more and no less than 50 cards.
2. Decks must be inspected by an Official or opposing player before a match begins.
3. Each player starts with 50 health points.
4. The first player to have all of their health points reduced to 0 will lose the match.
5. There are 5 card classes: Song, Ally, Trinket, Talent, and Weapon.
6. Cards can only be first played on or after their designated turn number.
7. Warsongs must be 90% complete to activate their effect.
8. The first player to arrive to a match may call the coin toss.
9. Whomever wins the toss must take the first turn.
10. A turn lasts for 1 minute.
11. The victor of a match may keep 1 card from their opponent's deck.
12. A player may forfeit at any time during a match.
13. Missing a match will result in a forfeit.
14. Players are to respect each other or they will be disqualified.
15. Players who receive external advice, insight, or help of any kind during a match will be disqualified.
16. Players are not allowed bet on matches they participate in.

30
Brightest
of The
Seven
4
4
9
Amber's

Rules of Engagement

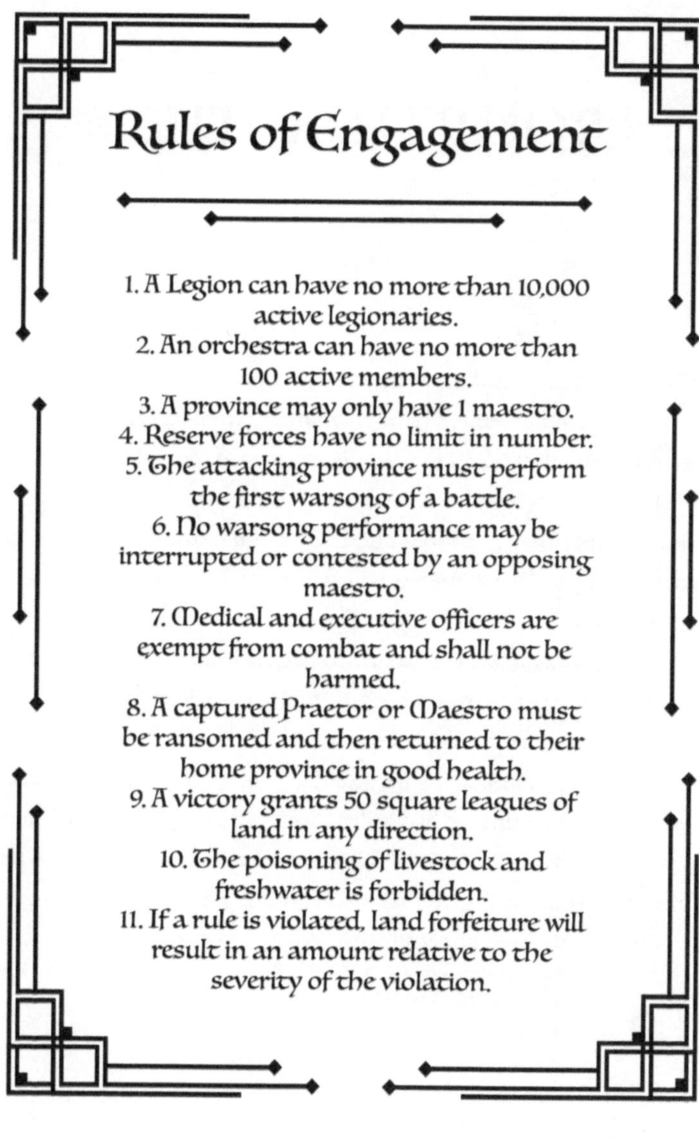

1. A Legion can have no more than 10,000 active legionaries.
2. An orchestra can have no more than 100 active members.
3. A province may only have 1 maestro.
4. Reserve forces have no limit in number.
5. The attacking province must perform the first warsong of a battle.
6. No warsong performance may be interrupted or contested by an opposing maestro.
7. Medical and executive officers are exempt from combat and shall not be harmed.
8. A captured Praetor or Maestro must be ransomed and then returned to their home province in good health.
9. A victory grants 50 square leagues of land in any direction.
10. The poisoning of livestock and freshwater is forbidden.
11. If a rule is violated, land forfeiture will result in an amount relative to the severity of the violation.

ABOUT THE AUTHOR

Riley McDougall grew up in Abbotsford, British Columbia, Canada. He wanted to be an animator from an early age, so he often spent endless hours in the quiet corners of his childhood home sketching elaborate action scenes or fantastical characters on every spare piece of paper that could be found. Over time, storytelling grew to become a much deeper interest which is why he enrolled at the Emily Carr Institute of Art and Design in Vancouver.

After receiving his Integrated Media degree, Riley began his career in the VFX industry and over the next fifteen years helped bring many of the world's most celebrated entertainment IPs to life. Riley conceived the idea of MotA in 2003 while attending a live DJ performance and hasn't slept much since. Thankfully, those restless nights allowed him to outline, draft, and design all 9 books in the MotA series. Please be sure that he is eternally grateful for you finishing the first and promises that the second is well underway.

Acknowledgements

I could never fully express enough gratitude for my family, friends, and colleagues who have shown nothing but unyielding love, insight, and advice at every stage of MotA's development. However, I can at the very least immortalize their names so that each copy of this book will also be a celebration of their support.

Allison, André, Andrea, Ashley, Briana, Cat, Conrad, Dan, Evangeline, Fran, Graham, Haiwei, JC, Jeff, Jen, Jinnie, Jonathan, Josh, Joyce, Kajsa, Katy, Kristy, Lindsey, Lottie, Megan, Michael, Nancy, Nick, Nicole, Patrick, Raf, Randy, Sandy, Sara, Tristan, Winter

It has been such a long road and I couldn't imagine having anyone else along for the ride.

With all my heart, thank you!